LUBRICATED CONDOMS

Millstone

Jeffrey Matthew Hopkins

HARD OAK PRESS LLC

2014

HARD OAK PRESS

ISBN: 0984567364
ISBN 13: 9780984567362
Hard Oak Press LLC

FOR ROBERT

"REMEMBER TO BREATHE"

The scene at the very beginning...

I have woken from a furious night of drinking, not knowing whether we ended up at the Crown and Anchor or the little bastard bar at the top of the hill, the name now escapes me; I only know that somehow I got home. I do not recall driving. My maid has informed me that the Ferrari is smashed into the lone tree on the property.

I am sitting here, and I am trying to put words onto the digital page. The whiteness of my iMac's screen is terrifying. I type. I erase. I type out a paragraph that does not make sense even to myself. My characters, I want to kill them all off. Marcus Hanley...I'd love to garrote him and leave him bloody in the gutter, but with him I trudge on. I've been contemplating suicide on an hourly basis. When it gets too intense, I go and look at housewares at Macy's, sometimes Williams of Sonoma. Ishmael took to the sea. I finger cutting boards to find my solace. Now the car is wrecked, starting to smolder in the front yard. Marcus is nowhere to be found.

I turn off the iMac unable to find any meaning in its small, glowing, detached, wireless keyboard. I find solace in my 13 inch MacBook Pro, late 2009 variant, with the sexy sleek aluminum case and keyboard that glows in the dark. When I sit with it on my lap, it warms my balls and tingles my loins like a talented stripper. I plug into Wi-Fi and do what it is I do when the feelings come on and I cannot take to the sea or take to looking at housewares. I surf porn. I've seen most all of my major fetishes before. My predilection now is big round asses. Doesn't matter the flavor. I don't care the shade. The bigger the better. To me they are the measure of a woman's fertility. I search for big white ass, big black ass, big Latin ass, and even find a few when searching for big Asian ass. When I tire of these I move on to big Indian ass, big Nepalese asses, big Arab ass, and find the videos to be mostly low quality home movies with out of shape sex practitioners. Still it gets my midsection heated. Warms my balls more than my MacBook Pro. I write in notebooks and transfer the scrawl to the computer whenever the spirit moves me. I have a problem though. For the past, oh I don't know how many years, when I turn my computer on, my thoughts drift to porn. My fingers click my mouse to porn. My free hand strokes my dong to porn.

Fortunately, or unfortunately, as of late, I've tired of porn. I'm depressed. I want the real thing. I long for it. Not that I'd ever hire a whore or an escort, or visit one of those seedy Chinky Chinky massage joints...I fire up Yahoo! Messenger and see if any of the numerous stroke buddies I've amassed over the years are online. They are all equally female, and all like to show me their tits, which are usually really, really nice for a woman who is so inclined to show them off for free. I ran into the usual ones who wanted you to go to a pay site so that they could charge your credit card $19.95 per minute of masturbatory bliss at which point they smoke a cigarette and start getting personal. These free ones are a delight. I don't know if they think I'll get into a relationship with them or what after they show me their knockers.

If I engaged in any significant labor, I would at least like to be paid for it. These women are talentless at marketing and sell themselves for cheap. They hang out in seedy dives with men of ill breeding. Bikers usually. I keep thinking to myself that if I mustered up the courage to actually go and fuck one of them, like they are always asking me to do, that it would be quite a *coup d'état*. Most of them have husbands, they are the property of someone that they say all the time they love, and then they voice their gripes and complaints to me about him, how he's so inconsiderate and such a pig, and then they show their tits to me and flick their bean on the webcam for a ne'er-do-well like me, while I tug on my beef for them. It doesn't seem a fair trade. One lady's boyfriend is in jail for doing something tremendously stupid, but she's waiting for him because he exerts some sort of control over her, who knows, but apparently he was a biker, and his name was Tyler McGundree, he had a great shock of red hair, wore a leather cut, had fists like concrete slabs, and according to her, had cock of epic proportions; her eyes just glowed when she talked about it like she were a girl talking about her favorite plaything, and it brought to mind that if this male specimen had lived in a more cultured time he could have been counted as a demigod cult leader of some sylvan orgiastic cult, but alas he was born in the 1970s at the very death of disco. He was in jail for beating someone senseless over something trivial, I don't remember. Rita, she told me once but then she pulled out those magnificent tits of hers, and well, I don't remember the rest.

lvlyritamm88

hi

mr_stuffington

sup

lvlyritamm88

whatcha doin

mr_stuffington

hangin' out

lvlyritamm88

whatcha gonna do today

mr_stuffington

dunno. I'm hung over

lvlyritamm88

go out last night?

mr_stuffington

yup. Crown. Drank a bunch. Marcus and I.

lvlyritamm88

fun

mr_stuffington

yup. You should come sometime.

lvlyritamm88

you should tell me next time

mr_stuffington

I didn't know you wanted to go

lvlyritamm88

you never asked...meet any chix?

lvlyritamm88

why not you?

lvlyritamm88

yeah right...you got 0 game 🌐

mr_stuffington

I know. Chix scare me 😊

lvlyritamm88

lol

mr_stuffington

I'm scared of women, isn't it pathetic?

lvlyritamm88

come see me. I'll help you get over your fear

mr_stuffington

can't no car

lvlyritamm88

broke?

mr_stuffington

no, I've got plenty of money

lvlyritamm88

lol silly I mean is the car broke?

mr_stuffington

yeppers...Marcus wrecked it. Absconded. I don't know where he is.

lvlyritamm88

omg!!!!! is he okay?

mr_stuffington

he's not dead in the car. So I think he's alright.

lvlyritamm88

oh no!! are you okay?

mr_stuffington

been better

lvlyritamm88

anything I can do? I
I'll come see you

mr_stuffington

let me see the girls

lvlyritamm88

lol
click on view webcam silly

mr_stuffington

I can never get this right

lvlyritamm88

click on make webcam available

mr_stuffington

I have mac

lvlyritamm88

lol...figure it out

mr_stuffington

there...

show me yours

lvlyritamm88 has started viewing your webcam.

lvlyritamm88

you first

So it began again. Rita splayed her luscious mammaries, and those tits were stupendous Mexican boobies, some of the finest I've seen. And she starts mashing them together, to the side, bouncing them up and down all the while making little sucky, kissy kissy faces, and occasionally winking. Should she want to turn professional, she could make a fortune doing this. She was only a few miles up the road, twenty at the most in Salinas, California, and I'm in Monterey. We could meet up, hell we could meet up halfway in a motel, but I was afraid we'd really have nothing to talk about after we got done screwing. That shouldn't stop you, Marcus would always tell me, that you didn't actually need to talk to them or get to know them and that was my major failing in life, that I cared too much about them. Marcus would have drilled her once, twice, perhaps after that point kept her around for a booty call. He would have been annoyed that she had kids who oftentimes would interrupt their mom and ask for something which would necessitate her putting those luscious tits away, sending the message BRB and make me lose the full length and girth of my erection. Beating your cock alone is no fun, no matter how powerful your ability to summon images from the spank bank. Porn stimulates loneliness, isolation, and masturbation. At least if I'm beating my cock while a woman is watching and pleasuring herself I don't feel like so much of a degenerate pervert, jacking off to puppets fucking on the screen. Pulling it to dancing pixels. Rita urged me onwards in that sexy, slight hint of an accent voice of hers. I bet she really was a number in the sack, but I'll never know. I'm way too much of a coward to find out. I felt the tension rising in my testicles and announced to her by typing with one sticky lubed hand:

mr_stuffington

gonna cum

lvlyritamm88

do it

come jam that big gringo cock in me

She threw her head back and laughed as I shot a streamer across my keyboard, most of which landed on the C key, which was quite odd because I'm usually a dribbler and this ejaculatory event was performed with me sitting down, working against the force of gravity. I sat back in the chair, smiling, breathing hard, sweat pouring down my brow.

mr_stuffington

lol

On the webcam, she looked a bit hurt. I heard a rustling in the house. Marcus. He burst into the room. My cock was still deflating, and still in my guilty hand.

"Jacking off again?" he shot.

Embarrassed, I covered up and closed the cam.

> **lvlyritamm88**
>
> where'd you go?

"Stupendous boobage on that one. You should go and fuck her," Marcus announced.

> **mr_stuffington**
>
> gotta run. Marcus is here

> **lvlyritamm88**
>
> oh okies...ttyl 😞

"It isn't that easy, Marcus."

"Dude. Sure it is."

"I've been working today."

"Oh yeah? How far did you get? Did you get to the part about me running amok through the Sultan's harem yet?"

"Not quite. I'll read you what I've got."

"Marcus reached between her legs to feel the moistness, and she shuddered once, twice as he brought his hands from a closed position, then opened them widely again grasping her oversized clitoris between his long index finger and erect thumb.

'Do you like that?' he muttered breathlessly, aware that the blood was very quickly leaving his brain stupefied.

Most all the blood in his body filled his double-sized cock and excited the heart, leaving his brain quite dumb.

'Grab it,' he ordered her as she quivered against him, her long robes splayed out in fifteen different directions giving her the appearance from above of being an intricately petalled flower centered on her wide open cloacae.

'No,' she implored, seeming as if she had gotten him to this point, only to leave him with blue balls, 'please me.'

He seized her by the buttocks, spreading them slightly so the cool breeze of the morning desert air blew across her exposed taint. She giggled.

'Oh, Marcus, my Marcus, you're such a man,' she said whispering into his ear and biting his earlobe gently, then harder, finally drawing a hint of blood. He laughed. Pain brought out the best in him, made him aggressive. He raised his head back like a dominant lion about to cleave the firmament of a naughty lioness.

'Do you think I'm worth it Marcus?' she asked.

'Yes, my dear, I'd gladly get my head chopped from my neck for you.'

'Then hurry up and do it.'

'I thought you wanted me to please you, babe?' Marcus said, both hands on her bod, kicking his legs to the side and laying on his back.

'Get on top of me.'

The Bedouin Princess obediently obeyed Hanely's wishes and lowered herself slowly, because it hurt, onto his strong shaft as girthy as the tent pole, which kept their tent erect, and the boiling Arabian sun from scorching their naked bodies.

'What will your wife, Veronica, think?'

What will your husband, Prince Abd al Faisal Abd al Ghanim bin Aziz Sulayman Mohammad bin Turki al Faswanamami think?' She just stared at Marcus with those big black eyes of hers, her eyes being the only thing he saw of her until he decided to give it the old college try.

'She won't find out.'

'The Prince may.'

'I doubt it.'

'You've cheated him. Stolen his treasures. If you didn't have such lovely blue eyes, as blue as the skies over Damascus on a bright spring day, I would have killed you myself.'

'You wouldn't dare,' Marcus said, slyly.

He flipped her on her back in one swift motion, thrust upward with his hips, and sank his shaft into her willing, lubricated flesh. She winced at first, like all women wince, on the feeling their first Moby Dick, great white whale, which in Marcus's case was slightly tanned from the nude beaches in the South of France, where his beautiful wife, the actress Veronica Dare and he had spent time in the past week while she received the Palm d'Or for her role in the United States soft core porn crime drama FROLIC. A movie in which the Hollywood Reporter had insinuated that she bedded most of the male cast, the director, the less aged producer, and some of the key grips, and definitely, most definitely the Best Boy. His wife was a tease, a flirt, and worst of all, there was also a very pernicious rumor floating about that she had turned him into a cuckold. Veronica Dare was seen several times in public with an NBA Power Forward. The child came out with unnaturally curly hair and a preternatural ability to tan, and Marcus was more than three quarters Native American, so hyper curly most likely wasn't in his woodpile. In fact, right now, while thrusting on the Princess of Arabia, his hair came straight down his back, right down to the center of his chiseled shoulder blades…a feature which the Prince remarked was quite queer, and mentioned this to the princess, who agreed, but she secretly thought it dreamy, and dreamed of running her fingers through it. This Bedouin beauty, whose name he suddenly forgot, while he approached climax and lay sweat bonded against her unbra'ed possibly DD boobs, against his well-formed muscular chest, and they climaxed at the same time.

She whispered into his ear, 'Marcus, my illicit lover, won't you leave her for me? Come here, stay with me. We'll stay near me at all times?'

'I can't,' Marcus said.

'Why not, lover?'

'Do you think I can really live in a tent, in this sweltering heat, without a shower, a refrigerator, eating dates and greasy camel strips for the rest of my days?'

'We don't live in a tent, we're only out here getting back to our Arab roots,' she said with tears welling up in her large, dusky, gorgeous eyes.

'Come now, I belong in a penthouse,' Marcus said coldly.

'I'll buy you a penthouse with my allowance,' she said.

'And be a servant among servants?'

The woman jumped up, quite naked, titties pendulously dragging at her, trying to pull her back to Earth.

'Then go back to your worthless whore of a wife!'

'Now, just wait!' Marcus said gravely, without yelling.

'Guards!' she screamed.

'No need for that! I'll take the penthouse!'

'Guards! Guards! This white devil is trying to rape me!'

'Shut up, damn you! I'll take the penthouse!'

The tent collapsed around them, pulled down by the wily guards who brandished scimitars, swinging them wildly around their heads like whirling dervishes locked for too long in the inner sanctum of some otherworldly Pasha. Hanely struggled with the thick muslin cloth that made up the tent, and now covered his midsection. The Princess stood up, bronzed and ferocious in the summer sun, quite naked. The guards froze.

'Get me some clothes you fools! And stop staring at my tits!'

Marcus's head appeared from between the folds.

'Meesha, darlin', let's work this out!'

One of the guards, seeing him indisposed took the opportunity to slash at him with his razor sharp scimitar. Hanley jumped to his feet and fended off the blow with one of the tent poles, which the swordsman chopped in two. He swung again, in full fury and force, so that this lust-filled infidel would be sent straight to hell for violating his sister. He was Abdul Aziz al Hakim, the brother of Meesha, *her caretaker when her husband the Prince was away. This horrible incident would surely fall squarely on his shoulders if he didn't kill the interloper. He wore a mask to hide his disfigured face, an accident from practicing falconry with an overzealous, untrained bald eagle that clawed his nose and ripped it off his face, thinking it was a desert vole."*

"Voles don't live in the desert, man."

"Sure they do. What do you know, Marcus?"

"You don't have to get all defensive, bro. Voles are woodland creatures. If you want to have some desert animal, make it a desert hare."

"A hare is too large. How could a raptor mistake a guy's nose for a desert hare?"

"Fuck it. Make it an Antechinus."

"What the hell is that?"

"A south Australian marsupial rodent. It's my totem animal."

"Totem animal?"

"Yeah, an animal symbolic of me."

"This story is set in North Africa."

"Make the Antechinus escape from a zoo in Marrakesh."

"Lame idea, Marcus. The story isn't about an Antechinus."

"If the story's about me. It's about an Antechinus."

"It won't fit."

"It will. It will fit perfectly with your book, my man. Don't you know about the Antechinus? It's one of God's bastard children, well at least the males of the species are."

"What's the matter with them?"

"Nothing. They're just following their program. Like all the little animals follow their program. The male Antechinus's program, like my program, because it's my totem animal, you see, is to fuck as many females as possible during their two week mating season. They don't eat, don't sleep, and don't even drink water. They just pursue the females wherever they're hiding...and they do hide, because the male Antechinus doesn't ask for it, he takes it. That is a point of difference between us...and the male Antechinus loses all of its hair, wastes away from exhaustion, all of its life force having gone into running around like a madman, producing sperm, and shooting it into whatever he can get his little Antechinus paws on. Just a first and final desperation spent in an effort to pass its genes onto the next generation. The most voracious of the male Antechinuses, or maybe they're Antechini...I don't know, pass their genes onto the most offspring, who repeat the vicious cycle onward and onward. Beautiful thing, isn't it?"

"So it pays off then? Dying to breed?"

"Yep."

"How do you know so much about this animal?"

"I'm an Antechinus, in human form. Like I told you, it's my totem animal. I, being three quarters Native American, had to have a totem animal. Wolf, bear, deer, tiger, lion, they're all boring...taken. My Native American name is Fornicating Antechinus. I'm an Antechinus trapped in a man's body."

"You're a man."

"Nope. I tell you I'm an Antechinus if I ever was an animal. I just happened to be born man."

"Wait, you're not kidding me are you? Thanks for wrecking my car, you twerp. How'd that happen?"

"Don't remember. We both made it back safe and sound though. You should cut the petty materialism, man. Life's an adventure."

"Still."

"I mean, what's the point to life unless you're balls deep?"

"There's plenty to do otherwise."

"It's not all that meaningful."

"Sure it is."

"No it isn't. It's merely a prelude to being balls deep."

"There's plenty to do out there that's not motivated by sexual conquest."

"It's a powerful force that you've been ignoring. How's the book coming? Dreadful as the first?"

"It's stalled, as you can see."

"I'll teach you my ways. Your book will be pure gold dust, just like the first one."

"What ways?"

"I'll teach the way of the Secret Order of the Antechinus, of which I am the one and only member. But you've got to promise me something. The Way of the Antechinus is meant to be lived, not written about. Just like life is meant to be lived and not written about."

"So, I live it then I write it."

"Yes, man! That's the way you've got to be. To be the opposite is to be inauthentic."

"Wouldn't want to do that, would I?"

"You did in your first novel. That thing was a monstrosity. Franken-novel. Hodge-podged together, electrified, and sold to bored and horny teenage girls nationwide. Then of course so the moms would have something to penetrate their daughters' psyches and maybe feel young again, they read it."

"It was a New York Times bestseller for fifty straight weeks."

"What does that mean?"

"It made a shit ton of money."

"Where's it going to be a few years from now? Nowhere. Your book won't have made you immortal; it had the life of a mayfly. Those immortal books are the only books that can possibly be called great, the books that kill the authors writing them, the books written for everyone and no one. Books by madmen."

"You aren't making any sense."

"You'll see. You'll learn the way and become a master. And you'll never really write, again; you'll live."

"But I want to write."

"No you don't, it's just a chore to make you be able to say that you're a writer."

"I have to."

"Yeah, I forgot, you're a slave to your agent and publisher. You don't have to be."

I thought about that as Marcus Hanely silently stood to his feet and glided into the living room, past the picture window that framed Lover's Point.

"I'm not a rich boy, earning my living from a trust fund; I've had to make every dime on my own," Marcus called as he sauntered through the kitchen.

"Tell me about it," I said. When he was safely out of the room, I opened my email, which was full of angry letters from my agent that I had not bothered to respond to.

Jackson,

Your second installment of the Marcus Hanely/Veronica Dare *Asymmetric Hearts* trilogy, and it will be a trilogy, per your contract, is due. Your concerns that the new material you are working on will not sell due to changing market conditions is preposterous, baby. You know that whatever you write will sell. You've got a built-in fan base. It will sell, Jackson, you've just got to get it to me. I hope you will see fit to put your magic hands to your keyboard and type me something out. You don't have to make it a masterpiece, just get it to me. Don't worry that you think you're selling bullshit to morons; I can confirm that your fan base, is mostly morons, but hell they're morons with money. Stop thinking that you'll elevate people through literature. It's entertainment, baby. I have to warn you though, that the publisher is *demanding* an additional novel in the trilogy by June. That's on June 1. Not June 2 or 3 or 4. I need a rough draft to give their editor in my hot little hands. Otherwise, I'm sure you know the consequences. The fans have been promised a meaty, thorough middle section and a pulse-pounding conclusion. Do not kill Marcus Hanely off, like you told me you were going to do. Let him and Veronica live a long and happy life. Hell, make them Vampires if you want. There's no reason to kill your character, and the best romantic character since, oh, I don't know who, Mr. Darcy in that Jane Austen book, just because you've come to want to write something else. See the trilogy through and write whatever you want. You don't have to worry about money. You just don't want your characters diverting to the publisher. They'll hire a gang of monkeys to write your next two books.

Salutations,

Roland Tannenbaum, Esq.

Tannenbaum Literary Agency, LTD

567 Madison Avenue

New York, New York

"Art without commerce is merely a hobby."

I slammed my computer top down without answering the email, sandwiching my semen between the screen and keyboard. I pulled a Gucci logoed handkerchief from my pocket and sneezed into it. Bright red blood streamed from my nose.

"You better get that checked out, bro," Hanely said with a smile, "could be something serious."

*T*he Sunday prior, I drove my bright red Ferrari down Pacific Coast Highway towards San Simeon, the palatial home of William Randolph Hearst, a man who started wars to drive newspaper sales. I was not going to a party at San Simeon; I was going to attend a party at a much larger sprawl, down the hill from San Simeon. The man who threw the party, Gibbon Fitzpatrick, was the most popular literary agent on the West Coast. It was not through his own effort of being a hyper-talented agent that he grew rich enough to afford the second largest home in California. He married well. His ultra-talented Chinese wife, who wrote and illustrated pithy books for children (and adults), is more wildly popular throughout the world than even the books of that plucky French aviator, Antoine Saint Whatshisnuts. Chances are you've never heard of them, but you have heard of Momo Chang. Her books, often numbering less than ten pages long, with a picture on each page and a single elegant, pithy little phrase on each page, retailing for 19.99 at most major retailers, and often on sale at gas stations and truck stops, near the DVDs and sweatshirts with funny sayings. Many said that the middle aged Chinese woman, who was as beautiful as Madame Chiang Kai Shek, a real porcelain doll, was actually the reincarnation of a dragon whose treasure was the collected wisdom of the Chinese people from ancient times, who had memorized all of the texts of this Chinese antiquity before they were burned by the First Emperor of China, Qing in his vain and utterly futile quest for immortality. She seemed to be made of glass when I saw her, her smile crystallized in an instant and then disappeared. Her husband, a round man, getting rounder from her musings and picture books, appeared behind her to extend me a warm, heartfelt (in his words) welcome. She came from nowhere in the 1970s in Shanghai, as if she descended in a ball of light from Heaven. Her husband, her agent and doubling as her PR man, did most all of her talking for her. She spoke limited English and could only smile and bow politely when any praised her works as pure genius. They were genius. They made you laugh, and they made you cry, all within the space of a single thought, a single sentence's space. I don't know how that was possible, but she did it. I wanted to bask in her greatness. There were rumors that she would be the first Children's Book author to be on the short list for the Nobel Prize for Literature in a few years.

I've often wished that I could write children's books, you know, cut right to the heart of the matter and really speak to the soul of the youth, educate them not to follow in the footsteps of adults, traipsing though trodden trails that should have been burned up long ago...I mean really speak to the children, but my lusts always overtake me and all I can write is just really bitterness and trite pornography. I need a woman to help me write. I need to roll off her post orgasm and write beautiful sonnets, but perhaps I cannot because there is no beauty in me. The composer of the most profound children's books ever is married to a wretch of a man. An agent, a professional salesman, a portly fellow who is usually drunk and red-faced, red-nosed, and ginny, hitting on the college girls who are his interns, telling them that they have literary talent so he can apprise their nether regions all the while his wife, his breadwinner, this saint, sits idly by pecking her works of genius onto the constrained keyboard.

You can tell the difference between today's charlatans and yesterday's saints, because today's charlatans fill the air with noise, while yesterday's saints spoke nary a word and showed their innermost hearts in action. She uses a MacBook Pro, the same one she has had since they first rolled out. It isn't hooked up to the Internet, and she doesn't see fit to have the newest and greatest ordinateur. Surely it will be a relic in the Smithsonian, similar to the notebooks of famous American novelists.

She writes in an all white room, and composes her universal metaphors for five year olds, tells about mysteries of the universe through the eyes of a panda bear that munches bamboo and waxes philosophically to passing Chinese farmers, on the nature of time, hopes, dreams, and how everything is your choosing.

I wish I had heard this as a child. I wish my mother had read it all to me. I was taught that in order to have choices, you must first have chosen. It was best to wait until retirement in a life planned from screaming bloody beginning, to tired and feeble demise. Best to play golf, as it got you ahead in business...have a snifter of twenty-five year old single malt scotch to take the edge off while you read the remainder of the paper that you could not finish that morning because your tie was not perfect, tied and knotted to the exact standards of the corporation who demanded perfection from imperfect beings, or else it would go tits up when it could no longer compete, and we'd all be out of a job anyway. So, fuck it. I write.

I long for the life of this Chinese woman. I want her skill in dropping golden nuggets from her mind onto gently rolling pages that pour, billowing from the printer, only to be chopped, efficient, and suitable for sale. And they do sell. By the millions. This concern always yanks me from my dream state, pulls me into the cold despair of a hospital-padded room, white in color, with flickering fluorescent lights.

How I long to rip the padding and stuffing, but I am bound by my contractual obligations: a slave, a knave, a typewriter-bound wretch fulfilling the dirty fantasies of couch-bound housewives who desire to become whores in training and live their lives through television. My novels sell by the millions too, but they are phony, arbitrary, contrived, desiccated of life, fit for puppets and puppet culture - string pullers and pullees. They are the fodder of public restrooms everywhere.

I will never forget the day when I read a review that my novel, *Asymmetric Hearts,* was "excellent bathroom reading material, because it loosened up the bowels like All Bran or Crunch Granola," and later on that month I found a copy of the book in the restroom of the local shopping mall, as if it were so unimportant, that it could be discarded amongst the tampon applicators. And why was I in the woman's restroom? The line for the men's was too long.

When in doubt you can always barricade the restroom if a woman catches you, run like hell, pull out an ID card and say that you're CSI and she's trampling a crime scene. My novel in the woman's restroom, abandoned like an aborted fetus! I snatched it up. Moisture from the sink had dampened its pages. I cried over the cheaply printed words; would one treat Dante or Virgil or Homer or even Mark Twain this way? I have never found this gang of gents at the bus station; they are always snatched up - gems. To write something like that is to be admired by the generations: a bright shining star to man's highest achievements and his highest mountaintop meant to remind us that we are collectively immortal. I do not believe in the power of death when I read these works. These were once men who are now bones, or in the case of Ovid - dust. My work will be dead and buried before I am dead and buried.

Marcus Hanely tells me that I must change my style. I should abandon the feeble romance genre for greater prospects of total irrationality, whatever that means. At one point he is telling me to abandon romance, at another instance he is telling me to just dive right in, as a diver would jump off a Mexican cliff for the sea below. He wants me to quit writing. He wants me to live. He wants me to live in total abandonment of reason, totally living in the present like a free radical in the bloodstream of an aphid which sucks the juices of a withering rose of winter and digests them into pure gold. He told me this over beers at the Crown and Anchor, where we sat smoking pipes in the corner of the outdoor patio that opened out into the street, where the revelers from an antique car show and auction snoodled their wine and discussed stock option chains and how their endowments were doing and how well they were endowed.

It was almost as if these people didn't believe that they would stink and rot when their luxurious lifestyles killed them in plane wrecks and horrible equestrian accidents. Hanely drank some top shelf scotch, and followed it up with a beer, something pilsnery, and we discussed the Chinese woman's philosophical picture books and how nice it was to meet her, and how she would probably one day with the Nobel Prize for Literature for writing children's books, which were written for no one in particular but for everyone under the sun.

"You know her pubic hair is like four inches long, right?" Hanely asked me as he quaffed his brew from a glass, which seemed to never get empty.

"What? How do you know that?"

"I knocked boots with her once or twice," Marcus said, as he snizzled his beer in great gulps, and leered at a college woman who could not seem to stop staring at us, err, him.

"What do you mean you knocked boots with her?"

"I totally boned her."

I had always thought her an unassailable fortress, impenetrable by vault or cock, however luxuriant it was. And Hanely's was luxuriant, a model cock for Encyclopedias, even in cross section. He hit the genetic lottery; he could have any woman he wanted. He was that authentic Romance novel cover boy, sans long hair and cheesy profile. I was friends with him, loved him even, because he always told the truth. He would never lie. It wasn't that he was such a pure heart that he could not tell a lie, it was that he had absolutely no reason to ever lie. Lying metastasizes out of weakness or a need to obscure the bitter truth from others, but more often from our very selves. Hanely was the perfect human being because he told you what he thought, and he told you this unvarnished ugly hag truth. He threw it right in your face and let you choke on it in a way made you love him all the more for revealing to you something which should have been apparent, but in fact had been obscured with the dirt of image and poorly thought fantasy.

"So, you really fucked her?" I asked him for clarification's sake.

"Yeah, man. The last party we were at. A month ago or whatever. While her husband passed out, that old drunk, I did her with my hand over her mouth from the back, at her writing desk. Then I put her up on it, threw her precious computer aside, and really gave it to her. She's not going to be the same again. All she did the whole time was look up at me and smile."

"No way! How'd you get her to...I mean what'd you say to her?"

"I asked her one question. I asked her if she was happy."

"That's it?"

"Then I cornered her, and said, 'I can make you very happy, if only for tonight,'" Marcus said smiling.

"Lame," I responded. "You know, I always thought that I would approach her from a literary perspective, discuss her picture books with her, and what they all meant."

"No way, bro, that's what everyone does with her. Everyone, including her worthless husband."

"Yeah, dude's worthless."

"You know, he married her while she was working as a waitress at a Chinese restaurant...the fortunes she brought him made him cry into his won ton."

"Lame," Marcus said.

"Yeah, it's in her memoir."

"It's still lame. She told me she feels like a slave to him and her publisher. She actually feels that way."

"She's a fucking genius. Everyone thinks so," I said.

"It doesn't matter. She hates what she does – sort of like you – only she's really talented."

I couldn't be angry with Marcus for his truths. Everything he said was brutal and blunt. His words were marked by brutality, not his fists, because God forbid if he ever laid into you he could knock your head off with a punch. He had tree trunk arms and was tall with broad shoulders. I don't think he ever worked out, at least I never saw him put up a weight. I have scrawny arms and no amount of lifting will ever increase their mass. I could work out for weeks and eat nothing but Kobe beef and my frame would remain lanky, pathetic.

Hanely and I were supposed to go to another party the following day, but as usual, he found an excuse not to go. He was sick of hobnobbing with celebrities and wanted to go out to Salinas to visit a friend of his. After much inquiry, he revealed that he wanted to go out and visit Rita and fuck her good and proper because I never was going to. I think this was a ploy to get me to go out there with him, maybe DP her or something like a shish ka bob, but I wouldn't. Her husband was in jail and was a dangerous man. Hanely invariably coupled with wedded women. Single women were way too much hassle (even the ones who claimed to only want to ball) and really wanted a relationship. "Suffer me to meet a woman who is gorgeous and behaves like a man, and I will marry her, if only to keep her with me," Marcus said.

A rabble rouser who sat in the corner mean mugging us with candlelight on his face screamed at Hanely as we passed by in the bar underneath the Horatio Nelson poster, a 1970s British souvenir, suitable for framing. I couldn't really tell if he was screaming at Marcus, or screaming at me, but he shouted, "Home wrecker!" I thought it was a womanly insult for a man and laughed, noting that his voice did not carry over the din of the crowd much like a drowning sailor scrambling for jetsam; rather, it was dragged to the bottom of the sea. Marcus did not hear him. We piled into my red Ferrari, "another cliché of your clichéd existence," Marcus called it, and he sped along Pacific Coast Highway towards my beach house, ever the drunken one, but no less drunk than I. Marcus was my permanent guesthouse resident, confidant, right hand man and pretty much sole source of my stories. He was my alter ego, the man who kept me sane as I attempted to create my literary crack for bored, boring house-wives the world over.

"You know what?" Hanely asked the next day, "After this party, you and I should take your car and go on a trip. You're always complaining about not being able to find inspiration by the sea. For fuck sakes, man, if you can't find inspiration here, I don't know where you'll be able to find it. You're not Hemingway for chrissakes; you should find your inspiration in the women that you're writing for. Go out into the world, descend from your lonely cavern of solitude and meet them. Write your fucking body of work, publish it yourself, let's park our bodies into your cherry red Italian cliché of a sports car and lets go out on the road, show up unannounced, take the bookstores by storm, toss all the other trash off the tables, show up and start a drunken orgy to rival the Roman feasts!"

It was Hanely's first mention of a road trip into destiny, not to be done on the lifeless arteries of American commerce, the Interstate highways, but to be done at the behest of Marcus on the lonely Federal and State Highways that time forgot. Highways that criss-crossed the country like neglected varicose veins on the cankles of an obese American hausfrau. I don't know why he hadn't mentioned it before. It would be brilliant, an ode to anti-commerce, we were sure to pick up hordes of followers and cause drug orgies throughout the sorry middle class boroughs we passed, hellfire in our pockets. I asked him again if he wanted to go to the party and he asked me if I had ever met a woman whose pussy was made for my cock. I told him that I hadn't and that was who he hoped this Rita in Salinas would be, the perfect pussy which gripped his cock like a hand. I told him that the party was at the famous agent's ritzy San Francisco apartment and his future Nobel Prize winning Children's book writing wife would be there, the same wife that Hanely had introduced to Ishmael, his Moby Dick.

"She's a cold fish," Marcus said. "I've already dipped my wick in the wax and found it tepid."

"Frigid?"

"Tepid," he said. "She was a screamer too, and she let me stick it in her ass."

"You're disgusting. I thought you said she only smiled at you."

Peals of laughter. He walked out of the room laughing. He abandoned me. That morning I found him asleep on the beach with a bottle of French wine in his lap. The seals were eyeing him with caution, barking at him to please evacuate their territory. He did not stir. I kicked his feet to rouse him. He stood up groggily and gagged a few times. In his hands, he held a consumed bottle of Chateau Margaux.

"I wrecked your car," he said.

"I saw."

"I tried to drive it to Rita's but only ended up crashing it into that tree."

"Was I with you?" I couldn't remember. I don't know if it was from the booze the night before, but I vaguely remember following Marcus when he left, following him to the car. Driving to Salinas with him. I vaguely remember smoking marijuana with a woman, having a party with a bunch of other women. Snorting cocaine, or maybe something else crystalline. And I remember a bunch of faces of children watching us, before being told to go to bed by their mother. Then I remember Marcus taking on two of them, and me with the other, and then swapping. The last thing I remember was drinking nearly a whole bottle of tequila with them before Marcus and I piled into the car for home.

"I'm sorry," he said. But it was well worth it.

"I don't really remember. Just bits and pieces."

We walked back up to the car. It seemed to have been purposely driven into the tree, which would have been easy to miss, as it was the solitary hard oak on the entire property. The Ferrari was impaled around the massive scraggly oak, so much so that the tree nearly reached the windshield and the tires were bent upwards in a U shaped fashion.

"I hope you aren't mad," Marcus said. "I just relieved you of the burden of your clichéd existence. You're free, bro."

"No, you're going to that party with me tonight. You have to. You owe me one."

"How are we going to get there? I wrecked your ride. We going to take a taxi there? That's real stylish. Oh, I've got a good idea. We kill two birds with one stone. We'll go and buy something at the car auction that will suit us on our trip. Are you mad at me?"

Ever the peacemaker, I said a lie to him. "No, I'm not mad. How could I be mad at you?"

"If I were you, I'd be mad."

"Well, you're not me."

We took an unstylish taxicab to the Monterey Car Auction. I did not know what I was looking for, but whatever it was, I would be paying for it out of petty cash. Marcus was totally estranged from his billionaire father, who was last rumored to be being treated for cancer by some quack in the Nepali Himalayas. The last proof of life Marcus received was a scrawled letter saying that his father was being kept alive, and his life extended indefinitely on a diet of Yak milk and honey from bee's nests harvested from bees that occupy sheer faces of K2.

"God damn!" I screamed, as of up to the point the red Ferrari, albeit clichéd to the point of absurdity, even Marcus told me this at the San Francisco dealership where the Burberry suit and Ferragamo shoe wearing dealer was hustling me in and out of the cars, whose lambskin leather smelled like a new baseball glove. "Feel the power," that bastard dealer said as I coasted through the turns convinced that I needed exactly what he was selling me. Anyways it helped me forget about my morbidity for a while. Hanely was there the whole time, in the tiny back seat, reeking of his French cologne which bordered on perfume, but drove the women wild, telling me, "don't do it...get an American muscle car, if you really want the women to know how big your cock is you won't get an Italian hyper-engineered piece of junk that you won't feel comfortable doing a manly thing in, like drinking a tasty coffee beverage from Starbucks because you're too afraid that you'll miss your mouth and your plush kid lambskin leather will get stained. This car is a rolling death machine, man, all it is... is wholesale flight from your bitter mortality, get a goddamned muscle car and be on with it! Drive it across the state and revel in its exhaust. Drive it and scare the shit out of all these Smart Car driving vegetarians. Really wreck some shit!"

I told Marcus that I was not into wrecking shit and he told me that it wasn't an option for him. He told me that I would quickly regret purchasing an automobile that every half baked lame-o, newly rich and brimming with Internet gold, eager to show off and show up their neighbors would buy.

"You'd be better served by buying a pink one and plastering the Hello Kitty emblem all over it, at least you'd be somewhat original." He even went so far as to ask the salesman if the Ferrari was available in Pink, but the salesman just ignored him. Hanely was obsessed with being original and he began to lament that the world was entering a grave sphere of over influence and lameness from which it could, quite possibly, never be able to return from its dilution.

"It's like this," he explained to me, as I drove home in my brand new bright red Ferrari, and it seemed almost as if I were drifting off into sleep as he droned on and on from passenger seat. He almost seeming like some modern day truth teller, only I wasn't listening.

Now Hanely had wrecked my Ferrari, on purpose, wrecked my pride and joy, the source of my ego, an extension of my phallus, and a substitute for my very balls. He wrecked it around a tree, an oak tree estimated to be over six hundred years old. None of the hippie treeologists who guesstimated its age would dare count its rings like I wanted them to. In fact it was much, much older; the salty brine for its drink and the windy air had served to stunt its growth. A passing fact master, some old bastard who had read too many books full of fun facts about California, and who just so happened upon my property one morning as I was watering the gardenias told me that the massive oak was probably around nine hundred years old, and had originally served as a meeting spot for the original California Indians. They used the tree to do all sorts of Indian things, and then Hernando Cortes and his gallant group of iron clad Catholic psychos used it as target practice for their blunderbusses before they used the California Indians as target practice after trading seashells and gonorrhea with them. Now it was the final resting place of a Ferrari, which looked like a crinkled, disposed of Dr. Pepper can washed up on the beach or a crude Yuletide log ornament.

*S*o here we were at the Monterey Auto Auction, an event that happens once a year and attracts all sorts of people with the common denominator of being fabulously wealthy from all over the world. These are the people who forgo real estate auctions because they are far too boring and instead buy and sell expensive automobiles like they are the stock certificates of blue chip Corporations. As the cab came, as bright yellow as the morning, out to the high rent district as the cabby called it, this cabbie schmuck gasped when he saw my cherry red Ferrari around the tree smoldering. I know he gasped for the Ferrari and not the tree, my toolbox modern Ferrari all wrecked, was dearer to this bourgeois ruffian than the ancient oak. When the cabbie looked at the tree, he probably saw end tables.

I sat in the front of the cab while Hanely sat in the back and glared at the Cabby. I watched Marcus, askance through the rearview mirror. His glare was a moldering glare. He did not speak, he really only spoke to women and often told me that he'd found other men to be trifling bores who were only eager to talk about the weather and football, as if they ever had a moment's control over either activity.

The car auction was a very prominent affair, an affair we were in no way dressed for. It was not so much a black tie affair, but it was a gaudier the better affair. One gent dressed in a plaid crushed velvet suit, with Abraham Lincoln top hat. His madam, gribbled onto to his arm like a clinging cat, wore an entire corporate farm's worth of an unidentified small animal as a coat.

Children, possibly rented from the local bougie community, struggled to hold the massive train from the ground. Saudi Arabians wore their ridiculous looking traditional garb and talked loudly on gem encased cell phones. That we showed up in a taxi cab caused more than a few of the patrons in the lobby of the Portola Plaza to turn their noses up, and that was not to look at the heightened airs of the place and streamers announcing the auction fluttering from the ceiling.

People from all over the world were there and would be well dressed so that the auctioneers would take their foolish bids seriously. These people flew private planes and private helicopters with personal assistants bearing nearing infinite expense accounts and held in their pockets fancy 45,000 dollar pens with diamonds and jewels all over the hilt like they were some sort of ceremonial sacrificial dagger of an oriental God, and not just the new God who demanded checks written legibly and sufficient accounts so they did not prove rubber. Many of the automobiles were ferreted away to showrooms in the Middle East and Mother Russia where they would spend the remainder of their existences totally drained of the fluids necessary to proper functioning, baked under heat lamps so their impeccable finishes would not blister and fade.

Hanely and I sat next to two well-kept women who announced to a short grey man that their husbands sent them on a mission to purchase American muscle cars, which had suddenly become quite fashionable in the Ukraine. These babes were perhaps Scandinavian, I believe, or perhaps from Norway or Sweden or one of those other Baltic Countries that I have never traveled to out of fear that I'd get kidnapped and my kidneys would be sold on the black market.

I have always travelled about in terms of age-old romanticism, but I always end up missing home. Whenever I go anywhere, whether planned or not, and no matter how I get there, I am sorely disappointed. The photographs are always nicer. I don't know how to let Hanely talk me into this; I should have stopped off at the Honda dealership and cut my losses. The money situation is fine. *Asymmetric Hearts* is a modern American Romance classic, probably soon to be taught in college courses on Postmodern Feminist Theory.

Hanely stared lasciviously at the Norwegian, or Russian, or Belorussian, or perhaps Polish women as they discussed the differences between the Super Bee and the Challenger, Copa SS, the cam stroke, manifold differentials like a couple of smug automotive engineers. I stared at him, and then I stared at them. One caught me staring and smiled back.

"And what are you here for?" she asked me.

"A car."

"I know that. Which one?"

"Don't know. A muscle car, I think."

"Oh, nice. Us, too. What do you do?"

"I'm a writer."

"What do you write?"

"Novels. You may have heard of it."

"Is it translated into Ukrainian?"

"Ukrainian?"

"Yes, our language."

"I'll have to check with my publisher," I said sheepishly.

"I'd very much like to read it," she said, smiling, blushing almost.

She was by far the most beautiful thing in the room. Her friend, roundish and older, but still hot, in a churchy, lunchy, school marm, two-beer doable sort of way, kept nudging her. I thought Hanely should speak, but he sat there like a deaf mute, looking at the cars as they came up on the block. I ran out of things to say, and the two Ukrainian babes just sat there looking at me, smiling. It grew uncomfortable. I left, excusing myself, telling them that I had to go to the bathroom. I pulled Marcus with me into the shadows with one hand on his shoulder.

"You have to run interference on that big, fat friend for me," I implored.

"I don't feel like it, really," he said.

"When you feel like getting laid, I've got no problem helping you. I help you," I said.

"I don't need your help. You know that."

He didn't intend his barbs. He always told the truth.

"You want my suggestion? We should leave those broads alone, just look at them, dripping with jewels, and from the Ukraine? What sort of industry does the Ukraine have for them to be that rich? None. I tell you they married rich. They're mobbed up from the looks of it. They probably have big, brutish bodyguards secretly watching them at all times. Mob bodyguards. Assassins, even."

"How do you know they're mobbed up?"

"Just look at them. Why didn't their husbands or boyfriends...hell, probably their pimps come here? The FBI and Interpol probably want them, my man. I've dealt with these types before. Nothing but trouble."

"When have you dealt with these types of people?"

"My aunt, she bought a Cadillac off of some of them," Hanely said.

"When? I thought you said she bought it off a dealership."

"It was owned by the Russians. Financed by the Russian mob. No shit. It was."

"The dealership in Santa Cruz?"

"Yep."

"Those are Armenians," I said.

"Anyways, Central Asians," Hanely said, pushing me backwards into the light.

A man wearing an ascot, puffing a fancy looking pipe stared at us like he'd just caught us making out. Marcus and I walked past him, and Marcus blew the man a kiss. The man pretended not to notice, tugged at his ascot, adjusted his pantaloons, and kept blowing sweet smelling smoke all over the hotel lobby. No one bothered to tell him to stop because he was on the Hotel's board of directors and had the last unfortunate soul who tried to tell him, a janitor with five squirming children was fired for trying to educate him on the Clean Air Act, and legal statutes of the State of California. We went into the pisser. The urinals, few and far between, were all employed. I ducked into a stall and whilst pissing, found the following inscription:

EPICS HAVE NINE MAIN CHARACTERISTICS

1) Opens *In Medias Res*

2) The Setting is vast, covering many nations, the world, or the universe

3) Begins with an invocation to a muse

4) Starts with a statement of the theme

5) Contains the use of epithets

6) Contains long lists

7) Features long and formal speeches

8) Shows divine intervention in human affairs

9) Stars heroes that embody the values of a civilization.

Underneath this, the description of *In Medias Res*...the Story begins at the mid-point or a conclusion rather than a beginning.

I shook my head and zipped my ding-dong back into my pants. Hanely and I walked back into the crowded hotel amphitheater, which reeked with perfumes like some crowded third world bazaar without the barkers, without the strange, exotic danger, the women who smelled like spice and painted kohl under their vacant eyes, without the children playing games I cannot comprehend. No, it was all very safe and devoid of any mystery.

I took my seat next to the Ukrainian women, who pretended not to notice. One of them, the short, roundish one had Googled my novel *Asymmetric Hearts* and just started gushing to me, "You're the author of *Asymmetric Hearts*? I have read it in Ukrainian! Beautiful Ukrainian!" The lovely Slav who I had my eye on, but I assumed Hanely would steal from under my nose and end up bedding, while I was stuck with the big, fat friend, put her hand on my leg while the bidding started, smiled and winked at me. Her not so hot friend said to me, creepily with her sort of Eastern European Soviet brownish teeth, "You know, Mona has always had a thing for writers, ever since she bedded the aged Boris Pasternak." She put her hand on my other thigh.

"I'm not that talented," I said, as her hand made its way up my thigh nearing my center of gravity.

"You're a writer...talent is no matter," BFF said with a smile. I flexed my leg underneath her crushing, meaty hand.

On the block, appeared a Ferrari Spyder from the 1960s, driven by an old man with a bright red Ferrari hat on. The lights scattered off the perfect red paint job.

"Apparently," the announcer, a husky masculine baritone with a spray on tan and spectacles said, "the same car belonged to the famous recording star, Burt Bacharach."

This tidbit elicited some ohs and ahs from the crowd. The strangeness of the amphitheater began to creep into my battered consciousness, and why do I start to get all woozy, like an accordion that played the same nauseating note, ground out by a maniacal jumping monkey chained to his overbearing, grinning, sadistic master? Why do I get all drunk when large sums of money are tossed about? I am sure it is the same feeling that I would get if I recited an epic poem in front of this very audience and they cheered and clapped and reminded themselves that they were mortal and no shiny hunk of steel could remove that fact from their lives.

The Ferrari glittered on a central dais, rotating, so the spectators could get a view of all the angles and how the light bounced off the sexy chrome. A bidding war between a man with money to burn and a man with less time than money erupted. A Saudi sheikh, or perhaps minor Prince, wearing a business suit, nodded like a whooping crane at a proxy, who bid for him with confidence, while the Prince smiled like a buffoon. When the bidding reached over five hundred thousand dollars, a few of the audience members gasped. The old oilman from Texas did not hold his sign up again and sat down to shake his head underneath his ten-gallon hat. The Prince nodded and smiled when it was announced that he was the winner. He bought several more cars that evening, and then retired to his room to call in his bets on the horse races.

Hanely urged me to bide my time to see what the Ukrainians were bidding on so that we could impress them. He communicated this to me with his usual nod and wink, reserved for moments when he wanted to run a game much like a diabolical jester making plots against the crown, but there was no crown, but only his royal impulse to fornicate as often as possible with as many different women as possible. It's Hanely's seeking after infinity, much like these people avoid the plague of mortality by purchasing cars in the excitement of an auction. Hanley does not have much more to speak of. His father disowned him for being a ne'er-do-well.

The Marcus Hanely I have written of in my fictions, the man I met my sophomore year of Princeton University, when I was a foolish business major, deranged and wanting to chug a bottle of cyanide I copped from an organic chemistry laboratory. The liquid cyanide was meant to add a cyano molecule to a blue dye were fabricating from base components, and I stole this cyanide, secretly wishing my own private Jonestown. Hanely met me in the library, and I eventually learned that he inhabited the dorm room next to mine. Quite a coincidence.

He approached me in the library and later came into my dorm room unannounced. He found the bottle of diluted cyanide on my desk. There was only one reason why a person would possibly have cyanide outside of a chemical laboratory setting, and that is to poison themselves or others. Hanely reached down and grasped the bottle and poured it into the sink, after which he sat on my bed and said, "Let's talk, man." Some music poured into my room from the hallway, and to me it sounded like all dissonance and noise, but it was all the rage with the youth. I didn't speak a word to Hanely and just hoped that he wouldn't report me.

"Change your major, bro," he said matter-of-factly, in the blunt way I would become accustomed to. "And get some pussy, pronto...doctor's orders." Then he turned to me again saying, "Well, unless you like dudes or something."

"I don't like dudes. I mean I'm not attracted to them. I like women that way," I said.

"You haven't had any around here, unless you're humping one of your professors or something. I've never seen one visit you."

"I'm no ladies man," I said.

"Don't worry. I've got a patented method that I'll come to show you, if you'll just, you know, hang out with me sometimes."

"I guess."

"We'll go out tonight, and you just watch me."

And I did. I watched him for the remainder of my college experience. And I'm still watching him to this day.

Hanely gave me that same wink and nod as he did back then and moved in on the svelte statuesque, very married, so he said, to the Ukrainians, mobbed up, hot gangster-ess, I'm sure whatever he did it was going to be excellent fodder for Book Three of the trilogy, sure to sell five million copies for Godknowswhat reason throughout the world.

The car just driven up snapped me back to reality: a Silver Aston Martin, like the James Bond Car. Marcus shakes his head no as he works his hand up the Ukrainian's leg. She's blushing. Another Saudi Arabian engages in a bidding war with the Asian who seems determined to purchase the silver car. The Asian is dressed up in a black tie like some Tong Opium Gang Triad boss, and a translator does his bidding for him. The price gets up to an absurd 750,000 USD.

Some more timid souls in the audience gasp, enraptured by the callousness. A few get up and leave, waiting for the cheaper automobiles, there is no way they will be around for the crown jewel, a Grey Ghost Rolls Royce, expected to garner over three million dollars. I read that this particular Aston Martin had a patched up bullet hole in the right passenger door. A vicious looking gang of Norse looking Viking gentlemen ferociously battle-axe their way into the bidding for the Aston Martin with a 900,000 USD bid. Another Saudi minor prince is shocked at their assault and turns red as an oil refinery plume. Going once, going twice, sold to a cellular phone conglomerate chairman from Sweden.

I scanned the audience of this assembled conglomeration of boring fashionable and rightly painted women and decided that if this was America's finest, the one percent, then we're all doomed. We made a mistake somewhere in setting up and maintaining the game and came to think that the premium talent under the sun was taking a small pile of money and designing a machine, or providing a good and service to turn it into a larger pile of money. We went wrong to think that skill in this, per-haps because it pays the bills, pays for brick and mortar establishments, which reflect our culture; we thought that these people were the highest among us. These rich folk. And I am here to tell you that I've been in the bathroom of the Portola Plaza during the Monterey Car Auction. They stink and piss and shit just like the rest of us.

Hanley's fingers are perilously close to the Ukrainian's wet folded skin. Her face is beet red, and she is showing no signs of relenting. She excuses herself and whispers something towards his ear, and then she departs, staring at me. My fingers are some-what moist by the heat, and I wipe them on my pants.

"Bid on the Copa SS," he tells me.

"Oh, the Copa SS is a nice car," the fatty Ukrainian tells me, as it's wheeled to the stage.

"Where are you going?" I ask Marcus as he gets up to leave.

"Taking care of business. You know," he says with a smile.

Resentfully, I did not bid on the Copa SS. The Ukrainian did and won.

Up next, came the 1969 Pontiac GTO Judge, black with orange racing stripes. The Judge glittered electric disco on the podium, looking like some thrusting cock of an automobile God spinning round and round, mesmerizing me. The bidding started at 10,000 USD. I announced 20,000 USD. I had to have it. The fucking thing hit like a bullet. It was the opposite of a Ferrari. It was a man's car. I stood up with my paddle in hand, and raised it high, not releasing it until 75,000 USD passed. I was now in a bidding war with a third unremarkable Saudi with a talent for spending money. We passed 90,000 USD.

"I've a question!" I shouted.

The auctioneer stopped his civilized banter.

"And what is the question of the distinguished gentleman in the bright orange Cardigan and brown slacks?"

"Does it run? What's the gas mileage?"

The amphitheater erupted in laughter.

"You can't be saying that you want to drive it, good sir?"

"I do."

A muffled gasp went up, muffled for the impediment to good trade, and the shock and awe that the vision of me actually driving a car purchased at the Monterey car auction promised.

"You actually want to drive this car?"

"Yes, I'm going to take it on a road trip. What's the problem with that?"

"Sir, there are only a few of these cars in this condition remaining. This is an all-original 1969 Pontiac Judge GTO with all of the original parts. This car really belongs in a museum, preserved for posterity."

"Why are you selling it then? Come on, man, it's a car! It's meant to be driven!"

There were more shocked gasps. I looked around the amphitheater. The glaring spotlight focused on my face. I brought up to block the lights, and said, "350,000 Dollars."

The Saudi, either the third or the fourth, I couldn't tell them apart, seemed to enjoy joining in the spectacle. "400,000 USD," his interpreter said meagerly.

I glared at his assistant. There was no way this guy would own this piece of America. The Chinese little man joined in the fray, sensing blood in the water. I raised my pallet and jumped up and down, stood on my chair, the Ukrainian wailed like a little Eastern Bloc chickadee singing of freedom in the dead winter of Kiev, all high-pitched like, I thought out of delight, but I had stepped on and mashed her hand. The barker flew into a rage and screamed, "Protocol! Sir! Protocol!"

I dashed to the floor and tried to calm the frantic Ukrainian, but she slapped me with ham hock hands and sent me reeling into a gang of large men from Zimbabwe, fucking headhunters, no doubt, in the way they grabbed me into their arms and hauled me out of the room into the lobby, but not before I yelled, "500,000 USD! There is no way you foreign brigands are taking this car out of America! Men in Detroit made this fucking car! It's going to stay here!" They threw me into the Portola Hotel lobby and bolted the door, all the while giving me mean headhunter looks and brandishing toothy grins like daggers.

I raised my head up just enough to see Hanely in the elevator with the tall, gorgeous Ukrainian damsel and the doors closing on him forcing her, rather willingly into the corner of the lift, a term I employ that's borrowed from the Brits, and I am quite the Anglophile. That motherfucker pulled a fast one on me and left me to rent my own room where I would sleep for the night while he was rutting on the bitch three generations out of a cave, mobbed up and all. Why women didn't see through him is beyond me. I woke up in the morning, gazing out at the courtyard of the Portola Plaza Hotel to a knock, knock, knocking at my door. My final bid, I learned, before the Zimbabweans threw me out of the auction, had triumphed and knocked all rivals out of the hunt because they saw the auto as an investment, and no one had ever paid 500,000 USD for an American muscle car. There were simply too many of them, but this one was mine. It would stay in America, where it would be appreciated where it belonged: on the goddamn open road. When I came to and moved to open the door, I saw Hanely sitting in a chair by the wet bar.

"You get it?"

"Did you get it?"

"What do you mean?"

"The ride. Mona told me you won it."

"I don't think so. They tossed me out."

"Well, your spectacle made the others back down. They figured you'd probably murder them or arrange their assassinations if they bid any further. They decided an utter two-fisted maniac, hot up in blood, was not worth bidding against. They'd rather live than have you lose out on your car."

"No way."

"You said that! Don't you remember? I'm surprised you weren't slapped in irons and taken to the police station."

I flipped on the news. There was no mention of any disturbance, like it didn't happen; forces allied against me, to rob me of my media exposure, good or bad, expunged almost the entire record.

"But you don't want any media exposure," Hanely said.

"The fuck I don't," I said.

"Come on now, how many interviews have you turned down? Why, you didn't even go on the *Oprah* show, and when you went on a lesser show, you didn't show up at the last minute, forcing them to book Jack Hanna and a bunch of geriatric chimpanzees."

"I went on *Oprah*, you fuck," I said.

"No you didn't."

"I did. The experience was harrowing, like being held at sword-point near a cliff at the base of which is a deep pool of sharks, poisonous snakes, and hives of killer bees. If you want to torture me and extract any information, I will gladly give it, just don't put me on the couch next to that woman and her legions of adoring fans. Her positivity perplexes me. There cannot be that much good to spread in a world which is so fundamentally rotten and fallen."

"But you don't believe that either," Hanely said.

"I do. Fundamentally. It's rotten."

"Then why don't you drink cyanide, put your head into an oven and deep breathe in your death, why not take a long walk off of the short Santa Cruz pier into those shark infested waters. Swim dressed up like a seal, a hasty snack for a Great White Shark. Fuck HIV ridden prostitutes right in their AIDS infested asses. Why don't you do it?"

"I won't," I declared.

"Why not?"

"Suffering is beautiful. The distance between suffering and yourself is your art."

"Can it. You aren't an artist."

"I'm a one story purveyor of schlock, romance, clitty ticklers for bored and horny housewives," I said, looking into the mirror at the lines on my face. I looked out of sorts, hair frazzled up like Jimi Hendrix without the talent to keep it curly, wearing the same shirt I had worn for fifteen days at least. The same ratty cardigan, which was beginning to smell musty like an old book. I needed a shower desperately. I realized I probably didn't lock my front door to my beachfront home, and now swarms of illegal immigrant Mexicans from roundabout Salinas were probably settling into my place, rifling through my cupboards, cracking open Modelos and laundering their Chivas jerseys in my elegant machine.

"Should I kill myself?" I asked Marcus, with no hint of joking.

"You live like a goddamn Puritan man, no fun in your existence. Might as well get it over with," Hanely said.

"Whatever."

"You're hurtling edgewise off a precipice. Shimmying towards it. Sliding towards it. The heroic measure I took in wrecking your fucking Ferrari was only the first step to bring you back to some sense of yourself, man. Fucking snap out of it!"

"I will," I declared gingerly.

"You had better. You're getting to be quite the drag, man. I mean, tearing up the damn car auction, what the hell is wrong with you?"

"I got out of control. It wasn't my fault."

The knock, knock, knocking at the door again.

"Don't answer it. It's probably that Russian Mafioso's wife."

"Ukrainian."

"Whatever, let me look," Hanely said. He turned to me horrified. "Fuck it's him. And he's got two big goonish Armenians with him."

"Wait, they're probably Chechens come to chop my head off for diddling his wife. I'll bet they'll chop our cocks off and stuff them in our mouths first. Oh, shit," I said and made to answer the door.

"Wait! Don't answer it!"

"You'd better climb out the window. These guys look like they mean business."

Hanely was the master at climbing out of windows. Sometimes naked, sometimes with his pants around his ankles, sometimes half-mast, often times at full attention like a disciplined soldier. And he jumped out of the windows of royalty and famous beds alike. He pummeled the rich slits of industrialist wives and oil derricked the dugouts of oilmen's maidens and took the maidenheads of their daughters often on the same day. And now the Russians were here to exact their vengeance on me, a humble romance author who only desperately wants to create something beautiful in the world. I answered the door slowly, waiting for the chirp of their silenced Makarov pistols to end my bitter existence.

The hugest of the huge goons said, "We're here to take payment for the car you purchased last night."

"And what did I purchase exactly?" I asked him, much to his dismay, and he felt uncomfortable answering the question, as if it were a breach of protocol.

"The 1969 Pontiac GTO, Judge," he said.

"Quite a steal, right?"

The little man did not respond, verbally. He merely nodded.

"Shit," I said.

"How will you be paying, sir?" The little man in the suit said with the air of a mortician.

"Let me work that out. Why the fuck did I let Hanely talk me into this?"

"Will you be paying with a cashier's check or credit card, sir?"

Instead of thinking sometimes, I blurted statements out that were better left to thought.

"Hanely!" I declared, not calling for him, but merely trying to curse my fate and lament the fact that he got me into this and then abandoned me, like he usually does.

"Hanely? Who is that? Will he be providing payment?" The little man inquired, and what he really meant to say was, "PAYMENT! PAYMENT! PAYMENT!" and have the two massive goons pummel the shit out of me.

"We will gladly accept your payment at anytime, sir."

"I know. I'm working that out."

The two goons just shuffled on their feet and held their hands out in front of themselves, around their crotches, I think because they had a morbid fear of getting incapacitated in a fight by taking a knee to the genitalia, or because they had seen tough guys in the movies act that way. The hugest goon in the two-man goon squad looked Eastern European and dumb, but the furthest east he was from was the Eastern side of Pittsburgh, Pennsylvania. My phone rang, it buzzed heartily against my right testicle in my pocket, and a chirp followed the buzzing. The two big goons stared at my midsection and looked up in time to realize that they probably shouldn't have been staring at my crotch.

"Sir, please stop tarrying," the little man said in as husky a voice as possible, "our customer needs to leave. His private plane is waiting at the runway and he needs your payment. Time is money, sir, please give us the convenience of your quick payment."

"Okay, well, I don't want to keep him waiting," I said. At any moment I expected Hanely to burst in the room to surprise the bill collector and his goons.

"You enjoy how I busted that auction up?" I asked the men.

"It proceeded without a hitch, sir, we don't know what you're talking about."

"I handed him my plastic Visa Black credit card and saw his eyes light up. He had a device in his hand attached to an iPhone which would pull my credit card information off the card, and blast it over the heavens of 3G to a waiting computer, which would check my credit card information and balance and encrypt the data back to the device, which would tell this guy whether to issue an order to the goons to start stomping me for making a false bid. My phone rang again, chirping in my pocket, the two goons, hired muscle who were dressed up to look like sales assistants, did not look at my pocket this time. The little man looked up, delighted. The transaction went through.

"Your account was debited for bill of sale for 47,000 dollars, sir. Where would you like to pick up your receipt?"

"That's it?" I asked with shock, having expected to pay much, much more.

"Yes, the 1969 Pontiac GTO Judge sold for a total price of 47,000 dollars. That was your bid. Are you disputing this? If you are, we can watch the tape."

"No, no dispute, I just remembered, err, a larger price...no I'm not disputing it, no need to see the tape." I started laughing as he handed me my Visa Black card back. It's not like five hundred thousand dollars would break the bank, but my sister would have some severe words for me about spending such large sums of money at once. Now I had nothing to worry about. I laughed again. This seemed to make the goons uneasy, so I laughed again as I asked the little man where my keys were at.

"Right here, sir. I was about to give them to you," he said backing up, trying to make his way toward the door without turning his back to me, like I was some sort of circus lion they had walked in on. I've often seen the same behavior in the movies when people are leaving the rooms of people condemned to the insane asylum. He held the keys out to me, like he was giving a rabid dog a steak, and then dropped them into my hands. The key looked like a souvenir and was on a furry rabbit paw keychain.

"Does the car have fuzzy dice?"

"No, sir. The car comes as is. You can purchase the fuzzy dice yourself if you want them."

"Where's the nearest place I can get them?"

"There's a Pip Boy's near here, or a NAPA, or an O'Reilly out in town."

"I want some red dice with white dots, like they have in the Las Vegas Casinos."

"Sir, I'm sure they have them at those fine establishments," he said not wanting to seem rude, but also wanting to get out of my room as soon as possible. You could see it all over his face. I set him at unease. He'd probably talk about me to his goons in the elevator, saying how all these rich types that he had spent his entire life serving were nothing more than a bunch of fringe psychos.

"Well, sir, do enjoy the car. We must be going."

I shut the door on them. My phone rang again, but this time I answered it. I didn't bother to look at the caller ID, if I had it would have saved me a bunch of hassle and heartache. The voice on the other end was distressed like she had just misplaced a baby.

"Father's dying," the voice said.

I gulped quickly, choked back the emotions that threatened me, "Dying, like it's the end?"

"He's battled the cancer for as long as he can, Jackson."

"Where's he got it now?"

"All over."

"Hannah, where are you at now?"

"Sheldon and I are with him. Come here now."

"Don't know if I can do that. The book and all."

"Jackson, you have to come. He's told us he needs to see you."

"He's not still smoking, is he?"

"Yes."

"Well not much to do about it now," I said.

"Jackson, are you coming?"

"I'll get back at you."

The voice on the other end didn't say anything. I probably sounded rude and insensitive, but it didn't change anything.

I didn't like my father. I mean he was a good enough person, he clothed me and kept me fed until the time when I was supposed to go off to college and follow in his footprints, that well blazed trail he paved for me at country club parties, and the supper club, the business he established, where he had a creepy portrait of himself in stark black and creamy blues, looking like a puritan undertaker, or Death himself, and the artist even included in the painting my father's trademark cigarette, because when my father came up men were men and could smoke in public and women were women and boys were boys and didn't ask questions they didn't want the answers to.

The cigarette didn't cut through the stress of a life lived in blind pursuit of the American Dream - well you could say that he had achieved the American Dream. He was dying in an enormous house, and this was not only his one and only house, but really the house he was choosing to die in, his favorite house, with a private medical staff and on-call painkillers. My sister, Hannah, the woman on the other end of the line, said that my father would probably lose consciousness soon, as the cancer was "all over." It was probably in his brain as well, metastasizing through his body, gaining its nourishment from the blood and healthy tissues, strangling the veins, killing the host and itself, nihilism as a bundle of cells.

I didn't want to see him. I didn't want to see how horrible he would look, wasted away by at least a year of the disease, worst of all fighting bravely for no reason at all other than to stave off death for another day. And death for him would be a reprieve, a relief. I called my sister back. I found the courage after sitting there on the mattress and listening to see if Marcus Hanely would come back into the room from the balcony where he had been hiding. I was very frank and unconcerned when I spoke with my sister on the phone.

"I will consider coming," I told her in hushed and gravely tones, trying desperately to make it seem that I had not the slightest concern about our father's predicament.

"You'll just consider it? You need to come."

"Can you just put him on the phone?"

"Jackson, come here. He can't speak, really. He lost his voice a few days back. He writes messages now on a little pad of paper. It will have to be soon, if you're coming. Please come soon. I know your relationship with father was strained, Jackson, but please come...."

"Nothing of the sort!" I said fiercely, interrupting her.

"We've grown quite close, since I've been taking care of him," Hannah said.

"You mean, arranging his care," I said. "You aren't exactly his chief surgeon."

"Yes. Arranging his care."

The bitch was trying to get at the money from the will, trying to ingratiate herself to him and get him to sign everything over to him and her schlep husband Sheldon. I wouldn't bother to tell her my feelings. She probably knew them already. I hadn't talked to her for at least a year. If I had just let the phone ring or tossed it down the toilet when she called, I could have saved myself tons of trouble. I could have remained in my isolation, my writer's block, and my cynicism could have grown like a weed in my soul to a level of unmanageability heretofore seen only in total misanthropic hermits who lived alone in the woods in the outer reaches of Montana. I was not a misanthrope. I loved people...at least that's what I told myself.

I met Marcus downstairs in the lobby. He sat in the faux library bar in which they had a bunch of junk and forgotten old looking novels on the bookshelves, probably purchased from some reader of junk fiction's estate sale or maybe the flea market. His head was buried in a Knitting magazine. He dropped it as I passed by and followed me.

"The Russian hit men gone? Did you manage to convince them that I wasn't around? Did they get anything out of you?"

"They weren't Russians. They worked for the auction company."

The front desk lady looked askance at me, with her arms folded across her lap. She raised her lip as if to say something and then just let it fall unsaid in a frown. As I departed the double doors that whooshed open, I glared at her. A car pulled up into the roundabout, and skittish Hanely dove behind a faux Roman column expecting a hail of gunfire from late KGB issue Makarov pistols and Czechoslovakian Skorpion machine pistols. It was not the KGB; it was Mr. O'Shaughnessy with his two overgrown goons again. He held a copy of *Asymmetric Hearts* in his hands, which appeared to be a first edition. "Can you autograph this for me? My wife absolutely loves your book, and I drove all the way home to get it before you left."

"Sure," I said. "Glad she's a fan."

I scrawled 'YOU TASTE LIKE HONEYDEW' and signed illegibly, but not quite and O'Shaughnessy stupidly looked at my signature and closed it up, snapped it really crisply like he knew what I wrote, but when he held out his hand for me to shake it I know his wife would get the blunt end of the surprise. I almost wished I had put my number down with my signature, out of hopes that she would call on some late night while Mr. O'Shaughnessy was out with his two goons making collections and that he would come home and into the room while I was mid-stroke on his plump wife, and I would only hear the shotgun shell being racked into the chamber before blasted my head and sent my brains all over the wall, ending my miserable existence, but also bringing about his own ruination, a double death. Hanely was man enough to bed multiple women during a single day, he could be in the back door while a woman's husband left the front door, on his way to whatever tediously boring office job he did to buy stuff for the kiddies, all the while Marcus Hanely was making his wife feel like a million bucks well spent making profit. I've never know him to have been caught, but I was pawed from my fantasy by the realization that my own father this very moment was suffering and dying in some dumpy home on the outskirts of Denver, Colorado, or was it Omaha, Nebraska, or was it Peoria, Illinois. No one could keep much track of him these days, and I hadn't bothered to ask my sister where I should actually go. The old bastard had so many homes all over the place that I should have probably asked her. I only assumed that he was going to choose the one in Denver, Colorado, to die in, but maybe he wanted to see the view of the river and the changing trees in Peoria, Illinois, or maybe, just maybe a big cornfield in Nebraska. He could have been outside of the United States too, but not likely.

O'Shaughnessy sped off in the automobile, holding in his hot little hands, which are used to adding and subtracting figures and grubbing up credit cards, my first novel, my illustrious novel complete with my dripping famous author's signature on the front cover flap. The book went from being worth about 20 bucks to being worth, oh maybe, five times that. Think of how much it will be worth when I'm dead and gone, or in the position that my father is now in. Hanely stepped back from the faux Roman Column assured that the former KGB hit squad was not in possession of Makarovs, which they were looking to ventilate him with.

"Close call, bro," Marcus said.

"No, that was the bill collector. He was a fan."

"You call that guy a fan? He had pure profit motive written all over him."

"His wife was a fan."

"I bet, probably one of those bored and horny hundreds of housewives who absolutely loved your first novel."

"Fuck off, Marcus."

"Believe me, I tried," he said with a smile and exploded into peals of laughter.

"We've got to find my car," I told him.

"There's probably only one Pontiac Judge around here. It's probably parked with the rest of the cars, under something, in case of a hailstorm."

"I doubt that. Insurance probably stipulates...."

"You've got the keys, right?"

"No, it's a robotic car. We don't need keys."

"Score!"

"Of course I have the keys, right here." I showed him the keychain with the dangly pink rabbit's foot.

"You got to lose that keychain, bro. People are going to think you're queer."

"Fuck 'em."

"Well at the very least we have to thoroughly check the car to make sure the Russians didn't put a bomb into it."

"Ukrainians."

"Yeah, whoever. We got to make sure those third world fucks aren't trying to assassinate us."

"Why would they want to do that?"

"Not only are the Russians tremendous novelists, they're also tremendous plastiquers."

"Why do the Ukrainians want us dead?"

"If I told you the things I did to that woman...my god, you'd want me dead, too."

"We should probably get out of town, then."

"Sooner, rather than later."

"Yeah, we're going to drive to my dad's house."

"Which one? Ha!"

"He's dying."

"Oh shit, sorry. You're going to say goodbye, right? Stake your claim?"

"I don't give a fuck about the money."

"Right. Well it's about time he croaked; he's been hanging on for years. Creepy."

"Six months," I said.

"How do you feel about it?" Hanely asked.

We walked up to the tent of cars, each one unpurchased or unclaimed and gleaming. They reflected the light off the seashore, which crashed and beat the rocks three hundred meters beyond the edge of the back patio. The wind blew my edgewise hair onto my brow. My visage reminds me of my father's own youthful appearance in photographs. He was a handsome man. He came from a time when the world made sense and he would grab me into his young, strong arms and his blue eyes would look just like the blue of the horizon, the blue of the connecting point between sea and sky. I stop, stand in the exact spot and Hanely walks forward toward the car we have purchased, a dead thing really, with the keys hot in my pocket. The car, parked by its lonesome, dead black and blazing orange, it was sure to elicit some stares and screams when we drove this hell wagon up the road. But I suddenly did not care about the means of conveyance we would take, I just knew we had to get there. I spent the last five years since the publication of my novel *Asymmetric Hearts* being a right selfish prick, alone, isolated, not fielding a phone call, sitting in an all white room, trying to mimic the genius of Momo Chang, staring at the sea, watching the whitecaps crash against the scraggly brown rock, composed itself of millions of little dead creatures, millions and millions of years dead. Why this planet should stink! Even the ground beneath my feet is rotten, decayed vegetable matter and dead animals getting constantly consumed and shit out, and they all had their time under the sun, and I have my time now and I'm wasting it! I'm wasting it!

My cell phone rang; it rang with the vibrations against my leg, as it had shifted since I started walking. I did not want to answer it, fearing bad news. I looked at the caller ID. It was my agent. The right bastard always saw fit to interrupt a moment of transcendental beauty with his petty marketplace schemes and the need to talk business. He zapped me from my metaphysical speculations on beauty and life and death and the organic totality of all life, a possible connection between everything, the secret to love, of the face of God, interrupted...smashed to doomsday by business. I answered the phone as Hanely kicked the tires to the Judge and looked underneath the frame for foreign objects and wires, which might indicate detonators attached to C4 or RDX and wired to the starter.

"Hello," I said.

"Holy Hell, Jacks, you're downright impossible to get a hold of," he said all Harvard Yard tied and suited up. He was probably talking to me from the speaker-phone of his Bentley. The background seemed all washed out and refined noise. He called me Jacks from the first time he met me. These efficiency types spoke in mono-syllables for fear that oxygen would start costing them pennies and lying would soon have to be written off in taxes.

"I'm embarking on a really creative period, so I have to be hard to get a hold of," I said, non-committal and sort of monotone, but on purpose.

"Yeah, Jacks, you just stay in that creative mood. I'm just letting you know that *Asymmetric Hearts* has been translated into Latvian and Russian, and the Russian publisher wants you to do an appearance."

"Where?"

"Somewhere over in Russia. I don't have the specifics yet."

"Should I bring Marcus with me?"

"Funny, Jacks!"

"He hasn't been to Russia, yet," I said, smiling at Marcus who immediately began giving me the sign for who the fuck is that. "I tell you what Mr. Tannenbaum, I really have to go and see my father. He isn't doing well, so we'll be disposed until he, well, uh, dies."

"Oh dear, Jacks."

"Yeah. Should be soon."

"Oh I'm sorry."

"No need. He's old."

"Where will you be going, Jacks? If you don't mind me asking."

"No problem. I don't know yet. Don't know where he's hiding out."

"Well is it possible that you can come here to New York City and meet with me before you see your father? I'll fly you first class."

"Can Marcus come? Can you get him a first class ticket, too?"

"Uh...."

"I don't fly, bro. I don't want my balls touched on or any ionizing radiation in my scrotal area."

"Yeah...on second thought, we don't fly. We'll drive there after I get done with my father. I'll be in touch."

"Jacks, we really have to talk, man!"

"Sorry, just no time. We're getting ready to leave any minute now."

"Wait, I'll fly you to your father's, then fly you out here."

"Nope. It's settled. We're driving."

"Just make sure you make it on time."

"To my father's?"

"Yeah, Jacks. Of course."

"Don't worry. I'll drive like a madman, Mr. Christmas Tree."

"Ha! Hilarious! Tannenbaum. Christmas Tree. You're a funny guy, Jacks. I wouldn't expect anything less. Hah, hah, kidding Jacks. Be safe."

"Thanks."

"Sorry to trouble you, Jacks, but uh, just how far are you on the sequel to *Asymmetric Hearts*?"

"Ahh, the real reason for you calling me comes out. No need to act like you care, you should really just be more direct and businesslike."

"Sorry, but you know, Jacks, the publisher is putting tremendous pressure on me. That's what I do. I shield you from the publisher."

"Okay, great. Tell them you're making progress."

"Are you making progress?"

"Sure, Mr. Tannenbaum."

I lied. I wasn't making any progress on some cheesy romance novel at all. In fact, it was the farthest thing on my mind.

"Yeah. Mr. Tannenbaum, tell them that I'll be more productive once my dad finally kicks the bucket."

There was a silence on the other side of the line. I enjoyed weirding Tannenbaum out. I could just imagine him fidgeting behind his big mahogany desk or behind the wheel of his wall of a Bentley, wondering how he would pay for it without me meeting my deadline. *Asymmetric Hearts* yielded for him a beautiful wife, a newborn son, while my genius only gained me miserable outings on talk shows. He got to enjoy the benefits of taking his ten percent; I wish I could cut him out of the equation. Slice him off at the knees with a samurai sword. Hanely kicked the tires again and hopped into the backseat. The leather, or perhaps it was vinyl; I had not felt it on my posterior yet, crinkled as I entered the car by opening the door. The hinge needing oil squeaked highly, like the shriek of a schoolgirl upon seeing a famous band member. A security guard ran up to us shrieking and waving his arms like a madman hell-bent on ritual murder.

"Run him over!" Marcus ordered.

"What the hell are you doing?" The security guard yelled.

"It's my ride, dude. Back off."

"Yeah, you fucking rent a cop, get lost," Hanely, added.

"Let me see the keys."

I showed him, and then placed them into the ignition. The engine roared to life after coughing twice. Then it died with a gasp.

"They don't keep any gasoline in these cars. Just enough to get them on and off the trucks."

"Damn. Where can we get some gas at?"

"I don't know. A gas station? Most people don't usually drive these types of cars out of here."

"I'm not most people. How do they get them out of here?"

"They hire teams of people to push them onto the back of big padded semi trucks who transport the car to wherever the people who buy them want them transported."

"That's no fun."

"That's what they do."

"Cars are made to be driven."

"Women are made to be ridden!" Marcus added from the backseat.

"How much for you to get us some gas?"

"I can't abandon my post."

"Come on, we'll watch these cars for you."

"There's an Amoco a couple of blocks from here. I'm sure they'll sell you a gas can for fuel."

"Sure, man...make us walk, just make sure no one steals our ride," Marcus said.

The man ignored him, like he lacked a chip in his brain to understand or respond to sarcasm. He was probably just above Marcus's level.

Marcus could be quite an asshole when he felt that someone was inferior, which I think was most of the time, but it was often tolerated because he looked like a Greek god. People just shut up when he spoke, almost like he wasn't there. They were that terrified of him.

We spilled out of the car in a huff and walked the three blocks to the gasoline station. The attendant claimed not to have any empty gasoline cans, but would gladly sell us gasoline if we got the can somewhere else. We asked him the closest station, and he claimed it was a Valero, at least seven blocks away. Hanely suggested that we hail a cab and tried unsuccessfully to hail one. I called up Yellow Cab, and a nasty one appeared a few minutes later. Marcus was dismayed that his efforts failed. Must have been no female drivers that day.

"Don't worry, they were all busy," I told Marcus as I piled in the front seat and he in the rear.

"The other cabs?" the cabby asked.

"Yeah."

"Yep bunch of drunks need rides home, and it's only three in the afternoon. Don't drink that rot myself."

"It's poison, bro, liver rot, and you can't get it up anymore when you drink too much."

"Yep," the cabby said.

"I stopped about thirty years ago, well my brother claims I got my lifetime's worth of drinking in the first fifteen years!"

He rounded the corner, and we had the full view of the seashore. Women with children draped to their breasts waded in waist high water.

"Don't go in the water much," the cabby said. "Just part of the food chain!"

He talked incessantly.

"Don't get out much either, now that I think about it. Don't need to. I've got television. She keeps me company like a woman, but only says nice things to me. Got my dog, too. I take him to the beach sometimes, so he can get in the water. I'm just content to lay there in the sun and watch the waves come crashing in. You know my dog pulls out the Jellyfish sometimes, he don't get stung none," the Cabbie said.

The cabbie pulled into the Valero, and rang up the meter, and the lousy seven blocks cost us seven fifty. Before I could tell him to wait, he sped off, perhaps in search of a new fare. The man running the gas station, Abdullah, had a beard and a broad nose and smiled at us as we walked into the store. We didn't happen to be threatening and didn't have shotguns and ski masks on. Hanely pointed out the gasoline cans, and Abdullah told me he was from Egypt and loved California, and that the weather was nicer than his homeland, but the people were not as nice. I slapped a five in his palm and noticed how small the bill looked in his meaty hands.

"Let's walk back to the car auction, bro," Hanely said, feeling like stretching his legs out after being in the cab all scrunched up with his legs around his shoulder blades like he was a massive wine cork. "Let's walk on that trail by the beach, better yet, let's walk on the beach, maybe we'll meet some babes."

"No way. They're all home right now, at least the ones of substance, eating their Arugula and having mimosas. What do you see in these women around here anyway?"

"They're like driftwood, man. The ones not from here, they're looking to score. The ones from here are looking to score, and by the time they wash up on shore here, they're just primed, man, ready to be stripped and polished. I don't even have to talk to them."

"You don't have to talk to them anyway. If one's drunk, she'll usually just grab you, and you'll fuck anything that moves."

"No I won't."

"Sure you will, you're the terror of all cunts, the pulverizer of beef curtains, damager of drapes no matter the room they grace."

"I won't fuck a man."

"Come on now, did I call you a queen? Aren't you a tiddly bit bicurious when you look in the mirror, you narcissist?"

He walked forward in a huff and left me to lug the can by myself.

"Why are you so sensitive?" I called to him.

"I'm not. It looks like our car ran out of gas. It looks like we're broke. Image is everything."

"Image means dick."

"It's everything to women. Tell me I'm wrong."

"You are broke, Marcus. That's the truth."

"Hey, we can't look broke though. It's everything to those babes out there."

"Fuck 'em. Who wants 'em?"

"You don't?"

"Not particularly."

"When's the last time you got laid?"

"Like when? I haven't seen you with a woman in a while."

Another lie. We had gone out to Salinas together. I wanted to tell him that was because he stole most of them and then would tell me in the morning that they weren't that good, and I thought he rubbed his prowess in my face to the extent that I wouldn't even talk about being attracted to a woman without him running leaps and bounds ahead of me, pulling up her skirt with his preternatural arm and conniving her in a matter of moments that the best thing for her to do is be impaled by an out of work, penny-pinching misanthropic womanizer who would probably – no, certainly – never call her again. Why did it matter to him to pursue whoever I lusted after in my secret heart? What was he proving? A point? Marcus seemed so self assured as he walked, at least thirty feet ahead of me, acting like he did not know me, stopping to bow briefly and Shakespearean like to two rollerblading ladies who smiled at each other as they rode past his hulking frame. Marcus was trying to avoid me like I was afflicted with some plague that only poor people have, and even though Marcus was broke, and didn't have a real dime to his name, because he had the courage to turn his back on his billionaire father, he had all of his needs taken care of by the string of women he strung along. He was always careful never to be in the same place as them and told them that he was an importer, a businessman, who traveled up and down the California Coast selling designer lighting to trendy boutiques and even convinced the San Francisco Giants to purchase lighting from his company, awarding him the one time bonus of 15 million dollars on the contract. This was a wondrous fib, a colossal lie. He became so practiced in this routine that he would, go so far as to learn the specifications of concert and stadium lighting, the lights and all of their frequency levels and candela powers that he would have been a convincing actual salesman of lighting. That position would preclude him from being a total petulant scumbag.

Funny. I had never really heard anything that Marcus said to a woman, all of his victories would be self-proclaimed, and I only saw that he would whisper something to them and they would leave together. Quickly. He would tell me about some babe he met, that he was passionately in lust with, that he already 'nailed', in his words, not mine, and that a few days later he felt that he would be all by himself all over again, because there was some small flaw with her such as one breast was slightly smaller than the other one, or his dooziest of doozies he told me that she had a highly annoying laugh.

"But you made her laugh, Marcus," I would say.

"I know, but she laughed at everything I said, and I think it was her way of compensating for having an emotionally unavailable father," Marcus said.

He was a pop psychologist, and while he could read a person's soul, he was ill equipped to explain anything at any great depth. He just had an intuitive sense, especially about me. He walked ahead and turned a bend, which passed through seaside vegetation, down a hillside, and onto a brown and mucky sand beach. Marcus walked to where the surface and the sand met and kicked his feet into the water like he was looking for something underneath the surface of the sand. Sometimes I felt that he was missing something, he was a substitute father ever since that stern lecture he gave me about drinking cyanide in my dorm room. When I walked up to him, he was visibly shaken.

"You see this beach here? It's empty. It's dead. Yet, still it has more than I do," he said.

"Whatever, man. Stop thinking too much. When you decide to do something, you'll be great at it."

Conscience is the seducer's ultimate enemy. Marcus was getting soft. I saw evidence of his deterioration as a horny purveyor of trim everywhere. There was soon to be inspiration for my second novel, I would be as dry of ideas as the dead driftwood that graced the littered beaches of Northern California. I couldn't allow Marcus to lose his graces, his wonderful God given gift to breed, or at least practice at it, the fusion of the body of a Greek god with the sex drive of that plucky South Australian marsupial. And who was I to think that what Marcus was doing was wrong? Maybe I was just jealous of him. The tales of his exploits made women in the forty-eight continental United States do a finger tap dance on their collective clitorii for hours.

While the pornography of men is visual, that of the stronger sex is programmed by words, and therefore only a Cyrano such as Marcus, coupled like mating baboons screwing in the Savannah with his absolute lack of any sense of wrongdoing, he echoed that all is fair in love and war.

He would have made an excellent general or conqueror, but he was born eons too late. We continued our walk, leaving moist footprints in the soft sand, not saying much of anything. When the gas can got heavier, I switched hands to the hand I normally masturbated with and found it had more endurance for lifting heavy objects than my weak hand.

Hanely's hands were equally strong, because he never masturbated. He had no need to practice that lonely and pathetic art, he said. But the art is not lonely, for I am a participant with myself, and I am delving into the limits of my sexual consciousness without the associated moanings and quibblings of having to please a stranger or loved one, or so I told myself at the time as I was four beers into an eight beer night and a hangover the next morning. That was day five of my latest ten day binge, where I usually forget everything that happens and Hanely reiterates story after painful story of his conquests to me, and I fiercely write in notebooks the very next day over lunch and margaritas.

When we got to the car, Hanely jumped in the backseat again. He never drove, except to wreck my secretly hated Ferrari. I don't know if he even has a license to drive or if he believes driving with his knees while gagging a flight attendant on your gherkin is appropriate for achieving orgasm. He never drives, not even from the airport parking lot, and his pockets always seem to have a copious amount of money, and he dresses in all the best clothing from all the best stores, the ones with all the strange girls with piercings and tattoos all over their pasty skin. I am convinced that he might be a gay hustler because women don't need to pay for sex; they can go to any bar, any auto repair shop, any college campus and immediately become the pincushion if they so choose. The men have to scrounge and pay, and lie and cheat, and if they so desire, go slumming, though I refuse to do it.

I poured the gasoline into the automobile careful to avoid sloshing MTBE on the black finish. Never start a novel without a title in mind, and never start a car that has been sitting for perhaps years, without first allowing the fuel to work its way through the assorted tubes and pumps that make the car operate. I don't know their officially agreed upon terms, nor do I care. I jumped into the front seat and revved the car engine and pressed the accelerator.

The black and orange trimmed Judge sounded like a chorus of bass singing demon children, and I laughed with delight at the security guard's anguished face, perhaps he lamented his choices in life and how he would never drive a car like I was driving. Perhaps he placed an extreme value on the car he drove, like most Americans, which was most likely inferior to the car, which I now drove. Perhaps he was appalled at my decision to drive the car away, to drive it at all, and instead wanted to insist that I treated it as a delicate paperweight. Whatever, I don't care, and I laugh at people who tell me that I should not drive this car cross-country, much less wreck a Ferrari at a whim. Hanely and I are of the same mindset. We would rather use weak moralism as a placemat because it was the appropriate size. I gunned it and tore through downtown Monterey to the horror of the inhabitants who mainly looked up from walking their little dogs to see what they thought was some notorious Hollywood insider up for crab claws, and instead they saw me clutching at the wheel with murder in my eyes and Hanely demonic in the backseat guffawing.

"Which way?"

"Don't you want to go home first and pack something?"

"No, we've got to hit the road and hit it hard."

"I'll stop off at the house, I've got to pack."

"No, we'll buy clothing from gas stations and truck stops, just live off the fat of the land."

"Where's your dad at? That will determine everything. We'll be traveling out into the great unknown, getting information for your great American romance novel, and visiting your dear old about to die, dad."

"I'll have to call my sister."

"You keep avoiding her."

"Just call her. No going home. We're not taking anything with us."

"Why not?"

"I want this journey to be a pure expression of an individual's search for freedom."

"You want to be truly free, you're going to have to kill me," Marcus said.

"I wouldn't do that, Marcus."

"I know. I'm just playing."

"I'll kill you, then," I said.

"So, no clothing."

"Yes, we buy what we need on the road, and in the meantime, I write."

"Sure thing," and I go about getting your stories for you, just like old times.

"Just like old times, bro."

"We kill two birds with one stone...."

"I know you told me," I said cutting him off at the proverbial pass before all sorts of meaningless baloney spilled out.

"...We see your father off to Valhalla or Heaven or whatever you Leman's believe in, and we find and fornicate with as many women as humanly possible, all the while you record it in your celebration of human life and possibility, *Asymmetric Hearts 2*."

"Please, I'm not doing another *Asymmetric Hearts*. It's dead."

"If you want to keep this lifestyle of yours, bucko, you're going to do it."

"Good ole Marcus Hanely will regret ever being born. The literary Marcus Hanely, of course."

Marcus Hanely wasn't exactly the best code name for a secret agent, but then again neither was Marcus Hanely suited to be a secret agent because he could not keep his dick in his pants. I abandoned my research into tradecraft when I realized that all a secret agent needed in fiction was a well chiseled face, chiseled biceps, a killer smile, a Walther PPK, or in Hanely's case a semiautomatic weapon of unspecified caliber that had mother of pearl grips and shot golden bullets straight into the hearts of women everywhere. He disarmed arch villains by getting into the pants of their wives, sisters, girlfriends and at the end of the novel, the forty five year old mother of the Terrorist Abu Mohammad to whom she revealed his fiendish plot to blow up Mecca and blame it on a gang of Crusading Infidels. World Crisis averted, with plenty of steaminess. Sex will cure all your afflictions, including old age.

In the entire time I knew Marcus, he did not really age. Nary a hair fell out of his well-tousled head. I, on the other hand, am falling to pieces, the wind blowing my hair through the window reveals a growing bald patch which will mean that eventually I have to be one of those creepy young bald guys who have to cover up for genuine baldness, with faux baldness and artificially pumped up muscles, because a skinny bald guy only looks like a concentration camp victim or cancer patient.

I pulled into the long, windy driveway after pressing my security code and made note of the crumpled Ferrari in the corner of the property. A family of seagulls had made a nest of it, squawking wildly at the perturbations in the leather and one got to sit in the plush leather seat, which served as a sort of throne to an uncrowned king amongst them. Wastrel, I am, but at least I don't bring other people in the world to share in its misery. My maid smoked a cigarette on the front porch, one of those long spindly fashionable death sticks.

"Call my sister at her number, 373 799 7095, and find out where she is. She's a disagreeable woman who will talk for hours if you let her, so find out where my father is and hang up. Remain noncommittal to me coming there."

"Yes, sir," she said, taking a few more drags off her slim cigarette.

"Consuela," I said.

"Yes, sir," she said, looking up.

"If I die, this place is yours. You and your daughter can have it."

"Why would you die, sir? Where are you going?"

"Wherever my sister tells you, and then possibly New York City."

"You want me to pack a bag for you?"

"No thanks."

"You better pack a jacket at least?"

"No. We have to be able to blend in with the enemy out there."

"What are you talking about? What enemy?"

"Just remember, no questions, and if I don't come back, the place is yours."

I went inside and looked underneath my mattress. I found the hollowed out space with my walking around money, totaling about three thousand bucks in hundreds, and a Colt Government Issue 1911 A1 pistol manufactured around 1911. The dealer even guaranteed that this particular pistol had belonged to an officer who had turned and run in the face of the last cavalry charge ever recorded but his discarded pistol was picked up by a plucky private who used it to gun down fifteen German war horses trapped in barbed wire. The pistol was great at putting things out of their misery. It had no real distinguishing marks other than it looked really old, and was a piece of genuine Americana. Still, I had never fired it. I bought it intending to blow away scores of bottles, like in an old cowboy film, but never really got around to it. I put the masterblaster in the back of my pants, because I knew that people often blew their dicks off by putting the pistolays in the front of their pants in the movies. I walked outside and noticed that Hanely sat lecherously in the backseat, ogling the maid, who pretended not to notice. He even made squeezing motions with his hands and licked his lips like a lecherous defrocked priest in a Chuck E. Cheese's, a politician rooting through a barrel of ill gotten war kickbacks, or a gouty man getting rimmed by a midget, happy that he didn't have to bend over fully.

"Stop it, sicko," I said as I piled into the car.

"Please don't go," Consuela said.

"I have to."

"Where is he? Did you call?"

"Denver."

I fired up the car and put it in reverse.

"Jackson," she said.

"What? You're acting like we're lovers or something."

She didn't say anything in response.

I backed up the car. "I'm scared for you," she called out.

"I'll be fine."

Hanely cheered me onward into our encounter with oblivion, the wide-open American road. He gleamed like a madman in the backseat, a backseat he knew and proclaimed would soon be full of women, babes of Montana, the Midwest, Utah, Poughkeepsie.

"We can probably get to Reno, Nevada, the first night."

"Drive past Tahoe?"

"Yes, through the damned Garlic fields of Gilroy."

"That route will take us through Utah."

"Godforsaken place."

"Absolutely gorgeous."

"Yeah, used to be a sea, that dried up."

I drove down Del Monte Avenue honking my horn at every woman we passed. Many walked dogs, pulling the leashes close, their obedient doggies minding their masters with noses to the hard ground. I longed to pull the babes' attention away that maybe one of them would want to run away with us, in our mad dash across the countryside, want to be both of our lovers, maybe at the same time.

"I got a plan, bro," Hanely said.

Anything that would come afterwards would be maniacal.

"Stop in Salinas, man."

"No way. We're not going to see Rita and her friends again. We want to get to Denver in one piece."

The coast ripped past us and I swear I could see dolphins amongst the whitecaps before we turned away from the sea permanently towards the interior. It was this interior where I conducted my surveys for my first novel, what the bored and horny Midwestern housewives of the world wanted to read. I advertised my survey on all of the Romance novel forums on the Internet and surveys poured into my email... romancestory@gmail.com. They thought it was a marketing survey, and I promised them that a future romance novel would be fashioned from their responses. I turned onto the 101, the interior went agricultural and I saw the poor migrant workers harvesting artichokes by the bucketful under the hot sun. California has the best land in the world to grow crops. It is a country in itself. You have lettuce, grapes, garlic, and artichokes, which were my favorite. If you put me in a tub of marinated artichokes, I would eat my way out of it, brine would coat my testicles and preserve them for future generations because I will probably never sire children. Women find me repulsive, and Hanely steals them all anyway.

"Say, why do you meet these chicks off the Internet?" Hanely asked.

"It's too easy."

"How do you do it?"

"I just post my photo, maybe a shot of me with my shirt off in the mirror, and they just flock to me."

"Well no shit, women flock to you in real life."

"The Internet is real life, it's just an interface, you need to stop thinking it's some virtual world."

"But people don't act like they do in real life," I said.

"Again, stop with the real life. It's a digital veil, man. That's it. You can pick out a psycho on the Internet just as easily as you can in real life."

"There, you said it, too," I said laughing.

"Are you going to stop in Salinas?"

"No."

"Why not?"

"I don't want to see Rita again."

"Why not?"

"Not after she introduced us to her nineteen year old daughter and her daughter introduced us to her in prison father's motorcycle and fucking Hell's Angels gear."

"Ahh, so what. He's in ten to twenty."

"He'll get paroled and come after us."

"Yeah, I don't want to see her anymore anyway. Her daughter's better."

"You sick bastard, you didn't."

"I didn't. Not yet."

"We can't stop. We have to push on. We're pushing on to Reno."

"Come on, stop."

A man whose penis is dead set on a piece of pussy becomes a wild beast, especially a testosterone freak like Hanely. He has permanent 'roid rage. Nature designed him to lay waste to the female populace. I am certain that if he were born in past millennia he would have been a most excellent Viking raider or Conquistador. However, he wouldn't have needed to rape and pillage the foreign babes; they would have delivered the men's heads on plates like that succubus Salome and made the funeral marches only after he breached the castle's defenses and sent the moat a gushing down the parapets.

We celebrate women because we wish to possess them, tame the wildfires, and in an antiquated mentality, we celebrate the prowess of men because we also wish to possess that prowess, and by that very prowess, possess the women. The hottie Helen launched a thousand ships and Achilles brought them home after first dying a horrible death, or perhaps it was Odysseus, I don't rightly remember. I just know that war provides wonderful opportunities for plunder. In this sense, Hanely was Achilles, and I was that sensible Agamemnon, secure in my knowledge of my rights.

"Stop in Salinas," he barked in an order.

"No."

"Fucking do it!" he screamed.

With the heat from his balls high on his brain, Hanely screamed, "JD Salinger used the word phony to describe people like you!"

"I'm no phony," I quipped in my defense. If anything Hanely was a phony, like most everyone today, a bullshitter. He bullshitted his way through life, and stupid women fell for him like they were dung beetles in the Savannah, glommering over a turd. If you listen and spit out opinions that confirm their preconceived notions, they will love you for it, call you a good listener, and fuck your brains out after 2.5 dates, one date, or no dates in the case of Marcus Hanely. I fucking hate him. I hate him. I hate him....

"Dude, you had better pull over this goddamn car," he said, and grabbed my arm. The car swerved, almost slamming into a minivan containing a family who looked at us out their glass aquarium in horror. The minivan actually went into the median and sent the sand flying into the air like an airplane lawn-darted into it.

"You fuck! You almost killed us!"

"No, I almost killed them back there!"

"Get your goddamn filthy dick beaters off me, Marcus!"

"No, stop in Salinas, man. I'm due."

The exit towards Salinas passed us by. When it was in the rearview mirror, Hanely glowered, his jaw twitched, like he wanted to murder me. He'd be in rough sorts now. He had to sit still now and be a passenger. Unable to get his daily fix of women, he'd just have to sit there and suffer. He reared back and punched me in the arm hard; trying to release whatever nascent sexual frustration he had built in his ball sack. Men turn to violence when their wills are truncated. He glowered again. I reached under the seat and pulled out my .45 and jammed it in his side.

"Don't you ever touch me again, you big fucking ape. We're going to go and see my father die. We're not stopping in Salinas. I don't give a fuck if the whole fucking Dos Equis and Corona Beer Latina Fuck Team is there giving freebies. We're not going there so you can get your rocks off with some married slut looking to step out on her Hell's Angel boyfriend. Give it a fucking rest."

"You're totally lucky your dad is ailing, or I'd take that gun and shove it up your ass."

I turned my eyes back to the road, and we came out of the rolling hills into the forest near Santa Cruz. I kept my eyes on the road ahead. I drove nearly to San Francisco before I heard a peep out of the backseat. I had almost forgotten that he was there.

Now, I don't often threaten my friends with loaded guns, but it has been a time of extreme stress for me. Hanely should have realized that. He was too demanding sometimes. I would hate to be a woman around him. Still, though, he had an uneasy charm about him. He was the basis of my bestselling novel, but I have probably told you that before. He did not ask me the reason I brought the piece. I figured that knowing Marcus and his penchant for trouble with the two Bs, the Bs that get men into trouble the world over, the source of all masculine troubles, and if a man could just cut them out of his life, he'd be a happy man indeed…booze and bitches. I don't know if we'll need my masterblaster. Had I went to Salinas, though, I might have. Salinas is loaded with banditos. Still, what's America without a gun, anyway?

I didn't consider stopping in San Francisco. I didn't have the patience to find parking and if we were to ever make it to Reno I would actually have to burn the road. The Judge guzzled and burned gasoline like an old pyromaniac boozer. I stopped just north of Frisco, at a Valero, chintzy on the outside, probably in a bad neighborhood. A crowd of gawkers came and looked at the car. The best way to make friends in these United States is to have an uncommon fancy car. It took fifty-five dollars worth of gasoline, 93 octane, and kept rising. I sensed the reek of gasoline everywhere around me, and if one of the gawkers had lit a cigarette then the entire place may have exploded. Hanely looked on from the back seat like a big, stupid child. It seemed he had developed a phobia of getting out of the car.

"Got a leak, son," an old man, dressed up like a hillbilly, or maybe he was a mid-northern California hillbilly said, with his thumbs thrusting his OshKosh B'goshes outward in self assurance. On second thought, perhaps he was a train fetishist.

I looked at my feet. Gasoline was pooling everywhere.

"Oh shit!" I yelled. I envisioned myself psychotically lighting a newspaper and throwing it into the gas pool, letting Marcus cook inside the car. Instead, I ripped the pump from the hole, angrily.

"You got to be careful with these old cars, son," the train fetishist said. "There isn't any natural reverse to them. The tank don't taper like the modern cars, boy. You better wipe off that gas, it'll ruin that pretty finish you got."

"I just got this car," I told him, when I really wanted to tell him to please not call me boy and ask him why he liked trains so much.

I walked into the gas station. A cheerful melody, I think it was an Andrews Sisters song, played in the background.

"I spilled some gas out there, man," I told the portly attendant, with muttonchops and a pomp, obviously a rockabilly singer or Elvis imposter.

"How much gas we talking'?" he asked.

"A metric shit ton," I said sheepishly expecting him to flip out and say he had to call a DHS Hazmat team who would have an EPA Adjuster declare the gas station a Superfund site, and I would have to pay for it all.

"I'll have to put some spill absorber on it. No biggie. Just pull your car forward."

"You got a towel? I got to clean up the car's exterior."

"Go in the bathroom. Paper towels 'r in there."

I walked into the men's restroom. The smell overpowered me, and as I entered I half gagged and coughed. Someone, some sicko, struggled in the latrine. I looked for the towels and my vision clouded. Someone, some nefarious degenerate, had drawn a large, veiny cock on the restroom wall and had written "Big Un" underneath it. I had no time to think about its significance, nor time to write underneath, "that's quite small." I don't know how I became so sidetracked in the shit storm, like I cannot filter the unimportant from the important. I grabbed, blindly, twenty or so towels, pulling them from the dispenser like I was pulling the guts from a great beast in an attempt to save a damsel in distress, but there were no damsels anymore and no real distress, only my own at the thought of the shit particles entering my body. A turd, a sizeable plunker, plopped into the toilet, and I bolted with my stash, perilously afraid to see the maker. I held the towels against my body, like a precious golden horde of ingots. When I went outside, Hanely barked at me from the window, "Should've went to San Fran! We should've turned off the 80 at Fremont!"

My reticence to driving to San Francisco was marked by wanting to see her again, because I had heard that she was there. Veronica Autobody. How many times had I headed up the 101 with her on my mind, burning in my loins, to be with a woman, not to have her, for any mere lecher can possess, but to be in her presence, enjoying her company, that's what we had: platonic love. But she said it didn't exist, and she drew me in close to her lips and kissed me in Sausalito. It was oysters that did it, a cliché, but a cliché with her, spewed from her lips was poetry. She kissed me as we walked back to my Ferrari. And Marcus called her a gold digger and said I should get rid of her. Hanely often said, do not seek out tame civilized women, you will find a wild woman and breed her to insure your sons are strong and immune to danger. Hanely's sons, his bastard progeny (if he had any bastard progeny), will eventually come to rule the world. Nature is his dictate, and the laws of attraction followed even in the smallest subatomic particles are his conscience; Hanely is one with the universe. Safe marriages are best to be cuckolded; safe marriages are artificial like saccharine and cheap like plastic, not sweet like honey and wholesome as a lion. The best gold is rough-mined from jagged rocks. So I say, I should follow Hanely's dictates, stick and move and love and lust like there is no tomorrow, otherwise I will end up scared of my own shadow, not looking into the intensity of the sun's corona and the beautiful day, but focused on my own small, insignificant little shadow. I will come to dwell in the shadows. The strong dwell in the sunshine and dance naked on beaches unafraid of their sinewy bodies. They are children of warmth. I would give everything to be released from the bonds of my prison and step outside my own mind.

"We've got women to plow in Reno," Marcus shouted, urging me to get in the car.

Maybe it was the gasoline fumes that sent me on my wild tangential. I had wiped clean the car's surface, and came to just as fatty Elvis waddled to put down the fuel absorber. I pulled the car forward, and then gunned it, leaving the tires smoking, and Marcus laughed great roars from the bottom of his hellish lungs and flipped fatty Elvis the bird.

Six hours later we were in the desert, speeding towards that imaginary border with Nevada. We left the clustered hell of material cities and all of the strip malls behind. When we hit Reno, Nevada, we would stop at the first flop house we saw and work our way from cathouse to cathouse sticking and moving until the sun came up and we sped across the boring states of Utah and Wyoming, until we headed south towards Denver. I wish we would have flown sometimes, but that would mean being jammed slammed into an airport with the rest of the piglets, strangled and corralled onto the plane and shumped off through the air over the desert and mountains and how much we would have missed, and of course, I couldn't bring my gun or anything remotely dangerous with me, not even a lighter, and I didn't slightly even look Arab. Hanely's assortment of dildos and butt plugs, anal beads, ticklers, Symbian machines, penetrators and sex toys would have surely been confiscated.

For fuck's sake, airports suck. They are hell, bought and paid for in the name of efficiency and convenience, anathema to any artistic sensibility, loaded with corporate art and junk to shuffle tourists out quickly. They are the repositories of art school projects and similarly, Tic Tacs, bric a brac bullshit.

The automobile is the quintessential American invention, and the road trip, with these two males fucking their way across the landscape, is even more quintessential. Hanely and I are modern cowboys, maybe even pirates, more piratical than any outlaw biker revving his all beef rocket hell-bound across the prairie. There is safety in numbers, and Hanely and I only have each other and Samuel Colt living underneath my front seat, so that I can kill at least seven of the bloodsuckers before I have to reload. Thank God we didn't pick up any of those boring biddies in Monterey, keen to nest and offer two maniacs a modicum of stability.

"Turn on the radio, bro," Hanely said.

He seemed to have forgotten that I had just shoved Sam Colt in his face and wasn't in the mood to take his orders. He was contrite in fact and maybe he didn't want the entire West Coast Chapter of the Hell's Angels after him, nipping at our heels after he dipped his well-worn wick into the Salinas Hell's Angels Chapter President's wife. He would get over it and forget all about my refusal by the time we got to Reno.

I flipped the radio on. All the FM channels seemed to be playing the same thing: bland rock. The only good channel you can find on the FM anymore is the lonely college channel, and in order to find that you have to be near an actual college that does not attract drones seeking corporate jobs, which are few and far between. And there was none of that to be found. All of these channels were corporate, spewing pay for play spunk as fast as the computer in COMMO NODE CENTRAL could zip them out over the airwaves. A new hit, christened by the masters was merely added to the shuffle and given a tagline so it would play more frequently, at least once an hour, lulling passengers to sleep with the faint recollection, when the song played again, of "hey, didn't we just hear that?" I hope in the future that there is only one channel that plays only synth pop rock fusions and rap music that reminds me how fun it is to fuck a beautiful woman, as if anyone needed reminding of that. Most everything I hear is watered down or lame, unable to walk on its own, dead, shellacked, with no life: a massive blob that eats money and shits shit for people to pick up and declare treasure.

"No man, turn on the AM, bro," Hanely said. "FM is lame."

Hanely's word for mostly everything he said or heard, jobs he didn't want to take, as if he ever even applied for them, women he no longer wanted to see because they had passed the obligatory first fuck session, was *lame*. Everything he didn't like or enjoy, even the women he labored at seducing were lame and were discarded like cheeseburger wrappers licked clean of ketchup.

"Can't I turn on NPR?"

"Those motherfuckers don't have an affiliate out here in this wasteland; besides, I don't feel like listening to something national. If you want to hear the pulse of an area, you listen to the AM, man."

I flipped the selector on the old radio. I would have to ruin the resale value and purchase something I could stick my iPod into. What greeted our ears with delight, was a preacher. He was talking about death and the good life, but not in those terms. That is what his rant boiled down to, but the packaging was apocalyptic fire and brimstone. Hanely and I laughed out loud at this desert madman, who probably wandered off alone at some point, eating locusts and honey from the dripping hives of wild bees and getting his beard and cardboard clothing full of knots and gnarls before he came to the worldly wisdom he sought and gained the ability to preach to the choir so effectively and utter such hilarious nonsense that sent Hanely and I to the very edges of our seats in laughter.

"I wonder what this guy looks like," I said, imagining quite a pied piper.

"Does it matter?"

"I bet he's short and squat and has a two-inch-when-erect cock, and that his wuv-ley wife has left him for a traveling circus performer when she saw him packed into his tights and that he secretly adores fucking chickens."

"Yeah, religious types can't be trusted around the barnyard animals alone. History is one big entrenched pattern of psychosis and repression. That's Freud, I think."

"Yeah, man."

"Let's find something sunnier," Marcus said.

"What, Marcus? Is this getting you down?"

"I'm a horrible sinner," he said with a chuckle.

"I'll change it once he gets to the point."

"We'll just listen to the static."

"Oh he just talked about abortion and moral faggotry."

"Gays don't make babies. Leave 'em alone," I declared.

//...You're out there driving' your automobile and you don't realize that you're heading' off to...to your DOOM, you're driven' off of a cliff after which a never ending fall, straight into HELL and the clutches of SATAN you'll land burning! REPENT gentlemen, REPENT of your sins and ask the lord our gawd jeezus kah-riest into your heart and he will show you the true path, the one path, the righteous path into HEAVEN, Jesus is your savior. Let us read in the book of Romans.... //

"Turn this shit off, find some rock channel. That's my shit. Put some fucking Allman Brothers on," Hanely said.

"Let me see if I can find it. Hold on. This motherfucker is taking calls on the air. I'm going to call and see if I can get on," I said.

"Yeah, call up and donate some money to him."

I dialed on my iPhone 4S, the number. It rang and rang and rang. I pulled the car off the interstate to a dusty side road, where an abandoned gasoline station that looked like it last saw a customer in the 1940s stood ominously, but about to blow over. Tumbleweed bumped into it and stopped.

Hanely looked like he wanted to get out of the car and go investigate the ruins, but he was waiting for the outcome of my telephone call. Someone finally picked up: a female, with a husky voice, "Reverend Billy Meyers Praise Hour."

"Put me on with the Reverend."

"What's the nature of your request? Do you wish to make a donation?"

"If it will get me on the Reverend Billy Meyers Praise hour quicker...I'm a huge fan."

"Donations are no guarantee that your prayer request will be answered or that you will be able to have your testimonial played live on the air," the female said in a senatorial voice, like a record player.

"Put me in the queue, then," I said.

"Sure, you are position 47."

Reverend Billy Meyers continued railing against "faggotry" and all other types of sin, but mostly against "faggotry," even describing how he had saved a young woman who did "abominate and unconscionable things to her body with an oversized cucumber, for using food for sexual gratification, which God designed as the nourishment of the body was not only a crime against nature it was a crime against the everlasting and Almighty Gawd that saw fit to give us this cucumber as nourishment. The woman was only fit for the fires of Hell with the blasphemers and idolaters and other practitioners of that dreadful plague pulling America into the swamp, that horrid practice of moral faggotry...."

Apparently the queue was whittled down by the type of prayer request because another woman got on the line and asked me the type of prayer request I was making, who it was for, so being an author I was able to think up a great story to tell her that would surely get me right to the top of the pile.

I began, "I am a man who had my first homosexual experience at a Styx concert in 1988 during the Mr. Roboto encore, my hand brushed up against the peckerwood of the man next to me, and it lingered there, seemingly with a mind of its own and the next thing I knew I was engaged in all sorts of lusty gay acts with this gentleman in the back of the touring bus that my church group took to go to the evil rock concert in. He came with a group from his college, and it was a Christian college, and I think his name was Frank, or Tom, or Dave, I don't remember. I have been blessed not to catch the homosexual punishment of AIDS, but God has punished many of my family members for my disgusting sins and transgressions, so I finally realized that God wanted me to deliver myself from my heinous ways. The lawd helps those who help themselves, right? And I prayed and prayed and prayed and prayed and became nearly unable to move, and this happened over four or five days and I didn't eat nothing or drink nothing, really no water at all, and then I started eating mainly just Campbell's soup out of the can without heating it up, and by the 8th day I actually saw what I consider a vision of God and I heard a voice that said, 'You love women.' And I collapsed and when I awoke, I screamed, 'I love women!' And I remember I saw my first woman, I mean really saw her like a heterosexual man would see a woman, and I really looked at her various womanly parts, and I felt a powerful lust for her, and I was overjoyed that I no longer felt the urge or compulsion to see the sweaty bodies of men, I no longer gain an erection by showering with men in the gymnasium...."

"That's quite enough, sir. Why do you think the Lord healed you? It wasn't your own willpower?"

"No, it most definitely, positively was the Lord. I tried several times on my own to no avail."

"Reverend Billy is very active in homosexual conversions and will probably be very interested in your method," she said.

"Great. I'll help him end this scourge in any way I can, even if he wants to test my blood and DNA to see just where this evil came from," I told her, sounding very serious.

"I don't think that will be necessary," she said with a chuckle of the self-assured.

"Well, give us your name, sir."

I looked over at Marcus and shrugged my shoulders and mouthed the word, <<name>> to him. I motioned at him with my hands to try and get him to supply a name.

"Jose Montalban," he said with a sneer. I shook my head, no.

"Frank Geherty," I shot out with.

"Okay, Mr. Geherty."

"No, please, call me Frank."

"Okay, Frank, I'm pleased that you're going to be next after Reverend Meyers speaks with a little old lady with a question about Charles Darwin."

The Darwinist dilemma this old lady faced down, in the twilight of her years, and introduced by a grandson with a wunderkind gift for scientific exploration was summarily handled with a postulate of creation science that made the intelligent design of the universe, a place in heaven for her, and some meaning in the void all the more present. Meyers was certainly a miracle worker. The audience cheered and applauded. The woman on the other line told me to wait, and that I would hear one solid tone at the one minute mark, and three solid tones, after which I would be live on the air. I waited.

I heard the three tones, indicating I would be live, in the auditorium, with my voice piped into the tens of thousands of congregants. I looked at Marcus and gave him the thumbs up. He rocked back and forth like a little kid waiting for Christmas presents; sure he would get the red fire truck he had lusted for all year for.

BEEP BEEP BEEP

"Caller you are live on the Reverend Billy Meyers Hour of Prayer."

The feedback through the radio was enormous.

"Son, son, please turn down your radio. What are you in your car?"

"Yes, Reverend Billy," I said.

I hit the radio volume knob and nearly knocked it from the moorings.

"Son, please go ahead with your prayer request."

"Reverend Billy, I am a sinful man. I am a horrible wretch of a man. You see I have this demonic disease in me, from the age of 18, I have had an overwhelming urge to couple with other men, and I have been coupling with other men and living with other men and going to discotheques with other men, where we only wear underwear and grope each other's bodies and sometimes we...."

"Son, son, you are obviously suffering the wages of sin. You are blessed in that you realized the error of your ways. Son, let me tell you that you are not alone and that I,

Reverend Billy, have cured men with your similar affliction, your disease. I prayed with these men and guided them on the paths of righteousness, the paths of a decent Christian life, and a life with women, where they love women, and many of these men actually get married to women and love them. Son, you really need to tell us what led to your conversion, your willingness to open up you impure heart to the fountains of Jesus's love."

"Reverend Billy, my boyfriend, err, I mean my sinful relationship recently broke up with me and abandoned me for a younger man with a bigger - well you know - and he left me all alone in the world. My parents tossed me out of the house; my family members all disowned me for the life I was leading. I thought I couldn't help myself, Reverend Billy."

Marcus was nearly hysterical; he was crying he was trying to hold his laughter in so hard.

"My sinful ways caused everyone in my life to abandon me. I mean, I must be wrong, Reverend, I must be."

"Well, what is your name again?"

"Frank, Reverend Billy."

"Well, Frank, blessed child of the Lord Jesus Christ, your eternal Lord and Savior, all you have to do is let him back in. Let Jesus's love back into your heart."

"How, Reverend?" I asked, feigning innocence and a genuine concern for my mortal soul.

"All you have to say is, 'I let you, Lord Jesus, into my heart. Wash over my iniquities and heal me, Jesus. Make me whole!' Please son, pray with me. Frank, please, son, wherever you are, bow your head and pray with me."

"My head is bowed, Reverend," I said.

"Say it with me, Frank. 'As a sinner and a horrible practitioner of the black dark arts of Sodom I lived an utter falsehood, which would have condemned me to the fiery pits of hell. I have realized the error of my ways, and I seek repentance and healing in the love of Jesus Kah-Rist.'"

"This cure won't be easy, Frank. It never is easy to walk the path of the Lord, the path of righteousness; it never is easy to walk the straight and narrow path, my path, the Lord's path, the path of all these blessed people in this auditorium, and the path of the people listening in. You must commit your life to Jesus Kah-Rist in full harmony with the Holy Spirit. Are you ready to do this? Are you ready to do this, Frank?" Reverend Billy said, sounding as if he were getting choked up a few times throughout his recitation from the teleprompter.

"Reverend Billy, I am."

"Pray with me, brother," Billy intoned.

"I'm ready."

"Dearest Heavenly Father who art in Heaven, we pray today for our Brother Frank who is mired in a life of unholy sin. We pray that through the glory of your holy name he will be spared the flames of hell that are now at this very moment nipping at his knees. Bow your head, Frank. Bow your head and pray that the Lord, God, blesses you."

"Lord Bless me," I said.

"Frank, scream it, wherever you are, scream away the Devil!"

I opened up my lungs, as Hanely was turning crimson with laughter, holding onto his ribcage. "I'm going to fucking piss myself," he said, barely able to contain the whisper.

"Get behind me SATAN!" I yelled.

"Yes, Devil, get out!" Billy yelled.

"Get behind me SATAN!" I screamed more forcefully out in the middle of the desert on the Nevada/California border underneath the overpass.

"Out, SATAN! Out!" Billy yelled.

"I'm cured! I'm cured!" I screamed.

Reverend Billy jumped to his feet. "You are a free man, Frank!"

"Reverend Billy, I've got one question."

"What is your question, my son?"

"As a just recently minted heterosexual, where can I find a quality piece of pussy in Reno? I mean, the urge is overwhelming!"

Hanley could not contain himself; he burst into hysterical, maniacal laughter. I echoed his onslaught, guffawing into the phone.

"What?" Reverend Billy gasped.

I hung up the phone, slammed it in the glove box. We had about 70 miles to Reno it was approaching dusk. Apollo's chariot galloped fleetingly to the west, overtaking the bright blues, painting the desert behind us with curtains of night.

Nighttime danced in front of us like a dark lady, as she sashayed and wrapped our pea brains in her dusky embrace. We both had the itch, the spreading lust that starts in a man's mind and fills up his being with the prospect of a guaranteed triumph. I believed it was the same feeling that high Octavian had when he vanquished Marcus Antonius and his lover Cleopatra at Actium; he ruled supreme and the people of Rome declared him a god, cheering him like a modern day football player.

I imagined that Marcus and I were triumphant generals, about to meet our apotheosis. Maidens would rush from the crowd, bearing their full breasts, unlike the women on our military campaign who had to learn to love us and cried rivers of tears at our departure, worshipping our busts in our absence, we had promised to return. We would find the first cathouse on the long string of pearls that lined interstate 80 towards Denver. We would stop and have our pink, bursting in the door like two cowboys loaded down with money after driving our quarry to market. All of the women would abandon their old men and greasy lecher clients and fight over us, tearing out their hair. We drove onward into the dark desert night.

"Search for these whorehouses on your phone, man," I ordered Marcus. I was now the orderer, and he the passenger/navigator in this hell wagon to nowhere.

"You know I don't have a phone," Hanely said.

"God, you're a cheapskate."

"Give me some money from using my stories in your books," he said.

"What? You've never asked for that before," I declared.

"Yeah, pay up, motherfucker."

"I've supported you for years."

"Nah, I've supported you for years. You're a basket case, man. How many times did I talk you down from the edge?"

"You aren't being fair, Marcus."

"Fuck it, pay up. Life isn't fair, twerp."

"Lick it, Hanely."

"Fuck yourself."

"Get fucked, Marcus. I should leave you out here in the desert to die, motherfucker."

"I'd make it out of here. I can get through anything."

"I know. You'd track me down and bludgeon me with that beef stick of yours."

"You'd like that, homo," Marcus said, glowering at me like a demon from the backseat.

"You want a slice of the action?"

"Yeah, ten percent of the sales of your next novel. I mean gross, not net, you cheapo."

"Let me call my agent."

"Yeah, do it. Call that dick licking homo up and put it on stone tablets. Ten fucking percent."

"Do you have to curse so much?"

"Only to make my point."

I grabbed the phone out of the glove box, swerving across the middle lane.

"You maniac, watch the road! Do you want to get me killed?"

There were no cars it seemed for miles. "Maybe I can roll the car, get you ejected, flip right on my wheels again, and keep on driving. And the buzzards will pick your bones clean."

Marcus laughed, slow and maniacal, he was used to this game of us describing how we would murder each other. It was nothing novel. I dialed my agent. The phone rang and rang and rang before it went to his voicemail. He was chipper as usual; it came with the territory of selling sleaze disguised as literature to publishers. His voicemail had taken on an even greater polish, and now it sounded like an insurance salesman's voice. Beep!

"Dippo! It's me, your meal ticket! Listen; let's cut Marcus in on this deal. He either gets ten percent of the gross of my next novel or he comes clean with the fact that he gave me all the fodder for my stories. Oh, yeah, that may cut into my profits, but I don't care, I have money to burn, man." CLICK

"You know the reason you write such successful romance novels for females is because you have a female brain."

"No way. It's because I understand women," I said.

"Yeah, you're a dude with a female mind. Don't worry about it, Sally."

"John Jacob Jingleheimer Schmidt. Motherfucker stop calling me Sally. You don't know anything about psychology, you idiot. Did you even get past the sixth grade? Or did your fucking retarded Okie oilman, drunk-ass poon-crazed father go to jail and you had to leave to go to work and support the family, eventually making your way to Princeton University on a lacrosse scholarship, which you learned at Church Camp for Injuns, where you befriended me, your only dude friend in the world? And you say I have a female brain? Maybe it's you with the female brain. You're so used to hanging out with them. If I've a female brain, you've a female brain too."

"Bite me, man. You female-brained writer, don't be mad. You write to relieve yourself of the estrogen. Your pen drips it."

"I write because I cannot stop writing, and it's either stop writing or kill myself and I'm too much of a coward to kill myself, so when the poison stops flowing from my female pen, it will flow into my gullet. What talents do you possess, Marcus, besides bedding women and dropping panties? Where's your great drive?"

"Pull over here."

"Why?"

"Down this crossroad."

"Why?"

"Don't ask. Do it."

"Why?"

"Don't ask why, just please do it."

"It looks desolate, abandoned. What the hell is down there?"

"Paradise, dude."

"Yeah, right. This is a road to nowhere. The place looks like a dump."

"Fuckwillickers, you're a fucking pussy," Hanely said.

"No, I'm not. Where the hell are you leading me?"

"We're going to a place I've been once or twice, a long time ago. You know, with my grandpa, the long haul truck driver."

"What is this place?"

"A whorehouse. A hidden flophouse. The best whorehouse just outside the country of Reno, my man. Where the women burn your soul and your wallet and leave your cock cindered. I was 14 and good old gramps took me to this dusty ass place that reeked of booze and perfume and stale cigars. The card's flapped through Death's skeletal palms to the table. The stakes were high. Grandpa lost the title to his 18 wheeler, and at 14 I fucked my way through the entire stable twice and the madam while grandpa tried to win back his 18 wheeler with the smelly mattress and the cunt juice stained cab back from Mephistopheles the Barber, the card dealer. The pile of gold and war bonds, a trove of Rolexes, and various defunct stock certificates and the table lined with the carcasses of has been real estate executives and whatever other moths were drawn to that flame of easy money. Easy money, damn I hope this place is still open. It was heaven. It was paradise. It was the Candy Land of my youth. My grandfather spent a full four days playing cards with Death before he fully lost everything, down to the last crumb on his plate and whiskers in his forked beard. He got his prowess from his grandfather who battled off nymphs and stroked his goat legs whilst waiting for the cards to fall, whilst I discovered my true vocation in life in that place, and this was, like, just in 1984, and so many women wore leg warmers and did not take them off in *flagrante delectio*, even when I, obviously somewhat under-age, manhandled them and declared that this one, it was on the house. God, I hope this place is open, memories of sweet youth that only grow older, fainter with recollections, vigor sufficing to reimpose its lusty malefactions upon warm, unwormy live bodies. If the women were still here, they would be well over fifty."

We parked outside the building, which looked abandoned. Nary a sound was around, not even the howl from a lone coyote. Neither was there any light, not a star's pinprick of light pierced our corneal frame.

"If I remember correctly, gramps said we had to knock just a certain way. I forget it now. Finesse is required here, but the rutting brawn comes in handy later. It was a rumbling knock. My grandfather's fist was the size of a damn bowling ball. What was it? Oh yes, a one, a two, a three."

The door opened. Smoke billowed out into the stale, dead desert air. The inside was a majestic shade of neon purple mixed with strobe light in which water from jet nozzles spotted intermittently, floating, undulating, like cum shots in outer space. The women inside, all gorgeous, Aztec princesses, the most beautiful of their tribe, women you would gladly immolate your greatest hopes in the baby's breath of a second just to touch, speak with, caress them, feel their nether regions, flick their buttocks like a Jell-O mold to see if they are real or just a television programmed marionettes.

The air smelled of perfume, not cheap perfume, but rather a biblical frankincense and myrrh mixed with orange, sandalwood oil, and a hint of clove. I smelled marijuana, which one of the women puffed from a long peace pipe. She looked ravenously native and glared at me as I passed, so much so, that it sent a shiver down my mortal spine. It seemed the whole perfume of the place has a well intentioned damask rose covering up and unfortunate reek of senescence, like rotted peaches, or cutting into a blackened, sickly, rotten pomegranate when you expected bright red bliss.

The over ripened fruit, lazy and heavy in the dusky summer air smiled sweetly to him from the corner. She was dressed in an Amish girl's outfit, perhaps a milkmaid, or horse whisperer. Absurd. Rumspringa was over and there were no communities around. She sat next to the Indian smoking the marijuana peace pipe looking like some oversexed Thanksgiving montage. The Amish lady bore an A on her DD chest. Hester Prynne! How long I had jacked off thinking about her big puritan titties, at least one thousand times during my Freshman Prep School English class. I walked up and jabbed the puritan in the side to get her attention.

"Oh Mister, you didn't need to do that. Most of you guys just smile and wave," she said.

"Sorry, I'm uncouth. I haven't the slightest idea how to behave around women. You see my mother abandoned me to join a circus at a young age. She wasn't young, I was. She was middle-aged. Apparently she loves Italian trapeze artists."

"I'm sorry to hear that."

"I'm sure. How much, babe?"

"Stuff doesn't work that way here."

"No?"

"No, we're not whores."

"What are you, then?"

"Women," Pocahontas said with a hint of anger in her voice, otherwise she looked stoned and bored.

"Oh, I'm sorry, my friend told me you were whores," I said.

"Your friend is wrong," Pocahontas responded.

"He told me he fucked the whole lot of you skanks way back when," I said over the throbbing bass. "Where's the dance floor?" I asked.

"What did you say?"

"Never mind. You mean I have to talk to you both?"

"Where's your friend?"

I looked around. Hanely was nowhere to be seen. I figured he was already balls deep in someone or something, upstairs rutting away like some Grecian satyr with his banana cock and balls like oranges, probably giving his partner in their crime the time of her life. I didn't hear anything, though.

"What kind of place is this?" I asked.

"This is a professional poker center."

"Oh yeah?"

"Yep. We're just hostesses. Don't worry though, a lot of miscreants bust up in here thinking we're whores. They usually end up broke and with blue balls. We won't fuck you, but we'll sure as shit play some strip poker with you."

I instantly thought back to the illicit game on my father's computer and the 8-bit women who played strip poker with me in the wee hours of my fourth grade mornings. I never had the opportunity to play it in real life, but I figured that I was a master of the cards. I had a sudden urge to play it again. I felt I owed these professional hostesses a turn of good fortune for assuming them to be whores. It was always an old habit of mine to assume. Pocahontas hated me now, it was written all over her face, but she was so cute, but not nearly as cute as Hester Prynne. I listened for signs of Marcus Hanely.

My phone rang. I did not answer it or pull it from my jeans pocket to see who it was. It vibrated comfortably against my sack. Phone calls could wait. Hanely, the only person I truly cared about in the world, didn't even have a phone. The freedom!

"So you biddies want to play some Poker?"

"Yeah, how much do you want to start with?"

"Two-fifty a game."

"Sure. You want us both?"

"No, Pocahontas can stay here. I don't like her attitude."

"If I may kindly play with you, our fine-haired, feathered friend can stay on and play," a well-dressed gentleman said to me.

"I don't want any new friends," I said.

"I assure you, I'm not your friend, and I'm not your enemy. I'm nothing to you. I'm just a man looking to play a game of chance with the owner of the 1969 Pontiac GTO outside."

"How did you know it was me?"

"I watched you park it, I watched you walk out of it, and I watched you walk in here."

"What do you care about me for?"

"What's not to care about? You know our friend here is famous, ladies?"

"What're you famous for?"

"Doesn't look famous to me," Pocahontas said.

I didn't answer, and shame wormed its way to my face.

"Come on, tell them, Mr. Leman."

"Nah."

"Why don't you tell them? You should really exercise less humility. It isn't becoming. Ladies, this gentleman here is the famous author of the novel *Asymmetric Hearts*. Jackson Leman."

They looked at each other like the name really didn't ring a bell for them.

"And who are you, sir?"

"No one in particular, but you'll know me soon enough. Let's play first."

"Well, if you're going to interrupt our threesome, you might as well tell us your name."

"I'm not interrupting. I brought Pocahontas here with me," he said blowing a great cloud of cigarette smoke towards me. I didn't recall seeing him smoking, but there was the lit cigarette, dangling between his long, skeletal fingertips.

"Isn't that right, Pocahontas?" he asked, chuckling, raspy like the old Marlboro Man.

"Yeah, I remember you wanted to leave me all night in the lobby with the creeps," she muttered.

"We're the creeps around here," the stranger said.

"Not I," I responded.

"Sure you are. I read your novel," Pocahontas said.

I laughed.

"Did you read this nutbag's novel?" the stranger asked Hester Prynne.

"No, I don't read," Hester said vacuously, mesmerized by the television in the corner. She pulled her phone from her middle-tits and stared blankly at the screen, which made her face glow like a witch performing some secret incantation. Asking her if she had read a novel was like asking an insurance salesman in Tahiti if he sold much snowstorm insurance. It was like asking Hanely if he cared about a woman's feelings. This babe was post literate; a product of the Internet generation, the Nintendo generation, a PlayStation kid, a kid raised on teleprompter churches of God the Image.

"You ever read anything?"

"Oh sure, the newspaper sometimes," Hester said sheepishly. God I wanted to fuck her. I didn't care what she had read; I just wanted to feel myself in her. Sure I'm a writer, but it didn't get me anywhere with the ladies. I'm a writer. I'd rather be a scoundrel, a knave, a cutthroat with a pen, a sick little dilly whacker, a pickle hider, balls deep in a poker den, like Marcus is at this very moment, coupling while I coupled socially, intercourse with bores. I can hear the grunting. I think he's fucking a poker hostess upstairs, getting sweaty on the couch, dribbling.

I put my hand on Prynne's leg. She pushed it away. Was it my approach?

The stranger laughed. I glared at him. I put my cards on the table.

Aces and twos. Quite an impeccable hand. Definite tit producing material here, and I said, "Good sir, just who the hell are you?"

"I've a message for you from your father that I'm bound and determined to deliver. There's quite a bonus in it for me."

"Oh, so you're a private investigator."

"No, I'm a private hire. A privateer. Not an investigator, I don't uncover happenings, I make things happen."

"Oh, come off of it. If we're playing then you're spilling your name."

"Trade secret."

"A nickname then."

"Hmmm...I don't have too many friends, and you can't give yourself a nickname."

"Well, fuck, you've got red hair, you ginger. I'll call you Red. There, I just gave you a nickname, friend. Red, deal."

"Damn," Red said, "and I had such a good hand."

Hanley walked in, naked from the waist down, he hid in the shadows so no one else saw him, but me, and smiled. His body glistened like he had been sprayed with a fine mist. But he hadn't. It was fuck sweat, from screwing.

"Where were you?" I called after him, but then the waitress entered the room topless, with pasties over her nipples, boobies jangling back and forth.

"Hold your horses, cowboy," she said.

"I want a scotch. My friend Red here, he wants a Scotch too," I said to her.

"No thanks," Red said.

"Sure buddy, have a drink on me. Or four or five," I said.

I looked up. Hanely had secured additional pleasures. I thought this wasn't a fuck shack, but a poker shack.

"I thought people couldn't screw in here," I said to Hester Prynne.

"Not usually, depends on how much you pay. A girl can wager her maidenhead if she loses badly enough."

"Yeah, or if we really like you, we set the prices."

"What the fuck! Let's do it!"

"You're not our type."

"Can't we just play Poker?" Pocahontas asked.

Red dealt. Aces and twos again. Pocahontas chuckled. Her turn to call. She took two cards.

Red winked at me. I felt he was holding something fierce. Hester Prynne's hair fell out of place. Tousled. My prick jumped in my pants. I took two cards. I had nothing in my hand but randomness.

"I bet my shirt," Pocahontas said.

"I bet my pants," Red said with a frothy grin.

"My gloves, or my bonnet," Hester Prynne wagered.

"Yeah, get that A off your chest and show us those Milkers," I said.

"I can bet that, but I won't," she said with a smile.

"I fold," I said, and tossed my cards in the center. Red called and then produced three Aces. Hester took off her bonnet. My prick did a somersault. Pocahontas removed her jerkin, made of leather; perhaps deer hide, and put it on the floor in a heap. She had a red bra on.

"That's totally out of character. Why don't you take it off and let your long injun hair cover those mammaries?"

"I don't want to. One article of clothing at a time, stud. That's the rules. You going to just fold all the time? Nothing hazarded, nothing gained."

"No. I'll play when I'm dealt a less shitty hand."

"You've got all the cards; you just have no idea how to play them. You quit. You're going to quit every time."

"Nope," I said. She was right, able to see through my soul. I was a coward possessed of intractable cowardice.

"Our friend here is timid, unsure of his opponents and what they're going to bring to the table."

"No I'm not. I really don't know how to play."

"What's the worst that can happen? You end up naked and embarrassed?"

"I've got nothing to be ashamed of," I said.

"Play then," Red said.

"Deal."

Red shuffled, and his long bony fingers clicked over the cards like ice picks on a glassy ice swan, corpulence of the beautiful and sublime, beating the cards lasciviously in the middle occasionally. I watched him deal, unimpressed. He shuffled like a madman would, with no end in sight. Haphazardly.

"Come on already," I declared.

"When it's your turn to deal, we'll see how you do," Hester said.

I was starting not to like her in favor of Pocahontas, who actually took time to read my novel. Underneath Prynne's bonnet, which lay in the corner, carelessly tossed, wadded even, her hair was hidden sexiness, mysterious, but out in the open it was the opposite: plain, as plain as a wheat field in Kansas. I could see the allure of Amish women in the romance novels. I considered making Veronica Dare an Amish girl gone wild on Rumspringa, but Hanely reined me in, saying that she should be a bad girl gone good, not the tired cliché of a good woman turning cockslut. He was right. I nailed it. I winked at Hester Prynne. She picked up her cards and buried her face in them like it was a mathematics textbook, and she a bountiful mathematician.

"Only I deal," Red said. "That's the rules."

"Whose rules?" Pocahontas inquired.

"House rules," he said, running his tongue over his teeth, malevolently.

"You don't work here," Pocahontas said.

"Sure I do. I work anywhere I want to. Tonight I choose this place, because my friend here, you know him, the foremost genius of Romance fiction, or so said *The New York Times* book reviewer in 2005, when his mega-epic, *Asymmetric Hearts*, was released. I had thought every woman in the United States owned it, but I guess it skipped your generation, Adulterer. I deal. Mr. Leman here writes books, but you two ladies look pretty and strip when you lose, play poker, and probably fuck on the side."

They looked at him flabbergasted.

"I write poetry," Hester Prynne said.

"No way. I don't believe you. Show me," Red quipped and yawned.

"I do," she said.

"What a poetic answer. Recite some poetry for us then, Prynne. Or should I call you Emily Dickinson, Ms. Sappho?"

"Who?"

Red laughed sending throngs of sickly smoke into the sky. He tugged at his cigarette.

"You don't need to know much to be a poet; you just hear the rhythms on the air. It's the language of life," Prynne said.

Red guffawed and choked on his cigarette.

"Yeah, Red, you don't need to know a bunch of crusty dead poets to be able to write poetry."

"So says the Romance section," Red quipped twirling his burning cigarette in his fingers.

"I studied more of it," I said.

"What do you write for then?" Red asked.

"Purely money now, unfortunately, but I will be a great artist, someday."

"Like Nero was a great artist, a suicide artist," Red said stroking his stubbly face. I could see it was a red with wispy grey stubble, not to be expected in someone who seemed so young, yet so old at the same time. I suspect he'd been to war, or engaged in a stressful MBA program to earn his dashes.

"Let's stop arguing and give the poet her due," I said.

"I don't have much prepared, just this short one. My epics are at home in notebooks."

"Premonitions of doom pay electricity bills and buy timeshares in Nassau

I wait dazed for oblivion sleep forgetfulness and a swinging scimitar singes my soul

Burns my memory

Immolated on altars of gold forgotten

My mind is dross mislaid barren

Time dawdles on

Knitting

A black and gold spider stitching dusky death in moonlight." Hester Prynne said.

"Nauseating," Red declared.

"Keep it up, Hester," I said.

"It doesn't matter," Hester declared.

"Correct," Red said.

"Deal," I declared.

"You'll fold," Red said.

"No way."

"Deal," Pocahontas said harshly.

"Alright, dealing," Red, said to appease the native.

He threw out the cards. I picked up my hand.

"Pure fucking randomness!" I shouted.

"You've got a hell of a tell," Red said, laughing.

"I told you!" I yelled at him. I tossed my cards in the center.

"Nothing to develop? Work on?"

"Not a damn thing."

"I think you're scared to get naked," Hester surmised.

"You got a wee one, stud?" Pocahontas asked, with a little laugh.

"No, my dingus is immense, capable of splitting the most loosened up claptrap snapper into five equal portions of pie. I'll pull it out right now, my long lance, and run you through. Fuck you all. I'll just strip and get it over with, you mongoloid fucks!"

"No! What's the point of the game then?"

"The point is there is no point to this game, Hester Prynne. Just pull those titties out, Hester. Whip those fuckers out and make them a hot dog bun for my lascivious dong."

I whipped it out of my pants. Pocahontas gasped. I jumped up on the table and helicoptered two or three times with my pants around my ankles. I felt glorious, like a conquistador of some junky island who cock-smashed the natives.

"You maniac!" Red screamed, "Get off the cards!"

"I won't, cheater! I won't, you fucking rigged, death-dealing old cretin. Stare at this! Stare!"

"Get down!"

"Get the bouncer!"

I jumped from the table, pants around my ankles still, around my holy shoes. I needed a new pair.

"Get back here, Pocahontas!" I shouted.

"I'm getting the bouncer, you nut!"

Hanely stepped out of the shadows. "Fuck, put your cock away," he said, still glistening and naked from the waist down himself.

"Where are these whores? I want to blaze behind your trail! Sow my weeds in your fields! Where are they?"

"They're worn out. They don't want you. I'm sorry, they told me so. Why don't you pierce the Puritan? That would be fun. I bet you've already alienated her. You're an idiot. The smartest idiot I know. Let's go! Let's get the fuck out of this dump!" Hanely said, bounding downstairs as the bouncer was coming up. I yanked my pants up, but my schlong still sat exposed. I gingerly folded him into the seams of my trousers.

Red put his hand on my shoulder. "Let's go, bub," he said.

"Where?"

"Your father wants me to bring you back. Or make sure you get back to where you need to be in a timely fashion."

"What if I just said, 'I don't want to see that idiot?'"

"No choice," Red said. "Orders are orders."

The bouncer bounded to the top of the stairs breathless. He was overworked, an ape with no neck, a killing machine, a pulverizing psycho with tattoos and a flattop.

"You're the fucko who whipped his dick out?"

"I am," I said calmly. "I put him back in my pants."

"I'm going to stomp the shit out of you," the bouncer announced.

He made to grab me. Red pulled a large silver hand cannon from his coat. One of those big, evil-looking bastards with all the industrial knobs. Old fashioned. Cold Steel. Unglamorous, not ergonomic. The bouncer soon bitched up.

"We're leaving. You call the cops, and I'm going to come back here with a flame-thrower and roast you. I'll bring a pack of wolves to eat your charred carcass, and whatever they can't eat; I'll eat the rest. Get the fuck out of my face, you overgrown, born eight centuries too late linebacker from a Division Three football team!"

"Goddamn you're poetic," I said.

Red pointed the gun at me. "Move," he said.

"Sure thing. This is too much!"

"Hester! Come on! I love you! Come with us!"

"She stays here. There'll be no lovemaking on my watch."

"No fun. You're going to be a severe drag on our operation."

"Just walk!"

"I'll go back, Red, but only on my terms."

"We get there in two days. No more, no less."

"Why so soon? That isn't in our plan."

"I have to be there at the appointed time."

"We're on a savage journey."

"No we aren't."

"Yes we are."

"Hanely and I are on a savage journey."

"Oh, so then it's true, what your sister says. You're totally insane."

"What?"

"You've lost it. You've gone off the deep end. Point of no return. A total break."

"Why do you say that?"

"Oh, you don't know do you?"

"Don't know what?"

"You drove here alone, Jackson."

"No, I didn't. Hanely came with me from Monterey."

"Whose idea was it to leave for Denver?"

"Mine. I have to see my father."

"Whose idea was it to stop here?"

"Marcus came up with it. I had no idea this place existed."

"Look around you. Where is he?"

"In the car, waiting for us now."

"I assure you, he is not in the car."

"He is."

"When did you meet Marcus Hanely?"

"My sophomore year at Princeton."

"Where?"

"In the library. Then he was my dorm suitemate."

"A short amount of time after your mother took her life."

"What? Yes! Yes!"

"That was a particularly black year, was it not?"

"Horrible. I nearly joined her."

"How?"

"Oh I had my method all figured out. Was about to do it, when Marcus knocked on the door."

"You actually heard a knock? Or he just came in?"

"I don't remember."

"I know it may seem real, but he isn't real. He's a phantom. A schizoid delusion. He's as real as your own mind is real. He's a construct you've placed on the world to give it some order or sense."

"He's my friend. He's real."

"I don't doubt that either. But he's not real."

"How old are you now Jackson?"

"Thirty two."

"For eighteen years now, you've harbored this hallucination."

"He isn't a hallucination. You're the one that's insane. I'm fucking out of here."

"I'm coming with you. We'll talk to Marcus together."

"You'll see."

I cruised downstairs past the quaking bouncer. It was hard to see a big man shattered, crying like a sad clown in the corner. The bartenderess, a sexy tattooed woman cradled his head like a baby near her tattooed breast. I laughed as Red walked me out. He waved at the bouncer with the hand cannon. In my mind I was formulating an escape. I would drive out into the desert with Red and Marcus, and when the old drooper started to nod off, I would pull out Sam Colt from underneath my seat and blow his brains out. We'd bury him in the desert, Russian Mob style.

Marcus was waiting in the backseat. Red piled in the front. He would help me. When Red got in the front, I don't think he saw Marcus in the back, waiting patiently like a pit bull.

"Nice car," Red said.

He would think my car was nice because he was a worshipper of the stupid present, a glitz and glam man, enamored with toys like a little boy. I bet he watched *Dancing with the Stars*.

"Marcus," I said, "I'm going to drive this old gent out into the desert, and then we're going back to Denver to see my poor unfortunate father, dying now of cancer, or extreme old age or whatever it is he's gotten into over the long years. Probably a trunk full of deceit and shady business deals."

Marcus was remarkably reticent. He just stared back at me.

"You're quite his opposite," Red said.

"I wish you'd tell me your name."

"My name's unimportant, my status is not. Just know that I'm your father's right hand man, his most trusted servant-... err, employee, and that's why I was dispatched to come and find you, track you down, bring you back."

"Right," I said, turning into the dusty road that would lead back to the Interstate.

"You see that, Marcus? My father actually wants to speak with me! All the time we were at Princeton University together, did he ever come to visit? Once? Did he ever show his great globby, red-cheeked embarrassment in my dorm room? He kept the coffers filled, all right. It was his way of delivering affection...a paycheck! His little gold plated love endowments and little disbursements of cash. Why, Red, did my father ever tell you the story of what he did when I was a child?"

"Did to you?"

"Did he bugger you?" Hanely asked. "It would explain a lot."

"No, he didn't," I said looking over my shoulder.

"Uh...he didn't tell me anything, though we do keep it business."

"You're his faithful employee. We're all his faithful employees. Anyways...."

"You were saying?"

"I was lonely. I wanted a friend. I met a kid from my school and invited this kid to our palatial home. He was a smart kid, at the school on a scholarship, not the son of a scion or a senator. He was poor in fact. Well, each time father would have the butler take us out on the town we'd have the chauffeur take us to the mall, take us to the movies, pick us up like a couple of princes. This happened for months, the kid became accustomed to it. We were best buddies. Finally my father went away on business and his credit cards with him. My friend came to the house, after seeing all my rooms, after playing all my games; he asked me where my father was. I wanted to know why my friend wanted to know where my father was, and he told me that my father had not paid him that month's salary. I asked him what he meant, and he said that my father thought that he was a good influence on me and had been paying him to stay around. And that, unfortunately, because my father had not paid him for that month, he had studies and other things that were more important and pressing on his time, he could not hang out with me. He left. He walked home, and when we passed each other in the halls of the school he just shook his head. I implored him to come and be my friend, and he said that he neither liked me as a person, nor could he be my friend, that I was a spoiled idiot, and he was glad my father stopped paying him because now he had time to go after the girls and do all the normal things a 14 year old does. See, we're all his employees, each and every one of us."

"I've a wife and kids to take care of, one in college and one in high school," Red said.

I almost felt bad that I would have to shoot him in the face when we got to an easy, secluded location.

"He uses my stories, my conquests as fodder for his books that housewives devour as if they were cupcakes or bonbons, not bitter, but syrupy and sugary with a feel-good feeling that lasted for at least a day after reading."

"You're too harsh, Marcus," I said looking into the back seat.

"Look," Red said, taking on a serious tone, like a forest park ranger warning of the pitfalls of bears and avalanches, "I'm no doctor, but I think you need serious help. There is no one in the backseat. It's you and me out here alone."

"Right, Red, you won't even tell me your real name, and you expect me to trust you. Perhaps you're also a figment of my imagination, and I'm out here all alone just talking sweet nothings to phantoms. Why won't you tell me your name?"

We passed lights on the left; a small city buried in a desert valley, forgotten about, a beacon to weary travelers. It glowed, probably visible from space, an insignificant nothing where the people laid about their lives hoping for better days, sunnier pastures, better and more entertaining cable television programs, or for their favorite team to be declared the winner of the Super Bowl after an undefeated season. I turned toward the town intrigued by the possibilities.

Hanely piped up, "Been here once. With my uncle. This place has one of the seediest bars known to man. I think it's called the Black Hole, maybe the Flying Nun, or perhaps it's the Speckled Hen or Horny Toad. I don't remember. Needless to say, I've brawled there. I've punched more than a few sets of teeth out there and smashed ladies' noses flat. I've thrown wild haymakers that caught the meanest bikers unawares."

"You hear that, Red? We're going to the Flying Nun, or the Horny Toad, the Finical Antechinus, whatever the name of Hanely's favorite bar is."

The car lurched onwards, my death wagon across the desert. It was apt. I was speeding towards eventualities, things that had to happen. I was hastening my father's demise.

I fear it. I feared seeing his pallid skin and sunken cheeks. I feared seeing people weep over him. I feared the reading of his will and the tons of lawsuits.

"Turn left here, bro," Hanely ordered.

I gunned the Judge and kicked up rocks along the side of the road that smashed off the black finish. Red winced, obviously a connoisseur of cars.

"Take it easy," he said.

"Nope. Must get home. Doctor's orders. I speed when I want."

"Yeah, gun it," Marcus yelped with glee from the back seat.

I stepped on the accelerator. The Judge responded, and it sounded as if demons stoked the pits of hell beneath the hood. I blasted the radio. It was something cheesy with a female singer wailing about lost love, totally *inappropos* for our manly conquest of this humble burg. I sped into the valley; the white lights surrounded us with their splendor. The sights did not equal their rival, the lights. The place, by night, looked as if crude bunglers designed it, a mining town that sprang up overnight and never changed since the silver ran out in 1943. The signs on businesses were stupendous great glowing bubbly bastards in disgusting cursive urging morons to partake in some sacred communion with the interiors of their walls.

IDA'S ANTIQUE FURNITURE JEROME'S BAIT AND TACKLE WAFFLES AND MORE CRAZY CARL'S FURNITURE,

all groped for us with their incandescent light bulb signs. I was on the point of despair. Perhaps the wretched bar had burned down, perhaps the bartenderess, as fair and buxom as Hanely described her, had knocked over an oil lamp with her huge titties and started a conflagration which sent derelicts and bikers running out of the place with their oily hair on fire. Perhaps she went to bed with a fat cancer stick hanging fatally from her neck that slid between the peaks, into her valley and caught the bed sheets, drapes, and upholstery on fire. Perhaps it was talked about in the town *SLEEPER* or *PICAYUNE, LAND THAT TIME FORGOT JOURNAL, FLYOVER STATE GAZETTE.*

Hanely slapped me on the right side of the head. His blow stung like a bullet on the slapping end of a cop's vicious leather sap, not like one had ever hit me, for I'm a pretty good and decent law abiding citizen, but Hanely sure has. He's wrestled cops in far off locales, battered sheriffs, thrust and parried with deputies, outran the secret police in dusky third world shitholes. He's mad, mad with life, and I'm his bitter companion, the mere chronicler of his deeds, deeds to rival any man's, born or dead. Had Hanely been born on the Peloponnesus Archipelago way back when, surely no one would have heard of the deeds of that noble Alexander, for Hanely would have cuckolded Phillip and poked his other eye out. That slap meant turn right. Red looked agitated now and demanded I tell him where I was going to take him, as he probably sensed his impending demise. I turned viciously right, and then left, each time Hanely slapped me on the side of the head, throwing Red against the door.

"Should I wear a seatbelt?" I asked, laughing.

"You aren't worth it," Red sighed.

"What do you mean by that?"

"The bonus money. You aren't worth it."

"Oh, why not?"

"You're mad."

"I'm not. I'm perfectly sane. We're just going for some liquid refreshment right quick."

"I don't want any beer."

"Then have a whisky and soda, a bourbon, a mojito if you can order that in this one horse town. Just don't be a bore. Don't be boring, and we're in love with you and with life and living. We want to squeeze every precious drop from our mortal bodies and teach others to do the same. We're off to proclaim the gospel according to Marcus. Don't you be bored. You're alive, Red; you're a man. Life has no place for boredom, no time for boredom, or boring fucks for that matter. The bored are the boring. They can all go straight to hell. They can coin their currency and pay their piper to escort them to fun land. They can all rot in Disneyland, in cinemas, at the shopping mall, glued to their televisions. You're coming with us, Red. You're going to not be bored for the rest of your weary moneymaking days, however short or long they may be."

"I was told to bring you back, that it was easy, that you'd come like a lamb."

"I'm not a lamb for your slaughter, Red. You know Hannah doesn't know me anymore. My sister doesn't know how much I've changed. I'm no longer the little boy under her thumb. You can't make me submit. I'm going home willingly, but I'm going on my own terms."

"Turn the car around. Get on the interstate!"

"We try not to drive main thoroughfares because they're not only the veins of capitalism, they're corridors of boredom where everything is the same, carrying the lifeblood of America and its cancer cells throughout this great land of ours. We blaze our own trail, Red. We look through the underbrush and watch the daisies bleed. If you think I'll go your way, you'll have to kill me first and drag my stinking corpse back, and my father and I can be buried together. If you think I'll love what you love, Red, I won't. That will never happen. I'll fucking kill myself first."

"Well said, bro," Hanely said from the rear.

Red looked out the window as the cars zipped by in the opposite direction and the storefronts flickered into the distance.

"Time to time, Marcus admits that he's tired of life. What does he do? He goes on an adventure, which is what we're doing. It's unfortunate that you should track us down to come here and be a leech on our progress and some sort of fun-meter set on dismal, to suck the very marrow from our bones, to put the alligator clips on the tips of our third legs and deny us our place amongst the stars and constellations."

"You are fucking insane," Red said.

"I'm really not."

Madness would be killing him, to liberate us from him, from the onus on our progress that he embodied. That would have to come later. If I could find someone to do it for me, all the better. I would gladly pay them handsomely. I would convince someone at the bar to do him in; if it were the hole of cutthroats and thieves, knaves and villains that Hanely remembered it to be.

We parked in a despicable little spot nearest to the farthest point away from the door. There were a few motorcycles in the parking lot, which was no longer the sign of a good time. Geriatrics had taken to forming riding clubs, so an AARP convention was looking more like a Hell's Angels conglomeration day by day. However, there may be a few assassins amongst them in the crowd. The bar's name, was the Ogilvy. Totally unlike anything Marcus remembered from his youth, still he told me that it was the same building that the nefarious bottle-breaking bar inhabited. I burst in the front door, followed by Marcus, with Red taking up the rear like a whipped, whiny puppy.

"Old people!" I screamed, scanning the crowd. They looked up from what looked like Bingo cards.

"This isn't the right place!"

"Nah, this is the one, just got churchified."

The band, a hired gang of mooks in horrid suits stopped their song. It did not sound like a record being ripped from its platen, as you often see in the movies, but rather the song just fizzled out. No one was listening anyway, and it was just background noise. The lead singer, a pimply face impresario of some fifties nobody made an announcement that their next song would be an equally obscure shuffle rock ballad. They burst into song. It was all over the place. The drummer had no rhythm, but still it was danceable by the mingling geriatrics. A few old people slowly rose to dance. They clung to each other to hold each other up and wobbled. It was pathetic, but still I watched on. A foul blast blew in from the door, which Red, mesmerized by the Bingo game, or maybe because he was actually amongst compatriots, had left open to the nighttime chill.

"Red, shut the door, or these old bastards will catch their death."

I scanned the room for a possible assassin for hire with whom I could conspire to off our nuisance businessman and sell him off for the inevitable. The women in the room smiled, like the way that old biddies smile when there are healthy young men around, or the way that they smiled when they patted the heads of children in the shopping mall and acted generally creepy, saying things like "God's little miracles." This place was absurd. Why weren't these oldies off in the old folk's home not gambling away their savings in this den of iniquity? Why weren't they tending grandchildren and spoiling them? Why were they wasting the precious last moments of their lives in this dump? The Ogilvy in BFE, Nevada? Perhaps it had life at one time and the young men came here to court the young women, but all those people had since died or moved away.

"You, come to the bathroom with me!" I yelled to Marcus over the din. He had taken a seat facing the door, keeping his back to the horror show band.

"Get a bingo card, Red. Live a little."

Red raised his hand and asked the waiter for a card and was told the Bingo card cost one hundred dollars.

"Bingo!" an old blue hair yelled, showing that there was, in fact, hope in the world.

The restroom smelled like bland Mexican decay. I thought I noticed a twinge of citrus on the atmosphere from an overpowered air freshener. I whipped my cock out of my tight jeans and pissed violently into the urinal. Hanely did the same. An old man, a dinosaur, the king geriatric tended to the bathroom, clicking a pen as we pissed. I felt his eyes burning me.

"How are we gonna lose this square?"

"There a window in here?"

I looked around careful to avoid missing the mark. It had been some time since I pissed, and my bladder now gushed my golden gift to the Ogilvy. The odd bathroom attendant whistled to himself. There was no window; the bathroom was a dark, dank pit of hell. I think the bathroom attendant lived in here and might have made his bed beneath the sink. His clothes looked rumpled like he slept in them. I wanted his story.

"No window in here," I announced.

"Nope," the bathroom attendant said.

"What are we going to do?" I asked Marcus.

"Don't worry, boss. Got some nice Aramis over here. I'll give you a spritz or two," the attendant said.

"Save it."

The whoosh of an automatic air freshener mocked us. The room smelled of sickly cinnamon. Baked, like in apple pie.

"That's awful," I declared. I finished and tucked my meat in my trousers.

Hanley concluded as well and slammed his Moby Dick back into his pants. I tossed the man a ten-dollar bill. His face lit up like Christmas, and he suddenly looked like a child; the pallor left his formerly sickly looking cheeks. If I had to guess, he had to be at least 120 years old.

"Thanks, son," he said.

"I want your story gramps, from birth to bathroom."

"That ten will just get you the first chapter," the attendant said.

I laughed. I liked this guy. "I've got pockets full of loot. I want to hear all of it. You see this pig here? This is the man I've been getting my stories from, and they're all stale and used up. Why, I bet you've got some whoppers."

"How many women have you bedded?" Hanely asked.

The man started a shuffling on his feet, tapping his fingers together like he was doing a field sobriety test. "Don't know, rightly. Lost count at 365."

"Not counting the whores. Whores don't count...you know the rules."

"Yeah, no whores," I said confirming Marcus's assertion.

"Well, then it's more. I've never paid for trim, never bought it, never connived with dinners and roses, never promised the world and delivered oysters. I've been adept at pinching the ones in heat with cheeks all red and flush, ready for the rut. You could call it my gift, gents," the bathroom attendant smiled and said.

"And how's your gift faring these days?" Hanely inquired with a laugh.

"Not well, boys. Not well. Hasn't been the same since 1973. Why, that's the year of my fifth and final divorce. If you're smart men, you'll never marry. You'll never let a maid tame you, never let a woman clip your wings. Some suckers in this world say a wife makes a man better. Why, that's news to me. She was my ruin...my downfall."

"Have you got any children? Grandchildren?"

"Nope. None. Not even none that I don't know of. The good Lord saw fit to bless me with sterility, no hungry mouths to feed."

"Some men would consider that a curse."

"A curse? What manner of man said that? A fool, I tell you. Only a downright fool would choose children over travel, seeing the world, fighting in wars, dying young. I tried. I tried hard not end up a desiccated old dumper, but I wouldn't ever take my life by my own hand. Nah, I ran at machine guns and rode the wildest horses hoping to take a header sometimes, but I tell you what killed me quicker...marriage. I've tried my hand at that and kept getting burned, but I kept sticking my hand right back in the fire. Five women tried to tame me, but they put me in a cage. Oh, how I would rage at night in the bed next to them while I could have been out on the prowl. I'd fight my natural urges. I'd think to myself, Willard, be a good boy, lie here beside your wife. She's yours. It started to feel like a tomb and not a bed."

"Yeah, it's a great institution for fools. We think random, lusty encounters generate the fiercest bloodlines."

"Maybe true, maybe not. Who knows, really? I only have my own tale to tell. My own self to know. There isn't a shred of patience in me. The moment a woman started her program of civilizing me, started building her nest, I was out the door. I fled in terror, screaming into the woods. It was the same with my father and my father's father before him, but luckily I was born without the productive spheres nested between my legs. Luckily I couldn't pass on misery issued forth by me into the world. I could enjoy the act, without the unfortunate consequences, and I enjoyed it well. Like a petty thief who poisoned the guard dogs, but stealing nothing of significance."

"I delight in wrecking marriages," Hanely announced.

"Why's that?" Willard said.

"I don't know. Nothing in the world delights me more than soiling another man's property. Only crime excites me, or the possibility of crime. Once it enters my brain, it cannot go unfulfilled. I must bring it to fruition."

"You're a cuckoo," Willard quipped.

"Nah, I don't desire to plant my seed in another man's field. I mean what's the point. I send it sailing over her shoulder to rest in the furrows of her back, the wrinkles of her face, a sort of free rejuvenation cream."

"You know, I lost my first wife to a man like you. That woman I actually really loved, but she loved me reciprocally. If I was up in blood, lusty at the bat, she retreated. When I retreated, she came on strong. Fucked up wiring in her. I thought I was too firm. I turned off the tap. Perhaps she thought I didn't love her anymore and had to find another source. She came up pregnant, a task I could not possibly perform. The doctor tested me, looked at my spunk under his microscopes but couldn't find a single mover. I asked her the culprit's name. I begged and pleaded with her, I had to know who had done the deed. Was it a rival from my office? A so-called friend? She told me it would best if I didn't know. Sometimes knowing the truth is too painful, so she spared me. I left her off at the bus station bound for her home, she was going to go back and live with her mom and dad. I dropped her off, and I carried her bags to the bus. I was such a gentleman, still. She gave me her wedding ring and engagement ring back and told me to find a woman worthy of my good name. I told her I thought she was worthy in the past, and she told me not to think, just do. And I have never been able to live up to her demand, not in my seventy seven years."

"So what brought you to the bathroom, pops? From birth to the bathroom, that's what we want, my friend; here's a pocket full of gold, and he'll pay you handsomely...he pays for good stories. Don't let him lie, though. He's a thief of stories. He takes on your experience like a vampire; drains a victim of blood...stories are his nourishment. He takes them, polishes them, and makes them marketable. He'll publish it as his own, and his pen writes gold. His periods? They're diamonds. Commas are bits of rubies. Just watch him. He's working on a second novel."

"How much are you willing to pay? If you can beat this measly wage, I've got nothing to hold me here. Had a little dog, but the doggy up and died."

"That idiot, Red, the businessman, he's out there gambling. He won't let you come. We'd have to get rid of him. Say, do you know any poisoners or hit men we might hire tonight to dispose of him?"

"I won't be party to murder. If you want my stories you can have them, but I've never killed an innocent man, if you want to get rid of him, why don't you just tell him to leave?"

"We're prisoners against our will."

"Two young men like you both? Get out of here."

"You're a killer, then?"

"Only whom I've had to. You know people trying to kill me. I'm trying to kill them; they're trying to kill me. War. I've served in damn near every forlorn conflict that dotted this stupid little world in this last half of the century. Till I crapped out. Just a hired goon with a gun, I was away over in those zones all the time. A life of adventure my boys. Sort of put the cabash on all that tomfoolery. Got to get legit about it all today."

He pulled out a towel and wiped his hands with it, like he was trying to wipe away something that we could not see.

"Cologne?" he asked.

"I suppose you're done talking to us, in that we're planning a strange end for our caretaker," I said.

"Just put some money in the basket," he said.

"Do it, Jackson," Marcus said.

"You promise your stories are good?"

"They're the best you'll ever get. You can smelt them into bullion, but I'll give you the pure ore. For now they're just one, but I'll have to mine my memories. What kind of stories do you want?"

"What kinds of stories do you got?"

"I mean, what type of book are you looking to write? A history? A comedy? A mystery? Fiction? Non-fiction?"

"I'm just trying to write it. I don't know. It doesn't matter."

"He's already squeezed me dry, every last drop," Marcus declared.

"Has he now? Smashed the young berry, now he's trying to get dust from an old rind?"

"I doubt that, pops. You seem spry."

"I feel magnificent. Now make me an offering. You want my stories, don't you?"

"How much do you need?"

"Well it has to be much more than I've got in my basket right now."

"You've a buck, and it's lonely."

"Well do your best then."

I took off my timepiece: a magnificent, marvelous, Swiss movement, a limited edition by a master. I tossed it with a chunk into his bucket. "There," I said. "Now you've got all the time in the world."

"You have more of those?"

"Nah, it's one of a kind."

"Gee, thanks."

"The most he ever got me was a hot meal," Marcus lamented.

"You're off a bit."

"Aren't all great artists?"

"Who said you're an artist?"

"He is, of sorts," Marcus added.

"Hmmm..." the bathroom attendant said, looking me up and down.

"Why are you thinking?"

"Who's to say you're not a maniac who'll abandon me out in the desert, or a psycho who gets his thrills by doing old men in?"

"I'm not. You'll have to trust us."

"Why are you having second thoughts?"

"I've been at this job for so long now."

"Smelling other people's shit. I can think of a worse fate."

"It's an honest living."

"Bah. So are we. Probably the two most honest people you'll ever meet."

"Your friend, the meathead. He doesn't look right."

"I'm perfectly safe."

"You coming or not?"

"Where are we going?"

"First off, we have to see Jackson's father off."

"Where's he going?"

"He's dying."

"Jesus," Willard said.

"His dad's not that good."

"Sorry," Willard added.

"It's okay. We came here in hopes we'd find some brave and loose women, but instead we found a companion on our journey that life is itching to take us on. Come."

"We have to be to Salt Lake City, Utah, by sunup tomorrow," I declared.

"That's quite a ways."

"I know. I've got a fast car."

"What are we doing about Red?"

"We should dismiss him."

"It isn't possible."

"It might upset our new buddy."

"What's wrong with him?"

"He's like a boring voice of reason. Who needs that?"

"Yeah I suppose you're right."

"Any way we can sneak out of here?"

"I could take you out the back. You could leave your friend here."

"Oh he's no friend of ours."

We walked out of the bathroom, all three.

"He's content playing Bingo."

"Let him play. We'll just leave him here."

"He loves money."

"Who doesn't?"

"Let's go and get in the car."

"We'll sneak out back while his glittering golden dreams distract him."

"BINGO!" Red yelled.

"It's better than killing him."

"This place will kill him sooner or later, or he'll just fade into the wallpapering. Become another fixture."

We slowly snuck out the back door. Red did not look up, mesmerized by the numbers that the maniacal little man pulled from the never-ending basket.

"BINGO!" A blue hair yelled.

"He hasn't looked up once."

"Oh no, he won't, no matter how much he wins or his posterior aches. He's in that chair, making divots for the ages, holding it down until he can no longer play and someone else takes his place at the Bingo card."

"One in, one out. That's the rules," Willard said, and left the Ogilvy with a smile on his face.

"Stop tarrying. Red will catch us. He'll wake up from his trance, and he'll realize his omission."

"Does he have a gun?"

"Of course, who isn't armed these days? He's got a great masterblaster underneath his professor's tweed."

"Who cares? Not much use to him now. Got to play by the rules at the Ogilvy."

The air outside was chilly and getting chillier. The sign to the Ogilvy was off, and the placed looked like it had been closed for years from the outside, like one of those ramshackle businesses hanging on each month by a thread, but the party inside was gathering steam. The wee caller turned the wheel and the numbers fell out, and the blue hairs stamped their bingo cards with a ferocity forgotten in all other facets of life. Time lingered in the corner, taking long drags from her cigarette, staring at the butt marked with lipstick from her crimson lips.

We piled in the Judge. Willard laughed at his new freedom. Of course it tasted sweet.

"Now talk, old man, and don't stop until we reach the Great Salt Lake," Hanely implored him.

Desert melted into canyon, and canyon gave way to valley, and cacti screamed past, hands upheld to heaven and the stars, their flaming patronizers. And Willard spoke. He started at the beginning, talking in a feeble whimper, and he spoke in his ferocious roar and all the points in between were the death valleys and apexes of his life. And there were many. His life had shape, and he told his story well.

"I was born in 1922 on a dirt farm in Northern Oklahoma. It was a dirt farm because not much would grow there, and we had to pick and borrow and beg for our food. Now eight children, that's a lot of farm hands on a viable farm, but ours only grew dust. Dust from dust, and when winter came my only memories were of cold and hunger, sucking the marrow from bones, thin soup, a real schooling in suffering. We moved west. Hell, I don't remember walking so much in my life. I was only about ten or eleven, tall, gangly. I'm convinced that's the reason I'm so thin to this day, and maybe the reason my loins never produced, all that starving coming up. My fast growing' years were spent so hand to mouth. Why, we'd pass families on the road, and they'd look at us like we were aliens just landed from some of those weird tales books, landed like a flock of locusts. We kept heading west until we hit the sea in California. Have you ever walked from Oklahoma to California?"

"No."

"Ever walked much of anywhere?"

"No, can't say that I have."

"Nothing teaches a man or a boy more about himself than walking until you're exhausted, then picking yourself up and walking some more. I don't mean walking around the corner; I mean walking across the country. You know, like I used to walk when I was in the army, walking with a bunch of other young men, just like a bunch of American gypsies into nothing known. All we really had was our hope off in that war, and our hope in walking to California."

Willard's stories blended into one great tale of desperation and walking to escape the travails of life. He even surmised that the reason that kids didn't have any drive or ambition these days to do anything real was because they never learned how to walk well.

"And you made it to California?"

"Yes, of course. Wouldn't be here if I hadn't of. There wasn't any stopping, straight to the sea. No quarter for Okies. If you're rich, you're loved. People don't care if you've been fleecing them for years. You're broke, you so much as steal a pickle from 'em, and you get the talking' end of a shotgun. No questions asked. You're trying to figure something out, and people assume you're a thief. You might as well turn to thieving if everyone always assumes it. That's the worst crime in this place, being poor. Living' hand to mouth, you're invisible. People will just look right through you."

"Look through you?"

"Yeah, like you're invisible. You don't exist. We wanted desperately to exist. That's why we walked. We didn't have a truck. We walked. We dropped our possessions, and they were not very many, along the way. You think someone wants to buy a whole mess of silverware that isn't even silver, or some ragtag clothes? Nah, you can't take it with you, you're better off just dropping it. Thing is, no one wants to remember the lean times. No one looks back on them times in fondness, like they generate memories people think is worth remembering. They don't even celebrate the lean times in the good times, and don't remember what they did to get through it all. They're forgotten and so is all the lessons 'bout getting through those tough times. But there is one thing I know about history."

"What's that?"

"It's always repeating' itself. Times get plenty, the fat grows on the bone, and when times get tough, we suck it off. We forget how to make a single chicken feed 20 people. You forget what dog and muskrat and 'possum and raccoon taste like. You forget how to prepare it. No one cares for the past's sufferings. In that way, the whole mess of humans is like a single human. We blot out the past pains we went through. We don't remember the pain; we only remember that we were in pain. We remember our triumphs with fondness. Triumphs don't teach us shit. All you have is another spectacle, you don't learn nothing when everything goes the way it should, because everyone is so content being happy with the result, you forget about the struggle to get there. You memorialize the heroes, but the dross, the laborers, the human is forgotten in favor of the gods."

"Tell me about your mistakes then," I said.

"Oh, I've made a ton. A whole heap of mistakes piled up in a long life. But it's just a mountain you've climbed. That's all my mistakes are. They're all behind me. Some of my sins would make a pirate blush with shame. Never murdered. Didn't need to. But I killed a plenty, when I went to war. I should have stayed in the real Army. That was my calling, I think. But instead I got out to chase the money. You know, some men aren't suited to build a civilization. Some men are only suited to be called on to tear one down, and the Army's a good place for them. Tear down other civilizations so they don't tear ours down. I joined up in 1940. I wasn't afraid. It seemed a good steady job. Y'all know what happened in 1941. Until then the Army was three hots and a cot. Weekend liberty. A different cutie pie every weekend. After that, two hots or whatever you could scrounge up and sleeping' in a hole."

"Where were you?"

"North Africa, France, Germany. Got out right before Korea. Couldn't see much of a point in going' there. Wished I would have stayed in."

"You were in North Africa?"

"Yep. Killed Nazi scum there. Killed them in France. Killed them in Germany. They only wore different uniforms."

"Fuck, Marcus, we've got ourselves a regular hero here."

"Yeah man," Marcus said, gazing out the window.

"Our friend isn't much for war stories. He's a fucking hippie. You know, make love not war."

"Oh, I agree with that sentiment," Willard said.

"Fuck that hippie shit."

"You've never been to war, Mr. Hollywood."

"War is hell," Marcus said, still gazing out the window at nothing.

"It's Romantic, you know. Knights and squires and bravery and honor and field nurses and recovering from mental and physical wounds and all that."

"And don't forget the smells. Rotted corpses and the fear shits and your friends getting blasted to human hamburger. Speaking to a guy one minute and asking him how the wife and child and mom and dad are doing, and the next minute helping him hold his entrails inside and promising you'll tell his mom and dad the unvarnished truth of what he did because he didn't believe the Department of War would get his medals home to him. And that was the last thing on that young man's mind when the lights went out. A little medal."

"War is hell," Marcus said.

"Oh yeah, you're a writer. It's all setting for you. All one big objective setting, something to be overcome, to be survived, to come out on top of. There will never be an accurate description written of war. The emotion cannot be captured. It's impossible. There are too many things happening at once. Some men are terrified, some men love it, and some are numb permanently. Far too much stimuli. It would come off as pure numbers, arithmetic, and that isn't what people want from an entertaining read. They want to think war is thrilling. It isn't. Sex is thrilling till you get too much of it. War isn't thrilling. It's just a time of my life I want to forget. I won't talk about it. I'll talk about love affairs, beautiful women, failures in love. You can't learn anything from War, except how to fight other wars. From discussions of love, you can learn everything."

"Yeah, maybe. A romance in a war story makes for a great read."

"Fuel for fantasies," Willard said.

"A fuck in a bunker," Marcus added.

An old song came on the radio, a sort of dance song replete with trumpets. It came on randomly, like we passed into the invisible threshold of the radio waves from the city approaching in the valley, sneaking up. Creeping like a glowing caterpillar sandwiched between two peaks. I rolled the window down. The chill had disappeared, and heat belched in the car like from a blast furnace. Raging, cosmic winds blew into the car. Hanely could have been scorched.

"Stop at the gas station. I've got to whizz," Willard said.

"We only left your bathroom an hour ago."

"When you're old, see how often you have to piss, and how long you can hold it for. I'm telling you, unless you want me to turn this car of yours into a jaundiced aquarium, you better pull over."

AN ESSO GAS STATION

Starring:

Marcus Hanely, Cyrano de Bergerac, sans bulbous nose

Willard, The ancient vagabond

Jackson Leman, Wayward Romance Novelist

Nascha, Gas Station attendant, a portly Navajo woman with the most beautiful face in the world.

Various interlopers, hangers on, gauchos, psychos, tarantulas, and blowing Doritos Chip bags.

Marcus: Cut it. The engine's loud; it's disturbing the old folks.

Jackson: Who hangs out at a gas station anyway?

Marcus: Look at them all. Just waiting around here like a gaggle of monks waiting for the Eucharist.

Willard: They're all lined up like they're buying lottery tickets. I just hope it's not the line to the bathroom.

Willard: (to the line) Is this the line to the shitter?

Man in Hat, Bandalero: No shitter here. You'll have to go into the desert, water a cactus. Watch out for snakes, tarantulas, and bats, old man.

Willard: Good God. We pay for gas, we expect facilities. I'm going off into the desert, searching for the promised land. If I'm not back in 15, nah, say 20, send a rescue party.

Marcus: Customer service is null and void these days. What are you gents waiting for?

Chorus of men in line: Our chance to talk to her. (They point)

Marcus: Got a girl turning tricks in the bathroom. It's a right nasty place to do your business. Royal Flush. Disgusting.

Jackson: No way. You've debauched plenty of bathrooms.

Marcus: Never paid for it though. That's filthy.

Chorus of men in line: She's not for sale. We wish she were. We'd give anything for her. This woman is a virgin. The best one going. The most beautiful woman on the planet.

Marcus: Psshah, in these parts? You'd be lucky if she has all her teeth.

Jackson: Why? You never know. Menelaus found Helen in a clam digger colony. Your most famous fashion models come from the slums of Rio, children of whores and foreign tourists. One thousand times mixed.

Marcus: Pure blood is for the butcher. I'll take my babes muttley, a gypsy for me, a gypo with wild hair and loins on fire, a greasy one, prime for a shower. Let's have a look at her.

Chorus of men in line: You can all wait your turn. We're in line. Buying beer, asking her for a date. She claims she's waiting for the prince of her heart. Whatever that means.

Marcus: Could be you or I, my good sir.

Willard: Back from my piss, gents. Everything came out all right.

Jackson: I'd thought you would have gotten lost, for sure.

Willard: Give me some credit. I don't have dementia yet.

Jackson: Let's go.

Marcus: Not without seeing her. A man should never pass a beautiful woman by without making a pass at her. Rule 103.

Willard: I agree. Life's too short.

Marcus: If you fail, you stuff her in the spank bank of hopefuls. These pricks won't let us in line and from the looks of it; some have been waiting for years, all sun burnt and crusty.

Willard: You idiots, what's the only thing that will hold a man's attention besides a beautiful woman?

Marcus: A more beautiful woman? There aren't any around.

Willard: No, you fools. The car. An ultra rare car. Our car.

Jackson: Go get it, Willard. Here are the keys. You bash it, you're dead. Marcus and I will brain you and bury you in the desert.

Willard: I can't drive it.

Jackson: Ha! So it's up to me!

Marcus: Make the announcement.

Jackson: Gentlemen, my associates and I are with the Royal Society of Anachronistic Automobiles.

Marcus: You idiot, no. What my friend means to say, gentlemen, is that we are both purists of a sort. We buy American for America types, and we are here doing a study on the pure joy that a 1969 Pontiac GTO Judge brings to a crowd of fellow Americans. This car, my good men, is one of the rarest North American muscle cars, and my faithful friend and I are driving it cross country to spread mirth and glee to the masses, as well as attempt to get as much pussy as possible before our inevitable demise.

Jackson: And we're raising money for CANCER. I mean, CANCER RESEARCH.

Marcus: No we aren't. But we are on an important mission. Now my assistant Jackson here will be bringing up the Judge for your perusal. Any of you fine gentlemen who want to sit in it, pose for photographs with it, or touch the vinyl seating will be free to do so. We only ask that you keep sharp objects away from the interior and that any of you sun burnt gentlemen will refrain from sitting inside until your peeling subsides. Who wants to see it?

Chorus of men in line: We don't believe you.

(A car engine, full of timbre, bravado, and a twinge of doom sounds in the distance.)

Marcus: Here it comes now, gents!

Man with Hat, first in line: Sounds like a Ford Mustang or Pinto!

Marcus: You will eat your words, good sir. Okay, Mr. Man, just for that comment you can just look on from a distance, while the others get to touch the car.

Man in sweatpants, 5th in line: You should have gotten a COPA CHEVELLE SS, sucker.

Marcus: Easier said than done. What do you drive, Johnny Walker?

(Jackson appears with the Judge. The men of the chorus gasp.)

Marcus: You see! We delivered! Now you come forward, but don't touch. Don't get your grubby dick beaters on the finish. If you do, we'll remove your prints and ensure your prosecution. The long dong of the law will smack you upside your head. Willard, manage this freak show. Jackson and I will go inside to claim our prize.

(The men crowd around the car.)

Marcus: Jackson, now! Follow me into the shop!

We busted into the shop trailed by a contrail of desert dust like we were fighter planes. The assorted riff raff of the desert, gauchos, day laborers, fire chiefs, off duty cops, shop stocker boys, all vying to win the heart of the lovely Nascha Otekah (OWL SUN MAIDEN), had just flaked out at seeing a one of a kind classic car. Willard continued to distract the suitors by lifting the hood and letting them finger the engine. I discovered behind the counter, surrounded by plastic bullet proof caging, potato chip bags, five hour energy drinks over whose shoulder an alive with pleasure advertisement clock from before my birth featuring a man with a 1970s porno moustache and a babe with no discernible posterior tick-tocked with the wrong time, thousands of rainbow colored disposable lighters, trapped in there in her little cubicle of commerce, the most beautiful woman on the planet Earth at that present moment. She was slightly chubby, smacking on pork rinds and a coke.

I gasped when I saw her. I put my hand over my mouth. My dopamine receptors fired and up took the beauty. My god, I thought, she should be a model for sculptors, that she should be anywhere in the world but here in this dump, this nowheresville surrounded by all these goobers and mongrels, one of them bound to win her heart when she gets too bored and tired and lets down her guard and lets him drive a big ole shiny new truck with mud flaps that compensated for a tremendously shrunken pathetic little pee-pee, hung like a desert fruit bat who suffered from malnutrition, or a wee man who was wee in his mentality as well who would only beat her and turn her into a leathery old woman in no time, but would also succeed in pumping his worthless genes into such a prized receptacle.

Then it occurred to me as I browsed the magazines, oh my god, I was in the tits and ass section, what would she think of me now? She would think I was some sort of pervert. I stumbled out, staggered past the round boobies, the Spanish rags and the stroke books into a more appropriate section. I picked one out and browsed it.

Hanely stood by the beverages and goaded me onto the prize, "Come on dude go up there and make a go at her. Remember what I said? Never miss an opportunity to make a pass on a beautiful woman. Married or not, single, young, old. Don't miss it. That is the lesson for all men, my man. Haven't you ever seen a short, ugly guy who has a gorgeous, vivacious Amazonian on his arm?"

"Yeah, I always assumed he was packing a meat missile in his pants."

"Well he may be, but first he has to go up and talk to her."

I made my mind up to approach her. But then, I saw it.

A rack of books. One of those circular spinning shelves loaded to the brim with literary Doritos. Trash fiction. You know the kind that idiots may buy in a gas station in Nevada for 4.99, disposable like the rest of the junk in the store, comfort food designed to fill you up but not providing any nutritive substance. And who did I see lining the shelves, but my handsome mug! An old photo of me with the suit and tie on looking all officially writer-like, and the nauseating cover art, pink and lavender with two intertwined hearts and Marcus Hanely in wild pursuit of Veronica Dare, he naked from the waist up, and her in a ripped shirt, probably ripped by his man hands, or running through bulrushes. The novel was called a masterpiece of late romance literature, the quintessential piece of masturbation fiction with length and girth and veiny importance, a triumph of the English, dusty, forgotten, the clits rubbed, moved onto bigger, thicker, better, newer escapades. I grabbed it. I whipped out my omni-present pocket pen. I signed a salutation:

To the Finder of this book, you are about to read the most beauti-fully written, yet disgusting piece of inveterate trash ever published. You will discover no deeper meaning. It will leave you with an illogical notion of manhood and maidenhood, but hey thanks for your money.
Happy Clit Thumping,
J. LEMAN

ACT II. THE NAVAJO GODDESS DISCOVERS MY CRIME

Nascha: Hey! You can't write in the books! What are you doing?

Jackson: What? I didn't write in the book.

Nascha: You did! I saw you! You did! You wrote in there damn near close to a paragraph. I'll call the police!

Jackson: Miss, I'm the author of the book. I was signing it, for you, you read don't you?

Nascha: Not really. I don't believe you.

Hanely: Sure is. Show her your ID, Jackson.

(J. Leman pulls out his wallet, and flips the book around)

Jackson: See? It's me. I wouldn't lie to you. Jeez, you're gorgeous.

Nascha: Still, if you wrote in the book, you have to pay for it. And thank you. Thank you for your compliment.

Jackson: No problem. Say, you don't ever get bored of working here?

Nascha: Of course I get bored. Who wouldn't?

Jackson: You're destined for greater things. I know it.

Nascha: Just because I'm pretty? Because my face looks nice?

Jackson: You look more than nice. You're the most beautiful woman I've ever seen.

Nascha: You're a famous author aren't you? Why don't you go hang out with actresses and models?

Jackson: I've given up the phony life.

Marcus: No, damnit, you idiot; these women want to be actresses and models! What you have to say is, "I have and none of them hold a candle to you." Stop playing the forlorn artist...chicks dig money and power, man. The only chicks that dig a skinny little twit artist are hippies who smell and don't shave, and hipster chicks that are frumpy and confused. Tell her you'll help make her famous. She'll be on your dick in no time.

Jackson: Well, I mean, I've met plenty of models and actresses, and frankly, miss, none of them even hold a candle to you. I also have friends in the industry... *I'm sure they'd be happy to pick you up out of this third world in the midst of the first world dump and splash your face on advertisements a face without a name, a beautiful body who never speaks just stares and makes little girls feel bad that they weren't born you all powerful succubus of the shopping mall! You black hole of the almighty dollar! You high priestess! They will feed you saltines and you can marry a quarterback you can cuckold him with a famous person! As famous as to your liking and your fame will increase and you will never die you will be an immortal capable of smiting entire cities with your hand! Just a wave, really! Or maybe, just maybe, they will slap you on a casting couch and use you until you're good and worn and they decide you're much too ethnic for leading roles and Native American movies are played out and you can breed with white bread and dilute you heritage in hopes that your granddaughter can be exploited by the industry you failed at, better to marry a smart doctor and settle down to being a kept woman than ever try and grind your soul into pure stardust, you'll be happier, but ultimately you'll be happier with me.*

Nascha: You okay? You kind of zoned out on me.

Jackson: Here allow me to give you a business card. Please stay in touch.

Hanely: No, you fucking fool. Look at her eyes. She wants you, man. You could probably convince her to close up shop and take her in the restroom and fuck her good and proper.

Jackson: No one does that in real life, Marcus.

Nascha: Whom are you talking to? Who's Marcus?

Jackson: Over there by the soda cooler.

Nascha: You're here alone.

(Jackson spins around)

Jackson: You're saying my compatriot isn't real? He's on the book's cover. I was there when the artist painted him.

Nascha: Well, you and he may have been there, but you're the only one here right now.

Jackson: That bastard! He must have slipped out while I wasn't looking or was talking to you, lovely.

Nascha: That's him there on the cover? No, I would have noticed him come in. You came in alone, stopped at the skin mags. When you noticed you were looking at them, you looked up at me to see if I had noticed. You said a few words to the soda case. Then you walked up and started writing in the book. I do believe you wrote the book, I mean your picture is on it. It looks old though, like you've aged a lot since then.

Jackson: I published it ten years ago.

Nascha: Jeez, that must have been a rough ten years.

Jackson: Please come with me. Leave this dump.

Nascha: This dump is my home, sir.

Jackson: Come with me.

Nascha: I can't.

Jackson: I can't leave you.

Nascha: Most all of these losers say that.

Jackson: I'm no loser.

Nascha: Is that your car outside?

Jackson: It is. It's a 1969 Pontiac GTO Judge. Want to take a ride out into the desert with me?

Nascha: Looks like those guys are about to start stripping it for parts.

(Jackson looks out the window; the mob has ripped Willard from the automobile, one of them stands on its hood. Willard is hanging on for dear life to the steering wheel.)

Jackson: You motherfuckers! Shoot them, Willard! Shoot them!

Willard: I don't have a gun!!

Jackson: You! Hot stuff!! What's your name?

Nascha: Nascha.

Jackson: Nascha, distract them!

Nascha: How?

Jackson: I don't know! Pull out your titties or something.

Nascha: No way!

(Nascha grabbed a shotgun from behind the countertop and ran outside, racking a shell into the chamber. The men stopped their stomping and looked upwards, towards her.)

Nascha: All right, you idiots! Leave this man's car alone or I'll call the cops and they'll haul all of your worthless asses to jail. And if any of you worthless mother fucks harasses me again, I'll blow your ass away. Be gone! Get the fuck out of here!

Men: But Nascha! We love you! You are our dream. You are all we talk about, all we think about, our highest hope.

Nascha: I'm sorry. We're closed for business. Get out of here.

Jackson: Come with me.

Nascha: I cannot. I'll call you. Make sure you answer. I will not call twice.

Jackson: My phone will be glued to my ear, beautiful.

Hanely: Good going, chump. You got a friend for life. The most beautiful woman in the world, and she's your friend. How cute. Make sure you set up a play date with her you pantywaist, you handholding rammer, and you wimp.

Jackson: Enough, Marcus, enough. Stop your reproach and get your big, dumb ass in the car. Where were you hiding anyway? You abandoned me in my time of need.

Marcus: Sorry, I took a stroke book into the bathroom. Nature called. Looks like you did fine on your own, stud muffin.

Willard freed himself from the last of the ruffians who melted into the desert night and slithered away like rattlesnakes into whatever trash-strewn burrows or trailers they called home. They slithered back to wives and abandoned girlfriends, spurned lovers and flames kept weak through neglect, rejected by one better they implored to be let back in by shouting promises and beating on their chests. Make no mistake ladies; a snake drags himself on his belly because his legs have been chopped off by defeat. Defeat him twice and he becomes a worm, thrice and he shrivels to nothingness, a black hole of no escape.

I jumped into the driver's seat, and I yelled to Nascha, "I will never forget you! Never forget me!"

With Willard in front, and Hanely sprawled, exhausted in back, I gunned the GTO. It roared and scattered the remnants of the cockroaches. I hit the lights, brazen specters chopping through doom. I looked in the rearview mirror. Nascha held her shotgun out in the darkness. We sped off, our mad party, towards the East and Great Salt Lake.

Willard moaned a cloistered little moan of slow boiling death. More a lament. "Should've fucked those whores you knew about in West Wendover, Marcus," Willard said.

"Someone didn't want to stop. Says we might've run into Red there."

"Red's back at the Ogilvy wasting his life. It will be years before he leaves. Did you see a clock in there?"

"Nope. No clock. No sense of time. No windows. He's as good as dead. He'll never have the inclination to look up and wonder where we are. He's got more money to make, so he'll stack the chips to the ceiling, staving off his opportunity to cash out. He'll keep putting it off and off, and off and off, off and off, into the future. His money will come to fill the entire room, suffocate the other patrons, fill all the available space with gold, and he still won't be able to cash out. Did you notice there was no cashier? They're all doomed. Flytrap, what goes in doesn't come out," Willard said.

"Sure thing, old Willard boy, but Red's happy, that's for sure, and he's out of our hair."

My phone rang. My heart leapt. It could be Nascha, calling already to declare her love for me. I answered, my heart full of light and mirth.

"Hello?" I said.

MR. MAN CALLS ON THE TELEPHONE FOR THE OLD BATTLE AXE, PROGRESS

Mr. Man: It's me, your agent, we haven't forgotten about all we discussed, have we?

Jackson: Just what did we discuss? I've had a trying couple of days. Father is dying, don't you know.

Mr. Man: I just got off the phone with your father's nurse. It seems you've not arrived yet. They are quite concerned that you won't make it in time.

Jackson: If they're concerned, they can call me themselves. They have my number.

Mr. Man: They say you're not answering. They knew you'd answer my call.

Jackson: I'd rather talk to them than you. What are you really calling for?

Mr. Man: Found any inspiration out on the road, good sir? I hope you have. I really hope you have. The folks at PARENT CORPORATION are getting nervous; there has been talk of ending your production line if you don't produce a sequel. Tell me, don't you like the nice things you have? That nice house there in Monterey? That gorgeous Ferrari? That gorgeous girlfriend of yours?

Jackson: I've abandoned the house to my Colombian maid. The Ferrari is wrecked. And my girlfriend? The one you set me up with? She didn't last three weeks. I guess my publicist stopped paying her to swizzle my stick, so she's probably back in her former eastern bloc country living like a princess. Who knows, who cares?

Mr. Man: Oh. Well, how much progress have you made on a sequel to *Asymmetric Hearts*?

Jackson: Not much. I've met the most beautiful woman in the world though. Much more beautiful than Veronica Dare. Much more beautiful than your model wife who I bought and paid for with my phenomenal best seller! Now you'll get a sequel to *Asymmetric Hearts* when I shit you a sequel! Until then, leave me alone. I'm in a period of bereavement. Tell that to the PARENT CORPORATION.

Mr. Man: Jackson. Listen to me. Can you just send me a single chapter? Just an intro to let PARENT CORPORATION BOARD OF DIRECTORS not to think you're out there flapping in the breeze? Please? Send me at least five pages. Just let them know you're a risk worth keeping around on the books. Let me assure them that you're on the same team, that you're willing to play ball, Jackson.

Jackson: Come at me with a non-sports metaphor; they're injurious to my ears. You're a fucking literary agent for chrissakes, not a sports agent. Come at me with a goddamn literary inspired metaphor and I'll get to work. Otherwise, you can fuck yourself...I won't do a goddamn thing. I won't type so much as a sentence.

Mr. Man: Do you think you're great? You think you're some sort of gift to literature? You're not anything without us. We'll own your persona! Own your image. We'll pay some ghostwriter to turn out your crack rocks for the bored and horny housewives.

Jackson: You can't do that!

Mr. Man: Have a lawyer go over your contract. An independent set of eyes. Have a whole team of lawyers look at it. And while you're home in Denver, Colorado, go ahead and have a little peek into your father's warehouses, if you think you're so fucking special. Go ahead and do a little investigation into Leman Global Industries Warehouse Way, Number 1480 C, Warehouse 17. Look in Warehouse 17, boy. Just you go ahead and look in there, Jackson. Then tell me that you both hate your father and that you're a literary genius.

Jackson: What's in there?

Mr. Man: A surprise. You should probably call me when you come to your senses about your future literary endeavors. And you had better shit me a chapter soon.

Jackson: Now you've got me intrigued. I'll send you Eros, Mr. Man. I'll send you an obese Eros, unable to fly, let alone shoot an arrow.

Mr. Man: Just send it to me. The Editor can polish it up.

Jackson: A chapter? I'll send you a book. I'll write like the annals of time depend on my efforts. Hanely! Take the wheel! I'll write!

<<HANG UP>> UHH UHH UHH.

Hanely: Let the old man drive - switcheroo!

Jackson: You ready, Willard?

Willard: (flabbergasted) For what?

Jackson: Switcheroo!

Willard: You want me to take the wheel?

Jackson: Just slide over me.

Willard: No way! I'm not doing that. No way in hell.

Hanely: Come on pussy. Get over there. You know you want to drive this fucking pussy wagon. Get over there Willard.

Willard: No way! Why don't you just pull over, and we'll do a Chinese fire drill like civilized adults.

Jackson: I'm only doing 90 Willard. Come on this car is very stable.

Willard: It sounds like a fucking warthog coming through the underbrush after its kinfolk.

Hanely: Ah, you and your Okie sensibilities. Fuck it. Pull over when we hit Utah. The Bonneville Salt Flats. We'll let Willard drive there. He can take over. I need to ogle babes, and you need to write this fucking schlock romance novel to get these New York psychos off your back.

Willard: You want a love story? I've got plenty of them.

Hanely: You know any Amish love stories? Ever fucked a Pennsylvania Dutch?

Willard: No, sorry, mine are pretty tame.

Hanely: Don't worry. My friend here will take your tame love affairs and turn them into fiery gold dust, like you bedded Sophia Fucking Loren.

Willard: Can't say that I have.

Hanely: Well no shit Willard! Just tell us. Tell us about your first time. Please, Willard, enlighten us, you kinky old fucker.

Jackson: Leave him alone; if it makes him feel uncomfortable then he doesn't have to do it.

Willard: You grandiose humper, you're damn right I'll do it. I'll tell you every last lascivious detail of my life from the first to the last, with a bunch thrown in between. Why I've stumped more women than you've ever talked to, queer bait.

Hanely: Me?

Jackson: Me?

Willard: Both of you put together, you wet behind the ears little twerps, making me watch the fucking car while you louse up an operation with the most beautiful woman on the planet. Why, in my day I would've had her in the backseat while you two idiots fought off the mob outside. She would've come with us.

Hanely: Whatever.

Jackson: We'll see when we get to Bonneville.

Willard: Drive on you lily livered, magpie eating, one suit wearing, brown underwear stained, idiot. If you had a brain, you'd take it out and play with it, while asking directions to the playground.

Jackson: Willard, why don't you just sleep? Go to sleep.

Hanley: Why'd we pick this guy up?

Willard: I got that idiot businessman off your back didn't I? Goddamn kids losing respect for their elders. Back in my time, I would have cleaned your clock.

Hanely: Well it's not your time.

Willard: Your time was up about five years ago. It's my time now. You know why the world sucks? Because young idiots like you are in charge of it.

Jackson: Believe me, Marcus isn't in charge of anything. Don't let him fool you. He's got so called executive looks, a full head of hair, and a great build. Why, he could donate his sperm to fertilize a rich cunt, but he's got empty spaces upstairs, man, nothing but vacant housing, a housing bubble. Marcus's head is a housing bubble. Hilarious!

Hanely: Sure thing, Jackson. Tell me why all those women go home with me time and time again.

Jackson: Look at you. You've got nothing on your mind to dissuade them from taking you home. The less you talk the better. They don't see you as a mate. They see you as...

Hanely: As what?

Willard: A fuck, my boy. That's it. You're a fuck to them like any fuck slut you meet on the street, but you don't get paid.

Hanely: Sure I do.

Jackson: How?

Hanely: That one old broad bought me a motorcycle.

Jackson: No, she let you ride the one she was paying off, because she had a Marlon Brando fantasy. Where's that motorcycle now?

Hanley: Repossessed.

Willard: Oh damn! That sucks, never had anything taken from me. I paid all my debts, never been a debtor, never went under in a business. Come in with nothing, leave with nothing, I say.

Hanely: It's okay. The bitch cornered me.

Jackson: You told me outright that she paid for it. That she wrote a check for 15,000 bucks to the dealership.

Hanely: She did. I guess it was only a down payment for services rendered.

Willard: How much did you owe?

Hanely: 2000 bucks or so.

Willard: And you couldn't pay that measly sum off?

Hanely: Nope. Never made a payment.

Jackson: I told you he's broke. Broke as a joke. He has no hope. No skills other than looking pretty. No means to apply, as all the jobs are beneath him. It's the product of being too handsome for the good of anyone. He thinks he can get by on looks alone.

Willard: I know the type. A user of women. A babe that never left the tit. Milks women for all they're worth. When he sucks them dry, he moves on. A handsome hack. A parasite.

Hanely: I'm no parasite. I please all those women. I show them the best time of their lives.

Willard: Has a woman ever killed herself over you?

Jackson: Like Ophelia'd herself? Drowned in a pond by a willow on Marcus's account? Probably dozens. But no, I doubt it. He's too stupid. He's a male slut, no more, no less. A drill bit. Good for a spin. That's all.

Hanely: Millions of babes balled in my young life without a word edgewise. You know, stick and move, stab and poke, and roll on.

Willard: Don't you want to find a wife?

Hanely: That's the death of me, old man.

Willard: How do you know? You haven't tried it.

Hanely: My pops said it was the death of him. He was another lascivious fucker of babes. The motherfucker showed up twice: my conception and my thirteenth birthday. I wouldn't try something I knew was bound to fail.

Willard: It's tough for a young man to grow up without a father.

Jackson: You're right.

Hanely: No it isn't. It just forces independence. Dimwitticus here has been trying to escape the curse of being a rich man's son for the past 32 years, and now he's just sort of drifting back to the epicenter to see his poor papa perish, a papa who never had time for him when he was growing up.

Willard: Have some respect for our friend here.

Jackson: It's true. I grew up, raised by tutors and nannies, I barely saw the old bastard. When he was home, he was chiding me for not doing better in my studies. You've only just read the *Complete Works of William Shakespeare* he says. Just? I was 10. The bastard has the *First Folio* in his library. The original. It makes for a good businessman to be able to discuss a wide variety of topics. 'You never know what will spark someone to sign a deal with you,' he would always say.

Marcus: His house is a museum. Who's going to get all that crap when he kicks it?

Jackson: Don't know. His will is sealed. Maybe he'll dole it out to girlfriends. Only had one ex wife. Plenty of girlfriends though.

Willard: Ex wives are the banes of a sane man's existence. They drove you crazy when you were with them, but for a woman to become your mortal enemy, to go from sharing your bed to plotting your murder with a notorious outlaw, who just so happens to be in possession of the biggest trouser sausage this side of the Mississippi, Pantaloony Baloney!

Hanely: What the fuck?

Jackson: One of your wives plotted to murder you?

Willard: (clears throat) Yep. Didn't do anything either. That was just for being around. Some women would rather be a widow than a divorcee, no matter the speed at which they remarry. Ole Wild Tom McGundree rolled into town and bedded her, hot little piece of ass, she was. If you ever do marry, Jackson, marry a troll of a woman and keep her fat.

Hanely: He will; that's all he goes for. Find the biggest bundle of joy in the room and glom onto her, climb her like Everest. Right, Jackson?

Jackson: That's universal gravitation, man.

Willard: Attraction is the unifying force of the universe.

Hanely: What?

Willard: It goes along with your hypothesis, Jackson. The best types of people are created by lust. Animal attraction. No fighting it. Not even the churchmen with all their pronouncements and fatwas and bullshit can fight it. Yep, Tom McGundree bedded my wife, good and proper, well enough for him to convince her to take a large insurance policy out on me and cut the break cables of my 1953 Buick. Kind of dumb, because we lived in Iowa at the time, the car rolled to a stop in an empty cornfield.

Hanely: The bastard. Did you shoot him?

Willard: Caught them in flagrant dee leck tee o, buried to the hilt, pommel horse style.

Marcus: Froggy style.

Jackson: What did you do?

Willard: Ahh, got good and drunk. Didn't even announce my presence. Threw the floozy out of my house and called the sheriff. Tom McGundree got away, took my wife with him. Heard he dumped her a few towns down the road when something' else caught his eye and made him forget all about her. She made an attempt to come back, but there's no real coming back from that.

Jackson: Women should be faithful.

Hanely: Don't agree with that sentiment. I love sluts. Just think if women weren't built to fuck and take dong like unrepentant monkeys, then none of us would be here.

Jackson: They aren't sluts any more than you're a man whore. You're built for one thing too, my man...sowing seed in foreign fields.

Hanley: I was blessed to shoot blanks too. All fun, no responsibility. If I were born with functional balls, my offspring would probably be able to have family reunions in a football stadium.

Willard: You too, eh? How'd you find out?

Hanely: I just know.

Willard: The doctor looked at your spunk under a microscope?

Marcus: Nah, I don't let it fly in cups.

Jackson: Onanist!

Willard: You ever stuck around long enough to find out?

Marcus: Not really.

Jackson: You're probably a walking clapfest.

Hanely: You're just jealous.

Jackson: Elko, Nevada. Five Miles.

Hanely: I know an excellent whorehouse there. Legal of course. Say Willard, when's the last time you had your carrot snapped?

Willard: I don't remember. 1984 maybe?

Hanely: Shit, Ronnie Reagan was in office the last time you dipped your wick in a hot fudge sundae. Going there might do you some good. Got any pressure in the fire hose? We might have to stop and get him a Viagra.

Willard: I'll just sit there and chat the girls up, like a proper gentleman.

Jackson: Most of 'em need a father figure.

Hanely: Yeah, Methuselah, get 'em on your lap and let them work out their problems with you.

Willard: Your womanizing will catch up with you. You quite possibly, no, you have, spread misery and waste in the world. You probably have scores of little bastards who look just like you out there, terrorizing playgrounds. You should settle down and let a woman tame you.

Jackson: That would require him to be tamable. This man is a beast. A force of nature. Pure energy.

Willard: You ever had a woman leave you because you couldn't produce a child? You know how that feels?

Hanely: I don't feel any less of a man, so why would you?

Willard: We're from different times, boy. A man was someone who got married and had children.

Hanely: So, one wife left you for an escaped convict, and one left you for a virile man?

Willard: Yes, it's a goddamn curse. I didn't do anything wrong, ever. All I wanted was a son. (Sobs slightly)

Hanely: It's a blessing. I have nothing to worry about. Come on, Willard.

Jackson: Leave him alone you boorish fuck. How do I get to the whorehouse?

Willard: Cathouse. Don't call them whores. That's an ugly word.

Marcus: Women have kicked you in your teeth for your whole life. Why do you still respect them so much?

Willard: It's all we have. Ties between men and women. The rest is just blackness, oblivion. Stuff. Just a few women have treated me wrong. I don't know, maybe wolves raised them. Maybe they made horrible decisions in moments of weakness, maybe they wanted a child just as much as I did and they left when they saw they were chained to an incapable man. Why are you such a simpleton,

Marcus? Oh, I know, because you've been born gorgeous, God's gift to women. We all know you've a dong the size of a dwarf's leg between your legs and your dangler produces instantaneous orgasms in every woman you deign to slide it into. Well, on the outside you're a good-looking man, you're handsome, you're gorgeous. I'm sure your doting mother fumed over you. I bet she told you that your daddy was coming home for Christmas every year. I bet you missed out on a lot. You clung to your mama like a scared little monkey, alone in the wilderness. You've been clinging to her since then in the visage of every woman you meet and use. Every woman you manipulate, every woman you convince that you might stick around and then just disappear on them the first time you start to have feelings for them, just like your old goddamn dear old pa did. It's a goddamn shame, boy. A goddamn shame.

Hanely: Stop moralizing on me like a damn Reverend.

Willard: Truth hurts, Marcus. It hurts badly. You're a goddamn black hole of a human being, not even light escapes from you.

Hanely: Whatever.

Willard: That's all you can say. Whatever. Whatever happens, happens. Idiot.

Jackson: Where the hell is this cathouse? Elko's going to pass us by while you two have this therapy session.

Willard: Ain't any therapy session, Jackson. This guy needs an exorcism. Who knows, maybe he's Lucifer himself. Where did you meet this fucking psycho?

Jackson: College.

Hanely: Yeah, I saved his life. Made him the man he is today.

Willard: How?

Hanely: Found him at his lowest and built him up. Boy here was about to drink cyanide before I showed up.

Willard: What the hell were you going to do that for?

Jackson: I wasn't right in the head. I don't know. I was confused.

Willard: Well good thing you didn't do that, eh? Aren't you glad?

Hanely: Of course he is.

Willard: Why don't you let Jackson answer?

Jackson: Yes, I am. Marcus has been here with me ever since.

Willard: He's leading you off a cliff. Don't you have other friends?

Hanely: He doesn't need any, really.

Willard: Why don't you let Jackson answer for himself? Shut the fuck up, Marcus, and let the man speak!

Jackson: (silent, eyes fixed on the road) Where is the whorehouse?

<<PRESLEY'S PUSSY PARLOR>>

The building was boxy, the curtains drawn, there were no silhouettes in the window panes and the place was drab yellow clapboard, built in the 1920s to be the office of a dentist who lost his practice in the mining collapse and did the natural thing heading further west to fill the cavities of the stars. The only thing, which would show that there were women inside trading comfort for cash, was a red light bulb on in the front porch decorative light. The place had changed owners to become a bar, a hangout of bikers and notorious youth. In 1978, the clapboard tavern put up the red light. Floppy breasts and squishy asses with big bushes between the legs gave way to taut bodies and scrawny little sorority girls hooked on dope, which gave way to Mexicans and girls hard on their luck, but they all smiled, all the time. Plastered on their faces were smiles. A few giddy boys waited outside, having to ring the bell to enter and announce their presence. An older woman dressed in a slinky, yet elegant red evening dress appeared and inquired how they all were and told them very politely to furnish some form of identification. The youngest looking one of the two produced an ID car from his ass pocket and gave it to her.

"Doesn't even look like you, kid," she said.

"We've got money."

"Sonny, 21 or older, we sell booze here too. Why don't you try one of the other places? We're not selling anything for you," she said.

"Please, lady, we're almost out of gas."

"Fill up your tank and go some place cheaper," she said.

"You look old enough to be in here," she said to Marcus, Willard, and I.

"Young, dumb, and full of cum," I said.

"Do you have any Viagra for my elderly friend?"

The woman looked puzzled.

"Don't need it, you young prick," Willard said.

"Want to come in? There's a two drink minimum."

"What's on the menu?"

"Come inside. We'll discuss everything."

We were ushered into a hallway; dingy and cluttered like a Tijuana alley. I think it was to dissuade the faint of heart and Mormons from entering the pleasure chamber. She opened a door. I felt my temperature rising and could hear my blood pressure and heart beat in my ears. Marcus strode forward, walking with the madam, his hand loosely on her waist, migrating south with each stride as if by force of gravity. She made no attempt to move it. He gave her rear a few squeezes and smiled back to me, and still she made no attempt to move it. You were a real man if you could fuck the madam, Marcus always said. It was his forte. Sit there and look bored until she came up to inquire if he was having a good time. No, but I could be, wink, wink. There was a reason some women were just madams. Queen bees, Marcus would say. Just like mom.

The madam opened the door. To all those who witness these presents: greetings.

From the outside, the place of ill repute looked plain, perhaps to distract your mega-church-going public who seem to be drawn towards glitzy, glamorous things. On the inside, the décor was anything but plain. There was a central circular recessed floor, marble in color but not substance, with pink tapestries on the walls. Couches lined the recess of the floor, magenta in color, a style of the 1970s (perhaps the last time this room was decorated), but who cared about the decorations in a cathouse as long as the women were hot and willing? The place could have a dirt floor and straw to flop out in, for chrissakes. A third world fuck house. The same throughout the world, heaven.

I had never been in one but I listened to Hanely's stories about them and imagined them to be just that, a little slice of heaven, or whatever the current cliché is. Anyways, this place had an organist. What a quaint touch! She sat in the corner on a small organ, like the types that tended to play Christmas carols in a vain attempt to hawk the pianos in Midwestern shopping malls. The woman was buxom, sitting there at her organ playing ditties that may have been popular right after Willard left the Second World War. These ditties Willard recognized immediately and began a strange little shuffle stomp. He shuffled his left foot in front of his right and stomped, stomped, stomped his boot on the ground and really danced well for a geriatric. Hanely sat down and ogled the madam. He fingered her over to come talk to him, but she didn't seem the least bit interested and just stared off into space.

"I don't care about the rest of these ladies," he said. "I've only got eyes for you, madam! Name your price, and my friend here will gladly pay!"

I shook my head no to her and felt the cell phone vibrate in my pants pocket, again against my balls. I looked at it, a text message for the world's most annoying agent.

> ARE YOU MAKING ANY PROGRESS ON THE NOVEL?

I texted him back.

> I'M DOING RESEARCH. FUCK OFF!

Little seconds later, the cell phone vibrated. I looked at the caller ID, hoping it was the world's prettiest woman, Nascha.

The caller ID read MR. BALL BAG. This was how I stored my agent's contact information in my phone. He was probably very offended that I told him to fuck off. I rejected the call and turned my phone off.

Marcus sulked on the circular couch, unable to get the madam's attention.

"This here's the way to a woman's heart, boys," Willard said, doing his old man shuffle, as he worked up a bit of a sweat.

"It's my wallet!" Marcus shouted at him.

"You mean my wallet," I said.

"You going to do some research here?" Marcus asked. "If not I say we get the fuck out of here. Willard's having too much fun. He might have a heart attack or something."

"No such luck there, stud," Willard said, out of breath.

The madam approached me. "I've got to get the ladies down here, they're sleeping. You came in kind of late."

"Sorry, ma'am," I said.

"Tell them to do some stretching exercises," Marcus said. The madam ignored him, obviously thinking he was a boorish individual, not paying him any heed.

"She's dealt with rude ones before. It's obvious," Willard said.

Marcus sulked some more. I had never really seen him thusly rejected. He probably was plenty of times, though I had just never witnessed it. Willard sat next to me, out of breath, dripping sweat.

"Can't you have fun, Marcus?" he asked.

"Shut up, old man," Marcus said, sulking.

"You'll forget all about that old lady when these young girls come out."

"I doubt it."

"Mommy issues," Willard said smiling.

"And daddy issues. He's all fucked," I said.

"Both of you dick lickers can lick a dick," Marcus said angrily.

Women began sauntering into the room, dressed in hooker costumes. I would pick the one who looked like she least wanted to be there and purchase her services. But I wouldn't touch her; I would only talk to her. She was the fifth one. She walked with a bad posture. Her makeup looked hurriedly put on. Marcus leapt to his feet and did his best to get the attention of a tall blonde, who also wasn't having it. The madam must have warned them all about the uber good-looking idiot downstairs. The blonde, bored, walked upstairs. Marcus followed her.

The little brunette tried to smile at me when my eyes went over her. I looked at the redheads, blacks, the one Asian who looked like a veteran of somewhere. Nope, it was the brunette. I wanted her life story. I wanted to mine her bitter heart for nuggets of gold. I wanted to know her cares, her hopes, and her dreams. I wanted to understand the heart of this woman. I stood up. I took her by the hand. She seemed shocked that I was going up with her. I grabbed her by the waist and smiled at her. Her visage did not float higher in the least.

Willard called to me, "I'll just wait here with all of the ladies. Don't you two escape out the back window and leave me here."

"No worries, pops," I called back to him.

"What?" the young brunette asked.

"Ahh, nothing," I said. "Where's your room?"

"Take a shower first," she said, more like a command than a request.

"Why? I'm not going to do anything."

"Why are you coming up here then?"

"Oh, I'll pay. I just want to talk."

Inside her room was decorated like a teenage girl's room. I do not know if that was intentional or if this was the teenage finger-bang fantasy room where the girl always stopped you when it got too hot and heavy and said, "You don't want to wake my parents." Men probably came here to recapture a youth they left a long time ago. Most probably wanted her to play like she was a lollypop-sucking nymphomaniac. Either way, in the light she didn't look the role, not excited enough to act the part of Lolita, nor was she happy enough to be responsible for the photographs of pop rockers and movie stars all hunked up and sweaty. A light glowed in the corner. She remotely dimmed it and took off her top. Her breasts were mostly areolas, but firm. She tried to bring my hands up to cup them. I sat on the bed, the only place to sit. She sat next to me, almost on top of me. The comforter was pink with light red polka dots. She looked up at me and asked me to make myself at home, stop being so nervous. I removed my jacket. I wasn't going to do it.

"Why don't you give me a hug, stud," she said, disinterested. It was all so sad. She didn't appear nervous. Just bored. Depressed maybe. Maybe an IV drug user. Smack head. Maybe she had HIV. They don't test for that in this godforsaken country. Shit, I'm not going near her. Don't want her hands all over me. I moved further on the bed from her.

She moved from her spot on the bed, stood up and started walking, as sexy as she could, towards me.

I gasped. "What are you doing?"

"I'm going to sit on your lap. You look nervous. Is this your first time with a hooker?"

"No. I mean, yes. I mean, not really." I stammered like a fool. "I've been with hookers before, I swear. I do not live vicariously through my friends, well my only friend, who is now really giving it to the tall blonde."

I can hear schlumping through the wall. In case you were wondering, that's the sound of two heavy bodies colliding over and over again. It sounded like a generator or some other well-machined performance. His pure ability clashed, mutually opposed to my pure fear. Why couldn't I just let go and really give it to this little one the way Marcus was wrecking the slut in the bed next door? It didn't help that the little one was trying to smile and each time I looked at her she just seemed to look sadder and sadder. She reached over and touched me. I recoiled with a gasp.

"Get your hands off me, miss. Hey, don't be so pushy. What do you want anyway?"

"What do you want? You're in a brothel."

"Nothing on the menu."

"You actually just want to talk to me?"

"Yes. That's it."

"Awww, you're a saint."

I heard the sounds of schlump-schlumping from next door, or down the hall. It became a fixation for me. I couldn't concentrate.

"He's really giving it to her."

"Doing what?"

"Laying pipe. He's a pipe laying fool."

"I don't hear anything."

"You can't hear that? I must have supersensitive ears."

She laughed.

"Take those pants off," she said.

"Don't tell me what to do, miss."

"Take 'em off."

"I don't feel comfortable doing that."

"Don't be ashamed, baby."

"I'm not ashamed. I just don't feel comfortable right now."

She reached her hand up my leg and worked it towards my wang's tip. I shuffled back on the bed away from her, like a pre-pubescent boy at a grade school dance.

"Oh, don't be embarrassed. Haven't you been with a woman before?"

"Yes, um, of course."

The woman next door wailed like someone was murdering her with a knife.

"Jesus, he's really giving it to her."

"Pull your pants off."

She thrust her breasts in my face. Sweaty, heavily perfumed. I gagged a bit, unable to breathe. I pushed her off me, backwards onto the bed. She flopped and bounced a couple of times before coming to a rest, with her arms splayed out, titties mashed to the sides.

"What's wrong with you? Be a fucking man and do me."

"I can't right now," I gasped, as Hanely made the whore orgasm next door. She was grunting like a pig, and he screaming something probably profane that I couldn't quite make out.

She ran her hand over it again. I bet she thought I didn't think she was pretty enough.

"Please stop," I muttered.

"What's your problem? You're with a hooker."

"Why do you say that about yourself?"

"That's what I do. Now pull your cock out."

She took off her stockings, and lay on the bed, rubbing her pussy, splaying it open, and trying to excite me. I didn't want to look. She flicked her hand across her landing-strip, down into the wetness. My mind of its own wanger started to respond. She found the glans through my jeans and tickled it.

"Come on, stud," she said licking her lips. "Pull it out."

"Lady, unhand me."

"You're so very strange. Come on, pull it out."

"No. I don't want to, and really, you can't make me. I'm going to sit on the floor in a minute. I just want to talk to you. Can't we just talk like two civilized adults without sex getting in the way?"

She turned the light down low.

"I'm cold," she said.

"Cover up with the blanket."

"I need man warmth. Most of you guys are over and done with by now."

"I'm different."

"You're strange. What's wrong with you?"

"Nothing. I don't feel comfortable."

I heard Hanely get up from his room and heard other voices in the hallway. I think he was negotiating another woman. I didn't hear movement in the room next door. Marcus may have actually murdered that whore. I had the sudden urge to check on him. I rushed to the door and opened it, looked into the hallway. No one was there. It was empty.

"Come back to bed," she said.

I sat down on the floor with the door open.

"Shut the door, please."

I pulled it closed. Quietly.

"What do you do?"

"I'm a writer."

"Hence the need to interview me. You going to use my stories, Mr. Writer?"

"No."

"Have you written anything before?"

"Yeah, a novel. It was pretty successful."

"What's it called?"

"*Asymmetric Hearts.*"

"No fucking way."

"Yes."

"You wrote that?"

"Yes."

"Oh my God, really?"

"Uh huh."

"Veronica Dare is my fucking hero."

"Really?"

"Yes, she's a hero to women everywhere."

"I thought I wrote her as a pushover."

"No way. She's a hero."

"I don't remember."

"What do you mean?"

"I wrote that book to save my life."

"Huh?"

"Yeah, sometimes you have to write things down. Besides, she's fiction. She's not heroic."

"She is. Thank you for writing her down."

"I haven't been in the mood that I have to write anything down for a long time."

"You're rich."

"I know, when an artist gets rich, they start to suck. It happened to my friend Bill, too."

"Bill?"

"Shakespeare. He quit and became a moneylender."

"I didn't know that."

"Yeah, he was a usurer."

"What's that?"

"A loaner of money at an excessive interest rate. A loan shark."

"I never knew that."

"About Shakespeare?"

"Nah, what a usurer was."

"When you get rich, you start to suck."

"That's not true."

"I think it is. If you fall in love with money, you put it before all else."

"What does money get you? Shit. Stuff. Stuff that other people can see. Stuff that other people will value you for, or judge you for. I prefer to be judged on the basis of my prodigious talents."

"Wait! Aren't you rich? Didn't your first novel sell something like five million or six million copies?"

"Seven point five million in the first run. One hundred million globally."

"Oh, I stand corrected," she said.

Her bare breasts gleamed like small globes in the dim light. Hanely was at it again. This woman that Hanely rutted on groaned differently, this one more high-pitched, possibly foreign. I looked away from the lady I was with, who looked at the clock. I think she was hoping I didn't see. I didn't care.

"Why do you only want to talk to me?" she asked.

"You're beautiful, but I don't believe in all of this."

The woman wailed like she was being bitten in half by a crocodile, and Hanely let loose with an ejaculation of various curses, each growing in intensity and disgust, with her ending up yelling, "Yeah, you big-dicked mother fucker, you drive me like a bus! You split me in half, you big greasy fucking stud!" in some foreign accent, which sent shivers, down my spine. The chick I was with was unperturbed.

I let loose with a laugh. She joined me, with a sort of nervous laugh that dissipated the more I laughed. She grasped my hand. I felt the tension melt in my soul. I asked her the questions that I had always wanted to ask these ladies of the night.

"Why are you a whore?"

She took her hand off of mine and recoiled distantly. In her eyes she appeared to be walking through the mists perhaps. I expected that she would be forthcoming and say that most of them liked their line of work that they were into it. They approached it with the pride of a skilled artisan. I read somewhere that most of them were sexually abused by sickos at a young age, forced to do horrible things, and that it was the only way they could experience intimacy. I heard from someone that every "easy" woman, you know the women men call an easy lay, you know one of those women you should just go in and out of for no charge at all, just pick up from a tree, somewhere like a shiny apple, those women like the women that Marcus Hanely frequented, I found out that most of them were sexually abused growing up and they never really got over it, just used that emptiness to chase fulfillment, and that it came in the form of plugging up holes, both physical and emotional in their lives. I felt for them. I really did. I imaged we were perpetuating that cycle by being there, listening to Marcus fuck the whore in the next room as well, listening to how she actually seemed to be really enjoying it and hearing her shudder in orgasm. Marcus would probably brag later about how he never left a woman without an orgasm. His claim to fame. I still waited for her answer. I looked directly at her. Stared into her eyes. She looked away. Then she looked back at me. I had struck some gaping open soft spot in her armor. I don't think anyone ever asked her that question before, and maybe she never asked herself.

"Well, why?"

She laughed nervously, defused the situation.

"Do you really have to know?"

"Yes. I'm trying to study the souls of women."

"Get married then. You can't learn anything from me. You can't study me. In order to learn the soul of a woman you should get married to her and be completely open and honest with her to the point that you are one person. I can just lie all day to you. I've never understood the men, the repeat customers who come in here and expect to find some sort of salvation, the starry eyed ones with a lust in their hearts, whose faces are painted with apprehension, much like the way yours is right now, expecting wisdom from a whore, expecting to mine the soul of women by talking to one of us, like there's some universal essence to us. You know what wisdom is? If you would have come in here and did what you're supposed to do. Be a man, shut the fuck up and put your back into it. You've a lot to learn before you're really ready for the world. There's no way in hell I'm answering the question 'why' for you. Do you think I like asking myself that? Why do you do what you do? Why do you write books? Do you think this profession of mine is a choice that I deliberated?"

"I don't know. I'm trying to get next to the bottom of it."

"Stop observing life and just live life."

"I don't see why the question is so difficult. I mean, I didn't mean to make you feel uncomfortable."

"Money."

"Money? You do it for money?"

"Of course. You expected something noble? Like I'm studying sex and the human male for a graduate school project?"

"No, I guess not. It's just sort of boring."

"It isn't boring. Why do you write? Answer that for me. Why do you write?"

"I'm filling up the empty spaces. Fighting emptiness."

"It's inside you though, right?"

"Yes, I've filled it up all my life."

"Empty. Incomplete. Searching for something, anything, anything to take your mind off of the feeling of emptiness."

"Right."

"You don't fill it up with money, or drugs, or women. You fill it up with stories?"

"Yes. I haven't been writing much though. I don't really want to write anymore."

"Why not?"

"Too demanding."

"Your writing is too demanding?"

"Well, my agent and publisher are too demanding. I'm afraid what I produce won't be as good as the first."

Hanely roared in the next room like a castrated zoo-pacing lion, high pitched and descending to a moan.

"You just have to do it. Why don't you just fire your agent?"

"That would be dishonest. I signed my name to a contract."

"We live an age of universal deceit. Pay the fee. Get out of the contract. Write to fill the emptiness, not for money. Money can't fill the emptiness, only creation can. It's all unfulfilling."

"Do you know about psychology?"

"Nope. No idea."

"You'll make an excellent therapist."

"There isn't therapy. Just self discovery."

"Goddamn, you're a saint."

"No, I'm not."

"I think you are. Patroness of parlor maids."

I laughed. Hanely ejaculated again, his bellows filled the hallways with mirth. God forbid he goes and grabs another girl. The girl I was with was again apathetic to the lusty sounds going on down the hallway.

"Time's up. It's been a pleasure talking to you." She put her tits away immediately.

I walked into the hallway, unfulfilled. I hadn't learned anything. Maybe I was obtuse, incapable of learning anything.

I went from door to door, saying, "Time to go, Marcus." I heard a few unintelligible grunts in response. I felt the peace Marcus was feeling, but not the mixed dread, knowing that the Antechinus would return, seeking future unfulfillment in situations that could only lead to demise, like a taught guitar string plucked, vibrating, settling to zero.

"Marcus. Let's go."

I walked down the stairs. I noticed a sign that I did not notice walking in.

MIND YOUR MANNERS!

NO INSERTION OF DIGITS OR APPENDAGES INTO ANY ORIFICE WITHOUT PRIOR CONSENT OF THE LADY.

My cell phone was dead. I walked the lady downstairs. Willard sat between two ladies, who laughed and told jokes, while he sat there, quite stoic.

"Having fun?" I asked.

"Yeah," the girls bubbled. Willard just smiled.

"That you making all the noise up there?" Willard asked.

"Marcus."

"This guy was a talker," the girl announced.

"No dancing?" The girls asked in unison.

"Don't feel like it much. Much more can be said with words."

"Marcus missed out on a great deal of life being a bumble bee, roaming from flower to flower in search of a hint of sweetness that did not satisfy," Willard said.

"He's no dancing bee, he's an Antechinus," I said.

"A who?" All the girls said in unison.

"An Antechinus. A south Australian marsupial rodent. Looks like a rat with a pointier nose. The males fuck themselves to death during the course of one breeding season. The females lead long happy, hippie lives in a birthing commune, where they raise all the young in some sort of communal, Marxian bliss."

"You're saying you're going to screw yourself to death?"

"No. He wants to."

"Who?"

Hanely bust downstairs, disheveled, pants on, barely strapped up, his t-shirt on backwards, dripping sweat and fumbling with his shoe. He sat on the couch next to the girls who sandwiched Willard and wiped the sweat off his brow. He winked to the madam, who ignored him, and ran his fingers through his hair. Even then, he did not appear ridiculous. It could have been an advertisement for some avant-garde fashion designer. Our clothes get you laid.

Marcus, in my mind, is the greatest scumbag ever born. If he were born ugly, there is no way he could get away with half of the hare-brained schemes he comes up with. If he was unable to talk to women, unable to convince them that he was going to stick around maybe even for just another go perhaps he would be seen as the brooding, quiet type. A simmering maniac. If he was born with a wang, less elephantine, muscles less chiseled, perhaps hair even slightly balding or slightly out of place, but no, God or nature or whoever or whatever you call it had conspired to let him wake up with nary a hair out of place, with a non dysfunctional dinghy dongy and a different young, beautiful, hoodwinked lady groggy liddy and frumpy as he sneaks out of her apartment or house or if he's really lucky, guest house to her mansion.

Women never call him when he's in the midst of his delivery. They never call bullshit. Sometimes it's goddamn frustrating to watch. You want to walk up while he's away in the bathroom or whatever seedy little bar or eatery you're in and tell them – "leave! Run while you can! This man is a black hole that not even light escapes him and neither will you, but you don't because that would not be right and proper in this world of established rules and procedures of men. If you did something like that, you are going against the established order and brotherhood and could be possibly construed as being in league with them" - the women!

"We got to leave right now? Can't we stay?" Marcus asked with a slight demand of extra time on his fucking furlough.

"My dad's kicking the bucket. We've got to go."

"It's always about you, isn't it?"

"Awww. We're sorry," the ladies said.

"Get to the car."

Marcus helped Willard from out between the sandwich and ambled to the car. I, of course, would be stuck with the bill.

"Looks before age," Marcus said leaving the building more like a phantom after having drained all his energy away.

"Hope takes a back seat to progress," Willard muttered and climbed in the back seat of the Judge.

I paid our bill, placing it on my Visa. I didn't bother to even look when I signed it. I'm sure it was exorbitant, and I was good for it. I just worried that my sister would take offense to me spending thousands of dollars on whores. Next to the credit card machine, a sign calmed patrons, declaring, "All purchases billed as "Plumbing Services."

The girls waved goodbye, and Marcus blew them kisses from the front seat. The engine turned over once and exploded into the rumble guts we had become accustomed to. A couple of the girls stood on the porch in their nighties and squealed giddiness, maybe because that was what they were schooled to do. I couldn't tell anymore.

It was a short jaunt to the Interstate. I know we didn't want to use the Interstate system, but it was necessary if we were ever going to make it to Denver on time. Elko faded behind us like a herpes blister. All that was ahead was blackness and the pinpricks of light. Willard snoozed, sometimes snoring. Hanely stared ahead. I wondered what was on his mind.

"What are you thinking about Marcus?" I asked.

He took a few seconds to respond. "Nothing. A blank slate. I feel at peace."

"How long will the peace last?"

"Not long. It never does. It fades quickly, more quickly than before."

A sign passed, LAST CHANCE FOR GAS 70 Miles. I looked at the tank. Three quarters full.

"Should I stop?"

"Don't need to. Maybe Father Time needs something."

"Don't wake him. Let him sleep."

Willard's head lolled.

"You ever noticed how old people smell?" Marcus asked.

"No, I haven't man," my eyes were glued to the road.

"Like fast approaching death," Marcus hissed.

"Yeah, well, you'll get old too."

"Not me."

"Yeah, you will, unless you kill yourself in a car wreck or die of AIDS."

"Nah, man, I've already envisioned my death."

"You're sure of it?"

"Yeah, I'm sure. I've seen it play before my eyes thousands of times."

"How does it happen then?"

"I'm walking out of a McDonalds, or In N Out, or Fat Burger, or Five Guys, or Koo Koo Roo, or whatever fast food restaurant I just wolfed down a burger and fries in and blam! I get shot."

"What? Why?"

"Who knows? Maybe one of the jilted husbands or lovers of the women I've dallied with takes sharpshooter classes. Maybe some of my ex girlfriends teamed up to do me in. People are able to organize on the Internet now for nefarious activities. I'm telling you, I've got contracts out on me."

"Hence your concern with the Russians."

"Who knows who else is after me?"

"No one is after you, Marcus. No one cares, man. Infidelity is all the rage. You could probably get a Reality Television show. Marriage Wreckers or some such shit."

"I'll have to find somebody eventually who will pull me out of my misery."

"Yeah, you'll fall in love. Can't be a brigand your whole life."

"Sure I can."

"Were you ever in love?"

"It's a disease, man. Mental illness."

"No it isn't."

"Sure it is. The most pernicious folly of man."

"Baloney, Marcus."

"Have you ever been in in love? Sure you have, you sucker."

"You know I have."

"Hopeless crushes. You should really go talk to one of those women one day. Grow some balls. Friend them on Facebook."

"Whatever. You're going to shame me for your stuffings. Your speech causes lust; that's it."

"I get the job done."

"Salt Lake City is pretty far."

"The most boring city on the planet perhaps for a guy like me. Mormon babes, they don't budge."

"Not an inch," Willard said.

"Go back to sleep," Marcus told him.

"Keep your eyes on the road, lad. You've been tossing all over it," Willard told me.

"Go back to sleep, Willard."

"You'd think you'd be sleeping right now, having paraded around with those working girls the way you did," Willard muttered.

"Fucking energizes me; it doesn't tire me. I am not a male lion, gramps," Hanely spouted.

"He's an Antechinus," I said, hands ten and two on the wheel, driving old man style onward toward oblivion. The phone rang in my pants pocket, buzzing unheeded against my manhood. It soon ceased its beckoning.

"The Great Salt Lake to your left."

"Can't see. It's too dark out," Willard said.

"It's like a big pond, only salty."

"It's the remnants of a huge inland sea that dried up like millions of years ago. Must've smelled awful."

"Yeah, rotting fish and whales and sharks and turtles for miles, all flopping about, wondering where the water went. No one to toss them back in."

"It didn't dry up overnight."

"Anything to do in this city?"

"We can tour the temple complex," Willard quipped.

"Are you fucking kidding me?"

I hurtled onwards.

"It's the dullest city on the planet. Voted nine times out of ten in a poll of twenty-somethings in some newspaper out here somewhere."

"Most dull? That's idiotic. It makes no sense."

"Dullest."

"Bunch of dullards."

"I'm sure they have fun somehow."

"They've got basketball out here."

"Total bores, man."

"I'm sure there's something fun to do."

"We're on our way to see my father, you misanthropes. No more stopping, save for gas."

"Your dad's a trooper, man, holding out to see a son who doesn't love him."

"How old is he?" Willard asked.

"Oh, hell, I don't know. I think the old bastard sired me when he was fifty-something."

"How old was your mom?"

"Nineteen."

"Must be nice being rich...young babes flock to you. Rich honey, even old, catches all the flies."

"Or a famous artist."

"Yeah, like Picasso. Nineteen year old Italian babes as your concubines when you're old and crusty."

"Talented honey catches all the flies."

"Who needs talent when you're famous?"

"Jackson, can tell you all about that," Hanely said with a laugh. "He's got to finish his second book to cement his reputation as the paramour of bored and horny house-wives everywhere. Then he'll have to beat them off him with a baseball bat."

"Fuck that. They'll get another novel out of my cold, dead hands."

"God damn, I've got to piss," Willard said.

"Let's pull over."

"You idiot, we're nowhere near Salt Lake City. Your GPS is all jacked up."

"Pull off for gas."

"We're in Psychoville, Utah. This is how all cheesy horror films start man. The old man has to pee. Then he's the first one to get fed to the wood chipper. Too bad there aren't any babes with us. We could at least go out fucking."

"I need gas."

"You're not on E."

"What city is this?"

"This isn't a city. It's the middle of nowhere."

"Bonneville Salt Flats State Park."

"We're nowhere near Salt Lake City! Fuck!"

"Pull over, there's a gas station here."

"Looks abandoned to me," Willard said.

"They're sure to have a pisser."

I parked. Hanely hopped out of the car like a sheriff leaping down from his tall horse. The desolate wind whipped around the car and smelled of a great, bleak nothing. An eagle screamed, or perhaps it was just the wind whipping through the iron works of this gas station.

"It's open?" Willard shouted over the wind.

"The light is on. No one is here."

"Maybe they're in the freezer. Bound and gagged. Saw that one on Unsolved Mysteries one time."

Marcus opened the door. A bell tinkled. Assorted knick-knacks lined the shelves of the island. My eyes were drawn to a shirt that hung on a rack closest to the absentee cashier. Two wolves howled at the moon, gray shirt, with purple glitter surrounding them. Could have been for a woman, but she would have to be pretty butch.

"I'm getting that," I announced.

"It's your money. Where's the cashier?"

"I hear some whistling from the back," Willard said.

"Murderers often whistle when they dismember people," Hanely said with a laugh. "It's just the wind."

A man appeared from the back. He looked surprised, like we had just interrupted his late night happy time.

"We never get any customers," he said.

"Today's your lucky day."

"Need gas?"

"No."

"Good. I ain't got none."

"Double negative. Means you've got some."

"I don't."

"That's all you had to say, my friend."

"Say. I've got a problem. Seeing you're a young fella, you might be able to help me."

"Besides having no gas and being a gas station?"

"Yeah."

"What's your deal?"

"Oh, no deal, just a problem."

"Yeah, shoot."

"We've got a real creepy dude here. He won't leave the place."

"Besides you?"

The guy looked at me deadpan. I changed the subject.

"We didn't see any guy outside."

"No, he lives here."

"Where?"

"The apartment out back."

We walked in a group out the back of the store, kicking salt dirt clods and Pepsi cans out of the way.

"Watch out. He's a goddamn madman."

"You rent this place to him?"

"Yeah. Behind on rent. He won't leave, told him to. He told me to call the law. There ain't no law out here."

"So there's a law then?"

"Nope. None. Man's got to be his own protector."

"So you're calling us."

"I'm telling you, the guy's sick."

My phone rang again. Fucking agent. I checked for general purposes, just to see that he was still interested in what I had to say, which from this time forward would be fuck off, piss off, blow it out your ass, and perhaps a photograph of my middle finger or hairy asshole texted to him. The goddamndest annoying prick on the planet, and he thought he had me by the balls.

"What the hell is going on in here?"

A man, naked from the waist down held a bible in his hand, reading passages aloud. Stacks of Bibles lined every nook and cranny of his otherwise non-spacious little hobo shack of an apartment, officially intended to raise the population of Smith's Balls, Utah from two to three.

"Put some goddamn clothing on, Bill! You've got company."

"Bill Dickel," the man said whipping around and reaching his hand out to shake Hanely's hand.

"Dill Pickle?" Willard asked confusedly. He couldn't hear anything from all the commotion caused by the television in the background and the massive rustling stacks of Bibles, which occluded his vision from the big-bellied, half-naked man who wore an AC/DC t-shirt, cowboy boots, and nothing more.

"Where the hell are your pants, Bill?"

"Reading Leviticus. No time for pants."

"Jeez, this guy is mad," Marcus announced.

"I don't think we should mess around with him," I said.

"If you'd take him off my hands, take him somewhere with you, I'd be really appreciative."

"He's got no pants on."

"Where you headed?"

"Salt Lake City, parts beyond."

"I've got to get to Salt Lake City. Got to get my Bibles to a buyer there."

"Where the hell did you get all these Bibles?"

"Sent away for 'em. You wouldn't believe all the people trying' to get the word of God to you. For free."

"Mail order?"

"Yep."

"Every single last one of them?"

"Yep. All free. Didn't even pay shipping and handling. Figured I'd be able to resell them on eBay, but no one's buying."

"It's a damn shame," Willard said.

"The end is near," Bill Dickel said, seriously.

"Maybe your end," Hanely announced.

"What do you got against me?" Bill asked.

"I like the company of men with pants on. Why don't you put some pants on?"

"Reading' the Good Lord's Word gets my blood hot. I get all enraptured, start speaking' in tongues."

"The guy's a madman," I announced.

"That voice!" Bill erupted.

"What?" I asked.

"Your voice! I've heard it from somewhere. In a dream, I swear it! I've heard your voice somewhere before. Somewhere...I can't quite place it. But I know you."

"He's a famous author," Hanely said, having picked up bible to read aloud, "Stay me with flagons, comfort me with apples for I am sick of love...blah...blah...I charge you, daughters of Jerusalem, by the roes, and by the hinds of the field, that you do not stir up, nor awake my love...well these skinks can awake my love any damn day of the week! We'll know them all in the biblical sense."

"Quite," Willard said.

The gasoline salesman adjusted his red apron.

"Coward!" Hanely said gravely, looking at him.

"Hey, I didn't come out here to be berated."

"What are you idiots doing out here?"

"Thought we might be able to get some free gas out of the deal, but the salesman doesn't have any."

Dickel stopped pacing back and forth through the stacks of Gideons placed Holy Bibles.

"What a second," he said.

"What are you getting at, sir?" Willard asked.

"Wait just one clown second! I know your voice. I know where I heard it."

"You watch *Oprah*? This motherfucker has been on that show a few times."

"Do you see a television in here, butt nugget? I don't. I see a stack of Bibles and a radio."

"What do you listen to on the radio? Not much substance anymore nowadays. Not like way back when you had all the good voice actors and actresses playing' in the serials, bunch of rot now, hippity hoppity stuff, women acting like sluts, slutting it up for a buck and applause," Willard said.

"I listen to the radio evangelist and televangelist preacher, the illustrious Reverend Billy Meyers Hour of Prayer. I never, never, ever, never, ever miss an episode," he said with a smile. A knowledgeable smile.

"Never?" Marcus asked, looking at me with a wicked grin on his face.

"Never, you godforsaken heathens."

He picked up a bible from the top of a stack, fingering it gently as if he were looking for a verse of scripture.

"Willard, start heading towards the car. I'm sure you don't want to get involved with what's about to happen."

"No more stops, Marcus, goddamnit," I said.

"I'm the only one whose going to be goddamning around here you bunch 'a miserable heathens. I heard what you said to Reverend Billy, you damn peter-puffing, post-stroking, homosexual abomination."

"What?" Willard asked with shock on his face.

"Willard, you'd better get to the car, and get her started up. We'd best be getting out of here," Marcus said.

"Oh, no," Bill Dickel, the pantless wonder, said. In the ten minutes they had stood there, he had yet to put on his pants, or even look for them. His phallus hung low, lower than most men of his height, which I could guess was 5'3". He was a wee, creepy, well-hung man. And he just caught me glancing at his junk.

"You're a meat gazing' queer!" he yelled.

He whipped the bible at my head, a telegraphed blow; I dodged. I batted the second bible away to the floor. The third came, and then an onslaught of thrown and flung Bibles.

"Go, Willard, go!" Marcus shouted, afraid one of the would catch our geriatric friend and send him off to meet his maker with Exodus stamped into his mortal forehead. The old man shuffled out of the screened in door, and ambled across the darkness toward the car.

"You guys!" he called back.

Bill Dickel hurled more at us. Marcus deflected Bible after Bible like a hockey goalie, with his big tree trunk arms. Dickel started to get winded, gasping for air now.

"Stop it, Bill," the gas station attendant yelled at him.

"Aww, Craig, let me be, and let me dispense the Lord's Justice on these Sodomites!"

"I'm no Sodomite!" Marcus yelled in his defense.

Dickel hit Marcus square in the face with a particularly meaty Bible. Marcus stumbled back through the screened in door, grasping his nose, which dripped bright red blood.

"Strike one for the Lord!" Dickel shouted and did a little happy dance, his ding-dong flip-flopping around.

"Jesus!" Craig, the gas station attendant screamed, and grabbed Marcus, holding him back.

"That son of a bitch. I'm going to kill him," Marcus screamed.

I actually had the means to kill Bill Dickel underneath my seat. My WWI Surplus Government Issue .45 Cal Samuel Colt 1911 Model pistol, wrapped in the greasy handkerchief, which I used to clean it off with and oil its parts. I thought about getting it for a moment which turned into a fantasy of me briefly chasing a half naked Bill Dickel through his stacks of ill-gotten Bibles, shouting wildly, perhaps catching him with a huge round right in the buttocks, and laughing with glee as he bled out all over the floor. I'd then bury him in his Bibles, and be on my merry way.

"Bill, I didn't mean anything by what I told the Reverend."

"Why'd you do it then, you damn homo ape-loving monkey's uncle, motherfucker?"

"I did it to be funny. I don't know why. I'm sick I guess. I need attention."

"All you damn bastards nowadays trying' to be funny and all, trying to get a moment's worth of notice, and no one's remembering' that the Lord's always watching and not given' any heed to the Lord's immaculate word. That's the reason there's so many of you homos running' around."

"You know what, Bill? I'd probably pay more attention to the Lord's word if I actually had a Bible."

"You got no Bible?"

"No. I don't. I've never read it. Never really been to church, really. You see, my family is into the church-of-what's-happening'-now. Moneymaking."

"Well, damn. You don't say. I've got plenty of them here. Seeing' that they don't sell too well, you just want to take one?"

"Sure."

"You've got to promise me, if you take one, you've got to read it."

"Have some faith. I'll read it, Bill."

He held one in his hand. A big, long bastard with a leather cover. One of the special Gideons ones that you gave to someone whose family member died. It was supposed to provide comfort in a time of bereavement. He took it from the position where he was going to hurl it from, right around his ear, and he held it out to me, arm extended, a peace offering. I took it from him, and held it to my side.

"Read it," he said, "you may just get cured of your lusting after men. See, holding' it there in your hands, you got no real urge to stare at me."

"Thanks. I will read it. Why don't you put some pants on and come talk to your landlord. He's got something he's been meaning to discuss with you. You've saved my soul, Bill Dickel. You've done the Lord's work today. Now it's time to handle your business."

"I guess you're right. Hey, on your travels, why don't you tell people to stop off and buy one of Bill's Bibles?"

"You'll have to get this place in order, Bill. A Bible store isn't befitting a crummy little apartment, and most shopkeepers, if they want to stay in business, wear pants."

"It's kind of in disarray, I know. I've been praying so fervently for any business and also for the Lord's return. I really forgot to pick up after myself, so I apologize. I bet it's quite disgusting what you fellas walked into."

"It's okay. Go with God."

I left. Bill emerged right behind me. Craig, who revealed himself to be the owner of the LAST CHANCE GAS CORPORATION, Bill's apartment, and the surrounding 100 acres of Salt Flat, suitable for nothing, not even fancy coarse salt on the account of its lead content, summoned the best law enforcement he could find: his cousin Ned and his cousin Ned's overly large Mastiff German Shepherd mix, Nellie. Now, Nellie was pregnant, and if there's one thing I know about bitches that are pregnant, it's that they are killers. Ned was coming with the Deputy Sheriff from the next town over, Brigham's Beard, and they were speeding this way. They were coming to arrest Bill Dickel and quite possibly just drive him deep into the Salt Flats to do him in like some old Western movie. I wasn't about to have any murders on my hands. Times like these called for an intervention. The partners in crime and I concurred, that Bill should come with us.

Bill Dickel, now with gabardine trousers and a belt on, Marcus Hanley, besotted with mirth, his bloody nose healed but his pride and ego wounded, Willard, a leather bound bereavement copy Gideons Bible, and a Samuel Colt underneath the seat were all packed into a 1969 Pontiac GTO Judge, and we sped off to the East, away from the Last Chance Gas Station, which should have been named the No Chance Gas Station.

Having accomplished our mission, we sped off with a tank of Gas that Willard managed to siphon out of Craig's old truck. We all had wolf t-shirts on, which we stole in the ensuing hubbub just prior to our agreement, though Marcus Hanely was reluctant to take Bob on as a passenger in our trip to Hell. Marcus, of course, had on the most flamboyant T shirt: a bright orange mother, showing a black male wolf engaged in a wolf mating dance ritual with a gray female wolf. Marcus told us that he swore the black wolf was male because the artist, most likely a disgruntled art student upset at having to draw perhaps the lamest form of Americana, the wolf T shirt, drew a brilliant red rocket on the black wolf, right above its copious ball sack. I don't know why exactly the artist drew a red rocket on the wolf; however, it could have been for the purpose of realism. Wolf shirt connoisseurs did not appreciate cartoony wolves.

The red rocket barely peaked through the skin surrounding, which brought me to another point in this great tired brain of mine, a point which I had previously discussed with Marcus Hanely over oysters and brave, prodigious amounts of beer at a rich man's Cantina in Carmel, California: the subject of male circumcision. All your human's rights groups had been up in arms about wayward tribes of people hacking off the delicate, tingly bits from females and I agreed with Marcus that it is a horror of which I would never partake, but there is also another horror going on unabated, the disfigurement of thousands of male children in hospitals, by doctors, everyday. Marcus brought up a fine point: he being quite hung and very uncircumcised, that one doesn't need the extra skin to stimulate a woman's naughty bits on the upstroke and down stroke. He did offer the following advice: Gents, if you're packing a gherkin, you know, a tiny clit tickler...go on look in your pants...your sons are also likely to have wee ones and you should give them a fighting chance. However, if in your pants you're smuggling a long dangling dong, a slut beater of massive proportions, aesthetics would dictate that you chop that rascal because who really wants to see a ginormous aardvark dingle dangle between a man's legs?

Hanely was uncut because his mama was indigent when he popped into the world, and he was born at a Catholic charity hospital who believed that cutting the male member was best performed by rabbis and other people who were deluded into the practice. He was much too cowardly now to do the deed.

Bill Dickel revealed that he too was uncircumcised, but even though his apartment was dimly lit, everyone could tell. Willard did not care to comment on the issue and dozed in the front seat, until a question burned him long enough to ask it.

"Where you going, Bill?"

"Oh, suppose I'll be going about as far as the Great Salt Lake City, the Promised Land, you know, where you fellas are headed."

"We're on our way to Denver so Jackson here can watch his old dad pass on."

"Oh, dear. He's got cancer?"

"Yeah. How'd you know?"

"Just came to me."

"It just came to you?"

"Yeah. In my head. I heard, 'cancer, cancer.' Like I heard it on the breeze."

"We have ourselves a regular psychic here."

"Don't know all that; I just get intuitions. I'm having another one. You don't want to be going poking about in any warehouses."

"What about a warehouse?" I asked.

"Some things in our lives are best, well, left unexplored, hidden. Some things you shouldn't find out on your own."

"You know what's in there, don't you?"

"Yep."

"He's a regular psychic," Willard said in marvel.

"Save, I get my powers from the Lord while others get theirs from below."

"He isn't a psychic," Marcus bellowed, his head out the window, brown locks blowing in the shifty desert breeze.

"The word psychic implies that I am channeling powers beyond my ordinary comprehension and those of others. I am doing no such thing. I'm merely using the gifts the Lord saw fit to give me at my conception."

"Fruit loops," Marcus said.

"I'm not crazy," Dickel said with a toothy smile.

"You're not crazy? Then why were you alone, without pants, in that wreck of an apartment with those stacks of unsold Bibles? Wouldn't you have been able to predict that your business selling free Bibles was going to be a tremendous flop?"

"No. That wasn't the point. Being in that house there put me in the path of y'all," Dickel said matter-of-factly, like he was announcing the sunrise.

"In my path?" Marcus asked with a sudden hint of concern, taking a shot with his voice that blossomed with anger.

"Yes. I've been sent by the Lord to exorcize the demons from your mortal soul, where they cling like leeches. God, he had big plans for you brother, but you just, well, pardon my expression here, I'll say it in words that you understand. You just fucked up in life and went to seed. I don't blame you for this, Marcus. I blame your mama."

"Don't bring my mama into this. She was a good, good woman."

"Oh really, Marcus? Was she really a good woman? Why tell us, Marcus, I'm reading your soul this very moment, and I don't even have the benefit of laying hands on you, tell us about the day you were seven or eight and you happened to surprise your mama and her friend up in the barn. Tell us all what happened. Marcus, know to tell a confession is to gain mastery over it. Mr. Marcus, I'm sure it will do you and do your soul some good to tell us all."

Marcus remained silent. Dickel continued poking and prodding him from the backseat, sinking his insults into the rocky son of a bitch, Marcus. I had been his best friend for years, and I had never been able to so much as scratch his shiny veneer with an insult. It all rolled off him, deflected, parried, battered, and bandied away like a professional tennis player hitting lobs. But what did I really know about him? His psyche, his interior was heretofore impenetrable. Nothing. I knew nothing about him, save the stories he told me of his actions. His thoughts, his private innermost self. He never shared that. He shared his saucy bedroom stories, his cheap conquests, and it had always seemed like a desperate escape from himself - those wild conquests, those headlong rushes into madness, benders of months at a time where I wouldn't see him, and he returning with wild tails of bedding the buxom brides of powerful men. It was a covering over, and Mr. Bill Dickel, itinerant preacher and failed Bible warehouser and salesman was about to reveal it in whatever infinite jest and sickness Hanely was motivated by. That Antechinus, that death instinct so wired tightly into him that it suffocated any other ambition. I was interested in hearing the outcome of Dickel's maniacal sermon.

"I will exorcise the demons from your world weary soul, the Lord Jesus Christ put me in your direct path so that I could turn you from a hollowed out vessel, a black pit of evil, a damn black hole of a man and make you fully into the colossus of humanity that the Lord saw fit for you to be. In you, he built a beautiful temple...."

"How much money do you want, Dickel?" Marcus asked, trying to distract Dickel from his onslaught, and shut his mouthpiece.

"No money, Marcus. I work for free. I've been waiting on that lonely stretch of highway there for some time."

"Why didn't the Lord direct you to me in Monterey? You could have easily found me."

"Yeah try the local high school girls' volleyball practice," I said laughing. Willard cackled.

"I was told to stay put, to wait it out, and I would receive a sign," Dickel said.

"Just like most prophets. You do a ton of waiting," Willard said.

Dickel's eyes went white and he proceeded to tell Marcus his past, present, and future. "I see a whole lot of nothing, Marcus," he said with a moan.

Marcus laughed. "I see your past, present, and future, too. A lot of masturbation."

Dickel's face dropped as if the Holy Book had been ripped up for toilet paper and marijuana cigarettes in front of his eyes. He sneered, a hypocrite sneer.

"Oh, Bill, do you want to fight me?" Marcus said, egging him on. "You want to fight me, don't you?"

"I'm not going to fight you, you arrogant prick. I'm here to cure you."

"You're a faith healer, then?" Willard asked from the front seat, curiously.

"I'm no faith healer, but what I have to tell Marcus may bring him some solace and cause him to end his horrible, sinful ways."

"Never," Marcus said.

"His ways aren't too terribly sinful," I said gripping the steering wheel as shit passed, flickering by like white hot love, cooling in the distance with time, sizzled like a white fire steel woman and then cooled quickly to blackness.

"Sure, my ways are sinful, Jackson. I'll admit it, that this hypocrite here, who was jacking off to scenes from the Bible, whether it be Salome dancing for Herod or maybe David spying Jezebel in all her glory, this sick fuck was, in fact, jacking off to the Bible. Either that or he was mining the corridors of his memory, the memory of church parishioners or of choir directors, or god forbid, organists. We're all human, right, Bill?"

Bill put his hand on Marcus's shoulder. His eyes flickered again, otherworldly like. He appeared to be in a trance. I surmised that this was an act, but there was no collection plate in the car.

"Get this homo off me," Marcus said, half joking, unsure of what path Bill was heading down.

"I'm no homo, just the person who's going to set you straight, Marcus."

"Remember the day you saw your Mom and her friend in the barn, Marcus? Remember your cousin? Polly? The game you played with her after that?"

Marcus's face flushed Crimson. I saw it in my rearview. Even in the darkness, I could tell he was raving mad. Or nervous. Perhaps both. Dickel got really close to him and began to babble.

"Marcus, Marcus, your cousin Polly really loved you a lot didn't she Marcus? Or maybe you loved her, and she was terrified of you. Why don't you tell the people here what you used to play with your cousin Polly when your mom used to watch you both, and she would run off to the barn with her friend?"

"What did you used to do, Marcus?" Willard asked.

Marcus was silent. Glowing with rage.

"I understand the shame and frustration you feel, Marcus. I know what you felt watching your mother in that barn. And I know what you felt when you asked your cousin Polly to do it with you. You didn't know what you were doing. And when your mother caught you, what did she tell you?"

Marcus remained silent. Now rocked back and forth in his seat a bit.

"Come on Marcus, what did your mother tell you?"

This was the first time I ever saw Marcus Hanely at a loss for words.

"'Bad, bad, boy! Bad, bad, boy!' Am I right? And she beat you! She beat that lust out of you, when you learned it from her! And how did that make you feel, Marcus? You felt all guilty? Like every time you were with a woman, you really wanted to love her, but you heard the words 'bad, bad boy! Bad, bad boy!' over and over again?"

"So what!" Marcus screamed at Dickel.

"And Marcus here, instead of listening to his mother, went off in search of her, went off looking to make amends with every single woman he came across. From the prime young age of twelve, right, ole Marcus?"

Marcus exploded in rage. "Shut the fuck up, Dickel! Pull this fucking car over! Pull it over!"

"No way! We're going to keep driving," I said trying to keep my voice down, trying hard to not add to the explosive atmosphere in the car and stay a calming influence over the war that was about to take place in the back seat. Dickel and Marcus began trading blows. I don't recall who swung first, but they were now punching each other.

"Hey, you two! Simmer down!" Willard yelled and feebly tried to get control by thrusting his bony arms in the mix.

I yanked the car hard to the side of the shoulder and spun out on the crystalline surface of the salt flat. There were no cars to be seen, no one to call the police. The sun was just peeking up over the horizon in the direction of our destination, and the sky was growing as blue as an ocean above our heads. A lone eagle, or maybe a vulture, flew in the distance, a wary traveler.

We all spilled out of the car for the ensuing battle royale. Willard gasped at the blows they landed on each other's faces. For being short, Dickel was a hell of a fighter. Marcus tired. Dickel began landing more than Marcus because even though he was a man of God, a preacher, a faith healer, partaking of some sacred covenants, he had actually taken the time to learn how to fight. Someone taught him along the way. Marcus outweighed Dickel, and had more muscle, a greater reach, but the bafflingly incapability to know how to use it; the most he ever fought with was a plus-sized model who took exception to him leaving her after a one night stand. Dickel easily dodged Marcus's blows, which declined in intensity with each one tossed in wild, willy-nilly haymakers.

Soon, after Dickel landed another square in his face, Marcus was whipped. He sat there shaking his bloody head, hands enmeshed in the salt, ass on the ground, exhausted. Dickel did not celebrate. Rather, like an old sport he graciously offered the vanquished condolences, as if Marcus's sinking ocean liner's worth of pride receded in its wake. Marcus continued just shaking his head. Dickel offered him an outstretched hand, much like the creator giving life to Adam in the Sistine Chapel ceiling painting. At first Marcus refused it, and he shook his head in a vehement no. I did not consider it at first, but perhaps he was not shaking his head at the drubbing ass whooping that Dickel handed him, but at the words and images that Dickel had conjured up in the car.

"You're right, man," he said. And then Marcus cried.

We piled in the car again as the sun rose on our strange differences. No one spoke. I could hear Marcus respiring through his swollen nose in the back seat. His nose was quite possibly broken. Dickel sat there, stone-faced. We drove past a sign that read, Salt Lake City, 90 miles. No one made mention of going out and seeing the sights when we got there. Willard asked me if I had heard anything about my father's condition. Old people are usually the first to inquire about the health of the infirm while the youth have other things on their mind, other things like youth and the prospects of love. I replied to him that I hadn't heard anything, nor did I really care whether we made it there on time or not.

Willard looked at me and said, "Son, you know we can't choose our fathers, we can only choose how we act towards our own sons."

"I don't have nor will I have any children," I told him.

"But surely you want a woman in your life."

"I could care less."

"You'll get lonely. Old age is terribly lonely son. I don't care how many books you've written, they can't come and visit you on a winter's day, they won't insulate you against the chill of being totally alone and sick, and old."

"Is that what you're scared of?"

"If I wasn't scared of that, I wouldn't be human, son."

"Why have you taken to calling me, son?"

"I like you. I don't have any sons, anyone to impart my wisdom to. I tried a few times in my bathroom, but people just wipe their hands of you."

"Ha. I'll listen, Willard."

"You want my advice? Find a woman. She doesn't have to be a knockout, just make sure she loves you. And you love her. Find one you can't live without. If you find yourself thinking about her more than five times a day, then you should strive to stay with her the rest of your life. This is advice for any man. Listen. That woman you're thinking about in your mind? That perfect one, the perfect fuck, or whatever? She's a phantom. That woman with perfect tits who never talks back and never has a hair out of place and fucks you right six ways from Sunday? She's only an aide to masturbation. Stop comparing everyone to her, or you'll be alone. Soon you won't be able to even get it up to jerk off to that ghost."

"I had her. She was in my life, but she wouldn't see fit to be with me."

"You've never mentioned her before."

"I know. I don't like to talk about it."

"You were married?"

"Nah. Mainly a passing infatuation that I haven't recovered from."

"You'll find another woman. You can't keep a good man alone for too long," Dickel said from the back seat.

"The prophet has spoken," Willard said.

"Where's he going to meet her?"

"Oh, I don't know, maybe he already has," Dickel said confidently. "You'll be swept off your feet, my man. A good woman is calm winds for any shoddy, seafaring vessel."

"When I lay pipe, I'm at peace for maybe five minutes post orgasm. That's the most peace we men can squeeze out of this world. After that, the little wants start cleaving my soul," Hanely said, breaking his contemplative silence.

I rather liked him when he was silent, when the focus of attention wasn't on his big, handsome, hulking frame, his man meat. Silent man meat cowed by superior logic. Hanely clawed his swollen edge.

"You hit me good," Marcus said to Dickel.

"You needed hitting," Dickel said tugging at his lap belt.

"I've seen it all now," I said.

I looked at him nursing his eye in the rearview mirror. Willard sucked his teeth the way that old men did, forming little divots in his cheeks like depressions surrounded by droopy-fleshed cliffs. Dickel dozed off next to Marcus.

Marcus stared silently ahead, fingering his facial wounds. These three peccadilloes, brave musketeers, and lancers snored into the wild-eyed sunlight. I stopped only once, for coffee, the black rich substance that fuels my fantasies at a junky blank town peopled by only juvenile delinquents sporting concert t-shirts from bands with suicidal and drug addled lead singers. Their faces should have been sour, but they were as blank as the landscape that surrounded them. One of the children looked like he wanted to ask me a question; it seemed to burn and bubble up within him, in his forehead covered with acne and a mess of what looked to be pure black hair. He was a coward like me, afraid to talk to people like a normal human being. My mind screamed for coffee when we passed each other, and I noticed that he looked at least half Mexican. Maybe three fourths.

"Gettin' on to Salt Lake?" the Lady behind the counter asked me, perhaps just to make conversation and punctuate her day with meetings with random strangers or perhaps because she was one of those genuinely nice people who really did care about where a complete stranger was from and where they were headed. Her name was Margaret, at least that is what her nametag read, and the T was beginning to rub off. Perhaps that's where she grabbed it every night from her pre-fab dresser drawer. I'll never know, because I didn't have the courage to ask her. Marcus Hanely, ever playing Cyrano, would have me inquire why the nametag was rubbed in one corner. At least, he would offer the question, and it would give him ample time to stare at her 45 year old tits, which looked like they had had the benefit of at least two children, now probably full grown, maybe the punks hanging out outside, greedily sucking from them.

"Got any children?" I asked, without officially realizing the creepy non-sequitor.

"Doesn't everybody?" she asked. I turned my back on her to pour my coffee, which came out nearly purple in the reflected incandescent light.

"I'm on my way to Denver," I told her trying to make up for my previous blunder. I don't know why I felt the need to put up such an appearance for a complete stranger and now everybody seemed a stranger to me, perhaps because I never really talked to anyone, hung out with anyone, and instead spent all my time in the vain struggle of writing when nothing really real would come out, getting Marcus's now poor advice on life and love, words of a madman hell-bent on self destruction.

"You all right?" she asked, with a genuine look of concern, not for myself, but perhaps for her own safety.

"Just tired. Got a long trip ahead of me."

"Long drive down to Denver."

"No, I'm making it with friends of mine. Lucky guys always get to sleep, and I've got to drive."

"Why don't you switch out with them?"

"I don't trust them enough."

"They're you're friends."

"I know. But it's my car. They don't have to drive it."

"99 cents," she said, it really seemed like she was trying to get rid of me.

"Where'd you get that awful shirt at?"

"A place down the road."

"I didn't know men wore that shade of purple."

"Now they do."

I paid. I raised my hand like a knight of old and bid her adieu. She smiled, strangely as if she had just spoken to the strangest man of her life and was glad to be rid of me. No doubt she got her fair share of oddballs. Good thing my photograph on *Asymmetric Hearts* did not look like me too much anymore. She was of the prime demographic to have read it. The two kids were smoking some ditch weed joint near the side of the gasoline station. It smelled awful. On second thought, if she would have known I was the author of her favorite novel, a provider of hours of clitoral stimulation, I could have made love to the attendant in the bathroom, Hanely style.

I looked back when the door jingled shut, two and half seconds worth of warning if an armed gang stampeded into the place. I guess that's what the bells are for. Ringing out the dead. The death knell. Ding! Dong! The bells we rang at my mother's funeral to signify the soul had gone to heaven, and how I was supposed to pray for her soul to make sure that it got to heaven. Plenary indulgences or something like that. I never did. I had never inquired of a single soul. I will Google it from the safety of my father's den when I go to watch him die.

Speaking of death, I'm not afraid of it. It has no power over me. Life is shit enough, I won't miss not being here to second anything. I thought about the .45 underneath my seat, safely hidden from view and prying fingers. It would be instantaneous. Instant nothing. I beat that morbid thought about my mind while the two weed zombie kids asked me where I was going.

"Denver," I replied.

"Got room for two more?"

"Nah, car's full," I said as I got in.

They looked at me with puzzled glances as I slammed the door and sped off. No one stirred inside. They slept the sleep of men worn out from a hard day's work, but they had not been working, only shoveling high the bullshit and stacking it to the ceiling, making great bullshit castles in bullshit kingdoms for themselves in nice geometrically pure piles, so that it looked nice on the outside looking in. But it was still bullshit and it still stunk and it still filled up rooms in mansions and trailer parks. I looked at the three of them, Hanely snoozing in the back, bull-shitter extraordinaire, par excellence. Every time he talked to a woman in earshot of me I wanted to cry foul, BULLSHIT! I wanted to tell her the truth about him, that he did not have a genuine strand of DNA in his whole body, that it was in his DNA to lie to get whatever he wanted, that it was his duty in life to drop panties. I would have, but the women didn't seem to mind. The man to his right, Dickel, the religious psycho, bull-shitter from front to end, from head to his forked devil's tail, I couldn't wait to be rid of him. Once we arrived at the funeral parlor, or wherever this nutter was going, I'd give him a swift kick in the ass.

I looked to Willard. He was the only one who seemed genuine among them. And he was a tired, probably about to die, old man. Willard did not snore like the other two. The breath vibrated from his sunken cheeks. I watched him for proof of life occasionally, otherwise I would have seen fit to declare him dead and bury him in the desert. I passed another sign, declaring SALT LAKE CITY 30 mi. Dickel farted in his sleep, vibrating the vinyl. It was loud, crude, and voluminous. He muttered something. I could not wait to be rid of him.

Speaking of Salt Lake City, I despise the Mormons and their secret underwear. I don't despise them for being Mormon; it isn't a matter of being against a religion. I despise them for their certainty. Their "we know the world is this way" outlook. Isn't part of the beauty of life to struggle against a great unknown? To blaze your own trail? Okay, no one knows what life will bring them. With a religion you should be certain of your responses. I don't want to be certain about my responses. I don't want a way of life that others have proven tried and true. I want to live my life.

Hanely came to, and the others as well as the din of the traffic increased. I also inadvertently hit a grind strip when I went off on my daydream.

"I think Mormon women are gorgeous," Hanely said.

"Got a lot of German in those wide hips," Willard quipped.

"Full bosoms," Dickel said.

"Blondes," Marcus said, adding to their collective fantasy.

"I don't dig on blondes," I said, with brunettes dancing somersaults in my head, all the black haired damask beauties belly dancing like they must have to greet the Crusaders when they weren't dipping sword into flesh like a great gang of Frankish disinherited psychos.

"I take it you haven't seen the full magnificence of the Mormon temple?" Dickel asked.

"No I haven't, doesn't make much sense to see it."

"It doesn't have to make sense. Nothing makes sense. All that matters is that you have people who are willing to donate themselves and their wealth to make something that will stand the test of time."

"Nauvoo was a good start."

"It's greater than that."

"You start a cult, and it's easy after all."

"All religions are cults. Look at all the recent ones...Scientology, Mormonism, Jehovah's Witnesses, Shriner's."

"They're all cults."

"I'll tell you what, anything that inspires people to get off their lazy, good-for-nothing asses and do something magnificent is fine by me," Dickel said. "The natural place of man is seated on his ass, following the path of least resistance. Hell, the only reason most of them participate at all is because they want to be comfortable. And what's inspiring today? What built the Notre Dame? What built Angkor Wat? What build Chichen Itza? What built the pyramids? What? The Mormon

Tabernacle? Have you heard it? Have you listened to Bach? What can inspire people to this level of grandiosity and genius? What today? Television?"

"Professional sports. Look at the auditoriums they build. Jumbotrons. Complete cities within cities."

"But what do they inspire people to do? Do they inspire people to greatness? Do these sports auditoriums, with their beer lines, and their piss troughs, do they inspire anyone to anything?"

"I don't know."

"They worship themselves, they go through the motions. They're emotional about it all. I don't get it."

"It's an echo chamber for these athletes. Is this the highest type of human being?"

"No, it's the one who has the most press coverage."

"Who cares? It's all phony and plastic. All of it. From sea to shining sea. All rayon and cardboard, all one guy selling it to the next guy in the cheapest way possible. You make a buck now, you're golden, your idea, however profound, however enlightening, if it doesn't appeal to the shrivel-brained masses, to the great bubbling ferment of youth, you're wrecked. In the eyes of the media, who gives a fuck? I don't."

"You're sure you don't, you has-been? You should take up dancing. Can you tap dance? Can you shake your hips? Dig yourself up out of the grave? No comment is needed here; you're a has-been, my man. The best part of your productive self ejaculated upon the scene in a big splash, like, four or five years ago. You've produced nothing memorable, nothing truly heart-wrenching. Your novel is an eight second crack cocaine fix. Hell, I even bet no one in this humble city knows your name, Jackson Leman. I bet they'll say '...who?'"

"Joe Smith," Willard said, "if that isn't the plainest name going, I mean their prophet could have been Johnny Doe."

"Prophets don't nominate themselves; the Good Lord does the choosing," Bill Dickel said.

"Baloney, Joe Smith chose himself. He knew he was a prophet. He knew it between his legs."

"Talk about a sex fiend," Willard said.

"If you're not married, it's a sin, and the prophet gets more than his fair share. Can you imagine the amount of hardcore frontier pussy that guy Joey Smith got? All those hot young women that he laid pipe to and convinced they were doing the lord's work? And whatever came out of his mouth was holy. That's power, man. That's charisma. Why, I doubt that even you, Marcus Hanely, I doubt even you could convince that many women into leaving their husbands because they weren't holy enough, arranging divorces from them, kicking them out of the group, and making it seem like you just didn't want to make a wagon rut with the little biddy. Oh, yeah, don't forget about beautiful daughters. Can you imagine the power of this holy fool?"

"There is no possible way to have that many women and not drive yourself bat-shit crazy running around all over town keeping them separate. Religion, my man, crushes female jealousy, floods the great plain of their sex drive, and teaches them that their natural inclinations are sin. Three cheers."

"Ahh, who gives a fuck? What are we going to do here?"

"Drop this guy off, be rid of him, bum off to Colorado, and get there in time for your dad to croak," Hanely said.

"Have some respect," Willard said.

"Get off this exit," Bob Dickel said. "It'll be good to be rid of you heathens. Haven't you learned a damn word I said, Marcus?"

"Don't care."

I ripped the Judge across four lanes, cutting no one off, really, and nearly colliding with a church van, no doubt, LDS, right in front of the exit, thus cementing our reputation in this great land of being demented. Cell phones whipped out, most likely dialing Utah State, Beehive State Troopers, with stun guns ready to shock our balls. The Judge ripped and sent the black asphalt flying, and we scraped past a Koo Koo Roo Chicken and Milkshakes-N-More, Fatty McFatt's Burger's, twenty random Obese-ologists with names from countries far beyond and a few Smiths and McCormick's, a few "get ready for your Mission" training centers, and Pizza, Pizza, and More Pizzas, all of which clung to the Interstate like barnacles to the legs of a pier at low tide. The west was no longer wild; it was just like everywhere else. Shitty.

"What time is it?" Hanely asked.

"Too early, man. I'm conking out."

"Let's get some coffee," Willard said.

"After we drop the boring prick off," Hanely said. "He's chick repellant."

"They'll smell a lecher like you a mile away, Marcus," Dickel said.

"Once we get rid of our moral Oral Roberts compass here, we'll be on our great adventure again," Marcus declared.

"Some adventure you're having. Seems pretty boring to me," Dickel said, Hanely and him parrying to trying to get a last word in.

"By the cock, these things start small and grow," Hanely said laughing. "And our phallus will be stupendous and inspiring."

"We're going to the only tit bar in Salt Lake City," Marcus said triumphantly, and then followed with, "Uh, are there any tit bars in Salt Lake City?"

"Where's it at?" Willard asked.

"Somewhere in the boring suburbs probably. Those women suck money like leeches suck blood," Hanely said.

"Cock teasers. At least a whore gets you off. We'll be left with blue balls. Maybe they'll tease Willard so much that he gets a heart attack."

"Let's go off on the wrong side of the tracks and find a sleazy one with a buffet dinner."

"Tits and pot roast," Hanely said licking his lips.

"No tits here. They have to wear pasties," Dickel said.

"And how would you know, Mr. Bible Beater? Or should I say, Dick Beater? Dickel dick beater! Because you go into them, to sell them Bibles?" Marcus asked, laughing.

Every antagonistic bone in his body was now aimed at Reverend Dickel before he departed the car on his merry way. Dickel pretended to not hear at first. He had already given Marcus a shellacking and didn't really need to get into a war of words, just kick his ass again. Maybe Marcus, about to be liberated from his oppression, was getting progressively ballsier towards Dickel on an exponential curve. He probably wanted to sucker punch Dickel in the jaw as we drove off.

"It's right around here," Dickel said. "My church, I'm always losing track of where it's at."

"How do you know they only wear pasties, Dickel?" Marcus implored.

"I minister to many of the ladies who work the jobs in those dens of sin," Dickel fired back.

"No. I think you go and partake of them just like the rest of us."

"I do not."

"Sure you don't," Hanely said.

"You aren't married," Willard noted.

"Yeah, Dickel, you never mentioned being married. Usually you religious types just gush about your little wife, I think so we don't think you're a homo or something," Marcus said.

"My wife, she divorced me many years ago. Claimed I was too religious for her. I wasn't to her liking. Actually, she just wanted to go be a loose woman. Slut," Dickel said. We should have just let him talk and let all his invective towards women out.

"Can't you find a good woman at your church?"

Dickel snapped back in his seat and screamed at the top of his lungs at Willard, "The house of the lord is for worship and fellowship, not to pull the latest bit of tail down!"

"Oh, I disagree, Dickel. Churches are houses of fornication, fair and simple, as long as you pay the entrance fee, it's game on. Why do you think most people go to Church, Mr. Reverend? Or are you even a Reverend? This is a recent development for us."

"The church is right here on the left."

A ramshackle little doublewide trailer greeted them, the yard unkempt and over-flowing with debris, the sign, conjoined of yellow metal letters, fake gold, a favored color, said THE LORD'S HEAVENLY ALTAR CHAPEL, though the O and R were missing from the word LORD, making it look like L D'S.

"Who's LD?" Willard asked.

"Laurence Dickel," Marcus said.

"Marcus, you dumb mother fucker, his name is Bill."

"Bill, Laurence...whatever, same-same, still a douche," Marcus said, rubbing his injured face.

"No, she's in need of repairs, but the Lord will abide," Bill Dickel said.

"How many parishioners do you have, Mr. Good Reverend?" Marcus asked, twist-ing the screwdriver in the wound.

"All I have to do is make a few telephone calls."

"You've never had a single parishioner here, Dickel," Hanely said with a tone of accusation in his voice, brusque, he even waggled his finger at Bob.

"No. I had plenty."

"Dope fiends and hookers?" I guessed.

"They're still God's children," Dickel said sheepishly.

"You holy fool, you've got to minister to the rich man! Do you think deadbeats built up all the great religions of the world? No, man! You've got to build your temples, then turn to charity. No way. The deadbeats start them, then you court the rich, make them feel guilty for being rich, make them think they'll find favor with what-ever deity you create, and let them donate their worldly possessions to you to build up magnificent palaces of worship that you also happen to live in, and it all counts as even more evidence of the worth of your religion."

"I'm no fool."

"Sure you are. Look at this dump. The only person who's getting ministered to here is a deadbeat crack head who has a few screws loose."

"They're still children of the Lord," Marcus. "Tell me, what do you believe in?"

"Myself. I don't need anything that you have to offer. You know why religion's a failure in this world nowadays? Dickel, you want to make one guess?"

"The people don't believe in it anymore. It no longer scares them. People aren't afraid of what they can't see. We're explaining more and more every day. We've explained religion away," I said to the maestro with the busted noggin.

"Partly, Jackson. But Listen! Come on, dear, good, most holy reverend father of the First Ramshackle Crack head Whatever Denomination Church of Greater Salt Lake City," Marcus said.

"Don't call me that again. Who cares what you think. I surely don't. I'll be on my way."

I hopped out and opened up the door for our distinguished guest. It creaked slightly, a groan, like an old man getting up from a long Rip Van Winkle slumber.

"Needs WD-40," Willard said.

"My point exactly!" Marcus shouted. "Today we live in a phony world of our own creation. We're taught to value brand identity and labels. We're obsessed with an image, while in that older world people were obsessed with rules, with manifestations of power. Nowadays we worship what we've created. It's gone way past the tipping point that not a day's thought have to be on that big bad scary universe out there. Where it used to be filled up with a phony God, now it's filled up with phony products. No need to think!"

"Consumers. That's the new laypeople."

"I'm talking about the people who make nothing really new. The hangers on in the merry go round of life. People who the producers keep throwing bones to and ever demanding newer and shinier bones," I said.

"Nowadays we worship what we created instead of worshipping what created us," Willard said.

"If it exists," Hanely added.

"You hear that, Dickel? Your days are over, man! And you're too blind to see it! Worship something like money or invention, and stack it to the ceiling. At least you'll be able to die someplace warm, in something warm. You're a failure!"

"He kicked your ass, Marcus. You probably will know better to instigate a fight with him in future," Willard said.

"I don't need to fight him directly. I'll just keep nibbling away at his confidence."

Dickel walked away, head proudly erect, looking towards the front door of his church, which as falling apart around him. He turned. "Marcus! What do you believe in?" he shouted. "What do you believe in?" Dickel asked again.

"Not going to answer him, Marcus?" Willard asked.

"I don't have an answer. I don't know."

I peeled out. Dickel waved to us, polite as ever, and Marcus looked back to him and shot Dickel the middle finger, long and pointy like, and waved it up and down so that Dickel saw it.

Willard was perturbed. Fuming mad. "Why didn't you answer his question?" Willard asked.

"I had nothing to say to him. Whatever you do say, it's wrong to him. He's made up his mind, and that disgusts me."

"But you didn't say anything," Willard muttered.

"What's it to you, old man? I just told him how the world was. You question. It answers you in silence."

"He didn't ask you how the world was, he asked you what you believe in," I said.

"Yeah, who cares if we've stopped thinking the world is an infernal cesspool and we're going to go to heaven when we die and everything will be grand, and life is struggle and its misery compounds daily and weekly? Who cares?"

"The man asked you what you believe in."

"I don't even know what that means."

"Something to think about, at any rate," I said speeding through the middle of perhaps the most boring city on the planet. We passed a 3D IMAX and a large shopping mall. I had never been to Jerusalem or Mecca or any other purported holy city. I'd been to Rome, but that was ancient history. Rome was a blast.

"This place was founded by a man with sixty or so wives," Marcus said.

"Bring 'em young," Willard said with a laugh.

"Belief is so powerful," I added.

"So I guess it doesn't matter what you believe as long as you have people to follow along with you."

"Leader doesn't mean anything special, only that you lead."

"Don't you believe in yourself, Marcus?"

"Shit, man, I don't even know."

"A crisis of faith," I said. The car approached the on ramp. We had passed no less than three McDonald's, two dozen Auto Zones, 14 shuttered Mom N Pops with ghastly boarded up windows, two separate Dancing Windsock Men, probably a thousand car dealerships selling twenty thousand cars each, thirteen or fourteen blocks of strip malls each with a jewelry store with a adjective or name in front, the most quaint being Zazzy Zazzman's Jewelry, which had a Rolex sign out front. Nowhere was there a sign with a huge phallic idolatrous emblem saying, LOOK HERE, BUY! The Mormons, I think, relied on word of mouth advertisements.

"Where are all the signs?" I implored, and darted across a few lanes of traffic, only cutting off one minivan, hopefully not with too many children on board. The soccer mom swerved and missed our rear fender by a long way. I did not look back to see the outcome of the poor decision I had made.

Willard gasped, taking his cues from the driver. Raindrops started hitting the windshield. In my panic for signs, I missed the onramp, and had to do a U-turn in a no U-turn zone. I scanned for police, and didn't see any, so I just went. I gunned it out in front of some light traffic, most of it SUVs.

"Pull off into this BP," Marcus ordered. I could not see the sign, it's comforting green and yellow exploited butthole corporate logo, which normally guided me to its comfortable roost, so I relied on Marcus's navigation skills. I only cut off a couple of drivers. I was no city driver, no way. If we didn't get out of this place soon, I would probably end up wrecking the Judge and sending a few Mormons packing off to be king of their own planet. I parked in the spot nearest to the door and killed the engine. As I got out, I noticed a bird had shit on my paintjob.

"Better take care of that," Marcus said.

"Fuck it," I announced rather loudly.

An older woman, saw fit to judge me as I walked past her.

"Crazy," she muttered under her breath, not thinking I would hear her or perhaps wanting me to hear her.

"Oh, sorry ma'am, sorry for cursing like that and offending you. I normally don't curse in public, but my friend unnerved me."

She immediately got up and walked away, without a word. Maybe it was the way I was dressed in my hunter gear and purple wolf T-shirt. Perhaps she took offense to my confrontation of her confrontation, and feared escalation. I walked inside the store, and Marcus followed.

"What was that cunt's problem?"

"Don't know," I said softly.

There was nothing out of order in the entire shop. Everything, everyone was pristine and white. I grabbed a couple of candy bars and went to the register. I think Marcus went to the shitter to drop a deuce. He cleared his bowels whenever he could. It was a habit of his – "can't be walking around like John Wayne, full of shit," he used to say.

"Nice ride," the clerk said. She was slightly pudgy, cute face.

"Thanks," I said to her with a smile.

We stared at each other for a second. She smiled back at me. I felt like I was supposed to say something witty now, like she was expecting me to talk about the car, brag slightly, but I couldn't think of anything.

"Well, take care," she said, smiling at me again.

"Okay," I said, and backed up towards the door, staring at her. I turned to go. My Cyrano was, as usual, taking a shit, nowhere to be found, probably fouling up the shitter for the cute young girl to puke in.

I exited, and the door twinkly ding-donged, and I saw Marcus sitting in the passenger seat. Willard and he had done a Chinese fire drill.

"I thought you went inside with me," I said to Marcus.

"Nope. Been here the whole time, man."

"You sure you didn't go to the bathroom or something?"

"Nope. Been here the whole time, right, Willard?"

"Yep."

"Shit, I must have been imagining some things," I said.

"You've been driving too long. Why don't you take over Willard?"

"I can't drive. Gave it up in 1973."

"I won't drive," Marcus said. "Remember what happened when you let me use the Ferrari?"

"Shit, I've got to keep on pressing there."

"Get some coffee."

"I'm all caffeinated out. It only makes me sleepy, anyway."

"Slam an energy drink. It's the American way."

"Fuck it. We'll press on to Denver."

"All we have is to go south and then the Western part of Colorado. Too easy."

"We stay north, we can see Wyoming," Willard said.

"Who wants to see Wyoming?"

"I'm telling you, going south and then east through Colorado is faster."

"We can go due east and then south for about fifty miles to Ft. Collins, and then further south down the 25 to Denver."

"Pull out a map."

"I don't have one."

"Marcus, use your phone," Willard said.

"I don't have one."

"He's too broke," I added.

"How can a man like me work when I've got plenty of friends to provide for me? Why, I'm just like Socrates, spending all my time in the company of my friends, setting them on the right and true path."

"You're nothing like Socrates," I said. "You're the anti-Socrates if you're anything. The man was profoundly ugly and wise. You're handsome and as dumb as a fucking ox."

"Don't be mean. I might be forced to drink Hemlock."

"I've had it with him," I declared to Willard.

"Why?" Willard asked.

"Why?" Hanely asked like he was suddenly confused.

"You're all talk, Marcus. That's all you ever do. You're just like a voice in my ear. You talk and talk and talk and while away the day with your magnanimous speeches, and then you always abandon me in my hour of need. You're not there for me when I need your silver tongue, or else you swoop in and steal the women like a wily fox in a henhouse. All this, and you claim you're doing your best to help me."

"Step on it," Marcus said.

"I won't go anywhere."

"We need to see your dad," Willard said.

"I don't need to do anything."

"You should go and see your father, Jackson. Believe me, you'll regret it if you don't, and as an old man, I know, you don't want to live with regret later in life. You want to have accomplishments. You want to have people around to share them with."

"Always the voice of reason, coming from the back seat."

"I think we should drive as fast as we can to see his father before it's too late," Willard said.

"Blah," Marcus responded. "You don't even know what his dad is like."

"If I had children, I'd want to see them and tell them everything I wanted to tell them in life, but was too much of a coward to say or too busy working to provide for them materially. But I don't have children. The good lord didn't bless me that way."

"Drive," Marcus ordered coldly.

"No," I said.

"He'll drive, when he's good an' ready."

"I won't drive. Marcus, you drive. I'm sick of it."

"No. I can't drive."

"You aren't drunk this time."

"I don't care. I'm going to enjoy the scenery. If I drive, I'm going to the first titty bar available, and I'm going to get some big pasty covered titties in my face."

"God, is that all you ever think about?" Willard asked in disgust.

"Of course it is. When your dick worked, wasn't that all you thought about?"

"That's enough, Marcus. Drive."

"No. I'm going to enjoy the scenery. I'm not going to drive."

"The guy obviously can't drive."

"Fuck it! He's driving!"

The old woman and old man walked their little dog from the dog park, faces aghast at the spectacle unfolding in the car. Marcus sulked like a crybaby, as I yelled at him.

"You better fucking drive!"

"No!"

The old man shook his head from side to side as his wife walked past the car, her hands full of scratch-off lottery tickets. I made sure to wave to them, and they picked up the pace towards their RV, dragging their little Pomeranian nearly five full feet.

"You two are making a scene," Willard warned. "They probably don't take too kindly to violent oddball strangers around here."

"Who says I'm an oddball?" I asked.

"Keep your voice down. They're starting to point."

"Fucking drive! Why have I been driving this whole time?"

"I don't know, Jackson. You like driving. You like fast cars. It was my decision for you to buy this car. You know, the quintessential American muscle car for the fucking quintessential American fucking road trip. A fucking struggling to write Romance novelist and his male inspiration out on a road trip to find more inspiration in the great Wild West. How fucking romantic is that? That's epic."

"Jackson, you wouldn't struggle so much if you'd just lose this one trick pony of a friend of yours."

"Can it, Methuselah. If I wanted comments from the geriatric section of the hospital we would have gone there and gotten in the family waiting line. Sit in the back, and shut up."

"I've got plenty of stories, you young idiot. You just keep drowning me out with yours."

"Fine, tell us some of your stories, Pops McGillicuddy. Wow us with your brilliance at taking the panties off of Joan of Arc and some flappers. Tell us how you laid pipe to Amelia Earnhardt and how you were so good she forgot how to navigate."

"Start the car, Jackson. We've come to an agreement. You're the driver. I'm the passenger. Willard here, he's the talker. He's going to entertain us the whole way to Denver. I want to hear old Willard's war stories, every last one of them. I sure hope you can impress us, Willard."

"Hold on. Hold on, gents. I was a little lax earlier in my description of myself. You see, I feel, well, I know that really every man has an ideal self, the self they really want to project to the world and they have their real, fallen, Earthly self, the animal self, the self that society has trained them to be afraid of, to loathe, to suppress with all the weight of their moral fiber, the self that certain men – Marcus here included – in very slim company can get away with because they are either ravenously handsome, endowed with a quick wit, or in my case, endowed with something else," Willard said, gingerly.

"Yeah, right, this guy's saying he's hung like a Shetland pony, baseball bat style. My ass, he doesn't even fill the crease in a pair of jeans," Marcus said with a laugh.

"I didn't say that, Marcus. You're a fool. You think the only way a man can be endowed is by having a Moby Dick between his legs, but I'm talking about the gift of gab, the seducer's art, the ability to talk the panties off even the most steadfast spinster, schoolteacher, or nun. The gift of the silver tongue, the knowledge of the psychology of women, knowing exactly they want to hear, when they want to hear it," Willard said.

"Bullshit," Marcus said.

"Bull nothing, boy," Willard said pointing his finger into Marcus's face.

The black car swept into the outskirts of Salt Lake City heading east, passing a full thirteen gas stations that looked just like every other gas station. America, the place where everything is the same, no matter where you go, only the scenery is different...if you can find a place to view it from that isn't occluded by business signs and advertisements. I'd love to see a poetic mountaintop or a sunset without having to crane my neck through five-dozen billboards and signs for fattening food. The people are starting to cook down into homogenized slurry too. It started to get to me as I just thought about it and listened to Marcus and Willard argue with each other like two little kids. It wasn't Willard's fault. This leg of the journey was supposed to be devoted to listening to stories told by our elder, but Marcus kept interrupting him, ripping on him, not letting him speak. Soon he wouldn't be able to tell stories anymore.

PURGATORY OF THE DAMNED

"Why don't we stop anywhere?" Marcus howled in fury, gripping his testicles as if they were on fire.

"A fine man, that Brigham Young," Willard added, thinking out loud.

"No. We move on until Denver and Dad, and then we go anywhere you want."

"Haven't a clue," Marcus quipped. "It's getting dark."

"Right, damn. Not even a moon in the sky."

The sun lay down on the shopping malls and strip malls and homes that looked the same, as if a God had flipped the switch on the sleepy, boring place. I assumed it was just like the beginning of the Universe before, "Let there be light," and all that hullabaloo, and poof there it all was, this time only in reverse. Small lights dotted the countryside fouling up the desert evening, we too were lost like the desert moths plunging headlong towards that false bliss of those lights ahead of them, but we were plunging towards darkness. The Judge, she coughed and sputtered, 93-octane fuel gunning in the carburetor.

"Sounds like the old girl might need a tune up soon," Willard said.

"Now he's a car expert besides a lady killer," Marcus said.

"Yeah, Willard, you never really began your stories."

"This youngster kept interrupting me, so I got into looking at the scenery."

"Baloney. I'm calling your bluff. Bathroom attendant doesn't know shit."

"Come on, Willard, spill it. I saw how you had those two whores eating out of the palm of your hand back there."

"He did?" Marcus asked.

"Yeah, you were otherwise detained."

"I think he even made of them cry," I said winking at Willard.

"Those were tears of joy," Willard said.

"I saw it with my own eyes."

"What does a woman want most in the world, Marcus?" Willard asked, from the safety of the back seat.

"I don't know," Marcus answered with a facetious tone and a phony smile of a cherub smeared on his face.

"Come on, you do so."

"No, I really don't," Marcus said winking rapidly, doing his best cutesy routine.

"But your talents indicate that you do know what they want."

"How do you talk to women, Willard?"

"You should know, Marcus. I mean, after all, you're a handsome idiot."

"What do you mean by that?"

"I mean that you're good at looking good and sitting there, and your other talent includes looking good and sitting there, and you're also talented at looking good and sitting there and never opening your mouth because you have nothing to say. You're a male what's-her-face. That black haired bimbo, what's-her-face."

"What's-her-face?"

"Yeah, what's-her-face. It's on the tip of my tongue. She's married to some rapper, what's his face? I just can't remember."

"Drawing' a blank, too."

"What's-her-face, eh, well it's not important, but what I'm telling you is that a woman will talk all day long because she must, and you sitting there with that blank, handsome look on your face, pretending to be listening and occasionally saying, 'Uh huh,' and never really throwing her train of thought off by trying to say something smarter than her or correcting her in any deficit in her knowledge, it makes her think that she has a man who is willing to listen and really understands her. Plus, don't forget that you're really good looking, so she doesn't hesitate to trust you, and that you're not the brightest which means you won't ever break the illusion for her by saying anything intelligent. You're a mirror for her, and in the end she's only going to do what it was that she had in her head to do from the beginning. She only needed to convince herself and hear herself, a woman envelops, a woman welcomes in, and she knows very well what she is doing the entire time she is doing it, always thinking ahead, always projecting herself and her wellbeing into the future – 'will I be taken care of? Well, will I?' And as long as she can tell herself yes, then you're golden. And she tells herself yes in regards to you before you ever open your mouth, and you don't need to open your mouth. You're like a male what's-her-face."

"Sophia Loren."

"Nice try. No, I remember her well. You know how many times I beat my dick to her in foreign, hostile countries?"

"Well, well, well. Spoken by a wise old Socrates!"

"Socrates was a homosexual," Willard said. "A wise man, yes, but he was a boy-loving old fool."

"He never must've had a woman to tie his mind in knots."

"Oh no, he was married to a woman. He just preferred the company of men."

The Judge thrust into the darkness, grinding asphalt under rubber.

"You see," Willard continued, "some poet said that whatever women may not lightly have, they crave, they cry for that all night long, all day, and so that begs the question 'what do women really want?'"

"Women want love," Marcus said.

"No they don't," Willard responded resoundingly.

"A woman wants the opposite of what a man wants," I replied, feeling myself ever the wiser than Marcus Fuck-face Hanely.

"And what's that, then?"

"Love!" Marcus interjected, like a charging bull darting into a crowd of red ker-chiefed nuns.

"No, they don't," Willard said bluntly.

"What do they want then, Mr. Romance Novelist?"

"The opposite of men. Men want to have every woman in the world at least once, and women want the one man they choose, whether he loves them or not."

"Women choose their choice. Men have no power over this, a man acts blindly, blind will of ejaculate, you know, determined like...women have free will...men do not."

"That's a fucking far-drawn conclusion."

"Let me ask you, Marcus," Willard said, pulling his tweed hat tight onto his fore-head. "All these women you couple with, did you make a choice to sleep with them?"

"Of course I did."

"Really?"

"Something else did not lead you down that path?"

"My cock and balls? Lust?"

"Sure. Whatever you say," Willard added.

"Who made the choice in that endeavor?"

"I did."

"Bullshit. You aren't the receptacle," Willard said.

"What?"

"You didn't make the choice, you were guided every step of the way by the woman who chose you as her partner. I will tell you what Hanely, you could get laid at a nun's convention, but first that nun has to break down a whole lot of vows and societal conventions and mishmash in her head about her position in life before she ever lets you past the gate. She had to have that preconceived notion that she was going to go down that path before she ever put herself in that position, and then you would just be the male to play that role with her. No man has ever been charming, where a woman was not there already to be charmed, where he has not been allowed to be charming by some little miss guiding him the entire way. The only error these women have when they couple with you is ever possibly thinking that you could turn your attention away from the wiles of all the other women. That is all they should be concerned about. You think a man's life is warfare? Marcus, a woman's life is doubly warfare. Not only must she lay traps for the man she has chosen for her love and hope that he takes the bait, she must eliminate all of her female rivals in the meantime. Why, Marcus, imagine if all the men in the world were eliminated save for one. Let's call him the prime stud. The world of human affairs would still go on. If all the women were eliminated save for an Eve, we're done for. Would female jealously still exist during the time of prime stud? Would Eve become a queen, or be trampled underfoot by the battle of brutes?" Willard said, panting towards the end, and fell back into the back seat. "There is much more to say, much more to question. I've lost my way...can we stop off at a pisser? I feel like I'm about to float away again."

"In the purgatory of the damned, women have only one choice. A woman is in heaven when she's the only one around and she can have her choice and there are no other women around to beat her to it, to slut it up and get all the attention of the feeble minded men," I said.

"Where did you get that from?"

"You want to see Armageddon?"

"No, what is it to you?"

"Put one beautiful babe in a room full of 300 men who haven't been laid for a while and see what happens. She has already marked who gets past the gate. The only one with freedom in that entire situation is her. She gets to choose who her choice is."

"The men have no other option but to fuck her though."

"This woman is gorgeous. Of course they don't have a choice," Willard said.

"She's the only one with a choice."

"Turn the tables. Lock one stud in a room full of 300 women, and make him me!" Marcus declared.

"My friend, you'd truly be in hell," Marcus said.

"Hell? That would be heaven!"

"No way! You know what would happen?"

"A torment, a firestorm, all the pent up furies, rages, jealousies, all the women would have to choose you, they would be forced to choose you, you alone, and they would set about denying the other women of being able to choose you."

"Or they would just all dyke out and leave you there to beat your dick alone in the corner," I said.

Willard burst out laughing.

"My friend, once you cede that women are utterly in control, you will be much happier."

"I'm happy as it is," Marcus said.

"But you're still suffering from the delusion that you're actually responsible for what happens," I said.

"I am," Marcus said.

"How?

"I put myself in certain places where women are."

"That's a laugh," Willard said.

"You should see this guy slink around Monterey, looking like driftwood until he washes up on some Belle's table."

"More like a sea monster, stalking them from the depths," Marcus said.

"They lure you in, Hanely, and you take the bait," Willard said.

"It's a misconception that foolish men have, that they're soundly in control of their futures," Willard said.

"When you're in your twenties, you're focused on getting enough experience in the sack to please a woman. In your twenties you're a twerp. Your thoughts revolve around a career, building your resume, climbing the ladder, stepping on the heads of your competitors, increasing the size of your bank account, having a threesome, meeting hot moms, fucking older more experienced women who will be grandmothers twice over by the time you reach your thirties. In your thirties you feel like you have the experience and it's all about teaching younger women the ropes. Your old flames are now too old for you and no longer burst when you are near them. Now you see fit to plow fresh fields, your tastes border on the exotic, you cannot get the taste of exotic fruits like mango and papaya from your lips, darker skin, skin of different hues is tantalizing, you're drawn to women with accents, and you..."

"Marriage is a prison built by a man for a woman."

"I wasn't finished."

"In your forties you want something real, so you call up your old flames, you meet them. Their kids are grown, and yours are unknown to you. You meet in their minivan behind a grocery store in your hometown when you're back for a visit, but it still wasn't the same as you remember when you were young and free and sex was new and dangerous and light and full of life. Now you did it to cling to life, to rip yourself back from your growing sense of frustration and ennui."

"Pity, the lady who feels forced to marry then."

"It's rubbish, hogwash."

"You think all women are beautiful, Willard? You think they all have a choice?"

"They are," Willard said.

"They marry out of weakness."

On the right we passed a shiny, neon sign.

> Repent now or you may find
> yourself in:
>
> # HELL!

"You know what Hell is, Marcus?" Willard asked.

There was no response.

He continued, "Hell is my first marriage."

"You cannot force a woman to love you. She'll only end up hating you more, her hatred for you will grow day by day, the pressure will build, you see because she's not talking to you until you feel the floor of your home is covered in tiny eggshells which will fracture at the tiniest step in the wrong direction, and you second guess everything you do or say, and you know what the cause is...."

"She's a cunt."

"No. She gets along with other people. You're the cause. And it's not your actions. You've done nothing wrong really, but you've done everything wrong. You're just plain wrong. It's you. It's your person, your manhood, whatever it is. She hates your existence. And it's just you. She didn't really choose you for herself."

"Why did you marry her?"

"Her father liked me. He and her mama put pressure on her. At the time I was selling cars for General Motors, making a nice, fat commission. She was the most beautiful thing I ever saw. Hair like midnight, eyes that would pierce your soul. Tits like tits like tits...I can't describe those things, if you ever want to show some Martian why men loved tits so much, all you had to do was pluck off her bra and he would be a true believer in the First Intergalactic Church of Holy Human Tits. If you ever wanted to slow motion and stop time for a crowd of men in a diner, you'd take her in there and let her do a couple of strolls looking for an empty seat."

"A nice pair, then?" Marcus asked.

"Stupendous fucking tits," Willard repeated.

"But she hated you," I reminded him.

"Yep. Hated me. Wanted to have nothing to do with me. Ran away with a no good, two-bit car thief and ne'er-do-well. Guess she thought she could change him, but she chose him."

"What happened to her?"

"She's got oodles of kids and grandkids and lives in New Mexico. Once she got away from me she found her stride and did what God blessed her to do."

"Fuck that, she left you for another man," Marcus said.

"She did not. She hated me, I told you so. She was freeing herself. I had really nothing to do with it. It's impossible to force a woman to love you. There is no compulsion in love. She has to choose to love you. It isn't a...oh he's not so bad, I'll love him type decision like when you rationalize to yourself to fuck an ugly chick," Willard said forcefully.

"Maybe if you spoke with conviction to her," I suggested. "Women love conviction."

"Even if it's bullshit," Marcus said, smiling.

"Right. Like Marcus here is only capable of stacking bullshit to the ceiling."

"You think I'm only capable of stacking bullshit to the ceiling?"

"Yeah. You're a baloney artist. You're so talented at it that you've forgotten you're ever even doing it. You're a perfect bull-shitter, swimming in bullshit up to your neck and loving it, taking it in like it was fine wine, bottling it up for everyone to enjoy a taste or two."

"You're a bullshit artist too, Jackson. The biggest. The best, for fuck's sake. You're a romance novelist."

"I create art!" I exclaimed.

Marcus laughed out loud; doubling over as his guffaws filled the ancient interior of the Pontiac reverberated off the windows and overcame the still blowing air conditioner.

"You create art?" Marcus asked rhetorically, with his hands held out as if he were panhandling for some more art from my lips.

"I do! I make life worth living on this wretched planet!"

"Bullshit!" Marcus exclaimed.

"Fuck yourself, Marcus! Why did I even bring you along? All you do, all you ever do, is belittle me, put me down. And what do I do? You see this car? My art bought this car, that Ferrari you wrecked? My art bought that, too!"

"You know the truth, Jackson, and don't you try to hide it. You know the ugly little buried truth."

"What's that?" Willard asked. Interrupting, shivering from the A/C crackling and washing over him, sending is teeth chattering.

"Tell him, goddamnit," Marcus demanded.

"What do you have something to tell me, Jackson?"

I remained silent. Marcus tapped his hand against the dash in frustration. Maybe a minute passed before he lashed out, "You were already rich! You act like you're some self-made Richie Rich, but you're no self-made man. You're no once-starving artist! Your dad is fucking Prescott Leman III for chrissakes. Not exactly a fucking janitor by any stretch."

"I've heard that name before," Willard said.

"Of course you have, Willard. After this poor unfortunate's mother died, his father devoted himself to worthy causes all over the world."

"Yeah, like making money."

"Oh, boo hoo. Your father became more interested in worldly business affairs and less about the petty pursuit of a relationship with his children whom he barely knew anyway. Come on, tell the truth. The only thing you're upset about is having too much money to kick around and people not thinking you're really real, because you've never really had to ever lift a finger a day in your life."

Marcus was about to push a final straw. Oh, I don't know why I kept him around, why I ever invited him on this trip, why I ever let him be my friend in college, and why I didn't just drink the cyanide that I stole from the lab. Instead, I let the fool flush it. Twenty years is a long time to be depressed and waiting for the slightest inclination to push you over the edge. I don't know why I listened to his advice. These things I am thinking as we hurtle down the Interstate past big 18 wheeler Peterbilts and Volkswagens which could crush us all in a heartbeat with the flick of a wrist, all in order to watch one of the richest men west of the Mississippi mind you, and there are some rich ones, my father, captain and previously scion of industry, a man who knew exactly when to buy low and sell high and who always played by the rules up until my mother met her maker, leaving me with various governesses and butlers in locations where I was free to develop a powerful imagination, and it was my wild imagination which pays my bills, not my damn father. He doesn't pay for shit. Never has. And he won't in the future either because he'll be dead.

We sped onwards towards Denver. Mountain peaks loomed and retreated. Driving through the mountains at night is like standing in a dark closet with giants. Willard's teeth chattered, but he never complained. I liked the old man. Marcus Hanely, dear old Marcus Hanely, would not allow him to finish his story about the women he has been with, and Willard claimed to speak the truth, and you know what, I believe him. I think Willard's method would work. It was Marcus's method to envelop them in a shroud of bullshit so thick they cannot see the exit. To pile on the bullshit until his purpose is fulfilled and then beat a hasty exit without leaving too many tracks as to where he was headed. Willard's method came from a bygone world that women created because their tolerance was not very high for bullshit. Marcus's method fits quite perfectly with the world where people are in love with falsity, shimmering images, stupidity, afraid of their own shadow, cloak themselves in ennui, and dream of what's-her-face. In this world, of advertisements and global signs, Marcus, the underemployed ne'er-do-well who could open his mouth and weave magic rainbows yet who was too uneducated to be a lawyer or Madison Avenue executive, was, in this world, a king.

We drove all night long to the very outskirts of a two horse dusty town just beyond the four corners. Name was Yellow Jacket, Colorado, or some such shit. Maybe it was Cortez, maybe the area where the two burgs met up and shook hands and said here's the middle ground between us. The name of this locale escaped me, and I don't really recall seeing a sign that posted any sort of name or any population density.

Google searches came up with, "Are you sure you typed that correctly?" Needless to say, in my long discussions in the car, I sort of took the long way. No matter. We were bygones anyways. There was a Gulf Oil Company that looked as if it had not received a shipment of gasoline or window decals, Red Bulls, or cheap DVDs since the creation of the Mouseketeer Club, and at one time was the near midway point of a journey that saw a young man from Peoria, Illinois, already possessed of a sizeable family fortune, on the path to becoming a multi-billionaire. That was my father, but this is neither here nor there. This is my story. He's only dying in it.

This fact was not recorded in the history books, and it was a minor aside to the entire endpoint of humanity, but this gas station, laying in disrepair, where we now lay, had at one time given that hard journeyer a moment's solace and a nice clean bathroom to upchuck in from the sheer nervousness at all the freedom he faced.

That's how this crazy world worked; people wrapped their hopes and dreams up in knapsacks and started on their own journey. They rode buses, planes and drove cars to places they intended. They stopped when something held their attention. They just packed up their knapsacks and marched off, their heartbeats counted the hours to their deaths. But they never stopped to ever listen. Here we were at this abandoned gas station trying to cop a few gallons of gasoline to get us to the next town, which we did not know the name of, but was hopefully an island of modernity complete with a lubricated condoms machine in some cherry smelly air freshener, Vienna sausages in the can, Dinty Moore Beef Stew, and a microwave to heat it all up in.

"Place looks abandoned, like a fucking ghost town," Marcus said.

"Place looks awfully abandoned," Willard echoed.

"Yeah, it looks as old and cared for as you," Marcus said laughing.

"Where are we?" I asked.

"Shitsville, Colorado."

"No such place."

"I christen thee Shitsville," Marcus said, with his dong out, pissing on the old pumps that had been totally stripped clean by looters.

"Why are we here?" Willard asked.

"We need gasoline," I said gravely. The Judge was sitting on just above E with nothing but more Shitsvilles looming on the horizon.

"Why didn't you stop anywhere else before now?" Willard asked with an inquisitor's thirst for knowledge.

"I'm looking for inspiration. I'm feeling in a very creative mood, and I wanted to stop in a place with character."

"Shitsville's got character all right," Marcus said, shaking and tucking and zipping up his pantaloons.

"We don't need character. We need gasoline."

"What kind of place doesn't have gasoline?"

"Places that no one goes to or whose managers embezzled all the money for whatever drug these people do out here. Christ, this is the pits. No places have gasoline, not on this forgotten highway."

"You might try further down the road," a voice said from the shadows of the Gulf Oil Company garage, now cluttered with parts of various trucks, enough to assemble one large monster type truck without the crushing tractor tires.

"Who's there?" Marcus asked.

No response. "Show yourself," I said.

"Oh, no one in particular."

A man emerged, tall, gaunt, dressed in mostly black, with an air of dignity about him like he had been places and done interesting things, with a black fedora on his wizened face, who looked to have stayed in the sun too long, either here or somewhere else, double baked. His skin was the color of French Fries, not sure if they were McDonald's or Burger King in color.

"No gasoline here, buddy."

"Why not?"

"The trucks stopped coming. We couldn't really pay in advance...we asked them to come every two months, but the management just went ahead and pulled the plug on the operation. I'm sort of mopping things up around here, if you will. Yes, I like the sound of that, mopping things up."

"Like you're a janitor?" Marcus asked.

Willard laughed. "No, you fool. He's cleaning up the messes, making sure everything is tidy and nice and neat."

"Don't look too neat to me," I said.

"Getting her in line for a buyer," the man quipped, wiping his hands on an oily rag.

"Someone's actually going to buy this heap?" I asked.

"Oh, we'll see."

"You're fixing cars?"

"No. I don't fix cars. I'm appraising this place for a buyer. I sell and buy properties. You see, haven't sold any around here for a while, so it's a buyers' market. No one's buying though. But still, it's a buyers' market."

"How much is this gasoline station going to cost?"

"Don't remember. Hell, I don't even know if the original owners are still alive. Why? You thinking about buying it? That why you're poking around here?"

"Nope. Can't say that I am. Say, what's your name?"

"My name's Avalon. Richard Avalon."

"Suppose I'm happy to meet you, Mr. Avalon. Now you know anyone who actually has gasoline around here?"

"Suppose I might."

"Well, will you show us?"

"Us?"

"You've got someone else with you?"

Willard and Marcus were nowhere to be seen.

"Must've wandered off somewhere."

"Yeah, I'll show you. Depends though."

"On what?"

"Whether or not you can make a deal."

"Shit," I said under my breath.

"Sure enough, just take us where the gasoline is. We'll pay top dollar."

"Top dollar, eh?"

"Yeah, man, mucho dinero."

"They probably don't want your money."

"What will they want then?"

"Probably a go at Willard's virgin ass," Marcus called.

I looked around. I didn't see him.

"Say, where can a fella get laid around here?" Marcus asked again, still eerily out of sight.

"Goddamnit, man, show yourself," I said.

Avalon just stared at me, queerly.

"You want to know where that gas is? Better be speeding your way out of town."

I heard Marcus and Willard's voices again, muffled this time, seeming to come from the garage. Only Godknowswhat they were into. I walked past Avalon towards the garage.

"What are you checking out back there?" Avalon asked, with more than a hint of concern in his voice.

When I got close to the garage, the voices appeared to be coming from behind the garage. I walked around it. There was Marcus and Willard, best buddies all of a sudden it seemed. Marcus had his arm around Willard, and Willard was cackling like an old crow, delighted at the prospect of fresh road kill.

"You coming?"

"Where we going?"

"Off to find gas."

"You sure he doesn't want to steal the Judge?"

"Come with me."

"Nah, we'll sit this one out."

"What? Why?"

"Got the good word, man. Willard knows a place."

"What? Where are you going?"

"We'll meet you somewhere."

"I can't stay here! I've got to get home!"

"I'm on vacation. I'm in no hurry."

"God, you're so selfish!"

"Just wait for us at the gas station. We'll find you."

"Damn you. You're going to choose pussy over me?"

"Hasn't it been that way for a while now?"

"But we're together on this trip. You have to come."

"Wait for me."

Avalon came from around the corner.

"No," I said.

"What?" Avalon said.

Marcus and Willard walked off towards the town in the distance, down a hill, into a gulley and disappeared into the mixed, tangly vegetation without making as much as a sound. I stared at their path of departure for a moment.

"What are you looking at?"

"Oh, nothing," I said, noting that my friends had abandoned me for some random stab at a good time. They abandoned me, Jackson Leman for what's-her-face, Miss Random, or Mrs. Random in Marcus's case, out there in BFE, Colorado, mountain town. I could only hope that mountain lions cornered them and tore them to shreds. Perhaps wolves. Grizzly bears or Indians, if we hadn't killed them all.

Avalon walked off. I followed him, eagerly.

"Where we going to get gasoline?" I asked.

"You want the easy sell, or the hard sell? How much money do you have?"

"Plenty. Just no cash."

"That's rough. Must have cash around here. You've got none."

"No. Just credit cards," I said, not about to let him onto my Niebelungen horde underneath my seat. I didn't know this brigand from Adam.

"Yeah. Good luck with that one."

"What do you mean?"

"No one takes credit around here. Just greenbacks."

"Well, then, how are we going to get gas?"

Avalon just smiled, and said, "All right, easy sell or hard sell?"

"I've never done an easy thing in my life," I said, lying.

"Okay, we'll do this the hard way."

I drove, and Avalon rode shotgun. When we pulled into town, the Judge was just about tits up in the way of petrol. Not that I had given the car a name or that I even considered the car female, but I knew that was tradition to call cars, boats, and fire-arms female names; a strange replacement for the real McCoy. Avalon was the one who reminded me, when he piled in the front seat and said, "She's almost out." We parked. We passed bikes, scores of them, red and blue, red, white and blue, chromed out and polished, interspersed with a few post apocalyptic beaters, but most iced out, none showing a wide array of neglect. Eighty years ago it would have been horses, but the dirty bikes, the beaters, replaced the animals, which showed a similar neglect, bony and starving. The place reeked of leather when we opened the door, and all of the leather clad men and cackling women looked to us, strangers, and they knew it.

"I'll get some gas. You head inside and make yourself comfortable."

I sauntered in and crept in right up to the bar like a wanted gringo cattle rustler in a wild Mexican cantina.

"What can I do for you?" the bartender, an oldish man probably hovering around 60, but who was possibly a 40 year old who didn't take care of himself and drank too much in his off time, asked.

"Three beers, please," I said, expecting Marcus and Willard to come waltzing in at any moment from Marcus's sexcapades and Willard's vicarious voyeurism. I told them that I would meet them at a gas station...but we were nowhere near a gas station. In fact, I don't think there was a gas station in this entire damn town. It was just a place to pass through, dump off some money and some jism in. Cash flow and gene flow. In fact, on the way in, I noticed nothing but boarded up windows. Hard to see out of.

"You planning on doing some heavy drinking there?"

"Nah. Expecting two friends."

"Well, hope they're not too long. I'd hate for a man to have to drink warm beer."

I sat, busy ogling the biker ladies. A few had taken to dancing without rhythm, looking like cheap dried leather marionettes as they bobbed and swayed drunkenly to the music, which popped and cracked from an antique Wurlitzer in which the neon lights had either malfunctioned or had been stomped out, punched out, or headbutted out. Still they flickered randomly and with more rhythm than the two right about over the roller coaster apex towards old age and oblivion babes. Their tits both fake and still slightly overcoming gravity, were nonetheless stupendous.

"Why do you look so nervous?"

"I do?"

"You do."

"Oh, I don't know, I guess I'm terrified of people in leather."

"Leather?"

"Yeah people wearing leather."

"You came to the wrong place then. What're you scared of? Bikers?"

"Had a few run-ins. Mostly terrified of the Salinas, California Hell's Angel Chapter."

The crowd looked to be pushing the upper boundaries of the geriatric. Still, some of the old bastards sitting in darkened corners with candlelight on their fierce wooly beards and braids gave them the appearance of being Viking marauders. And wherever I looked, I saw older, greasy men with young babes.

"We're friendly enough people around here, unless you cross us. That makes Lucifer's Prairie Dogs real upset."

I smiled and pretended to look around the bar, looking for something to change the subject away from burly bikers beating my brains in. I spied a poster on the wall with Avalon's mug on it.

"That guy is getting us some gasoline; my car's bone dry."

"Ahh, yeah, our old buddy Dickie Avalon. I wouldn't trust him. He'll probably sell you gasoline-scented water. Taste that beer you're drinking?"

I had not yet begun to drink. It took a swig, it was slightly bitter on the tongue, watered down. I grimaced.

"That beer's from him."

"He told me he was a real estate agent," I said.

"He's all things to everyone, a real jack of all trades. Have a toothache and are willing to get it taken care of? He's a dentist. Got your old lady in the family way? For the right price he'll fix that for you to or at least introduce someone to you who can and then extract some twenty percent finder/fixer fee. Ten percent from both parties on account of fixing them up together. God forbid he ever introduced you to your wife or something. Might be charging something else on a bimonthly basis. Guess he's an attorney, too."

"Attorney?"

"Yep. Handles all sorts of disputes. Charges for that too."

"Strange."

"Funny thing is, he's only been here for a month or two. Just sort of blew in to town with all the answers. Right when he came, the market totally went to shit, like anything he dabbled his fingers in turned to worthless. King Midas's opposite."

"Why do you have his photo up then?"

"We love losers in this place. That's from when he ran for mayor a couple of weeks ago."

"He's been here a month, and he ran for mayor?"

"Yep. Ran on the ticket of being tough on crime and a business reformer. Well, we don't have many people here really, so there's no crime, and I'm about the only business left in this place. Only reason I stay open is catching all these retired bikers on their runs."

"There's not even a name on his advertisement," I said. The poster looked creepy, Avalon's big undertaker mug sort of staring at you, looking through you, imploring you "Vote, Vote for me."

"See what I mean? The guy says, whatever, you don't need to put your name on the sign. People will see my face and automatically remember the times I've helped them out and vote for Dickie Avalon because the guy's a gem, a real fine, upstanding citizen."

"Sounds pretty dumb."

"Right on with that. Plus the emmer effer owes The Nursing Home Rejects some dues, and he took Pee Wee's Harley out for a spin and wrecked the forks on it something fierce."

"So I take it he's not liked around here."

"Not until he pays up the 750 he owes them. He's not welcome here. Plus he owes me money I fronted him to start a bicycle repair shop. Thought mountain bikes would be all the rage, and we could make this some sort of start off point for mountain bikers that would become world famous. But look around you. There aren't too many mountains too close to us right here. But still, he imported all these fool fancy bikes, some of 'em cost more than a decent chopper, and then lost the whole damn place in a few short months."

"Sounds like a fool," I said.

"Just smell the gasoline before you put it in your car. Who knows what old barrel he dug up out in the desert? Could be surplus from World War II. Alien shit. Who knows?"

I finished the contents of the beer. Next time I would ask for a bottle. With the water content of the draft, it ended up being half a beer. I eyed Hanely and Willard's promised beers greedily. They'll be here any second, I said, always trying to be the nice, equitable gent.

Sweat beaded on the glass like the beer was a fat man doing hard labor in the sun. I eagerly waited for the ching-ching of the door and for those two rascals to come in and join me. Smoke from the biker's cigarettes tickled my throat. I suppose that there was some ordinance against noxious cigarette smoking inside, but there were no local authorities to enforce it.

One of the bikers, a tall grizzled man with a wispy black beard and knife slash wound across his face bowlegged shuffled up to the bar and plopped down on the faux leather seat, which whooshed the contents of the air out, bringing him more down to my eye level. He sat there and just stared at me, sort of curling up his lip. He lit up a cigar he had been chewing on and blew the smoke into my face. Not once, but twice, so I knew it wasn't an accident. I just smiled at him. I started guessing in my mind where he got the knife wound at. Prison riot. Vietnam. Detroit Auto Factory. Catholic Boy's School. All the possible scenarios did not bode well for me having to fight this guy, because my fighting skills consisted of running fast and throwing well-aimed rocks. It's not that I'd ever had to do that, but that's what the way I would fight this horde of psycho grandfathers. He kept staring. I looked away and started at Marcus's beer. I'd have to apologize and buy him another.

"What are you doing here?" the biker asked.

"Oh, nothing really, drinking a couple of beers, waiting for my friends," I said.

"Usually people who come to bars try and socialize. Try and meet people. You looking to meet people?" the biker asked.

"No. Just waiting on people I already know."

"You know, you look stuck to me."

"Maybe."

"You ain't too talkative."

"He's got a biker phobia," the bartender quipped, whilst wiping mugs free of their remnant foam.

"Really? You're scared of us?"

"No."

"No?"

"I mean, yeah, I guess."

"Come on...what's there to be scared of?"

"There are about one hundred fifty of you in here, and one of me."

He laughed. "We're harmless. Come on and have a beer with us."

Just as I was about to get up off my semi-comfortable bar stool, light glared off the mirrors, and the door to the establishment opened. A young woman, with a shadowy profile on account of the parking lot lighting behind her, burst into the barroom, much to the delight of all the geriatric bikers who hooted and hollered like the Great Ape House at the San Diego Zoo on banana day. Ridiculous swine, I thought, and then she hit the light where I could see her.

I gasped, much like I gasped when I saw that other hot Navajo woman what's-her-name. This woman didn't look Navajo, rather Italian, maybe northern Italian, somewhat Roman-like. She turned on the old Wurlitzer, something by Otis Redding maybe, or Lou Rawls, plenty of horns and guitar and a sultry soulful black man singing about the good old times in the bad new times. It surely wasn't Marvin Gaye. The bikers cheered her on when she began to dance in the center of the barroom.

The older women, who paled in comparison to her, immediately sat down. This young lady was not even wearing leather, rather a tight T-shirt, and a black miniskirt that looked like it had been painted on her. She pulled one of the old men up to his feet, a right lucky bastard, and whirled around with him until he was out of breath, only tossing him to his seat when the old lecher tried to steal a kiss from her. He stumbled drunk to his chair, with the guffaws and arm punches and backslaps of congratulations coming from all directions.

"Who is that?" I asked the bartender.

"That's the slut daughter of Dickie Avalon, Vanessa."

She spun and gyrated to the music, seemingly in her own world, focused on something not in the room, but inside her.

"Does she come here often?" I asked.

"Nah, first time for everything though. Her old man's probably up to something."

Vanessa walked up confidently, boot over boot, sashaying her hips all kitten-like. I looked to the biker next to me, who made to jump up and get in her way as she bee-lined towards me, but she pushed him backwards like all the rest and said, "No, not you."

She grabbed me by the waist and grinded her big tits into my face, forcing me to bend my head to the side so I didn't disrespect her, and she said, "You."

I looked up into her dark eyes, made darker by the dim light of the bar. They glowed red, briefly, like she was some foul succubus, but then I realized that was probably just the reflection of the Pabst Blue Ribbon or Schlitz sign in them. I could have mistaken it for a flash of passion if I just wasn't so logical. She pulled my head out of her volcanic boobs and said, "My god, you're Jackson Leman, aren't you?"

"Oh my god! Jackson Leman!"

She had stopped her dancing. She stood in front of me smiling like a little girl. She wasn't a little girl, maybe 19 or 20 at the most. But a woman. You know why.

"This is Jackson Leman everyone!"

"Who?" The bikers shouted, nearly in unison, and someone called, "Shut up and dance!" They glared at me, some shouting obscenities like I had just sat on the remote and turned off the Super Bowl at the final play of a game tied 7 - 7.

"The author of *Asymmetric Hearts*. It's, like, only the best novel ever written," she declared.

"That's not shit we've ever heard of," a burly man, who looked to be the leader of this malevolent gang of geriatrics said.

"You know me?" I asked.

"Of course, silly. I've only read your book like 35 times or so."

The Nursing Home Rejects started to get rowdy. Like a great conglomeration of AARP members only offered prescription drug coverage with co-pay, they were incensed and this wasn't something they were going to write their congressmen about. A few of them stood up, looking menacing, taking their teeth out as if they intended to pummel me.

"You better pull those out, or this place might get ugly," the bartender told her.

"Dance!" the crowd roared.

She stood up. "Fine!" she yelled. "You bastards want a dance? You've got a dance. But only for two songs. After that, I'm taking Mr. Leman and leaving with him." She turned around to wink at me. "And I won't be held accountable for any of your pace-makers zapping you or heart attacks."

She ripped her shirt off violently. Glorious tits upheld their bargain with gravity. The crowd went wild. Something fast played on the jukebox. Time seemed to stand still. It was like she was dancing for me. She ignored everyone else, dancing for them, working the room, but it was only me that she looked at, winked at, made little kissy faces towards. At any moment, I expected Marcus to waltz in and steal her attentions from me. My pocket rocket thumped with every wink, every little kiss. She finished by waltzing right up to me and aggressively forcing her tongue in my mouth, much to the howls of the assembled old gentry.

"Let's get out of here," she said. "Dad should be just about done."

"What's he doing?"

"Come with me."

"I'm supposed to wait for my friends."

"Would your friends wait for you?"

I stood up as she put her shirt on. "I don't think so," I said.

The knife wounded gentleman glared at me. "She's gonna leave with the twerp!" he announced.

"That's fine words for a pal," I told him.

At the door she announced, "Women love literary men, you old washed up nobodies. If any of you wrote a bestselling book that I've read over and over and over again from the age of 14, then I'd let you in my pants too. Until then, have fun riding your hogs."

Before we could get out of the door, the bottles started flying. The sexual tension built up, ejaculated itself in the form of that good old violence which creeps into situations where men's blood is up and there is no release, or none befitting what they see themselves as. Old rivalries amongst the geriatrics that simmered exploded. There were several gangs present, which had their heydays in the 1960s before being ridden out of town by tougher, mobbed-up gangs. She pulled me out just as a bottle nearly smashed my face. The Old Hens started fighting their one time arch rivals the River Cocks on the Block, the Reckless Ones fought the Rolling Thunder Outlaws, the Whirling Dervishes, a gang of Arab retired dentists and doctors from mainly Egypt, but a few from Jordan as well fought amongst themselves. Beer bottles flew and blood spewed like a crescent of fiercely ejaculating cocks. Lucifer's Prairie Dogs were the toughest gang going. When they stood up to rumble, the place quaked like the San Andreas fault.

"Bolt the fucking door!" Dickie Avalon yelled to us, shouting orders now like some battlefield commissioned private cum general. He held a clear plastic tube in his hands and reeked of gasoline. I looked down the line of assorted choppers and boppers and low riders with ape hangers all chromed out. Their gas tanks were open. Avalon had committed the ultimate sin. He had siphoned the gasoline out of the tanks of the most notorious gang of geriatric riders west of the Mississippi. We were in trouble. We had to leave now. There was no waiting around for Marcus Hanely and Willard to come stumbling up with their pants around their ankles. I looked over at Vanessa, who smiled at me, an evil smile. She would be all mine.

"You used your own daughter to cause a diversion, you sick fuck," I said, grabbing her by the hip, much to her delight.

Avalon didn't hear me. He was busy dumping his collected gasoline into the Judge's tank. A few bullet holes came through the barred door. Vanessa screamed and we ran to the car.

"Get in!" Avalon yelled, as the door started to come off its hinges, with the weight of a battering ram improvised from a wooden Indian and collective strength of fifty burly seventy-year-old functional alcoholics behind it. Avalon was in the driver's seat. Maybe he was intent on stealing the car. No harm. I was in the back seat with his daughter. Avalon gunned it, peeling out as the first oldies burst into the light of day, and found their gas tanks drained. We rounded a corner, and a few shots came in our direction. Vanessa reached down and squeezed my cock through my pants. I jumped back a bit. She had a smile on her face, and her eyes seemed to be searching out plans in her mind.

"Your dad's looking," I whispered to her.

"He doesn't give a fuck," she said as she dove backwards and spread her legs apart. I noticed she wasn't wearing any underwear. Total hair pie. I leapt beside her. There wasn't much room in the back seat. We were nearly on top of each other. It was nice to have someone driving instead of me. Vanessa grabbed my head and tongue kissed me again, biting my upper lip.

"Get those tight ass, high thread count, immaculately tailored jeans off," she demanded.

I fiddled with the belt as her father sped to the onramp.

"Keep your eyes on the road, pops," she said.

"Fuck," Avalon announced, looking in the rearview mirror.

"Don't peek," she said.

"This is so fucked up," I announced softly to her.

"Shut your mouth," she said, squeezing hard on my dong.

"Goddamnit, wait until later," I said motioning to the man driving, her father, with my head.

A bullet impacted the back window, shattering it.

"Fuck!" Avalon yelled. Suddenly I realized he wasn't talking to us.

"Daddy, you obviously didn't siphon all the gasoline."

I peeped my head up. Avalon swerved as more shots came from the geriatrics. Thank God it was shots from a pistol fired from a motorcycle. The next couple went right. Avalon seemed to know what he was doing, fine motor handling skills for a real estate agent.

She squeezed my cock again. "Goddamnit," I said. "Wait until later."

"He's about ready," she said with a smile.

We passed mile marker 308, and the bikers started to drop off. Probably out of gas. The gas in the lines had cooked off. The Judge, full on their energy like a vampire, growled like a tiger cat in heat.

Vanessa tugged it and squeezed my balls. I batted her hand away.

"Jesus, your dad is up there," I said.

"Listen, I don't give two shits whether my dad is up there, and he doesn't give two shits whether I'm back here, so fuck it, Jackson, give me this."

Avalon turned on the radio. Loudly. Some country came on.

She managed to work my prick out the top of my pants.

"God, that's only half of it?" she asked in delight.

"Put it away," I said, shuffling to get it out of sight. I could see Avalon's eyes in the rearview mirror. She flipped around and licked my glans, flicking her tongue across it. She put her lips around it and squeezed the base. My god, this was happening. She half blew, half jerked. It was loud. Disgusting.

And that's bit of nostalgia for the old West...
Where the men were men and the women know best
Who the men are
Who the men were
And that's recompense for a time long dead
Where the women were all Annie Oakley
And the Men looked like Buffalo Bill
And I miss it all, but still
It's not coming back
It's not coming back

The perfect woman lay there with her mouth full of skyscraper, unable to bring words to whatever she was thinking. We'd just met, but I felt a kindred spirit with her. She had brought me to the point of being about ready to dribble a few dribbles down her throat, because I'm a dribbler, not a shooter, though I wish I could, but my kegel muscular contractions are subpar according to the California Pornography Actors Guild standards. The money shot was rising, creeping like I think she sensed it too, because she pulled off me, and asked, "You love me, Jackson Leman?"

"What the fuck?"

"Do you love me, Jackson?"

"Sure. I love you."

She squeezed it and pumped the blood back, the wilting rose, invigorated. I also have that problem. If it's not getting attention it dries up...constant tongue action, that's what I need. I pushed her head down on it, taking control. Fuck her dad up in the front seat. Another song came on the radio.

I ran in
You done ran out
You slapped my best hunting' dog
Right up on his snout
You're a trifling woman
But I give the devil her due
Baby I'm leaving'
I'm through with you
Gonna pack up my 18 wheeler and head out on the forty
Head out California way, gonna get me some sun

But I know I'll be back
I know you'll call again
And I'll come running
Just like a faithful dog
That's all I am
A loyal pooch
A faithful mutt
Ain't any aspirations in this buck
My woman's got me whipped
She's got me crawling on all fours
Back to her cheating door
Back to her cheating door

The old creep up front kept driving, tapping his hand on the steering wheel to the music. No sudden moves. I wouldn't want his daughter choking on my cock. I started breathing heavily again; the mountains loomed like grease fire smoke to our front. Colorado. The color red, like blood from a nicked nut sack, bright, beautiful in the sunlight. Fuck, I wish Marcus could see this.

"Marcus!" I yelled.

"What?" she asked, looking up at me from around my shaft, which partially obscured her eye and was partially obscured by her black hair.

"We left my friends back there!"

"What are you talking about?"

Avalon looked back. "Eyes on the road, Daddy," Vanessa said.

I felt panic. I grabbed my dick and slammed it back, firmly in my pants.

"My friends! You made me forget my friends!"

"What friends?" Vanessa asked.

"My friends! You made me abandon them back in that town! We've got to go back!"

"Settle down, skipper! What friends are you talking about?"

"I drove to the town with two men. Your father saw them. Two men, Marcus Hanely and a guy named Willard, from Oklahoma, originally."

"There was only you in the car, Jackson," Avalon announced from the front seat. He turned the radio off.

"No. I came here with two men. We have to go back and get them."

"You were alone when you talked to me. You drove up alone."

"Pull the fucking car over," I screamed.

"Wow, just cool it, man," Vanessa said, now sitting against the opposite door, staring at me like I'd told her favorite store plummeted out of business and there would be no time to pick through the remainders.

"Turn the car around!" I screamed. "Dick, you better turn this fucking car around."

"Daddy, this guy's a fucking lunatic."

"We knew that. Mr. Leman we've got to get to Denver."

"You're not riding with me until we find them."

"Marcus Hanely, I've heard that name before," Vanessa said.

"You've got to get to Denver, Mr. Leman."

"Why the hell are you suddenly calling me Mr. Leman?"

"Marcus Hanely? The character in your book? You mean the guy in your romance novel? The character?"

"No. He's my inspiration."

"Marcus Hanely is real?"

"Yeah. Of course he's real," I said, with my voice trailing off. "He's been my best friend since college."

"What about Veronica Dare? She's my hero...could I meet her?"

"She's fiction. An amalgamation of every woman I've wanted to fuck since the third grade, when I didn't really know what fucking was. She's got the smarts of Ms. Polly, my second grade private school teacher, the tits of our Latin maid Rosaria, the eyes of a woman I spied in a Victoria's Secret catalogue in 1993, the hands of this lady I shook hands with during the 9th inning of a San Francisco Giants baseball game, and I guess, the soul of my dear departed mother."

"Jesus. You writers are fucked in the head. I wanted to be a writer after I read *Asymmetric Hearts* for the 27th time, but I decided I'm not fucked up enough to be a writer, and I like living too much. I like people too much. I like to be around them too much. I can't waste my time writing."

"You either do it or you don't. Practice makes you good. Kind of like sucking cock for you."

Avalon glared at me from the rearview mirror. I glanced under the seat, the butt end of my .45 masterblaster had shifted into view, moved from the greasy blue bandana I had it wrapped in. I rested my hand on it. I was about to make sure they turned around and picked up Marcus and Willard.

"You're an asshole, Jackson," Vanessa said, having had the time to process a rational response to my comment on the probable amount of dongs she'd had between her teeth without biting down on them.

"Turn this car around right now, Dick," I said, trying to get as much gravel and menace into my voice as possible.

"No can do, Mr. Leman. We've got to get you to Denver as soon as possible."

"You're riding with me?"

"You're riding with us now."

"Bullshit, you fucking businessman," I said.

"Since when is businessman a pejorative?" Avalon asked.

"It's always been. But it's a necessary evil, you evil fuck. Now turn around this car before I get hostile."

"Death is the most necessary evil and business makes life go round. Why, without death, life wouldn't rejuvenate, wouldn't be fresh. Businesses fail, they die, new ones crop up, fertilized by the ashes. So it's mimicking life, monsieur. It's beautiful. It's a beautiful cycle. We aren't turning the car around. You're riding with us to Denver."

"Sounds like I don't have a choice. Say, who do you work for?"

"I'm self employed," Avalon said smugly.

"Oh, really? An independent contractor, then. Thought I was worth more than that." I grabbed up the gun. Vanessa gasped when she saw me pull it from the back seat.

"Me, I'm an artist," I said, and thrust the gun at Avalon's head. "Now turn around."

Avalon laughed. "Art isn't sold at grocery stores, Jackson. Diversion, that's what sold at grocery stores. Diversion and potato chips."

"I'm an artist."

"You're a businessman, just like the rest of us," Avalon said.

"I know who you work for. You all work for him. If that's so, you work for me, too. So turn this fucking car around. We're going to go look for my buddies."

Avalon laughed, and flashed a toothy smile, "Your wish is my command, sire. I am your faithful squire."

"Do you really need the gun, tough guy? Now that you've figured us out?" Vanessa asked.

WALLY WORLD

"*Y*es, I need the gun! I'm a villain, a rogue, the man in black, a god damned satanic minister, and I'm going to shoot you both if you don't turn back for my friends."

"When I met you, you were quite alone and lonely," Avalon said, not breaking a sweat, seeming to almost enjoy having a gun pointed at his head. Maybe he knew that I wouldn't use it. Well, I would. I swear I would.

"Turn around," I said. The gun was shaking in my hand. Visibly. Everyone in the car could see it.

"You're some tough guy author," Vanessa said, laughing.

"I'm tough enough."

"I'll turn around, Mr. Leman, but you had better get rid of that thing you're holding. The only person you're going to use that on is yourself."

His words settled into my mind as he found a dusty turnaround, an island of abandoned commercial prosperity, now turned into a half-junkyard playground for a few overweight children. Who knows if they were ten or fourteen? I shook my head at them, and the kids stared like aborigines, never having seen a car, or never having seen a special car. Our car was pretty special, distinguished. I gave the finger to one of the kids, a big fat bastard with an outgrown buzz cut and freckles, whose beady eyes looked like little suffocating globes in his jowls, which poured over his cheeks. I shook it back and forth and smiled at him, as if to say I dare you. He offered me two back, whilst shaking his fat belly, busted out underneath his tight striped shirt.

"That was uncalled for," Vanessa said.

"Just be glad he didn't decide to throw rocks."

We were back, driving the way we came, back towards the town that modernity forgot. Or maybe it was a town that forgot modernity, forgot or grew tired of the incessant change that the living must undertake to keep one foot ahead of oblivion.

And I began to muse out loud about my missing friends, saying, "I wonder where they went, are there any whorehouses with cheap parlor tricks in town?"

Avalon piqued up. He looked like a man in the know. Hell, his daughter probably worked at one part time, when she wasn't power-cramming and seducing deadly bikers.

"Put the gun away, stud," Vanessa implored me.

"Not until we get to town," I answered.

"We're headed that way."

"You know how to shoot?" I asked Avalon, my voice trailed off out the front window.

"Not really."

"Yeah right, daddy knows all about guns," Vanessa said coyly.

"My daughter and I were just passing through this town, and I tried to make a little money from speculating on the local real estate market. I got into it real deep, just a few days before the bottom went out."

"Oh, gambling the company funds, then?"

Avalon looked at me out of the corner of his eye, like he was somewhat ashamed. I changed the subject to keep him talking, to keep the mood as cordial as it could be with a gun to someone's head.

"It's alright. You people aren't paid enough probably. What? Did you lose your shirt?"

"Shit, my shirt, my pants, my underwear! Vanessa's all I have in the world."

"We're making money off the rent, daddy."

"Yeah, Vanessa, for as smart as you are, you have no idea how the world really works. I'm still millions underwater. The bottom of the ocean."

"I bet the pressure's intense."

"If you knew how the world worked, daddy, we'd be rich. We wouldn't be trapped out here in BFE."

"Give me a break, you spoiled brat."

"At least we make the money off the rents."

"That pays the mortgages for now."

"We've bought up half the town."

"The old folks, suckers, they're all jumping on our reverse mortgage bandwagon."

"You're despicable," I muttered under my breath, looking out the window to see if I could see a red light. It was broad daylight and we were in Colorado, so there wasn't likely to be one. You never knew.

"You're sure there aren't any trailer park flophouses around here?"

"You go turning over rocks out there, you never know what might crawl out," Avalon said, bemused.

We drove past the boarded up downtown, returned to the scene of our crime and passed the bar where the bikers had chased us from. The bikers had departed, but a few skeletons of bikes that had seemingly been lit on fire remained.

"Never return to the scene of your crime."

"We aren't practiced criminals."

"Too bad Marcus isn't here. He'd have schooled you."

"Could you stop bringing up your friends?"

I looked at the desiccated downtown. There was nothing. Even the washing machine store, former glory of a corner, stood empty; save for a bleached by UV rays, plastic cutout which adorned the street side window, looking more a tombstone than an advertisement.

"This place is fucking dead."

"Tell me about it."

"Where the hell is everybody?"

There wasn't even tumbleweed on the road. The winds must have diverted them to more fitting blowbys.

"Well, not only did I buy up the mortgages of most of the homes here, but I encouraged some corporate anchors to come into the luxury outdoor shopping mall I encouraged some farmers to invest in."

"A luxury outdoor shopping mall? Here? How the hell did you swing that?"

"Financial alchemy, my man...by taking out mortgages on the all the properties, I managed to acquire, sometimes double, triple mortgages. This place is right by the interstate. I guess I gambled, thinking that tourists would come here to the mall and that I could start paying off the mortgages with the jacked up rents I could charge."

"You're an idiot. You've got to have a demand before you supply something."

"Nah, you just have to advertise. I didn't figure that into the budget."

"Daddy's not a good businessman."

So yeah, cities, we think they're part of nature, but their ultimate energy source is nothing like the sun; it is money. Look, you can see from a helicopter where the money flows in the organism, all the nooks and eddies it piles up in, where it ultimately flows, where it is shunted like a mystical force, the lifeblood and thrust of men's ambitions. Go ahead, look!

I looked out the window as the glorious little city full of lights came into view as it approached dusk, all abandoned, dead, save for the lights that emanated from that great beyond past the dingy little homes. Avalon's Mecca, full of stores where no one could afford the merchandise, floating above water, barely, bolstered by what little credit the commoners in the surrounding hinterlands had. And still they bought and spent and tarried, entertained by the race, thinking themselves fortunate, better off than the neighbors to the left and the right. And their path to Heaven was paved in cardboard boxes from big box stores and plastic bags and packaging and road signs to heaven, which gave way to advertisements and what was termed healthy diversion.

"Well, we're here," Avalon beamed.

"Lovely isn't it, Jacky?" Vanessa asked, expecting a response.

"It looks safe," I responded.

"Has its own security force. Ten part time guards on rotating shifts," Avalon said, bursting with pride.

"Where are we going first?"

"I don't know. Where could they be?"

"Some friends," Avalon said whipping the Judge into one of the ample parking lots. The lot looked nearly deserted. There was an RV stopped there, maybe to dump the contents of its poo tank. Avalon looked at them and told his daughter, "Call the security force and have these freeloaders run off."

"Oh, daddy, maybe they're customers."

"I doubt it. They're looking for a free place to sleep."

Several cars were parked in one section of the parking lot. I could make out for sale signs on them all. Some were store bought, but most were scrawled on bits of cardboard scavenged from a grocery store.

"You own these cars too, Avalon?"

"Oh, you know, people are out of work, they need money, they got equity to pay for cars out of their homes, and they can't afford either the cars or the homes anymore. So here they sit, waiting for buyers."

"That seems to be this whole damn place, waiting for a buyer."

"It's a buyer's market."

"I guess so."

"Where are your friends at?"

I thought about it really hard, but drew a blank. Then a flash of inspiration came to me, "Say, do you have any stores which cater to cute girls here?"

"Girls?"

"I mean women, from the ages of 18 to 40."

"We do," Avalon announced without thinking too hard about it. "The anchor store of anchor stores."

"The one store that will survive anywhere," Vanessa piped up, grabbing my hand into hers.

I looked back at her, and she slinked away and shot me a coy half smile. We rounded the corner of the desolate storefronts, which formerly housed good middle class brands like Polo and Black and White and Biggun's Plus Sized Dresses, and Mumu's By Design but were now quite kaput. The shops now were just a façade, but behind the little shops, which were abandoned of customers and was a sort of rind around the real show, which radiated from within a massive parking lot, was a place where cars actually congregated and flocked like some Billy Meyers sermon was emanating from within. I looked across the bright parking lot and saw an all too familiar sight.

"Fucking Wally World," I said.

"Right on. If they're anywhere, they're here," Vanessa said patting my ass swiftly.

"You think there are cute ladies in there?"

"The cutest," Avalon said.

We walked through the jam-packed parking lot. Carts intermixed with cars and nary a single one was where it was supposed to be in the cart return. A gorgeous young lady, well less gorgeous than Avalon's daughter, but equally capable of taking my phallus into her body, walked past me wearing a bright orange day-glow vest: protection against crazed tweaked out motorists dashing here for more pseudoephedrine to use in their home bathtub chemistry experiments. She smiled at me and said that I should have a blessed day, because I was now in the Crusty Mountain, Colorado Wal-Mart, probably one of the best places on Earth. She actually said it like that. I looked at her tail end to see if there were wires coming out...she had to be a robot, just had to be. I laughed out loud. I could not control it.

Usually, I try to be stoic, but because the situation I found myself in struck me as so absurd, I could do nothing else but laugh about it. Laughter is much better than letting things get so bad and negative that you buy a high bullet capacity assault rifle and run around gunning down random strangers in a shopping mall. Better to just have a laugh at it all, and let the freaks run about their own paths. Who was I to call them freaks anyway? That would be me exercising my own judgment on the whole population out there. Impossible. I'm the only freak here. Judge not lest you be judged. Tears welled in my eyes. Every time I laugh at it all, I laugh at myself. I passed another pathetically fat couple, carts loaded with bags. It was Friday, or the day I reckoned was payday round these parts, and it was evening. The only draw in town drew people like flies to a sticky glue trap.

"You know, Avalon," I called to him as we made our way through the maze of errant shopping carts and fat people and chewing gum and dog shit and enormous SUVs that you could barely see the fat people over. "You've given all these poor souls something to get up for in the morning. Something to drag these tired huddled masses to work to work. Product. Things to buy. Things to acquire. You're the new Messiah, Avalon! Before...God filled the sky, but now it's an empty space, much like a television screen without satellite service. People's minds have always been on work. They used to spend what little free time they had thinking about what people always think about, perhaps they didn't in contemplation of the most high, maybe it was what used to be the most low. Sex. Don't know why that is, but now they just try and decide what to buy. It's sort of sad."

"It isn't sad. Slaving your life away for nothing to stay in the same place, now that's sad. I'm offering these people a chance at the American Dream."

"Freedom," Vanessa said.

"No. Comfort. If you offer a man a risky but free existence, he'd rather choose a comfortable cell where he's got pretty girls to wait on him hand and foot, and 555 channels of the same thing! Nothing! Tons of stuff to buy."

"You're a genius," Vanessa said.

"No way, I just tell it like it is. Your father is a very rich man. The richest."

"No way," Avalon said, seeming to choke back some tears of regret.

"Surely you're a very rich man, sir."

"No way," he said walking ahead of us, gaining in speed. We had to hurry up to catch up with him. "We've got to get out of town before a lynch mob kills me. I'm in default. Banks are going to start foreclosing on all these people's homes. It's falling apart. The whole rotten enterprise."

"All in a couple month's time. And you're a fraudster, too?"

"No. I swear. I offered them cash for their homes. I picked up their mortgages thinking this place would really take off, but hell, was I wrong."

"When are the banks coming?"

"I just missed the first payments this month," he said clutching his throat as if the stress was killing him.

We walked inside the cool building. It seemed as if everyone and their grandmother were in the Wally World Megastore, walking through the aisles, eyes glazed over. A fat momma yelled at her kids to stop staring and keep walking. I walked from Avalon in disgust. This man would perhaps single handedly ruin the entire town. I thought about telling everyone of their impending doom and what was in store for them when the bank came to collect. Giving people money for their mortgages, and then collecting rent from them...it was ridiculous, despicable.

I walked up to customer service. A young woman stood there, gabbing on a cell phone. I waited, staring at her for at least a minute while she finished up her conversation with, "Sure I'll text you." She finger-fucked her phone and texted the lucky person on the other end while I asked her for her help.

"Can you page Marcus Hanely for me?" I asked.

"Are you serious? Is this a joke?"

Perhaps I had found yet another reader of my *Asymmetric Hearts*.

"No joke, miss. My friends are missing."

"But you're having me page a fictional character."

"I didn't ask you to page Huck Finn or Ishmael, for fuck's sake."

"Uh...who?"

"Never mind. Marcus Hanely is real. So what if he's in some book written by some prick, but that's my friend's name, so please page him. He should be here with an old man."

"What do they look like? I'll call ahead to one of our other desks," she said as a text message came in and she wrote a detailed response, holding a finger up in the air to indicate that she was most important in this dialogue, and I was a measly third.

"Hanley's big, strapping, handsome. No other way to describe him."

"Just like the guy in the book," she said.

I looked at the collection of ugly baby and fat lady photos behind her, and it came to me. She was blowing me off, and not in a good way. Rage bubbled within, "He's a real fucking person. Now page him!"

"Okay, jeez!" she said, vapidly.

"Paging Marcus Hanely, would Mr. Marcus Hanely come to the customer service department?"

The girl looked lonely handling returns all day, stuffed into this small room. Her blue vest didn't fit properly, or she gained a tremendous amount of weight. Still, she wasn't fat, just on the teetering point where you go either way, either falling into morbid obesity or a sudden urge to become a cross fit psycho and work out four times a day. It depended on if her compulsion was food or fitness. All it would take was one good knocking up; maybe her compulsion was fucking, but I don't know how many suitable partners she could find round these parts. Vanessa waltzed up.

"We wait," she said.

We sat down on the blue colored bench. Vanessa put her hand on mine. A fat woman with a month's supply of fattening pills disguised in various donut boxes and chip bags and an island of crack vials disguised as Romance novels with big buff boffos on the cover gripping sexy maidens, sensuously ready for the final stabbing walked past. Wally World didn't carry the female snuff romance novel where the swarthily handsome male lead is in reality a stock market bilker and real estate investment fraudster who seduces older women with his virile cock and then stabs them to death with his carbonite steel blade in one two three thrusts that he learned in the Special Operations Community.

No, hers were all Prince of Arabia fare, studly farmhand beds sultry rancher's wife, and the classic devastatingly beautiful princess kept captive by an old crone of a woman who lives in the woods who spies devastatingly handsome forest ranger through her window one day while the old crone is out gathering roots and herbs and the like for some witch's potion. Stupid shit for kids, but this lady, with her wee eyes and bulbous face stretched to the point of insanity, seemed to be about on that level. But I noticed as she passed, something peculiar in her cart, at the very top of the mountain of discounted grocery store trash, Frito Lay snacks, various foil bags full of greasy fat inducing sludge was a copy of *Asymmetric Hearts*, with a new cover, which said on it in bright Big Red Letters, underneath the priced 30.99 in paperback, DELUXE FOIL BOUND LIMITED EDITION TENTH ANNIVERSARY RE-RELEASE.

And inside the deluxe foil bound limited edition was a 9 volt battery that sent power to an actual flashing red light gaudy heart, which a small sticker said was guaranteed to last as long as the reader held the book to their own chest and their own heart beat in synchronicity with even pulse and pump of lifeblood, and that the steamy scenes in the book were so steamy and inducing of clit thumping in your, well woman as this woman was, large n' lonely perhaps, that the book could foreseeably stay charged forever. Pulsing that red glow into the lonely nights from here to eternity.

Who knew, maybe the woman wasn't that lonely and she was in the clutches of some deranged BBW fetishist, or maybe just a plain old nice guy. She had no children in tow, which is strange for this demographic. This copy of *Asymmetric Hearts* was rare enough to be printed in the millions and sold in Wally World everywhere. I suppose the bastards would give me a dollar per book sold, and they even went against my wishes and put a genuinely dopey photo of me on the back cover. My name was big and pink in wispy little bubble gum letters, suitable to titillate teenagers. The heart was made purposely off, asymmetric, slightly askew at the very top of its rounded protrusion and printed to stick out from the page.

The artist's rendition of Marcus Hanely intertwined, like a helix of DNA around the female protagonist Veronica Dare, who looked back at him haughtily, her angular face pursed at the center, a beauty mark over her upper DSL. I recalled telling the artist to make the lips even fuller and describing Marcus (who could not be at that particular session because of an appointment with an ophthalmologist's wife) in infinite detail. Then Vanessa opened her big mouth. I have a mantra that I live by, and it is, *The lower your IQ the louder you speak,* which is why I try to remain silent most of the time. My IQ is through the roof.

"Ma'am!" she shouted to the big fat woman.

The fat lady ignored us, thinking us solicitors of donations for some poor kids with cancer or perhaps some church of god-knows-what.

"Ma'am!" Vanessa called again.

She turned her bulk towards us, "Why, yes, young lady?" she asked with a look of fear on her face at having a perfect stranger approach her in public. In the United States, according to the media reports, that only meant one of two things: they wanted your money or they wanted to grind you into tasty human burger.

"I see you've got a copy of *Asymmetric Hearts* there in your cart," Vanessa said coyly.

"Oh no, don't," I said to Vanessa, knowing where she was going down this rabbit hole.

"Just be quiet, Jackson, this woman is a fan."

"Jackson?" the woman said, looking at my face with more than a hint of recognition.

She picked up the book out of her cart and looked at the back cover. Her fat face lit up and shook like a slot machine gone buck wild, but instead of dumping coins and tokens she dumped, "Ohmagawd! Ohmagawd! Ohmagawd!" Each ohmagawd gaining in intensity and volume until it couldn't be contained. She did it, she exploded, "Everyone! Everyone! It's Jackson Leman! The author! The author of *Asymmetric Hearts*!"

She came closer, closer, and even closer. Jesus! I had longed for fame! If everyone loved and worshipped me, I would be content. These were the thoughts of that under-grad idiot who had no understanding of real life, when I put pen to paper and gave birth to this stinky turd of a novel this crushing fatass loved and adored. I gasped. She grabbed me and squeezed. It felt like a fucking anaconda was preparing me as a snack pack.

"Good God! Get this walrus off of me! This woman has anaconda arms!" I wailed, pushing, getting free, and falling back to the seat.

"Mr. Leman! You must autograph this. It's for my mother. She's dying. She's, well, sick in the hospital, but she just loved your work. My God! It's a miracle that I would be on my way to see her with the novel that she requested to keep her mind off the horrible chemo she's going through and that I would run into you, the best author in the world and in this place! Come look everyone! It's Jackson Leman!"

A crowd began to form. Vanessa squeezed my leg. A woman shouted, "Is this your wife, Mr. Leman? You're a lucky man!"

Vanessa retorted before I could say anything, "I'm his lover! One of many!"

"What's he like in bed?" the woman asked, laughing. Vanessa gave thumbs up. The crowd began to vibrate on its own with women clawing and elbowing. They blocked all the exits. I was trapped.

"Alright, alright, form a line!" Vanessa yelled like a perfect cop. "One at a time!"

"What are you doing?" I begged of her.

"We should at least properly monetize this experience. It's one of those golden opportunities in life," Vanessa said.

"You're always thinking about money," I yelled to her over the din. The crowd grew agitated, like a gaggle of hens gyrating their way to the precipice of a feeding trough. Some of the littler, cuter ladies, whom of which were in short supply here, were elbowed to the rear by bigger mama jammas. A lady with at least FF tits thrust at least 10 inches of cleavage in my face. I gulped sweatiness, gasped for oxygen. I looked up to see if Marcus was anywhere in sight. Nothing. The crowd grew. "Whoozit? Tim Tebow?" I heard a man yell.

"Can you sign this, Mr. Leman?" they cackled one after another.

"Me first! I'm the one that discovered him here! And my mom's in the hospital!"

They started elbowing each other violently. I heard the Wally World dispatch on overhead speakers come across with a code that may have meant a riot was about to break out and to summon the National Guard, or it may have meant that a new truck-load of product was awaiting unloading at the back gate and all hands needed to report to unload it. It was probably the former, and at any minute I expected contracted security guards to burst in from all angles and start spraying people with fire hoses and other non-lethal means of crowd dispersal, possibly beating us with Nerf bats, shooting rubber bullets into the fat crowd and then tazing us if we refused to disperse.

"You bitches had better form a line, and each of you better have twenty bucks ready! We don't have change, so you better have exact change!" Vanessa screamed.

"Do you take Debit?" A lady inquired.

"Where do you want to swipe it? In the cheeks of my ass?" Vanessa asked.

The women looked up, aghast. Vanessa put her arm around me, and shot the women a look that said - if you come at my man with anything but a pure heart, I'd chop your fucking throat out. It screamed, "I'm a tiger." My cock got instantly hard. Not strip club hard, it was I-had-to-have-her-now hard. I started feeling woozy. This had not happened in a while.

The women formed a line behind the one with the sob story, after she and big tits pushed and shoved each other for a while. Vanessa solved that problem, the little minx; I liked her more and more every second that I was by her side. Her father, who appeared like a shark who favored money instead of blood, came when the first woman handed over her Andrew Jackson. He diligently collected the money as the women passed by. I practiced a new signature out. I wrote in sweeping Sharpie pen, which we happily acquired for free from one of the many abandoned checkout lines:

Not my usual signature, I swear. None of the women wanted the signature personalized, for it would hurt the possible future resale value, until a dear old lady came up to me and asked a question.

"Mr. Leman," she said, sort of fidgeting, "you write of Marcus Hanely's escapades with such vigor. The ladies in my book club think that it can't possibly be fiction and that he has to be real. Is Marcus real, and is he letting you use his stories?"

"Well," I began.

Vanessa interrupted coldly, "Of course he isn't real, ma'am, what a silly question. Jackson Leman is just an immensely talented literary artist."

What a laugher. Marcus would have doubled over if he heard that one.

"It's a shame then," the old lady continued, "because if I was younger, I'd let him do the horizontal mambo on me any day, bury the pickle in the pickle barrel, or as my granddaughter Marjorie says, bump uglies. I don't think a man's member is too terribly ugly, especially if it's a big, veiny, swollen specimen like you're always describing Marcus Hanely's dong as. Glorious! Makes a woman really regret getting past her prime."

"What do you want ma'am?" Vanessa asked, getting to the point of being rude.

"Just personalize my autograph for me. I don't see myself selling it on EBay or anything," the old dame said with a smile.

"What do you want it to say, ma'am?"

"Well, I don't know. Just write to Edna and say something nice about me."

"Oh, goodness," Vanessa said.

I thought a second and wrote:

A woman should spend her golden ages
Not in the company of book pages
But in the arms of a stud with three legs
Two for moonlit walks upon the beach
One for parting the curtains of her peach
To have a man like Marcus Hanely
Takes gold driven through the bitter wages of lust
Earned, stretched, counted, plated on dildos made stainless
And Antiseptic
Dow Corning plated, ribbed for her pleasure
Magnetized and divided
One in being with the ding-dong
Through Hanely's ding dong all things were made
His balls shoot fountains of creamed corn, baptizing the humble masses
Sprayed on the tits and asses of maidens everywhere.

I didn't even bother to sign it, just handed it to the old bag and told her that the inscription was a poem that I had written when I was in my sophomore year of College, incidentally right after I met Marcus Hanely, though I didn't tell my secret to anyone let alone some old dingbat from Wally World in Western Colorado. She looked to be descended from the slope browed miners who panned for gold and fucked red skinned beauties in their off time. I instantly regretted what I wrote. The remainder of those women waited patiently while I wrote patently degenerate things in their horrid little novels. One I told to actually learn to read by reading the classics, not stupid bullshit designed to sell and placate the teeming masses. One woman told me I was very witty, so I wrote in her copy of Asymmetric Hearts that if the masses think you are witty then you are shooting blanks from your pen.

Of course, I didn't sign my actual legal signature to any of these degenerate little writings, so there is no way for any of the birds to claim it was I who disgraced their purchases, which is what they did. They read my inscriptions and immediately claimed to customer service that I was not, in fact, Jackson Leman, but rather his evil doppelganger, a real character from the plotline of a sick, twisted Romance novel. Only a dastardly schmuck, could have come up with the plot to defraud so many hard working women by posing as their favorite author and bilking them out of their hard earned pay for an autograph, which, incidentally, I never even provided; just made them hate me. And when I said Hate, I mean these women came back, in droves, to tar and feather me. A whole five of the women lodged such a fierce protest that the Customer Service girl got overwhelmed and called for the store manager, a portly fellow named Mr. Burnridge, to come waddling up to the front of the store.

"You're the one claiming to be the author Jackson Leman?" he asked in a slightly annoyed and annoying, nasally, rabbity voice, that is if I imagined a bunny rabbit actually speaking, like calling the police for help...and there was no real vigor or force of purpose behind his words to actually intimidate a fellow man, let alone a shoplifting child. Vanessa, my saucy feline companion, sexual tigress, whatever she was, started in immediately on Burnridge's lack of testosterone.

"Of course he's Jackson Leman, you twerp. Look at the back cover of the book, and look at my beautiful Jackson," she said. She was always finding time to flirt, even at the age of 19 or 20 or 21 she had mastered the art of always letting the man know she was thinking about him, maybe something she learned from her dear old mama. Mine taught me how to always doubt and how to hate my father for always being gone.

Burnridge looked at the back cove and then looked up at me, his reading glasses pushed down to the tip of his red nose.

"Kind of looks like him," he said, "But we never have signings without the publisher's first express written guarantee that there will be at least 750 persons in attendance, publicity paid for by the publisher," he stopped and pulled out a thick Wally Word rulebook, dog eared and coffee stained. "Ah, yes, and legal attendance says that authors cannot charge money and are only allowed to sign their name to the novel, or book, or magazine. This is to prevent unfortunate incidents like the one we are having now, that was caused by you."

"We didn't cause anything. Jackson was only expressing his literary muscle by writing those inscriptions, a hundred years from now, they'd be museum pieces. Those women are just too blind and stupid to see that."

I laughed. This was no snicker. A maniacal, evil even, world domination laugh erupted from my gullet. The women looked up at me aghast. Their superhero author was insane.

"You have to give the money back," Burnridge said to me.

"I don't care. Give it back, Dickie," I said.

Avalon was nowhere to be found. I scanned the aisles ahead of us feverishly for a glimmer of his black suited frame. The prick had left us, abandoned us, ran away with my money, and my car keys. The son of a bitch was probably at the edge of town by now. Would he be that scummy to leave his own daughter? Maybe he was looking for this opportunity to get rid of her.

"Where's your dad at?"

"I don't know. He was just right here," Vanessa said.

Burnridge glared at us and said, "You leave me no choice but to call the police."

Wally World security guards appeared, after they received their cue to enter the stage. They streamed to the front of the store, butter softies, ice cream soft serve dripping in black uniforms, wheezing to the scene of the crime, as if they expected a terrorist attack. Their fingers were on their tazers, twitching, itching.

"Where's the perp?" The head security guard asked.

"Right here," Burnridge said pointing at me. I backed up. Vanessa grabbed my hand, then without saying a word, she ran off in the direction of the doors. One of the rent a cops asked, "Should we get her?"

"No, we've got him."

I tried to follow her. Hearing a pop, I felt a searing jolt of electricity in my ass, which buckled my knees and then BLACKNESS.

JAIL CELL

When I came to, I groggily discovered that my cellmates were the two swinging dicks who had so rudely abandoned me to the wiles of the nymphet and her overlord prick of a father. I am dead sure he stole my ride and was halfway to Oklahoma or wherever he was going to take that insatiable tramp of his. Willard slept on top of the bunk beds adjacent, and Marcus sat on the bottom, staring at me. I threw my shoe at Marcus, but missed him squarely. He did not budge. I supposed we were stuck. Willard slept on top of his bed, perhaps afraid to mess the sheets, as he would probably have to remake the bed. Marcus didn't bother firing my shoe back; he just moved further to the edge of the bed, staring at me.

"Where'd you run off to, boss?" he asked, in a pleasantly suprising way. This was unbecoming. I expected him to be enraged. After all, I left him in quite possibly the worst city in the United States in terms of getting laid by the female population.

"I was looking for you guys. You probably should have waited for me," I said.

"You probably should lick my long, lascivious dick," Marcus yelled. "You left us. You abandoned Willard and me to a fatal suburbia or death by wolves!"

"You're blowing it all out of proportion, Marcus. I went into a tap for a single beer, and you guys were supposed to find some gasoline, or whatever the hell you guys ran off to do. Did you find your warm fuck hole? I figured you were balls deep in some housewife or lovesick granny."

Willard snoozed, his cheeks flapping with each breath.

"Listen to him sleep. Been out in the hot sun all day long, sleeping like a baby," Marcus said.

"Where did you go? Ran off with a floozy? Was the circus in town? Did you get it on with another trapeze artist?"

"Jackson! Shut up! When you get a clue, speak! I'm not talking to you any more, until we get to your father's house."

I turned around in my bunk. I faced the cement wall and studied the contours of the mortar work. It was sloppy. I didn't want to look at him. The amount of power that he exerted over me was appalling. After we got to my father's house, I was going to unfriend him forever. He made my life hell. No one was ever good enough for him. He was probably the most judgmental being on the planet Earth. A real bastard. It is almost as if from his very essence, he was designed by some foul being to make me miserable. Some evil demon sent to deceive me. He was a tick that had burrowed so deeply into my soul that it would be impossible to remove without removing a large part of myself.

I turned around again, careful to avoid the condescension of the ceiling, and watched him, as he slept with his back to me. He mimicked my own previous posture. He breathed in and out. Willard did the same thing on the bunk above him. They were like brothers, one young, vital, impeccably dressed with the stolen booty of ten hopeful women, goods all purchased on credit, and Willard was old, withered, dressed shabbily in the same bathroom attendant's outfit I found him in. Willard had the soul of an angel and embodied the qualities I thought best in the world: a sense of justice, of fairness, hope even. I've never known another man as wise as him. I guess that came with his years.

I only wish his voice was not drowned out by Marcus's snide remarks and out and out buffoonery all the time. I don't know why we listened to Marcus, maybe because he was young and good looking, and had all the hallmarks of a "leader". He held us in a spell. And what does it mean to be young and particularly good looking? It means you should remain silent and be admired as the newest best thing. Your youth and vigor admired in its unspoiled nature, best left alone like a new jagged mountain peak or admired from a distance like a purple thistle.

Hanely was unbridled passion. Dionysus. Dangerous. Deadly. Why could I not tap into some of that energy? Was it forever lost on me? Was it due to my upbringing as the only spoiled son of a rich man, who in turn inherited his own window into the world of the upper 1% of earners, definitely not the upper 1% of goodness, like his own father before him had earned by virtue of his birth? And so on and so on, all risk takers, all moneymakers?

Maybe we were so used to making bets with money that we had actually forgotten how to gamble with life. It was as if money formed a greater reality on top of reality, easily accounted for: a great phony, descriptive mask for what was really happening. I rarely, if ever, broke into the bitter limits of philosophy, preferring to instead be an artist and live, not to think about living. But that was all a laugh. I was as much an artist as Marcus Hanely, this great sleeping clod, was a morally upright, productive member of our great society.

My musings on the state of nature and the fetid garden that man had planted all over the great green Earth caused a great drowsiness to come over me. I dreamed, not a dream that normally strikes when I've had too much beer in the gullet and lack of pussy on the brain, this dream was something else, there was a great racket all around me, it was as if I were floating in an ocean, but there was no water. A merry puppeteer was pulling my strings, and I was going nowhere.

In my dream I saw my father as I remembered him. Busy, full of life, full of energy. I called out to him. He did not stop what he was up to. He was busy digging holes into the ground. He pulled something out of his pocket and placed it neatly into the hole. The broadside of the valley he had descended into from the mountaintop was full of holes; they dotted the landscape as far as my eyes could see. Each hole had a little pile of Earth next to it. The Earth appeared a great sieve or colander for straining the boiling water from cooked noodles. I walked up gingerly, and I could see in each of the holes that my father had placed a small, faceted object. I bent down to see what it was and in the fog and mist I could not see anything. I scrounged in the hole filling my hands with warm filth, and my hands clasped around each object. I pulled it out in front of my eyes and held it up to the dim light to see what it was.

My father walked ahead of me, always 20 or 30 paces ahead, dropping the objects into the holes. The soft, wet Earth, warm...stinking. A flash of light. My father looked back to me, and bade me with a wave of his arm to come, follow him.

"Daddy, Daddy!" I called out to him, "Where are you going?" He smiled a great smile, the expression that I only saw of him when he was leaving our home on business, headed for his private jet, having left mother and I alone in the company of butlers, governesses, and gardeners, like we were just two other servants. She always asked to go with him, and he always refused, and said that where he was going was no place for a woman. Mother would always get upset and scream at him, because the business manager said Father was going to Paris with one additional guest, a buxom female, and my father said to her for her information it was the head of Operations for Western Europe, a West German I'll be traveling with and mother always said, "oh are you fucking her too? Let me guess you wooed her on your yacht."

The visions left as soon as they cropped up, and I continued to follow my father who queerly bent down and scratched out a hole with his wheel-worn hands and manicured fingernails. I followed him by the familiar trail of his cologne, which he would change at the drop of a hat if he ever smelled it on anyone else in his entourage, just so you can tell the ladies you meet how special and important you are my mother used to say through the bitter tears and father would always retort that anyone he came into contact with already knew that he was an important man, he was born into it, and mother told him that was the problem with aristocracy that it didn't guarantee the best got anywhere only that the scum stayed plaqued onto the surface of power sucking up the sun's rays and killed off everything unfortunate enough to be born below.

Father told her to shove a sock in it and he would be home soon. I kept following him into the light, the sunrise, I looked down at my muck and filth covered hands I turned the object over my hand and uncovered the thing from the muck. I spat on it as I watched my father at his work digging the hole, covering the hole up again. I rubbed the drying mud from the object – plastic. *What the fuck?* I held it up to the daybreak. It was a doll's head, a baby doll's head, hideous, deformed, with bugged out eyes and a swollen, blackened tongue like a plague victim.

I gasped and shouted to my father, "What are you doing?"

He looked back to me and smiled that smile that he shot at clients he had just sealed deals with and spoke, "Jackson! Don't you think it's time you gave me some grandchildren?"

I woke up drenched in sweat, unsure of my surroundings. I looked to the bunks next to me. Marcus and Willard were no longer there.

"Sons of bitches!" I yelled.

The cage rattled. I looked up and saw Dickie Avalon standing there, tapping a tin cup on the bars, "Spare change, sir?" he asked, and laughed.

"What do you want?"

"Here to bust you out, Jackson!"

"Where'd my friends go?"

"What friends? Oh those friends?"

"They were just here."

"Looks like Vanessa and I are the only friends you've got."

"Vanessa..."

"Upstairs sucking off the day shift guard," Avalon said smugly.

"Your daughter, Jesus..."

"The girl has her charms, and there wasn't any other way to get you out," Avalon said opening up my cage with the key.

The door rattled open. Vanessa trotted downstairs, "All done, Daddy."

"You two are sick."

"We're doing what we have to do to accomplish the mission," Avalon announced.

"What mission?" I asked, half dazed.

"Oh, never you mind that," Avalon said.

We made our way upstairs. The guard sat there at his desk, his pants around his ankles, his little dick looked like a thimble in a forest of hair.

"I feel sorry for you," I told Vanessa.

"Don't!" she said fiercely.

The guard glared at me, and hiked up his pants. He tossed me the keys to the Judge along with my wallet in a plastic bag marked PRISONER POSSESSIONS.

"Shit. You mean I had them the whole time?"

"Yeah," Avalon said as he grabbed the keys from the bag.

"Where'd you go?"

"To the bathroom."

"Yeah, right. You were off looking for someone to scam. What did you do with the money?"

"Got your car out of impound."

"Didn't your daughter do that?" I asked.

"No that only got you sprung," Avalon said.

"We've got to get to Denver by nightfall."

"You want to drive?" Avalon asked.

"No."

"Sit in the backseat with me, Jackson," Vanessa implored.

I ignored her.

YES, BUT IS IT PROFITABLE?

I walked to the car which had been towed to the impound yard and sat squarely in the passenger seat. Vanessa glared at me. Dreamy eyes even when enraged. I could just kiss her. What is it about beautiful women that make me want to mortgage my soul for their embrace? I begrudgingly climbed into the backseat with her; or rather, I acted as if I were begrudged, even though my heart began to skip a beat whenever I was around her. She was one of those women who were much more than a pretty face and tits and ass, she was much more. I couldn't quite determine what yet, but I decided that I liked the way I felt when she was around me. The most gorgeous babe in the room, she made heads turn off their swivels and other women would ask me if she was my woman and not respond afterwards.

It was as if we had dated for a long time, and I think she may have been at least 1/4 Colombian because Avalon, the swankster, probably spent time down there at one point. I figured that I should at least ask, because the body language she put off indicated that she wanted my stink all over her. How did I know that Avalon wouldn't leave me in the middle of the desert with a bullet in my head or worse yet, just abandon me to starve to death in some wretched black mountain pass like the Donner party? Only I wouldn't have any wagoneers to eat. I looked up at Avalon, the coy businessman in the front seat, driving the beast my hard earned money got Hanely and I.

Wait. Why was I always including Marcus in almost all of my thoughts? The son of a bitch abandoned me, but does that mean I should even think of him again as one would forget an acquaintance or another annoying pest that one met in an alleyway somewhere? Marcus and I had been together for years. Ever since I discovered him in that Princeton University library, after I found out that my dear old dad had donated a lovely chunk of money for a new Natatorium or horse track or Mathematics building or something he didn't even want named the Leman Building and instead had it named after another famous Alumni because he didn't want it to damage my supposed (and real) fragile eggshell ego.

Well, I'll tell you, the only reason my father paid a huge sum of money to get me accepted to that pretentious dump was to boost his own ego and be able to tell the other over inflated cod pieces and pool boy cuckolds at the country club who thought they had the entire world on a string because they inherited oodles of wealth from way back yonder days of yore and fickleness, that they wouldn't be able to tolerate me going to a state school and father did what he did because he could get away with it, quid pro quo. Only I wasn't supposed to find out about it. Just bury it deep down inside. The thought of it just enrages me!

When I started writing, that's when I finally got out from under his uber successful boot and began to make my own way in the world and didn't have to listen to him or his wonderful advice, delivered by proxy through counselors. He had stacked money from here to China, tripled it and paid no taxes. I think one of his stellar refineries employed about 3/4 of a certain province of Russia – Svetlanapovistan or something like that – and it was all coming to an end, or at least he would have to step down as chairman of the board and appoint someone to act in his stead, maybe my sister's idiot, born of middling money husband who married rich, Sheldon. I'm sure that's why Sheldon married her, to marry into the most powerful industrial family in the entire West because he got his MBA from Harvard University and all his beautiful connections, he would have to work his way from middle management all the same. He was great at stepping on faces.

Those connections wouldn't get him to the top of the shit pile fast enough. He needed a helping hand. My father was an idiot, and my sister was doubly an idiot. The last time I saw my father, like 10 years ago, he told me that my sister reminded him of my mother. I asked him what that was supposed to mean, and he didn't even have an answer, he thought I knew, like I was clairvoyant. My father often assumed that everyone around him was on his same wavelength and could determine and act on his thoughts before he gave them as spoken commands. You had better be moving before his lips started moving.

Rich men don't ask favors, they issue orders that you had better follow if you want to be continually able to buy your toys to keep up with them. You're better served just dropping out before you're so deep in their pocket that you can't crawl out.

I felt a hand on my dong over the top of my pants. It was Vanessa's hand, and she was smiling at me. I'm sure that she wanted something. Her eyes glowed, mirrors to the skylight. I think I was falling, slowly, well, being led down the path to actually, perhaps, have feelings for her. I took her hand and moved it off the bacon. I'm sure her father probably directed any affection she had for me at me, and he wanted to get at my nearly infinite sum. We drove until we reached a battered road sign that read...

DENVER 97 MI.

*W*e were getting close. If there was a time these two would off me, Hollywood dictated that it would probably be right now, so they could both do me in, in a rural area with no witnesses and have plenty of getaway routes. You could never trust a failed businessman at the helm of anything. It was like trusting a failed ship's captain who had crashed into a dozen bridges to guide your cruise ship to safe port. A businessman was only good at one thing: turning small amounts of paper into larger amounts of paper, and if they weren't good at that, they weren't good at much of anything. Put Dickie Avalon here up for humanitarian of the year award; he provided so many people so many jobs. These businessmen, they claimed to have grandiose dreams, were the prophets in the desert of a new era, but in the end they were only concerned with dollars and good cents. Avalon at the helm, I've often had the reoccurring feeling that we were about to drive off a cliff.

She put her hand on my peckerwood again. I politely moved it off. There would be no seduction today. Today, God willing, in three hours, thereabouts, I would see my father, one of the richest men in this land filled with rich men and plenty of debtors acting like rich men. I would see my father croak, because in the end, everyone croaked, no matter from starvation, obesity, or just super advanced old age.

Still, the old bastard had a rightfully good life. He married his sweetheart from another powerful family, he eclipsed them, he came to hate every moment of his enforced marriage...never let anyone know about it and just drove on throughout his days. He stayed gone, building up his business and therefore the world. His business was like a ship, and the world was left in its wake. He gave his son and daughter everything they could possibly want, save for any affection.

Affection came in the form of a healthy paycheck at the end of the month, or bi-monthly should you so choose, stock options, and Christmas bonuses based on good performance, or perhaps a Christmas pink slip if you were dead weight. Now he was going to croak, and I was supposed to come running. Or maybe he already croaked. That would save me the fit of having to cry and act all bereaved in front of him.

I supposed when I got there I would probably clean him out of the remainder of his excellent scotch, have a few cigars from his humidor, provided the help didn't smoke them up, and just sit back and watch the chaos and calamity unfold.

It's not like he cared that much when my mother croaked. He made an appearance but did not appear to be traumatized in the least, save for trying to salvage his public reputation as captain of industry when his beloved wife did a very unwomanly thing and blew the top of her head off with a platinum plated pistol at our home. It was an open and shut case. I don't even think the police investigated it, because my father, like the Pope, was both infallible and beyond reproach. All of the details that the public did not know...my father's philandering, his chronic absence...all these things, the marrow of scandals; they would be buried with him.

Truth is, she couldn't take any more of his philandering. You're golden in this world until you're caught fucking the help or interns, in the case of politicians. Hell, you could even plead that you had a sexual addiction now, but back then it was expected that you were a man's man and could keep your woman in check with a golden tiara now, a pearl necklace then, and matching Rolex watches on lovely occasions when your secretary reminded you that it was an anniversary.

Really, my mother became just another accessory: someone to be paraded around in front of the media, at charity events. Mr. and Mrs. Prescott Leman III. Thank God my father saw fit to name me Jackson. I returned from my fit of reminiscence. Getting closer to home, the more powerful the visions became. I would have to distract myself to keep them from overwhelming me.

"Wally World? Are you kidding me? Of all the places to get me into an impromptu book signing but the most art unfriendly big shyster complex in the free world," I said to Avalon, who gripped the wheel and weaved in and out of the miniscule traffic on the highway.

"You aren't an artist, Jackson; you're a damn hack if I ever saw one. Why, you couldn't even write your way to first place in an English poetry contest with illiterate Bangladeshi fourth graders."

"You don't know shit, you failure."

"I know a damn hack when I see one. You're all dried up, kid. You don't have a single sentence left in you. Your books are gathering dust. They're phony like you are. Mass marketed ploys, bent and used up. So what if you've made tons of money. So what if you've had a bunch of fans. You aren't what you set out to be. You aren't an artist. You're suffering, but it's all self-imposed hogwash. You aren't suffering from any genuine emotions. You've taken on the weight of a world on your shoulders with your fingers exploiting crevices, finger banging your way around, acting like you're never going to get old and croak like dear old Dad. Jackson, don't you think there were a reason, and a pretty profound one to get home and see dear old Dad? Like maybe, just maybe he wanted to tell you something important before he passed on?"

I gulped. It might be true.

"Step on it, Richard," I said.

"Daddy, don't be so hard on Jackson."

"This man here needs to just grow up. Artist? Shit, you wouldn't know art if you were in the exact center of the Louvre. You're a spoiled little talentless hack."

191

"Piss off, Dickie? What have you written?"

"Doesn't matter. I'm not a writer. I'm a businessman. Maybe not a good one as of yet, but I'm learning. You can't claim to be a writer. Writers write. You haven't written a damn thing for over ten years."

"I'm planning to."

"When? You aren't planning shit! Maybe if you financed your whole being, took it all out on credit, you know, put food on the table by writing, then you'd have the urge to be more productive. You know how I pay for my daily bread?"

"Uh, no. But I'm guessing it has to do with Vanessa going into bars topless and you holding out your bowler hat."

"No way. I move goods and services around. I'm a businessman. I conduct business. It's what I am. It's what I do. Just like you claim to be a writer, but you don't write. You've written nothing recently. You're a washed up has been."

"You aren't a businessman. That's why you're running away from all those dried up properties you've been trying desperately to keep afloat. What are you going to tell all those poor kids when they're out on the street for Christmas?"

Vanessa cut in between us, "Why don't you both shut the hell up? You're acting like a couple of babies, each blaming the other for nothing. Just face it. You're a loser, Jackson. Daddy, you're a loser, too. I'm with both of you, so I guess that makes me a loser by association. But you know what? That doesn't mean I don't love both of you."

I glanced over at her. "You're young. You have a future," I said.

She looked back at me, and stared at me with her green fuck-me eyes. My midsection boiled. What was I waiting for?

"Pull over at the next stop, please," I asked the driver.

Her hand moved up my thigh.

"Don't you want to see your father?"

I lied, saying, "I've got to see if they have a charger for my iPhone. I can't just show up unannounced; his security staff is liable to shoot us. My phone's been off for a couple of days now as we've been driving across this apocalyptic hell of the West. Not a damn iPhone charger to be found anywhere."

"Whatever. You had plenty of opportunities to get an iPhone charger."

"I heard your phone buzzing just a second ago," Vanessa said, stupidly. I glared at her and put my finger to my lips.

"Look!" Avalon declared, "Wally World!"

"You motherfucker! If you pull over there, I'll blow your fucking brains out!" I screamed at him, reaching under the seat for the .45.

"You're a madman, Leman," Avalon said grinning. "Are you getting all this, dearie?"

"Please, stop anywhere but Wally World. I don't feel like going to jail again."

"Hard pressed, buddy. They're everywhere. Why didn't you get one at the last Wally World we were at?"

"You were too busy pimping me out. Why didn't you just drive off with my fucking car when you got me tossed in the slammer?"

"Moron. I gave you the keys. Anytime you leave a man's vehicle, you give him the keys. It's an unwritten rule."

"You did not. You kept them."

"I tossed them to you, and you caught them. Or were you too busy getting lovey dovey with my daughter to realize?"

Vanessa's hand slid further up my leg. I slapped it away. These two were in cahoots about something.

"Just go somewhere that I can get a damn charger, Dickie."

Avalon laughed. He seemed to enjoy driving me mad. He pulled off at the next exit, beyond which another consumer paradise loomed, treeless, loaded with hatchbacks and minivans: receivers for the large boxed items that the large people loaded out of large, big box stores. Those that weren't stuffed full of goods and services were teeming with screaming brats. It was a Sunday, the first or second of the month, following the biweekly cash disbursement, like the spitting of bits o' worm into the mouths of baby birds, from god-knows-where these people worked.

I imagined some old penny pinching cretinous boss flipping nickels, not wooden of course for they must be spendable, into the hands of dolers, rakers, and dream masters. I looked to Avalon. I looked to his hot piece of ass daughter who had nothing important to say. I dreamed that I stuck my long, fat cock into the American Dream and fucked her well. We had an ugly child with no eyes. Perhaps we named it Hope or Care. I gave up. Avalon was in the driver's seat, and his sexy daughter was in the back seat with me, tempting me. Still she did not speak, or maybe she had nothing important to say, or maybe I was too busy staring at her dannies to even notice. She just groped my staff like a blind person waiting for the streetlight to change. I shook her loose.

"What do you know...another Wally World!" Avalon announced, with a timbre in his voice like he was proclaiming the Second Coming or a Eureka! Scientific discovery on par with dark matter.

There was nothing else in sight. The rest of the strip mall was abandoned, save for a Chinky Chinky All You Can Eat Buffet, which fat people poured into with looks of murder in their eyes and a few overloaded souls managed to escape to pile into their SUVs to head to the sunset. The no name buffet had an enormous pulsating sign over the top that said

I guess it was supposed to be visible from the highway, to call people with hunger pangs and sate them with no other alternatives. My view of the enormous sign was partially obstructed by a family of hogs. I suppose they were people who prayed and hoped and loved but to me they looked like hogs, smiled like hogs after withdrawing from the slop bucket, and they made sounds like little squealing, contented piggies. They piled into an SUV and drove off in the direction of the largest house on a hill. They were successful hogs, because when they parked their hog-mobile at the top of the hill, they jammed their carcasses in front of a television with the appearance of a movie screen. It was so large you could see it from the Wally World parking lot. They were watching the TBS Evening Movie, Short Circuit, interspersed with Jumbo Pizza commercials. Hog Heaven. Wally World: a paradise of infinite proportion. They built their hog home in view of it. I returned from my fantasy to the cool Wally World air hitting my face and the immense grandeur, like a medieval Cathedral, sucking me from my detachment. And I noted, that 9 out of 10 medieval persons would prefer shopping at Wally World to worshipping in the Notre Dame and the Black Death. Overwhelming luminosity. I gasped.

I began my search for the iPhone charger, and Vanessa galloped behind me trying desperately to hold my hand. Every second I walked forward, the bile of fear rose in me. Not for the infinite choices and finite capital, but that she would say something else to get me into an impromptu book signing. We skirted the clothing. A hideous woman holding an equally hideous child, all googly-eyed, lardy, and red, holding a half-eaten, unpaid-for candy bar, and the woman a verifiable hag and breaker of cameras, looked our way as we passed.

"Ugh," Vanessa said. "Who fucked her?"

"Your guess is as good as mine," I answered, taking note of her brushings with Nazism.

"They should stop fucking," Vanessa said. "Someone should make them stop breeding."

I made to change the subject. "You know, my friend Marcus told me that the human race will continue on and on and on until all the stars burn out."

"Because of love?"

"No. Because fucking feels good."

"Well, she should stop."

"Are you going to make her?"

"She should get her tubes forcibly tied."

"Court ordered condoms," I said, not agreeing with her, just seeing how far her rant would continue.

"Sterilizations. You could perform them here."

"Uh, okay. Her crime is being poor."

"Poor, beautiful people can live," Vanessa said, and laughed.

And they think I'm psycho. I had to change the subject. "Let's find the iPhone charger. Why can't this place be simpler?"

"You've been in one, you've been in them all. Don't worry. I have one."

"Why didn't you say anything?"

"I wanted some time alone with you."

"Uhh...why?"

She brushed my cock with her hand. I slapped it away.

"Don't you get a hint?"

"I don't want a hint," I said, doing my damnedest to play hard to get.

Electronics. Always smaller than the rest of the sections, always in the back of the store, drawing you in, saying, "Hey, big spender, you shopped for electronics. Maybe you have money. Maybe you just wanted to go ahead and purchase a fishing rod, too, or maybe another high-ticket item on the same day. Put it on credit." The store clerk, one of two in Wally World that day who wasn't busy restocking shotguns and shower curtains or slapping merchandise back on the shelves as soon as it came down and made the cash register maintainer go Zink Zink with a laser gun, twirled her fingers through her heavily hair-sprayed hair, and I walked up and parked my caboose at least within the peripheral vision of this normal human being. Another patron and her own iPhone distracted her, and she switched between that tiny screen and the screen of life.

I cleared my throat. She looked up at me. Changed the channel. She moved her lips together to spread the lip-gloss evenly.

"Whatchoo want?" she asked.

"Uh, excuse me?"

She looked at Vanessa, who now tried to put her hand in my pocket.

I slapped her hand away again and luckily the girl did not see it as Vanessa's through the pants hand job (TPHJ) was occluded from her vision by the countertop.

"You need something?"

"An iPhone charger."

"That's, like, down the aisle over there," she said brusquely pointing towards non-descript aisles loaded with lap top cases.

"They locked up," she said.

"Uh, do you have a key?"

"Yeah, you gonna buy it or just look?"

I laughed. Vanessa made a little whispering noise with her mouth, a signal of impatience or frustration, perhaps indigestion.

"My dad could be croaking at this very moment. Could you please get me a damn charger?"

"Shoot. All right, don't get all lippy n' shit," she said underneath her breath. This generation thrives on phony confrontation: video games, Internet wars, and massively interactive passive arena fantasy football. However, confront people about something, and they'll say their witty retorts with a whisper.

Vanessa made to start a fight, but I brought my finger to my lips. There was more use for this clerk to be had.

"Sorry, it's just a charger. Is there anywhere I can plug this at?" I asked, trying to distract her into being helpful after our previous near blowup.

She thought. "The woman's bathroom should have a plug, you know, for changing babies and all that."

"What do you need a plug for changing babies for?" Vanessa inquired. I sensed there was about to be a fight between them.

"I don't know. I always figured that's what they was for."

"Maybe it's for a hairdryer."

"What, after you wash your hair in the toilet?" she asked.

"Desperate times call for desperate measures."

She returned with a charger and held it out, a small Lucite box befitting a diamond ring. It was minimalist packaging in its purest form. Packaging bliss.

"You want it?"

"I'll take it."

She rang it up. "31.07 with tax."

"What?"

"Don't worry you can afford it. I've got mine if you don't want to buy it."

"No. It's the damn principle here. That thing couldn't have cost more than 5 cents to make."

"So does everything. Do you want it or not?"

"Yeah. I guess I'll pay cash."

I reached into my crocodile wallet. No cash. Where did it all go? Surely I wouldn't have spent over 500 dollars on wolf t-shirts and stupid hats. The fucking cops must have robbed me. I never signed a damn custody document when I entered. I would never reveal my Niebelungen horde beneath the Judge's seat to them.

"Try my credit card," I said.

I reached for the slot where it normally was. Oh comfort...when it pushed back on my index finger and I knew it was there. Not the case this time. I only felt the cold, dead reptilian skin, reworked into a high dollar Italian wallet. Ferragamo, I think.

"Oh shit," I said out loud.

'What, dear?" Vanessa asked.

"I've been robbed. The fucking cops in that BFE town back there robbed me!"

"You need to call and cancel your cards," Vanessa warned me.

"How can I call up and cancel my cards when I can't even purchase a phone charger? The number is on the back of the card! I can't Google it! I'm fucked! I'm finished!"

"Calm down, or I'll call security," the employee said.

"Sorry."

"I'll pay for that," Avalon said, walking up from the DVD section. He must have taken the other way around, avoiding the clothing section all together. He had shaving cream on his face, must have stopped to shave surreptitiously in the sundries aisle.

Avalon reached into his wallet. A look of exasperation came over his face. He turned the wallet over on the counter. A movie stub and an Indian head penny fell out. The penny whirled around and around on its axis, finally settling on the ONE CENT showing.

"Robbed too!" he announced.

"Who could have done it?" Vanessa asked.

"Those old bitches! The women at the book signing! One of them must've robbed both of us."

"And left our wallets? My wallet is about 3,000 bucks, new," I announced.

"Well, why don't you list it on eBay and get us out of this jam we're in," Avalon said murderously.

"I can't, no phone."

Vanessa looked like she wanted to announce that she had a charger, but wanted the lie to persist with her father.

"Avalon, just come clean! You know you robbed me and robbed yourself to make it look like a clean getaway. Give me my money and credit card back, and we'll call it even."

"Bullshit, sir! I may be a horrible businessman, but I've never been a thief."

I spied some credit cards in his wallet. His wallet looked like a third world shanty town, there was so much used plastic stuffed into it.

"Why don't you pay for it with cards?"

"Can't. They're maxed out."

I stormed out past them, calling out to him, "Avalon, you piece of shit! You and your whore daughter can walk from here on out!"

"Hey! I'm no…" Vanessa made to say, as her father slammed his hand to her mouth.

Then he did it. I saw him run past me, towards a woman who carried a copy of *Asymmetric Hearts* clutched against her ample breast, a shield, girding her rotund, spilling over her pants body, in the parlance of the Greeks, a muffin top par excellence. This was the uber deluxe limited edition Love Box edition, which she placed amongst the Ore Ida fries, sandwiched by two pints of Ben and Jerry's and some Hormel Double Fried Microwaveable Chicken Wings. He approached her and whispered to her and pointed towards me. She turned the back flap of the Love Box, and a look of instantaneous recognition and gratification came over her face. Three hundred pounds of lard bucket started undulating down the aisle towards little me.

"Mr. Leman! Mr. Leman!" she yelled.

I started backing up like you're trained to back up from a charging hippopotamus: make yourself big and back away…quickly. I tripped over my feet and fell into the hosiery, tangled in yoga leotards that were the size of one man tents, two sizes too small for my pursuer. Good God, I thought, if she catches me she'll smother me in double Gs! She'll wreak havoc on my torso!

"I'll sign! I'll sign!" I screamed, and hoped it would placate her.

The commotion attracted the attention of the other women in the store who decided to buy my book, all of them sensed an immediate investment or perhaps because they were fans. Some waltzed over, but many picked it up and came running, crazed looks in their eyes, like it was an forty percent off oxygen sale at the end of the world blowout. I became a Romance King Orpheus. The women were scratching and clawing at me, threatening to tear me apart. They huddled around mashing my hair, "Me first, me first!" they screamed.

"Form a line you…cows," Avalon said the last word under his breath. He held out his bowler hat. "Drop a ten in the hat, and get an autograph only. Drop a twenty in the hat, and Mr. Leman will write you a personal message, though I don't recommend that because it will make a resale on eBay very tricky. But hey, who wants to cheapen this once in a lifetime opportunity by only getting an autograph? Get something to pass down to your children's children's children!"

I wanted to get out of there as soon as possible because I think Cherry Surprise back there in Electronics may have called the cops on us.

Avalon went too far. "Drop a fifty in the hat, and Mr. Leman will quite possibly, we don't know, he's very shy, but with the famous romance novelist's consent, he may deign to give you lucky ladies a kiss on your rosy red cheeks. Isn't this a treat? Of course for one hundred dollars, we will be willing to discuss privately what Mr. Jackson Leman will do for you, provided you tip appropriately."

"No way," I announced. "No kisses. No after dark surprises! No personal

messages. You get the, *John Hancock* that's all."

The ladies didn't seem to mind. The first one in line asked, "Was this planned? We didn't hear anything about this on the radio."

"No. Totally unplanned. Totally unscripted. For the first time ever," I said as I signed her book FREDERICK T. PUMPERNICKEL.

"Are you married?"

"No," I signed her book MORTIMER McCALLISTER, ESQ.

"Is it true you're writing a new Marcus Hanely/Veronica Dare murder mystery romance? That's what *Publisher's Weekly* said."

"No. They lie. Marcus Hanely is dead," I told her and singed, CHAS PERIWINKLE.

I read on Wikipedia that you got inspiration to write your first novel while walking the lonely corridors of the Princeton University Library."

"Nah. It came to me while I was on the shitter in a Seven Eleven or maybe a WAWA in Hoboken. Can't really remember," I said smiling as I signed her book PIMP DADDY WOO WOO.

"Why have you not been on the Oprah Winfrey Network? You've been on her show a few times when it was on daytime, right?"

"I've never been invited," I said and signed her book ROBERT MCGILLICUDDY, COCKMASTER.

I said everything with a snide little smile, just to keep them from opening the book. I was making all their dreams about meeting an author, which kept them up at night finger-banging their lonely genitalia to what Marcus Hanely would be like in bed, or maybe I would be like in bed, and I shattered them. It was Marcus they wanted to see, lonely, lost, dashing Marcus. They cared nothing for me. I was only the mouthpiece that gave Marcus expression. He was what they wanted. To them he was a "what" because he was an object of their imagination.

To me he was little more than a reporter who told me of his sexcapades, someone who taught me how to follow along and make myself scarce, to record the words and deeds, and to print books and print money. Only, it didn't work out and it wasn't going to work out because I didn't feel like playing the game anymore. I really didn't feel like participating in it. I didn't know what I wanted to do. I suppose I won the lottery when I was born. I would give it all up to do something genuine, create something really real, to just be able to feel something again!

I signed the last five books and fielded their stupid questions, all related to bullshit that my agent and press agent had planted in the media to keep them ravenous for a sequel and to make sure that these women all understood that Marcus Hanely was dead and gone and probably lost in the desert with the wolves eating his liver out of his ribcage. Sorry, but that was the way things went. In the meantime, I suggested they read something trivial by either Nicky Sparxx, or JD Robb, or someone else whose pen dripped estrogen in sloppy piles all over the page. I signed these last five books without looking up. I signed them...BOBBY PIMPLETON,

BARTHOLOMEW GRASSYTUNES, WINFRIED GREENSLEEVES, SAMMY BAMMY BO JAMMY FEE FI FO FAMMY, and JOHNNY KINGSTON THE PIPE-LAYING PLUMBER.

By the time the ladies alerted the security guards, who were sleeping near the dumpsters in their little micro SUV, we were running out of the place with over two hundred dollars. We hit the road hard and stopped for gas at a dumpy little cash-only gas station, seen them once and you've seen them all, or perhaps that is a prejudice of mine that this gas station was not worthy of reporting on. The attendant was older, and I felt sorry for him. This was near the I-70 about 40 miles from Denver.

I reached into my pants pocket. The Visa Black was there, hidden among the pocket lint and week old receipts that I saved for no reason. Whoops. When I touched its hard plastic, I felt that old comfort return and settle in my bones like a kiss from a long lost lover.

DISCUSSION OF LIFE AND DEATH, with JACKSON LEMAN taking the side of LIFE and the businessman RICHARD AVALON taking the side of dead, inanimate things and market activities:

Avalon: Why aren't you in a hurry to see your father pass on?

Jackson: Most fathers and sons, perhaps they love and respect one another, but my father and I had a different sort of relationship. I was always wondering where he was, and when he was at home, he was never there mentally. Maybe he was off having adventures in his mind, thinking about facts and figures, and I tell you what, that guy had every single asset of his enumerated down to the thousandth iota of a cent. He knew what was making money and what was sniveling, receding, dying as he used to say. For him, making money was life. Money had a life of its own.

Avalon: Yes, a businessman through and through, though his business seems to be much, much larger than my pauper's mills and ramshackle debtor millionaire's homes. How'd he get his start? Inherit his wealth like some lackluster silver spoon? That's how all the real richies get their money: a bit of capital and an inborn genetic compulsion to make it grow, or maybe a mechanism to balance risk. Risk aversion isn't present in these holy fools. Sometimes they bet the ranch and lose it all, houses included, but when they win, they win big. How much do you stand to inherit?

Jackson: Now that's prying. I don't know, and I don't care.

Avalon: Surely you must care a bit.

Jackson: Nope, don't care at all. I stopped caring when I was about fourteen years old and mom died. Dad acted like she was a nuisance. You know, people talked, thought dear old dad had something to do with it. Not that he pulled the trigger of the heirloom platinum pistol, but that he drove her to it. I don't remember. I was a kid. I remember the funeral. No one talked. Everyone was draped in black. I remember that my sister wailed out loud and one of our aunts, who since joined my mother, tried to comfort her. I guess my sister and my mother were closer than my mother and I. I always tried to be closer to my father, but that was impossibility, and after my mother died I felt totally unfulfilled, alone. After that I didn't have much to do with anyone; I guess I sort of entered my own world.

Avalon: You're still in your own world.

Jackson: Who are you to talk?

Avalon: Just an observation.

Jackson: You don't appear to be a very astute student of life and personality.

Avalon: You see that young woman sleeping in the back seat back there? She's my life. Ever since her mother ran off, we've been together, traveling, doing our thing...

Jackson: Defrauding people? Sending your daughter into seedy places for a titty diversion while you rob them? Some father you are, Dick.

Avalon: Come on, now. What would you do in my situation? Shoe-stringing yourself along, trying desperately to find a home, but you're welcome nowhere?

Jackson: You're not welcome because you're a fraud and a huckster. A flim flam man. A snake oil salesman with no salesmanship. People see right through your half-baked, chock-full o' nuts schemes with a steaming regularity. You're a dunce, a vagrant, and a whoremonger. Hell, you probably really only own the clothes on your back, and you probably stole those from off the rack.

Avalon: We weren't born into wealth, with the ability to become the world's most fraudulent author of trite rubbish ever devised for bored and horny housewives, which is a fraud in and of itself...

Jackson: I'm changing my style. I'm no longer a romance novelist. I...shit. I don't even know what I am.

Avalon: I think you're bat shit crazy! You've got a good product line. All you have to do is feed your fans, and they will eat it up. Keep shoveling your idiot pamphlets at them, and they keep forking over the cash.

Jackson: I already have cash by the armful. I want to make people think.

Avalon: (breaks into hideous peal of laughter) You know the problem with that? You can't just immediately assume a person will have the intellectual ability to comprehend what you write. We're living in a swamp, man! Write for the frogs and turtles!

Jackson: It's unfulfilling.

Avalon: It's enriching. Hell, I don't know, write bullshit. Highly original bullshit. Write bullshit for morons and use that to finance serious works that plumb the bitter depths of the human experience. Write those works under a pen name. JOHN FLANNERY or something like that. Just don't fuck up something when you've got a good thing going.

Jackson: Bah! Artists take tremendous risks!

Avalon: You're no artist! You're a businessman, a brand name. A household brand name! Why, have you ever looked at your contract? Have you ever had a lawyer independently review it? Go over it with a fine tooth comb? How do you even know that you can write another thing that isn't in accordance with your dear publisher's wishes? I bet you can't. Hell, you could write something so profound that it shifts the course of history, and it will collect dust in the remainder bin because no one now will buy it, or the few who do will be madmen like you. You're a failure, Jackson Leman.

Vanessa: *Asymmetric Hearts* was profound. It spoke to me as a woman, made me see men for how they really are: creatures meant to be manipulated, tricked, molded, made great, or destroyed if need be.

Jackson: I wrote nothing of the sort.

Vanessa: (waking up to join the conversation) You did. It spoke to me. That's the mark of a great writer. There is no unity of message in his work. All persons see all things differently, take a piece of the work, and carry it with them.

Avalon: The only thing Mr. Leman's writings stimulate is the clitoral hood of middle aged housewives, women who see Virginia Dare, that female version of Marcus Hanely, who is equally phony, as a pale version of their former selves, before they chose poorly and chose a real dud of a man to take to bed and husband. You know, for what they thought was love. Love is for the birds or for the pages of a story. It doesn't happen in life. It's only description. It's felt, perhaps, but its just brain chemicals. When the chemical is isolated, chemists will make it in a synthetic process, bottle it up, and sell it at the Wally World pharmacy for all those lonely hearts out there. In a fortnight, you'll be out of business, Leman. Better start writing action adventure novels or designing the story lines for video games. The only people who will be able to sell books are the already famous, and with their deaths, literature will die. Or, perhaps you can ghost write for them.

Vanessa: Jackson is a famous author, daddy.

Avalon: Oh, I plumb forgot.

Jackson: It's not just love I can write about. There's the other prevalent theme of literature: overcoming death or approaching death. I can help people overcome their fear of DEATH.

Avalon: (grins creepily, stares right at Jackson Leman as if he can see right through him) Death you say? And what do you know of it? And how will you help people overcome a fear that is so intrinsically wired into their little primate consciousness, into their little brains? What makes you think that you, for all purposes, a miserable hack, can write your way around it?

Jackson: I didn't know you felt so strongly. I won't write my way around it. I'll write through it. It's all comedy.

Avalon: Death? Comical? I've never heard that before.

Jackson: You've never died. Yes, of course it's a comedy. Death's a bungler, always fucking up.

Avalon: Death always meets its mark. It owns what it rents. Dust to dust.

Jackson: Bah! Whatever! Everything old must be swept away. Death is a dust broom employed by an idiot child. Sweep away the dust! It is not powerful. Life is the real power. Death gets rid of the extra packaging.

Avalon: It also kills freshly bloomed flowers, ripped athletes by the hours, senators at the height of their political powers, washes away infants like spring-time showers carry silt and grime to life's river.

Jackson: You're amazingly poetic, for an idiot.

Avalon: So you're off to see your rich daddy die.

Jackson: If he isn't dead already.

Avalon: Oh he's probably clinging to life, waiting for his first born to acknowledge him before he rides off into the sunset. How did he spend his golden years? In the company of grandchildren? Taking pleasure trips to couple with foreign maidens who love old money?

Jackson: Counting his money.

Avalon: He must have an elaborate tomb laid out, architecturally sound, geometrically proportioned.

Jackson: The tallest pillar in the cemetery. But I don't know. We never discussed it. Maybe he's building a pyramid to himself.

Avalon: It will crumble, fall into the sands.

Jackson: Oh, he'll build it in some farmland somewhere, just so they curse his name when it shades the sun from the farmer's crops.

Avalon: Was your father a religious man?

Jackson: Very much so. He counted money all day long.

Vanessa: Where will the service be?

Jackson: God knows. Wherever is cheapest. I'm sure he's building a palatial tomb, just like the other world's bores who want to be remembered by their sarcophagi.

Vanessa: You're awfully hard on your father.

Jackson: You were never his son.

Vanessa: Guess not, but still. He's your dad.

Jackson: He gave me life, paid my way through most everything I ever did. You see how that could be cause of some resentment? But he can never claim my writings. He can overshadow all else in my existence, but he can't take what I've written away from me. When I write, I'm free. Every dime I spend of his binds me closer and closer to him, he calls to me, "What is owed, shall be repaid." It's a constant reminder.

Vanessa: Your father and my father would get along splendidly.

Avalon: It's a shame. I'll never get to meet the great Prescott Leman. I would have asked him so many questions.

Jackson: Here's a tip. Want to be rich? Start rich! If you can't start rich, then don't spend more than you take in. Only use credit when you must and only buy something with a guaranteed profit margin and revenue stream within 15 years, eh...maybe thirty. Oh yes, and don't spend lavishly on weddings, especially your own daughter's! They are only a way to show off and act out. You're better off giving your daughter money in the form of a dowry. Those are my father's rules of life. Financial rules. The guy was an absolute penny pincher, par excellence, and bore! Horrible bore!

Avalon: And genius. Don't forget genius. The man knew how to attract talent and retain it.

Jackson: Blah, blah, blah, buzzword, blah blah blah. Fuck you. You're a bore too, Avalon. Is that all you assholes think about, really? How to make a fucking buck? How to make three from one and five from two, multiply and subdivide infinitesimally, expand, subtract, count on your fingers like a five year old?

Avalon: You're quite hostile for being a businessman yourself.

Jackson: I'm no businessman.

Avalon: Suit yourself, businessman. You produce product. You sell it to the masses. It sells well, your stupid books. You've generated a revenue stream. Hopefully you invested it into other worthwhile endeavors. You would have done this if you wanted to be successful. Mind you, by worthwhile, I mean profitable! Take profit while you're young, and philanthropize when you're about to kick the bucket. But by all means, funnel those profits into other worthwhile endeavors. It's freedom.

Jackson: Blah, blah, blah. You butcher the mother tongue like a badly equipped three fingered, or should I say cloven-hooved, jackass.

Vanessa: Would you two just shut up and enjoy the view?

Jackson: There's nothing but blackness and stars out there.

Avalon: What of them?

Jackson: They aren't for sale yet. Just this little hunk of granite we're on.

Avalon: Granite and marble and gold and diamond and feldspar and rubies and sapphire and oil and permanganate and oil and oodles of plastic and plaster-of-Paris and concrete and iron ore and uranium....

Jackson: Blah, blah, blah, boring! You're putting me to sleep.

Avalon: We move mountains to get at them, to keep it all going.

Jackson: Well it's all bullshit. Sorry.

Avalon: If he wants to live like a pre-historic savage, be my guest. Vanessa, there's no helping him.

Vanessa: Don't you want to buy some sweet girl a diamond ring someday?

Jackson: Not a chance in hell.

Vanessa: What's your problem?

Jackson: I'm going to stare at the stars and make a wish.

Vanessa: What will you wish for?

Jackson: It's a secret. I'm sorry. If I told you, it wouldn't be a wish; it would be an assertion, a hope, a dream, and an endeavor. For now it will remain unknown and remain a wish.

Vanessa: I'll make a wish, too.

Jackson: I want you to sing something for me. A song, but make it your own song, not something floozies sing these days.

Vanessa: I don't know any.

Jackson: And you fashion yourself a poet? And you don't have a song? Why, I met a hooker, err, card player in a den of sin at the very edge of Nevada who had more of a poet nature than you. You first have to suffer to write beauty....

Vanessa: Are you saying that I should become a hooker, and that only then I can write beautifully?

Jackson: No. Just practice. Sing what's in your heart, milady. Don't think, just sing.

Avalon: My daughter has a wonderful voice.

Jackson: Can it and drive. You've already spoken enough as is. Just let your daughter sing, and don't say anything! Sing!

Vanessa: I don't know what to sing.

Jackson: Just sing what is written in your heart. Sing past all the rubbish and things and rotten decayed hopes and pickled dreams of paths others desired for you that are stacked to your heart's ceiling. Sing me a song. Hell, it doesn't even have to rhyme. Just sing something.

Vanessa: I can't think of anything.

Jackson: Damn you, don't think. Just feel and sing.

Avalon: Honey, just do it.

Jackson: Richard! Can it! Let your daughter do this without your interference.

Vanessa: Well, okay.

Jackson: Sing!

Vanessa: Mother and I walked the seashore, just talking

Covered in foam from the waves

Back and forth

Back and forth

She said I once was a little girl too

And the sun was warm and the grasses

Covered in dew

Now all is working and life is nothing but amends

No time for passion not any time for friends

Spirit a flower for the buzzing wiles of men

I once was a little girl too

Head full of posies, diamonds, and pearls

Hair done up in curls

And grasses covered in dew

I once was a little girl too

I once was a little girl too

No cares, no wares, no shimmering potions

And grasses covered in dew

Now all is working and life is nothing but amends

No time for passion no time for friends

Spirit a flower for the buzzing wiles of men

Avalon: Bravo! Bravo! See? Doesn't she sing wonderfully?

Jackson: You heard, but you didn't understand her words.

Avalon: The words don't matter. The voice matters. It was beautiful, honey.

Vanessa: (Silence, looks confused) I have to go to the restroom.

Avalon: You just went.

Vanessa: I really have to go.

Avalon: Okay, I guess you can't piss in a bottle.

We pulled into another dusty mountain town, utterly boring. The view would have probably been nice, but it was night. Underneath the flickering streetlights, I saw that there was another Wally World, and a strip mall with some chinky chinky buffets next to it. One was called WOK TIME, and the other was called CHINA BUFFET, as if that was original in the least. I figured they both served about the same thing. BIG STOP is where we parked, and Vanessa rushed inside to use the restroom.

The BIG STOP employee, a kid I didn't wish this type of boring work on because he seemed to be precocious, at least in the way that he checked out customers who looked suspicious, as we motley three who came in bedraggled and tossed about the road were. Or maybe it was our car that he was checking out, and the fact that we were an older man, a young, gorgeous woman, and a middle-aged, leering, lecherous weirdo. That's me. Maybe he recognized me from the back cover of my novel. I doubt it. His staring became uncomfortable. I thought that he might be trying to tell me that the bathroom was a pay-for-play enterprise. I asked him how far it was to Denver. Avalon ran to the men's restroom as he clutched his gut, with an exasperated look of volcanic anguish on his face.

"Denver?" he said, coming out of his trance.

"Yes, Denver, you know the biggest city in Colorado."

"Oh, I know, my family's from there, moved out here for more oportuniteee..." and he said it just like that, his voice trailing off like he had just realized that he really didn't find any opportunity out in these sticks and that he would much rather be back home watching the Broncos.

"Did you find it?" I asked. I asked just to rub salt in his wound.

"Can't say that I have. It's 25 miles, by the way."

"Thanks."

"That young lady there with you?"

"Yeah."

"She your wife?"

"Nah. Just a friend."

"Really?"

"Why? You want a go with her?" I asked him. His face perked up, like he was shocked.

Vanessa walked out the restroom, drying her hands on her pants.

"No paper towels in there," she announced.

"Yeah, man. Fifty bucks. Pay up," I said.

"How much for the coffee?" Vanessa asked.

"For you, free," the attendant announced.

"Gee, thanks, sweetie," she said in response. "Where's daddy?" she asked me.

"He's around, probably stealing some shit, the kleptomaniac. Nah, he's in the bathroom."

The attendant perked up. Vanessa grabbed her coffee and proceeded to walk out the door.

"You missed your chance, bub," I told the attendant. "Hey, do us a favor. Lock that old fuck in the men's restroom for a little bit. We have some business to attend to."

Vanessa and I sat in the car, admiring the psychotic insects that buzzed and beat their brains against a partially obscured floodlight, which illuminated an ad for cigarettes. I thought, if they could comprehend what they were doing, they would be totally ashamed, declare that their God was a sham, and retreat to their insect homes. I breathed in her perfume, which smelled like musty orange peels and a slight hint of Parisian sewer, but the rich people's sewer, not the slum dweller's sewer. I could tell she was looking at me, waiting for me to make some sort of move.

Her hand brushed my leg. It sent a bust of blood coursing through my body. Maybe it was a dump of brain chemicals that caused me to feel so giddy, quite possibly love. I don't know what power she held over me, but previously I did my very best to ignore it. The hand brushed my leg again, not an accident or a coincidence. It was purposeful, intended to arouse me. She could not see me blushing like an 8th grader who conned his way into senior prom with the hottest girl in school. I breathed deeply.

"What's your problem, Jacks?"

"What do you mean?"

"Stop answering me with questions and answer my question."

"I've been answering you with questions?"

I looked into her eyes. Her eyes glowed the green of anger, or maybe it was the reflection from the BP sign next door. I saw the contours of her face; fiercely angular, just barely discernable in the darkness like some lusty undiscovered country of dancing natives in the distance. I smiled. The OPEN sign reflected off her pupils, splaying them red and willing. Land ho! I smiled, a fierce smile. She attacked. Grabbed me, hopped over the seat and onto my lap, grinding her pelvis onto my cock.

"Papa has spastic colon," she said breathlessly, forcing my hand across her nipples and deftly removing her Victoria's Secret Bra with one hand. "He could be in the bathroom for hours."

"I made the restroom attendant lock him in there, if he finishes early."

"How'd you do that?"

"We're best buds."

I gasped for air between her tits, they were slightly sweaty and perfumed, not overly flowery down there like stripper tits, but more like wholesome tits, you know what I imagine French milkmaid tits look like after she's all sweaty from milking cows in the dewy Bretagne morning.

"It just comes on him, these attacks it's from working too much," Vanessa said, quivering.

She hiked up her skirt around her hips. "Put your goddamn hands on my ass," she ordered.

I rested my hands on her hips. She took my hands and moved them onto her firm, yet plump, ass. It felt like an ass that had done plenty of squats. When I get in situations like these, my mind starts to race. She moved my hand down, right in line with her poop chute. I tried to pull it away, but she held it there. "Stick a finger in my ass," she demanded.

"Eww. Why would I do that?" My cock was throbbing. I think the head had grown a head.

"Because I like it. Now do it."

I decided to sacrifice my pinky for the cause. Revolting. I slid it in her starfish. "Now take your thumb and jam it in me."

"Where?"

"Where do you think?"

With my other hand, I assessed her thighs. They were muscular, not like the thighs of a tennis player or soccer player, maybe the thighs of a college cheerleader from a good school in the PAC 12, like Cal Berkeley or Stanford, definitely not some school for schleps like Oregon. These were highly educated thighs. Smart. Full of substance. But she was probably a PAC 12 cheerleader who had let herself go just a bit, and had become a housewife to some power mad West coaster. No cottage cheese, pure vegan thighs. She guided my hand to her drippy, wet love triangle. My pinky popped out of her bottom, and I apologized for it not being long enough.

"Shut up, you worm," she said, and then tongue kissed me until I couldn't breathe; the dry desert air had really dried my nose out.

Her muff was shaved, maybe waxed, into a small palpable triangle, like the Bermuda Triangle. I'm sure I would get lost in there, point of no return for my dong. We would have to see. There was no prophylactic between us, but still she fished Ahab out of my pants and pumped him a few times with a tight fist to make sure he was ready for spelunking. There is a story about Ahab and the first girl Marcus and I ever bedded together while at Princeton, which I will not tell because this one, this moment of time, she has just slid my beef stick inside her and is now making that half pleasure half pain type face that I so love and admire, like she was getting a shot from a nurse and sucking on the best lolly pop of her life at the same time.

I'm not saying that I'm particularly well hung. I'm a long way from Long Dong Silver or Lex the Impaler, or Pedro Norte, Richard Longley, the Porn Star formerly known as the Mad Stabber, or even Gabe "Gutcrusher" Willis, Bobby "Back That Ass UP" Bowman, Donny "Diaphragm Poker" Norris, or ...or any of the other really well hung, dorky porn guys. Should I be a porn guy, I would recite love poetry to these women while I made tender, passionate love to them. They all look just so happy to be getting laid. You should really approach it like you did them a favor. Then we'd really be in love on camera, and you could see it gushing out of all of their pores. But, my dong rather isn't a baby's arm holding an apple when flaccid or erect. It's rather like a garter snake attempting to eat a cherry, and a small, malnourished garter snake at that. But I've been told it's pretty big. I really have been.

At Princeton, a girl told me I was living large and in charge, but she was tiny and Asian. Most of the time I'm overshadowed by Marcus's tremendous phallus. Marcus could be a stand in for Priapus at the local Greek festival. He's that spectacular. And why am I thinking about Marcus's cock when I'm supposed to be concentrating on making this fine specimen of woman, who's now bouncing up and down and pausing to rhythmically grind on my wang, come? Vanessa was really pummeling my cock and wheezing at the same time, and I'm getting really into it, but I can't help feeling detached, watching the door, making sure Dickie Avalon doesn't come strolling out whistling, only to catch his daughter in flagrante delectio with me, a rogue. My spearing answers each of her thrusts, an exclamation point for every one of her sentences. We are like a gigantic perpetual motion machine; my vibrations cause hers to vibrate and we are soon in harmonic motion. I'm thrusting with all of my might and she's working up a scream, I can feel her body tensing, so I decide to touch one little button in her to see if I can push it over the edge. I reach around her hip and on the down stroke, jam my thumb in her brown starfish. She shudders. And I explode. We heave together, in the front seat of the car, passenger side. Our sweat mingles, and the cool desert air wicks it away as soon as the pore spews its contents to the air.

I look up to see Richard Avalon, red in the face, in a heated argument with the gas station attendant. The attendant is a sickly shade of purple rage and Avalon seems to be making protests, not like he's angry, but like he's really, really nervous. The attendant is exhorting him, thrusting a mop and a broom his direction, shaking a pink and white container marked CANI CIDE at him. And I just went back to Vanessa and tongue kissed her until I felt her squeeze me like a death embrace from a boa constrictor. I didn't want to run. I only wanted to run over the healthy cliff with her into the churning yellow and lavender sea below where the octopi could mash our bones to suck out the fucking marrow and suck the jelly out of our eyes. She pulled her lips off mine and started mashing back and forth again, and within what seemed like an eternity but must have been only a good thirty seconds, I flamed her with both barrels of testicles, spurting full bore. She climbed off me, leaking.

"Hell, I needed that," she said as we shared breaths. I looked up and noticed Richard Avalon, now less visibly enraged and more timid and put in his place, hand the broom and mop back.

"Your dad's coming," I said, as I tucked away my pogo stick, which was more like a melted and overly masticated gummy worm, and rolled down the window to dissipate at least a hint of sex from the car.

Avalon got in the car and slammed the door just as Vanessa adjusted her shirt. It was sort of awkward, us all being in the front, but Avalon, he was a control freak you see, and he just had to drive.

"You want to get in back?" He told me, more like an order than a request.

"What took you so long?" I asked, after we had performed our mini Chinese fire drill.

"Well, that's something I'd rather not have you ask or have to discuss, because it's of a private nature, but since you've been so gracious with my daughter and me, I'll just tell you about my little condition, err, problem, nah...condition the doctors call it. Hey, why does it smell like fast food in here?"

"Fast food?"

"Yeah, like overdone burgers and fries or something like that."

"I don't know. Maybe my buddies and I left something under the seat."

I felt under them, playing off the fact that Vanessa and I had been making the beast with two backs. I'd never even considered that it smelt like fast food, but perhaps that was the almost universal appeal of the midsection expanding, gullet stretching filth. I felt the 1911 again and picked it up, placing it in my waist band for a rainy day or if this prick decided to off me on the approach to Denver, realizing that my car is tits and not wanting to go back to riding the bus or bumming rides off friends and family. The gun would do just nice in arms reach. I put it in the back of my pants, because I know that people blow their dicks off if they put it in the front of their pants. It happens in the movies quite frequently and it is usually hilarious.

"You were saying something about your condition?" I asked Avalon, wanting him to tell me something detrimental about himself, instead of acting forthright and puritan all the time, a real obscure prick.

He spoke. He spoke at length. I learned all the ins and outs and mostly outs and intricacies of a wheat gluten allergy combined with a spastic colon. He warned me to eat plenty of soluble fiber and to take supplements of it, even, and if he had been doing that as a young man, he probably wouldn't have coated the restroom with his outspewings the way he did. That, and the young attendant locked him in the restroom, forcing him to respond in such an aggressive manner. He told me he warned the attendant that he would do it, unless the attendant opened the door. I guess the attendant took to watching us, until he heard the explosions and rumblings.

"You see when you've got a spastic colon, the pain is intense. It makes you feel like all you want to do is die."

"That's much of life, forgetting about death, Dickie," I said matter of factly.

Vanessa gasped, a thin amount of air escaping her lips, much like a corpse breath when the diaphragm finally gives way. "What?" she asked, queerly.

"Face it, Dickie ole boy, one day you're going to die just like my dear old Dad who is desperately clinging to the light as we speak. So step on it, man, and no more stops until we get there."

"No one said anything, Mr. Leman," Avalon said, as he gripped down on the skull's head shifter and gunned the car well past the speed limit.

Vanessa shifted in the back seat next to me. She looked at her father uncomfortably; her eyes a bit misty, as if she was searching for something to say to beat back the thoughts that I introduced to her mind.

"I don't think its true, Jacks. I mean, it can't be true. People do things because they love life and they want to survive."

"Ideally they would. But nope. All I see all around me is a wholesale retreat from the inevitable, a clinging to life, not a powerful embrace. A tepid, clinging, weak little hold, like a young boy grasping the wrist of his mother, terrified to go off the curb and onto the bus to take him to his first day of school. We live in absolute terror of the unknown. It coats everything we do with its blackness. But it isn't really black; it's just our perception of blackness. It's nothing, really. Nothing at all. It's just a getting rid of the old, this dying. A sloughing off of the tired and worn out. It's a demonstration that no matter how much you elevate yourself over your fellow men, over material, in the end you come crashing back to nature. You're trapped. You're stuck. You're alone in your fight."

"Like your father."

"Yep, just like him."

"Think that's why he wants to see you?"

"I don't know why he wants to see me. I'm just coming because he requested me. You think I would have come if he didn't issue me a summons? It's not me that has to deal with it. He has his reasons. He's the one that's dying. He's the one that's lived his life and made the choices he's made. Do I have to see him off to his final rest? Is that what I owe him as a good son? I haven't seen the man for ten years or so."

"That man made you, Jackson. He's your father," Vanessa said.

"Would be better that I had another one."

"Why's that? As a father myself, I know that all fathers, no matter how dismal, at the very bottom, they love their children."

"They love that they've created something. No more. They love only this."

"You don't have any children. How do you know?" Avalon asked.

"And neither should my father have had any children."

"You'd be damning yourself to oblivion," Dickie Avalon said.

"So be it."

"You don't think anything matters?"

"I didn't say that."

"You don't think you matter?" Avalon asked.

"You do matter, Jacks," Vanessa said, interrupting.

"Okay. If you say so. Why? Because Jesus loves me, this I know?"

"No."

"Why then?" I said angrily.

"I don't know," she said sheepishly.

"Listen. I may not care about a whole lot, but that doesn't mean I'm one of those guys that is going to damn everything and say nothing matters. Just because I think the world is worthless and vile doesn't mean that I'm going to just off myself...take a machine gun into a crowded mall and spray the place down...those people are *fucking cowards*. I decide the world is a worthless place; I'm going to decide to do my damndest to make it worthwhile, by *doing something*. What I do, that's the only thing that gives me any sort of meaning. And I create it for myself. So don't you, little missy, tell me that I matter. I decide that I matter. Call me a fucking nihilist. I'll just tell you that I have a nihilistic confidence in my ability to hone my abilities that I care about. You two don't need to tell me shit." I said as I heaved and sweated in the backseat like a madman about to have some not minor fit.

"You don't need to get all upset about it."

Little did Avalon know that I had just plowed his daughter. He drove my car, the whole time thinking that I am a decent, upstanding citizen, when I have just finished with his little girl, his own flesh and blood. I had my way with her, much like I would have had my way with a Coca-Cola, Pepsi, Monster, or Red Bull, had I so chosen to. Still I do care about her a little. I would have saved the can I suppose. I don't think he would care if I just announced the fact that we had been scrumping and bumping uglies in the front seat, that I did deposit my seed in her, and I did not ask if she was on the pill, nor did I bother to purchase a lubricated condom from the greasy bathroom that he just shitstained, because I don't care about the outcome. It sort of just happened, just like I sort of just happened, and Avalon sort of just happened, and so did Vanessa, this car, the interstate. They all happened. Well at least the interstate and the car were planned. Even if you plan to have a baby, you can't choose which sperm fertilizes which egg. It's a beautiful, and entertaining crapshoot.

Somebody looked at someone else and said, "Hmm...want to make something?" or lust just took over and the same blind, dumb force that made hydrogen molecules stick together, made all these people stick together and keep the whole mess going. In the great grand scheme of things, me siring a child with Vanessa and I hope to God she isn't as fertile as a Mexican, the death of my father, the publication of my upcoming works, the survival of the planet Earth throughout the eons, not much of it mattered, when taken from the extreme macro view. That extreme macro view of existence, when the Earth is viewed as dust particles among shiftless dust particles shaken up in a beaker, importance dwindles to vagueness and then blinks out. I am the opposite of that dumb man who cannot see the forest for the trees. I cannot see the trees, because I am lost in a forest. I guess I am suffering from Macrovison, from flying too close to the sun at too high an altitude, where the air is thin, and not much remains to even breathe. Why slim my spectrum down?

Avalon interrupted my train of thought, saying what all fathers are supposed to say when a man comes calling for his little girl, "You've taken quite well to my daughter." Followed by, "What are your intentions toward her?"

I looked out the window to the lights of Denver in the distance blending with the mountain sky, like the area where the man-made muck from the river washes out to sea. I tried to imagine the mountains with nothing coming, nothing going on about them, just a pristine wilderness that no men had ever touched. Avalon grunted to get my attention.

"Yes?" I asked.

"I mean, you and my daughter seem to have taken to each other. You're quite the item, you two," he rephrased it again, a voice of hope against all the darkness that surrounded us. It was probably only the darkness that I perceived, and these two simple comfort-seeking souls were spared it. So, I decided to give them hope. I had a slight inkling of a feeling towards her, but you know I had just banged her out and that was bound to fade, but still I did like her, maybe crossing the threshold of me starting to have more serious feelings for her, I think.

"Yes, she's nice," I said as if she wasn't sitting right next to me, her hand on my thigh.

"Just nice?"

"Yeah, nice," I said.

"You could say something sweeter, maybe, Jacks," she said.

"I can't think of anything right now. Sorry." I said, feeling like a hopeless mess of contradiction, words with no focus, longings without any real intentions, drives with no boundaries. And then I saw the actual reason for my scattered mind state just laying off exit 75, west of Denver.

"Take this exit, Avalon."

"Goody, so we're almost there."

"This is where dear old dad lives, then?"

"Yeah. It's real private. I'll show you the way."

Avalon brought the Judge down the low, winding exit ramp and onto the Mackie Road in Leman, Colorado. We passed two hobos who were headed west, perhaps towards the warm and homeless friendly communities of California. They were standing on the exit ramp, thinking it was an entrance ramp, and if someone would have picked them up, they could have traveled east, back to the chill and homeless doom of Chicago, New York, or Philadelphia: good cities where being homeless is obviously either a curse from God, evidence that you are a failure in life, or that you are economically non-viable and there would be no parties bidding you good riddance as you rode the rail for greener pastures. These two gentlemen were too drunk to notice.

I won't know their story, because I didn't stop to talk to them. They could have been rocks on the side of the road. But when we passed them and my reflections started as they automatically do when something pierces this great wall I've built up and actually trickles in and makes me realize something important about myself, what I realized was that if I didn't have all this capital behind me, that if I wasn't born rich and won the lottery the day I was born, I would probably have been worse off than those two hitchhiking hobos, because at least they had each other, and my friends had just up and abandoned me.

We passed on the right a small general store which marked the "secret entrance" to the hardball road, which looked like a road out into the wilderness to people not in the know, but was frequently traveled by black SUVs and other sinister looking vehicles driven by sinister looking men in military type uniforms who sported moustaches. This hardball road wound through a canyon for about 15 miles up to what was my father's favorite getaway home out of perhaps hundreds of secret lairs throughout the world. This was his largest home, his most remote, with all the conveniences of living in the most industrialized and freest nation on the planet. Others were hovels and safe houses, nothing to write home about, or suitable for a postcard.

"This doesn't look like much of a road," Avalon remarked.

"It's no road. It's a driveway."

"Longest damn driveway I've ever seen," Vanessa said.

"My father's spread has its own zip code."

The passage was different than I remembered, more overgrown with trees, as if the migrant gardeners had been let go on furlough or quit en masse. We were entering a wild habitat in which bears and wolves found refuge. Vanessa tensed up and gripped my hand.

Avalon negotiated the twists and turns in the dense forest. His lights cut a saber-like, serpent's tongued swath through the black fuzz, and illuminating sharp, jagged angles of rock and pine trees that seemed to howl in the night. Vanessa gripped my hand even stronger. This was a horror show.

"Who would have thought, my dear, that when we set out from that dismal little place we called home just a few short days ago that we would soon be guests in the home of one of the most successful industrialists in American history?" Avalon asked his daughter, beaming with pride, probably hoping that a visit to the shrine of the guru could somehow teach him to stack coins more effectively, count beans at a faster rate, and polish gold and silver to perfection so that it was all the more shimmering and gleaming when he too rested on his deathbed.

"You probably won't be allowed to see my father. I take it he's under doctor's orders to have no visitors, unless of course he's already kicked the bucket."

Avalon negotiated a hairpin turn as we continued up the mountain. On the right, we passed the first of my great grandfather's mines. It was abandoned of course, the main vein had long ago run petered out, and it was now a boarded up ugly eyesore, like a huge fistula in the side of the mountain.

"You're your father's son. You could probably secure me an audience with him."

"What do you want to talk to him about? He's really weak."

"I'd like to ask him his secret."

"There is no secret. I'll tell you that. You were either born with it, or you weren't. Talent only gets you so far. You can have lovely ideas, ennobling ideas, but without the capital to bring them to fruition they would just stagnate. You can have all the capital in the world, but if you don't know how to employ it, or harness it for beautiful notions, it will be wasted.

My father's secret? He knew how to hire talented people with beautiful ideas, to hold them to his bosom and nurture them, or bilk them, I should say. Why? Because even though these people had ideas that could have launched new enterprises, they joined the establishment of my father.

Why? Because they were afraid. He was established. They were afraid to go against the established authority. So they settled into being his well-compensated slaves. Sure, they were well paid, but their ideas? They were trademarked with the Leman Global Industries logo. Now when people think of these beautiful inventions, they don't know who the actual inventor was. Hell, it could have dumped forth from the brain of a computer. They signed non-competition clauses in their contracts. Idiots!

Their contributions elevated my father's net worth and Leman Global Industries market shares and loaded my father's pockets with more Gold than God himself could count on the seventh day. He'll tell you his secret all right, if he is still among the living, and that's there is no secret. Anyone who tells you there is a secret is a fool or a damn fine salesman, and my father would be looking to hire them. You want my advice? Don't buy."

"As we get closer, the security will be much more aggressive," I told Avalon.

"Who do you have working up here?"

"Dad hired some former South African Special Forces, real mercenary types, a few years ago to be his private security contractors, body guards, thugs, intelligence collectors...I guess their reach is long and wide."

"Why South Africans?"

"I guess they're dependable and out of work now that they're not bashing the skulls of blacks and flaying them for speaking up. They're vicious. One of the perks of being a multibillionaire is that you can have other people do your dirty work for you. Mind you, they're watching us now. Don't make any sudden movements."

We traveled another mile or so at the steep grade. The Judge chugged along. We rounded the bend, and a massive deer jumped out in front of the car, bounding with antlers flexed forward toward the other side of the road, toward an illogical gash in the vegetation fashioned by a person who could best be described as a nut, bent on taming untamable, wild nature. Now the gash was overgrown with vegetation, as if the teams of Sri Lankan and Bangladeshi nationals must have gone on strike or have been deported for being suspected terrorists and were driven in droves from the Denver Airport, whole planeloads of little brown men carrying hatred in their hearts for capitalism and my father's corporation in particular and would be protesting it from hot little capitals the world over.

Who knows? Maybe they were sitting in their little servant's quarters playing board games, because my father was too feeble to inspect the grounds anymore. He was too feeble to travel. I know that. I'm sure he would have much rather kicked the bucket in Brazil or his estate in the French countryside. The deer froze. Avalon stopped and flashed the high beams. The deer just looked at him like Avalon was a pest and he was head honcho of these here woods. The animal, the big dumb bastard, flicked its tongue at us once, twice, and just stared.

"Get the fuck out of the way!" Avalon shouted out the window at the creature who belonged there more so than we did.

The deer backtracked the way it came, stopped again and nibbled some fresh shoots in the concrete sidewalk. Father had a sidewalk constructed up the mountain so he could take scenic nature hikes with women who were not on their periods. Signs were posted approximately every 100 meters that stated:

DANGER! DANGER!
MOUNTAIN LIONS AND BEARS!
DO NOT WALK HERE IF YOU ARE
MENSTRATING.
YOUR CHANCES OF BEING
EATEN

ARE　　　　　　　　**HIGH!**

Whoever wrote the sign was an idiot, but we let it slide. We had never seen any bears, but what we needed now was an aggressive bear or mountain lion to chase this deer from our path.

"You should shoot it," Avalon said.

Too easy. I could shoot the big, beautiful bastard. Or I could get out and shoo the wild animal away. Shooting it would draw the guards, who had big ass hand cannons and rifles and really knew how to use them. We would be no match.

"I'm not going to shoot it," I told Avalon.

"Why not? You chicken?"

"I discharge my gun here, and this place will be swarming with South African mercenaries in no time."

"Just get it off the road, Jacks," Vanessa said.

I exited the car, grumbling, and kept the gun in my waistband, just in case the bastard charged me. I looked back. I had left the door open. The dome light illuminated Vanessa and her very dopey father, who peered at me in terror. I bet they hoped

I got gored and trampled so they could do a yooey and keep my car, after they left my carcass for the wolves to pick apart. This mountain would be my grave. I approached the deer with my hand out, the other hand on the .45 in my pants just in case the bastard got smart. It grunted and continued nibbling.

"Get out of here!" I shouted to the deer, like a landlord evicting an unruly, broke tenant.

The deer looked up at me. "That's no way to talk to an old friend," the deer said and continued nibbling.

Shocked, I drew the pistol.

"What's with the gun, buddy?"

I looked back to Avalon and his daughter who were making motions with their hands for me to just shoot the damn thing. They seemed to be arguing about something, too, with their faces all flustered. Avalon kept glancing at his watch. I could not just kill a talking deer. It wasn't even deer season.

"Watch out for those two. He who seems like a friend is really an ene-meeeeeeeeeey!" the Deer said and bounded off.

"Fuck, I've lost it," I announced.

The deer poked its full rack out of the woods. "Get to your fahhh-ther. Leave these two somewhere. Do as I do. Run away..."

It pranced off, tail flicking against the moonbeams and high beams.

I walked back, gun still in my hand. Vanessa and her father gave notice that I was approaching and stopped their arguing. I climbed back into the car. Having been out in the wilderness, the car took on a whole new smell. It was not a new car smell; it had been through too much use. It smelled of old air fresheners, sex, and a wee bit of booze, a tinge of marijuana, and almost a cheap grandeur, like a ton of money stashed in an old musty shoebox.

"What were you two arguing about?"

"Oh, nothing," Vanessa said.

"Seems to me like you two were arguing while I was out talk-...I mean shooing that deer away."

"It had nothing to do with you, Jacks," Vanessa said quietly. She was a poor liar. Maybe it was because she had developed feelings for me.

The insects screamed, a chorus, no, an orgy of gyrating thoraxes. Vanessa's hand went back to my leg to rest at the very tip of my glans. A delight, but not quite the whole affair. It was starting to feel real, it really did.

We turned the next bend and the sky lit up like Christmas. Two figures, a large man and a frailer gentleman who held his head cocked to one side and a crumpled hat stood in the distance in the middle of the road, shadowy figures. As we approached, Avalon made no signs that he was going to stop. His high beams struck them. It was

Marcus and Willard trudging up the middle of the road! Avalon was going to run them over!

"STOP!" I yelled and grabbed the steering wheel to the side. The car hit the curb and lurched to a halt.

"What the fuck!" Avalon yelled.

I lurched out of the car. "My friends! Good God, my friends! I called to them, running towards them. "I thought I lost you!"

Just ahead of us was the first South African checkpoint. The guards looked thrilled at actually seeing someone approach. Their hands were on their weapons, and they looked at us quizzically guard-like.

Willard appeared haggard. Emaciated, he breathed hard like he was near death. Hanely was strong as he trudged the hill to the checkpoint as if he had just gotten done fucking the queen of some distant, exotic land whom everyone had warned was unassailable and impossible to seduce. Circe cast a spell on him, and made him deaf.

"Marcus!" I shouted. "Don't you recognize me?"

Marcus turned and shook his head and continued trudging up the hill.

"Marcus!" I shouted again and made to run up to him.

"Marcus, did you forget about me!"

"Stop!" The guards at the gate shouted to me.

I looked up. Their flashlight equipped black machine pistols were leveled at me and their flinty eyes were full of murder.

"Who the hell are you? A huge guard shouted to me in an accent I couldn't fully comprehend.

"You aren't South African!" I stated confidently, not quite aware of the peril I was in.

"Hands up!" The other guard said with a French accent.

"What happened to the South Africans? Marcus!"

"You will be shutting up now, monsieur," the dark Frenchman said. I think he was an Algerian or Moroccan. An Arab. A regular unliterary, soldierly Albert Camus. I had created the perfect diversion. Hanley and Willard slipped past the guards unscathed. I would probably be taking one for the team.

"Who are the people in the car? Friends of yours?" The French Guard flashed the flashlight in their direction.

Avalon exited. So did Vanessa. "Ehh, yes," I said quietly. "They'll be leaving soon. They gave me a ride."

Avalon and his daughter walked up to the guards confidently. They snapped to. "Monsieur Avalon. Mademoiselle Dupree," the guard recited, rendering salute.

"What the hell?" I asked looking at them. Avalon had a great grin on his white mug, which looked quite sinister all of a sudden underneath his black bowler. Vanessa couldn't look at me. The Eastern European's hand brushed my .45.

"Gun!" he shouted.

I put my hands up in protest. The Frenchman, out of instinct, put his rifle butt into my temple. The last thing I heard was Avalon shout, "No!" as everything went white, a shade of white I had previously only seen in...

DREAMLAND.

Stars wash over me -

(Some sort of dreamy song begins to play)

A boy plays a flute, he may have angel wings and a large bulbous red nose from drinking too much gin...DRUNKEN CUPID...inept at shooting his arrows into the right persons...love erupts all over Denver, Colorado, as DRUNKEN CUPID, all ginned up, little Lothario Cupid sprays his mini gun arrows from the mountain top

"Stop please, sir," I tell DRUNKEN CUPID.

"If everyone is in love with someone and that someone doesn't love them back, don't you think that's a wonderful state of affairs?"

"Unrequited love all around...two helpings of disappointment. Why in one genera-tion, we have born the most profound poets, musicians, and thinkers. We will start a golden age, my friend."

Cupid loads his minigun for another helping of love and disappointment, and pulls the trigger

-2 doses for you sir, and shot of wrath for your missus

Stab the mailman full of love for the mayor's wife and her full of lust for the pharmacist who dispenses pills by the handful to increase the length and girth of the pricks of elderly churchgoers whose pricks fell out of favor decades ago

There is a purpose to nature and violations introduce absurdity

I recall a philosophy professor telling me this once, but I was too stoned to take note.

That was Princeton University in the year of our Lord 2001. Then someone burst into the room. I believe she was a secretary there in the Philosophy Department. She was shrieking something about the World Trade Center being hit by airplanes. I guess her husband worked there. Hence the emotion.

Cupid flapped his wings close to my ear, and it sounded like the buzz of a pair of hair clippers plugged into a 220-volt outlet. He whispered to me, "Your love petered out, and how can you write about love if you've never loved? Can a blind man sing a song about the sun?"

"I have heard enough about love to know that I want no part of the pain that slices you and leaves you gushing wet, hot blood all over the sidewalk. And who says that I never loved, Cupid? Maybe your memory is faulty."

"I don't know. Maybe you have."

"My love is deeper than any love you could ever impart into me. It is my free decision. It does not strike down like an arrow shot by a petulant winged boy. It is time, position, and inclination. Physics and will. Love has no object. It cannot objectify. Only greed objectifies. We enter into love as equals. There is no seller and buyer. There is no marketing plan. No diamond is as brilliant as a mere pebble you discover in a lover. When she touches it, it becomes molten."

"Cupid. I once knew a little black haired, black-eyed girl whose head bounced up and down each time she took a step. She appeared puzzled every time that I saw her pass me by in the hallway on my way to English class. I wanted to ask the girl her name, but I could not muster the courage. She was a dream, and she floated through my days without knowing it. I saw her smile, but once, at a young man who tripped up the stairs. Schadenfreude. It made me love her even more for her silent cruelty. That night I tugged my meat and thought about her beating me with the slim switch of a tree, perhaps a weeping willow. It would sting ever so slightly. I imagined her standing over me fully clothed. I could not visualize her naked, she was too pure to ever let the sunlight kiss her neck. I resigned myself to cowardice and I dropped the course, so I would never have to see her again."

"You're a fool. When in doubt, say something foolish. It should come naturally. Do something foolish. Stand out from the wall and make yourself known to her. You are going to die. Remember that. In oblivion there is no love. No dead man writes odes to decay, and no woman bears fruit beyond the bounds of the living. I am love. I am life. You needn't embrace me. You're already me, just realize it."

I woke up. My sister, Hannah, and her husband, the money-grubbing Sheldon, Marcus, and Willard stood over me. My dream was over.

"Marcus?" I called.

"Good God, it's more profound than ever," Sheldon said.

Marcus stood in the corner, looking smug. He didn't bother to respond.

"Where's dad?" I asked, my head still pounding from the skull-crushing goon squad's treatment of me.

Hannah did not speak to me. She just stared. She was still beautiful, with her brown hair and brown eyes, though more than a slight pall of worry sought to wreck her outlook.

"All he wanted was to see you, Jackson," she said matter-of-factly.

I swallowed. Then asked the most logical following question to her morose statement, "Is Dad still alive?"

Sheldon snorted a brusque response, "I don't see what he sees in you. I mean, you haven't even poked your head in to say hello for ten years."

Hannah cut him off. "That's enough, Sheldon," she said.

"I don't understand why you all are so upset," I said in my usual passive aggressive tone. "Where is he?"

I tried to sound like I was getting down to business when these people were just interested in discussing the past. They could put me on trial later.

"Don't worry. He's still alive. He's strong."

"You told me he was on the edge of death. You told me he was laid out on his death bed."

"He is on his death bed. Sitting, not laying. The doctors think he has a few weeks left."

"What the hell?"

"We knew you would take your sweet ass time getting here. We called you really early."

"Oh, thanks. Now what the hell am I supposed to do for the next week?"

"Jackson, you can be so insensitive."

"Hannah. You know as well as I do that you're acting like a saint because you might hope that there is something in it for you in return."

"How dare you!" Sheldon yelled, in a display of real theater. I just laughed at him, which made him more furious. The purple nearly became a shade of eggplant. He coughed and had to take a breather.

"Your brother...he's enough to kill anybody."

"Oh, so that's why you made me show up? You wanted to accelerate things a bit? Get your payments quicker? Maybe end up running the show?"

"That's enough, Jackson. You're impossible!"

"Nice to see you, too, sis."

Marcus stood in the corner. Willard twiddled his thumbs. I cued for them to say something, by waving my hands around.

"What are you waving at?"

"My buddies."

Hannah and Sheldon looked at each other like they were suddenly very afraid to be in the room with me.

"Jackson. Give it up," Sheldon said. His black suit made him look like an undertaker. He was an MBA from the Harvard School of Business, which did not mean that he actually had any talent for business. In fact, his only talents lay in spending money. He was like a stylish woman in that regard, never buying anything on sale, waiting patiently until some Italian power tailor or the fashionistas announced a new style of suit at New York Fashion Week. He then did his best to ensure the style would catch on by wearing it as often as possible so that he could be viewed as something of a trendsetter, though he wasn't much to look at. He was somewhat pear shaped, but that too was a trend he wholesale trudged along. I think he did all this fashion nonsense so that he wouldn't feel so all-alone in the world.

He was allergic to human sweat, I believe. My sister, she had to be cuckolding him. I mean, just look at him. Thirty-two, already bald up top, and just butter soft. All I really had to do was say the word, and Marcus Hanely would make mincemeat out of him. That, of course, would be saved for a later, hopefully much later date, when I really needed to pull that trump card out. You know, when Sheldon, Marcus, and I were alone somewhere out counting stars or shopping online or something.

I had no idea of this man's other pastimes, but I assumed from the looks of him that he wasn't a fan of fasting or pushing away from the table. I don't know what my sister saw in him. Maybe it was because she could control him so plentifully, or he ensnared her in his sticky web of frivolousness and stupidity. Apparently she enjoyed a silver-tongued, snappy dresser over a real man.

Sheldon glared at me like he wanted to see my end. I think he decided to put on a display of making peace, but really wanted to rub salt into my wounds. Wounds that he could perceive in me, because he was far too blinded by others' weaknesses to see his own gaping, hemorrhaging faults.

"How's the new novel going?"

"It's coming along well. Really shaping up. Going to be putting the final touches on it soon."

"You realize it's a family concern now, right?"

"What do you mean?"

"Well, some people close to you, business associates of yours, they're quite concerned. Let's just put it that way, and leave it at that."

"Oh. You've gotten a call from someone I should probably look at firing?"

"Well. Yeah. You know, at first I wasn't going to tell you, but we all feel that it's in your best interest to finish the series of novels you're contracted to finish."

"So, my agent's violated all the statutes of being an agent, and he actually contacted you to put pressure on me?"

"Of course. You're part of the family business now."

"And you're part of the family business, Sheldy?"

"Of course."

"You aren't part of this family."

"Hannah, excuse us. Please get your brother and me something cold to drink. Have the maid bring it, or whatever."

My sister slavishly responded and complied with his wishes. Gone was that happy girl I knew and grew up with, playing in the sand at the beach while our parents fought in the vacation home. I suppose we all had to grow up.

"You know, this family has much to do with your success, Jackson. It's high time you started realizing that."

"Baloney. I did it all on my own."

"You're quite wrong. The Jackson Leman pen name is now a registered trademark of a subsidiary of Leman Global Industries. Anything published under your name is now owned by us."

"I'll write under a pen name then. Michael Flannery. Tommy Van Der Veer. Boris Markanov. I could come up with names all day long."

"Yes, yes, but don't you want to know how it all happened?"

He was such a snide little prick.

"It isn't true, and really, I don't care."

"Oh, but it is true, my man," Sheldon said, delightfully wringing his hands together, doing his best ape imitation of an evil genius with a Harvard fraternity mouth.

I decided to call his bluff. "Show me, you fat fuckface," I said.

Marcus laughed.

"You hear that, Marcus? I called Sheldon a fat fuckface! Funny, huh?"

"Who the hell are you talking to?" Sheldon asked, pointing his fat sausage finger in my face.

"My compatriot, my brother in arms, my closest advisor and dear friend, Marcus Hanely," I rattled off confidently.

"The male love interest in your first novel?"

"I can't believe you've actually read it. Thank you."

"The synopses are all over the Internet, and are you serious? You're talking to Marcus Hanely?"

"Yep."

"Fuck, you're bat shit crazy," he said with a smile. "I love it."

"What? I'm not crazy. He's standing right there behind you."

Sheldon waddled around to look. "Nope. Looks like a wall to me...."

"Marcus! Pounce!" I ordered.

Hanely just stood there, same smug, shit eating grin on his face. I'm surprised he didn't follow my sister out into the kitchen to have his way with her. Those were his rules though, and he did have rules: no sisters, no moms, and no daughters of compatriots. Of enemies, it was all fair game, like a Mexican soap opera, and Marcus would nearly always play the villain. This was a different situation, because Hannah wasn't just my sister, but she was a real enemy's wife.

Sheldon cackled. He erupted into teaming magma bursts of laughter and became a veritable Pompeii, burying us in his thick, heavy, burning spite.

"He's right there! Behind you! Are you blind?"

"Jacky, Jacky, Jacky, you live with a great deal of illusion. Or should I say, hallucination," Sheldon said suddenly becoming gravely serious.

"Don't you see him or the old man?"

Hanely walked toward the open door with Willard in tow. Willard appeared to be on his last leg and walked with his head toward the ground, shuffling as if the weight of this place were about the crush him.

"Willard!" I screamed.

Sheldon whipped around, quickly for a fat man, and waved his hands through the air. "Nothing...nothing...nothing...."

"Why the hell are you doing this to me?"

"I think you know, Jackson. It's high time you grew up."

He wanted me to think I was insane, so I would go fully bounding towards that path. He wanted me to totally implode while my father was alive, so my father would change the will. We didn't know the contents of the will, but Sheldon was probably certain that I received the lion's share. Primogeniture! If he could make me totally go off the deep end while my father was still extant, maybe that could force my father's hand to write me only some small house, where I could sit out my days muttering in the shadows and not have to worry about paying any bills on my own. I'd be a slave. An invalid. I couldn't let this idiot do that to me.

"Focus, Jackson," I said, hoping it would become my mantra.

Hannah entered with some lemonade. She never liked to trouble the maids to do anything that she could do herself, and most of what she did was a labor of love. Even when she was a little girl, she was always making nice with the help. Our mother, she was a basket case, and I think Hannah being raised by the maids who had their own share of stories of life's toils made her more able to cope with all that happened to our little family. Hannah learned to cook. She learned all about silverware and hosting dinner parties. She would have made a much better man a lovely wife, but instead she chose this douche bag with no redeeming qualities.

"Why did you do it, Hannah?" I asked her.

"Do what?"

"Why did you call me and say that father was on his death bed?"

"We haven't seen you in ten years, Jackson. Ten years! Dad *is* on his deathbed. He isn't going to get any better. He'll never see grandchildren from either of us. First there's me...then there's you."

"It's not my fault."

"Do you need an invitation to everything? And when we did invite you, you always claimed to be hard at work on your novel. So it was really strange when your agent called us up and told us you hadn't provided him anything over that long time."

"See, it's all about the money."

"Jackson. I care about you. You're my brother. I love you."

She did look sincere. Still, I couldn't trust her until I found out Sheldon's true intentions. The way she looked at me, hurt me, and I wanted to agree with her.

"Hannah. I...yeah...I feel the same way. You know that. I tried to get here sooner, but my traveling companions got in the way. I swear. I tried to get here."

"Oh, the employees you showed up with. Yes, they did a good job."

"Employees?"

"Come on, you know it. You called them on it when you first met them. It's all in the report."

"Report?"

"Of course. Any Leman Global Industries employee dispatched on a mission files a report, so they can earn their bonus for mission completion."

"Vanessa?"

"You're talking about the girl? Yes, she's an employee, too."

"Did she write a report about me?"

"Nothing stunning. Just the facts," Sheldon said.

"That little bitch," I said, and noting how Hannah winced, quickly apologized. I'd play Sheldon's little game.

"So they weren't father and daughter?"

"Of course not. They were playing a role."

"So was I."

"You weren't. It's all evidence."

"Evidence of what Sheldon?"

"Your continued mental infirmity."

"Jesus, it's worse than we'd imagined," Hannah lamented.

"Jackson, you take after your mother. Degenerative schizophrenia with chronic hallucinations. It's only going to get worse unless you treat it."

"I do not."

"Face it. You've been mad for years. Stark, raving, Tom O' Bedlam mad, and it's no act."

"I have not!" I screamed. I coughed. I heaved and spit up a black substance, like choking bile. Unable to breathe, the room started spinning. My sister shrieked in horror, out of genuine concern maybe, but I think I heard another laugh escape from Sheldon's distended gut.

DOCTOR *GILROY*

*T*ake a boy who's literary and teach him to write a corporate memo

Take a man who's a born poet and force him to design greeting cards

Take a man with a penchant for math and make him account for every penny

Stick him in a box, and soon he will be sawing logs

Teach a boy he is what he buys

Dull and blunt his ability to ask why

The why is not important; it's the bottom line when all things are corporate

Do as we say, not as we do

Take a pill when you're feeling blue

Unstripe the tigers and muzzle the wild dogs

Stick him in a box, and soon he will be sawing logs

A poem attributed to Jackson Leman, written at the age of 13 or 14, photographed and used as evidence in Doctor William Gilroy's treatment, this eminent psychiatrist to the stars.

Dysfunction is blunted to a dull nubbin by excessive amounts of cash at your disposal. If my family was broke, there would be certain reality television show producers beating down the door of our trailer offering us up as a testament to how fortunate you are not to be us. You dream of your riches while we dreamed of your ability to have a quiet serenity. Life is grand when you have limited possibilities. You have a choice to just be nice to people. We have to hire scores of attorneys to do our business. Niceties and niceness has always interfered with our bottom line. We stood poised to inherit billions of dollars and be instantaneous additions to the Forbes 400, but our conscience never developed much more than our ability to participate in the economy. It was never a question of whether we should do something or not.

It was a question of whether or not it made good fiscal sense, and we hired advisors to tell us this, and we trusted them, because we paid them exorbitant salaries. Father was involved in so many shady, underhanded deals through shell corporations and probably underworld deals in third world countries, greased hands with palm oil, paid money to warlords, paid them whatever they wanted for favorable mining rights and a chance to get at precious natural resources. I really had no idea what I was walking into.

Plant life only needs the sun, water, and nutritious soil to grow. Human life suffered under the factor that it needed a fourth factor to foster growth and development. It's a good idea, but I ain't doing it until you show me some money. I spend my time doing what you want me to do, you part with some of your ability to make other people do what you want them to do, and you hope that in the end, you have more of an ability to make more people do what you want them to do, provided you choose that and not buying one of from among the thousands of luxury goods and money traps in this world. Father never gave his time to us, and he always left money on the dresser when he left.

You know, when my sister and her husband Sheldon came at me with the knowledge that Avalon and his daughter, I mean...those two employees... were sent to apprehend me; a mission that the previously dispatched Red had failed to do. I should have known that it was best to stay away from this place.

Sheldon wasn't the least sneaky about his intentions. I should have known at that time that my family would stop at nothing to bring me home. One errand boy averted, I should have known they would have sent more. There were probably hundreds of them out there looking for me, when I was finally brought in, like some wanted outlaw. It would have been best just to turn around and go home, let my father die in peace, and avoid the situation altogether. I let them all get the best of me.

Not that I haven't been a completely trusting person in all facets of my life, but perhaps I put the trust in all the wrong people. Like a blind gardener, I watered the weeds and neglected the beautiful flowers until they shriveled up and died and fertilized the weeds. Well, I saw that sometimes a thorny scragglebush has bright beautiful blossoms, and sometimes a plant that you believe and hope will produce a magnificent flower and delicious fruit, in the end, turns out to be nasty like milkweed. Toxic, in fact.

My sister, Hannah, was one of those people. No, not toxic. She was a person with such an intrinsic goodness that it blinded her to seeing people's faults. If she saw their faults, it was only towards an aim of helping them to improve. She had poor decision-making skills because most of the facets of her life became overgrown with this capacity for goodness, or rather her goodness shown such a bright light on her being that any negatives just washed out.

When Hannah informed me that this very morning our family friend, my head-shrinker, Dr. William Gilroy, and my confidant for, oh, five whole years from the time of my mother's suicide to the time I went away to Princeton University as a legacy admission, would be flying directly from the trenches in Detroit in order to give me a psychological evaluation. In Detroit, he did his own self-imposed penance for bilking my family of millions in purported treatments while he knew the patient (me) was a recalcitrant case. He now aided in psychoanalyzing the burnt out victims of the Detroit automotive off shoring of jobs. I was not a candidate for a job, nor was I on trial. For once and all, they wanted to find out just what was wrong with me.

Why did my own sister order a complete physical and psychological profile of me? I discussed the prospects with Marcus, who confided in me some very important information that I had missed out on while Marcus, Willard, and I were separated.

He laid the whole damn plan out to me.

While searching for gasoline, Willard and Marcus came upon a man who purported to be an agent of Leman Global Industries Security Division who was looking for a former agent by the name of William Meriwether. The agent showed Marcus a photo of the man, who Marcus told me was the man I called Red. The agent told Marcus that William Meriwether was a former employee of the Leman Global Industries Security Division (LGISD), but had been terminated for "impropriety" a couple of years back and that he was extremely dangerous. Someone, the folks at LGISD had no idea who, had hired William Meriwether to track me down and perhaps do some injustices to me. Who knows who these people were, or what their plans were for me. Marcus assured me that no one in my family sent Red after me, and that Red had surely "dropped the ball," in today's sports centric parlance, instead of getting a "slam dunk." At any rate, Marcus told me, I had better watch my back. By the time that Willard and Marcus finished talking to the agent, who really wasn't interested in apprehending me any more than he was in finding Red, I was gone, nowhere to be found.

Marcus also informed me that the motorcycle gangs in the bar were scouring the entirety of the West for the Judge and its occupants. No one better dare touch a Biker's ride; it's like messing with his old lady or daughter. They, too, had contacted some more nefarious individuals than themselves and had organized a contract to be put on my head. Luckily, they really didn't know who I was. Marcus told me he would be heading out on another one of his wild adventures, because this place was far too docile for him, and my sister would never give it up. He had tried with a few of the younger maids, too, but they were also clapped up pretty tight and professional. He said they giggled like schoolgirls when he made his amorous advances, but that was about it. Before he left, he told me that he would be back before long. When he walked out the open door, I had a feeling this would be the last time I saw the likes of Marcus Hanely in a long time. Willard and Marcus would ride out into the sunset for sure.

In walked Dr. Gilroy, no rap-rap on the doorframe, and he could have really surprised me if he had waited a couple more minutes, because after Hanley left, I had an overwhelming urge to tug my beef. The doctor put all those flights of fancy to rest. Good ole Dr. William Gilroy, my psychiatrist since I could remember. Rather than talk to me, my father hired this expensive dolt to follow me around for an entire year after my mother's untimely death.

I suppose he wasn't that bad of a guy. I mean he was a fellow human being. Unfortunately, he became like any other employee of Leman, an employee in perpetuity. If you show that you are serving a purpose then father would keep you around on the payroll. Once your purpose is fulfilled or your contract period expires, you will be informed whether or not your contract was being renewed. Gilroy had to give my father a full briefing of my treatment progress every month to justify his existence as an employee. During periods of contraction and downsizing, he became especially nervous. There was no way he would make as much money as my father was shelling out in private practice, and now he only had one patient...someone who was not damaged in the least, but someone who was young, naïve, and very open to the powers of suggestion.

For safety's sake and to avoid any future lawsuits, which may result from my untimely demise, Gilroy recorded all of our conversations from the time I was 14 years old and the unfortunate incident happened, to the time I was 19 years old, psychologically cleared, and ready to attend my legacy admission to Princeton University. You know, I may seem obsessed with saying I'm a legacy admission all the time, but it was a point of contention between my father and I. I would have rather wanted to go to a state school that I could get into on my own merits, but father would have none of that. "No, you're going to Princeton," he would roar. Gilroy never really asked me how that made me feel.

Sometimes when I was feeling pangs of ennui, I would pick the lock to his quarters when he was out on the town reveling in his fancy car, and I would review his notes on me. These brought me the greatest amount of entertainment. It was much more entertainment than television or going out and spending money ever could have given me. I started to tailor my performances to cause this guy consternation. Any dream, the more bizarre I made it, the more bizarre his speculations about my interior state became. Most all of the notes stated that I was on the verge of a complete breakdown, that I was a fragile egg and he was an acid bath for Easter.

Sometimes I would change his observations and save them over the old reports that he had typed into his computer. The guy's password was 123456, for chrissakes. This caused him great fits at the end of the month when he prepared reports for my father that said, "The boy is totally cured! Miracle!" and self deprecating statements that I would write in the reports such as, "I could probably help this kid out, if I knew what I was doing and wasn't a total charlatan." On a nearly hourly basis, I was required to report my mood to him, what I was feeling at the precise time he asked me. When I was indifferent I would tell him that I was contemplating suicide. When I was contemplating suicide, I would tell him that I was happy. For an entire week straight I told him that I was an overflowing infinity of bliss, when I was really feeling quite empty inside. I composed lovely poetry as evidence, which he burned in his room's stove. Destruction of evidence that I was on the road to recovery. Recovery meant he would be out of a steady, easy paycheck.

Something troubled me about my mother's suicide. It wasn't the fact that she took that way out, that she didn't love me, that she abandoned us. It was that I was the person to discover her, and I swore as I walked in the room, I saw someone leave the room through the adjacent French doors. The person was a shadowy figure, and by the time I managed to catch up to him or her, he or she had bound off into the woods.

I told this to my father, who pooh-poohed me, and I told Dr. Gilroy, who claimed that it was an aberration of a troubled young man who was suffering symptoms of Post Traumatic Stress Syndrome at seeing his mother dead and bloody. I maintained that I had seen someone to everybody, and they laughed it off or dismissed it out of hand that someone could just sneak onto the Leman Family Compound with security greater than Fort Knox, murder the Mrs. Leman in her private quarters, and abscond from detection. Foolishness, they all said. Still, I know what I saw. It was no hallucination. The person was wearing black with a green ski mask.

The good doctor asked sheepishly how I had slept. During the night, he told me, I had been thrashing around in my sleep, and he was forced to give me a mild sedative to help me rest more peacefully.

I told the doctor that I really had no complaints, except that I was not allowed to see my father. I was quite good, by this time, at lying to the rat. The good doctor said that given my current state of mind, I might upset my father's fragile health and send him off from the shadows of the valley of death, to full blown dying, and that no one was ready for that right now, so it was best I kept my distance until the good doctor could set my mind on an even keel. In my mind, the old bastard was going to kick the bucket anyway, so hastening him in his demise would only do him some good.

"Come on Doctor, what's the real reason that I'm not allowed to see my poor father? He only wants to see his one and only son. That's all he asks."

The doctor did not respond immediately and the look on his face, one of deep consternation, suggested to me that he was chewing some deep, dark secret over and over again, in deliberations over whether to tell me what he ruminated over. This man needed some softening up. So I asked him how long we had known each other. I adopted the role of the timid patient, the role he was used to seeing me in. That was, until the first well calculated words came pouring out of his mouth like salt in old wounds.

"We met right after your mother's death," the Doctor began, "and I was brought in to try and console you, because your father didn't know..."

"What? He didn't know how? Say it like you mean it Doctor...we are old friends. He didn't want to take the time to deal with his basket case son, just like he didn't want to take the time to deal with the son's basket case of a mother. I'll tell you what. We weren't born basket cases. He made us this way. He paid for what he got in the end. If that man took a fraction of the time he spent traveling around and inspecting his holdings and doing god-knows-what and spent it with us instead, perhaps some normalcy could have spawned in the family instead of a bunch of half jacked quacks and lunatics settling here. Let's face it Doctor, my problems are quite insignificant. I'm doing well for myself. I'm a bestselling author with another book on the way, whenever I get around to actually putting it down on the computer. Unlike my sister, god bless her heart, I don't really have any real addictions to speak of, other than I really enjoy booze every once in a while. But who doesn't? I'm quite unflawed doctor, like a magnificent A-clarity DeBeers Diamond."

"When's the last time you spoke to Marcus, Jackson?"

"Marcus...Marcus...Marcus...hmmmmm...Marcus. Doesn't ring a bell. I don't know. Had to have been over five years ago now. Why? Do you think he's a bad influence on me?"

"He's a fiction. An illusion. A hall -u -cin -ation. He's a character in your novel, *Asymmetric Hearts*. No more, no less. You, in your years of self imposed exile, you've fashioned him into a real person in your mind. He's a delusion. Quite fixed, and hopefully not permanent."

"Marcus is as real as you or me."

"No, Jackson, he isn't real. He has no vitality. I know he exists on paper, much like Nicholas Nickelby, or Captain Ahab, or Hamlet, but he's no more a real Dane than you and I are real Danes. Tell me something. Does Marcus Hanely ever do anything that doesn't involve some sort of secret intrigue known only to you?"

I thought about it for a moment. Marcus had never really done anything public. He never held a job. He never sang karaoke when we went out on the town. He never, ever even ordered a drink. I offered him a drink, and he always refused. I always thought that he ran off with a particular woman because I saw her leave, and I saw him leave. I thought they were being very discreet about their shagging, but on the other hand, most of the people who hooked up in bars made out in front of everyone. I told myself that Marcus Hanely was a true gentleman who didn't ever make a scene. I never really ever saw him talk to a woman in public.

They always seemed to make eyes at him, and he would follow them out when they left. And funny thing was, he always sat in my way, so the women would always look at him, and not me. But, if he was a phantom, that means all those women were looking at me! I only heard his stories after the fact. Suddenly, all the comfort that Marcus had provided me for all these years disappeared. Not even a slight trickling of the dam happened before it burst and the floodwaters of despair and disappointment washed over my soul. I cried.

The doctor told me that it was okay to cry. That this was normal when a fixed delusion is discovered by the owner to be false. He told me the next phases I would feel would be a profound emptiness, and following that, a horrendous, soul gnawing fear. I passed through the emptiness phase rather quickly, having felt it before and knowing that it had no power over me. The fear...it had me shaking. I wretched in the corner off the edge of my bed.

"That's it, Jackson. Get rid of him. He isn't real. He's a fantasy, a figment of your harried brain. I take it that if you would have spent the time putting his imagined exploits on paper, you would have the fodder for 10 or 15 books, but see, you never really believed him. Instead, you wasted your time chasing the phantom, courting him. It isn't time lost. You will just need a great deal of talk time to weave your way out of this convoluted web."

I sobbed. It was if I had been informed that my best friend had died. It was worse than if he died. I was just informed and came to realize that he never existed. His perfection. His poise. All fictions. He was too good to be true, and he was dead, evaporated into the mists of this psychoanalyst's verbosity. Dr. Gilroy, for how much of a hack he was, had a compelling argument. And think about all the women I missed out on talking to! The doctor kept talking, weaving a tapestry to try and bring me to reality. Okay...granted Marcus was a figment of my imagination, but Willard? Gentle Willard? He had to be a figment then too! And Bill Dickel...the Bible Salesman! A figment! Nothing more than phantoms! What the fuck is real?

"Who did you drive here with?"

"I guess I drove myself here."

"Whoever had interaction with Marcus Hanely did not exist."

"I had interaction with Marcus Hanely."

"My point exactly. In your state of mind, you were barely functional. It's a miracle you made it here without getting lost in the desert. Tell me. You were captured at the front gate with an antique WWI Colt M1911 pistol. Where did you get it?"

"I got it at a firearm's auction."

"You aren't allowed to purchase firearms. We had you blacklisted."

"I gave them the money in cash, and they handed it over. They were all too happy to give it to me. Even told me where I could buy the bullets for it."

"Why did you bring the pistol with you?"

'The roads are dangerous."

"No they aren't. What sort of thoughts led you to bring the pistol?"

"Listen. I don't remember. I had just bought it. I thought it would bring me a level of protection that I wouldn't have without it."

"Your maid called us and told us you brought it along. You had us all terribly worried that you were planning on doing something..."

"Crazy? That's why you dispatched all those bumbling fools to find me."

"They found you."

"Send a fool to find a fool."

"No one said that. They are very well trained."

I looked at the Doctor long and hard. A smile came over my face. The crow's feet that developed around his weary eyes demonstrated that this man had suffered a lifetime's worth of problems. His patients' problems became his own problems. Maybe I had judged him too harshly in the past. Something dawned on me. This man had spent much of his professional life with only a few patients. Right now, the Doctor looked like he considered his life a total failure. I smiled even broader, showing off some teeth. I'm sure it was quite a maniacal smile.

"What are you smiling about?"

"Does there have to be a reason for everything, Doctor? Can I not just smile and enjoy your company, old friend?"

"There is a reason for everything."

"No, there isn't."

"Fine. Let me reiterate. Every human behavior is the product of a rational thought process or the product of an irrational impulse, which itself is the reason for a particular behavior. I asked you why you smiled. What is the reason behind your smiling?"

"I just thought about something."

"What was the thought?"

"I'd rather not tell you. It was humorous to me, but I'm afraid it would be lost on you."

The Doctor's expression changed from one of curiosity to one that headed downhill.

"More of your games, Jackson?"

"Nope."

"I know you used to break into my quarters."

"I didn't. I resent your accusation."

"This whole place is wired for sound and video. Didn't you know that?"

"Really?"

"It is. Your father is quite the security-conscious individual."

"So there are tapes of the entire house?"

"I was only given access to my own private quarters. I thought some of the maids were altering the records for some strange reason."

"Well, I apologize."

The Doctor sat there in his leather chair, a leather backed lush chair that was much more comfortable than my steely bed frame, which I was still tied to like I was some sort of axe murdering maniac.

"Can you untie me?"

"Cooperation gets you untied."

"Am I a prisoner here? In my own house?"

"You were captured by the gate guards with a gun. They're considering you a danger to yourself and others."

"Since when do the gate guards have the final say?"

"They don't. I do."

"I'm no longer the boy you used to badger on a daily basis, Doctor."

"No, you're a man now."

"I'm an accomplished author."

"Right, about that..."

"Oh? My agent called you to harass me about a new manuscript, too?"

"No. Since we're into telling the truth, I figured we should tell the truth to you about your career as a novelist and your millions of fans."

"I am a novelist. I wrote *Asymmetric Hearts*. It's for sale at Wal-Mart. I saw it there. You can't take that away from me."

"Oh it's all true."

My sister and her husband entered my cell.

"Why are you holding me here?"

My sister had a genuine look of concern on her face. Sheldon looked as smug as ever when my sister wasn't looking and faked concern whenever her vision passed over his big fat face. I still don't know what she saw in him. I would have to ask her the first chance I got, meaning sans smug idiot. I didn't want him misconstruing my concern with a reason to write reports about me. I would call her somewhere private. The garden perhaps. Father had a lovely garden that we used to play in as children. Sheldon folded his arms across his man boobs. His Harvard University MBA kept him well fed.

WAREHOUSE #17

"When can I see my father?" I asked the Doctor. Perhaps the good Doctor would intercede on my behalf and get me an audience. Even for me, the eldest (and only son) getting an audience with my father growing up was like getting an audience with the Pope.

"It's probably not for the best that you see him now. He's very fragile, undergoing constant treatment for his condition."

"What's the point? The man has to be ninety two years old."

"Ninety seven."

"Jesus."

"Longevity runs in your father's family. But we know what was in your dear mother's."

"Yes. Of course."

"Right. We do."

"What's this about anyway?"

"What do you mean?"

"Why hold me here against my will? Sheldon and my sister had something to do with it, right?"

"I'm not at liberty to discuss all the aspects of your treatment with you. I only know that we're going to try to bring you back to reality by showing you all of your delusions. If this doesn't work, we may have to take drastic measures."

"Like what drastic measures? You're going to have me committed against my will? Do you know what sort of media shitstorm that will cause?"

"That has been discussed."

"I'm an adult. My sister and her husband don't make my decisions for me."

"I'm sorry. When you were caught with the firearm, you came into violation of certain stipulations of an agreement, the one you signed when you reached the age of 18 and went out on your own, that you would do nothing to bring discredit upon your father or the family corporation, Leman Global Industries."

"Oh yeah, the one that said I wouldn't bring tarnish upon the precious Leman name, any of the brands we manufacture, or any of the subsidiaries. Basically, the 'be a good boy' clause. How close to disowning me did my father come?"

"Disowning you for what?"

"When I changed my studies from business to everything else I eventually took?"

"You mean when you up and declared yourself a novelist?"

"Yeah."

"He encouraged you, of course, as would any good father."

"Encouraged me? The last time we spoke he said it was a piss poor idea. Real piss poor."

"He's responsible for your literary success as much as he's responsible for bringing you into the world. Let's just say you were a pet project of his, from a distance."

"He didn't give a shit about my literary career. I did it all on my own. I found my own agent. I wrote the damn manuscript myself."

"Sure, you wrote it. But your father helped nudge it on the path to literary success."

"Success?"

"Book sales. You know, success."

"I don't understand."

"We couldn't allow a member of the Leman family to be a penniless writer...a failure. You had to be a success. Everything your father touches is a success. *Asymmetric Hearts*, with his goading, became an instant success. Tell me, did you think for one minute that your father played no role in your success?"

"No. He didn't. He couldn't have cared less."

"I forgot, Jackson. You're one of those types of guys that need evidence. You don't accept anything on blind faith," he laughed. "Except in following your little buddy, Marcus."

"What kind of Doctor are you?"

He just smiled.

Sheldon and my sister walked in. "We've arranged a little field trip for you."

"This agreement is over when my father dies, you know that. I'm leaving after that."

"Just come out to the car with us, Jackson," Sheldon said, with his arms crossed like a real tough guy.

"Are we going to a Nuggets game? I want to see Carmelo play."

"He hasn't played for the Nuggets in years. Stop being a smartass."

They unstrapped me. I needed no coaxing to leave with them. I floated to the SUV like the forlorn ghost of some failed, hack writer still clamoring for the attention of the living from my dusty grave. Armed guards brandished small compact machine pistols as they guarded me, with blast furnace intensity in their violent sun glassed eyes, scanning for threats. We moved in concert to the convoy of Black SUVs.

My sister had glazed over eyes like she had been crying. I wanted to ask her what was wrong, but I couldn't find the words because my nemesis was also in the SUV with us, and my concern fused into my growing rage at the very sight of this swollen prick. We packed into a fleet of SUVs, black ones, real sinister and governmental looking with the LGI fancy logo on the side. It was a simple, sophisticated logo, really, unchanged to one of those modern Internet friendly logos, and my grandfather, after he inherited the biz from his father drew the logo on a beer soaked napkin. It was that simple.

The convoy snaked its way through the Denver streets toward the warehouse district. I recall when I was a child, perhaps four or five, maybe older, I cannot fully remember my exact age, that I declared to my mother that I was going to be a writer. I did this whilst tugging on her shirt, so it must have been when my mother towered over me, so I must have been three or four. I had taken fondly to watching my father working in his study, surrounded by books, great leather bound books with gold lined pages, and I recall asking my father how these marvelous things came to be. He never really read to me because he really did not have the time. I recall him telling me that people wrote all these books. I asked my father if he had written any of these books that were on his immense shelves - oaken and lined with gold name plates that I could not read. He told me that he had not written any of the books.

I asked him why he had not written any of the books, and he told me that people who write good books have something important to say, otherwise the books they write are forgotten about a few months after they are written or at most a few short years after they are written and these books turn to dust over time because no one prints these books anymore.

I asked my father whether he thought that he had anything important to say, and my father seemed to get annoyed with me, his face reddened, his hands tensed on the book he was reading, and he told me that he does very important things for the world every day. I took this as a sign to leave my father alone in his study and was always apprehensive about pestering him in there. Often I would just watch him at his study from the door, or sometimes I would climb up the shelves to the second floor and sit in the corner and watch him work.

I would watch him pour over the volumes. I don't recall what they were, but he would often read books that had large prints of paintings in them. It seemed he read these more than anything else in the library. Sometimes I would look at them. They were paintings of religious figures with their faces twisted and contorted in Agony, paintings of maidens with looks of mirth on their faces and round buxom bodies, and paintings of fruits and vegetables and dead animals sitting on tables.

I never got the courage to ask my father why he was looking at so many pictures of paintings. I asked my mother. My mother told me it was because my father was spending some of his hard earned money being an art collector, but we would probably never see the paintings because he always kept them in his places of business to bring joy to the workers and clients.

I asked my mother why he didn't have any in the home, and mother told me it was because he always put the business first ahead of everything and that I would understand when I was older and ran the business myself. I told her that I did not want to run the business and would rather just write, because I felt like I had something important to say, or maybe I would paint. My mother laughed. It was not a cruel laugh or a spiteful laugh, but more a laugh of surprise and shock. A nervous laugh. She said to me that the Leman men do not write books or paint because they are too busy with business to pursue those trifling arts.

The prick, Sheldon, woke me from my midday daydream and shocked me into the reality of the warehouse district. Our gas-guzzling SUV belched emissions that would choke the feral kittens that darted in and out of trailer connexes with contents that had not seen the light of day as of yet, but which were most likely from China.

Life comes in fragments. Memories of memories that are only assembled when a pivotal moment is about to dawn and bring its full weight to the forefront. The star is about to take the stage. In reverse, it is hindsight. Going forward, clairvoyance. I call it being a student of human nature and knowing that people tend to behave in the future how they behaved in the past. Unless someone is a true madman, because madmen are unpredictable. I learned most all of this in school when I got my worthless, impractical, and utterly eclectic education. I looked at Sheldon, who right now seemed very content letting the rumors swirl around; at least he was in the limelight.

"Where are you taking me, Sheldy? Off to the Stock Exchange? I didn't know Denver had a board of trade. Are you betting your wife's inheritance on cattle futures in this Western cow town? You can subdivide the world to the smallest infinitesimal pieces, you can chop it into vapor, sell it off to the highest bidders, but you cannot even see your nose in the front of your own face without a mirror. It's a sad, sad day, Sheldy. I don't know what you're up to, but I'm not buying it."

"You will," Sheldon said, and taciturnly croaked like a sea urchin being yanked up from its rocky home by a hungry Japanese skin diver.

"Sure, Sheldy. What drugs did you give me back there? What dope has that foul family doctor masquerading as a headshrinker? What smack, coke, weed, pharmies, has he forced down my gullet? I'm remarkably able to think clearly for the first time in a long time. Is it something experimental? Am I a foul test subject? Are you doing human experimentation? Call *The New York Times*! Am I an Algernon for your pharmacopeia? I don't recall signing a consent form. You're in breach. You're all in breach! You're doing human experimentation just like some gang of Nazis! What are you up to?"

"Calm down, Jackson. We're not up to anything."

"The Doctor told us he would get very paranoid now. It's this phase of his cure."

The SUV convoy whizzed by the warehouses. I remembered what that lily-livered douche bag, the Agent Tannenbaum had told me...that I should look into a certain warehouse. "Are you taking me to warehouse 17, Sheldy? And what am I going to find there?"

"I don't know, Jackson," he said, focused on my sister, who now had tears in her eyes. She tried to sob silently.

"Why are you crying, sis?"

She remained silent, as silent as the doors of the abandoned, gaping warehouses we passed or maybe the ones with the crusty FOR SALE or LEASE signs on them, ones that were full of life once, perhaps around the year 2000 or 2001.

"Can't you see, oh sister of mine, that this hubby of yours is leading you astray? And why are you doing this, Sheldy? Oh, let me think...father is dying. That's what my dear sister told me over the phone. Father is going to go the way of the Dodo and dinosaur, taking the great leap into the unknown, carving an epitaph on a tomb, sailing off into a sepulcher, commissioning statues like Ozymandias..."

"Shut up, Jackson. You're only making matters worse on yourself."

"What matters are worse, my dear sister? Do you think I care about father and his money? I've my own money! I'm a novelist, remember! I'm a very successful novelist! I'm a writer..."

Sheldon chuckled. It was a smallish chortle that could have escaped from his lips quite on accident. The driver twitched, perhaps sensing the karmic disturbance in the cabin of the luxury SUV, which reverberated off the Madagascarian rosewood paneling, a substance that I thought was banned from import into the United States, but somehow these pricks got their hands on some and decided it would be a good decorative feature in our GMC SUV. They acquired enough for this sickly fleet of SUVs and probably leveled the trees with axes made from the bones of some endangered Asiatic Ibex.

I should like to think that "rich" people were socially responsible creatures, caring for their own fellow man instead of designing nets to further entrap them and shake out the contents of their pockets. And it was unfortunate...Sheldon probably could have contributed greatly to society, but he went to school when the great vogue amongst brainiacs was to go into financial mathematics with the view of being an MBA and hedge fund manager.

These were men who could probably aid greatly in noble pursuits such as finding the cure for cancer, discovering mathematical algorithms and making advances in physics to increase man's understanding of the natural world. Instead they sunk their hooks and wrapped their minds around the world of men, the economy, and turning a small pile of money into a larger pile of money. No longer having the courage for noble endeavors, they declared moneymaking the noblest of the endeavors. It is an artifice. It is not real.

So was Sheldon's chuckle...petty. He was a petty man, obsessed with money and making a bigger pile of money from a smaller pile of money, and the pile would always be small to him. Greed. That was his religion, his way of life. He was a member of the cult of the spendthrift. He got a charge from it, a rush, like someone would get from climbing Mount Everest, but that too was played out. He got the same rush that the bastard pirate Christo Colombo got when it was formally announced to the great European Courts that he had sailed west and bumped into something. Sheldon discovered new ties made with exotic fibers, tailored suits for fat boys, buttons milled from rare woods and rare bones from rare animals, indistinguishable on sight from other, cheaper buttons, but known to the owner...that they had a suit with a button, held in place by a single middling rare wool thread or alpaca nose hair was in fact one of the last of its kind.

Sheldon usually looked marvelous, but that could not change the smug look on a face with eyes set too close together, pretty much an inch from perfect symmetry, and a nose that, though altered with rhinoplasty by a highly skilled and well compensated plastic surgeon from some unpronounceable small country, some ten-thousand pound brain who could have used those God-given hands to heal the actually sick instead of mentally sick, but they, whom decided the best way to wealth was to serve the rich with rhinoplasty and Botox. I think he was probably one of those Doctors whom would join some cause to repair the cleft palates of poor third world children, but only when he had enough money to retire comfortably. Levels of comfort, like amounts of money were never satisfactory, so he would continue mortgaging his future.

People really believe that time is money, but go ask Nathan Rothschild what he thinks about that notion. Dig up his bones and hold a séance. Ask Billy Shaggy Beard if he was happier a playwright, or usurer. How I hated Sheldon! Everything for which he stood, which was nothing other than his own droopy, lumpy, soft self, I hated. And he hated himself...so I guess he was doubly hated. I have never said that I hated anyone before as much as I genuinely dislike my sister's husband and how every time his luxury Gulfstream G7 took off, I wish it would crash into the side of a mountain or a plummet into some mega church hosting the Southern Baptist's convention, immolating a few hundred of them, but sparing the children. Children can and do change. The adults are the ones that leave me thinking and worrying.

Sheldon, oh Sheldon, just what seed was planted in you to make you such a creep? Many may think the same thing about me, I mean, a person who would give up mostly all of what I've had handed to me just for an opportunity to write some of the thoughts that are perambulating through my brain down on paper for a posterity that is not guaranteed? I'll tell you why. Writing is one of the only pure endeavors left anymore. As far as art goes, the temptation to follow is it's most strong amongst "writers," so when something truly original and daring comes along, it is a breath of fresh wind that kindles fires for generations. When a character comes alive on the page, they become one of your constant companions, a source of strength to draw on in times of trouble, a bellwether, someone who actually lives. Someone we cannot imagine not being in the world. I say this now, but whether like all true philosophy, the real test is whether or not I can make it my way of life and live it.

Sheldon coldly ordered the driver, again nondescript save for his dark sunglasses, which were stunning, and his OJ mad stabber gloves, to turn into the parking lot to Warehouse 17. The doom-faced drivers parked the convoy and the security directorate secured the building with the wondrous efficiency of a gaggle of Marine Corps privates. I was impressed, as a civilian, with their lethargy, their lack of precision, and general apathy, quite possibly apparent in the me because we were in the nicer section of the warehouse district in a major metropolitan area in the United States, and the Arab section of town was quite small, the most terroristic looking people being several miles away in Aurora. Still, rules were rules and they had to be followed. It was even more comical the few times my father, Sheldon, and Hannah attended professional golfing events and the SWAT team walked with them down the narrow fairways of the most exclusive of the exclusive enclaves of White America, Augusta National.

"One last time. What are you going to show me, Sheldon?"

"Be patient. Patience is a virtue."

"Okay. We'll see, then," I said and crossed my arms.

Sheldon opened the door and disappeared into the bowels of the warehouse. A few Secret Service rejects followed him in, equipped with night vision goggles. I heard the all clear shouted several times. The garage door, a really massive iron or steel door that looked like the door of a Air Force hangar housing an ultra expensive, ultra secret, jet test plane, opened slowly, grinded against itself, and sounded like a tank tread on steel plate. It creaked against the walls of the building, and shouted a warning. I could not see inside. I looked at my sister's face. She appeared concerned. She noticed me watching her and looked away, as if she did not even want to see any reaction from me. Her hands tensely gripped her coat, like it was a medical apparatus to measure her remaining life force.

"What's wrong, Bean?" I asked her.

"I'm sorry, Jackson. I really am."

"For what?"

The door shuddered shut, like a creaky old man suffering dementia coming to rest at a fork in the hallway of an old folks home, undecided as to whether he wanted the bathroom or his room or even which way they were. The lights cracked on. I peered into the glimmering warehouse expecting to see ingots stacked on top of each other. However, the warehouse was full of books.

"It's full of books," I said.

"That's it, Jackson!" Sheldon called out.

I walked forward. Towards the first stack, about to ask him what books there were, and thinking them textbooks, maybe my father had diversified into becoming a textbook manufacturer too, and then I saw the red covers, the dust jacket. A few were upside down, and my photograph was on the back page.

"Why...it's..." the words trapped themselves in my throat. Tears welled in my eyes and my throat was on fire.

The sheer immensity of the stacks, some of the books dusty and dog-eared as if they had been haphazardly stacked, briefly leafed through on a bus or train, and finally discarded. The stacks were at least ten feet tall, and as I ran around the warehouse and grew winded, they covered the area of football fields. I ripped books from the stacks. They were all mine! *Asymmetric Hearts*! First fucking edition! It could only mean one thing. I wailed. I crashed into a pile taller than me. It tottered, barely budged. I hit again, with my shoulder.

A book from the top of the circus tent crashed to the bitter concrete floor. My photograph remained, smiling on the back cover, the front pressed to the cruel, cruel cement floor. Hell seemed to open up around it, with all its broken souls and brimstone clutching dead fingers to drag me down into my doom. I would have willingly gone because I had to look at him. I had to answer to him. Sheldon. Standing there.

Gloating. There was a smile on his face, plastered there and growing wider and broader as my own despair grew. I took some deep breaths, and with the air filling my lungs, I finally worked up the courage to ask him, "Why?"

"There aren't any family members who aren't a success."

"It was for your own good, Jackson. You should be a success."

"But don't you see! I'm not a success! This is all one great big illusion! I'm not a success! My success was bought and paid for! Purchased on credit!"

"It was an investment in your success!" Sheldon yelled back at me, wheezing, trying to catch up with me as I ran around the warehouse like a madman, pitching books onto the floor.

I pulled a lighter from my pants. A nice Zippo. I don't remember where I got it.

I struck it.

"What are you doing with that?"

"I'm going to burn this place down! It will go up quickly! There's so much shit piled up here to feed the flames! You utterly sick fools! How did you expect me to react to the truth?"

"The truth is what the people out there think! They think you're a multimillion novel-selling author, and father's little investment in your enterprise established you in that truth! They don't know the actual truth!"

"It's a fraud! A fucking fraud! I wouldn't have wasted so much time! Not writing something new! Resting on my laurels! I would have tried again and again and again and again until I got something good! I would have filled up the drawers and cabinets of my house with scribblings! It would have been a better fate than this revelation! Damn you all! Damn you! Why the hell did you have to show it to me? Why?!"

I knocked over another pile of books and kicked them, and sent them skittering across the slick concrete floor.

"Father's dying, Jackson."

"I know! Well, I don't know! You haven't allowed me to see him!"

"We wanted you to be free of your little delusions. We wanted you to know how much father really loved you."

"I'm going to fucking burn this place. I'll burn it in another way. Jackson Leman is dead! He's as dead as a fucking Tyrannosaurus Rex! Extinct! Never again will Mr. Leman set foot near a pen. Never again will Mr. Leman see fit to drag a risky run across a hate filled blank and fill it up with life. You bastards have taken the will out of me. You've crushed it. And you wonder why I never came to see you bores. You fucking horrible, dead bores. Take me to my father so I can bid him adieu. Then I will bid you all adieu."

I stormed out of the warehouse, kicking whatever piece of cowshit was in my way, throwing my arms in an attempt to break my way through the stacks of rotted rubbish. It might as well have been stacks of newspaper with a headline that no one would ever care about: "Famous Author is a Suicide." I reached the SUV and piled into it, slamming the door.

"Drive, you bastard. Take me to my father."

"Can't go yet, sir. We have to wait for Mr. Grimbone."

"Sheldon? Fuck him. He can walk his fat ass home. What? Is he calling the shots now?"

"Appears that way, sir. Don't really know who's in charge."

The subcontracted Wacky Hutt security guardsmen were made to sign non-disclosure agreements about what they had seen in the warehouse, as if it was a secret test airplane that I had so vainly hoped it was, stamped PROPERTY OF US GOVERNMENT, and not some piece of shit romantic trash novel that purported to be authentic literature, as if I had any idea about what that term actually meant. Literature! Shit! We write because we must. Otherwise, we're skin bags. Lonely little bags of skin that blow swiftly in the breeze to some final destination. We're tumbleweed! Snails that carry our works on our backs like shells. Writing leaves a snail trail in the dead dust. Better than any marble monument ever could.

Better than any pyramid could embolden someone's soul. I had been failing. Taking journeys inside myself, drudging up memories that were better left to the slimy under rocks. It is *tres difficile* being the eldest son of a multibillionaire industrialist. Everyone expects you to take over the reigns and be as brilliant as your father and his father before him, and his father before him, an infinite fucking regression of brilliance terminating in you. You've got the DNA to be a profound business thinker.

If my father would have furnished me with a happier childhood, maybe I wouldn't have seen fit to become a random scribbler. And what do I want to write now? I want to write the truth. I want to write something that unburdens me, teaches someone how to carry a burden, and then the burden disappears. What a terrible burden it is dredging all of this up, casting off invisible chains in the name of some freedom which itself could be just another chain, and now, is only a word that people toss around like a Wham-O Frisbee!

I go off on these little diatribes, and I always find the means to escape inside myself when the pressure becomes too great externally. And the pressure builds inside me like a floodwater dammed up behind concrete. There really is no stopping it. I cannot stop from going off. And how do I go off? I go shopping. Sometimes I do something foolish like wrap my Ferrari around a tree. I drove drunk and cruised down Pacific Coast Highway at a speed that far exceeded the posted recommended speed on some of those hairpin turns. So what? If I would have hurtled off the cliff, I would have only killed myself.

I believed I had lived a full life and experienced as much as I was meant to experience. I have not written a goddamn thing for ten years, and I call myself a goddamn writer. I'm nothing. My only talents are spending money and looking at blithe, insouciant girly men's magazines that forecast trends and tells me how to be a part of fast retreating history. The warehouse was evidence enough that I'm a hack who is reliant on marketing. And the market has dried up. No wonder everyone is screaming for a new novel.

Sheldon informed me in the car that I would be forced to write a new novel if I did not produce one. They might even steal my name and ghostwrite the novel by committee. He wondered if I read the ultra fine print of my contract, the same fine print that the lawyers for LGI drew up when I thought I was getting my first book deal from the fruits of my own labor and I could finally step outside the enormous shadow my father cast for me. Sure it was smart on my part to order all of the marketing strategy polls and write something that women wanted to read, but now, I was more interested in writing something "real," whatever that meant. Hell, I guess I would determine that as Sheldon said I would be forced to write another novel, well I could write something that no one expected, something completely unsellable, something actually novel, something daring, something bold! Something authentic.

Something that would establish me as an up and comer in some sort of literary community, something that would really get people to stand up and take notice...if that was even possible anymore. I was, after all, a faithful employee of Leman Global Industries, as Sheldon repeated over and over and over to me...barely registered above the blasted heater that shielded us from the frigid Rocky Mountain air and made us get clammy skin underneath our alpaca wool coats. I tugged at my calfskin gloves lined with cashmere and shearling blend, of course, as my hands were overheating beneath them.

"Can't you turn the heat down?" I asked Sheldon, half expecting a punch in response.

"I can't do that because your sister is very susceptible to cold, Jackson," Sheldon quipped, and he looked at me like he expected me to know that my sister had turned into a wimpy hausfrau since she married him. Hell, she used to play outside with me for hours.

"Of course she's susceptible. Since she married you, she's always been susceptible to anything even remotely uncomfortable. Why, you should have grown up with her, Sheldon. I doubt you would have wedded this very same woman if you knew how unfinicky she was when she was growing up. She actually used to like to play in the snow and dirt. This is the same kid who used to plan our family vacations to exotic locales since the time we were either nine or ten. Every year our parents asked us where we wanted to go, and I would say Indiana or California, and my sister, your wife, came up with wazoo shit like Macau and Fortaleza, Brazil! You remember Brazil, right, sis?"

"No."

"Come on, Hannah," I said. "You have to remember. That's the year everything changed."

"Brazil?"

"That's right, Hannah."

"Like it's my fault!"

"You chose the setting!"

The radio crackled and a song came on. Sort of poppy, rocky, with a bit of a rappy, hip-hoppy interlude thrown in.

People who are in Hell invent the very word selfish...
You were told your entire life what happiness was...
We live on our thoughts and choices...

Poppy shit. Something Sheldon probably whistled on his way up to the 38th Floor of the Goldman Sachs building to meet whatever prick was in charge this week or his investment advisor or whoever the Hinwi ran into first. Sounds like Henry spoken by a boy with a lisp. Success inherited or hard come by. Hinwi. High Net Worth Individual. I made that up. Me. No other word for us rich assholes.

The Sun Shines for us. NO!
No! Matter what we done
So Girl come here and Give me some!

The Moon is Luminous
No matter the mess
We've made our own lives
How many times we've cheated on our wives

The stars shine and will for all...time!
When planet is cold and dead
And the Diamonds and Gold and Iron have all been mined

Girl, I look in your eyes
Girl I look in your eyes
Girl I look in your
Mascara dripping eyes
And tell you
It's okay
It's alright
Don't need to fight
Just love me
Just love me

Only the song was slurred to render the lyrics unintelligible to the casual listener, the rock riff was catchy. The singer sounded like he might be on heroin, or had just gotten off heroin and was enjoying his three years of pop stardom. The heroin addiction made him edgy and dangerous to teenaged girls.

"Change the station."

The driver complied, putting the radio on scan. It went through the news. Some crazy right-winger channel, all security, gold gold gold, and personal Armageddon shelters complete with a Bible and a kiss-your-ass-goodbye instruction manual. Then it hit the classical channel.

"Stop there," Hannah said. She had always appreciated classical music. I must admit, it calmed my nerves. The car became serene almost. I decided to stir the shit pot to see if it would stink.

"You ever tell Sheldon about Brazil?"

"No. Why would I tell Sheldon about Brazil?"

"I don't know. Maybe it came up in conversation."

"No, I didn't tell him, Jackson. I wouldn't tell him. You're the only one hell bent on airing the family's dirty laundry."

"Maybe I'll write a tell-all book," I said.

"If you actually could write something, that would be a miracle," Sheldon said.

"No. Don't bring up the past...it's dead."

"Jeez, sis, you're like Mrs. No. Always saying no. Come on, this could be therapeutic talk therapy for us."

"Goddamnit, Jackson! Shut up!"

"Come on, sis."

"Honey, why don't you just let Jackson tell me?"

"It's horrible."

"Oh, so the truth is horrible, now is it? I think it's more horrible living a goddamn lie for all these years."

"It is horrible. Not everyone needs to know it."

"You need to come to terms with it. I obviously need to learn how to deal with it. Why don't we all talk about it?"

"Not here, Jackson. Goddamnit, the driver's here."

"You don't even know his name. Come on, Sheldon will make him sign a non-disclosure agreement."

"No, Jackson. Not here. Shut up!" Hannah said, her voice begging to boil over into a scream.

I laughed. Then I said with a hint of malice in my voice, "Then you and me and pops need to talk about this."

She breathed in deeply, exhaling with a sigh.

"Father can't talk much anymore."

"He's barely alive then."

"Yes. Barely."

"I have to go see him now. You've cured me after all."

"Don't worry about that," Sheldon said.

"Shut the fuck up, Sheldon! Who the fuck are you anyway? I demand to go and see my father! Take me to him. Right now!"

"You aren't the one making decisions around here, Jackson. I am. When you get to see your father is when I choose to let you see your father. You'll probably be the gust that blows the old man over into his grave. Why, seeing you...you broke his heart by not coming around for so many years. He had to find a replacement for you...you...."

"What?"

"Prodigal son."

I laughed. It was hearty belly laugh with a fair bit of timbre in it. It felt good. I'm sure they thought it was the laugh of an evil genius. A manly laugh, in my book. Not the least bit evil, like Sheldon's little sniveling, miscreant laugh. He sounded like a juvenile delinquent who had just fleeced some porno mags from a neighborhood 7-11 and proceeded into the alleyway to read them in half fear and half unbridled joy, happy that he got away with it. If you put your hand on his shoulder suddenly during one of those chortles of his, he would probably die of shock.

"Please..."

"You've had everything handed to you, Jackson. You haven't had to work for a damn thing. Do you know what my parents did for a living? Do you? My father was a cop, and my mother worked in a dress shop."

"And their son is a thief. First he stole my sister's heart, and now he's trying to appropriate my father's wealth. I know what you're up to, Sheldon! First time I met you. You see. You've got golden doubloons for eyes. They gleamed whenever the discussions of wealth or net worth or any of those high falutin' financial terms you pricks discuss over cosmopolitans at the queer bar come up. It was like you were in charge of polishing the gold yourself. I know your plans, Sheldon. I know them. I'm going to help you out."

"You don't know me," he said.

"I do."

"No, you don't. You don't know how much I love your sister. You weren't even at our wedding."

"I didn't get an invitation."

"We sent it."

"I'm sure you stuffed the envelopes. Really got all sweaty when you did it. And what the fuck is a wedding? Just a way for two schmucks to show off and for some purported holy man to reflect on how wonderful everything is. It's a bunch of bullshit. An illusion, just like everything else. People think the hard part is over. You've found the guy or gal of your dreams. You get hitched. Tied together. In the eyes of society, you're allowed to make babies and it isn't tainted. It's kosher. It's a happy event. Everyone is all smiles. You share the sonogram pictures with all your friends. They look at it to see if there's a little prick or vajayjay. You circle the little dick using Adobe Photoshop and email it out saying 'IT'S A BOY' in bright blue letters, because that's the fucking boy color. Everyone emails you back and says congratulations. I think that's because that's what they're supposed to do. It's all jolly and fun. You take photos of the little bundle of joy with his baby bonnet on. He looks cold, tired, sometimes scared. People say congratulations again. You smoke some cigars you managed to rustle up from Cuba. They smoke well. One of your major life's hurdles has been surpassed. You've surmounted the obstacle of breeding. Whoop-dee-ding! You've ejaculated in a warm pussy and your little spermie found its mark. Lovely. Congratulations! If it wouldn't have been you, it would have been some other lucky bastard who hit the lottery and married my sister. She's been around the block. Then you look around, Sheldon, and you realize that everyone you know is doing the same thing. It's all so quaint. All the kiddies are so cute. They look like a combination of their two parents. It's a fucking miracle. But sometimes a child doesn't look much like his father, and people talk."

"Yeah. People talk," Sheldon said.

"They wonder and remember that she did go on that business trip for a couple of weeks. 'At least the kid isn't dusky' they say, 'you can tell by the hair and skin tone,' but still they ponder the situation, because maybe some wily fucker got in the mix. Maybe while papa was away on business the wife felt lonely. Maybe she got close to someone from her office or from the charitable organization she donates money to. This is the stuff of romance novels, man! Or her tennis instructor...all the old clichés. Maybe she ran into someone while she was pulling her car into the shopping center. Maybe, just maybe, it's your brother's? Maybe...the scenarios go on and on. That's the ultimate fear of man...even more so than losing his testicles. It's a double death, monsieur. It's the ultimate of wasted time. The thought that your children could possibly not be your own and you've been lavishing your bounty on a child who would have just as easily been the child of any two-bit whore and sailor in any port of call in the world. A random deposit. A total violation of the sacred and holy order that you have entered into. A crumbling block of society. You raising the bastard offspring of some schmuck."

"Where the fuck are you leading me, Jackson?" Sheldon asked, nonplussed.

"Your wife, your lovely little wife all damsely and maidenly and pure, allowing said schmuck to jizz in her. Something you thought...you were taught required planning. So you waited. You schemed and maneuvered until you found the "right" girl. You married her. She was yours. And some prick waiter beats you to the punch. That's a deed that can't be undone. That's the goddamned end of civilization."

The driver chuckled. The prick actually broke role.

"What's so funny?" Sheldon demanded of him.

"Nothing," the driver said, maintaining an almost military decorum.

"No...please, tell me. What's so funny?"

"The guy talking. He's completely nuts."

"Want to sign an affidavit stating that?" Sheldon asked him, then looked back at me, and winked.

They took me home. They put me in my room. During the night, Marcus came to me in waves.

"You have a despairing view of life, Jackson," Marcus said to me in the darkness of the room where I was trying to sleep. The thorazine, casually administered by Dr. Gilroy must have been wearing off.

"Go away, fucker. You don't exist."

"I do. You gave me life."

"But you're not living. Fuck, I'm nuts. If they see me talking to you, they're going to have me committed for sure."

"That's what they want to do anyway. You're a burden, a malcontent, and a source of poor family press. If you bothered to listen to any of their criticism instead of being lost in your own world, you will realize that they mean you no harm, my man. Any fool knows that."

"God damn you, Marcus. Where do you come from?"

"Your mind, of course. You invented me. Gave me life."

"You're just a character in my novel."

"The doctor knows best."

I put my hands to my head. It was throbbing. My mouth was so dry. Thorazine.

"Life is so entertaining with you around."

"You don't have to say goodbye, Jackson."

"What do you think I should do?"

"Refuse the medication. You're an adult."

"I don't care if you're a figment of my imagination. Where's Willard?"

"I imagine he's somewhere in that massive, perturbed brain of yours."

I heard a knock at the door, medical style. Dr. Gilroy entered quickly, doctor style, floating around...disembodied.

"Who were you talking to?"

"Myself, of course. Just planning out my day, seeing that there's no one else here in the room."

"Why were you talking to yourself?"

"I suppose I was just thinking out loud."

"You haven't been talking to him any more have you?"

"Who's that?"

"Marcus Hanely."

"No. What do you think? That I'm fucking nuts?"

"No one ever said that, Jackson. I just want you to know that Marcus is a delusion, a misplaced affection for your father, your id, something of a hallucination that has become the focal point of your entrenched sense of reality. And when realities are altered profoundly, as yours has been, the hallucinations can reassert themselves vigorously. Jackson, you have to know, and be aware that it's only your brain's defense mechanism reasserting its hesitancy to change. What you need is time and the drug therapies. You have to give the medication a chance to work. Please promise me that you'll do that."

"You're with them, doctor. Have you signed any affidavits against me?"

"With who, Jackson?"

"Them! The people trying to take control of the corporation after father passes away. You know, my wretched sister and he horrible husband."

"Have they tried to harm you somehow?"

"Yes. They have. They showed me the warehouse with nothing in it but copies of my novel. They were trying to send me over the edge."

"How did seeing that make you feel, Jackson?"

"I can't say that it pleased me. What's been done is done. Can I right my mind, Doctor?"

Gilroy paused, "The medication and rest is what you need."

He handed me two of the smallish purple caplets and a glass of water. I noticed he was shaking with a slight tremor when the water entered my field of vision.

"What's wrong?"

"Oh, you know. Getting old."

"It doesn't matter," I said.

"Why's that?" the Doctor asked in a scholarly and analytical way, taking no offense ever to my comments.

"You've done what you wanted to in life. I'm sure father's paid you well to look after his defective son. I'm defective, right down to my mitochondrial DNA. I got the craziness from my mother, you know. Crazy bitch."

A look of horror came over the doctor's face. He shook his head and put it down as if he were trying to stifle the flow of tears.

"Your mother was my patient even before you were born, and the woman wasn't pathological in the least."

"What do you mean?" I asked. "My entire life my mother has been painted as a kook."

"She was an overstressed woman, but there was no significant pathology in my findings."

"She wasn't crazy?"

"No."

"Why'd she kill herself then?"

"It doesn't make any sense. Her last few sessions she mentioned filing for divorce from your father, and then she up and did that. No one expected it. She didn't display any of the warning signs...didn't even act depressed. She didn't seem suicidal to me in the least."

"Strange."

The Doctor administered a shot to me. I winced as the needle drew into my arm.

"What is that?"

"Something for your treatment."

"What drug?"

"An antipsychotic. You'll need regular injections to keep the hallucinations at bay."

"Regular?"

"Every couple of weeks."

"There may be some side effects. Increased paranoia, agitation. I can give you some other medicine to help you out with that."

"Yeah, Doc, pill me up."

He handed me a bottle of small capsules. Lovaramin. Take one tablet daily on a full stomach.

"Follow the instructions on the bottle, Jackson," the doctor said. He handed me another prescription in his scrawled writing, got up from his chair, and walked towards the door.

"Be seeing you, Jackson. I'm sure of that."

"Take it now?"

"Just take it."

He walked out. Nearly as soon as he disappeared, my brain produced an image of Marcus Hanely. Flickering. Irresolute.

Sulfurous fumes belched forth from Hanely's britches and shirtsleeves reeking how I imagined hell would.

"Damn, you stink."

"Can't help it, bro. It's hot where I'm at."

"Where are you at?"

"The convoluted recesses of your brain. Man, this place is a cesspool and cobweb-filled junk pit. A hell. What the hell is wrong with you?"

"Now even you've started in on me. I've no friends in this world."

"Why aren't you breaking down that door and demanding to see your father? That's what Marcus would do."

"What Marcus would do? And why are you speaking about yourself in the third person now? You sound like some sort of professional primadonna athlete or other idiotic nut bag," I said out loud.

"Marcus can't refer to himself as a subject. You're the subject. Marcus is a mere figment. A perturbation of your brain chemistry," the disembodied voice said.

"I'm talking to you, Marcus."

"No you aren't, Jackson. You're engaging in soliloquy. You're lathing to yourself, grinding yourself down, mano e mano. You're a grade-A nut bag, ball bag, testes holder, a modern man or whatever that means. You see, Jackson, I don't exist, I'm a character that you created to get yourself out of a bad situation mentally. Jackson, I don't exist. Get that through your thick, perturbed mind. Get it through there now. Beam up to Scotty or whatever you need to do, Jackson. There are games afoot, games invented by madmen greater than you, madmen with access to capital, madmen who hold the linchpins of the world, the levers of power. Sheldon cannot be allowed to take over your father's business. He's an idiot, and he'll ruin the business, run it aground. He's not even suited to run a popsicle or lemonade stand. The kiddies would be in arrears. They'd lose their college funds. Some people are just born losers and swindlers. Trust your gut on this charlatan here. I may be a figment of your addled imagination run amok. Maybe you should trust the doctor on this one. Just take the medicine and silence the hallucinations."

"That would mean silencing you."

"No. I'd still be a part of your thought process. They would be your thoughts, like they've always been your thoughts. Jackson, I'm a part of you. You created me. You let me take control. You don't need me anymore! Your enterprise doesn't need me. You've made me as real as any Hamlet. Boy, now just take the medicine and think up what I might do in one of your stories. Just think. Just write. Hell, your mind made up all I've done thus far. I wasn't there, and I swear to God, neither was Willard, nor the itinerant bible Salesman, nor anyone we've met save for a few people. The corporate police officers, they were real. As real as a punch to the face. No doubt hirelings of your brother-in-law to beef up security around this farce. Take the medicine, Jackson, and abandon me. Live your life without hallucinations. Abandon your illusions, because illusions are the stuff of life. That way, you'll be one of those writers who write on the side of death, grasping for the light. Don't fear the nothingness, Jackson. Embrace it. Write from it. Write from the point of view that you are already dead and you so miss the world of the living that you buttress it against that cold, viscous world of your visions.

"What did you say, Jackson? That life is but a brief moment? A mere speck of dust in that great maelstrom of infinity? Well, goddamnit, that speck had better be as bright as a star, if for no other reason, no, no, not for fame, because it fades heartily to dust and is dependent on other people to notice, and not for money because you've got plenty and it's only a security blanket in your old age, and who wants to live just to save for when you're old, it's just for a means of keeping tabs...when the only tab you can ever say is that time is fleeting and I will not last forever. Use your time, Jackson. Make it your own! Write for those who come after you. Let them know what was on your mind during this time, because you can step out on the street and get crushed by a bus, no matter if you had the intention to write the most profound works of poetry or the cheesiest romance novels, your world came to nothing. Cast your soul into the world in your little unwanted children! Be done with it!"

I declared to Marcus, but more so this was more a declaration to myself, because the medicine had yet to burn into my brain, "I'm going to renounce my fortune that my father has stacked it to the ceiling. I'm going to be an artist. I'm going to abandon the world and find myself. Damn everything! Fall away! Fall away! Stop clinging to me like little needy rug rats. I've nothing! My talents! That's all I have truly. I will write until the pen slips from my cold, dead fingers! Be gone, Hanely! Be gone! Slip fast to the bitter depths of hell where my soul is fast to join you!"

Marcus burst into a puff of smoke and flames, and a smile was the last thing I saw written on his face as my brain took on a sudden calm. The medicine had melted in my gut and attached itself to synapses, or whatever it's mechanism of action was. I don't know. I didn't read the dosing contraindications.

"No one will believe me. I'm mad. What is the difficulty with Sheldon managing things? What is my great concern? I will take my briny bits and rocks and trees and cobwebs. I will retreat with my time and the energy of my youth. I won't play their foul games. I won't fall into distraction. I will become who I am. Jackson Leman. Creator. Madman. Or is it madman creator?"

I turned the handle on the lock of my humble room. They had forgotten to lock the lock, or there was no lock on the door to confine me. But I won't dwell on it. I'm done dwelling. I want to live. The world, she is created for me. I was born a rich boy, but like St. Francis of Assisi, I renounce those riches. Like Napoleon Bonaparte, I renounce mediocrity as the way of slaves contented to mortgage their lives for a bit of time to do what someone else has fabricated. I'm done with it all! I'm dead! I'm dead and buried!

I walked past two stunned guards. "I'm going to see my father and you cannot stop me," I announced to them.

The guard did not know what to say because no one had briefed him on what to say. He could follow no script, as this eventuality had not been thought up. I walked past him so easily. I am sure he would be punished and possibly lose his job, but I did not care. My father needed me.

I found my sister in the palatial hall, weeping. She gasped when she saw me, as if she suffered the fear that I would murder her.

"I'm not going to hurt you."

"You already have."

"How? If I did it, I did not mean it."

"You did! You mentioned Brazil! You know how it makes me feel, you bastard."

"I'm no bastard. I know my father, I think. But maybe it's time we talked about Brazil," I said feeling a lump steadily growing in my throat. "I did not want to talk about it, but I felt for the sake of our shared experience and in order to stop blaming ourselves for all that befell our family afterwards, after this horrible tragic event...and we were only children! What could have been so horrible, so..."

"Mother persisted in her delusions of thinking that father was a nice, perfect husband without fault, with ravishing good looks, it only made him that much more appealing to the women in the village, down below the vacation home," Hannah said.

"Our house there...do we still have it?"

"It's forgotten. Probably gone back to jungle, tangled and tormented in the vines. It was a beautiful place when we took care of it. White. Sunny. You could pick your breakfast from the trees. Mom was so happy there. It was her favorite place in the world," Hannah remarked.

"I remember that. Dad was absent. Meetings with the folks at Vale. Mining concessions or something like that. He never talked about his activities, really. He would come into the house and depart suddenly, like the crashings of the ocean," I said.

"Our father is a scoundrel," Hannah said and then corrected herself looking downwards, "But he's a man."

"I remember what I saw. You didn't have to run off and tell mother about it all," I said.

"I didn't know any better," Hannah said, remorsefully.

"Delusions come crashing down hard, and leave their bearer with nothing. They cause your time you thought was well spent to contract and whatever future you envisioned to shrink and dry up to nothing like some beautiful rose that gone black and dead. You suddenly realize you're quite naked and alone in the world, an opportunity to rebuild yourself without illusion, or just sink into the mire of the swamps from which there is no escape. Sister, we flit above the surface like birds. Hannah, we fly boldly into the future, or else we sink. Mom couldn't escape that. She wasn't strong enough, I think."

"Mom was very strong. You wouldn't know. You were off in your own world from birth. Sheldon's the same way."

"Why do you put up with it?"

"You have to keep up appearances in this family. You know that."

"I keep up disappearances."

"Disappearances, appearances…it's all the same. You're playing your role. You're a reclusive artist. Got it. You care only about yourself. Got it. Stop blaming me for what happened to mom! Goddamnit, Jackson, we're in this together!"

"What did happen to mom? You act like this was totally against her will! Forced on her!"

"I don't know, Jackson. I just don't know."

"Hannah. Mom was no suicide. She was murdered."

"How do you know that?"

"I don't know. I just saw things that no one else did."

"Oh, like that's a surprise."

"This was real."

"Sure."

FLOR DE CORCORAS

A sunlit mountainside, jungle trees intertwined psychosis bearing all types of fruits, pomegranates, mangos, tropical fruits of all shapes, sizes, colors, ripeness levels, picked upon by South American monkeys, not so much cute as they were considered pests because they would also steal into your home and steal shiny objects, be it a piece of foil, a diamond ring, or Faberge egg. Capuchins would steal the eggs benedict from your breakfast plate if you turned away from them. For some reason they loved the hollandaise. The Conquistadores thought they looked like monks with their colorings...those same monks who invented Cappuccino. Somewhere a woman is singing a song in a language that I cannot understand, and her voice is sweet with a husky resonance and dripping with all the nectar of the verdure canopy where monkeys rape and jaguars stalk and stupid peccaries from perched treetops too tall to climb by man....

My sister and I follow the sound of this woman's beautiful voice abandoning our mother on the patio and looking back to see if she was concerned that we had unlatched the white-washed stone gate and crept to the edge of the jungle where the woman's voice beckoned, trailing upwards off the leaves. Mother was reading a National Geographic and was immersed. We followed a logger's trail, or maybe a miner's trail, but either way we figured it was a fortune hunter's trail through the jungle, a deep gash through the slashing and groping trees. It was approaching ten in the morning. The humidity was full bore. Father had not come home that night, flying his plane away on business with representatives of Vale Mining Corporation who wanted to explore the strategic possibilities of strip mining certain locations that geologists had said may be or quite possibly could be laden with a material quite useful to the burgeoning semiconductor businesses my father was now heavily invested in. We walked through the beautiful fantasyland of screeching monkeys and diving birds, the paradise of green. We walked further into the heart of this fantasyland, and it was real.

I remember the smells of the place, never to be recreated by Hermes or Guerlain or some other Frenchy fashion houses, not one in a million years, all smells now lost to us forever. I held my sister's hand as we followed the woman's voice. I did not know if I was dreaming. I held my sister tightly at the roars and groans of the canopy, which light barely trickled through. Strange shapes, like little men, men creaking and groaning and bobbing up and down. Monkeys, these capuchins without the fortitude to steal into the houses, which remained wild in the jungles with as much curiosity as a human child, sat eyes wide with wonder at us. Ahead the woman's voice grew stronger, sighing, bowing towards the heavens above her song I did not understand. I was a young boy, and I did not understand. My sister and I looked at each other again, each of us imploring the other, asking, "should we continue?" And we did, being naturally curious, being children about to be baptized into the pools of deceit, unaware.

I suppose my father was all well and good to spend his family vacation in the gross pursuit of the flesh, the love of the local maidens, affairs of the heart. He would have been a talented conquistador, but decided to get married at a young age. I suppose this would have been too good for father, now playing jungle love at our vacation home with the maid, a woman half mother's age or perhaps underage. But this was Brazil in the 1980s, plus she was more than her fair share of mulatto, and no one would have cared either way.

The steamier part of seduction is finding a willing partner. And Ane appeared to be willing. Very willing. She was naked from the waist up and splayed from the waist down, opened up. At least my father exercised enough chivalrous virtues to allow her to prop her ass in the front seat of his decommissioned military jeep while he rooted on her from the standing position. Ane noticed us at first and screamed, "The Children!" in whatever broken English she could muster, and my father said something foolish like, "No kids, no kids, I'll pull out...". I don't quite remember but in retrospect it would have been a funny one liner, like something dead Marcus Hanely would have said to the hot home wrecker. My sister tugged at my arm for us to go, but I stood in awe of my father's great sweaty back and buttocks wondering just what it was he was doing there with the maid who incidentally caused me to achieve one of my first ever girl induced erections while seeing her whip the mashed potatoes, a motion which transferred from her arms to her hips and ample behind. I suppose my father noticed too. My sister pulled me back into the brush but not before Ane got my father's attention enough to watch us scamper off.

My God, I think I heard him say but we were already running. And he gave chase. I looked back at him laughing, and he wasn't angry, but mostly looked afraid. I had never seen him that way. We thought it was a great game that father was playing with us and the most attention he had paid to us, playing with us, maybe for the first time ever. For he was usually away or in his office at home with the door closed, and it was usually the maids like Ane or whatever nanny we had at the time who paid us the most attention. If all else failed, mother would sit with us, and we would pass the time listening to her complaints about father, but mainly we were told to be thankful that we were born with what mother called wealth and privilege and power and weren't being raised by parents who never saw us because they had to work two or three jobs just to be able to put substandard food on the table. And now we laughed and cackled and crashed through the jungle back to mama who waited patiently by the pool with a whiskey Manhattan, freshly mixed by our butler who always traveled with us.

The monkeys howled and tossed some sort of seedpod they didn't want to eat but instead weaponized in protest of us taking over their jungle and driving them from their homes, rapidly expanding outwards, overtaking the monkeys and fruit tress and all the decent clearings where a married man could take his underaged lover for a nice midday plowing, well father never caught us and we made a hell of a game out of it, and we laughed the whole way home and burst into the courtyard laughing and sweating and carrying on that mother immediately thought a vicious jaguar or baboon, even though those were endemic to Africa, had given us chase and terrified us, and we screamed and yelled the whole time laughing that father, and the maid were chains us because we caught them we caught them we caught them doing something and mother demanded to know what they were doing and Hannah said they were fighting trying to get unstuck from each other because they must have gotten stuck together.

And mother's eyes turned to horror and she screamed, "Where! Where is your father!" And I wanted mother to join the game and I said I didn't know, but Hannah told mother that he was out in the jungle, follow me mommy, and Mother and Hannah took off out into the jungle, mother snagging her long shirt on the brambles and choking vines and getting all in a fit with the vines grabbing at her and holding her, ripping her clothes like mini rapists until father appeared and I watched all this from a distance, as I climbed up on the tall wall to our place and watched mother shrieking and Hannah start crying and my father with a look of emphatic denial with his arms outstretched like he was trying to make himself appear bigger to a vicious dog or animal about to attack him.

And I saw mother pick at the bush at her feet holding him at bay, and she picked up a hearty stick and set to beating father and screaming and hitting him, chasing him all the way to the gate where he actually fell down, and the dirt stuck to the sweat on his face, and he looked up at me the whole time mother called him a real piece of shit, a rogue, worthless scum bag. And from my perch, I just looked on and watched and didn't cry like my sister was crying her eyes out and just took it all in, not really feeling much of anything.

Mother packed all of her bags and took my sister and me to the airport and said that father could just stay in Brazil with his whore and if he ever came back home to Colorado it would be a miracle if she would ever let him back into our house again. Hannah and Mother cried, but I not really understanding anything told them both that I would love to stay in Brazil with father and his whore and make sure that father was okay, but mother just looked at me in disgust and said that I would probably end up just like him. Then she and my sister left, I tried to follow them, but my mother wouldn't talk to me, and Hannah just looked at me and stared and cried.

I tried to make amends to my mother. I cried. I wailed in public, so much so that the locals at the airport stopped and pointed as I apologized and begged my mother to love me again, promising that I wasn't going to be anything like my father. But she held my sister close and just shunned me and didn't talk to me anymore, not until I cried myself asleep in a chair next to her and my sister woke me up to tell me that the plane was there.

My mother told me that I could just stay here with my father, but he probably wouldn't be very happy about it because I would just get in the way of all the time that he and his whore had together, and if I wanted to stay I would have to get back to father's on my own but I would probably just get kidnapped if I was going to wait for him to come get me and taken by some horrible people out into the jungle and never be heard from again. The stories of Hansel and Gretel being fattened by some horrible old crone came pouring into my mind, and I recanted and said that I loved my mother and wanted to go home with her even though I really wanted to stay and walk in the jungle some more and maybe ask my father just what he was doing with the maid who made me feel so funny.

Father came back eventually, but mother never really talked to him again. She traveled to less and less of the house, eventually barricading herself in a small section of the room, refusing to see anyone. Then came the gunshot and the strange man that I followed out into the woods. It could have been my father. It could have been any-one. After the police left, my father talked to my sister and me and told us that mother was very selfish and she made a selfish choice. He told us that we would have to be strong and help each other after the funeral. He told us we had to watch over each other because after the brief respite at burying our mother, he had business to attend to.

SEEING THE OLD BASTARD

"**W**hat are you doing outside anyway?"

"Take me to dad."

"Jackson, he isn't in good sorts."

"That's what I've heard from all of you people. How bad dad's doing. You called me here to see him, now let me see him."

"I don't see the point of continuing this charade much longer."

"Why were you crying? Feeling guilty about confining your own brother, sissy?"

"Jesus, Jackson, you forget everything a minute after it happens. I just told you that you made me relive Brazil."

"Must be the meds you've got me on. We can't run from our past, sis," I said as I made an attempt to hug her.

She pulled away. "Just follow me, and don't touch anything."

"No touching what? Father's art collection? The priceless vases? Or are they pronounced VAHZEZ...isn't that how Sheldy pronounces vases? VAHZEZ? The beautiful Ming Dynasty VAHHHHHHHZEZZZZZZZZZZ...a tired cliché. Every rich man has one...and countless Persian rugs and a dozen Faberge eggs. Why, they're so quaint. I'd love to smash them all right under my shit kickers, sis. I'd love to burn this whole place down to the ground. Of course though, only after all the servants, squatters, physicians, trainers, exercise physiologists, chefs, phlebotomists, florists and whoever else pop put on staff is a safe distance away. I'd love to rig it all with explosives and laugh and flip the switch and cheer. I may be an arsonist and firebug, but I'm no murderer."

"You aren't an arsonist either, little brother. You're just a horribly confused man with too much time on his hands."

"What would you have me do, sis? Scour the world like a playboy looking for the next best thing? Fight crime with the vast wealth I've had at my fingertips? I'm Batman! Rich people are bored...that's the heart of it, that's what made dad want to traipse around fucking hotel maids and unsavory ladies the world over. Oh, I'm sure they tasted good, but you know, the whole cheating on your wife thing..."

"You don't even know the first chapter of that man's biography," Hannah said.

"Dad's?"

"Yes, dad's. Who else would I be talking about, Jackson? Marcus Hanely? There's a laugh. Your imaginary friend."

"We don't speak anymore," I said and shook the bottle of pills at her. "This is my insurance against Marcus."

"That's good. Just make sure you take the medicine, or Marcus could come back with a vengeance."

Secretly, I wanted him back. I wanted him to teach me how to saw off a shotgun in his spare time so that I could blow Sheldon in half with it. Probably not exactly in front of my sister, but I could see it now, walking into the Yacht Club with the shotty obscured by a newspaper saying, "Hello, Sheldon!" while he looked up from his mai tai or Bellini or whatever prissy drink those Harvard Yard MBA faggots drank to decompress from a day's worth of lining their pockets with fees and brokerage costs and whatever other scams they made to fleece us artists out of our daily bread. BLAM! Both barrels at the same time. Double aught buckshot right in his face.

Ole Doctor was right the drug they had me on might be producing violent visions, but alas, Hanely was dead and buried in the crypt of my mind, and Willard was dead and done and buried too. I can feel the blood rushing through the vessels in my head, and I swear one of these days my blood vessels are going to rupture and I'll just slump over and that will be that, just blackness, just blinking out. I try not to dwell on it, the D word as we walk up to this massive oaken staircase that slightly spirals heading upward and is ornately carved by artisans in either Turkey or somewhere in Italy. I asked my father's butler in passing one time, and he told me it was the same difference.

"He's lucid, but only caused by the medicine he's on, otherwise he'd probably be comatose. It's all very sad."

"Sad, sad, sad, sad, sad, sad, sad, sad, SAD! I'm sick of hearing how sad it all is. Why, if everything that people say is sad struck me as sad, I'd be buried under an ocean of tears. You gotta live, babe."

"You're an asshole."

"Maybe the invalid will croak and we can all get on with our lives. Do you think I'm sick, because I just want him out of the way now?"

"Most people keep that to themselves, these secret wishes."

"They're the really sick ones."

We came to the entrance of the large hallway, at the end of which would be where my father's immense sickroom was, complete with his deathbed.

"I must warn you, he's been a little strange as of late. It's probably a side effect of the lucidity medication."

"You're so matter of fact in your characterizations of my father's mental state."

"Well, you'll see for yourself, little brother."

As you walked past, the lighting in the hallway was specifically designed to illuminate the portraits of Leman family members in a sort of ghostly procession, almost as if they were illuminating the souls of the faithfully departed. Generations of Leman men were displayed, even back to the so called old country, French Huguenots, I think, at least by their collars which marked them for massacre at the hands of Catholics, lacy and frilly, but mostly austere and boring with dark and foreboding skull caps on, large wooly beards, and eyes full of malice, as if someone paid them to be stern for their portraits. The privilege of money, and we had it even way back when, though in lesser amounts because banking was considered unclean and we made ours buying things at a low price and selling them at a high price, mainly cloths to make clothing out of, allowed father to acquire these portraits from whatever dusty private collections they were part of.

He found Leduc Leman's 1570 portrait in some sort of military uniform, we don't know which, but we acquired the arrest records from the local magistrate to realize that this gentleman was most likely a ne'er-do-well who so happened to sit for the painter's brush in an artist colony because the painter found his chiseled profile to be remarkable in the light of a Dutch morning. At any rate, the chump was hacked to bits by a cavalryman's sword in some battle that everyone, probably even historians who actively look at small, inconsequential battles in undeclared wars and minor border skirmishes, have forgotten about. We passed his portrait quickly. He had the look of a madman, a marked absence of fear with a real sense of humor at life, a cherubic smile on his face, perhaps because at the time of the painting he was well within sight of the dancing gypsy girls. It must have been something in the water or rampant syphilis that gave him that look of abandon.

Anyways, as I passed these gangs of my blood men and kin, I had the strange feeling that all of their collective hopes, dreams, working for what they thought was a better life, clawed ambitions, loves lost and gained, were glaring back at me with those now dead eyes. I was the end of the line, a horribly diluted, deluded, spoiled, rich vagabond, addled beyond the point of comprehension and probably three degrees beyond fully baked psychosis. I actually started to feel guilty with each poor, dead soul I passed. And then we passed probably the final portrait, and it was of my father, painted by artist unknown. The portrait next to his was empty. There was a frame on the wall, but an empty, blank canvas hung in it as if the painter they hired to paint me had gotten disgusted with waiting around and climbed out the window to paint landscapes and never quite made his way back. Next to the painting was a brass plaque with a date of birth and a dash with no closing date to indicate that I was still a work in progress.

My father's was the same way, but we all knew the story. It would be filled soon enough. My father's portrait had that same madman's look in his blue, empty eyes. Oh, the eyes were the windows to the soul, glinting there in the sunlight, which appeared to pour in from the upper right corner. He sat at a nice overstuffed leather chair, with a pipe in his hand, I never knew him to smoke a pipe but in the other paintings he had the same black pipe as if to say, *"Ceci n'est pas une pipe,"* and *"Ceci n'est pas un homme, monsieur."* I stared at the black pipe in his hand as if I were about to discover for the first time that I was in keeping in the solidarity of my madman kin, would take up this pipe and go off into the world of business and make my mark on the world and brand it with an L.

Hannah opened the doors to the room. It smelled of antiseptic, like a hospital, but also hints of oak, citrus, and mint with a slight overtone of some type of mildewed wood. It was like we stepped back into the middle of the Brazilian rainforest. My father looked diminutive, not the former vibrant, hulking, thrusting mass I knew him as. He sat in the center of the bed Indian fashioned, looking quite like a Hindu Yogi. He looked up at me with an angelic face, framed by a halo, seemingly coming from nowhere but his baldhead, which gathered all available light in the room to it and concentrated it on the surface.

"Jackson. My boy," he said. "You came." He had a weak smile on his face.

"Fah...Fah...Fah...ther," I managed to get out before breaking down into tears.

"Son, where have you been?"

"Oh, out," I said, sobbing.

"Thank God you came."

I could not speak. I just looked humbly at him.

"I can't waste my time in arguments about the past. Past behavior. Past mistakes. Past activities. Past false hopes. Past hallucinations. Past recriminations. The past is dead. We are steadily sloughing it off from the new and vibrant, the gleaming, like a 19 year old woman's posterior, ahhh...its perfection, perfection, perfection...."

"Father!" Hannah lamented.

"Hannah, my dear, could you leave Jackson and me alone, honey?"

The door clicked shut as she departed. Father smiled at me. He looked quite sallow, skeletal, like death sat upon his lap. It was probably 6:30 in the morning. Father's view was an enormous paneled window that overlooked a valley breaking northwards to a majestic peak with snowcaps on one of them.

"Magnificent," I said.

"It's loaded with molybdenum," Father said.

I looked out the window past the stuffed Asiatic deer that father had imported because they were more majestic than the stubby nosed mule deer that frequented our property.

"What is?" I asked.

"That mountain you're staring at. It's loaded with molybdenum veins and probably gold too. Maybe even uranium."

"It looks like a mountain to me," I told him.

"We did a geological survey about 20 years ago, right before I bought this place. The board of directors wanted to mine the mountain, blast its top off and scoop out the precious metals. Some things are better left pristine, Jackson."

"It's beautiful," I said.

The sun eclipsed the peak, and the Asiatic deer scattered as if spooked by something.

Father coughed, dragging, dry, unproductive like the sound of a tomb being raked of its bones.

"Son, I'm not much longer for this world," he said.

"Father, I know...Hannah told me," I said, still looking out the window towards the lonely mountain peak.

"Son, I'm leaving everything to you."

I turned around. His words shocked me. They were totally unexpected.

"Why?"

"I'll give Hannah an allowance, but if that bastard Sheldon gets his hands on anything, he'll make Leman Global Industries into something after his own image. We'll become the purveyors of death, my boy. The board, they've already been trying to set the stage to orchestrate a coup against you, trying to get you declared incompetent, a mental patient, a nutbag, a literature buff with no other concerns, than foppishly writing drivel, which the company must then run out and buy in order to boost the idiot public's perception that they're onto a megahit bestseller that will change their life for the better."

"Father, I saw what you did for my first novel. It's horrible. Why did you do that?"

"No Leman is a loser," Father said.

The remark stung, like a slap in the mouth from mom. I stared at him.

"You didn't do your best. You want to be an author; you had better not write that type of schlock. It's unbecoming. Why did you put your real name on it?"

"My picture on the back of the first edition was taken in my senior year at Princeton University. I was looking all proper and Ivy League."

"You went to Princeton?"

"Dad, of course."

"I guess I've forgotten. Anyways, son...you're a fool."

"Why?"

"You're not doing what you want to be doing."

"I am."

"You know what I wanted to do?"

"No."

"You've never seen a hint of my true calling. Of course, it isn't business. Whose is? People whose passion is stacking paper bills to the ceiling, paper stackers and coin and bean counters are lacking in all the fundamental characteristics of what comprises a fulfilled and happy human life, because you see, my son, the moneymaking endeavor is never ending, its impossible to vacuum up all the capital that the world has in it, but when you truly have an original thought or an original idea, you add something to the world that didn't exist before. My God, son, you've done something wonderful. You know what I studied at my time at Princeton University?"

"No. I always assumed you studied Finance or Business. The Art of Expanding Limits and Maximizing Global Possibility. I don't know, I think since we never really talked while I was growing up, I've always just assumed things about you without ever getting the real answers."

"Philosophy. That's what I studied, and that's what I am. A philosopher."

"You've never written anything."

"I've had some damn beautiful thoughts. And I don't write. I do other things."

"Great. You didn't share them, so they'll evaporate to dust when you pass."

"They've gotten me through tough times, son."

"Maybe you should have written them down."

"I pursued other endeavors."

"Great, you're alone with your thoughts. Did you share some of them with the maid in Brazil? Did you read her some poetry? Was it easy to talk her out of her britches?"

Now it was dear old dad's turn to be silent. I imagined him strapped, bald headed, to a spinning wheel and I, his vicious progeny, throwing daggers and ineptly barely missing. I hated seeing him squirm, but maybe he had forgotten that I even remembered. He was responsible for my mother's death. I aimed for his heart, and threw my dagger.

"Do you miss mom?"

He didn't say anything.

"Cat got your tongue, dad?"

He grumbled a bit, sitting there, his beatitude somewhat dismayed. I saw him sink in the bed like there was a button he pushed that deflated the mattress.

"I asked if you missed mom."

"Of course I do. Of course. Of course. Your mother was a very particular woman, and I must say that I did love her very much, but I was a man, damn you, and a man's man at that. At least that's what people thought of me, and I had an image to maintain. My whole damn life spent, my money spent, all in the maintenance of the image bequeathed to me in the form of an inheritance measured in billions of dollars, an inheritance that will be yours, all yours, son..."

"Did you love my mother, or was she just one of your millions of possessions?"

"Your mother was a beautiful, beautiful girl when I met her. An heiress from an old, wealthy East Coast family. It was a suitable match. But still, I should have never been married to her. She was too good a woman for me. I should have been contented with my village girls."

"Did you love her?"

"Oh, well, yes I did, I think. I mean, I loved her at one time, but of course, that was what was scripted for me, I guess. The wedding was huge, beautiful, written about in all of the papers in the United States. The periodicals, broadcast radio...it was all over the radio waves, the idiot box wasn't yet invented, but I guess...I was at the time."

"You didn't. You didn't. Your entire life has been a sham. Have you ever loved anyone?"

"I think...yes, I think I have."

"You never loved Hannah and I. You can't claim that you did. We barely saw you; you have to...you have to tell me the truth. You're going to die soon. You're going to perish, and you can't just sit there like some saint and continue to lie to everyone about your actions, father. Your actions tell me...."

"The past is dead and buried, my son...."

"It isn't, goddamnit. The books may have been signed and closed out, and you made your money, but the past isn't dead and buried. You may have forgotten about it all, you may have arranged for the debris to be swept and tidied by one of your servants, swept under an antique Persian rug, but I tell you it's all still there It reeks, and you can't tell me it doesn't. The past isn't dead and buried. It isn't. It won't die with you, damn you. Hannah and I still have to live in this world you've made for us. We still have to carry the weight around while you're quietly laughing in the void."

"I won't be laughing. I won't. I want to apologize. I'm making you my sole heir, Jackson. I'm doing it for a very important reason. It isn't arbitrary. It all has logic and purpose behind it. I haven't done anything arbitrary. Nothing ever. I swear."

"That maid wasn't arbitrary?"

"Always with the maid! Are you still going to hold that over my head? I've done far worse, son. Far worse. Are you going to tell your children's children the story?"

At that moment, I had a vision of myself with a faceless woman. Together we lay somewhere in the sunshine, and the birds sang. The children, also faceless, play in the waves of some white sand beach. There were no annoying seagulls to junk up the scenery. Then, ahead of the horizon, came a dark, black shape, ominous, like doom, and the children screamed and ran to my faceless woman. The grandfather clock chimed, and its tick-tock, tick-tock filled the room and echoed as I became more aware of it, it grew and filled the entire atmosphere, the sand bounced off the oxygen in the room that my father and I shared, filling the dead spaces. I looked at my father who was smiling ever so subtly, though it could have been a frown too, a frown of disapproval or a smile that he would soon be unburdened. Or it could have been fear working its way to the surface, cracking his stoic countenance. The dark, black shape continued to blot out the horizon, crept slowly. It dredged up the contents of the sea bottom as waves crested and broke on the massive void. With seagulls blotted out, it overtook the sun, and the last rays settled on its opaque black surface. To feel limitless possibility in your bones and the crunching galling surface, the blackness from which there was no escape. It overtook everything living, crunched my children into dust, my faceless woman staring off into the void with no definable features, fantasy, all disappeared in its wake. I gazed into the void and found a strange comfort in it. It stopped just ahead of me. Its contours were metallic, and with the smell of gun grease all around me, it halted in the wet sand and shrank to a manageable hand sized annihilating element and dropped at my feet. I picked it up. It became solid. In my hand was a handgun. As long as I didn't turn it on myself, I was immortal. Nothing would harm me. No harm – no real harm – would befall me, as long as I just moved through life. Until the bitter end, I would be just fine. As long as I didn't turn the gun upon myself and pull the trigger, all would be forgiven, all would be right in the world.

"You blanked out."

"I know."

"What were you thinking about?"

"Nothing. I forgive you. We all make mistakes. I'll keep walking ahead. I don't want your money. You can keep it. I don't want it. If you give it to me, I'm going to give it all away. I'm going to spread it all around like margarine on a piece of toast. I'll let it all melt. When it's gone, evaporated off, I'll get on with my life."

"You cannot allow my life's work to fall into the hands of these highwaymen, these lawyers, these bankers, psychos, the nuts, the ones who think this is all so damn important and grand. The worshippers. You can't let them make a foray into defense contracts. They want to make bombs, missiles, bullets, they want to make it and sell it all. You can't let them. You can't tarnish our family's name by giving them the means to do it."

"Where is that coming from?"

"I showed you the mountain. They want to strip it bare. They want to drive the animals and trees down the other side. They want to turn the mountain into munitions. The Earth artificed to kill the Earth. Suicide. They want to make steel tanks, bombs, airplanes, ships, and it's only a small facet of their plans. They want to do whatever it is that is popular and will make them a little chunk of profit, just a small, paltry sum. They don't care, just as long as it's more they put into it. They'll produce these weapons to satisfy the customer demands. War will beget war. Children will suffer and starve and hate their neighbors. The world will get hotter and hotter, and they will be lovely on their golden commodes, far from the actions, safely protected, pulling strings. Don't sully our name, Jackson. Don't let them destroy our family name. Be strong. Don't allow them to drag you into their artificial abyss."

"For God's sake, who are 'they?'"

"They'll come. They'll come to you with new ways of making money. They'll come and attach themselves to you like vampires, sucking the life out of you until you give in and you're too weak to offer any pleas of resistance. They'll come to you with offers of empire with stars in their eyes. They'll do it. They tried with me, but I was too busy for them. Why do you think I was gone all the time? I was keeping them at bay."

"Right."

"I was, son. I devoted my life to worthwhile causes."

"Your pocketbook."

"I devoted it to trying to preserve the best part of what we will leave behind for our grandchildren."

"No. You devoted it to your pocketbook and dipping your wick in exotic waxes."

"You don't know me, son. No one does."

"I never had an opportunity."

"Don't turn your back on your inheritance. Our family's legacy."

"I really don't want it. I won't though. I'm going to devote myself to giving it all away."

"You know, son, I said the same thing to my father, and I told him that I would never be like him, and here I am having the same conversation with you. The times changed, son. You're the only person I trust enough to not louse up the family legacy."

"What family legacy?"

"Do you know the only time we ever manufactured anything for the war effort?"

"World War II?"

"Right, and do you know what we manufactured?"

"No. The Atomic Bomb?"

"No. Faulty pants fasteners for the Wehrmacht and SS, through a phony German Subsidiary. We sold them in droves. We supplied the pants fasteners to the German Army and those scumbag SS men."

"Yeah, right."

"It's true. Companies on both sides of the War were selling stuff to the other side for money. Most of it was shoddy, defective, designed to explode at the wrong time. It was just very hard at the time to trace origins. Your grandfather had the brilliant idea of making a defective pants fastener, which was designed to work for a few weeks and then snap when the wearer was running. Do you know how hard it is to fight a war with your pants around your ankles?"

"I suppose it's hard to do."

"We did our part for a few weeks. The Germans got word. They shut down our little enterprise...took the workers outside and shot them, but not until we sold them tens of millions of corrupted fasteners into the system. It took them years to root out. Hell, I even think Herr Fuhrer's riding suit was corrupted with a falling down fastener. Sure, we felt sorry for the workers who were duped into thinking they were serving the Fatherland by working in a vital war industry...."

"You can't say that the mining doesn't end up in weaponry, serving as components. You can't say that."

"We've never profited off of blood. Well, the Dutch side may have profited off of slavery at one time, but that was just in the shipping side of things. A shipper will carry any type of cargo. I think they got out of it when it became unfashionable. We don't get involved in that anymore, and you have to make sure that all the sons of bitches out there don't get the company involved in that."

"I care nothing about managing the company. I couldn't care less if it was the last corporation on the planet, and it was the only occupation to keep me from starving to death. I don't care at all. The company could go tits up tomorrow. I wouldn't bat an eye."

My father pinched his face up like there was something besides cancer eating up his insides.

"You little bastard," he said.

The words cut a tremor across the marrow of my bones.

"What?"

"You ungrateful little bastard, you're acting like no damn son of mine," he said.

"Father, what do you mean?"

"Stop playing dumb. No damn son of mine would ever back down from his birthright. I didn't. I couldn't. And neither can you. You can't, you can't do it, Jack. You can't."

"I can, and I will. I'm stronger than you."

"My God, my son, are you really that mad? How did I fail in life that my own son, the flesh of my own flesh should be so damn dysfunctional? How did I screw up in life that badly, what did I do?"

"It's probably what you didn't do, father, and besides that I'm feeling better, being able to tell you this to your face, being able to tell Hannah and Sheldon how I feel about him, it's been liberating. Being able to tell you, well in a little bit, I'm going to tell you how I feel about you, really and truly. I feel nothing for you. I suppose you brought me into the world, perhaps by folly, I don't know, maybe you wanted a son desperately to carry on the family name or maybe to do your little dirty business, to keep up with the contracts and expand the business onward to infinity, and, oh, into I don't know, the Horn of Africa or wherever."

He stared at me blankly.

"I don't know father, there isn't any Terra Incognita anymore. The fucking Chinese are already there, and they're sucking it dry, man. It just isn't worth it for me to spend my every waking moment taking one pile of money and trying to figure out how to make it grow. I just don't care, father. I don't care about your filthy, dirty, bloody money. I don't care how it came about. I don't give two shits how hard grand-grand- grand- robber baron Bartholomew Leman, or whatever the fuck his name is had to toil, trapping beaver in greater freezing Saskatchewan. The Lemans were poor once? We'll go back to being poor when you are good and dead, oh father of mine. When you are good and buried, you write back to me and tell me whether it is better to be rich, or it is better to just be alive. You write me a letter, and you tell me that, father..."

At that point I could not contain myself, and I burst out in laughter, which my father in his doped up state must have mistaken for tears.

"Son, you know that I can't do that. I know I haven't been the best father to you. I know that every last second of my life, and I think of how to make it up to you."

"You can't. What's done is done. You can't make it up. Now I know they've pumped you full of drugs to make you cognizant enough to talk to me. I know they've done this so you could try and talk me out of walking away from this whole sordid mess, talk me into attempting to take over the stewardship of the company...father it's a mistake. I'm not cut out for it. We're not cut from the same cloth. You and I both know that I'm not. I'll only fuck it all up, and they will destroy me. They're going to as good as bury me. I think they're trying to convince you to lock me up, to commit me to a hospital or something. Father, just let it go. I'm not a harm to others or myself. Father, just let me go. I'll disappear and never try and interfere myself into Leman Global Industries business again. I'll divest myself. I'll sell Sheldon all my shares. He'll manage the company well. It's what he really wants to do in life. He dreams about it, salivates in his dreams for the shot. Sheldon will take the world's largest private conglomerate public, and I'm sure it will be a riotous success. They'll expand into making bombs and bullets, mining tin and turning it into projectiles. So what, we'll never win a Nobel Peace Prize. So what."

"What will become of you?"

"I'll ride off into the sunset in my classic car, head to godknowswhere, and wander the Earth like a more jovial Cain, spreading mirth and goodwill. I'll give away the proceeds from my stock sales. I'll give it away to people who need it, 'cause where I'm going, I won't need money."

"Anywhere you go, you need money."

I thought of the .45 hand cannon that I brought with me. The Wacky Hutt bozos no doubt had locked it up as evidence of my madness in an extra strong locker somewhere. I think it was still loaded. I had a lump in my throat the size of my bloody heart.

"Where are you going, son? To do missionary work? Are you going to become a Franciscan? You going to go for the holy orders? What are you going to do?"

"I'll become a dead author, father. I'll write about life from the point of view of the dust. We'll be strange bedfellows, father of mine, and my soul will burn through my writing. I might even change my name, I'll write absurd things, father. I'll dump it straight from my living brain onto the page. That's the only way our brains live on after we're gone. I'll do battle with madmen... the ones who play like they are sane, rational creatures, and I'll slay them. I'll chop their heads from their shoulders and watch as geysers of blood stain my page like Old Faithful. And above all else, I'll live. I'll live, and I'll do what I want in this life, and I'll live like there is no tomorrow because there really isn't. It's just a series of sleepings and wakings, sleepings and wakings, a long trudging to the final sleep, the final blinking out when the power company turns out the lights even though you've been so good, a diligent boy scout about paying all your bills. The final sweep. Dust. You've come out with far more than you went in with, you're bounce-passing me a fortune, father, and I must say, I respectfully decline it."

"Some people spend the majority of their life just to earn .0000099% of what you stand to inherit, son."

"Facts and figures won't sway me, father. I know what I'm giving up. I do it freely."

"Sheldon and Hannah will get everything, then."

"They can have it! They're planning something dastardly for me, I know! And guess what? I'll just refuse to play their game! That's my answer. I'll just say no. I'll give up the crown like that one Roman Emperor. Just give it up! I'll refuse to play! That's the wise answer. I'll be my own man, for myself. That's where we've failed as a species, oh father of mine; we don't know when to quit and just fade out. When a man is given a choice between power and being the slave of all his fellow creatures, or powerlessness and being a complete and utter nobody and not in the power of anyone, he cannot choose to be alone. He can't be a free nobody. Well I choose loneliness! I'll have a lonely, free heart, and I'll smile, and any tears I shed will be tears of joy at my freedom."

"There's no helping you. There's no helping you. You have to take the helm. You have to. You have to be the final approval authority for the corporation. Sheldon, he'll sell us out."

"You've given me ample time to think. I thank you for that. I'm not in the business of trying to please anyone anymore. I'm done. As far as you're concerned, Jack Leman is dead. His cancer stricken father, his sister, and a host of nannies that taught him to think for himself survives him. His mother died at her own hand, or maybe not, godonlyknows, and her only real crime was doing what other people told her to do for her entire life with her freedom so pared down that her maybe suicide was her only recourse. So goes the theory. You can't hold me here any longer. Tell Sheldon and Hannah that after you depart the scene, I will sell them my entire inherited holdings in Leman Global Industries for the princely sum of, oh, one dollar, and I will depart the scene. Or you can just cut out the middleman and leave all your assets to those spellbound fools. You decide."

"Jack. You can't do this. You can't."

"Father, you weren't strong enough to walk away. I am."

I turned my back on him. He moaned and muttered feebly as I walked out the rich mahogany and teak paneled door. It closed with a clunk, heavy in my mind. The carpets, they felt sumptuous on my bare feet. My hospital gown would not do for an escape. I made my way to the drawing room and my father's closet. That man, he couldn't throw anything out. He was a clothing hoarder. He must have had a fortune in vintage clothing. In this closet, white marble inlaid with gold and heavy with green velvet trim, I happened upon my father's wedding tuxedo, in its original form, wrapped in shrink wrap to keep the ravenous moths at bay. *Perfect.* It would be a great outfit to escape in. I ripped it from the shrink-wrap. Maybe my father was saving it for me to marry in, to find some lucky girl to bed and wed, to have children with, to laugh, and sing and fuck in the tender moments of the sunshine of my youth.

Alas, I never learned to tie a bow tie so I thought I would just wear the tuxedo sans bow tie or any other accouterment, a tuxedo without a bow tie is also not deserving of a cummerbund, so I left them hanging together like cast off, closeted lovers. My old bastard of a father never took the time to teach me to tie a bow tie because it would have taken maybe ten minutes out of his busy day, so I have been to weddings bow tie less. Thank God I don't have any real friends who might declare me best man. Thank God I have not been nominated for a Nobel Prize in Literature, because I think you're supposed to wear a bow tie, or a National Book Award, but I think you might be able to show up to that fandango in a t-shirt and jeans. For I hear that those are somewhat snarky formal affairs, much like weddings of royalty or coronations.

Papa wouldn't have to teach me to tie a bow tie, I could have just googled it now. One didn't even need a father to teach you how to play baseball or the other pastimes that fathers and sons took part in. Fathers are obsolete. There's mommies and Google now. I found a pair of my father's shoes, but my feet were a little narrow, owing to the genetic input of my waifish mother, and I am more partial to Viking women and warrior women, their bestial bodies, the stuff of pagan legends when women were wild and free and not the dainty Christian housewives we are taught to lust over in the television shows. I would have loved to have boned Boudicca.

The shoes creaked slightly, but father was a gentleman and kept his shoes safe and sound and in shape in cedar shoe trees, all thousand or so odd pair of them to include the shoes made of sharkskin and manta ray and all sorts of bullshit creatures whose skin is pliable enough to make shoes out of. His closet was a veritable woolen paradise full of suits from the 1960s and earlier, skipping the unnatural fiber period of the 1970s; there was not a dusky rose or yellow-colored suit among the rows and rows of navy blues, gabardine, conservative suits and ties. My father never discoed.

I could have chosen any one of them, but instead, of course, I chose my father's wedding tuxedo, hand tailored to be worn on multiple occasions by an old world tailor, maybe from Italy. Yes, most likely from Italy, because my father liked the finer things in life. His name, BRIONI, or least that was what the label said on the inside, by the inner pocket. I reached in and found the play bill for an Opera, by Verdi from the year 1962 at the Bolshoi or some such place, I don't know; it was in Russian and there was some Madame Comrade's lipstick on it, one of the best kept secrets of the USSR, but no doubt father discovered that Russian maidens were not all fat hausfraus who rode tractors and wore babushkas. You know my father jetted off to a rendezvous whenever the spirit moved him. I suppose I could do the same, but I'm a creature of habit, and I rarely ever left home unless Marcus put me up to it. Dead Marcus.

Well, you know, dead within the limits of being a totally imaginary character that I invented, but who ended up inventing me. Hell, he would probably show up just like he used to and offer up some profound and life altering advice like some Navajo sweat lodge guru without the peyote, and I would follow it because he is my best friend and all in all the advice was really coming from the perturbations of my own diseased mind. Maybe Marcus is my Id or my superego, if I was free to believe or subscribe in the theories of Sigmund Freud. Personally, I always found him to be entirely too sexual, and the only person in need of psychoanalysis was Freud himself. At any rate, Freud would have much too much to say about me, none good. Fuck him. He's dead. His theories live on and continue to plague my sensibilities.

Marcus may come, so let him come. I hope he leads me to wine, women, and song. I hope he leads me off a cliff. I hope he leads me somewhere, anywhere but here and what I do in the present, to somewhere where I feel alive for maybe once in my miserable existence. Father wouldn't be around to trouble me anymore, so I would live my life for myself and become well versed and practiced in the ways of love and practiced in the ways of love and generosity, a fucking modern day St. Francis of Assisi, without all of the mad talking to birds shit, unless the birds had breasts, little pointy chins, high cheekbones, and big eyes. I would have to harness my illusions and make them my reality. I wouldn't be scared to do it. I was good at manufacturing them; dreamy little wispy visions, and I would be good at following them because following them would be following my heart. I would say no to the naysayers and exsanguinate them.

They could sleep alone underneath their musty tombstones, underneath the cold, cold Earth. I would live in the sky. An Eagle! Marcus would be a guide for me on this dumb Earth, but no more. I will soar! I will renounce it all! All of it! I would leave, flying, with my head held high, no dog with my tail between my legs, whimpering, simpering about from trash bin to trash bin in a blind search for consumables. Oh you douche, Sheldon! Have it! Take it all! My loss is your gain. I know the path! I'm going to follow it! I'm going to fly!

In order to be granted permission to leave their little house of horrors, I decided to put it into writing that I would totally give up any share in Leman Global Industries and go about the rest of my life totally divested from the family business, unconcerned about the buffeting, or the successes it would have in Sheldon's idiotic stewardship. I was very certain it would fail totally and be in receivership after at least five years because Sheldy's talents in life include spending money fruitlessly and marrying rich, not leading a multibillion dollar international mining and manufacturing conglomerate. If he didn't run the business into the ground it would be a miracle. He failed at whatever he attempted to do, and he did not learn from it. He had the business acumen of a parrot, but parrots who were well trained by their owners could often say, based on the position of the sun, what the weather would be like, "Looks like rain, awwwwk, looks like rain...."

Dressed in my tuxedo, which I admit was a bit over the top; I entered their bedroom without bothering to give the doctor's knock. My sister slept soundly. Sheldy paced the floor.

"Jackson, what are you doing out of bed?" he asked.

"I'm escaping, old buddy, old pal, my big brother. It's not that hard. I'm not as mad as you thought I was."

Sheldon cowered, perhaps expecting me to start shooting him at any minute. Bullets would fly and puncture him, and I would be laughing my fool head off, ventilating the frescos behind him.

"I've come here to sign over my rights to Leman Global Industries, and then I'll disappear. She's all yours, douche."

"Have you gone completely insane?"

"I think you know the answer to that. LGI will be in full receivership in a few years. I'm happy to walk away from it and you both."

Sheldy motioned to wake my sister.

"Don't wake her. Just hand over the car keys."

"I don't have them. You'll have to see Wainright, Chief of Security."

"Where can I find him?"

"Guard's Barracks most likely."

"Goddamn, I'm on a tight schedule to go nowhere. Call that prick up and tell him I'm on my way."

"Stop by legal first and sign that paperwork."

"You've had it drawn up for a while now, right?"

"Better this way than the other way?"

"Lawyers keep the loot."

"Yes, it's better this way," Sheldy said, looking quite self-assured.

"Can Marcus sign over his shares, too? You know, I made 25% owner with a gift of preferred shares, should we go public. My lawyer has all the paperwork. My portion will be in his name. So I guess he'll probably hold onto that."

"You nut," Sheldon muttered, furiously but still under his breath. Though too much of a coward to strike me, his words were daggers.

"You will fail," I struck back.

He made to wake my sister again.

"No. Don't wake her. I don't want to say anything to her. Good riddance."

"You'll fail," he said.

"There is no failure in being an artist. So what if my books don't sell or no one reads them. I'll still have written them. They'll be as real to me as you or me standing here."

"You bag of nuts."

"Keep pouring it on, Sheldon. You're terrified. You've got what you've always dreamed of. A chance. You'll blow it though. Everything that touches your hands dies."

"You're not a good writer."

"The only sin in writing is plagiarism."

"You're a plagiarist."

"Call me a plagiarist again, and I'll cut out your liver and feed it to you, Prometheus."

"Who?"

"I didn't think you'd understand that reference, you foggy MBA. You didn't really learn business either. Don't worry. I'll stop by legal on my way out of this cesspool. You don't actually have those little lawyers at work now, do you? It's, like, two in the morning!"

"It's about six in the morning, actually. They'll be in at 7:30."

"I'll make sure I stop by there."

"You better. Things could get ugly for you if you don't."

"Right. I suppose you're telling me I'll be written out of my father's will. I don't care. You've won...whatever winning means. You're life's big winner."

"Get out of here, Jackson. Get out before you make me mad."

"Oh, I'm going. You don't have to tell me twice."

I stomped out, shuffling my feet, real dramatic like. The 1960s Italian leather shoes creaked like the lid softly going shut on a coffin and being reopened again over and over. I think old Sheldy wanted me to attack him. Walking away galled him, and he ran outside the door, shutting it gingerly, then running, bounding over to me in a surprising way for a fat pear shaped man, panting and huffing after me.

"You can't just walk out of here," he said, wheezing.

"That's what you want me to do."

"But you can't!" he yelled, and grabbed my arm, squeezing it tightly like a fat kid's grip on a candy bar.

"Get your fat dickbeaters off of me!" I snatched his weak, flabby arm away. Even though I'm young and svelte and frankly in greater shape than my unfortunately pear shaped brother in law, wrenching his arm from mine proved to be difficult.

We struggled.

"You cretin! I'm trying to leave! Do you have to be so dramatic in keeping me here?"

"You've got some trick planned! You're too damn cavalier about all this! What did you talk to your father about?"

"I didn't talk to him."

"Sure you did. I saw the tape, you shit!"

"Too bad, you didn't hear the sound. Roll the tape, fat boy, and learn to read lips!"

He redoubled his efforts.

"Nah! You're up to something!"

"You said it yourself, Sheldy! I'm a madman! Let the madman go away! You're getting what you want! Now un-fat-hand me, asshole! Get your filthy dickbeaters off me! Security! Security! I'll be forced to thrash you in a moment, you fat boll weevil!"

A couple of Wacky Hutt employees bound in the downstairs ballroom, both with what appeared to be tazers in hand (TAZER is a licensed trademark of TAZER INTERNATIONAL, INC. NASDAQ: TASR) and one with a flashlight looking quite like John Wayne. They ran up the stairs full bore and shouted, "What's the problem bucko!" in unison. I put my free hand to my eyes to avoid the glare. Sheldy did his best to yank it down.

"Arrest this man! If you're good for anything! Stick him in the hole! Ack!"

"I need to get out of here!" I ordered to them.

Sheldy said very directly, "Men, who signs your paychecks? Me. Look at them next time. Sheldon Grimbone! Well that's me. You need to arrest this man, here."

The guards looked confused. "I grew up in this home," I implored them.

"We've never seen you before, sir," the younger of the two guards said.

I broke Sheldon's grasp and made for the stairs. I heard the snap of the Taser and then my muscles seized. My legs locked, and I fell, face first, down the carpeted stairs toward the marble foyer floor, looking much like a ski jump gone horribly awry. The whole way down before it all went black, I swear Sheldon was laughing.

XXX**XXXXXXXX**XXXXXXXXXXX**XXXXXXXX**XXXXX**XXXXXXXXXXX**XXXXX
XXXXXXXX**XXXXXXX**XXXX**XXX**XXXX**XXXXXXXXXXXXXXX**XXXXXXXXX**XX**
XXXX**XXXXXXX**XXXXXXXXX**XXXXXX**XXXXXXXXX

I came to. I was in my father's room. Sheldy stood there, over my father, and tried his best to feign concern. He had a real boo boo bottom lip sticking out, and I think there were a few ersatz crocodile tears coming down his face. What a rammer. The family attorney was present and so was Dr. Gilroy. He had administered me an IV in my sleep. My bowels rumbled. Perhaps he administered an enema, too. Doctor was fond of those. "Never leave anything to chance," he would always say. Plus it was an opportunity to double bill my family 500 bones, 450 for the procedure, and 50 dollars for a five-cent disposable butt plug. I reached down and felt around. There was no butt plug in, so maybe an enema wasn't performed. At any rate, the prick was out of a job as soon as dad croaked.

Sheldon glared at me. Father, glassy eyed, stared off into the distance like he was waiting for worms or maybe looking at a chorus of angels. He didn't seem the least bit scared, just tired, really. He looked past the wall, as if into an invisible courtyard of his past where children played the games of childhood like there was no tomorrow.

"He needs some more of the drug to come to, honey," Sheldon said, choking back tears.

"Give it to him then, Doctor."

Gilroy said in his best gravely authoritarian voice, "He's had too much in the past 48 hours. Giving him any more will have serious side effects. He needs his rest."

"What's another dose? Will it make him comatose?" Hannah asked, crying.

"Ha! You rhymed!" I yelled, clapping my hands like a seal. Humor was the only way to deal with these madmen. I had to play the fool for them all, because that's all they thought of me. I had to play their game until they let me go.

Who was in on it? The Doctor? Most likely. The lawyer? My businessman brother-in-law? My sister? My dad? The goddamned butler, Chauncey? Who was in on it? I should have to murder them all! The guards? I would have to pay them off to turn against their masters. Coup d'etat! How much did they earn a year? Ten thousand bucks? Twenty thousand at the most? Lackeys! They didn't look underfed. They must have had a McDonald's allowance. Put her on the corporate account, eh? Big Macs all around. (Big Mac is a registered trademark of McDonald's Foodservice Corporation). Father was the only one who wasn't looking well. He looked a shade of death that I'd never quite seen before. Actually, some corpses I visited looked a few shades more healthy than him because they usually didn't have a horrible grimace on their faces. I don't know if he was in pain or what, but he was looking right at me, acting like he wanted to cry, but there were no tears.

The doctors hovered over him like flies on a garbage heap, not saying that father was a garbage heap, but rather saying that the doctors were licking him of money ever so lightly, tasting here and there with their long tongues, while deciding all the time to prolong his life as long as possible. Milk their sweet gig for as long as they could, even if it meant the suffering of my poor father. He was not just being consumed by cancer; he was dying of extreme old age. One of the doctors administered the contents of a blue vial in an injection. Immediately the color came back to his cheeks, sweetness overcame the pallor, and an ambiguous Mona Lisa smile replaced the grimace.

"The medicine is losing its effectiveness, Doctor," one doctor said to another doctor. I don't know which specialties they all practiced. To me, one white lab coat was as good as another. They were all plumbers and wastes of damn fine scientists.

"You know," I announced, much to the chagrin of everyone in the room, "we should really stop pumping dear old dad full of this synthetic shit. Anyone ever think about just cooking something wholesome for him...you know, maybe giving him an apple a day? Shouldn't we just let nature run its course?"

"No. You should butt out and leave pop's treatment to the professionals."

"The will hasn't been decided yet? Why are we prolonging this man's suffering?"

"Oh, it's been decided," the lawyer declared.

"Signed?" Sheldon asked.

"No, not yet."

"It's null and void then! Ha!" Sheldon declared, quite weirdly, with a giddy smile on his face.

"How do you know what it's going to say?"

Sheldon and the Lawyer, an entity who worked for a law firm, both the man and the law firm professional but utterly forgettable, and who's name I forget even though I saw him several times growing up and he always asked me how I was doing and was generally friendly...he was just the most non-descript person I really ever met, a lawyer in a suit, another man in a suit with a face and a neck who said legalistic things and got paid. After he said hello and goodbye, he sort of trickled out of your memory like a newt in Niagara Falls. He was boring. I don't know where he got his degree at, perhaps Monotone Law School or Tacky Suit U. He had on a particularly tacky suit, and white socks.

The suit was brown, or maybe gray. In this dim light, I can't tell and I'm still woozy from the tazing. My ass, where the prongs entered my skin, hurt. I rubbed it. Lawyer looked like a used car salesman in a suit he might have obtained from Goodwill, third hand. Maybe it was a Sears's original. I think it has gold buttons, probably with some sort of hokey crest on it. I think the tie was in fashion in Ronnie Reagan's presidency. A real Wall Street power tie back then that just seemed really lame nowadays. The tie was yellow, but looked like it had been worn by a whole host of smoking chimpanzees with the shakes, yellow with little brown scorch marks. He held three brown boxes from Fed Ex Kinkos in his arms, sort of haphazardly stacked. The last will and testament of Prescott Leman III.

"He'll have to sign it today. We can't pump any more of that chemical into him," Sheldon said.

Father wobbled a bit in his bed. Chauncey, my pop's faithful butler, erected a curtain around father. It was to shield him from anyone else who was not really invited to see him die. Some people were there, but only as cosigners. My father was an immaculate planner. That way people would hear of his death, but would not get to sneak an iPhone shot of his death mask. I would sign my share away. Sheldon and my sister would be the sole beneficiaries of the entire estate. Dad would probably have to give away a boatload of cash, maybe sell off some of his art collection to various mistresses, girlfriends, concubines, and outright hookers scattered in apartments throughout the greater globe. Dad always liked it rough, the environment that is, not his sex. I never knew how he liked that, other than outdoors.

The tougher the tenement, the more my dad loved it. He says that living amongst the poor inspired him. The butler, after the scaffold curtain was set up, left the room shaking his head. He looked at me and smiled a genuine, loving smile, one without malevolence. I doubted that he was aligned against me. The Lawyer entered the curtain sheepishly. Sheldon watched Lawyer with approval, a sort of delightful hope on his face like he had been waiting for this moment ever since he heard my sister was single. A sinister accountant peered over the ledger books, dusty, leather-bound, and cracking. He shuffled the papers. No one seemed to notice his presence there, but he touched them on the shoulder, one by one. Each in his stead, he made his way around the room, touching everyone on the shoulder.

"Just counting everyone here. Got to account for everyone," he said to me as he came and touched me on the shoulder. "There's one missing though. One missing. Yet to arrive," he said as he made his way past me.

I watched this man as he moved across the room, silently, like a snail. He was a dark man with a grimy beard, ill kempt, with tatters in his pressed, black wool suit. He held a hat in his hand. It was a queer hat really: an off green hat, sort of a color green like a pepper that just started to rot and go towards brown. A sickly green. He paced around the room and gazed at everyone with coal black eyes as if he were waiting for something to happen. Did anyone else notice this man? Who accounts for the accountant? Maybe a tailor, here to make the final measurement on a fine suit, Italian, but this gentleman looked a little Irish to me. Perhaps one of father's more eccentric legal professionals. Maybe his head of security? No, had to be an accountant. He entered stood inside the curtain with the rest of us when the Doctor called, "The cancer has spread to his brain."

The room took on a foul odor. I don't think anyone else noticed. The sinister man nodded in agreement and opened his dusty volume. He made a few notes and then closed it. He headed towards the door.

"And where are you going?" I called to him. He did not stop, and he did not look at me.

A man entered as he exited. It was another strange man, but this man looked familiar to me, like I had seen him before somewhere, maybe long ago, somewhere. He had one of those faces that were very apparent and you would remember it. He was skinny, like he either worked out a tremendous amount or ate heartily or he didn't work out at all and survived on oxygen and water. And his accent, when he announced who he was to the Lawyer who was the defacto bouncer here, was British. All I heard was the last name, Malvolio. I could not garner his position, but he moved through the room like a knife. He bent down and spoke to my father who whispered things into his ear. He listened. He nodded. He said yes quite a bit.

His position was most likely a Yes-man. And they were in no short supply in my father's organization, but who knew really what this gent did. He struck a fear into me with his familiarity. However, no one else seemed to know him or notice him much. Sheldon kept his eyes on the will, as if behind this great curtain, even though it was a full fifteen feet to bedside and my father's withered arms signing the page as this Malvolio talked to him and received orders or Godknowswhat...and I swear I've seen him before somewhere. Maybe he was part of the security detail that was assigned to me and who were always just out of sight. My father finished signing. The pen, some fancy number purchased for this event, fell from his hands. As if with signing, he had signed the remainder of his diminutive life force away. Lawyer bundled up the will and sealed it with thick tape. A smile came across his face as he realized that his work was done, and he could finally retire and spend his millions. Father gasped. He slumped in his bed. The Doctor came forward and felt for his vitals.

"He's gone," the doctor announced with a gravely voice more befitting an action hero than a man of medicine. It wasn't sensitive at all. More like an announcement that he was out to lunch than that he had died. Tears welled up in my eyes. I did my best to contain them, I really did, and it doesn't seem right that I should have spent most of my life hating him, but now it all seemed so petty. And to think that the last things I said to him were just designed to make him feel miserable and introduce a great amount of uncertainty when all he wanted was to feel certain that all he worked on during his life would not go to pot. I looked through my tears to Sheldy, who had formed an avaricious grin on his face, as if my only protection had just vanished. Sheldy was already barking orders.

"Make a press release, but don't release it yet. What's that called?"

"Uhh...an unreleased press release?" a writer, a member of the press corps, who came as soon as he was called said.

"A corporate memorandum," I said. "The only people who can write those are officers. I don't think you're an officer of the corporation, yet."

"Oh, damn it to hell. Just write it up and let me approve it."

"And just who are you? Good God, man! My father's not even cold for a moment, and you're already shouting orders like you run the place. You're not in charge of anything yet. I don't think you'll ever be in charge of anything."

"You said you'd sign the company over to me, uh, us..." he said, looking at his wife, who was still dumbfounded by the proceedings.

"Nah. I don't think so. Verbal agreements aren't legally binding, not on this scale. Plus, I was off my meds," I said.

Sheldon turned his shade of grape.

"Are you on dope?" I asked him.

"What? On dope?"

"Yes, you're turning all red, and that's a hallmark of being on dope."

"I'm not on fucking dope!"

"You look like you're abusing narcotics. Sis, does this guy take frequent blow bathroom breaks? How's your petty cash doing?"

"I'm not on any sort of drugs."

"You look like you're all sweaty."

"I'm...I'm just really stressed out."

"You should take a vacation until the funeral. Take some paid time off."

"Now you're telling me what to do?"

"Yes."

"You can't."

"Well, until we know the contents of the will, I will. You've got a lot bet on getting more than your fair share of my dad's fortune, don't you?"

"No."

"Sure you do. All your hopes and dreams. That'll be a hard fall, Icarus."

"I don't."

"Don't lie, Sheldy. You married my sister with that in mind."

"He did not," Hannah said.

"He did."

"You don't know anything about the love we feel for each other. You don't even know how to love," Hannah said.

"I do to."

"Jackson, you've no clue."

"I know what love isn't. You don't have the body language of a couple in love. I see you two together, and all I see is *American Gothic*."

"Give me a break. You don't have a clue. You talk out of your ass all the time."

"Jackson, why don't you just leave already?"

"Hey, the truth hurts. I'll tell you what, Sheldy. If you so happen to gain control of my family's breadwinner through some machination or just plain luck, you won't be happy, ever. You...you...you need more, more, more. You don't just want. Nah, this cancer has grown in you to become a need. It's ensconced itself into your soul. The taproot has wrapped itself into your heart. Without it, you'd be dead. You can't stop acquiring shit. That's what it is. You're carrying this virus around. I could care less about all that you need. I'll sink into the shadows. I'll live. I'll go about my own merry business. You, you can't walk away. You can't ever be unremarkable. You better hope you come out on top...whatever that even means. You better hope that happens."

"Slam dunk."

"Your use of sports references indicates a marked lack of intellect."

"Forgot, you're a writer."

"I'm an auteur. I'm going to be one of the greatest...."

"That's a laugh. The greatest authors who ever lived? Ha! You can never be as good as...those guys."

"You don't know any."

"It's not important. That's why I don't know any. Who cares anyway?"

"I won't even begin to argue with you. It would be like trying to debate the meanings of life with a video game-addicted, three year old cretin."

Sheldon broke out in laughter. I think it was directed at me. "Meanings? Who cares about meanings anymore?"

I turned around and walked out. I slammed the mahogany doors behind me, and they reverberated throughout the house, sound waves bouncing off the grand chandelier and sending the glass tinkling. It was a show off implement, just like this entire house. It was purchased from the former baronial home of some French prick that was born into wealth and authority in the 1750s and ended up losing his head during the Terror. It was another thing that I would sell off on eBay. I paused at the top of the stairs to see just who would come storming after me, and no one came. I could hear a commotion inside of the room, like someone was wrestling. I suppose it was Hannah tearing at her hair in grief over our father's demise. You know, for all it was worth, my father was able to teach me a few things during his lifetime. He taught me what it was like to long for someone or something to fill a void.

When he would come home, he would make his presence known to our nannies and the housekeeping staff, a sumptuous meal would be laid out, like the arrival of some Middle Eastern dictator to one of his many palaces. The sons of busy-as-a-bee men are left wondering what life and fortune will have in store for them. When my father would come home, and that is, if he actually ever made it home, it would seem to Hannah and me that Santa Claus himself were descending from the heavens. Father's coming home! Father's coming home! Hannah and I would tell each other, and then we would giddily prepare alongside the other housekeepers and servants. Like the other servants, when his plane was delayed or he had to be diverted to another business interest, we were upset that all of our hard work went to waste.

I may be batshit crazy, but I can deal with it. Writing will help me deal with it. Maybe I should try and get away from the whole Marcus Hanely thing, you know, maybe kill him off, make him die at the hands of a new character, or give him some ignoble end like getting hit by a bus, or die in some terrorist attack where he wasn't even the target, just some pathetic instance of collateral damage. I could bring back the female heroine; I mean she is the one that drove the buyers of *Asymmetric Hearts* anyway. They really identified with her, but I don't really know why. Maybe it was because she could so effectively keep the male mega-stud Marcus under her thumb. So what if my status as a best selling novelist is somewhat in doubt now. I'll just travel and write, and take pleasure in putting the words on the page, stringing them along or maybe bringing delight to some poor person who happens to be perusing the aisles of some dusty used bookstore and comes across my collected works. I won't force the numbers or manipulate the sales. That's for businessmen. They're the professional liars and massagers. They're the ones that convince people that something they're selling is valuable. Where does one find inspiration in this flat, boring, potato chip bag, beef jerky, and gas station infested nightmare of a country?

Do I sequester myself in some cabin far off in the woods where I can sit and stare out the window at some scenic vista that I'm taught is supposed to be real inspiring and I'm sure was photographed by Ansell Adams in stunning black and white at some point early in his career? Am I supposed to do that and open myself up to the possibility of being mauled by a bear in the pursuit of genius and inspiration in stringing words on the page to form meaningful and awe inspiring classics that will barnstorm and burn brightly through the generations?

Maybe I'm being too bold. Perhaps I want to take on too much. Perhaps I am trying to heave the heavens on my shoulder blades and thrust it ever higher. Shouldn't one try to do just that? The world is going to crush you. It's going to eviscerate you. You won't get out alive. Isn't life middling and boring and loaded with ennui enough without people making at least the attempt at doing something grand? I suppose I could give into the doctors and medicate myself into oblivion. I could seek normalcy and normal behavior. I could seek comfort, which many people mistake with peace, calm, and quiet these days. I'm the poster boy for internal conflict and frustration.

I say, let them play out! Let them smash off each other and intertwine! Let all your loves, lusts, hatreds, all your best sanguine elements come thrusting to the surface like so many Himalayas. At least you won't be a bore. At least you'll be slightly interesting, perhaps to the next fellow or next lady who sits next to you on some bus somewhere, who shares the space and breathes the oxygen, should you converge to engage them in conversation. They might just realize that in you. They might think you're dangerous, but being dangerous and alive is better than being asleep or dead.

You know, I've been told I think too much. I don't even know what that means, but all the people who have told me that, as I've noticed, love watching television. I tell them they don't think enough. It really pisses them off, and they go off sulking. My ability to act is lost in ratiocination. I'll tell you what, monsieurs and madams. It is time for me to start acting. Will I go off into a cabin in the woods, alone with myself, some lovesick Thoreau? I don't think so. I need to get out amongst them all. Burn the candle at both ends. Cut all the meat from the bone and suck out the marrow like a ravenous wolf. I want to eviscerate life and see what it is that makes it play. I want to report on that. When I'm dead, in a dusty tomb like my dear old dad, all that will remain is my dusty words, and I hope they will carry with them a brief glimmer of vitality. We shall see.

I half expected my sister to come wailing out of the room pleading with me not to go. In fact, I stopped in the foyer, near the front door and waited for her to come rushing up to me. That would have been the dramatic thing, but my sister, I guess, is not given to histrionics. I wanted Sheldon to come barging out, waving a cutlass or rapier with which to run me through or challenge me to a duel. I think the lawyers present had a calming effect on him and advised him just to let me go. I began pacing back and forth in the foyer, wearing a track in the Italian marble with my black leather Italian shoes, one size too small in length and too wide for my feet. Someone stepped out of the shadows, gripping a handkerchief, wiping down his eyes. Chauncey was once young and vital, fresh out of Butlering School, when my father hired him sight unseen on recommendations from the previous butler who left our employ to attempt to fulfill his dreams of starring in detective serials in Hollywood. I knew this Butler well. However, Chauncey was now older, more infirm, with tired eyes from all he had seen. I wanted to comfort him. He looked to have been crying and was more shaken up over my father's death than I was.

"Is the shock of it all preventing your grief, Master Jackson?"

I thought for a second. Nope, really I felt nothing. Like there was some great buildup of pressure that really turned out to be me thinking that there should be some emotional response. I lied to him.

"Yes. I'm waiting until I have private time to cry. You know I'm an incredibly private person. I'll wait until that time to cry and wail and wring my hands in shit."

He didn't hear me. He was hard of hearing and had great hearing aids in his ears.

"Where are you going then, Master Jackson?"

"Don't know. Wherever opportunity and that whore, Fortune, take me."

"Oh that's good. So you're going to Chicago, then. I shall see you there. Your father has left me something for my service."

"I really don't know where I'm going. Pick a direction, I'll head that way. Give me some guidance, man. I'm a ship without a rudder or helmsman. I'm waiting to see what I run into."

"You're not going to run into anything."

"My father was full of goals and plans, fully baked schemes and intentions, and look where all his scheming and plotting, planning and contracts and bills of sale and deeds got him? A lifeless corpse. It all comes to that. No matter what you do in life, it all comes to that, and the others will judge you and write up an ill-conceived epitaph because they never really knew you. Look, we judge my father harshly for his deeds, but we never really knew his inner intentions, we never really knew what drove him. He never told us, never shared. He provided, but was not giving of himself. You aren't your money, Chauncey. Your bank account cannot be stored in your soul."

"Then do what you want to do, Master Jackson. You're not in your father's shadow anymore. He's dead and gone, the grand old man..." Chauncey got a bit choked up. This man actually loved and respected my father for reasons that I could not fathom and did not have time to ask. I had to get on the road. "What are you going to do?" he asked. Maybe he wanted me to take him with me. I couldn't. Not possible.

"I don't know," I told him.

"Dear Jackson, do try and figure it out."

"That's just what I'm going to do, Chauncey. Thank you for your concern, so you know in a sense I'll be doing something. Even if I give away all the money I stand to inherit, even if I give it all away, say sayonara to riches, pay it forward, whatever, divorce myself from it, remove myself from the equation...."

"You can't be alive and remove yourself," Chauncey said. "You're living. Your father may be dead...you're not. You're like a son to me, too, Jackson. Now why don't you go out and live? Forget about dear old dad. You've got the money."

"I give two shits about the lure that fills the bowels of the Earth. I give two great buckets full of shit for the money. I despise it. I care about time more. My time, which everyone fills with the pursuit of stuff, so they can make a measure of progress. I could care less about all this stuff. You won't ever make me care about it."

He shook my hand with a Rolex wrapped wrist, a gift from my father, and said, "I'll remain here, Master Jackson. I'm staying here because I'm too old to travel. I'll watch whoever lives in this house."

"It may be abandoned. I won't live here."

"Well then, I'll make sure the house stays in order."

"Why don't you retire?"

"Can't think of much to do with my retirement. The house will always be open to you. Even if we have to smuggle you through the basement corridors."

"Thank you. You were my father's butler, a faithful servant, and a keeper of secrets, small and great. Will you still have a job with my degenerate sister and brother-in-law? Will you watch their children like you watched me? Will you allow them to ride on your back through the halls, a faithful steed like Bucephalus? Will you be there when their father won't comfort them? Get me my Doctor, Chauncey! I wish to see him! I wish to bid him adieu forever!"

"The Doctor, good sir, ran away with one of the maids."

"So he served my father, really, when I was his patient. His medicines kept me quiet, like a ghost, an apathetic little ghost. Drugged, doped up on thorazine dreams, free from outbursts."

"You quite possibly could have needed that, Master Jackson."

"I like your use of possibility, good old Chauncey. It's intriguing that you must be so inclined to be hopeful."

"I can be nothing else. We've nothing but hope, here."

"Well neither can I. That's..."

"And just who are you, Master Jackson? I know who I am."

The heavy wooden door opened, and Hannah emerged, running down the marble stairs like she used to do as a child; however, now she was running with a heavy burden like a rucksack on her back. I think it was probably regret.

"Are you just going to leave? You're going to run away and turn your back on your family?"

"What is with you? Why won't you just let me go?"

She walked down the final two stairs, and stood right in front of Chauncey like he wasn't even there, a transparent screen to be shouted through. Chauncey backed up and took position near the base of the stairs. He seemed to disappear in the shadows and become a part of that great house.

"Well, pardon us."

"Who were you just speaking to?"

"My father's butler. My surrogate father. Chauncey. You remember him, I suppose."

"Jesus, Jackson. Chauncey died maybe ten years ago now."

"What?"

"Yes. He's dead."

"He was just here! He was as real as the sun, the moon, the stars!"

"Jackson. You can't leave. You aren't stable. People will take advantage of you."

Hannah looked at me with horror. Her shock melted to sadness and she started to weep, pouring tears down her face.

"Jackson, what's happened to us? Why did we allow ourselves to be this way?"

"At each other's throats? I've always been this way. Full of delusions. As mad as a Denmark Prince with weeping willows for a crown."

"Could you drop your dramatic persona for just a minute. I'm really trying to talk to you here. Talk to me like we were kids again."

"I'm sorry, sis. The boy in me is long dead. Life is serious. The boy is dead, rotten, and dusty in a grave. I can't go back. Really, I can't. I've got my life to live, to live anonymously. Live by the pen, you know."

"Quit trying to be something you aren't."

"There's the rub. I can't find even a kernel of who I am in there. I don't know. I've failed. You do the same, Hannah! Take your own advice. You aren't a schemer. You're no Livia. Your husband, that petty castrated Nero, must have put you up to all of this."

"My god, Jackson. What do you have against him? You don't know him. You've never made an attempt to know him. You needed to know the truth! You needed to know the truth so we wouldn't lose you again!"

"Where's my doctor?"

"We had to let him go."

"The Butler told me he ran off with the maid."

"Drop the Butler."

"He ran off with the Brazilian maid."

"We've never had a Brazilian maid here."

"Never? Must have mixed fantasy with reality again. Nine parts fantasy. You should have seen her curves."

"The only Brazilian maid I ever knew..."

"Was in Brazil," I said with a smile.

Hannah looked at me, real penetratingly like. "We just had to go out into the jungle that day and leave mother alone to lounge by the pool. We just had to have adventures, you and me. We couldn't just sit quietly by the pool and watch mother read her fashion magazines. We couldn't just be quiet."

"We should have. I've always been afflicted with the most pernicious wanderlust, and you have too. It's in our DNA. That's why your marriage to that great Gibraltar of a man is particularly difficult for me to swallow."

"A woman's place is to make a home."

"Or wreck one to make one."

"Find yourself a good woman, Jackson. Settle down. Have children."

"Tried once. It's not really working out."

"Jackson, you're missing out."

"Build myself a mausoleum or another monument to myself and my finite horizon…I'd rather pitch barrels of gasoline into the burning hot sun, sister. No, my job isn't to do the mundane; it's to burn my soul. Suffer for the world and yourself as you wish, sister. I'll offer myself up as a sacrifice."

"No one will care."

"I can't enter into anything with that attitude. Of course they won't care. It's up to me to care. That's your problem. You've never given yourself up. You've never given up on other people."

"You've never shared any of yourself with anyone else."

"My mind is my own."

"You're delusional, Jackson."

"So be it. I'm a madman. I'll be a madman for life and living. I'll ride a pale horse. I'll gallop headlong towards destiny. Headlong into the fray. I'm absolutely scared of nothing."

"Your whole life is fear. You're so afraid that it never even penetrates you. You're so afraid that you can't be anything else. That's why you don't love anything. You have no mental space for love. Your fear eats it for breakfast. Tell me something, Jackson. The second you have even a kindling of love enter your frame, your overwhelming fears extinguish it. Have you ever loved anyone, Jackson? Ever?"

"I think I did once."

"You thought."

"I'm sure I'll find it. I'm sure it will happen, I mean. I mean, I think I'm ready."

"Just open yourself. Ask yourself when you meet anyone, 'is this person real?'"

"Give up my hallucinations? I've the medicine for that."

"Give them all up. Banish them."

"Jackson, who wrecked your Ferrari?"

"Marcus…."

"Jackson!"

"I did."

"Say it again."

"I did."

"Good. Admit it."

"Goddamn it, okay."

"Get angry with yourself. It's fine."

I sulked. I folded my arms. She was right. My mind was my prison. My nut-shell mind. Not this home, not my childhood, not Brazil, not Father, not Mother, not Marcus Hanely. My Mind. My Mind was the prison. The spider webs that bound me. I created adventures, so I did not have to actually adventure. I created friends to spare me the feeling of actually having them. I created the meaning to spare me the expense to my soul of actually building a meaning for myself. I didn't need self-help. I didn't need a professional evaluation. What I needed was to shatter this self-facing mirror into five thousand separate pieces. Not through drugs, not through booze, sex, butt fucking, not through shopping, but maybe just through some meaningful conversation through some shared experiences with my fellow members of the human race: people would look at me with suspicion, I suppose. I could, I take it, reveal myself through my interactions with other people.

"Hannah," I said. "I desire peace. I ask you for peace between us, peace and reconciliation. I wish that we could live in harmony with each other, but that isn't my business. I just want no animosity between us. Hannah, we've been through a lot together. We have. You know it. I'll always be your little brother. I'll be a wonderful uncle to your children. Right now I just need time."

"Okay. What are you going to do?"

"Drive. Write. Talk to people. Get out of my own head." *Kill myself.* I pushed the thought away as soon as it came.

"You may not see it, but people care about you. You have a marvelous ability to affect them in good ways."

"I don't know, sis. What I'm doing, it's going to be difficult."

"Just find out for yourself."

I embraced her, and then turned to walk out the door. A thought occurred to me.

"When are we burying father?"

"The press release already went out and should be reported in the morning news. I'm sure it's probably all over the Internet."

"I asked when we were going to bury him."

"I don't know his wishes. Father was terribly secretive."

Like a piss poor defense attorney, I left questions unasked. I supposed she would call me and hope I had cellular reception.

"When you open up the will, I'd like to be there."

"Where are you going, Jackson?"

"I'll tell you what I tell everyone else," I said to her. "I don't know."

I couldn't trust her husband, even though I had forgiven her for marrying him. He might dispatch an assassin against me to rub me out. You know, this was probably all an attempt to fish the information out of me, information that she would deliver to my assassin. No, I wouldn't tell her anything. Deflection, that's what it would be.

"Yeah, I'll have my iPhone on me." (iPhone is a registered trademark of Apple Computer, Inc., NASDAQ: AAPL).

I turned to walk out of the door, expecting her to stop me. She made no effort. I watched her climb the stairs, defeated. She probably thought she'd never see me again. Who knows where the road will take me. Maybe she never would.

My family? Those who weren't dead should be written off as dead. Those friends of mine? All imaginary. Finely tuned hallucinations. All the happy memories were nothing but wasted time. They were so real! Like I could reach out and touch them! Marcus and Willard, dear old friends of mine! Wayward souls, kindred spirits! What was the root? A profound gullibility? Had I not progressed beyond some childhood stage in my development? Was my growth as a person retarded somehow? Retarded from the infantile stage? Was I like a great big walking baby who invented playmates to cure my boredom and pain? I don't even feel boredom and pain. I don't feel much of anything. Did not my own brain supply the details so I could live vicariously through Marcus's actions? It was because I was too scared to actually live. Did I not want to become Marcus Hanely in my own life? Who was Willard? What did he represent? A need for restraint? The wisdom of the ancients? He was dead. Those were the thoughts that I had as I made my way to the Wacky Hutt guardhouse to retrieve my keys to the hell wagon. When the security guard finally found the envelope in the paragon of disorganization that was the guard house, even though it was air conditioned, the guards were busying themselves playing multiplayer shoot 'em up games: practice most likely. He handed me the envelope, and I found the keys and my iPhone, which had tons of missed calls and text messages.

"Have you all been joy riding in my car?"

"No, sir. Though I have to say, it's been tempting."

"Why's that?"

"The car is one of a kind. I'm surprised you're even driving it."

"Cars are meant to be driven."

I glanced down at his nametag: AINSWORTHY, written in black and surrounded by highly polished brass.

"What are you meant to do, Ainsworthy? Guard this post?"

"I guess so. Uhh, yes, sir."

"Surely there's more to you than that."

"I'm married."

"With children?"

"Yes. Two boys."

"Awesome. I've been thinking about doing that."

"Getting married? Don't."

"Why not?"

"Single's where it's at."

"It's empty."

"Do you have a girlfriend?"

"No, but they're easily obtainable."

Ainsworthy laughed.

I folded up a 100-dollar bill and placed it in the pocket behind the nametag.

"Thanks," I said.

"You're not allowed to tip me."

"I wanted to tip you."

"I mean, I can't accept tips."

"It's not for you. Buy your boys something nice with that. Promise me."

"Promise you what?"

"That you'll buy your boys something nice with it and won't just spend it on yourself. I know they keep you here for a long time with minimal pay. The boys will appreciate a gift."

"I can buy toys for my children myself. The hours aren't that bad, and I make a decent living. We're happy."

He tried to give me the 100 dollars back, but I held my hands up like he had just demanded my money or my life. I backed up saying, "You keep it. You keep it."

I turned from the guard headquarters and ran to my shiny, sparkling, most bad ass, new to me 1969 Pontiac GTO Judge. In the fluorescent lights of the main parking area, next to the Bentleys, SUVs, other real pretentious prick-mobiles, party car Lambos, and rarer 1960s Ferraris, the car looked like an original dream that I would have a hard time waking up from.

"Hey!" the Wacky Hutt guard yelled after me, as I opened the Judge door and was nearly getting into the front driver's seat. He ran towards me in a military, but unthreatening manner, holding what looked like an iPad in his right hand. (iPad is a registered trademark of Apple Computer, Inc. NASDAQ: AAPL). Startled, I looked to see if there was a perpetrator hiding in the garage, ready to cold cock me and steal my ride.

"You need to sign this letter of release and security affirmation statement," the guard said.

"Oh God, really? I'm part of the family."

"Hey, rules are rules. I didn't make them up."

"The guy who formerly made all the rules is dead. You can know that. The press release came out already. Feel free to post it on Facebook."

"Really?"

"Yeah, my dad croaked earlier today, may he rest in peace."

"Will we still have jobs?"

"I guess. As long as things need guarding around here."

"Thank God," he muttered and then snapped to a quasi attention that he had probably seen somewhere in a movie. A hint of recognition came over his face, "I mean, uh, sir, sorry about your loss."

"No problem."

Why the hell am I so humble? Marcus, or even Sheldy would have smacked this peon around. He's always been indignantly righteous with an air of superiority that most mortals only attempt to duplicate. Marcus that is, not Sheldy. Sheldy was a human ramrod. Fit only for a hole.

"What the hell is this I'm signing on?"

"An iPad."

"It looks cool."

"I know. You use your finger to sign. No need for a stylus. It's a much more advanced product than even a few years prior. It's really revolutionized our job."

"Can you write books on that thing?"

"I suppose so."

I read over the agreement...blah...blah...blah...blah...at no time in the future from my visit to the Leman residence, hereinafter referred to the Residence will I discuss anything that happened to me, I overheard, saw, enacted, no business deals, matters pertaining to other guests, types of furniture or furnishings, books in the library, what types of publications they subscribed to, photographs on the wall, as all could consist of forward looking statements which public release could have detrimental effects on future business prospects and deals pursued by Leman Global Industries... blah...blah...blah, the sheer and mortal peril of it all, god forbidding one of our little secrets got out. I glanced over the glowing screen, flicking my finger against the screen for at least a minute or two and watching the text fly by...blah...blah...blah. I saw the box for the signature.

"Just sign it with your finger."

"Show me."

"I can't touch it. That would render your signature invalid."

"Does the doohickey know who's signing it?"

"Believe it or not, it does."

I traced my finger in a hapless J, completed the rest of my signature while shaking at the possibilities of where and when this document would be used against me.

"You know, my father's dead. All of these precautions are of no use to him anymore."

"Until that information has been passed on to me by the proper channels, I cannot just take your word for it."

"I'm his son."

"Well, you don't constitute the proper channels."

"That's unfortunate."

"That's all I needed from you."

"I can be on my way now?"

"Yes."

"Okay, take care then."

There was an odd pause while we both waited for the other to say something to cut through the shell of formality that had hardened around us, not chose by us, rather like office buildings that we did not choose to work in but only found ourselves working in one day, from which no genuine words could escape. I guess neither of us cared too much to try. The guard did not even fall back on the old standby of discussing the Denver Broncos or what I thought of the old quarterback, Tim Tebow.

"So where are you headed to?" the guard asked. I immediately sensed a trap.

"Nowhere in particular. I just need to clear my head."

"Don't we all."

"How do you do it? I do it by driving with no aim in sight, long distances, and letting random things happen to me along the way. You know, see how many women I can bed, and stuff like that."

"Sounds fun."

"You can come with me, you know, and be my wingman."

"I can't."

"Oh, the wife might not approve."

"That's right. I need this job."

"Sad."

"What is?"

"Oh, that you can't come with me. I'll probably get lonely."

"I doubt that."

I just looked at him standing there in his black uniform and wondered what series of missteps or maybe non-beginnings had brought him to that point in life to be wearing the uniform. Perhaps they weren't missteps at all. Maybe it was all some sad plan. Sad for me, I mean, but not for him. He was employed. Perhaps for him, they were a series of happy fortunes to be acquired. He seemed to have a wife he adored. Maybe he was richer than me. My life seems wanton, insane. It is my life. I avoided his asking where I was going. No one has to know that. I didn't want repugnant assassins stalking my every move as I traveled about the country.

The Judge fired up nicely and I watched the dim lights of my father's estate twinkle into the starlight of nothingness as I wound around the mountain, this time aided by the force of gravity. Freedom. A sudden regret hung around my neck like a giant timepiece, tick-tocking me towards doom. I'd been dependent, kept, a good boy for so long. Did I really want to give all of this up? Had I ever actually lived before? Had I really lived? Or did all that gold stack up so nice and neat as to fashion me a great, golden jail cell. I stepped on the gas. My mind screamed U-turn! I fought it. I struggled against the urge to just stay there. The farther I got away from that epicenter, the less I would feel its pull. Still, pulling away was going to be difficult. The iPhone rang. It was Hannah. She sounded as if she had been crying.

"Are you okay?" I asked.

"No. Nothing's okay."

"What's wrong?"

"We're burying father in two days. Private ceremony in his hometown. Last Will and Testament reading will follow. You're expected to be there."

"Where?"

"His hometown."

"Where's that?"

"He's from Illinois. Peoria."

"Get the fuck out of here? Really?"

"Yes."

"I never knew that."

"You've never read his Wikipedia page?"

"No. Never felt curious enough to."

"You're an ass. A total ass."

"You're fond of redundancy and superlatives." I had to have the last word. "I'll be there." Then I hung up the phone and shut it off, and threw it into the back seat.

Prudence dictated that I should drive to the Denver Airport and board a flight, but I preferred to drive. Plus, I didn't want my balls groped. So...two days. That's all

I had to putz my way to Illinois. It sounded doable, especially if I sped in this hell wagon. I reached under the seat for my protection. Where my .45 should have been. It wasn't there. Nothing but crusty upholstery. The Wacky Hutt bastards must have misappropriated it, taken it, filled out a form of reclamation, and put it away in some sort of evidence room. I came to the main gate, revving the engine to draw out the guards.

"You! Guard!" I called.

"What?"

"Where's my pistolay?"

"What did you say?" the guard asked with a face hovering somewhere between perplexity and anger as he looked at me like I had cotton balls in my mouth or some funny foreign accent. And I did, because he was Fijian. I had to ask his supervisor, who walked out of the guard shack, twiddling his thumbs because he had been playing so much Xbox One (Xbox One is a trademark of Microsoft Corporation, NASDAQ: MSFT). You know I think the Fijian was actually dismayed at my somewhat brash attempt to get my hands back on my classic masterblaster, which when loaded and fired could cause massive damage to the human frame. It was loaded when I left it with them, and it had better be loaded when I receive it back from them. I think I had the safety on, but I cannot remember.

"You know, my man, I'd appreciate my masterblaster back and soon. You know this road is fraught with rogues and jackboots and thugs, though you, in the safety of your little transparent bombproof and apocalypse-proof cubicle, would not be able to discern that. Your little booth is temperature controlled, so I suppose so you will not have to break a sweat. Why, look at you, man. What have you been guarding? The local hot wing shack? You're butter soft, doughy. What could you stop? I'm not here with a hulking brute of a partner. I'm out on that lonely road alone, that lonely highway. Hell's highway. I'm the man of action, out there amongst the evils of the land. You'd better go ahead and pony up my masterblaster, and no, I won't take your little insignificant hand cannon in exchange. I'm very particular about my masterblaster. It won't go on eBay (eBay is a registered trademark of eBay, Incorporated an online auctioneering giant based out of San Jose, California), ever. In fact, I won't leave here, and I might just raise hell if you don't hand me my very own gun. Put it right here, son, right in my hand, right where it belongs."

He balked. Or maybe he was lost for words at the vigorous strength of my argument. At any rate, he didn't really reply at all, but instead just called up something on his radio. No one responded, probably because they were immersed in either watching a football game where godknowswho was playing or they playing some sort of shoot 'em up zombies game on the PlayStation 3 (PlayStation 3 is a trademark of Sony, Inc.; NYSE: SNE).

He pressed a red button on the Cisco Voice-Over Internet Protocol (VOIP) Phone (Cisco is a global telecommunications corporation based in San Jose, California. NASDAQ: CSCO) and then went to his Motorola Walkie Talkie. He couldn't seem to reach anyone to make a decision for him.

"You're cut off, hombre," I told him.

"What are you talking about?"

"You've lost communications with higher headquarters. You're all alone in the combat zone. A stranger in a strange land."

"They warned me about you."

"What did they say? And who are they?"

"Higher."

"Oh really. And what did they say?"

"They told me you're off."

"Lovely. I just speak a truth they can't handle."

"You want your gun? You've got to fill out a loss report."

"It's not lost. It was taken from me."

"Didn't you fill out a property control form when you checked it with the guards?"

"I didn't check it with them; they seized it from me."

"Still you should have filled out a property control form, ehh...."

"No! They took my hand cannon from me like I was a common criminal."

"Good luck getting it back without the reclamation form."

"Damnit, you gang of thieves! Answer me this, Bucky! For all that you're securing up here in this desolate mountain crag...how many legitimate threats have you actually discovered and repulsed? I mean...has there ever been an invasion of rogues or terrorists or migrant workers or hobos with chainsaws come up here to pester the family yet? For the amount of money you creeps are slamming pops for, skimming off the till, how much have you actually defended?"

"I guess you could say that we're all here just in case."

"We've got insurance!"

"We're your family's insurance policy."

"Baloney! Baloney! Give me my hand cannon! Shove the insurance policy up your ass."

"There's no reason to get hostile. Chill out and fill out the fucking form, you nut."

I glared at him. I wanted to rip his head off, maybe yank his own gun out of the holster like I'd seen in the movies and blow him and the Fijian away before they could summon aid. I discounted the amount of practice that such a move would take. I could try always try, but I'd most likely end up in the hospital or morgue. The Fijian looked itchy, like he was blazing for a fight. His face had a go ahead expression and his hand was already on his holster. I relented. I took the form and filled it out, but I scrawled my name almost illegibly. The form had some sort of caveat against illegibility, so I did it almost illegibly. I mean, I could barely read it. I made sure I faced away from the perturbed guard, who guarded nothing. It thought it was nuts to waste your time like that. However, not everyone was as noble as I was in my pursuit of the literary elements of life.

You know, maybe I, in my short life, had done things for money that they wouldn't agree with, like writing that schlock romance novel, but then again I didn't really need to do anything for money. Maybe this man, standing in front of me in his starched black uniform, working a stupid job that really didn't matter in the grand scheme of things, maybe to provide for a family, maybe he was much nobler than me. I usually didn't ask people questions about their intentions or what they were doing in a particular place at a particular time performing a particular function.

Maybe he knew. Maybe he was just drifting through life like the rest of us. So that brings me to the thought that has been lingering, which should have always been most prevalent to me, but has just been lying under the surface sort of percolating in my fiendish, unkempt brain.

Just who am I? Who am I? Perhaps that is the much nobler question that I should have asked myself a long, long time ago. But you see, I was lacking the courage for real thought. Or perhaps you could say that I was lost in thought but all of my thoughts were directed inwards. You could say that I was really bent out of shape really about nothing. I've got money. Tons of it. But what does it matter what I say to you? Shouldn't we all be asking these questions of ourselves? You know life is really light when you renounce the tremendous burden you carry about on your neck and shoulders and that's weighing you down, hanging about your neck like a millstone. And what is this millstone? It holds you fixed to the floor of your cave, wrapped around your neck. It grinds away your time. It makes nothingness of your one and only life, brosephus. When you should be grinding it away.

Nothing creates nothing, man oh man. Boredom generates boredom. You won't escape it. Not even with five thousand channels on your Google glasses. It sits there. Squeezing your throat like a constrictor. You put it there. You accepted it. You wear it like a necktie. Yeah man and woman, you're free all right. You can drown if you want to but I'm going to take my millstone and grind this all into dust. I'm making flour with mine. Flour out of all these dead and fossilized notions that the vultures and crows have all picked clean. I don't know. I don't know why this simple little loss form spurred me to all of these thoughts about myself. I mean, can I fill out a loss form for something intangible like my mind? My body? A loss form for all the time that I had wasted in that self imposed black hole called Marcus Hanely? Okay, I'm a rich boy. A rich boy. Like all the other children used to mock me, mock me that one-day I wanted to buy the sun. And they even butchered my last name to do it.

What are all my riches compared to absolutely not knowing what to do with your time? Not having to do anything, even? You think riches are a blessing? They're a curse. I should spend the entirety of fifteen lifetimes proving to you why. Plenty of men line rich tombs, and I bet if you would've asked them, they would have traded it all for a brief moment to walk around in the sunshine again. Unhindered, maybe off in some bright public meadow that no one really owns. You see, being able to walk around in the sunshine, that's freedom, and that's a blessing none of those dead and rotted and forgotten pricks can ever do again. So you see, I think I've become a dead man, walking around in the sun, knowing that I'm walking around in the sun and cherishing it, more able to appreciate this gift we call life at its basic element. I haven't lost it yet, or I wouldn't be reporting to you.

Jackson! Jackson! Jackson! LEEMUNN! ONE DAY HE HOPES TO BUY UP THE SUN!

And they all joined each other in mocking me, and I could just sit there and pout and cry and tell them how it was impossible for one person to own the sun because it was just a big burning ball millions of miles away that didn't burn for anyone in particular.

I filled out the guard's form slowly, making sure that I got all of the blanks done right and properly until I came to the largish blank for description. It said, in small, bold letters:

DESCRIPTION OF THE MISSING/LOST/CONFISCATED ITEM TO INCLUDE SERIAL NUMBER, YEAR OF MANUFACTURE, COLOR, APPROXIMATE DIMENSIONS, WEIGHT.

"Are you kidding me? The serial number? I don't have my masterblaster's serial number, man!"

"Damn. That may complicate things," the guard responded gruffly.

"What? Why? How many World War I surplus, ultra rare Colt .45 Pistols have you confiscated recently? Look, man! It's silver...steel, I think. It has a wooden grip. It's a typical .45 1911. It's the goddamn quintessential American Firearm, man! Are you kidding me? The serial number?"

"Chill. Can you remember any of the numbers from it? Any of the letters? We have to make sure it's yours."

"Good God, man! I don't remember! I've never studied it, you know, I mean, it's just a tool. I don't study it! I don't worship it. I don't really even finger-fuck it to clean it. I don't take it apart. Fuck, I've never even fired the thing. I don't love it. I didn't memorize the serial number."

"That's day one that you know the serial number."

"Oh, come on and just find it for me."

"You really want it back badly? How badly?"

"Are you trying to hit me up for a bribe?"

The guard paled. He shuffled on his feet and crinkled his crisp black uniform as he folded his arms, closing himself off to my bitter accusations.

"You ever get sick of being a liar? I mean, do you really do anything here? You don't add anything to the world. You're quite a bit like that potted plant there. It even does what it's told. Why haven't you ever considered doing something else? All you do is lie to yourself and to good people like me."

He looked up from his computer and said, real matter of factly without hint of malice, "You know, you're something else, man. You're a spoiled brat who's never done anything by himself, never lifted a finger for anyone else. You've just been looking out for yourself and feeling happy how you were born into this ridiculous amount of money...more money than anyone should have. Why, if I had your money, you know the things I would do?"

"What would you do? Waste it? Buy a bunch of fucking fancy ass cars? Give it to your wife, if you have a wife, and let her blow it in a bunch of boutiques?"

"Yeah, I'm married, man. Are you?"

"No. I wouldn't be."

"You're so negative. You can only see the negatives. Sure, I like this job. My family is provided for. But if I was rich? Hell, they'd be provided for from now till the rapture. I wouldn't have to put on this uniform. I could spend more time with them. We wouldn't have to worry about anything."

"You kidding me? You know why we hired you? You're here to take a bullet for us. Don't you know that there are people hell-bent on taking what we've got by force or fashion? Everyday some business out there is plotting warfare on our house. They want to dispatch assassins to do us all in, all because they want what we have. All the covetous nature of men is maximized by their stupid system...this damn cobweb that we're all trapped in. This sticky fluid that keeps us all down instead of lifting us all up. We hired you precisely because we've got tons to worry about. It's not as pressing as your biological concerns, but ours is for the very continuance of our worldly concerns. At the end of it all, does it matter that so-and-so was the best at delivering so-and-so service? It only matters that so-and-so's service got delivered. It matters that you're able to change with the times, that you're able to drop everything and switch gears. Yeah, we've no problem putting food on the table, but all of our problems very much outweigh yours. They bury yours."

"My child needs a heart transplant," he said very stoically. I could see the pain in his eyes. I didn't know what to say. It popped out. I know it probably sounded callous. The guard didn't seem to mind. I think he had been practicing his stoicism.

"Why?" I said.

"He was born with a hole in his heart. Blood without oxygen leaks into the pipe that is supposed to carry oxygen.

"Is he going to make it?"

Again, I was callous and I know it. I was gauging whether the guard whose name I had not even bothered to get or even ask about would not be willing to tell a perfect stranger or at least someone he had never spoken to before. I don't really know why, maybe it was because there was nothing really happening in my life on the emotional level, that from the age of 14, I had shut myself off from the slings and arrows of the world, from life, from all the beautiful splendor of life, to avoid the small setbacks, the hurts, the pains. Or maybe it was that my personal pain overwhelmed my senses so much that they frizzled, unable to gauge and make their way through the folly of the world, forcing me to march inwards to take succor from whatever fantasies my addled brain created. The brain isn't meant to exist in a vacuum. It needs the soft touch of another person, it longs for sharing. I wanted desperately for this man's story to have an effect on me, to break through the wall that I had created for myself, to draw me somewhat a shade outside of myself. It is not selfish. I can help this man just as he can help me.

I know what it is I need to do. I need to immerse myself in life to drink it like a vital liquor, like the tree of everlasting life. I need to have adventures. I need to burn the candle at both ends. I need to brave snakes, alligators, hyenas, lions, tigers, bears, sharks, evil men, public opinion, my own low opinion of myself, anything that can eat and destroy me before this elaborate ice castle that I've constructed implodes. I need a single bullet of feeling to melt my damn icy heart. My own father's death couldn't do it. Perhaps finding empathy with a complete stranger could. Maybe being open to it, being open to the experience of helping someone else, someone in need, would heal me and make me whole instead of just a spoiled rich boy and closeted maniac. I could totally take down the rotted curtains, the musty mildewed interiors, and step out into the light.

I zapped back into the conversation with this man. Apparently, even though we paid Wacky Hutt millions of dollars a year to guard all of the aspects of the going corporate enterprise Leman Global Industries to include all of the family members, themselves full fledged tax identified employees of the corporation and answerable to the chairman of the board, formerly my father, now the position was up for grabs, and even though millions of dollars were paid the actual guards on up to the elite special operatives that are involved in our convoys and other possibly more nefarious activities around the globe, these men make beans and don't even have health insurance that will cover something that the insurance company deems pre existing, which I guess means that if you are born with a calamity, just as I was born with megabucks, the insurance company can just wipe its hands of you, deem that you have a congenital problem, which isn't their problem, and bid you to have a nice and productive life, and go home and die.

If you could pay for it, you could try and prolong your life for as long as possible, up until the age when you just keeled over, full of tubes and pumped full of age extender medications, but god forbid you were a poor child. You were fucked. Now this little son of this guy who's name I still don't know was diagnosed with a congenital heart defect in utero, which means while he was still in the womb, meaning it was revealed by using a machine or something like that, I don't know; I'm no doctor. So they were given the option: they could terminate the pregnancy or have the child and deal with the consequences.

I don't know what I would have done if I was in their position, but this man and his wife decided to have their son, heart condition and all. So why should I feel obligated to help them out? Maybe obligation was too strong a term. I wasn't obligated to do much of anything in this world. I had the luxury to do nothing. I didn't need to work. Money was a means for us to buffet ourselves against nature, to convince other people through a form of coercion to hoist themselves above nature. It was man's ultimate thinking game; to think that we are apart from nature. A never-ending accumulation of manmade things was our mask against nature. Nature does not accumulate; she stores and spends in a constant inward and outward flow...waves crash, energy dissipates, and energy is returned.

This accumulation of money is a phony escape and false promise, which is never fulfilled. It's best for money to be like nature: for the wave to swell and crash on the shore, but the way in which this wave crashes is not designated by the distance and direction; it isn't a matter of mere physics or determined by the pattern of the rocks the wave bashes into. It is up to us. When I inherit my father's money and position, it is up to me. I'm going to help people, not just acquire more money. I'm sick of it all. I'll give it all away. Otherwise the money freezes in the clutches of people like me. Rich people.

Did this man here in front of me ever ask me for anything? This is just a situation that came up to which there was no easy answer...unless there was a great deal of money involved. The fee for the surgeons. The fee for the hospital. The fees everywhere. Well, I could just give him the money and break the cycle of fees. I wouldn't even want a blurb put in the paper to let everyone know that I was such a nice guy and was about to embark on a resurgence of my writing career. I asked the guard, "Why don't you have some sort of charity fundraiser for your son?"

"We want to do something like that, but we, we uh, really don't know how to do something like that."

"Easy. Just pick a date and time. Call people and tell them the truth of what you're doing, take a few photos of the sick little rug rat, you know, and pick a level of money you need to raise...ask for a few thousand over the cost of the surgery just in case the greedy doctors decide to jack up the price on you. And also try and get some donations from local businesses...they really like to let the local people know that they care, and what better way to show you care than having some adorable little sick kid's photo in your place saying you helped save his life? Hell, you could charge 500 bucks for a t shirt, 1000 for a poster, 5000 for a decorative plate, 10000 for a gold towel, cause you know the golfers can pay for it...if you got it taken with a celebrity, then you'd probably stand to make even more."

He looked puzzled. Could have been a under boiled rage. "It's going to cost 250,000 dollars."

I almost snickered, it seemed such a paltry sum, but I quickly stopped myself and started coughing.

"Is your son in danger of dying suddenly?"

"It's a small hole. But it's getting bigger. He's not thriving. He's getting weaker, which leads the doctor to think that there may have been other complications. It's only going to get worse. Deteriorate, the doctor said."

"That's awful. No kid should live like that."

"We're saving."

"You have other children?"

"Two boys. Everything happens for a reason, you know. Maybe this was supposed to be a trial for me. After two healthy boys, I was starting to feel mighty proud."

I suddenly envied this man. I envied his simple happiness. I envied his explanations and the fact that he had an explanation for everything. I envied his answers and his belief in them. I did not envy him having a sick child; I would never ever wish that on even an enemy. I envied his certainty.

I was uncertain about most everything, even myself, even my own uncertainty! Maybe this was a trial for me. Maybe the only certainty you can ever find in this life was the knowledge that you have helped someone. That certainty would be the first brick in a new castle I would construct in my soul. Not an ice castle of beautiful thoughts, as I had been constructing formerly. This would be a marble castle of good actions. It would set me on the path of getting out of myself. To do this, I would have to do something, which terrified me, and actually talk to real people who were strangers. I had to make sure to verify that they were real people. I had to banish anything unreal or imaginary.

Be gone, demon! I could think and act my way to sanity. I would search Wacky Hutt's records and find out where this guard lived. I would arrange for an anonymous donation to be affected at the hospital in Denver or whatever hospital this family decided upon. I don't care if they wanted Cedar Fucking Sinai. I wanted to give their son a new chance at life. I would help the downtrodden and unfortunate. It would be my calling in life. I would be wonderful. I would laugh in the face of death, because I would actually be doing lasting and permanent good in the world.

What else was there to do? Be a right rich bastard, holed up with my money, ordering stuff off the Internet? Go about collecting babes? Sit passively by and buy and spend my way to a ride on Charon's ferry? What little I could do, and it was little in the grand scheme of things, whatever little I could do to brighten the face of a child, I would do it. I'll let Sheldon worry about piling up money on top of money. I'll be the patron saint of lost and worthy causes. Why is it lost if it is worthy? Because no one even knows there is a glimmer of a problem. Why don't we solve problems by removing the conditions for their arising? I will never till fields that are incapable of bearing fruit.

So you can see that I am still lost in my own thoughts, but at least now I can see a faint glimmer of escape from the cave. Tired of these thoughts I was having, I handed the form to the guard, and I noted his name. BOKAVMAN. It seemed uncommon, especially round here. I decided to ask him where his family came from.

"You know, I don't know. I recall my father talking about it once when I was really young."

"What's your first name?"

"Dan."

"That's a good name."

He looked at me funny and didn't respond. When he turned around to digitally send the form to higher headquarters, I wrote his name down on a scrap of paper, along with the message "DAN BOKAVMAN. Boy needs a new heart." and I stuffed it in my pocket. All seemed right in the world. I had my intention, now I just needed to carry it out. Bokavman's boy would get his heart repaired, and the family would forever tell the tale at Thanksgiving and Christmas. The phone rang. Dan listened intently. He hung up the phone gingerly, like it was priceless.

"They've found your firearm. Someone will be bringing it soon."

When every human activity had a standardized and universally accepted process and procedure, the world would be a highly efficient, dark place. It would cease to have shape and become a completely flat, linear machine. Humans would serve as the electrons to move from one gate to another according to the heuristics and algorithms that they followed from higher. Without the hiccup, I never would have learned about Dan as a person. We never would have had occasion to talk. He would have been just another cog amongst cogs. A well-oiled machine. But that's so 19th century.

Just another gate in some massif that opens and shuts or passes the buck on down the line. Thanks be to god that there was no monitor to tell us to stop talking to one another. When it isn't necessary to see another human soul to accomplish your day's dirty work, there will be no compulsion to talk to another person. There will be a lingering want, but that lingering want can be medicated away. Someone who talks to another person will be off their meds.

Oh, sure, that want, that loneliness, will still occur in the minds of people, but some pharmie offshoot of Leman Global Industries will produce a pill or extended release medication, probably pink or purple in color, with a snazzy symbol printed on the outside...called LONESTREX or SOLITUDE available in 5-, 10-, and 15-mg doses, and loneliness will cease to exist. If you've never experienced the company of another human being, how is it possible to be lonely? Is loneliness written into us? Is it discoverable like chunk of gold in some flowing mountain stream? Removable?

Another guard appeared, more slovenly than the first. I made note of his name. O'DAY. He held my .45 masterblaster, sans magazine and sans bullets, in a red Biohazard evidence bag.

"What's up with the bag, O'Day?" I asked.

"We didn't have any more of the TC/15-9 evidence bags. This was all they had when you were brought in."

"Why'd you run out?" Dan the Man asked.

"They've been carting off Leman's documents in the other ones."

"Documents?" I asked.

"Lots of stuff being taken out of your father's personal papers."

"Sanitization operation," I quipped with a smile. Most likely chicanery by Sheldon. Whatever he was up to, it was beyond my care or knowledge. He could be searching for another more original copy of the will or maybe papers he didn't want ending up in the trash or some biography. Maybe my father was a poet in his spare time like that Lloyd's of London insurance salesman T.S. Eliot. Who knows.

"What kind of papers?"

"Just old yellowed papers. We were told to collect them and not read them. They made us all sign non-disclosure statements."

"Ah," I said.

Speculation in this matter is useless. Better to speculate in other matters like what the weather is going to be on July 3, 2999. Sheldon was capable of anything. He had probably already dispatched the assassins and they were busy sharpening their long knives and throwing daggers for my back. I had not even left the compound, and he was already plotting my demise. It was good that he was fooling with father's papers. It would make my escape easier. Could he have hired the Wacky Hutt guards to dispose of me? Maybe that was the reason they delayed the return of my masterblaster to me: to delay my escape and allow the assassins time to put on their dark uniforms. Now I had it in my hand, well, it was in the bag in my hand, and the magazine was out and the bullets out of it: a further delaying tactic. Now that I had it in my hand, my pistolay, my best buddy and companion, how the west was won, my peacemaker, with a little, oh, not so little, copper jacketed love shop, seven to a magazine and here I had four magazines in my glove box, all locked and loaded up, I felt at peace.

Assassins could come and do what it is they did, attempt to assassinate, but they would soon realize I was nobody's fool. I've come prepared, you foul miscreants, and whoever doesn't get ventilated, and perhaps I can up the ante and dispatch them against their former paymaster. That's at least how it usually worked out in the movies. Right now, I didn't feel like finger banging the gun: my gun, waiting for the worms, scared and timid like a child who's getting nothing but coal anticipating Christmas. I wanted to go and look at pretty girls and finger the masterblaster in my pocket. I want to live dangerously. I want inspiration. I'm finding none in these immaculate gardens and phony sweatshops maintained in my dear old dad's palace. Illegal aliens all over the place, or maybe they were green card holders; who knows. I bid my buddy, Dan, goodbye. He didn't wave, even though I was about to change his life for the better.

Where better to go in for the mingling, in these bitter winter days before the blah blah joy of Christmas than a place where there were more stressed babes per hectare, the highest concentration of hot pent up little bodies packed and double-stuffed into form fitting jeans and granny sweaters. Yoga pants!!! The mall! And not just any mall. The mall for rich people. Who wanted to deal with picking through lots of insignificant rubbish? I wanted to go to the place of gems. All of them would be shopping there, probably without lists, wildly slapping shit on plastic. They'd be quite easy for a man of my talents to acquire. Even though I didn't have Marcus around to goad me onwards, I'd goad myself onwards. What did I have to lose? I'd park my Judge where everybody could see me. Before I entered, I'd hit up the Sports Authority and buy a soft jock.

Not only did I not want to get kicked in the nuts by some grandmother fighting over the latest sold out video game or silk tie, it would make my already impressive wanger just that much more impressive in these vintage early 1960s tuxedo pants.

Or I could just turn in the tuxedo and purchase some tight, form fitting luxury jeans from the same mall. I needed a war plan. Did I buy the jock first? Or just stuff my sausage in it once I purchased the jeans? I'd need to try the jeans on. I'd have to ask the little salesgirl just how the jeans made my package look. I'd tell the little college-aged baby girl working there in the Sports Authority for her college book money that I was purchasing the jock to keep my cock and balls in place while I danced the rumba in Brazil, or maybe while I played soccer or something athletic like that. That would key her in that I was a well-traveled man about the town and not just another slob with a fancy haircut and jeans that I purchased on credit.

You know, most jeans won't fit me properly. I'm just that hung. I have to let my long wanger slide down my leg, where it rests cozily between my kneecap and thigh area. Amazing right? I swear to God, when I'm running Leman Industries I'm going to start producing third leg jeans, oversized wear for young urban professionals, featuring a cock holster...and actual third leg, but smaller...sewn into the crotchal area of the jeans to allow endowed men like me to let our wangers hang the way god intended. Attachment codpieces and legs could button on the front of the pants and of course it could unbutton for easy access for your ladylove...or man love; we won't discriminate against your particular preference. I'm thinking a nice, triangle-shaped piece of cloth, detachable, maybe made out of sweatpants material with vent holes for the hose beast contained within. I'm going to get R and D to get on this right away. It will be my first move when I'm running shit. This has the propensity to cause not only a fashion revolution, but also possibly a fashion bloodless coup. No more getting caught with your pants down. But wait, I don't want to run shit. Or maybe, I do?

We'll expand into business suits, exercise gear after that. Golf pants to follow. Some people exaggerate that a key component of foreplay is undressing your partner. Pah! These are the twenty teens not the nineteen forties. This is the new millennium, for chrissakes. There isn't time for all that undressing. If fucking didn't feel great, the human race would have perished eons ago. But fucking takes time, and time is precious. Time is money. Humans wouldn't have even made it one generation if it didn't feel good and wasn't totally natural. Women have always had easy access in the form of skirts, allowing them to slut it up all over the place, by just hiking their little skirties up over their rumps and naughty bits. Now, given the propensity of women to wear jeans, and very, very, very sexy, tight jeans at that, there is also a need for an easy access panel, sort of like the old britches that children used to wear to bed, so they could poo in the middle of the night in a poo-pan and not have to fiddle with putting their clothes back on. Kids are so stupid.

Maybe there could even be a built in merkin covering this easy access flap. I'm a true renaissance man. Not only am I going to do good deeds in the world, I'm going to change the world for the better by making that hottest of all human activities...all other human activities are window dressing...easily accessible, sanitary, utilitarian, beautiful...able to be performed at work during sex breaks. Getting laid by the secretary will take on a whole new dimension now that you don't have to rip her panty hose. I'll call the man's version CockOut!, and the female version some elegant E.A.P., sort of like E.A.T., but Easy Access Panel jeans. Beautiful!

Hey, brilliance is often not appreciated, but I would dare you to come up with something just as brilliant and revolutionary. When I go to the shopping mall, I would love to share my brilliant discovery with the managers and buyers at Nordstrom's and attempt to secure their orders for this revolutionary item. In order to avoid looking like a crank or madman, God forbid, I would have to have working models of the clothing, and possibly model it for them. I could stop by the Mexican shops on the way to the Richie Rich mall and try to sell them on the idea in my best broken Spanish. My brilliance cannot really be encapsulated in any language, even Spanish, which some old fuck at Princeton told me was the language of literary fantasy, mysticism, poetry, and of course Don Quixote, which is a much better read than anything written by God to include the Qur'an and the King James Bible.

Instead of thinking so much, like the trance I've just fallen into in the bitter cold, I'm going to will myself to be a man of action. I entered the Judge, turned the key, and listened to the Chorus of demons roar and tap out a maniac rhythm under the hood. I again waved to Dan, the man whose son I was about to save, goodbye, and he pretended not to notice, or else was too stoic about his guard duties to bid a fond and heartfelt farewell to a dear friend.

I DISCOVER I'M QUITE THE PIMP DADDY WOO WOO

*A*s I drove from the mountains along I-70, where our nondescript compound lies, and drove toward the city of Denver proper, I couldn't help thinking that the best years of my life were wasted in doing exactly what I was doing now. The passive thought, internally self-directed was like dumping treasures into a black hole. I wasn't improving as a person, because I wasn't doing anything to change, grow, or develop. If anything, my ratiocinations were making me implode, sucking me ever inward, like a self-devouring black hole that would soon make even matter, possessed of density, disappear. After that, godonlyknows what happened to it.

I had to break out of this nutty pattern I had established for myself. I really wanted to be around other people who would help draw me out of myself, and I determined during the course of my drive, that the best people in the world to help me lose my personal desire to implode, to go off into a bout of narcissistic self-loathing, self-destruction, which was really all for attention anyway, was to meet particularly feisty women. Young women. College women, set out to save the world, who might find me interesting and force me to open up to them at the same time. I wanted to find and fuck chicks who sported SAVE DARFUR and SAVE IRAQ T-shirts over their big collegiate titties.

The two universities in Colorado that a Princetonian like myself, albeit a legacy, knew about were the University of Colorado in Boulder, and the Colorado State University in Fort Collins, Colorado. Sure there were others, like the prestigious Colorado School of Mines in godknowswhere BFE Colorado, but I was only interested in girly girls who put out, not some woman who was talented at swinging' a pick axe or driving one of those big ass heavy duty mammer jammer Earth moving trucks. No. Oh, no. In order to meet those lovely ladies, I would head out into the city of Denver, probably also home to college-aged women.

They'd be home for the holidays, finals would be over, they would be all distressed with nothing to do, and definitely DTF, or down to fuck as my dear, departed best friend would call it. How would I approach these little biddies? First, I'd be wearing my breakaway codpiece pants, which was sure to be a conversation piece. Maybe I'll purchase a pipe and a cardigan, like any proper writer or man about the town should have. Immediately, the women will identify me with their dear old dad or a favorite grand daddy. I'll appear a stable father figure to them, and when they least expect it, whammy whammy, they'll be mine. I'll bone them like they've never been boned before and they'll forget all about dear old granddad. Being honest, I'm probably the farthest thing from stable.

When a woman asks me, "What do you do?" I'd have to answer her, "Nothing really," because that's the truth. If I follow that with, "well, you know, I have a lot of money," I'll come off like some spoiled rich kid, at best a drug dealer, or maybe a trust fund baby there to study Art History. The only type of women I would be able to pull then were the ones after my filthy lucre and not the ones trying to get into my lusty man pants to see what fills out my bulge. I want a genuine experience, not to pay for sex, even on a contractual basis. No thank you, missy. I'd rather just keep my dick in my pants if there's even a hint of wanting me for my roll. But they'll probably be able to tell that I'm akin to the Rothschilds. I mean, I carry myself like a prince, a modern day member of the Medici family, like Cosimo was my granddad himself. I have a top notch education that I do nothing with, and if I don't know something, I'm great at faking it or I go to the bathroom and look it up on Wikipedia or if that fails, I Google it. Knowledge is power.

As the mountains gave way to the lights of the valley below and the great cancerous cornucopia that is Denver loomed ahead in the blackness, I was reminded that Sheldon showed me that I'm not actually that good of a writer. That's something else I'll have to remedy when I'm on my way back East. I'll have to bust out the old laptop and tap out a work of brilliance that will silence my critics and make anyone who ever doubted me go off gagging with joy at having known me. They'll have nothing at all to say. You know, I think I'll write it about a young man who just returned from war and is traveling out West in search of the American Dream and some semblance of his old self. I suppose I should know something of the experience of war, so I'll have to spend plenty of time reading *The New York Times* and watching news broadcasts of Fox News and CNN to get a glimpse of what's actually going on. Oh yeah, this young man, recently returned from war will be writing a novel himself, stringing it out in notebooks as he heads West. Maybe he'll start out in New York City, which is where all the ships carrying all the troops home from Iraq and Afghanistan end up. You know, like that Alfred Eisenstadt photograph of that sailor kissing the hot nurse.

The troops get a paradise of a ticker tape parade and plenty of kisses and poontang from all the pretty girls who are so grateful that they went and destroyed their enemies and they can sleep well in their beds without fear of the savage cocks of the Arabs and Afghans raping them in their sleep. I mean, that's really how it happens, and I've seen it in more than a few movies. I'll have to look into the whole scene, maybe go to a club for veterans and talk with some real veterans who are overcoming adversity. The book would become immediately popular and immediately will be picked up by *Oprah*'s Book Club.

You know what? There would probably be talk of movie rights, right away. Let's waste no time with slapping this fucker up on the paper. I'm done as a romance novelist or at least the type of romance that is spawned at the behest of bored and horny housewives the world over. I would love to write Romance that even single women who are professionals, like doctors and lawyers, can get all jazzed up at and flick their beans to. You know, it would probably have to involve someone getting tied up or shit on. Powerful women love to be dominated.

Or maybe I could write some real high adventure that takes place amongst the strip malls and modern American landscape. This guy, whose name I will think of later, and I will have to go to all of these places that time forgot, these flyover states, and I'll have to brave the vicious death ridden highway, the folly of tried and impatient truck drivers, minivans full of screaming children non sated by even *The Incredibles* DVDs, people unmotivated to do anything but get from Point A to Point B as soon as possible and curse themselves for trying to find some sort of solace in the open road and not on a four hour plane ride. They'll think themselves, in their little fishbowl rides, these solipsist drivers who cut off 18-wheelers and send beef carcasses spilling off on ramps in order to get their next sip of gas into their Mega truck SUVs, and a little food in their bellies.

I'd love to be out amongst them. I'd love to interview them. I want to see what makes them tick! I'd love to see the ladies wearing shiny Coach riding boots, riding nothing, a passive observer, a passenger in life, looking out the fleeting windows of life at their existences whizzing by. All the denizens of the road, my compatriots, are already at a destination. They are self-contained as long as they have the geld for gasoline and their machine is mechanically sound, they have no need for anything else. They really don't have to talk to another single soul. They can eat out of machines if they choose or order a sandwich from one of the Automatons on the road that they don't bother to talk to but only order from. They can pay with credit/debit and sign sloppily and not have to wait for change. They don't have to speak to another human soul outside themselves. I'll get them to talk. I must.

You know, you cannot have solipsist adventures, not real adventures. You need other people for great adventure. I'm heading out into the great unknown, alone, no Marcus dead Hanely to be my security blanket. Gun is my insurance policy. I mean, I have auto insurance, but my life insurance is my .45. I really doubt I ever need to whip it out, but you never know. That's why I have it. So what, I don't have Marcus dead Hanely anymore, and I was living a complete fiction by spending all of my time with him and ignoring the real people I had in my life. Many people lead completely fictitious lives that they neither created for themselves nor do they realize they're leading them. They're sucking in oxygen, sucking up entertainment that passes them by. They're filter feeding. They're barnacles on this ship. Marcus Hanely was a creation of my brain, but he was my creation. I was always in control of him, though I did not know it. He is a part of me, maybe a part that I am in a way, maybe the sum total of my desires.

Maybe I can become him in a way or maybe I can fuse into that more perfected self. I want change! But you cannot go out for a walk hoping to meet your new self on the street corner or in the neighborhood bar. Maybe the path we take in life is only up to us. You know, nothing is written. There's no plan. It's best to plan to be open to new eventualities, explore new possibilities. You cannot meet yourself that you want to be and don this new self like a funny gorilla suit. You'll know the difference.

I'm going to follow my instincts. I'll destroy my rationality in order to be part of my environment and hopefully I'll grow strong and beautiful like my dead buddy Marcus Hanely. In order to die you must have lived. People will tell me that my Marcus Hanely ideal is evil, women will run out of bathrooms in public establishments throughout the country to warn other women to run away from me. Maybe self-help books will be written to escape from my newfound persona. Marcus Hanely recovery 12-step plan.

Step one, admit Marcus Hanely was a figment, a fictitious person, a creation of your perturbed and longing psyche. Maybe I'll be lynched. Maybe angry mobs will castrate me like Peter Abelard. Maybe I'll be forced to commit suicide...or maybe I'll do it willingly. I'll be a muscular stud amongst slight men. I'll project my persona like I'll project my cock through my detachable cock holster. It will be lovely; it will be grand. I snapped to, and I was in a part of Denver I did not recognize.

MY VISIONS OF ARMAMENTS

Miguel Cervantes, when he dreamed up Don Quixote in prison had nothing to lose. By having nothing to lose, he had nothing to gain. He published the novel, and his publisher fleeced him. He didn't make a dime on it during his lifetime. Nothingness is the handmaiden of literature. It is a rising up from nothingness, a struggle against the void that eventually takes us all. It is a tossing up of gems to life from the encroaching blackness of death. I would say that literature is a struggle against our animal nature, the interplay - the wrestling of Apollo and Dionysus, which begins in desire and ends in physiology, having the courage to write what comes out of your mind, polish it or not, and share it with others whether they like it or hate it or are totally indifferent to it. Indifference is the death of literature. It begins with a profound care for the living and ends with profound apathy of the opinions of others.

Madmen have been the leaders of the human race since the very beginning. Men with souls capable of entering the void, experiencing it, despairing not, diving deep by not diving at all, not emerging completely unscathed but learning how to cope by not flying from the fray. They are warriors who do not seem warriors.

I know my mission in life. I'll toss jewels and gold from the borderline, rip up the guts from the beast; I won't use myself for ill purposes. I won't allow myself to be used up. I'm getting older now. I should find a nice woman on my travels and wed her or at least live with her, make love to her on a continual basis, love her, provide for her. These thoughts are what swirl up from my brain. Also is the urge to make love to every beautiful woman I have ever seen...or to at least make the attempt to try them all once. I hope to come to realize the infinity found in the soul of a woman and find that it takes my breath away, removes from me any urge to leave and binds me, willingly to its sheer bright lightness and joy. I think this is possible for me. Love is the death of fear.

All it requires is openness, the death of fear. My warrior, he will have experienced fear beyond anything I have known. He will be unafraid of death. He will be a warrior of love for love and by love. He will have conquered mortality by losing that fear. He will only be concerned that he will not find the time to weave all the tapestries of his mind before the lights go out in the loom. The finite nature of our existence impels us to attempt to build an infinitely expansive pyramid in a finite time, stone by stone heaved into place, stacking stones to infinity. It can crush us if we rest the apex on our foreheads. Mile by mile, brick by brick, and oscillation of engine converted to rotational energy on the tires of the Judge, I'm driving forward. I'm behind the wheel. The shopping mall...I'll get there eventually. Don't invert the Pyramid!

What is my draw to these places? These bastions of consumerism? I really think that it serves as my incubator. I feel at home in the possibility of all that is offered for sale. If I wanted a new look, you know, a new me, it's all available out there, it's all priced to show me what new me is within my grasp, and for me, a hinwi (HIGH NETWORTH INDIVIDUAL), nearly infinite means are available. I possess the wherewithal to make a run on loafers at Hermes. You know what? I dress like a scrub, but the scrubby clothing I wear sets me apart from the best of the drones who think they need a damn label to shield them from the day. This tuxedo is out of character for me.

I don't get it really, did we come all this way, we as a species, drag ourselves up by the bootstraps, descend from the trees, forge ourselves through violence and struggle, fight battles with metal swords, butcher each other, invent things like the shiny automobile and atomic bomb, drive from coast to coast, put a man or men on the moon in shiny space suits with laser guns, did we do all of this just to hang out in shopping malls and piss away the hours sipping coffee?

I think that if I was born in a different era, and don't get me wrong, this is the best era ever to be fat and happy because it has the most material comfort and leisure so that the average person can watch up to 10 hours of television a day if they so choose. I'd choose to be born in a savage era. A Pre-Idiot Box Era. Television tells you all about the products that you can spend your money you earn at your unfulfilling job, rather than save it, if you so choose. None of the commercials advertise saving your money, Banks offer savings accounts but that is only because they charge a monthly maintenance fee. Maybe I'd choose to be born in a Post-Idiot Box Era.

I'm a tremendously positive person who has nothing but good things to say to other people, who builds and brings out the best in other people. That's at least what I've been told, for at least one time in my life, though I can't really remember who it was, maybe it was an aunt that told me that at a lake house that one summer when everyone got together way back when before we all got spread out to the winds, busy... too busy to ever stop and say hello to each other. You know, I think I've lost out on a lot by staying away for so long. I guess I had my own reasons to stay away from everyone.

I claimed to be working on my next novel but we all know that was an ugly lie. I maybe have written 200 hundred words and a different 200 words every time I sit down to write, but I just backspace it all into oblivion. I don't have writer's block because you have to actually attempt to write to be blocked. I've fritted away my wildest years with underserving fears. I've given energy to bogeymen that I could have devoted to creating something.

I turned into the high rent district of Denver. Cherry Hill. The Judge did not fit in amongst the Volkswagens with Colorado Native stickers on them, nor the BMWs with Greenpeace stickers or old Volvos with Dave Matthews Band stickers and little family-oriented "we have three kids and a dog and we're all happy" and "my son's an honor roll student at so and so prep academy" stickers. The Judge was bare. It was a pollution-belching man's car from a bygone, error-laden era, one of the last cars that prowled the highways and byways during the Vietnam War, back when a man could get belligerently drunk, turn the big-assed girls' heads, and maybe get them dripping slightly. I think the Judge upped my testosterone levels. I used to suffer from low T. I really did.

The Judge ate gasoline in massive drunken gluttonous gulps. It does 0 to 60 in, like, four something seconds. Its engine sounds like a chorus of malevolent demons singing dirges to an era, which valued anything but the boring science of efficiency whilst beating EPA regulators with a hammer. I wanted to hear the cries of horses as my brothers and I charged headlong into the fray, lances ripping through the flesh of our enemies, swords ready at our sides. I wanted to charge over a mud soaked field, terror ripping through my gas mask, sucking down oxygen to fuel my youthful folly and exuberance. I wanted to do something completely insane to the timid cows. I can be timid in my grave!

I can go there, unwillingly, kicking and screaming into the night. So, guess what. I'm going to park the Judge in a space next to the handicapped space so I don't have to walk too far to the entrance of Neiman Marcus. I'm going to make my way over to SAKS FIFTH AVENUE.

You know what? Given this neighborhood, the most fashionable accessory I can take with me will be my silvery Colt .45, which I cannot seem to make fit in the passport pocket of my vintage tuxedo. I left it under the seat. God, what a sight I was. I would undoubtedly be the only truly dapper man in the entire establishment, dressed in black tie, at ten o' clock on a Wednesday afternoon. I shuffled my feet to keep the tuxedo from bunching up around my crotch. I tugged at the fabric and shook my leg to free my cock and balls from their prison.

Sports Authority was nowhere to be seen, so there would be no jock for me. I shook my leg again, but still my longish phallus wouldn't peel itself away from my thigh. I grabbed my Moby Dick and tore him away, just as some soccer mom with a young kid in tow walked by holding her youngish child by the hand. She shot me a look like I was the most disgusting degenerate in existence. I shot her a sneer. I wouldn't normally have given her the time of day. I know an empty vein when I see one. I didn't want her calling the cops and me to have to get into a gunfight at the OK CORRAL in the parking lot of this rich hood, doody. Maybe later, but not right now. I'd letter let Betty Fucking Crocker go about her business. I had mine to attend to.

I felt drawn to the entrance of Neiman Marcus, like I was walking under the power of a trance and under no volition of my own. I walked past the neatly arranged cashmere scarves and handbags in cases lorded over by smirking personnel who tried to stop to ask me if I was there to purchase a gift bag for my wife. I've always figured that was a way to assess my relationship status because they found me visually appealing, handsome, in fact, debonair, a witty conversationalist once we finally talked, and, in general, highly beddable. I walked past them without saying a word. I didn't even shoot them a wolfish grin.

You know, I think they might believe that I'm a foreigner here in the United States on vacation, fighting the terrible ennui that I felt in my own country by heading to the wild west in search of cowboys and genuine experience. But who knows; we didn't talk. Much of the idle speculation nowadays could be settled and done away with if people got into the habit again of saying what they meant, being direct, and meaning it. Not wasting speech and vital oxygen in platitudes. Manners, of which I am fully endowed and cognizant, having been beaten into me by my mother and several governesses, are included in this. You can say the truth and not come off as uncouth or an uncivilized boor. You just had to practice your delivery and have a vocabulary exceeding that of a two year old. Being an uncivilized boor was all the rage. Idiots best entertain idiots.

I made my way past a portly security guard. You know, they only exist to call the real police force in case of an emergency. You take away their phone, and they're doomed. They also rough up the juvenile shoplifters for a little bit, you know, to soften them up for the real deal. He didn't even bat an eye as I walked past. A hat caught my eye. I stopped to look at it briefly. It was brown tweed. It wouldn't match my tuxedo, so I put it back on the rack. The hat was mediocre anyway. Not that I believe in extravagance, but mere mediocrity is tantamount to death. You know what? When in doubt, be bold!

Just middling and hacking away your time, lying to yourself by never asking any questions of yourself, your place in the world, your place, your life, your one and only life…maybe I am supposed to spread some sort of message of you're going to die some-day, just blink out if you're reading these words, and so will I, because I'm writing them. One day my pen will fall down from my hands, my head will slam on the table at which I sit, or perhaps the hotel room or car if I'm driving. The point is, something inevitable should not be terrifying to us. Death should have no power. It is nothing.

What should be terrifying is to just suck up, consume, muddy the waters for the children coming after us, laugh, fuck, get drunk, buy homes, go to school to be able to participate in the economy, and be able to get by day to day. I'm tired of just getting by day to day. I'm sick and tired of it. I don't wish to live in the present. I don't want to live in the future. I don't want to live in the past. I'm looking to be timeless: a human being existing inside of time, but my soul not tied to time. That's how it is supposed to be, or that's what those Churchmen say. I'll find the soul of the past and ride it like a wave into the future. I don't care. I've given up caring about much, but I care pro-foundly. I'll be gone. I don't see anyone else doing what it is I'm doing. I see phagocy-tosis of energy, waste, and dunderheads marching lockstep to nowhere.

They may think that I've gone totally mad, but I've never felt more comfortable in my own skin. I look good in a tuxedo, I thought as I passed myself in the mirror on the way out of NEIMAN MARCUS I never really noticed myself before. I was too busy slavering up to Marcus. I cut a nice figure, and I'm quite handsome. I always heard it from my mother, but that's what mothers always say. Women want a hand-some son to shoot their genes all over the world; that's why they couple with hand-some men. I walked and looked around at all the people carrying bags, jimmy-jawing to each other, laughing and frolicking like it was some meadow in the sun.

I looked at myself in the mirror again at the BROOKS BROTHERS where the saleslady, dressed in a yellow sweater and navy blue slacks, rummaging and arrang-ing the pre-Christmas sales table loaded with belts and ties that fashionable people in their right mind would wear. I spied a purple and yellow ensemble in small interwoven pattern flecked with gold. It lay, neatly folded, near a pair of black tuxedo shoes, sized, as I poured over them, looking at the clodhopper old shoes on my feet, my same size. I looked at my reflection in the patent leather shoes. The saleslady approached me, and I found her attractive. I wondered why she was hawking clothes and not doing something else, more meaningful perhaps. Instead of filling the air with speculation, I decided just to commit a cardinal sin and talk to a stranger.

"You got these in a 12?"

She looked down at them. "Those are a size 12."

"Ehhh. Oh, right."

"That's a nice tuxedo. What's the occasion?"

"No occasion, really."

"Hmm. You get it here? Trying it on?"

"No. Brought it from home."

She looked at me funny. "Why? I mean, it does flatter you."

"Oh it's my dad's. He wore it for his wedding in 1962 and probably several times to the Opera after that."

"Who made it?"

She looked at the label inside the jacket. She gasped. "It's BRIONI."

"So?"

"That's probably worth a fortune."

"That's nice," I said.

"You said it was made in 1962."

"On or around. Why?"

"Why are you wearing it?"

"Uhh...tuxedos are made to wear."

The shoes did not fit. "You have them in a twelve and a half?"

The sales assistant nodded and left, returning with an elegant cardboard box.

"One last pair."

"Oh, Thank God," the salesgirl said.

"How much?" I thought she overreacted. I wanted to temper the conversation a bit; it wasn't like we were debating politics or theology or something important. I was only buying shoes, and shoes on sale at that.

"Are you sure you don't want to look around at our other shoes, sir?" she gushed imploringly, really enthusiastic like...much too enthusiastic for what we were doing in our transactional relationship.

"No, I want these, but I want you to bottle all that cheer you are spreading and let me market it. We'll call it something awe-inspiring and make a fortune."

She smiled from ear to ear and blushed a little, and my smile mirrored her own.

"Where's your nametag?"

"What?" she asked.

"Your nametag, don't you wear them here? They do at SEARS."

She laughed. "You're going to great difficulty to ask a girl her name, aren't you?"

"I always take the rough road, the harder, more mountainous path in life."

"You're quite the poet. Handsome. You could model, do you know that?"

"No one has told me that before. Maybe you can discover me."

"Really? I know someone who could do your portfolio."

"I'm not really interested making a spectacle of myself."

"You wouldn't be. Just suits. Tuxedos. Things like that. You look good in that tuxedo. Why are you wearing it again?"

"To remember my dad and what he represented."

"What was that?"

"An age of sophistication and genuine feeling. An age where men did business over whisky, cigars, and call girls. You know, an age when lawyers were employed by someone and not striking out on their own causing mischief in the world."

"Uh, oh, okay."

"Yeah, he died a day ago now."

"I'm sorry."

"Don't be. He was home. He had a nice life."

"Uh...good."

"Yeah. He could afford to stay home. He didn't get carted off to some old folks hellhole. He died in view of the Colorado Rockies, something he always loved. You know, he died in his favorite home."

"Wow. How many homes did he have?"

"I don't know. I suppose all that will come out in the reading of his will."

"Oh, okay."

I don't know why I was telling her all this but she seemed like a genuine person. She wasn't really smiling much anymore, and she looked like she wanted to run away. Maybe it was my utter unconcern with my father's passing. She wasn't used to that. Most people were supposed to be all weepy-eyed.

"We weren't really close," I said to her.

"Uh, okay. Yes, I'm, uh, sorry about that."

Uncomfortable pause. Very uncomfortable. Probably more so for her. I didn't really feel it, but for a moment, you know, I wanted to pave it over. I wanted this woman to maybe have some sort of commonality with me. Maybe she lost her parent, a dog, a pet ferret, maybe a boyfriend succumbed at a young age. I wanted her to share some painful experience with me, I wanted her to share and feel what I was feeling. I don't know how I became so dried up, desiccated, a dead piece of wood floating in the great sea of life, beautiful when captured and polished, but still dead all the same, having fallen in the sea eons ago, drifting, serving as a landing platform for blue-footed boobies and pelicans, maybe chewed upon by a seal, drifting, waiting to wash up on some sunny beach, but unable to make any effort in that direction. And why couldn't I?

I snapped back from the thought.

"Yeah, I'll only be taking these."

She seemed puzzled at my sudden change of mood. I felt like I needed to run out of the store.

"You don't want help with anything else? A tuxedo shirt, perhaps?"

"I've a tuxedo shirt on, along with a cummerbund."

"A pair of cufflinks?"

"Got those, too, somewhere around here."

She smiled, still trying to make a sale.

"Have you a cardigan? A Captain Nemo type of sweater? Something nautical without an annoying coat of arms junking up my breast pocket?"

"Captain Nemo?"

"20,000 Leagues Under the Sea."

"What?"

"No? Perhaps a Captain Ahab sweater?"

"Who?"

"Moby Dick?"

"What?"

"Dear God," I uttered under my breath.

"I don't know all about that," she said sheepishly, looking as if she wanted to run, but still focused on the sale.

"It's a cable knit sweater, big buttons. It has a collar, kind of padded wool, not lambs wool, but not exactly itchy either. I've seen them with leather elbow pads too, they're quite fancy, those El Capitan Nemo sweaters."

"Saks might have them. They have everything."

"Too pretentious for me. I don't like wallowing in there. It's like going into a church. Everything seems hands off and sacred."

"Where do you do most of your shopping at?"

"Gas stations."

"Excuse me?"

"Truck stop Gas Stations. Pilot, sometimes Loves, Travel Centers of America, Little America, the Worlds Greatest Truck Stop, Iowa 80. Holy Hell, is there a great selection of Wolf T Shirts there."

She just looked at me, unsure of whether I was joking or not. Or maybe she was scared.

"Just the tuxedo shoes, and I'll wear them out. Can you throw these away for me?" I asked, putting the old shoes into the box. "Oh yeah, how long before these break in? Will I get blisters?"

"We haven't ever had a complaint about those shoes, sir."

"Don't call me sir. I work for a living, ma'am."

"What do you do?"

"My profession?"

"What do you do for a job?"

"I don't have a job. Just a profession. I'm a writer."

"What have you written?"

"Nothing of consequence, yet."

"Oh, okay. Well, you'll just have to keep trying. You'll make it someday. Just don't give up."

"You too."

She smiled. We had shared a moment of mutual positivity. If we were in a bar, I would have at this point asked her for her number to contact her at a future time, just in case any unforeseen circumstances such as other rutting bulls pulled this potential mate from the herd and away from me. At least I could call her and we could discuss her couplings over coffee, and I could listen to her complain about how she never met any good people anymore, then maybe we could go for a walk...her walking and talking and I bored out of my mind and lingering, hoping for an opportunity to either strike and ask her back to her place, or just bound away howling.

Either way, she'd be left with the impression that she might have spent two hours of her life with the strangest person she'd ever met. Better than being forgotten, yawned off, or discarded with the pre bedtime evening news. As she swiped away my plastic, all of this fantasy was forgotten, and by the time we put the card back into my wallet, all that was tangible was forgotten as well, even what she looked like, and I didn't even get her name. You know, maybe I would see what SAKS FIFTH AVENUE had to offer. I was in the mode of wasting time, and I think that a Captain Nemo sweater would look stunning with my wolf T-shirts. I had nothing to do, nowhere to go, nowhere to be for a couple of days. To many this would seem the luxury of all luxuries: Heaven on Earth.

It is what everyone secretly wishes for, you know, and I am probably right now the most envied and despised person on this small blue Earth. Everyone would love to be in my position: inheriting megabucks, possibly. No deadlines, nothing to do, no boss breathing down your neck, no commitments of any kind. I looked at the decorations in the mall and determined that Christmas time was fast approaching. Just another day for me, it would be. I wouldn't envy me if I were you. Life is all about those stresses and strains and broken bones and scrapes and love affairs and babies and envy, avarice, coveting the property of your neighbor and all the like. I was doing good deeds all over the place, and though I had yet to do a single one, I had good intentions. I know I'm going to. It wouldn't even be my New Year's Resolution. I just know I will.

Store corporate management hired elves to strategically place applications for credit throughout the line for Santa. This would stack this year's purchases on top of next year's purchases and assure the cycle continued indefinitely until the rug rats were at least 18 years of age and they were out on their own. I watched for a moment from the upper floor until I noticed people watching me, felt their eyes burning into me. I mean, it is not often that you see a man in a tuxedo watching the line to Santa Claus with some shit-eating grin on his face like he's thinking about getting in line himself. I take it that they suspected I was either a secret agent operating on behalf of some cabal of Chinese toy manufacturers to subliminally implant messages into the minds of America's youth, rendering them passive and inclined to fatness, so they would be easy pickings come 2030.

That, or they thought I was the paid organist who was supposed to be belting out Christmas Cheer, or the worst possible scenario, I was a pederast leering at the children, storing images in the spank bank for later. Not wanting to be lumped into that lowest of all human life category and have the blue-shirted, over-waddling security guards thrash the life out of me and toss me into the wishing well, I decided to beat a hasty retreat to SAKS FIFTH AVENUE, or the Cathedral as I call it: the Mecca of the Material Girl and well-to-do fancy pants to go look at whatever just so happened to jump into my field of vision and scream, "Buy me! Buy me!" If its quality was in greater proportion to the quality of items found at the Truck Stops, Visa Black and I would buy up all we could grab.

He stepped in, or rather slinked and slithered into my peripheral vision from his hiding place, or maybe just a point of admiration, albeit camouflaged from the view of the SANTA waiters and busybody credit serving elves.

"Leman," he wheezed at the first instant, coughing a few times with the dustiness of an ancient store coffin, perhaps holding the bones of a little troubadour or famous poet. It was quite lyrical how it flowed from his overly chapped face like he had been out in the wind with no protection. He had chapped lips, viciously chapped, and cold sores were breaking out in the crevasses and splits. Perhaps it was a non-herpes variant. Cytomegalovirus? Perhaps. Kissing and cunnilingus without dental dam caused both. This was the damned gentleman I saw presiding over my father's departure from this Earth, the one my father talked to. You know all the time he was there, this gent said not one word to me, and now here he was accosting me on my way into SAKS, a right fine store for his type. This gargoyle of a man, stringy-haired, clothing matted, the smell of chemicals like herbicides or something else belched out of Dow Chemical, Dupont de NeMours, Monsanto, or Anzo Nobel.

"Just who are you then?" I inquired of the gent who withdrew himself from his hiding place behind the fichus.

"Oh...well, who I am to you is to be determined, Mr. Leman. I was in the employ of your father for several years. I served him very well, traveled around the world on his behalf, you know, righting wrongs."

"Oh, you were his attorney, then."

"No, no attorney, not a legal eagle, or corpse stripping crow of a legal clerk. I'm your father's accountant of sorts."

"Really? I saw the dusty accountant there, walking around, with his great big book. You're not him. You mean father had a personal accountant and didn't go with some huge accounting firm to manage all the billions of dollars of assets of a global mining and manufacturing conglomerate?"

"Your father doesn't have a single accountant. I didn't see him. And I don't account for money, Mr. Leman."

"What else is there to account for?"

"Plenty."

"Like what?"

"Loose ends."

"You helped out in our textile mills then? You oversee our sweatshops in Asia? Gotta keep those little black-haired devil kids working on their looms, right?"

"No."

I couldn't help but notice his smell as we walked and then stood at the entrance as the wafting smells from the food court, the pizzas, the gyros, all collided with Cinnabon. His smell overpowered them all, crushing their collective smells to the ground and then holding it off the Earth like a foul wrestler.

"Goddamn, my man, don't you know you smell like a chemical factory? Anybody ever told you that?"

He seemed unperturbed.

"Don't you want to know why I've tracked you down, Mr. Leman?"

"Not particularly. Any and all of you representatives of Leman Global Industries can string yourselves up for all I care. I'm not budging from my declaration."

"I'm not here to get you to commit to running the company. I couldn't give a Good Goddamn whether you run the company or you just run around doing whatever it is you do."

"I don't do anything. I fancy myself a Romance novelist, you know, like one the olden days off courting the muse in the wild hinterlands of this great nation of ours. But I haven't actually written anything. And I just found out that my whole published career was a big fucking marketing farce. I don't even know why I'm telling you this. You're a stranger. Just who the hell are you? I recall being introduced to you once, but I don't recall your name."

"Right. You're right about your brother-in-law."

"I wasn't even talking about my brother-in-law."

"I engaged in highest level board meetings where that weasel was present. Believe you me, he'll stop at nothing until you're out of the way."

"For fuck's sake, I don't care about running the company. He can have it! He can dispatch assassins against me, maybe start some sort of smear campaign at *The Wall Street Journal* showing how I'm totally inept, unable to run the company. But we don't have shareholders to answer to, so who cares really? I don't want to run the company. Is that what this is about? Are you here to do me in?"

"The company will run itself. Always has. You know, your father was pretty much a figurehead."

This went against everything I have ever thought about my father. I wondered what he actually did. Still, the assassin didn't answer my question. I thought, do assassins usually talk to their victims? They don't in the movies, usually, unless they have to reveal who the villain is. I don't think this guy was here to off me. I wouldn't ask him, yet, why my father spent so much time away from us. I didn't even know who this prick was. He could be an imposter. Mal something.

"Why the hell is Sheldon so concerned with getting me out of the way, then? I've already agreed to step aside. I told them, I want nothing to do with Leman Global Industries."

"His obsession is his own. Just like your obsessions are your own, and mine my own. Look, he's already dispatched them after you. You were probably really smart to come here in public. Who taught you that?"

"That's what they do in the movies. Who's after me?"

"They're after us, Mr. Leman."

"Don't look now, but we're being followed. Come. Walk this way with me."

We shuffled off into the store quickly. He took me by the arm, whispering into my ear, real creepy like.

"Don't look at them."

"Who's following us?"

"The most unsuspecting of assassins. He's hired a real, real couple of professionals."

"Who are they?"

"He didn't hire a couple of thugs from the trailer park. Damn. I guess I'm valuable dead."

"Don't turn around, whatever you do. They'll know we're onto them, and if they know that we know, then they'll be able to alter their plans for you. We need to force them into a confrontation on grounds of our choosing. Best to let them just follow us for now."

"Why should I believe a word you say?"

"Tell me, did you happen to run into a man, older like?"

"Dick Avalon?"

"No, he's an associate of mine. And the girl. I sent them."

"Oh, thanks."

"Better a pretty girl to escort you home, huh?"

"Yeah, she was a real delight...and oh yes, there was a guy I called Red. He never told me his name."

"He had red hair? Tallish? Sloppy dress? Gambling problem?"

"Yes."

"Jesus. William Meriwether found you. You're very lucky to be alive."

"You know him? Was he one of the best? He claimed to have been."

"Meriwether's alright, mediocre, could have been great but he's got that gambling problem. He used to work for your father, but he up and quit. Went with another firm for more money. It's catching these days."

"What the hell does he do?" I asked, as we shuffled past the women's jeans neatly arranged in meticulous piles and lorded over by a small, frumpy woman. It was the style.

"He blows people away and buries them in the desert, last I heard."

"Jesus."

"You're safe for now. But you've got to worry. They've really sent the heavy-weights after us now."

I expected that two lurching madmen were following us. Russian. Possibly former Spetsnaz, maybe mobbed up. Jesus.

"Don't turn around."

"Why should I believe a word you say? I saw this in a movie once. The actual assassin acted all friendly until he got the people alone, and then he did them in."

"Come now, Mr. Leman. You saw me at your father's bedside."

"I saw Sheldon there, too."

"Did I not lean down and whisper something to your father as he passed?"

"I did see that. I thought you were an apparition."

"I told him that I would take care of you so that no harm ever befell you, just like I took care of him. Your father knew about Sheldon's plotting. He was gravely worried about you."

We hit the escalator in SAKS FIFTH AVENUE, always bright and sunny and glittering inside, ample space in the aisles. Loaded full of baubles and bangles and pantaloons and T-shirts priced for tycoons to wear out yachting. I turned to the gentleman whose name I neglected to get. I was always forgetting to get people's names and business cards, meaning I had no real aptitude for business, and no business being a businessman. I turned to him to say that he probably needed to purchase another suit while we were here because the one he had on reeked of chemicals and made him smell somewhat otherworldly like he had just ascended from the depths of helly, brimstony pits. It was some sort of choking smell, which I couldn't quite put my scent glands on. He stopped to paw at the women's scarves. The whole place was empty, save for a few wandering biddies. Maybe it was too expensive during the recession. Strange, I thought that people only purchased luxury goods during a recession so that they could act rich and lift up their spirits. So why wasn't this place busier?

"Where the hell is everyone?" I asked.

"These people have a massive reach."

"They could clear out SAKS a few days before Christmas?"

"Yes, quite possibly. Don't put anything past them."

"Who the hell are they?"

The unknown, smelly gentleman continued fingering the scarves, going over every seam.

"Buying something for the wife?"

"Just looking."

"Looking for a girlfriend?"

"Just looking," he said, the tone of his voice getting a bit huffier.

"Oh really, just looking. What are you shopping for? Planning on buying something lovely for yourself?"

"No," he said gruffly.

"Say, want to get a handbag for yourself? Why don't you get one? We can get matching ones, all monogrammed. Say what's your name? I wonder if it will fit on the buckle?"

"My name?"

"Yeah. What's your name?"

I remembered his name was Mal something.

"I haven't told you my name?"

"No. That's why I'm asking."

"Uh...your father always addressed me by what my friends call me."

The smelly man continued finger-fucking the scarves. He was drawn to them like a ravenous wolf to a fine steak dinner. He fingered them all, feeling them for make and material, and sort of licked his lips as he did it. He preferred brightly colored ones to the plainer Burberry and Prada. He loved the high thread count scarves. I glanced at a price tag: 450. Quite pricey for a snot rag. He seemed to be concentrating on something otherworldly besides the scarves.

"They're all so pretty," he declared.

"Fuck, you're strange. Are you going to buy one for yourself?"

He looked up at me with those rheumy eyes of an alcoholic, but he didn't reek of booze. He held the scarf between his index finger and thumb and made to wipe his wheezy face with it.

"You can't do that! You can't wipe your face on unpaid merchandise that you don't intend to purchase. There're no free trials at SAKS FIFTH AVENUE! You don't even look like you can afford that!"

He stopped himself in his compulsion and set the scarf down on the display table where it lingered briefly before being drawn back into position by one of the many surreptitiously placed SAKS sales associates who positioned themselves throughout the store to spy on possible shoplifting riffraff and movie star miscreants who got their kicks from the old five-finger discount.

I noticed a decrepit old couple who appeared to busy themselves in the overcoats, the man swaying back and forth all wobbly-like as he tried them on and the old lady occasionally broke her gaze from her husband and the beastly woolen overcoats to take a look at us. The old lady took a few steps forward towards me from across the department store floor and bade her husband come on. The old codger dropped the coat on the floor.

"Uh, sir...uh...I believe I've made them. Are my assassins really Abraham and Sarah warmed up from the deep freeze?"

The unnamed man looked up. "My name is Robert Malvolio," he said.

"Malvolio?"

"Right as rain. Don't let their advanced looks fool you. That pair are fucking terrorists. Best look this way. Don't let them know that you know."

"They know, all right! They know. They're walking this way."

"Why don't we just run?"

"You can't outrun them. You can try, but you can't outrun them. Your brother-in-law cared about you enough to send the very best. They'll pursue you to the ends of the great, green Earth."

"Let's get out of here."

"Not yet. This is the perfect place to fight them," Robert Malvolio said, still fingering the ladies panties.

"Jesus, man. Can't you tear yourself away from those things?"

"Pretty things, beautiful things, they move me so...."

I took him by the hand, or rather I grabbed his forearm with mine, his bony emaciated forearm, and bullied him away from the beautiful things. "Come now. Let's get something to eat. Don't you want to get something to eat, Robert?"

"Eat? Who needs to eat?"

"Obviously, you do."

"High metabolism."

"Yank yourself away from all these women's things."

"They're so pretty...pretty...pretty."

"Fuck, man. Death's walking across the store. They're slowly making their way over here. They're close enough to take a shot now."

"They don't use guns. They're more into swashbuckling."

"Piracy?"

"Like swordsmanship. Unless their MO has changed."

"I don't see a scabbard on them."

"Are you crazy? You can't walk around in public wearing a sword. People will rush and tackle you. A man with a sword at his hip means business, kind of like a man in public walking around with his cock hanging out the crotch of his pants. It's all quite phallic."

"Where's it hidden, then?"

"Stop it. Don't look at them so much."

"Where's his sword at?"

"Him? She has one, too!"

"Where do they hide them?"

"You see those canes?"

"Uh, yeah."

"Don't they look quite old?"

"It all looks old. Everything about them."

Malvolio didn't pull himself away from all the pretty women's things, now strewn about the floor and table from his rampant intrusion into their well-ordered symmetrical placement. His constant finger-banging was starting to upset the shop girl who waited attentively for him to stop his finger-wringing and weighing and measuring of all the highly priced brassieres fit only for Princesses and wives of cattle barons, pop starlets, actresses, and short sellers on Wall Street. She cleared her throat.

Unperturbed, Malvolio continued admiring the dainties, going over them with his fingers, inspecting the quality of the stitching and feeling the seams to see their tensile strength and whether or not they could be ripped. The shop girl cleared her throat again, this time louder. I looked up at her, smiled, you know, to kind of try to defuse the situation. She continued in her emphatic throat clearing. Three, four, five times. Finally she asked. Apparently that was the protocol. Clear your throat five times, and then ask the question, "Are you actually going to buy anything, sir?"

Malvolio quaked when she talked to him, like he had just popped in his pants. He stepped back from his lusty endeavors and started to blush profusely. Actually, it could have been more anger, not embarrassment. Malvolio didn't seem one to embarrass easily. His voice quivered, maybe with a mixture of both, but perhaps more embarrassment at being caught in that net, which gave away midsentence to a hostility. Perhaps it began as an inbred, or inborn hostility that gave away to a nervous acceptance that what he was doing was quite strange and now he wondered what she was actually thinking and what she thought of him in particular. Either way, we forgot for a split second about them, our pursuers.

"I was just admiring them for their fine weave, craftsmanship, and materials, miss."

"Oh, they are well made...," she said with a wide mouth and smile, which melted suddenly to a look of horror after a tiny dart appeared in her neck and before her eyes rolled back into her head, demonic possession style. She plummeted to the ground faster than the declining revenues at big box retailers.

"Good God, man! That's a new one! They've changed their TTPs!" Malvolio shouted and pulled the dart from her neck. We wheeled behind cover, in the form of three mannequins, just in time to see Granny bring the blowgun cane to her lips and shoot another dart, which impaled itself right in the fancy mannequin with hands on hips, modeling an overcoat. The barb whizzed right by my ear and sounded like the wee voice of a hummingbird as it flitted from nectar-bearing flower to nectar-bearing flower, warning the aphids of its approach.

"Old one has a fucking blowgun," Malvolio quipped. "Stay down!"

"Look out! The old bastard is flanking us, while the old lady has us pinned down. Fucking brilliant," Malvolio said, dismayed.

The ancient man hobbled his way past a bank of mannequins. They were silent but deadly; no one ever bothered to look up from their retail posts. It wasn't as if someone had shouted "Stop Thief!" That was sure to alert the store security. I swear, this entire place could be put into a massive vending machine. No need for people. A vending machine that boxed it and wrapped it and made it all pretty after you did the swipey swipe with your plastic lifestyle tether. Another dart impacted the glass with a tinkle and dropped to the floor.

"Damn! I asked my informant at the Destin Acres Senior Retirement home to inform me when these two psychos left their rooms."

"Where's the old man at?" I said, the fear rising in my throat, choking me off. Another dart came in. She was advancing forward.

The ancient bastard was on us. His eyes glowed hellfire, and he drew his sword from his cane. We backed up, back to back really, like you see in all the great films when the heroes are trying to get themselves out of a jam. Malvolio watched the old lady while I watched the geriatric swordsman, ever looking like death, not the reaper, just advancing, slow creeping death and all the racks of clothing and mannequins were not stopping him in his approach. He just kept up his incessant shuffle forward, skirting around the racks, not kicking them over. Silently shuffling doom.

It reminded me of a dream I had as a child. It was a reoccurring dream where I was playing with all of my schoolyard chums on the playground monkey bars. We were all taking turns going across the monkey bars, and I waited patiently until it was my turn. I was somewhat scared to go across the monkey bars, so I took a long time. The whole time the other children were mocking me, shouting "scaredy cat! scaredy cat!" I go, and my body is burning as I go from rung to rung. I go further and further to the other side, their taunts die out, and I celebrate inside. I drop to the other side, and I say to my chums, "See I told you I could do it."

No sooner do the words come out of my mouth that I see that my friends aren't there, but it is him instead, the old and decrepit man sitting there on the merry go round with a sick grin on his face like a chimo's grin, but I can tell he isn't there to bad touch me. I want to run. I want to run, but I have been taught to respect my elders. I call to him, asking, "have you seen my friends?" And he nods his head. I ask him where they went, and he says he really does not know, that all he knows is they are not here in the playground anymore, that they have left to go home, that they have left me, that maybe they did not like me anymore.

I looked up, and the streetlights had not even come on, so I knew they did not have to go home. Then he smiles, and he tells me, "you know, maybe all of your friends are dead and gone. Maybe they are all dead. In the instant that it took you to cross the monkey bars, maybe death he came for them all and dragged them off. Maybe I am death, or maybe I am just a very old man, and I scared them away." He smiled. His teeth were rotted out, and I saw just a gaping black nothingness inside him, no flesh, only an abyss, a sick blackness, and it crept out and penetrated into me so that I could not scream but only melt if I remained. I turned, and I ran. There was nothing but terror in me, and I tried to run, but my feet crunched through the pea gravel as I gained no momentum forward. I was sinking, and the old bastard he was catching me. But this is preposterous! I am young! This old fuck is catching me! Death! He is catching me!

The old lady made ready her blowgun and held it to her lips just as the old man, the same old man from my dream, stepped out with his mad stabber.

"Duck!" Malvolio screamed as the dart flitted in, and he grabbed and yanked me downward just as the dart whizzed overhead. Old man death wasn't fast enough. The old bag's dart embedded in his forehead. He looked shocked, his eyes fluttered for a second before the poison overtook him, and he dropped forward, coming to rest standing up, with his sword stuck into the ground.

"Would you look at that," Malvolio said as he shopl his head.

So much for their plan of flushing us into the open. So much for death's victory. Old woman realized her error and was trying to beat a hasty retreat, sobbing a bit on the way. A Shop Assistant, named Ingrid, recognized potential shoplifting indications in the old bag's demeanor, Malvolio, my new protector and companion, approached from the old bag's rear and grabbed her arm before she could plunge the poisoned dart in the young shop girl's neck and be about her evil old lady ways.

"Come along, mother," Malvolio said, wrenching the dart from her hand and pocketing it in his smelly suit coat.

The young lady looked relieved that she didn't have to do a strip-search.

"You've found our dear old mother. Bless you, young lady," Malvolio continued.

"Yes, thank you," I said.

"Our mommy gets away sometimes from the house, and she heads to her favorite store. Pesky servants, they're supposed to be watching her more closely. Guess who's not getting Christmas bonuses," Malvolio said.

I sensed the shop girl's confusion as she looked at the pair of us.

"Oh, you know, my brother and I don't look alike. Everybody tells us that they swear we must have different fathers. I look more like father's golfing buddy who was met with an unfortunate end in a yachting incident off the Cape of Good Hope...or was that the Straights of Magellan?"

"Mom was quite the whore," Malvolio interjected.

"She may have taken something without paying for it. We don't give her an allowance anymore."

"I assure you, Ingrid," I said reading the shop girl's brassy, shiny nametag, "she didn't."

"There's only one way to tell," Malvolio announced, dragging the old woman to the exit. We crossed the threshold with her.

"Did any alarm sound?" he asked.

"I don't hear one," I said, nodding to Ingrid, who agreed with me.

"I thought I saw her in here with an old man," Ingrid said.

"Oh, Good God. Mom doesn't have a boyfriend! Why, look at you, mommy. Out meeting men at your age. Why you aren't a day younger than 93, and you're still out trying to rope studs."

Malvolio looked at Ingrid. "Don't you ever loose it, missy," he said, licking his lips. She recoiled and called her coworker...the dead one...on her Secret Service style ear bud. We had to be out of here before the mishap was discovered.

"Well, we'll be going. Come along, mother."

"Okay. Take your mother. I must apologize for thinking she may have stolen something."

"You take care, Ingrid," Malvolio said deeply, "and Happy Holidays." He bowed to her, from the waist, and he put his leg out real medieval like. He turned and started in on his captive immediately.

"A murderer and assassin! But a thief?"

"Oh you," she said, exhausted. Defeated.

"Not a word, hag, or I swear I'll throw you onto the first floor. It's a long way down."

He walked with his arm around her, real supportive like.

"Maybe next time they'll send professionals, by the way," Malvolio said, then thrust his fist hard into Grandma's ribs. "Who sent you," he said to her fiercely but under his breath each time he punched her.

"You should take it easy on the old lady," I said, owning to my sense of justice and fair play.

"She's a killer. Don't you realize that? If she would have hit you with one of those darts you'd be as dead as that sales clerk back there."

The old lady winced, but still remained stoically silent, perhaps out of fear, or perhaps out of a sheer inborn unwillingness to speak to her targets. She may have been a true professional, like my newfound protector, my newfound friend. Yes, I said it. My newfound friend. You know the way he was holding her, roughly, but not too rough around the edges, it reminded me of the unease with which Santa Claus held the children of strangers, gingerly, but without too much affection lest he be paraded in front of Fox News and hauled off to see the judge for his chemical castration, or worse, be forced to shave his creepy beard and perhaps find a normal retirement gig like the greeter at Wally World...and you know why? The way he was holding her, could they be acting? Could they be in on it together? They could just be in on it together and knocked off the other guy in there, the ancient Methuselah, for the insurance money. This old lady could be Malvolio's momma for all I know. Maybe his wife. Maybe their plan was to lead me somewhere, the whole time me thinking that Malvolio would do her in, and at the very last instant when we were all alone, wham bam Malvolio turns the gun on me, they would go to guns and do me in, firing from the hip, perhaps taking aimed shots to compete, shooting up my carcass, practicing all sorts of trick shots and laughing that they had duped me. Then they'd head back to their taskmaster, my brother-in-law, the evil Sheldon, collect their paychecks, and head to Godknowswhat tropical country. What a shocking ending if this were a major Hollywood production.

I could just see my pissed off brother-in-law guffawing heartily when he heard of my demise. I could just see his fat, greedy, tallow-colored face full of paucity and poverty of intellect, dreaming about how he and Hannah would spend the holidays in some exotic locale that's safe for tourists. Go ahead and plug whatever local you want in for X...all the hotels there are the same. You could be in Bali or Argentina, and if you don't leave the resort you've basically been to the same place. They'd call this freedom, but it's an illusion because that's only freedom from fear, but not real freedom. I don't know what that is as of yet. They'd enjoy cocktails and mourn my loss with other tamed and boring couples, all the while Sheldon would be laughing on the inside at my untimely demise, laughing all the way to the bank. It suddenly dawned on me that I don't have a will, a final Last Will and Testament and if I suddenly croaked the entirety of my estate would probably sit in Probate Court indefinitely.

There would be no money left over to even create a museum out of my boyhood home that tons of people would most likely visit on an at least bi-yearly basis. No, I would have to create it with my own money, because no one was going to do it for me, not even the president of my almost defunct fan club, last active possibly in the summer of 2007, though now most certainly non-existent by now, after all what's the point of having a fan club for an author who hasn't been productive since about the year 1999, the year he graduated from undergrad, and set off into the wider world to conquer it by force of will or by foil.

More foil perhaps and more energy, but maybe now, especially since I haven't been exactly active since around that time, preferring instead to live the life of a popular reclusive author; however, without the fan base to even sustain that I was just really a washed up, lonely author, which aren't quite the sustainers of cult celebrity status. You know, had I done the talk show circuit indefinitely and totally pimped myself out, talked about rubbish until I was blue in the face and increased my popularity vis a vis the masses, then perhaps I could have declared myself a recluse in *People* magazine and say I was abandoning the world in the attempt to find solace in my artistic activity, that I was creating art and literature for art's sake. All I did by refusing to engage in this sort of behavior was ensure that whatever small amount of popularity I enjoyed was thoroughly stifled and buried like a plant inching its way to the surface for the precious sunlight only to be cruelly diverted by a cement slab from which no further growth upward was possible.

I could not even laterally escape. Father fucked that all up for me by dispatching agents of his Leman Global Industries, en masse, a great literary levee en masse, to purchase up all the known copies of the novel *Asymmetric Hearts* along with a PR blitz to make my name a household name. Of course during the media onslaught, I remained blissfully unaware of all these hidden machinations, just as I remain unaware of the machinations now, and the forces aligned against me.

If anything, now, I needed allies, and plenty of them...not phony allies like Marcus Hanely, God rest his phony, fictitious soul. To think that I made it all the way to Denver, driving on tanks full of delusion, in a car with a still leaky gas tank, with maybe half a tank of unabashed hope, irreducible to my circumstances...I'll tell you hope does not stem from my bank account balance or the credit limit of my Visa Black account. I don't revel in the fact that I'm tremendously wealthy. I only need to find some worthy end to direct my money at. I feel as though I'm some sort of stupid little marginalized Saudi Prince, 4999 heart attacks away from the throne, wiling away my days at Harrod's in London, outdoing all my cousins in buying up luxury goods, letting the world pass me by.

As I lost myself in thought, Malvolio and the old lady got ahead of me. I looked at all the posters hanging about, and we passed by Burberry's with some elegant coats and bags stationed in the front window surrounded and framed only by glass and marble, only about one inch thick, a façade really, which in the previous years and incarnations was a lady's boot store, a designer no one will remember though he made really fine boots, finer than the tacky shit which passes for craftsmanship now and is really tonned out in Chinese factories and shipped to Italy for the final label imprint, I think, only the label was made in Italy; so they aren't really lying.

It's only a matter of stretching the truth, and if no one asks the questions, it is the truth for all time. Above all that was this image of a woman with impossibly high cheekbones, a healthy jawline, and oodles of good, wavy hair. You know, no one knows or cares what is on her mind. She is not even wearing any of the products below her. The photo was taken probably some years prior and the model may even be out of the business, possibly married to some actor, football player, or investment banker, venture capitalist, or whatever other title people making it go by.

You know, these are the people we idolize today: the heroes...the people in the business of creating illusions and distractions. The football player, Mr. Sunday Entertainer, makes people long for the weekend away from their bitter office places. He sells jerseys and tickets and hopes and dreams from thin air. The actor plays a role written by a writer who spins words to pack seats, not caring about the consequences of his labor, as long as the tickets sell.

But the investment banker is the worst sort of sot in existence; he takes a pile of money, doles it out, and receives more money in return to dole it out again. With a talent for mathematics, he could spend his time in pursuit of the arcane knowledge for which Faust sold his soul and could build the bridges and space elevators and thermonuclear reactors of tomorrow, but is instead content counting golden coins one by one and trying to find a way to stack them to the moon with charts and graphs and numbers. As long as the numbers get bigger and stay black, it's good; life is good. He is the gatekeeper and guardian of the door to beyond nature, the world of men, the world that sucks nature into its black hole and builds an edifice, but that edifice is always crumbling and in need of repair. And men unknowingly spend their entire lives to build this edifice, to carve their name in these shifting blocks of sand, and they call it their will, and this is the most profound of all the illusions madmen spin for themselves. It all blows away, and their time in the sun comes to an end, and people do differently. As for me, I refuse. I walk through this modern day, a holder of secrets and knowledge of what will be the final activity of men. This buying and selling, elevated to a God, which is really just a foundation. I am a well-dressed, handsome madman in this marketplace and I know that death leads time to a precipice, hurtling ever closer and closer to an edge where nothing is written, is remembered, nothing practiced, nor spoken, nor thought.

My time will come to an end just as yours will, just as my father's has, even though he was one of the richest men in these United States, was one of the richest men in this world, and the United States will come to an end, and all of this, my voyages, my meetings, my conversations, may or may not live on in the hearts and minds of those I have come into contact with. I can't be sure, but if I were inclined to be a betting man, I say it is without much risk. They might listen for a moment or they may think me a fool and dismiss me to watch more television.

Something in the Burberry store caught my eye and I turned to tell Malvolio that I would be entering the store to take a look at it and possibly purchase it once I felt it, because I'm a tactile beast. I have to feel something in order to purchase it. I need to feel everything to make sure it isn't phony and plastic rubbish, disposable after a few uses, worked into useable form by machines programmed to be hell-bent on production 24/7. As I turned to Malvolio, he had his arm around the old lady, possibly interrogating her as to just who sent her. They walked closer to the guardrail separating the third floor of the wall from the empty spaces below. He pointed his nearly skeletal arm, wavy sleeve draped haphazardly off his elbow, which jutted sharply, bent 90 degrees, as he extended his arm to point to show her something on the bottom floor. He shifted, lowered his center of mass, and calmly picked her up by the waist and pitched her over the edge.

"Jesus Christ!" I shouted, to the horror of some of the bag-handed mall patrons who quickly dismissed me as the walked past.

The old assassin tumbled briefly through the air and splatted below in the midst of the Santa Claus display. A few screams shot up from the bottom floor.

Malvolio trotted ahead, quicker than I had imagined he could for his sleight frame, and bade me come with him saying, "We have to leave now!"

I caught up with him, and we speed walked like two excited marionettes beyond the crowds of people who seemed oblivious that he had just tossed granny over the borderline. The people who weren't texting or checking godknowswhat on their smartphones were busy talking to one another, little insular worlds within the world.

"What did you do that for?" I asked Malvolio, who had a grin on his face.

"I warned her I would do just that. I told her to tell me who sent her, but she wouldn't…not until the last minute when she felt herself going over the edge. That's when they all drop their toughie act and start to talk: when gravity takes over. It makes you sort of lose your inhibitions like drinking too much booze. You know, when they stare down at that floor. She must have thought I wouldn't let her go."

"So, what did she say? Who's after us?"

"It's strange. She didn't know. Right before she went over she says that one of her competitors called her up and asked her to finish a job for him. Says he just couldn't pull himself away from a game of bingo."

"Red."

"Mr. Meriwether. Used to be one of the best. Washed up now. We all get washed up with age. You no longer have that killer edge. People can jog away from you. Half of the assassination business is striking fear into people, making them panic, making them make mistakes."

"Who hired Red?"

"I don't know."

"Sheldon?"

"I doubt it. That guy couldn't orchestrate a solitary walk in the park."

"You're sick, you know that...dumping that old lady over the edge like that. Right in front of Santa Claus," I said as we hurried through the third floor of Neiman Marcus towards the entrance/exit and the parking lot where the hell wagon was parked.

"But I'm not sick. I'm here to protect you by any means necessary, my man. I was sent to watch over you by your father."

"Father's dead."

"He died as must we all, but you won't die on my watch."

"The cops are on their way."

"Probably. Panic hasn't set in yet. For all they know, she offed herself. No one on the upper floor tried to detain us. They'll roll tape and find out the truth. Holy hell, that tape from Saks Fifth Avenue will be hilarious."

"It will set in. You can't go pitching granny off the third floor of a mall and not have people notice."

"They must have already found the old man."

"And the young salesgirl."

"People are remarkably unobservant these days. The most powerful sense is the olfactory sense. They won't be noticed until they start to stink."

"Yeah, who wants a dainty scarf in winter? They'll be found. Probably before the day's up."

In the Saks Fifth Avenue store, we passed the statuesque old man death. The corpse formed a bizarre mannequin and really fit in with the rest of the motif, dressed in his suit, which was remarkably 1940s Duke of Windsor-style topped off with a charming Fedora on top and a dashing maroon scarf really waylaid and knotted to perfection. In life he was a daring killer of women; he rather looked like an ancient Sir Galahad mixed with an equal portion of headstrong gumshoe. I wondered if he had a pistol on him. Could be useful, but you know, I have always wanted a swordstick. I wanted to pry it from his hand, but it was the only thing propping him up from discovery until the rigor mortis really set in. I did pluck the dart from his forehead and tossed it underneath some tables, to make his appearance more natural.

"Check his wallet," Malvolio said, ever the professional. "It could give us a clue as to where he came from."

I patted the old dead guy down, feeling his bony legs underneath his suit. Finally I hit pay dirt in his inside jacket pocket. I grabbed the wallet. The man wheezed. I jumped back and screamed, "Oh shit."

"Corpse breath, you fool. It's oxygen leaving the lungs as the diaphragm relaxes."

"I don't know these things."

"You shouldn't. Normal people don't. Now let's get out of here before his fucking knees buckle and the store clerks come running."

We walked, rather hurriedly, towards the exits, not arm in arm, though Malvolio's arm kept brushing against mine, locking it in a near death grip as if to keep my pace at bay and at his nonchalant stroll. Every urge in my body screamed run. I found it very disturbing that he just pitched a grandmother off the third floor of the mall without a pang of conscience. Who knows. Maybe he was one of those killers who got torn up on the inside. When we burst into the bright December sunlight and walked across the parking lot towards the Judge, I asked him, once we were out of harms way for the three killings, if throwing the granny from the ledge bothered him.

"Of course not. It was either she or I or she or you and I at that point. You know that. Why should it bother me?"

"I thought we'd take her somewhere and give her a talking to."

"The old bitch threatened to scream. I had to do it. It was then or never. She screams and we get caught. You know how many ways she could have spun that story to the authorities? Two young punks accost and murder her husband in Saks Fifth Avenue. Why, she could have declared that we got into a fight over the last raspberry red cardigan with ox horn buttons, you know, some sort of Christmas shopping hijinks, and the old bastard had a heart attack. And guess what? They'd up and believe her. They wouldn't even bother with an investigation. No one would look at her cane. And we'd be all over Fox News. Did you see that sweater? It was reduced in price from 1200 to 500, and it was an exquisite Alpaca cable knit. I bet you'd look really Dapper Dan in it, my man."

"Will you shut up and concentrate on the task at hand?"

"What's that?"

"We're getting the hell out of here before this place explodes into a frenzy of reporters and they all roll the videotape and see you pitch granny off the ledge in an attempt to crush Santa Claus. All the police in the tri-state area will be dispatched after us. They'll probably give us sporting nicknames, and people will applaud when our shot up terroristic carcasses are displayed in front of the television cameras."

"Dude, don't worry. She wasn't young and hot. No one gives a fuck if an old lady decided to meet her maker the day before Christmas. If she was young and hot and disappeared, yeah, there would be a nationwide manhunt. Last seen...getting in a muscle car with two weirdoes...it would be the fucking crime of the century."

"Come on, man. You're rich. You can afford a good defense attorney. I can't. I'll have to turn state's evidence on you. You can pay for someone to dream up a plausible alibi. My public defender will probably make me plea out to twenty-five years of sodomy. Look at me; I'm slight. I can't handle prison. But guess what? That shit's not going to happen. I doubt we even see this make national news."

"But it was on camera."

"No way. The cameras weren't rolling. These people want you dead. They're going to figure out a way to get you dead and have it not be on camera. These people have a nearly infinite reach. You hide in a Chinese Junk off the coast of Hong Kong, and you better believe they'll find you and run a fat fishhook through your ass and go trolling for sharks. Shark bait before sunrise."

Fear boiled up and shrank backwards in my soul.

"Some other people who they wanted just up and committed suicide rather than face them. You knew, at least then, they had some choice in the matter."

"What else did she tell you before you pitched her?"

"Come on, you don't know them. You've never heard of them."

"Maybe I have. I've been around."

"That's a laugh."

"If you've heard of this gang of rogues, misfits, hired killers, philanderers, destroyers of all that's good and right in the world, wandering evildoers set against all order and light in the world, my God, man, you'd be dead already. Just to hear their name is to mark yourself."

"You know about them, and you've lived to tell about it. How the hell did you hear about them anyway?"

"That's another story for another time. You'll hear about it once I think you're safe and able to fully comprehend just what we're up against. You know, I think right now that if I told you you'd be sent running stark mad through the streets. You might have enough sense to not be naked, but you might just throw yourself in front of a train or train a masterblaster on yourself. I don't want that happening. You're too important for that."

"Where do we go from here?"

"Here's what we do. We have to take the most untraveled route possible to get to Peoria. They have agents everywhere who are always on the lookout for their targets."

"Who we dealing with? The FBI? CIA? NSA? DHS?"

"You fool, these people aren't the government."

"Who are they?"

"You aren't ready to know. Don't ask. You'll find out in time."

"They're everywhere?"

"Yes. Everywhere. Your father was a member."

"A member of what? Skull and Bones? The Rosicrucians? The Illuminati? The fucking Freemasons?"

"No! Stop asking! Get in the car and drive. Take 25 north to Cheyenne. Avoid the roads during the day. From Cheyenne take one of the little state roads through Nebraska and Iowa, then onwards to Illinois and your dad's funeral."

"Is it safe to attend?"

"Probably not. Might have to take a rain check."

"There are no rain checks for funerals."

"They'll have agents everywhere around there, but as long as you remain in public with a bunch of people who have your back, you'll be fine."

We finally made it to the Judge. A folded up note lay underneath the windshield wiper on the passenger side.

I opened it. "YOU HAVE ONE BADASS CAR!" it read.

"A warning? Who's it from? Who signed it?"

"No, it's a compliment."

"We'd better pray they're not on to us. It could be a code of some sort. A warning, maybe."

"Tell me it's not the Freemasons."

"No. No way. They've never been a force to reckon with. They've been much maligned by people trying to sell books and scapegoated, but in reality they're a bunch of old men and young guys who don't have any fresh ideas trying to get business contacts. What we're dealing with makes these gentlemen look like a highly refined knitting club. You know, their tapestry is life itself, but know this. We're dealing with consummate professionals. Not knitters, mate."

"Damn."

"Drive, man! Drive! Put Denver and the mountains behind you. Head north and then east if you want to survive!"

I floored the Judge. The wheels burned out and attracted the attention of everyone sitting at a California Pizza Kitchen outdoor lounge, covering them in plumes of black smoke. It occurred to me as I was well on my way towards Cheyenne with the suburbs behind and an open plateau ahead of us, that they were concerned about me crashing into their conveyance and couldn't care less about my safety in the matter.

You know, I was in this world all alone. Malvolio was my companion for the time being, but he was going to see fit to abandon me and prove himself totally unworthy at some point in our journey, and I would have to kick him out of the car, maybe shoot him or run him through somehow. I would try my damndest to avoid violence, though it was the American Way. I would try and avoid all that. I really would.

As the sun descended, Malvolio did not tire. Even though I was sick of driving, I didn't bother to ask him to take over. This way, I knew that we would at least end up where we intended without too many sidetracks. Still, the sidetracks were the important paths taken. You can't set out to have an adventure on the Great American Road, because you'll find yourself sorely disappointed when you end up looking at a bunch of road signs pointing this way and that, and like most of the other people on the road with you, who are hell-bent to get to some distant location in a fixed amount of time, you'll be forced to keep their frantic pace.

I was in no hurry to be like them. Malvolio looked contented sitting there, lolling in and out of sleep. There was a grace to him while he slept, an angelic grace that I cannot quite put into words. And they call me a writer. He was strange in his physicality, but splayed before me, he was trusting and as innocent as a poor beast of burden, bridled to his master's yoke.

If these people, Godknowswho they were, were that dangerous, wasn't it possible that he was one of them? Maybe even me? Maybe I was one of them, born into it, like my father, and I had just not received my invite yet. Funny. Father never mentioned them before. There must be entire vaults full of secrets that I have not been made privy to. In fact, there is only one thing I do know. Marcus, you don't exist. You are a fiction like Hamlet and Ahab, and Don Quixote, and all the other great characters of literature that will live on even when we are all dust. And perhaps when this civilization's ruins are discovered amongst all the gas stations and office buildings and these words are translated into some alien tongue, perhaps they will have a new life. And they will tell others of our most noble intentions, profoundest secrets, the height of the nobility that was men, and the basements of darkest devils and despair.

I don't know. I just know that I'm voyaging through a vortex of dust to some unknown destination with waypoints on the way where I will stop and can say hello and share in my journeys with the good and bad and indifferent struggling peoples of the globe. You may be insecure of your meaning, but my meaning is for me and me alone to know. Of all the places I have been, I have felt like just a visitor, a mere vacationer, and a passive observer. When I finally find a place that makes me, that makes me weep, fall to the ground and kiss it like I would kiss my long dead mother as I remember her, then I will be home. I will cease being tumbleweed. I will stop and grow roots. I shall not use the nautical clichés of being a ship without a rudder or a forlorn mast less ship of fools drifting out at sea as a metaphor for humanity. We are no longer a seafaring people, and all that is dead and tired. I'm no barnacle on Moby Dick's blowhole. That's for sure.

I'm a man with a full tank of gas that fills itself and an engine that always idles, never seizing. I'm a slave to inertia. Objects at rest tend to stay at rest, and objects in motion tend to stay in motion. I care nothing for a prime mover. I move myself. I'll keep moving until I croak from neglect. For me, the Lord is a forlorn concept, which removes personal responsibility from the equation of life. Nope, the Lord isn't going to help you. You're on your own. You can pray all you want, but they aren't being answered or filed away. The Lord doesn't have an inbox because it – only Godknowswhat it is – doesn't exist. Like I said, you're on your own. Being all alone? That doesn't scare me, not in the least. I know what I want. I don't even care if currency gets all devalued and the bridges fall apart. I don't care if the world descends into darkness. I'll remain a man with my gun loaded and my sword ever sharp.

It was around eight at night when we crossed the Colorado border into Wyoming. Right on the border, a redness glowed just behind a hill and looked eerily like some spaceship come to exsanguinate and vivisect cows or perhaps do milkings of male human seminal glands. As I sped toward the glowing redness, I glanced over at Malvolio. He stirred in his leather seat. The heat blasted over him, and he picked his trousers, perhaps dreaming that he was sitting on some foreign beach gaping at bronzed beauties while he himself was wearing a thong. I shrugged it off and instead reached over and shook him.

"Wha? How long have I been sleeping?"

"Bout four hours now."

"It took you four hours to get up here?"

"I've been taking everything in. Like the strange glow ahead of us. A strange redness rising in the north."

"What is it?"

"Don't know."

"Can't be good. Maybe it's the exhaust of an oil refinery or fracking operation. They're popular around here."

We crested the hill. It was not a spacecraft or oil refinery belching red death flames; it was a great red sign that read "THE CLOWN'S DEN."

"Stop!" Malvolio screamed.

"Not stopping."

"Stop, damn you, if you know what's good for you! Pull off at this exit. Don't you see behind us?" he said looking in the rearview mirror. "We've had a tail since Denver. How the hell did you let me fall asleep?"

"A tail?"

"Someone's following us."

"You were sleeping. How the hell did you know we have a tail?"

"I saw them. They're following us. Just pull off and see if they follow."

"The cars back there?"

"No, man, the bikes."

"The bikes were following us?"

"Yep."

"How do you know?"

"I woke up occasionally to see if they were still there."

"No, you didn't."

"I did. You were probably just too lost in thought and muttering to yourself to notice me up looking around to make sure that we were okay."

"You never woke up."

"Baloney. I almost never sleep."

"You slept for four straight hours. I figured you needed it."

"Well, damn you, wake me up next time. I'm supposed to be your bodyguard," he said frantically. "Now pull over."

I hit the exit. The cars kept going. I used to be a slave to inertia. Now I was a slave to Malvolio. The motorcycles followed. There were about four of them. I'll be damned. These bikers were following us.

"I made them coming out of the mall after us," Malvolio beamed.

"Could be a coincidence that they're coming here. What is this place?"

"Well it's out in the middle of nowhere, it's got a big glowing sign, and it's got a bunch of trucks in the parking lot and no windows. What do you think it is?"

"I don't know."

"It's the best titty bar in the world."

"Titties?"

"Yeah, you know what titties are? Breasts? Bazoombas, Jugs, Knockers, Fun Bags, Boulders, Flapdoodles, Dannies, Hot Dog Buns, Chebbies."

"Of course I know them."

We parked, far from the entrance, near the parking lot's exit so that we'd be able to peel out in case the bikers pulled out machine guns to do us in. They looked pretty harmless to me, but so did the elderly couple that tried to blowgun and slice stab us to death. I learned one thing about Malvolio at the Clown's Den.

I came to determine that Malvolio is an ass man. Through the course of the evening spent at the Clown's Den, also known as the world's friendliest gentleman's club, though we were no gentlemen, and rightly deserved, because neither Mr. Malvolio nor myself have ever been to a tit bar where you feel genuinely welcome, especially towards a handsome gent willing to purchase lap dances for his friend. I determined Malvolio in not only obsessed with dainty scarves. He is obsessed with ladies with large posteriors.

Mr. Malvolio is an ass man par excellence, and I must say that during the course of the evening I also came to appreciate the well-endowed rump. In the bathroom, I actually saw Malvolio piss and heard it splash against the urinal cake, thus assuring he was a real man, whilst I purchased two large condoms from the Lubricated Condoms vending machine and was happy to see them marked LEMAN GLOBAL INDUSTRIES, ensuring that I was purchasing a quality product and not some junky inferior brand guaranteed to pop in the snatch.

Malvolio theorized, and was always promulgating theories, most of them half baked, half fantasy, and half pseudoscience, that the reason the girls at the Clown's Den had so much, as he called it, "junk in the trunk" was either the perfusion of Recombinant Bovine Growth Hormone (RBGH) in cattle feeds at the world's largest cattle corral or the stench rising from it made for all the little girls in a hundred mile's radius who by just breathing in on a day in day out basis assured that they would have ample tits and ass by the time they were thirteen. These girls who worked here were at least 18 and had five years of growth. I had a perma-erection the entire night long, which was only reduced to a semi-Woodrow whenever I made eye contact with the bikers and found them staring back, confirming that they weren't there for the girls or to traffic methamphetamine. They were there to do us in, ignobly.

Malvolio came back from his 200 dollar string of lap dances to tell me the virtues of being an unrepentant ass man, that being intimate with, or in his words "fuckin'," a woman with a large posterior was the closest thing to heaven on the godforsaken planet and was akin to being the emperor of a semi-largish country with ample water, mineral rights, fishing rights (so it wasn't landlocked), a docile and happy populace who dedicated monuments to your memory, only unbridled for a while you were still alive, and they'd send their own big-assed daughters to do your bidding in magnificent, never drafty castles.

Malvolio, through the course of the night, burst into song at least once, when he saw not a dancer, but our waitress, our raven-haired beauty who was blessed by the rump gods from a very young age, which was Malvolio's theoretical postulate regarding this particular lady named Daniela who was just as sweet and nubile as the other ladies who inhabited the Clown's Den from the hours of dusk until dawn.

Ahh...Daniela...you have a faux mink coat on, why, I would trap the little bastards in the wild, grow a wild and bushy beard, live the existence of a wretched, starving, uncaring about my own welfare, just to be able to come into a cabin and get cozy with her in the warmth and have oodles of children, or if she already had children, take them all in and make them princes or even dukes of the kingdom on Earth I would establish with her. Then we'd have oodles of our own children, grow old, and die happy. It was a wonderful dream.

As she walked by, Malvolio prodded me to speak to her, perhaps because I was the one dressed up for the occasion and Malvolio, though he stood up later in the evening and declared his undying love for the virtuous and rotund in all the right places ladies, declaring it a great coup of nature to conspire that something you love could only get better and better and better with age, expanding outwards past its own previous borderlines, an investment you can watch grow, declaring his affinity as he asked her, her ethnicity, always wanting to trace out the contours of the crashing and breaking of the genetic ocean surrounding him, and discern which little pool he wanted to jump into.

As it turns out she was a mixture of German, Mexican, Native American, Dutch, that one of her grandmothers may or may not have been 1/4 African and there was someone from the Caribbean Islands thrown into the mix, no doubt a skullduggerous pirate, bent on raping and pillaging who plowed his stern into an Irish woman, quite possibly without asking permission, perhaps after asking permission, or perhaps receiving a wink that charged him, who knew...it resulted in a hot and horny half breed with a high Darwinian fitness and a talent for unlacing bodices from Aruba to the port city of St. Lucia, and ports beyond under assumed names, sometimes wearing an eye patch, never carrying the skin of a goat's intestine because we know that takes the fun out of all of it.

Ahh yes, how little we know of our ancestors! He was rumored to have died, much like Henry VIII, rotting from the legs up, poxy and wormy and still at the plow, serviced by one wench after another who had to gag themselves against the stench, no doubt, but I saw this gentleman's cod piece, so to me he lived a good life. This ne'er-do-well rogue, wannabe pirate, he left no property, no memories and was quite possibly buried at sea for the fish to snack on.

Daniela, a single resultant of his beautiful shot in the dark for days long dead, stopped from her duties for a brief moment, stopped laying beers and whiskey down for the numerous gents none of whom were as handsome, dashing, well dressed, or rich as I and all of the women in the place knew that for they could smell the cash dripping out of my pores, and they paid Malvolio and me, well, me really, the most attention. Of course I tipped them around 100.00 at a time in twenties that I pulled out of the ATM, nearly bankrupting the thing.

The girls, they ate it up. Not only were we rich, but we were dangerous, and there's only one thing that women love more than money and that's dangerous men...not men dangerous to them, but men that did dangerous shit like walk through lava flows and tribes of headhunters to get to them. Yeah, that ain't the only thing. I'm also probably the funniest, most dashing, and profound, philosophical, and swashbuckling swords-man to walk through the door, ever. I swear, the guy would probably take our photos and put them up on the wall. Goddamn, I wish I had that old geezer's swordstick, and I'm ashamed that we left it in the SAKS FIFTH AVENUE. It probably could have come in handy when the four bikers jumped up and started spraying the place down with Uzis, or whatever they were smuggling in their pants.

Someone had to be vigilant against these goons, and I kept my eye on them and doled out Malvolio money for lap dances like it was candy to petulant trick or treat-ers. The girls giggled. Daniela, according to her nametag, stopped serving up the beverages and took to sitting on my lap, grinding that sexy posterior into my crotch so that her cheeks spread right over my shaft, which firmed up and grew firmer by the second.

She started gyrating on my cock to the music, and I was nearly about to lose control and cream all in my pants and underwear and ruin my BRIONI tuxedo pants when Malvolio, exiting the FRICTION DANCE room, which is what the CLOWN'S DEN calls LAP DANCES (and I definitely recommend you go and get a Friction Dance from one of their big assed maids), Malvolio...he decided to rush the stage in his fury with semi wood that I could clearly see in his slacks, pitching a fucking tent, delivered up a song from the innate and unfulfilled perverse horniness of his mortal soul, spun for other souls to hear before disappearing into the dust of the moments, passed.

MALVOLIO'S SONG

Who will love the feeble lasses

Built like twigs and spindly grasses

Blowing in the winter winds

Blowing in the winter winds

Other men can conquer them

Men in love with boys and slim women

It's not for me!

They're not for me!

I love women strong and stout
Women possessed of that ultimate feminine clout
Possessed of the world at large
For you skinny babes I sing a dirge
For who wants them, and who needs them
That queer world of fashion can keep them

For hefty girls of gravity, I'll sing my song for free
I'll sing in summer, I'll sing in fall
I'll sing at any frozen winter's concert hall
I'll tack my 99 decrees on any fashion house's wall

Against those dictates of dressed up men
Disguised as death's cruel gaping grin
Only a strange fool will go against nature's bountiful blessings
Lulled towards sleep with death's cold caressing

I should rather pierce my arrow's shaft through the center of the sun
Than make sweet love to a skeleton
Should I find mine self in a foreign land
Trek across desert hell, death's jungle, to the Strand

And fail to find any ladies there possessed of weight
I'll go to my bitter rest home, I'll masturbate
I'll dream of women, real and round
I'll do it while I punch the clown
I'll succumb to a monk's unmanly fate
I'll give up my dream and die a forlorn celibate.

The lights went down for the third time in the evening, and the announcer, not your typical juice bar announcer because his voice was not that of a well-trained carnival barker but instead had a natural timbre that added a further air of reality to an already real situation, announced that there would be a three for one special in celebration of very special guests.

Malvolio leaned over to me sort of fatigued and declared in hushed tones that the best place to hide out from the agents of the as of yet unnamable menace would be in the VIP room. He suggested we invite the majority of the dancers that had thus far tickled our pickles and even one of the waitresses who was possessed of ass into the VIP room, but not all at once, meaning that we couldn't be in there together because if the bastards dispatched an assassin into the fray, they could kill two very important birds with one stone, and for safety's sake, even though he was hugely partial to lap dances, I could go first with the woman of my choice.

The woman of my choice, alas, was the waitress, Daniela, but she had not gotten over whatever fear or pride or husbandly control that kept her from showing that luscious ass in all its glory and opulence underneath the black light and strobes. I wanted to watch it bounce up and down in slow motion, and this thought grabbed me with such as specific gravity that my ding-dong responded immediately, throbbing against my tightie whities. Her titties were begrudgingly ensconced like two perfect and immoveable spheres in her tight black sports bra. How I wanted to see them drop and flop around, see the curvature to the nipple, flick them, and make them perky firm like gummy bears left on the dashboard on a cold day.

I stared at Daniela's tits again. There was a small amount of sag evident in them. I told Malvolio that I would much rather entertain the waitress and stay sitting down with her on my lap than take any of the other globbers who wanted to get paid to grind their plump asses on my ding dong. He could go into the back, and I would be fine by myself against any would be assassins.

"I don't know that you can handle yourself," Malvolio said.

And now, it was either I went into the back, dragged along by any little damsel waiting for her payout, or none of us went into the back, and we would lose the much coveted three for one special. I think Malvolio just wanted a go at my baby girl, my love, and the woman who I was going to plan on proposing to. I wouldn't be able to get enough of her; I knew this even though we had barely shared two syllables, let alone words.

"I can. I've got the battle scars to prove it. Sometime in the daylight I'll show them to you."

Malvolio laughed, "All right, all right. I'll be back. Say, got any legal tender?"

I reached into my pocket and pulled out an enormous, flagrantly disgusting wad of twenty dollar bills and slammed the pimp roll in his hand, the bottom one being quite greasy from being trapped against my thigh and acting the buffer between my thigh and right testicle, smashed underneath the weight of Daniela's sexy ass. I'm pretty sure that I saw an imprint of my glans (and for you neophytes that's cockhead) in the face of Andy Jackson.

Daniela shifted and sent my thoughts rambling across hilly frontiers and a sumptuous verdure valley teaming with fruit and honeybees, apiaries, pomegranates, melons, and her, waiting for me underneath a tree with nothing on but a crimson red sash and ruby red lipstick. The long and the short of it...she was perfect for me, boner inducing, and I so wanted to tell her so without fear of scaring her off.

I figured, perhaps I would be wrong and that she would want to know the truth, the whole truth, about me and where I was headed in life to determine if her future life goals could mesh with my own. I had heard once or twice either from the lips of Marcus Hanely, which were really my own lips, or perhaps in an episode of *Oprah* that I happened to watch in a hospital emergency room or home of a family friend, perhaps these very words I couldn't recall. I only knew that I had to be fast. I had to seal the deal before we had to move on. She could come with us and sit in front with me, or Malvolio could drive, and we could make out in the backseat. All of these thoughts were racing through my head. I would probably have to abandon her. This was the story of my life: running from these unrepentant assassins, hell bent on my destruction.

Malvolio walked past the sign of the VIP lounge that listed the rule. There was one rule to The Clown's Den friction room. No THPJs. A TPHJ was a through the pants hand job: that much coveted, though hard to come by, stripper hand job or meat tenderizer, as it is known amongst hordes of lesser men, because it eats you enough to get you ready for the heat, but not enough to let your juices leak out.

All in all, the cock tease was an appropriate name for the whole lot of it, and anyone with enough balls to name a "juice bar" the Cock Tease would be doing pensioners and college students everywhere a favor. I suppose strip clubs would plummet out of business if prostitution were ever legalized, or the strip club would just become a prelude as it is in other countries where people don't mind a good fuck every now and then.

This distraction, this line of thought and the weight of my future and only wife Daniela, her back blocked my vision from the front door just enough to prevent me from seeing six bruisers dressed in motorcycle jackets join forces with the four geriatric bikers who followed us, and these six bruisers were younger and had slicked back hairstyles that screamed I've done time, grey moustaches, without benefit of Grecian Formula that would have been appropriate on an all gay male revue pirate ship, their ripped muscular arms capable of smashing my head like a grape, and busting my ribs with their fists they probably strengthened by tearing the heads off of pit-bulls.

I only caught a glimpse of them talking to the owner, and I watched the way he shrunk back from them to know they meant business. My first thought in regards to them was that they were the assassins dispatched by Sheldon to haul my miserable soul off to Hell, battered, bruised, and broken like Christ. The bastards were the modern day Roman centurions who would crown me, your humble and virtuous narrator, with my crown of thorns, only my crown, fashioned cruelly in this place, would be the jagged edges of Miller Lite bottle caps. An ignoble end.

Yes, they'd probably crucify me outside on the big ass red sign, and Daniela would serve as my weeping Mary Magdalene, and this time she'd actually be there and not turning some trick somewhere. Daniela gasped when she saw them waltz in like mother-fucking conquerors and got off my lap immediately as if she had been caught in flagrante delectio by another lover or perhaps husband. Apparently she was, and apparently I had already asked her over the music if she was married, engaged, or "had a dude," and she answered, but I did not hear her authentic answer and just assumed she said, "Oh no, I'm all yours stud."

I asked her who these men were, and she told me that they were the meanest bunch of bastards outlaw motorcycle gang this side of the Mississippi and this side North of the Colorado River; the motorcyclists of greater Las Vegas being even more daring and more crude in their mayhem causing behavior. This gang, however, was an even more deadly gang of fisticuffers, brawlers, bastard baby makers, and mutineers in these glorious United States, though it was fiercely up for debate amongst the Latino Bikers Association of California and other associated groups of evildoers throughout these forty-eight Continental United States. What she told me last, really mouthed the words to me breathlessly, was that she was the "old lady" of the Sergeant at Arms of this notorious gang of misfits and outlaws, and out and out psychos. They were the Eastern Chapter of Lucifer's Prairie Dogs, not to be confused with the Western Chapter. We had made short work of those geriatrics back in Shitsville. These were their bastard children who grew up malnourished and none too bright.

"But you're not old at all," I said to her as the jimmy jammer got right up near us, looking all psycho in the face or trying hard to, wondering why his old lady was cozied up to a gentleman with my looks and my refinement in a tuxedo. Or perhaps that was what he was thinking. Anyways, he was cross-eyed with rage. When he was just out of earshot, I turned to her, actually turned my back to him, and said, "I love you. From the moment I saw you I wanted to be with you for all times. I want-," at which she pulled away in horror. I thought it was because of the strength of my admonitions caused her support system in her current loathsome existence to erode away at the foundation, and I thought she was going to declare her own mutual love for me, but instead she told me, "I agree. I don't know your name, but I agree. He's just a very violent man, you don't know the half of it." I could see that underneath her white concealer she concealed a vicious black eye that had just come past the black point and started turning yellow. It was still puffy. I started to abhor the sick little men who beat on women. I wanted to murder this fellow, but had to attend to more pressing matters.

I went to stroke her face, and he was on us.

Now it is my duty as an able-bodied man to protect the virtue of my sisters, be they mere flesh and blood and not full of evil compunction and malice like my real sister. She can get bent. Wherever the babes may be, and this is out of a genuine desire to see justice and truth in this rotten little world of ours. I hate seeing women harmed by scum. And by scum, I mean any man that is not I. Not that I would ever harm them, it is just saying that I am a lover of beautiful women par excellence without equal, taught by the noble phantom Marcus Hanely, now dead and gone into the vast recesses of my brain. These are the things that I tell myself to make the punches from bikers have less sting.

Now these gentlemen, and I use that term in the loosest sense because they are in fact scum, are from the notorious biker gang popular in Cheyenne and approximately five miles south of the border into Colorado, and they are mean and known by the name that strikes terror into Southern Wyoming and Northern Colorado, the land encompassing the area around Interstate 25, but not quite extending to Ft Collins, Colorado, and they are known as Lucifer's Prairie Dogs Eastern Division or the LPD Faction ED, known to the locals as the Lunatic Posse of Doofuses with Erectile

Dysfunction and some other pejorative terms that the local populace has assigned to them but would dare not say it to their faces for fear of getting fucked up like I'm about to be.

We all know that the prairie dog, portrayed in Mutual of Omaha Wild Kingdom videos seems a right docile beast, but people of the prairie know that is a plucky, plague-carrying varmint, creating entire civilizations beneath our feet with eons of lineages of prairie dogs and worse, networks of tunnels that erode the soil and cause hundreds of otherwise non-drunk, perfectly sane individuals to trip and fall in their holes while playing catch in their backyards with their friendly Labradors.

It seemed in slow motion that the dame removed herself from my tuxedo pants where I had hoped she would spend the remainder of her days. Her pigheaded, Lucifer's Prairie Dogs Sergeant at Arms boyfriend stomped toward us tossing a patron and the bare-tittied without benefit of pasties dancer giving him a lap dance aside like they were stick figures. She collided with the mirror and left a perfect boob print before falling to the ground, picking herself up, and storming off to the safety of her dressing room.

I stood up and felt something loosen against my pants. I had shoved the .45 in the back of my pants. I had actually been prepared and done something smart today. I reached around my unwrinkled dinner jacket and produced her in all her blued-over steel. The lights danced off her, and the dancer stopped her whirling about the pole, let out a scream, and dove off the stage covering her titties with her hands, covering them up as if she hadn't been dancing naked just a few seconds ago.

Gumbone, the Lucifer's Prairie Dogs Sergeant at Arms, obviously did not get the memorandum that I am not a man to be trifled with. As a civilian given to intimidating churchgoers since the days of shaking down the kid skinnier than him for his milk money, Gumbone had relied on his fists to solve his problems. Other biker gangs in the area, like their main rivals, the Holy Rollers and the Devil's Kittens did not carry hand cannons for good reason.

They were given to anachronism, whether they knew it or not. In their brawls, the most battered a person might get is a bashing with a non cast iron Teflon coated frying pan. The Lucifer's Prairie Dogs ate supper with their moms on Sunday night. Some accompanied their fathers to the VFW on Friday nights to take advantage of the twoferone beer specials on tap and listened to the war stories told by the old and dying generations before them. These stories emboldened them to great acts of chicanery. The people of the town thought them harmless at best and hoped that no on would ride through who had actually done seriously nefarious shit on the planet.

They never joined the military, like many of the other motorcycle clubs because they were too scared of Iraq and Afghanistan, too fat, too stupid, or too lazy. How Gumbone scored the big-assed girl who just so recently hopped of Jackson Leman's own lap was the gossip of the town.

Old men speculated that she was new in town and was just using him to get established, or didn't know any better. Some of the women speculated in idle corners of the grocery store that she had a poor self esteem, maybe because her father didn't love her enough, or show that love with hugs and kisses. They all figured that it couldn't last long, eventually someone would come ride in on a pale horse, sweep the beauty off her feet, and she would slam her chunky ass down on the rider's pommel of a 1996 Harley Davidson Soft Tail with Ape Hangers, bid Lucifer's Prairie Dogs, the Devils Kittens, and the Holy Rollers farewell and ride off into the sunset with a real outlaw.

Besides, this was the Lucifer's Prarie Dogs Eastern Division. Not the much more geriatric and experienced in the ways of violence Western Division. Avalon and I had riotously pissed off their Western Division as you very well know. They wanted us dead. Hopefully, the two chapters did not share intelligence, and I was not on some BOLO or on Kill This Man On Sight List. If I was, oh well, I was about to get curb stomped for having Daniela on my lap. I thought otherwise, and I had a plan.

Gumbone froze when he saw the gun come out. It was a natural reaction. Holding a gun in a public place is an awesome feeling at first. You're in control. You're the man. But then you start to worry that maybe other people are packing and want to be a hero. He had probably never ever before experienced this phenomenon of having a masterblaster aimed in his direction since he embarked on his life of toughguy-hood. By the time Malvolio left the Friction Dance Room to declare that it was the time of his life, Mr. Gumbone had wet himself, and his bowels were loosening up too. Gumbone's reaction to my hand cannon had an opposite effect on me. I turned into delivering lines imparted to me from on high, trailing into my brain, shot into my brain like arrows slung by Holy Angels of the Lord.

"Face down, good sir, right in that puddle you just created. No one told me there was a chance for rain."

Malvolio trotted past the dismayed and cover-seeking strippers, calmly smacking them on purloined asses, taking glorious advantage of the situation. Not a word of protest was leveled because after each slap that landed with a resounding pop, he delivered a single, crisp, twenty-dollar bill into their welcoming G Strings and boy shorts. He prefolded the twenties into little origami men and birds for an added accent, placed them right where it counted, near the naughty bits, made kissy lips to them, and trotted on his way.

"Amazing talent," I declared.

Malvolio joined me at my side, smoking a cigarette, blowing smoking greedily into the air, looking quite sinister and infernal, somewhat demonic even, stroking his chin at the remaining bikers who had their backs up against the wall, hoping that their comrade in arms, the only really tough guy amongst them, would not meet his fate at the prospect of a tuxedo-wrapped, gun wielding madman (for that was what I was this very day), and it was about to achieve ludicrous proportions at the behest of my own Sergeant at Arms, Robert Malvolio.

"You should beg, idiot, that I spare you for your transgressions against the good people of this fine establishment."

"Get on the microphone and try this, gentleman," Malvolio suggested to me.

I complied because, being head of my father's security detachment and getting father out of the trouble he managed to get himself into, meant that Mr. Malvolio had proven his fidelity.

I am arguing principles of honor in dishonorable times, a wretched time where the only point value of consideration is the cost of a thing and not even its shine. The emcee microphone had a nice matte finish, which had an almost glittering, worn patina on it caused by the emcee's acerbic grip at looking at all the pretty ladies. He had his face in the carpet, saying his prayers. I let him, and I even said to him, "I'm not going to shoot you," as if that was any reassurance.

I held the 1911 aloft and spoke into the microphone, not with that throaty strip club voice advertising the wares of Dallas, Mercedes, Shai, Jade, Diamond, Ruby, Summer, Isabella the Columbian, and Francoise the Josephine Baker reenactor from Trinidad, whom no one but I, the plucky anachronist, appreciated for her true artistry. They were all safe. I had no beef with them. I had beef with all the men sitting there, particularly all the idiots clad in leather who thought through corporate brainwashing and the intermingling of 40 or so odd years of popular culture that being tough, which was formerly earned as a badge of honor, could be purchased for 10,000 used or 18,000 new. Like a cowboy with a six-shooter, he knew how to load and shoot, and a horse he knew how to ride, but being a bad person took practice. It also took the willingness of people to look the other way and sigh, "At least it isn't happening to me."

Enough!

I began, "This turd here, dressed in leather, this leather-wearing pig in a blanket, chap-wearing fool will die this very night unless he recants his life of crime and promises, in his piss stained, I'm so scared underwear, and go straight...to help the elderly...to stop being such an asshole, and to break up with this lovely lady here."

There were no complaints from the crowd. Malvolio smiled, looking sinister, infernal again, now slightly psychotic in the limelight.

"So here I am, supporting the Single Mother's Association of America, and I'm accosted by this ape we have lying in front of us. For what crime? The crime of his girlfriend, for whom he is totally unworthy, sitting on me, a genteel gentleman of the gentry's, lap! Can I help it that I'm charming far beyond my ken would support? Can I help it that women see me as a provider and cannot wait to bed me? You know what we've been through? This man Malvolio can tell you, Malvolio, my compatriot and guide, and dear audience, he is only escorting me to the funeral of my father, a very, very, very rich man, which has me beset upon by assassins and all manner of rogues to include these motorcycle riding hooligans that we, my faithful compatriot and man at arms, Malvolio, this man, here who helped me apprehend this chump laying in front of us with our cunning and my gun...of course," I said, nearly out of breath, nervousness creeping into my mainframe, eager to see if any of the captive audience was making their way to the door or telephone. Surely some of the young ladies in the basement dressing room were making mad, frantic Facebook posts such as, "OMG. Psycho with gun at the titty bar where I work!"

Police were sure to be alerted, SWAT and Sheriff's deputies sent to rout us from our position. Still, right now, at this precise instant, it was eerily silent. No one dared speak. Perhaps, I was interesting to them, an attraction. Maybe it was the gun, which unknown to me, holds significant weight, even if it is just sitting on a table, unloaded, a mere tool to be picked up. I'm not even trained with the damn thing.

The safety is on, I think, and my finger isn't even in the trigger well. I'm holding it like my father's butler, who taught me all sorts of manners and manliness in lieu of my father's instruction. In a semi-threatening manner, finger near the trigger well but not inside, ready for action but not ready for the deaths of innocents, I listened for the sound of sirens in the distance and heard nothing but the whimperings of an overstuffed biker, whom Malvolio now pinned down under a stiff boot.

"What's this man to be charged with, then? You can't just keep us here all night long, you degenerate death dealer," Malvolio called.

"I really don't know. What's a good crime, good sir? Perhaps a violation of the sanctity of the universe? Or an offense against all in general good taste, or what the commoners routinely call 'acting a fool?' At any rate, this gentleman busted up, or at least attempted to spoil a night of merriment, by being a general bully without balls incapable of carrying the day against even me, quite possibly the weakest gentleman in here."

"Yes, but you've got a gun!" Gumbone yelled.

"I've got a gun, yes. It makes me such a manly man like a moustache or forked beard. That's what they call us, us gunmen. And we Yankees are crack pistol shots capable of William Telling from across the room. My charge against this man here is that he is a bully and an idiot who doesn't deserve the companionship of this lovely waitress here, who is more than her job, this big assed vixen, Daniela, and oh I was busy enjoying her on my lap, which might have been only for a tip and which shouldn't cause offense to this great ape of piss on the ground with his face buried in eons of stripper sweat and discarded chewing gum. I don't care for him or his manners."

"Shoot him already," Malvolio called. "Come down here and execute this evildoer. Shoot him in front of all these people."

"I don't think so. His crime doesn't warrant the death penalty. Just an apology and a pledge, in writing of course, that he will change his ways."

"He won't though. He'll shape up for a week or two and then fall again."

"He will. He'll swear it in front of all these people. They'll hold him to it."

"They won't, kind sir. You'll just have to do him in."

"I can't."

"You can't? You can't?" Malvolio roared.

"I'll have to let him off with a reprimand."

Malvolio tightened his grip on Gumbone's neck. He was too light. Gumbone didn't really seem to notice. He was sweating bullets in the red light. A few of the girls chuckled and then talked amongst themselves. They didn't bother to cover up. I stared briefly at them and then looked away, ashamed for them.

I turned back to Malvolio and said, "What do you want me to do with this man? You want me to kill him?"

"I want his blood on the ground," Malvolio said.

"Do it yourself, then. I won't."

I heard sirens in the distance, fast approaching. Apparently they thought I would go through with it and brain this dumb bastard in front of them.

"For fuck's sake, we have to go, Jackson."

I leapt from the stage and hurled my worthless carcass out into the midnight air. Like a smart one, I kicked over the starter choppers: just something I learned on my adventures. I should have lit them on fire. Down the bleak highways, cherries danced like mad fireflies swirling in a frenzy of fucking and dying. They entered the valley and disappeared into the depths like strange leviathans. The Judge gunned off road, lights out, I drove and Malvolio called out the large rocks that I should avoid. One chunked off the side. What did I care? It was only a machine meant to carry us to another point in space and time, not a hell chariot meant to convey my soul in to the afterlife.

"Next time you see an unfit male with some beautiful biddy, do him in, Jackson," Malvolio said. "You'll feel better about yourself. Such is the way of nature. Society tells you to preserve life, but society is responsible for all the warped and twisted beasts of this world. You smell that?"

"Yeah, it's the cattle pen."

"Society's responsible for that abortion, too."

"I can't do that. He got ample warning that he should change his ways."

"I doubt he cares about much of anything. He's smooth brained, a product of his environment."

"He can't help it, then?"

"Oh, no, he can, but thoughts might induce wrinkles on the brow and brain. They're best flushed away as soon as they drift in."

"Never to have a thought. Must be lovely."

"It probably is, but I wouldn't know."

"Leave it to the happy contented to seize the day. I'd rather stay in the shadows and scheme."

"I knew you would. That's why we're going to be such wonderful friends. The time between here and the road between your father's funeral will be very dangerous."

"I'm ready for anything. Lead on, Malvolio."

"First stop. Gun shop."

"Why?"

"We've got assassins and now bikers after us. We've got to get some hardware. Military grade, preferably. Got to get strapped."

"I've had bikers after me. They're no problem. You kick over their bikes and run or better yet, light them on fire. Then you get in your car and drive away."

"Those bikers are the tip of the iceberg."

"They're weak sauce, man. No problem."

"Who's the security expert here? Me. I know they're a problem."

"Yeah, right."

"Hear me out as you drive. You need to get out of those clothes and into something more sensible and less memorable. You want to wear black and play the villain? Fine. But you can't have these people remembering who you are. I suggest an alternative course of growing a beard, growing a mustache, shaving totally, waxing your eyebrows, shaving your head and letting it grow out again, applying polish, wearing a skull cap you can pick up for 3.99 at any gasoline station and think the old standby, Unabomber style hoodie and aviator sunglasses."

"I guess it's good I have you around," I said, driving the last little rocky patch before coming out on a rough and tumble road that led east and west to godknowswhere.

"Go east, my man."

"We should go west and pick up the Interstate."

"No interstate! They're loaded with cops and villains. You're to stick to these little roads. You avoid the police. You talk to no one. It's a good thing we're in the American Heartland, where you can be a total stranger as long as you can foot the bill. You buy your gas and your little knick knacks and shut the fuck up and do what I tell you if you want to survive."

"Roger that."

"Where'd that come from?"

"I saw it in a movie."

"Which one?"

"I don't remember."

"Funny. We are on sort of a mission here."

"You're right. Survive long enough to get to my dad's digging in."

"You never liked him much, did you?"

"You have to know and see someone to love them."

"He really loved you, Master Jackson."

"Really?"

"Oh, he'd just talk about you all the time on the road. You were his bright, shining star in a world full of darkness."

"When did he say that? He could have told me."

"Over scotch one night in some third world shithole where he and I did time together."

"You make it sound like prison."

"The pursuit of happiness is a prison. Money is a prison we've built to cage ourselves. It contains our thought and desires and makes for a tangible outcome, easily measured. We leap from stone to stone picking up little dollops flicked from the hands of our taskmasters."

"Not I."

"You're lucky, then. But now, you don't really do much of anything, do you?"

"Your father was a busy man of business. He was busy all the time. Busy-ness was his business. He knew nothing else. You know, I encouraged him to stop, retire, and maybe start an art collection. He couldn't. I don't know why. Maybe his father beat that ethic into him?"

"A man is only worth his ideas. Hermit crabs carry a shell on their back. Gorillas a fur coat. Canaries sing with yellow feathers on. A man is composed of his ideas, nothing else. A man with nothing on his mind is nothing. He's a slave to someone else's conception of the world."

"I think not."

"Don't believe me?"

"Makes sense."

"Then what're you going to do when you get your hands on that fortune and the reins of your father's sun chariot? Wreck it? Scorch the sky? Burn the backs of the Africans?"

"Give it away."

"Really?"

"Yes. I'm going to take it public, divest myself of it, and spend my time in merriment and helping people in need."

"I don't buy it. You're made for bigger and better things than miserable charity. You should start a business."

"And be just like my father? I'm an artist, you know that."

"Oh, really? You're an artist?"

"Describe the sunrise over there for me."

"The sunrise?"

"Yeah, the sunrise. You see it, don't you?"

"Of course I see it."

"Do you really see it?"

"Of course."

"Describe it for me."

"It's red."

Malvolio laughed, cackled really, somewhat a snicker or a snort, like he tried to suppress it.

"Are you laughing at me?"

"Nah, not at you. That magnificence, and you're an artist, a regular wordsmith William Worsdworth, and all you can think of, Lord Byron, is...it's red?"

"Well it is. I guess purple at the edges? It looks like a grand black eye in the sky."

"Don't ask me."

"My mistress' eyes are nothing like the sun."

"Do you think you can begin to capture the greater untold magnificence of this experience we're having? Do you think it is possible at all?"

"I really doubt it. But I'll try."

"Why do it?"

"I don't know. I guess I love it. I'm in love with each and every person I see. I'm in love with the Earth and this is all that I love because it's all that I know. People were putting all their love into this strange being called God and now that he's dead and buried they're putting it in this strange activity called moneymaking, and they're neglecting how strange and absolutely breathtaking it all is. I give two shits for God and three shits for moneymaking. He's not petty, that's for sure, and if he was watching over me and I was following his plan for me, I'd be doing nothing other than what I'm doing right now."

He cut me off.

"No, Jackson. What would you be?"

"Why do you say that?"

"You'd be writing. Instead of talking about being a writer, you'd actually be writing. Instead of discussing creating art, you'd be creating it. You'd be practicing being one. If you're practicing, you are one. If it sells, then you're a professional. If it doesn't then you pay out of pocket for your passion, which is what most people do when they buy their bullshit at the store. You don't shop for Burberry or buy a Bentley, you eat tuna fish out of a can and your beer is made of rice and the malt is marred with water, but that's not so in your case, is it, Master Jackson? You can afford to have your Bentley and a bookselling career. Lucky you are, monsieur. Problem is, I don't think you can write your way out of a paper sack, and if your dead old dad wasn't the silent majority stockholder in your publishing venture, you never would have gotten published and your manuscript would have set idle in the dingy drawer of some chest somewhere until it was purchased in some junk sale, all deemed junk, and used for kindling. Let's face it, not all literary works are meant to be immortal, and not all writers doomed to be in print for time immemorial. I think that the greater doom is instantaneous success and the promise of immortality without the wherewithal to see it through."

"You act like you know."

"Know what?"

"What you're talking about."

"You're right. I don't. I'm...how do you say...talking out of my ass."

"Flatulence. That's why the times stink to high heaven."

"They stink because no one cares."

"They stink because no one, not even a single person, tells the truth anymore, not even to themselves. They're looking for cues from someone else or worse, from the television."

"Who cares? Let them waste their time. The key is getting advertisements to them. They don't watch television. What are they going to do, cure cancer? Do complex mathematical formulas? Do aeronautical engineering? They need the fucking idiot box to cater to the idiots so they stop breeding. I mean, it's a prelude to fucking most the time, but maybe, laughing at the stupid jokes at the laugh tracks will make them not want to do it, but what do I really know? What do I know?"

"Not much of anything."

"I don't."

"You don't know shit about me."

By the time the sun came up, we were back on the interstate, headed towards Nebraska: Corn fed State. I guess it was considered a land of milk and honey at some point way back when in the past when how you grew your food actually mattered, but now is considered just another flyover state and cultural wasteland. The situation, me riding in the car with this, and I use the term loosely, gentleman, who has encouraged me to give up on my wildest dreams and go straight for a change, to chase a moment's security, but I would chase it, if it afforded me the time to write.

That's all we really need, right? Time to write? Is that what I needed? I doubt it. I have all the time in the world on my hands right now, but how have I spent it? How have I ordered it? I haven't! I've followed! I've made a mess of things. It's in my head, my skull, my hide, my time, my bones, and my fucking time! No one else could write what I'm going to write!

Malvolio seemed to know everything about me as we spoke, and I learned a couple of things about him. He was my father's chief of security from a few years before I was born, until now, when my father passed away. He probably had an access to my extensive corporate dossier, complete with all of the psychological reports written about me. Labels, really. Labels against originality.

Originality was the entire world, the only endeavor the Earth respected. All else was just replay and a great lot of baloney: tasks and traditions that became ingrained. Stupid people following stupid people in perpetuity, mimicry, the "it's old, it's good" mentality. Fuck it all. The world always longed for a great sweeping clean. It could do it to itself. It wasn't self-correcting with human beings since we had cast nature aside and financed the tower of Babel.

I mean, nature could weed out inferior species through the interaction of the environment and the species group, or some such shit I learned at Princeton. What did I ever learn there? Business principles like my dear departed father wanted? I think not. I watched movies and read books when I should have been studying for standardized tests like the GMAT. Why did I watch movies and read books? To distract me and to support myself?

When you've got as much inner tension and turmoil as I've got coursing through my veins, then you've got to find something. That was my lonely freshman and sophomore years, back before I decided to choke down cyanide like Wallace Carothers, back when Marcus Hanely had not come into my life. A boy needs a father, absolutely needs one, and if a young man does not have a father, perhaps he will invent one out of the air. I miss Marcus. Malvolio is a nice guy, but he lacks Marcus's charm, wit, and his controlling tendencies too.

"Master Jackson," Malvolio said.

I did not puncture my fierce ratiocination for a moment.

"Master Jackson...."

Again a drop of water on a pond.

"Master Jackson, snap out of it!" And with that, he gave me a pinch right above my hipbone, but it didn't hurt, just sort of tickled. It was a gay sort of pinch.

I looked over at him. With his skeletal face and his skin stretched over a bony substructure, he looked like death not fully cooked. Raw death as it was. And then he said it.

"You think too much. It's not a bad thing, but shouldn't you be creating something, Monsieur Artiste?"

"I'm thinking about that."

"Oh, you're thinking about writing something on paper? Tell me, Master Jackson. Tell me; if you took a sudden wrong turn and we ended up being devoured by giant radioactive ants or murdered by a clan of irradiated methamphetamine zombies, do you think your words, floating around in that great-addled brain of yours would ever see the light of day? Would they just drift out of your lonely coffin, all those poetic images and musings flapping about your tired brain, whimsical styling you've been putting so much effort into thinking about? Do you think that art will create itself?"

"I was going to get a MacBook Air at the Mall in Denver, but I ran into you and the old pair. My MacBook Pro has a sticky C key."

"I surveilled you. You walked past the Apple Store. Only thing I saw you buy was a pair of shoes from Brooks Brothers. Still caring what people think of you, aren't you?"

"No. I ran into the old pair and you."

"And you'll keep running into them. Not them, but members of their little corporation, err, collective if you will. You've got a laptop in your trunk. You don't need a new one."

"It's not up to par. Plus, I've hunted and pecked my way on that stupid thing for about two years now. It's got a sticky C key."

"What I'm telling you, young fool, is that writers write. That's the fundamental rule, Master Jackson."

"Goddamnit! Stop lecturing me!"

"There you go. Put that anger on the page."

"You're full of useful advice. I've got some advice for you, Robert. Let me concentrate on driving, and you worry about the security of this little operation."

"You're wasting time, Jackson."

"I'll get it out there."

"I'm not so sure about that."

"What are you saying?"

We crossed the Wyoming/Nebraska border. The scenery did not change.

"You've got tons of enemies. I'll do my best, but one will eventually get through. We may not even make it to the reading of your father's will."

"We'll make it."

"What's more important to you, you addled writer? Getting there or getting your words on paper?"

"Getting there and getting my words on paper."

"I could drive."

"Really? You'll drive while I sit in the passenger's seat and write?"

"Yes, I'm willing to do that. I've got to warn you. I drive really fast."

"You think I care how fast you drive? We'll pull over at this Kum N' Go and switch out."

The thought of actually having time, from Nebraska to Illinois, to work on what I hoped would be a fitting sequel to my first well-received by the few people who actually read it at first and then spilled over into the laps of millions of women all over the world novel, *Asymmetric Hearts*, the tale of the businesswoman entrepreneur Veronica Dare and her tangled love affair with Special Forces/spy/ love poet on par with Pablo Neruda/fucking business prince, Marcus Hanely, who wears a moustache in the book and is very fond of giving Veronica rides on it and he even has the proclivity of tongue darting the northern chocolate factory when the time was right and he had worked her pussy into a right twitching spasming slimy honeyed up salty miso. Only then was her guard let down enough to allow Marcus to slip a figure in or dip its tongue in her cute little sphincter. Mmmm.

The Kum N' Go was the scene of a sizeable crowd, and I had reminiscences of the last gas station goddess we ran into. These Gas Station Goddesses were within the scope of the possible, but highly unlikely on these lonely stretches on the planet, and if you find one, I should say that you offer her family goats and blankets and her a diamond ring and a rescue. Do it!

"What's the fuss about?"

"Assassins, perhaps?"

"No. They operate in pairs. Never mob action. That's amateurish. Too many eyes and lips to speak to the police."

"Flash mob?"

"Those are phenomena of cities."

"Why don't we just ask these people what's going on around here?"

"They're all dressed up like cowboys and that fucking creeps me out. Even the children. All little cowboys."

"Maybe an impromptu rodeo."

"Maybe a hanging."

"Pull over, kind of far away."

"You're going to confront them?"

"No. This isn't confrontation. I'm going to go up and speak with them politely. I also need to get some new duds."

"Yeah, the tuxedo is malapropos for this area. These people might take offense to it and decide to have a shooting gallery."

"Let's hope not."

I stepped from the car, which had already drawn enough attention to force people to spin their sunburned cowboy necks in my direction. One Brooks Brothers tuxedo shoe ensconced foot followed the other, and by the time I had cleared the door, and Malvolio Chinese fire drilled to the driver's position, the cowboys and cowgirls of mostly pear shapes, impossible horse riders, had swarmed up to us. They did not do so with violence, but rather curiosity.

"Why you wearin' a tuxedo?" one cowgirl asked, and she was quite the looker.

"I didn't get married in it, miss," I said.

"Well, that's a damn shame. Why are you wearin' it?"

"Ehh...."

Malvolio rolled down the window and said, "Because he's a distinguished gentleman and scholar, a modern day nobleman and scion of the aristocracy of the mind, milady." Then he humbly bowed his head to her and rolled the window up to a crack, which would allow him to hear our conversation and monitor it for possible plots against my person.

The cowgirl just smiled, and said nothing. A big brute bull rider of a man came up to us and threw his arms around the lady and said in a typical cowboy good guy fashion, "These guys givin' you trouble, Rebecca?"

"They're harmless, Ben," she said, sheepishly.

"They look like a couple faggots. They've got a nice car though. Must be rich faggots."

Rebecca frowned. I smiled at him. Malvolio cracked the window, further sensing that the peaceful situation was about to deteriorate into malevolent striking and chest beating gorilla combat. God, I wish Marcus was here to tell me what to do in this situation. All I could think of was flattery to defuse the situation.

"No offense, Ben, but those are a hell of a pair of boots."

"Sea turtle."

"No shit? Sea turtle boots?"

"Yup."

"How'd you get those into the United States? Aren't they illegal?"

"Yup. What do you care for?"

"I want to get something even more exotic. Maybe pterodactyl boots or something. Make some boots out of the last tiger or something like that."

Rebecca laughed.

"Why are you all out here like this duded up?"

"A fashion show for charity."

"Really? At the Kum N' Go?"

"Nah, we're just waiting for the bus to take us to the convention center. Gonna be a shit ton of booze there. No one wants to drive and get a DUI."

"I love fashion shows," I said.

"I love booze," Malvolio said.

"I bet you do," Ben said with more than a hint of malice in his voice.

"What's that supposed to mean?"

"You figure it out, buddy."

"What's the charity?"

"You figure that out, too."

"Ben, stop. These guys are nice. You shouldn't treat strangers that way."

"I thought cowboys were supposed to be honorable and just people. You're wearing colors befitting a sheriff, and you're acting like a guy in black."

Ben glared at me and started to slink away, back towards the crowd that was eyeing me with suspicion. Always eye a stranger with suspicion until they show they want to buy something from you was an unwritten rule of the prairie. It was still in full effect to this day. Especially if they dress funny.

"It's for a little girl who was diagnosed with a rare, awful disease."

"Cancer?"

"I don't know. I can't pronounce it."

"I'm sorry. How much are you trying to raise?"

"I think her parents need about a million dollars or so."

"Jesus, that's a lot."

"You want to come? Maybe bring your friend? They need all the help they can get."

"I can't go dressed like this."

"You're in luck. See that strip mall across the way?"

"Yeah."

"You got Winkler's Western Wear in there. They'll have everything you need."

"Nice. What do they sell?"

"Uhh...western wear? Like I'm wearing!"

"Are you going to accompany us?"

"Uh, my boyfriend wouldn't like that."

"Sheesh. Boyfriend. Tell him my compatriot and I are bottom chasers, buggerers, queers. He already thinks that. Let him think it."

"He's just horribly jealous."

"He's glaring at us right now."

"It's your car. It's probably how you look, too."

"How do I look?"

"Handsome," she said blushing.

"Why, thank you."

JEFFREY MATTHEW HOPKINS

"So I suppose you should just meet us at the fashion show. If you buy something really nice, you could be in it."

"I always try to look nice," I said and bowed to her. She giggled.

These people would be on my list of people to donate to. I would add them just under the Wacky Hutt rent a cop whose name I had written down. Following the EFT or whatever inheritance I was set to receive from my father's estate, I would immediately send my agents of do-goodery out into the world to track these people down, verify the legitimacy of their claim, and dispense funds to them. I would be a force for good in the world, aligned against decay, greed, sloth, and envy. Envy, add that to the list. I should start with her boyfriend and try and change his mind about how he treats this lovely woman of his, who in all regards, is a knockout and quite nice. You know, much of love and attraction is timing and position and mutual attraction of two individuals, and I am not merely discussing the beast with two backs and lovemaking.

A motorcycle roared past us, very loudly. We all stopped to look. Malvolio rolled the window down, ever vigilant. The guy wasn't riding colors. We were safe.

"Motorcycles freak you out?"

"Nah, just bikers. My good friend Malvolio and I have had a few run-ins with some bad guys. You know, I guess we just attract attention."

"Duh. You should probably lose the car and the tuxedo. Grow your hair out long like Jesus."

"I want a beard, but first I'm going to dress like a cowboy and strut my stuff on the stage, like a debutante."

"I bet you'll look really nice."

Ben shouted over at us, "Hey, Rebecca! Can you come over here?"

"You better go," I told her.

She looked downtrodden, upset, and like she didn't want to walk over to him to receive her berating.

"You know, you could always just say no."

"I can't."

"Rebecca, get over here!"

She slunk away, back to him.

Malvolio rolled the window down all the way.

"Jackson, we best be going."

"Right. Battered women always run back to the source of their abuse."

As she approached, he hurried her up by dragging her part of the way to a gas pump where he could ball her out liberally, partially obscured from the dazed onlookers who had grown quite used to their domestic turmoil.

"Isn't anyone going to say anything?"

360

"Not our lane, buddy. We aren't the police."

"Goddamn it. If he hits her, I'm going to execute him."

"Then you'll spend the rest of your days in the clink, and you won't be able to write or sit down because your ass will be so sore."

"Yeah, right. I can afford a great defense attorney."

"Plus, the dame will turn on you like Annie Oakley. They always stick up for their batterers."

"It's fucking insane."

"It's a way of some women."

"She's sweet like the memories of bitterest death recorded while alive," I said with a hint of sadness in my voice.

"God damn, my man, you aren't a warrior or even police. You're a poet, a tempest, a bellwether, and a fucking center of gravity. You need to drop this hopeless romantic charade and become what you are, my man."

"I am what I am."

"You're right. You're right. You're a god in your own right. You're a creator. You'll die, but you'll never die. You have an immense power. You see all these humble folks? They'll blow away like dust. They live, they love, they fight, they fuck and breed like bunnies, they go to college, they join the military and spray battled over towns with hot leaden bullets and blood, but do they live?"

"I think they do."

"They do, but unless someone records it, they die a double death when they pass. Some of their highest hopes are to be recorded by someone. To be on display."

"Why all this talk of death, Malvolio?"

"I'm here to protect you from it, Jackson, but you must get it through your crushingly dense melon that you will go the way of the dodo unless you take it upon yourself to prevent that."

"I write because I love it."

"But you love nothing, as perpetrated by your actions. You're probably the most apathetic little twit I've ever met, and don't get me wrong, you don't need to be. You're brilliant, but you're so fucking scared of ever getting hurt that you are afraid to even make the attempt. You're suffering from a goddamned deficit of will and manliness."

"Have you ever seen my manhood? He's spectacular. A real Moby Dick. Call it Ishmael."

"You fool, I'm not talking about your cock. I'm discussing your deficit of courage and care. Your pride, or lack of it, is an issue. Do you know just how fucking lucky you are do-gooder?"

"I think so?"

"You won the fucking lottery, double down when you were born."

"How so?"

"You despairing idiot, you're blind."

"I can see just fine. He's just about to slap her around."

"Fuck him. Fuck them. Just get in the car and listen to me."

"I don't follow orders well."

"Get in the car, Jackson," he said looking off into the distance.

"Ask me nicely."

"Please, get in the goddamned car."

On the horizon, dusty doom approached, like and army of ransacking, razing, rapist Mongol horsemen. As the dust cloud parted, I heard motors. These ruffians were no Mongols on horseback; this was an army of motorcycles.

"Oh, shit," Malvolio said.

"We haven't had an opportunity to get to the gun shop."

"Please, just get in the car."

I didn't need another word of encouragement.

Ben and his girlfriend settled down when the motorcycle group rode hellishly into the Kum N' Go, engines blazing, beating out a snare drum staccato, obviously in need of a tune up and muffler.

"What flag are they flying?"

"Can't make it out, they look to be elderly people though, from here."

"Could be a false front, a façade," Malvolio declared.

"They don't look dangerous," I added.

"Does a box jellyfish look dangerous? Does a lion cub look dangerous? No, but I tell you'll they're all killers. You do the underestimations at your peril."

A couple of the old bikers, rough and tumble looking fellows probably back in the day, looked as though their last successful ruckus, if they had ever been in a good knuckle dusting, was most likely fought bareknuckle or brass knuckled during the Johnson Administration. Some of the men had little war ribbons on their leather jackets, badges, and tiny insignia that declared to all in the know that they had performed admirably in some foreign conflict that no one now remembered nor really cared about nor thought about when they were barbecuing or waiting in line to pay for meat and booze at Wally World on Memorial Day.

These gentleman and all their various ladies represented a Vietnam, Korean, and even a few World War II veterans who proudly rode in sidecars and waved small American flags to passers by on the highways they traveled in their retirement. And here, my compatriot and brother in arms, Malvolio, thought they might be some offshoot of the Hells Angels, perhaps a retirement club for baddies or other outlaw motorcycle club entitled the Geezer Brigade or Old Dude Faction or some other such nonsense. Then Malvolio told me that he heard on that very day that a nursing home located in Topeka, Kansas, was set upon by a raging mob of AARP card holders, and those who could ride away were liberated from the confines. Whether this was true or just a product of his paranoid imagination was beyond my wildest guesses. I shrugged this off and told Mr. Malvolio, my paranoid, security-minded friend that if you really want to know the truth about something or someone, it doesn't require an investigation or behind the scenes speculation, which works really fine in scientific inquiry, but not that well in human affairs. No, if you really want to know something, you will just go up and ask somebody about it.

"What if they lie to you?" Malvolio asked.

"And why would they do that?" I bandied back to my paranoid buddy and engendered the game of philosophy.

"Because they're tracking us and sent more oldie types to throw us off the scent, you know, lull us into a false sense of security. They've done it before. How do you know that hearing of the demise of the two decrepit assassins, that this much larger cell wasn't activated?"

"Give me a break. We know who hired the old assassins. It was somebody who is used to paying for the best, and wanted to pay for the best in the business but doesn't have the wherewithal to release funds and who's only recourse is to issue promissory notes and IOUs. It's obviously my brother-in-law who is behind this."

"Maybe."

"Maybe he's gotten membership into the organization you won't tell me about."

"Maybe."

"I know so. When his plot to drive me mad and send me stark raving insane to meet my father failed or was rather foiled by me, he upped the ante."

"Thank God you've got me around. Now here's what we do. You go talk to them about our presence. Then we should probably attend that fashion show for charity. It's public. They don't need that sort of negative publicity of ransacking a charity. We should probably follow this same course of action all the way to Peoria, Illinois."

"Attending charity events? Hiding out in the open?"

"Aye. That's a good plan. No way they'd target us there. Plus, we might meet some nice people willing to take a couple of war weary vagabonds in."

"We aren't that war weary, Malvolio."

"You might not be, but I am. Life is strife, strain, and struggle."

"Only if you make it that way."

"Okay, enact the plan. Say hello to their ringleader."

"How do I do that?"

"Get out and say, take me to your leader."

"That's stupid."

"Look for the guy with the most bling on and talk to him."

"Agreed."

Again, I stepped from the car. Of all the Harleys that were parked, the vast majority were cruisers with the modern conveniences of radio and air conditioning. In my peripheral, I saw one older Harley, gunmetal colored with war wounds. A tall, quiet man with a salt and pepper beard and his matching colored hair neatly greased and pulled back into a pony tail sat on the seat of his bike, waiting for his tank to fill.

"Nice Fat Boy," I said as I approached him.

He looked up, seemingly puzzled. He took off his sunglass and said, "She's no Fat Boy."

"I apologize. I was just trying to make conversation. What is it?"

"You ride?"

"No. I mean, that's my car over there," I said and pointed at the idling Judge.

"Wow, she's a beauty."

"Thanks, yours is too."

"This bike has taken me from Tallahassee, Florida, to Seattle, Washington. Hell, I even rode her down to Mexico City one time back when it was safe...nothing like being alone in the Mexican desert with nothing but the heat of your engine and the heat of the sun and the smell of exhaust and the vibration. Man, the vibration is something else."

"I bet."

He looked at me somewhat crossly; maybe he was unsure of what to say. Then he said it.

"Dude, why are you in a tuxedo?"

"I'm looking for something else to wear. You see, this is the tuxedo my dad got married in, and he died just the other day, so I'm somewhat attached to it."

"Man, I'm sorry."

"It's okay. He lived a long life."

"Natural causes. I always said I wouldn't ever want to go out that way. Just sort of petering out. I was sure Vietnam would kill me. Nearly did several times. Ever been in?"

"Prison?"

"Nah, the military."

"Nah."

"What do you do?"

"I'm an author."

"Like, you write books?"

"Well, just a book."

"Might I know it?"

"It's for women."

The man laughed. He rolled his head back and let out a guffaw that reverberated off the Kum N' Go's canopy. People turned to look, he laughed so hard. Then he composed himself, adjusted himself in the seat, and stopped pumping the gas into the tank. He shot the nozzle back into its holder.

"You say it's for women. Well, a whole hell of a lot of women bought it judging from the looks of that car of yours."

"It did pretty well, but that was like ten years ago."

"You ain't written shit since?"

"Working on it. I'm trying to get some inspiration."

"What? Driving around? You should get a motorcycle."

"I'm headed to my dad's funeral."

"Well, hells bells. You're going the wrong route for inspiration. You should have come more of a southern route and totally avoided Kansas, Nebraska, Iowa, and the like. Where's the funeral at?"

"Peoria, Illinois."

"You're from Peoria?"

"No, dad was. I'm not really from anywhere."

"You're a military brat? Was your dad in?"

"Nope. Dad had money and kept us on the move."

"Why aren't you flying?"

"I don't like being groped, and I'm certainly not going to subject my balls to being cooked by a ball scanner. It will make me sterile."

The man laughed again, "You're funny. You know that?"

"No one's told me that before."

"You're funny as fuck. My name's Ray."

"I'm Jackson."

"Well, Jackson, we're about to roll out. But let me tell you, if you ever find yourself in a bind, you can call me. That's what The Old School Truants and I do. We help people out."

He handed me a card. It read:

RAY LEFEBVRE
PROBLEMS? SOLVED!

(318)-345-2318

I folded it into my wallet.

"That's what I do too, Ray."

He smiled. "Give me a call sometime, Mr. Author."

"I shall," I said and bid him adieu in the best way I knew how, a deep bow from the waist with one leg back.

He broke into another peal of laughter. "You have to be one of the funniest bastards I've met on the road," he said between rib splitters and sucking air like a man coming up from deep diving under water.

I about-faced and marched over to the car where Malvolio waited in the driver's seat. He rolled the window down and smiled widely.

"Ahh, aren't you the little charmer? I see you've made friends with them, but did you get the goods?"

"They're nothing to worry about," I said.

"Just what I'd want someone to think before I ran them through."

"Who runs anyone through anymore? You're quite given to anachronism, Malvolio. Why don't you just say blew away, shot dead, or stabbed with a corkscrew? Run through? You're so damn Shakespearean and you don't even know it."

"And what's so wrong with that? Don't you find it relevant to our situation at all?"

"Not really. I mean we're about to become bonafide cowboys."

"Right. Let me see what that rogue handed you. I saw him hand you something, now hand it over."

"Just a business card."

"Well business cards can be indoctrinated with all sorts of fast-acting neurotoxins."

"Don't you mean adulterated?"

"Sure, whatever, hand it over."

"You have to give it back once you find out it's okay."

Malvolio put on pair of rubber gloves he pulled from his pants pocket. He held his hands out like a child expecting to be given candy as a reward for good deeds done, and frankly I don't think he deserved anything like that. Reluctantly, I handed over the card. He held it up to the light like a fine gem.

"Inferior quality, probably Staples or some other superstore. Horrible design. Problems? Solved! That's a laugh, well if it were on cardstock similar to Crane's, I might suspect it could be indoctrinated, but this seems cut out from printer paper, and cheap printer paper at that."

"Adulterated...."

"Sure thing," Malvolio quipped and handed me the card back before asking, "He seem like an upright fellow?"

"He never stood up, he remained seated," I said half joking, trying to lighten Malvolio's security enhanced paranoia.

"No, I mean, did he seem like an upstanding citizen?"

"Yeah, Vietnam veteran. Seemed like a real adventurous sort, rode his bike...the beat up one there all across the country and Mexico."

"Mexico? He could have had contact with some of the drug cartels. We'd have to verify that wasn't the case before we ever made contact with him in the future," Malvolio said.

"You want to hire him?"

"A gentleman like him could come in handy some day, depending on what we need him to do for us. Remember this, Jackson, when you're running the family business, always be cordial to everyone you meet, because you don't know how you can use, I mean, employ them in the future, and believe you me, you want some of the people you run into to work for the firm in the future."

"I'm a writer, remember? Not a businessman. That's sound advice...I'll file it away and make sure that I use it to my advantage. You know...on second thought, no. I won't take it into consideration. I don't use people. I meet people because I want to, and I talk to them because they are interesting, not out of some phony fucking desire to get ahead."

"You're just like your dear old daddy."

"Drive, damn you, before I take offense and fire you."

Malvolio cackled, "You can't fire me, Master Jackson. I've got a lifelong contract, ha ha, signed in blood, ha ha! Of course your dear old dad was quite drunk and possibly malarial when he signed it, but you know, it's certainly legally binding."

I stared at him. His skeletal face was covered in pockmarks, possibly caused by some acne vulgaris as a teenager or maybe the remnants of some tropical disease.

After all, he said he followed my father everywhere, to the ends of the Earth, protecting him against Godknowswhat paranoid inventions he managed to cough out of that addled brain of his. It used to be the Red Scare when my father first set out into the world of buying things cheaply and selling them for a handsome profit.

Then with the fall of the Communist Bloc, it morphed into fearsome terrorizers who hijacked planes, kidnapped for profit, and then blew up buildings with truck bombs. Malvolio had seen it all. He was a battle scarred veteran in Leman Global Industries' global push and world wide reach, dealing in mercenaries and cutthroats, bribing rebel armies to conduct assassinations of obstructionist government officials, all the while operating in strict secrecy to keep my father's hands lily white. No wonder he was paranoid beyond belief.

He smiled heartily as if he knew that I knew what he was truly capable of if released from his duties and allowed to be a free agent again, and he gunned the engine, popped the break, and burned a tire screeching scorch into the parking lot. He drifted around the corner of the Kum N' Go to the horror of the assembled bikers and cowboys.

"Onward, Master Jackson! Time to purchase you some new duds. You aren't going to the Opera, after all! Time to get some shit kickers on to rival the riding boots of Alexander, my man."

"Fuck, you're dramatic, you mad old Shakespearean! You can't tell me you've never been an actor or circus performer at the very least. You've a talent for histrionics, but you're ugly. Hollywood would grind you into flour and make cupcakes of you. Drop all of this rampant paranoia and acting like a fool, and let's just live, my man! Let's just live!"

"What's life without security? Life without process and parameters? Without rule-following from birth to death? It's chaos. Pure and simple, boy. No, you need my stringent applications. You thrive on them. Don't tell me otherwise. I'll tell you to run off and play in traffic."

"What I need is a bit of fun."

"What you need to do is write."

"I'm spent. My mind is made up. My hand wants to put pen to paper or fingers to finger clicks, but my mind won't let it happen. I've a block. Every time I try and write my brain says no."

"Then pickle your brain with booze. It worked for many men who had your same ambitions."

"I'm already a depressive, and booze makes my apprehensions all the worse. I don't want to suck start a shotgun like Ernest. I need something uplifting."

"Bust your brain wide open with blow, or try that lusty maiden, methamphetamine."

"I think not. I'm not one for chemicals."

"Bury your midsection in some steamy tropical cove and emerge a modern day love prophet...that's what you write? Romance, correct? Write it with the aid of a woman."

The Nebraska countryside whizzed by. Malvolio had to be doing 130 MPH. Silos came on us like erector sets and disappeared, fumble fucking off into the distance. Corn machinery skirted fallow fields slated for strip mall pizza places on the minutes of county boards.

The Western World Clothing Store, huge by even Nebraska standards, stood like a pyramid in front of us, and the neon signs flashed BOOTS! BOOTS! Even during daylight hours. It was a mecca for polished, sequin-wearing, alligator boots and platinum stirrups and ostrich tack on Arabian horses, cowboys buoyed by vast oil and natural gas wealth and artificially inflated corn prices subsidized by ethanol for engines and corn syrup manufacturers. We parked near several enormous SUVs, possibly the owners or the patrons' vehicles. Only time would tell.

Again, I slid one alien Brooks Brothers tuxedo shoe out of the passenger's side and humbly walked up to the door of the establishment. A vast mural entitled, "How the West was Won," depicted cowboys fighting off hordes of Indians: any five-year-old Yankee boy's fantasy. I couldn't help thinking, with my modern sensibilities, that the mural was archaic and quite Disney-like in its representation of the savages with their bows and arrows, their Tomahawks, and their burnt red skin, exaggerated by the artist whose name was obscured by birdshit and a plaque proclaimed that the building was on the National Registry of Historic Places. The plaque declared that in the past, the building had been a supply depot on a military base that did Godknowswhat for the war effort of some hard fought but ultimately forgotten struggle against the Plains Indians.

The owner, Mr. Mitchell, who had since given up the Geist and met his maker, had put up spackle after spackle over worm rotted timbers, replacing them one at a time until the building no longer had a single remaining timber that was original. Shop girls came and went with rapid ferocity through the ages in this shop, the oldest western wear store this side of the Mississippi River.

The shop girl inside looked bored, and didn't look up as the bell tinkled signaling our arrival. She facebooked status updates, saying, "Bored lol" and "OMG just had the fattest customer eva tryin to squeeze into some size 6 wranglers, LMFAO." Some of the cowboy hats were gathering dust. The most expensive hat was an 800 dollar George Hermann original, perhaps formerly worn by Glen Campbell. Underneath Mr. Campbell's photograph, another plaque proclaimed, "WORN BY GLEN CAMPBELL, THE RHINESTONE COWBOY." Apparently, Campbell performed at the Tuscacola County Fair in 1982. I cannot independently confirm or deny that this hat was in fact, truly worn by the Rhinestone Cowboy, because advertisements are often lies. The are also plenty of Rhinestone Cowboys to go around.

So here we sat, Mr. Malvolio and me, because he refused to wait in the car and insisted on coming inside with me to be a fashion consultant and tell me what suit would befit a do-gooder. Definitely not black, or perhaps I could wear black, do good deeds, and totally upset the stereotype that black is associated with malevolence and evildoers. I don't find it a particularly reprehensible color. In fact, I quite like black, even though it is hot in the sun when you're riding a dusty trail and come in from the range sopping wet and angry. Perhaps I should purchase grey and call it a day, an admixture of the good and the bad in us all, a color of the moral nature of life, and I could dispense justice and act as the long arm of the law in the hinterlands and fly-over territories I stopped through.

Shop girl still did not pull herself from her social media even though she was quite alone, for long enough to socialize with Malvolio and me and perhaps earn a commission. Perhaps Malvolio turned her off. The store had made its yearly quota, so there was no real reason to go out of her way to sell me anything. I cleared my throat to get her attention.

Once. Twice. Malvolio did a little dance to get her attention. Still the girl did not look up from her small screen. I wondered if she was discoverable via Bluetooth. If so, perhaps I could send her a message to her phone and break the spell she was under. I suggested this to Malvolio, who proffered a complete absurdity to me. It seemed everything coming out of the man's mouth was more and more absurd by the moment, and gained in momentum and steam until he threatened to have his head explode. It flew out of his mouth like a wingless, featherless, song less canary, full of bombast but utter infeasible. He suggested I take a photo of my heaving ball sack and send it to this young lady, using this as a distraction so he could abscond with a full suit of clothing. He didn't have any money.

"I'll pay, don't worry."

"It's foolproof."

"You sick twist, why don't I just go to jail and lock myself up? I'll just go and talk to her."

I walked past the racks of dusty dungarees and denim jackets, stood right in front of this young woman and cleared my throat again. Her face was still down, gasping wide eyed at her Facebook page and all of her "frenz" and LOL'd a few times while I was standing there over here staring. I could have been some pervert or serial killer and she would have been oblivious to the fact that I was standing there. Her face was still down, gasping wide-eyed at the Facebook page, typing with her thumbs at the rate of about a thousand words per minute.

Text messages poured into her phone, and it buzzed incessantly. I could see she was listening to iTunes on her phone, downloading music, perhaps the latest album by Justin Bieber or Lady Gaga or some combination of kids hand-selected by a record company executive to corner the ringtones market. It all confounded her ability to hear my silent pleas for customer service. I stared back at Malvolio who urged me, with a hand gesture, to smack her a good one.

"Slap some sense into her," he mouthed.

I decided to just take my index finger and tap her ever so gently on the shoulder. You would have thought that I gave her a bad touch. She recoiled from me like a hairy tarantula had just crawled out of my half-eaten eye socket.

She yanked her headphones down and demanded, "What do you want?"

"Whoa, sister," I implored, "Me and my buddy need to get some duds."

"What?"

"Some clothing."

She sighed and put her phone into her tight red pants. It buzzed and beeped a few more times while she directed me towards the chintzy section. She laughed a few times to herself. I thought she had a psionic connection with her cellular phone and her brain had grafted onto knowing what status updates would be made before they were made.

Then I discovered the real reason she was laughing. The phone kept buzzing and buzzing in her tight red pants. Text messages poured in, vibrating her phone near her naughty bits.

"You're a popular lady."

She giggled back to me.

"I need to get something really nice. We're going to a fashion show."

"Everything we have here is nice."

"Get some boots first, bro," Malvolio said.

She turned around and looked at Malvolio like he was a newt or other small, shiny, easily crushable creature. Malvolio shot her a creepy, toothy grin. I think he even winked at her once or twice.

"Hey, you've got to base the outfit on the boots, right?"

She shook her head, not in a kind way, but in an I have superior knowledge type of way.

"I know what I'm talking about, girl."

"Look how you're dressed. What is that? Some sort of monk's outfit? Are you a knight or something?"

I laughed. Malvolio's face suddenly went blank. Like he was very, very angry. He sulked off without saying a word to station himself by the door amongst the hats that were losing their batting and generally decaying to form part of the dust that percolated through the room. The girl giggled again as her phone vibrated. It wasn't a text message, but longer buzzes.

"You going to answer that?"

"Nah, they can wait."

"Not worth talking to?"

"We just talk all the time. It's no biggie."

"That your boyfriend?"

"No, my friend Samantha."

"She from here?"

"Nah. She moved to Florida. Lucky."

"It's good you can talk."

"Yeah, so do you want to buy something?"

"Yes. I need to change my style."

"You do. What? Did you just go to a wedding or something?"

"No. Senior prom."

"Really? That's not for months. Where'd you go? What high school has their prom during the wintertime?"

"That was a joke."

"Oh, okay."

"Yeah, I'm here for a makeover. Both of us are."

"You want to go country from a city style? It's hard to pull off."

"Yeah, whatever gets me chicks."

"So you're into chicks, then?"

"What guy isn't?"

"Oh I thought you and the other guy...."

"What?"

"Yeah, usually if you wear anything besides this cowboy stuff, we think you're a...."

"What? Weirdo?"

"A gay."

"Really?"

"You know what we think about people who wear farming shirts where I'm from?"

"What do you think?"

"That they're a farmer. We're non judgmental. We accept everyone. We white-wash them, or they work in the kitchens of our restaurants, out of sight out of mind. And the hot women? We turn them into fucking movie stars. One day they're a maid, hanging out in a string bikini in their front yard, the next moment they're an actress in a major motion picture. You don't have to be able to act anymore, just look good. Fuck yes, we make fun of them. We call them rednecks. We claim to be an open society, us Californians, but we seek for everyone to be just like us. Bland, lame, spoiled. I'd be happy to dress like a damn cowboy out there. I'd be happy to walk into Warner Brothers with my dick hanging out of my tight cowboy pants, with some damn manta ray boots on."

Her eyes briefly glazed over but came back into focus when I mentioned expensive product.

"Ostrich is the shit."

"You have some?"

"They're pretty expensive."

"How expensive? That's a relative term."

"What do you mean?"

"What's expensive to me might not be expensive to that gentleman over there and vice versa. People have different spending capacities."

"Sure," she said blandly.

"They do."

"Yeah."

Malvolio had tried every hat on in the front of the store and finally settled on a hat with some turquoise baubles around the body. Why the hell would he settle on that one? Was he a colossal king of tackiness?

"So, he's the ostrich boots?"

"You got sea turtle?"

"No, they're illegal. They're, like, endangered or something like that."

She was cute, the way she said endangered, and I could see her comforting all the cute endangered animals of the globe, trotting through a field with snow leopard cubs, cradling a three-toed sloth, two by two the animals ran through this field with her, tongues lolling, some stopping to sniff the sweet nectar of flowers in full bloom. And then I see that this young lady is naked, hair, Nebraska cornhusking dirty blonde hair barely covering her ample breasts, she's chubby in all the right places, not too chubby, but just a little chubby, big-boned if you will, and I notice that I'm starting to get aroused. I don't know if it's all the flowers on the girl, her cornucopia she holds, or that all of the animals are living in harmony and she is the cause.

Malvolio is proudly wearing his cowboy hat, which goes well with the outfit he has tried on. It is nothing to envy or write home about and he stops by us and asks what I think of his selections, which really amount to nothing but fashion faux pas.

"That's a joke, right?"

His face tightens, and he looks shocked like I was being a petulant boy in ridiculing him in front of this young woman who I think he genuinely likes. He likes her because she hates him or at least has such repugnance towards him that it is obvious.

She laughed. Malvolio grew more despondent. He gingerly took the hat off his head; staring at the girl the whole time with his salt and pepper locks spilling across his forehead. Sweat rivers exploded across his forehead breaking through their blackhead and clogged pore-ridden skin. Malvolio, in the skin department, was not blessed. In fact, his only blessing was probably his paranoid brain, which suited a security twit like himself. He seemed to be endowed with no "good" qualities and no real talents that I could see.

He was a mediocre poet at best. He was the anti-Hanely, the anti-Marcus. He was the yin to Hanely's yang, but Malvolio was real, and Marcus Hanely was a beautiful, muscular, throbbing, pulsating fiction. God, I wished he were real. If he were real, this young, sexy lady would not be attempting to sell me boots, but rather, our boots would be locked in the throes of love, enraptured, perhaps in the back of the store. Perhaps up against the hat rack. I would be the rutting bull to her bucking bronco, or something like that. Malvolio looked on the verge of snapping. The sweat continued to build on his face, and a tiny purple vein became engorged and throbbed pointlessly in his temple. Then he calmly stated, with her feeling the full brunt of his calm "I want to kill you" wrath, but without it registering in this millennial child because she was not trained to pick up on social cues unless it contained an emoticon or lol.

"What hat do you suggest I get, milady?" he inquired.

She giggled, perhaps nervously, perhaps out of genuine glee. Who knew; we didn't receive the message via text message signed and postmarked with a lol. Soon humans will be able to breed via text message, but for now, sexting was a prelude to the real thing. Soon, it's going to be the real thing because touching is icky. I joined her in her laughter.

"Why don't you get the one in the case up there?"

"It looks too white for me, too dusty. It's also got a hell of a price tag," Malvolio said, walking over to the case and looking at the sticker.

"Oh, yeah, that is expensive," the shop girl chimed in.

"Remember what's expensive to a pauper is a pittance for a prince."

"Huh?" she asked.

Having nearly infinite capital at my disposal only buoys my soul. If I were a poor man, I would have died a penniless poor Tom in the streets, most likely a decade ago. People in college described me as eccentric instead of crazy, the weirdo rich kid who's father didn't give him enough attention growing up and who would probably go the route of his mother. Women who were attracted to freaks, not that I'm freaky looking, laid me. I'm just a great ball of despair grasping at life. I only see the funny things, the gallows humor.

When you live and are accustomed to leaving the light of day for a spelunking adventure into your own warped consciousness for a day or two, or several years in my regards, you get used to the darkness. Your soul longs for it, and you relish in loneliness. When you ascend for air and sunshine and to share with your fellow man, everything you say might be taken for granted, because it is said from an experience that they, the perhaps unthinking, unreflective peoples of the world, the lovers of the light, of flickering images on television screens, and mini smartphone screens, lovers with reckless abandon, the marchers of the great gross status quo, these peeps they shoot you with puzzled looks, and you recoil, descending even ever further into the byzantine depths of your mind's maze. This time better able to deal with the darkness, your eyes are more accustomed to the sight with scanty light, and your hand is better honed to drag up uncut diamonds. That's what I do. I mine the depths of my infinite soul for small, unpolished pieces of this beautiful infinity. I recognize them as such and polish them in the darkness, not knowing what they will look like in the light. I don't care. It's what I have to share with the world.

Mathematicians say that the number line can be divided into infinitesimal components, each representing a infinity unto itself. That's what I am then; my body is bounded in space and time, but my mind lives freely without limitations. I will think whatever I want. I will go to the rooftops and sing a song like a muezzin, but not to an abstract thought of a God. I will sing the song to and for myself and I will descend again into the murky depths to drag up beauty. I will not fear that Leviathan death, for it is nothing. We all stop singing sometime.

Father saw a national park as a profit center, endowed with bauxite, that aluminum ore, kimberlite, that diamond rich ore, deposits to be worked by people, an army of ants chewing away the tops of mountains to fashion spatulas. The Earth is a tool to be fashioned into our own image. I think not. Men decide in the confines of the city, they have absolutely no say over nature. They buy and sell. It's their way of life. It's their religion.

I looked at all the boots and became disgusted with myself. I saw manta rays gliding through the ocean depths, majestic. I saw caimans croaking in effluvial swamps, eating, burping, and farting in the sunshine happy. I see men not knowing themselves, bumping into objects, guided on journeys by advertisements, thrusting themselves forward for their god, commerce, and for his minions, commercials. I see them bow down to worship at the altar of Hollywood. I wonder, if there were no cameras and no moving pictures, no images, would men be able to survive now? Did they need some sort of direction to spur them into movement?

I am a slave to inertia.

Part of being an exceedingly strange, yet polite gentleman is going off on thought tangentials like this. It's absolutely free; you are free to think whatever you want without form, without consequences, save if you can deal with the beauty you dredge up. It's killed lesser men. They went out stark raving mad into the streets. The world is beginning to crush me into flour. I can only hope that I won't blow away in a bitter wind and that I may be used to get someone, somewhere in their life, through another day. I should become a poet. Is it a decision one makes?

Did John Donne wake up one morning and say to himself in the reflection of a basin of water, "Methinks I'll become a poet today"? Or did his soul, too, like mine need to burst forth or be crushed under tons of soil when his mine collapsed? I want beauty. I want self-created beauty. In a world of plastic trinkets that pass for permanence, my endeavor is a noble one.

Malvolio slapped me. The girl stood there in front of me, waving her hands in front of my gaze.

"Come out of it, man! I swear I'll start having to carry goddamned smelling salts on me."

I looked up at them, shocked. "What happened?"

"You stopped talking. Stopped responding."

"I went on a long journey. You know that you can voyage a lifetime with a single thought."

"Huh?" the girl asked.

"You were on a long journey while we're supposed to be on a long journey. Let's get these duds and get out of here."

"You scared me there," she said. "I thought we'd have to call you an ambulance."

"Nah. I just get detached. All these boot choices...it's what did it to me."

"Too many choices?"

"Yeah."

"I think you'd look super hawt in these red ostrich leather boots."

"Not super villain enough."

"Huh?"

"Yeah. Those look like the boots of a saint. Malvolio and I are villains through and through. Gangsters. Well, actually, we want to look like villains but be do-gooders."

"Oh."

"You have any black ostrich leather boots?"

"No, part of the charm is the feather rivets."

"Oh, the bumps?"

"Yah."

"Got eel skin?"

"No shit! That's a super villain boot if I've ever seen one!" Malvolio chirped. He had put his turquoise embossed lady's had back on.

"That hat isn't for super villains, monsieur. It's for ladies who go to bake sales and large rodeos without fear of a clod of mud flying out of the area and damaging their sequined shirts. You want a sequined shirt to match that hat, Polly?"

"Oh just come off it, Jackson. Come off your high horse. Can you do better? You pick me out a hat then, you dandy!"

"This one!" I pointed at the hat, all black Stetson with a striking taxidermied rattlesnake shooting out the front and a rattle in the back. It actually looked like the snake was thrusting through the hat at a rat or something. It was the perfect super villain's hat. Malvolio must have missed it on his first, cursory inspection. His eyes gleamed hellfire when he saw it, though it may have been the reflection from the red ostrich leather boots.

He dashed over to the hat, dipped down, and with bravado flipped it onto his head. The girl laughed, genuinely, with delight. At the same moment, I saw my ultimate super villain suit. It was an all black polyester number, which probably hadn't been taken off to be tried on by a patron since the 1970s, when good guys were all the rage. If Steve McQueen ever made an action film and he starred as a straw chewing gunslinger whose quest was looking for a discotheque, this would have been his outfit.

"Give me that."

"Don't you want to try it on for size?"

"Just go off the size of this tuxedo, miss."

I'm terrified of dressing rooms. All the mirrors, the angles. Usually I just end up staring at my dangling cock and balls in them and not actually trying on anything.

She bent down to look at my label. 41R. "What's your pants size?"

"I'm not taking my pants off for you."

Malvolio tensed up. "We got to get out of here, Jackson," he said.

"Why?"

"Because. We have to," he said motioning towards the door.

"Is everything alright?" the girl asked.

"We'll just get the stuff and go."

"Eel skin boots. Size 12. Black. Make it happen."

"The boots run a couple of sizes small," she said.

"10. Wide. I'm not so long as I am wide."

She didn't get it. She didn't get much of anything, and didn't know how to laugh without an LOL or LMFAO attached. Malvolio, that smug serious bastard, chuckled a bit.

"What's gotten to you?" I asked Malvolio when the girl was out of earshot, off rummaging in the back for my boots.

"I have a feeling something bad is about to happen."

"You're right. I'm about to spend 350 bucks for that absurd hat."

"You picked it out."

"I know. It makes for a good disguise."

"You idiot! You know we're driving a damn ultra rare, ultra mint condition muscle car with just some minor damage to its fender. Like that doesn't attract attention," I said.

"Not as much as that damn tuxedo you're wearing," Malvolio said.

"I'm getting rid of it. My only memento from dear old dad, and it's going in the trunk."

"Oh, come off it. You've led a privileged existence, Jackson."

"You don't say?"

"Yes, you have. You know you have. You have no idea what it is to actually work for a living."

"I do plenty of work."

"That's hilarious," he said laughing, barely able to avoid crashing into the boot rack. He laughed so hard, they started to vibrate in their berthing. "The only work you do is swiping your Visa Black card, which is then mysteriously paid off for you. You know how it's paid off? People work, they do this, which generates profits for your family's firm, which goes in turn to pay off your Visa Black card. I'm sure the management has even hired someone to do this for you. In fact..."

Malvolio's face went blank like he had just seen a carload of children careen off a cliff.

"What's wrong?"

"Your Visa Black Card. They're obviously tracking us that way."

"What should I do?"

"Cut it up. Don't use it."

"Uhh...I don't really have a bank account."

"Set one up."

"I don't have any money to put in it."

"Really?"

"Yeah. I've had this Visa Black since I was 12."

"What about your book profits? Where did those go?"

"I always assumed someone was managing that for me."

"Fuck, you're dumb. Well, shit."

"You have any money?"

"No."

"Didn't you work for my father forever?"

"Yes."

"Did he pay you?"

"Yes, of course."

"Why don't you have any money then?"

"Wage Garnishment. I'm accident prone."

"You've got bastards out there?"

"Summer kids. Summer here, summer there."

"Oh, really? I never took you for the randy cocksman."

"Fuck, he's my alter ego."

"Yeah, right."

"I'm fucking with you. People mess with me, they have accidents."

"Really?"

"Yes, really. I've done some pretty diabolical things in my time."

"The only thing diabolical about you is your face."

"My face shows no treachery. If you're on my list, you're dead before I can even talk to you. I'll kill you with a smile."

"You're an assassin then?"

"Among other things."

"Am I on your list?"

"Nope. You're on the Don't Kill list."

"How can I be so sure?"

"I'm talking to you."

The girl came back with my boots, a heavy load for her. She set them down on the bench and walked away towards the register. I helped myself to trying them on. They were snug against my feet, with plenty of toe space.

"They'll work," I shouted at her.

I walked, uncomfortably in my new eel skin boots. They had more shine than I anticipated. Malvolio pointed to his watch as I grabbed my clothing to change in the bathroom.

I looked in the mirror as I wadded up the tuxedo. I stared at myself naked. My body, slim, hairy, my cock, under rivers of hair, seemed beautiful to me. I almost wanted to go outside into the cold and have my uniform be Crazy Naked Man, but instead I changed quickly into my new duds. I gave it up. Malvolio donned his chapeau with the same bravado. He clapped enthusiastically when he saw me in my villain costume. I must admit, it was a great new beginning, and I was happy to be free of the ridiculous tuxedo. I was not, after all, going to the opera.

Buying the cowboy suit was perhaps one of the most liberating experiences of my life, akin to the first time I ever masturbated and guiltily wondered afterwards if God had been watching and shaking his great, massive head in shame, waggling his finger at me that was probably the size of Texas, much like I shook my head in shame at the zoo when our nanny took Hannah and I to the monkey house and said "No Look, Jackson," when the monkeys were doing their business. I peeled my hands away to see a chimp shoot a streamer of semen that arced across the cage and dangled from the branches of a faux tree like a Christmas ornament.

Later, in the cart, I kept asking the nanny to explain to me the significance of the event but she just kept turning red and saying she did not know but the monkey must have been diseased. Then she crossed herself, over and over again and told me to be quiet. I told her that I knew she had seen it because instead of gasping like some of the old biddies there she actually laughed a little bit. This made the nanny more uncomfortable and she turned even redder as the car rolled down the avenue.

When Malvolio and I got to the car, he checked it over with a small retractable mirror that he pulled from his pocket, ever paranoid about some assassins hired by a secretive cabal, and he told me that they could quite possibly be using a Mexican drug cartel as a proxy. In the car, he discussed his participation in the Lebanese Civil War, the First and Second Intifada, a few incidents in Northern Ireland, and some stuff that happened in Waco, Texas. It went in one ear and out the other. It seemed like Malvolio sought out strife, and strife did not fail to find him.

"Your daddy played the part of the pacifist really well, but he was Americanski through and through. Instead of solving his own problems that cropped up from day to day in a large global mining and manufacturing conglomerate, that's where I came in."

"Yeah, right."

"There's a lot you don't know, Jackson. I'd venture to say you don't know ninety nine percent of what went on."

"Uhh...maybe you can fill in some of the gaps for me."

Malvolio looked absurd, sitting there in his hat that came squarely across his brow, causing his stringy salt and pepper hair to shoot out the back like an after-burner of a polluting jet airplane.

"So, no shit, there we were in Burkina Faso, going over uranium mining service contracts with a corrupt minister of the foreign trade commission..."

"Burkina Fucking Faso!"

"Yeah, Burkina Faso. Some little African country that borders a bunch of other little countries in West Africa, I think. Hell, I don't know. I wasn't paid to do country studies. I was paid to cause bloody wars. You know, kick ass, as you youth say."

"I'm having a hard time believing your ass kicking tendencies."

"Oh, you'll believe it. You'll come to believe it."

"I might, but I doubt it. You're not much to look at. Ass kickers are always handsome. I could be quite an ass kicker."

"You've got one problem, though."

"What?"

"You're a pussy."

"Listen, don't call me that."

"You are. Why do you think your father retained me with his dying breaths?"

"Yeah, right."

"Don't you know the best people in my line of work are unassuming, Master Jackson?"

"Listen, stop calling me that too."

"What? Pussy?"

"That too! No. Master Jackson. It makes me sound fucking ten years old or something, and it makes you sound like a butler. That's what the butler called me."

"Oh, I've done that before. Butlered for a few years before your father discovered my other talents."

"I knew I recognized you from somewhere."

"You've seen me before?"

"Yes, yes I have."

"You were in our house, around the time my mother passed on."

"I wasn't butlering then. Your father promoted me."

"To what?"

"Who are we running from?" Malvolio asked. He was fond of answering questions with questions. It annoyed me.

"Uh..."

"We're running from assassins, rogues, a whole medley of evil doers. There might even be some legitimate terrorists, you know, farming out their talents for a buck thrown into the mix."

"I'm not following your logic."

"What does it take to catch a thief, Master...uhh...sorry, Jackson?"

"Some detectives."

"But who's the best detective?"

"A guy with a nice Burberry trench coat and a notepad?"

"Are you dense?"

"Hey! You're the one who asked me! Why don't you just tell me what type of person it takes to catch a thief? I've never needed to steal! I don't know any thieves. I don't know what it takes to catch a thief, you convoluted fuck!"

"Hey! Hey! I'm sorry. I've forgotten I'm dealing with Prince Charming. I've a flair for drama, and I thought you'd get it."

"Just tell me."

"A thief. A thief is the best person to catch a thief."

"So what are you telling me? You're protecting me so well against our pursuers because you're the same type of person?"

"Exactly."

"I don't buy it."

"Oh, you'll come to believe me."

I glared at him. His antics were quickly becoming tiresome. You know, the more I gave credence to his absurd proposition, the more we would be led down his path from which I really saw no escape. I mean, look at this guy. Just take a long hard look at him. He looks like death, and not death warmed over or whatever cliché is going now. In a weak sense, he is like death, like life's river had washed over him leaving him a smoothed out pebble in a stream.

Malvolio's scared of everything, afraid to take even the tiniest leap that wasn't planned to death from start to finish. Malvolio was a twisted creature of habit. He had a heuristic for everything, life descended to algorithms of habits. These were secret habits, security conscious habits, paranoid habits, and possibly schizoid habits. I don't doubt that the two old people were real; I just doubt that anyone cares about that as much to dispatch a Brigade sized element of assassins to kill little me. And to what purpose?

I think that's a basis for psychosis and schizoid behavior, that a person just thinks they're too damn important. They succumb to delusions that they're a knight errant, a do-gooder, the Messiah, a talented writer, a spy and assassin. They can't be content with just being someone; everybody's got to be so damn important. I'm a very important person, a VIP. No, I'm a VVIP. Very Very Important Person. Give me a break. You know, my father was never in the business of hiring subpar professionals; he left that up to the sub contractors.

Maybe I should hear Malvolio out. Maybe he had done some things in the past and he wanted a confessor, maybe the only other person who knew what he did in his life was now dead, about to be entombed in a cemetery in Peoria, Illinois. I made fast a pact with myself that we would make our way to Peoria as soon as Earthly possible, right then and there. I would hear Malvolio out along the way; I would listen to his stories. I would see and discover how my father had spent his days. And why did I care to hear this out? Why care for a man who only thought of his family as an afterthought, an "Oh, yes!" moment, "I have one of those." Or maybe it was a glancing thought when he sobered up in some third world bar and the sunlight struck his face and reminded him of the warmth of the world. From what Malvolio came to tell me, father appreciated the down and out and honkey-tonked his way across seven continents. And who knew?

Father paid Malvolio to cover his tracks. What he told me between the flat plains of Nebraska and the cornfields of Iowa and what he did, for excitement or maybe it was out of a sense of duty to my newly dead father, paying certain people a visit, many of them women. Pregnant women. Pregnant, like the humble lady that we came upon in this bumblefuck little town in Nebraska whose only claim to fame was the Tractor Supply shop it boasted in the center of town around which buildings that had not seen tenants since the early 1980s.

Ah the fucking eighties. That's when a Wally World opened up three exits down the I-80...you know you stick a Wally World in the middle of a rural area, it's almost like sticking a poison block in the middle of a densely wooded area. It's like an atomic fucking bomb, man. There is a kill off of a certain radius. The rest get radiation poisoning and die slow. The rural denizens have a choice to either go to Wally World and get lost or go to a store with slightly higher prices owned by people who know them and that they have known their entire lives. I don't know why they choose Wally World.

Convenience, maybe, that modern day whore of cost savings. They no longer care about their neighbors. But what they spent in gasoline to get to Wally World, that great cancer cell on the prairie, that genital wart, all those SUVs acting like red blood cells carrying oxygen in the form of cash dollars to the bloated tumor mass, that gas could have best been saved by walking to the mom and pop shop. But, what is familiar settles to the bottom as normalcy, which hardens into the mud of ennui...that bricky clay that allows no growth, not even penetration downwards. You're stuck, a mere placeholder, holding a place in the line, a position in the great march forwards. You can walk forward, even if you're marching lockstep in a circle, and blinders obscure your vision.

I'd tell you that I didn't appreciate the cushy lifestyle that my megabucks afforded me, but I would be lying. I don't flaunt it because that is not my nature to flaunt it off, to peacock around from town to town. According to Malvolio, I probably should have rubbed their little faces in my magnificence a bit.

"You can't take it with you, Jackson," he said.

"So tell me, Malvolio...."

"Yes?" He asked flashing me that toothy death-dealing grin with a glint, more than a hit of severe derangement in his eyes.

"Tell me what my father was like. I think I'm ready to hear."

"You're willing to pay attention and not get all sidetracked when I'm telling the story? You know, I hate repeating myself again and again, so I'm going to refuse to do it."

"I'll pay attention. I promise. Just tell the story. From beginning to end. Don't leave anything out."

"I'll try my best. That's all I can give you. Don't expect a miracle worker."

"You've been delaying for long enough."

"You know, you're probably not going to like what you hear."

"Just say it. I'm a full grown man, so just say it."

Malvolio smiled. Take everything with a grain of salt with this one.

XXXXXXXXXXXXXXXXXXXXXXXXXXXXXXXXXXXXXXXXXXXXXXX
XXXXXXXXXXXXXXXXXXXXXXXXXXXXXXXXXXXXXXXXXXXXXXXX
XXXXXXXXXXXXXXXXXXXXXXXXXXXX

You know, I found her. When my mother did the deed. I wasn't in the house yet. I was walking, quite alone in the fragrant garden behind our home when I heard the shot ring out. It was uncommon for women to shoot themselves. I remember the paramedic saying that. In our home, it could have been mistaken for one of father's vintage automobiles backfiring after the mechanic tuned it up. I ran upstairs, and I saw a man standing over her, looking down at her. He did not look at me, but when I made the smallest sound, he bolted. I ran past my mother lying there bleeding uncontrollably, bleeding out, and sort of mouthing words. Mah...Mah...Mah...I pursued the man down the stairs, but lost him in the hedgerows. I only remember that he was wearing black. A green ski mask. When I came to, the gardener was over me with the smelling salts. I heard sirens. He just dragged me up to the house while the medics poured out of the ambulances and the cops established a perimeter. My sister, five at the time, was whisked away with a maid, and screamed and balled her eyes out.

I watched with detachment. The police interviewed me. I told them I didn't see anyone. I don't know why I did that. I thought about the shot. I knew that my father had expressly forbidden anyone from setting foot into his office where he kept most of his important business information, and that's why it was so strange to see her in there with all the contact information for all of his business associates, his collection of artifacts from around the world, his artwork. This was his out in the open side, and still not even my mother was allowed access to it. I used to sneak in there as a child and sit in my father's chair, and pretended I was answering the telephone, and shuffled his papers around, but I always remembered to put everything back where I found it.

I was a sneaky child, full of myself and my ability to sneak around and discover things. I guess nothing has changed much; I'm still the same old Jackson, just wondering what I want to do with my days, still a sneak if you ask anyone in the family. But why did I have to sneak in there and see that?

Anyway...getting back to what happened. When my mother decided to do herself in...if she did...I don't know, I'm still puzzled over that...when my mother decided to take my father's reliquary revolver and go up into his office and blast herself...why did I have to be there? I can't say that anyone saw my mother's suicide coming. If anything, she was not acting depressed. She wasn't showing anyone any warning signs. She never attempted. She always had a smile on her face. She had even taken on a young Argentine tennis instructor. She was taking golf lessons, lessons in cooking from a chef from her favorite restaurant in California that she flew into a week at a time on my father's Boeing Bizjet.

She wasn't depressed. She wasn't in need of counseling. She wasn't in need of hospitalization. Did she just snap? Decide to call it quits? She could have at least said goodbye. Did a catalytic even take place? Did she discover the true extent of my father's philandering? Did she finally say enough was enough? Why not get a divorce and take him for half of everything? In my family there are deep dark entrenched secrets. I'm afraid, or at least beginning to suspect that most all of them died with my father. Why did I hate this man so much? Did I blame him for what happened to mom, who on all accounts was a beautiful woman, full of life, with so much life ahead of her? Did I blame him for that? Did I think him responsible? I go off on tangents because I think it keeps me from the truth.

"You know, there's much about your father that you don't know, son."

So now he was taking to calling me son.

"Of course. He was never around."

"Someday, I'll have to tell you about all that," Malvolio said grinning. "But for now, we've got a fashion show to attend."

"We didn't get all duded up to go nowhere."

The Judge screamed into the parking lot at the single largest single employer in the area, the Falconbridge, Nebraska, Anheuser Busch InBev Beer Distributor's warehouse. A small cohort of cars and an enormous flotilla of motorcycles, all chromed up, diamond dazzling the sunlight in our eyes, as if Big Baby Jesus himself had descended from heaven shooting moonbeams and sunbeams all over the place, were all parked haphazardly. A loud talking lady, dressed in an equally loud cowboy ensemble, purple and pink sequins on silver, busy herding cats, all equally dressed in annoying, garish and gaudy cowboy getups that would get them shot and scalped in seconds had the west not been won, herded the rootin' tootin' cowboys into their respective positions. To these people we seemed just a tiddly bit anachronistic, you know, possibly even capable of being Wild West morticians, our appearance was so dour. Malvolio, in the sunlight, looked downright gloomy, and I looked like the reprehensible villain of a low budget, poorly scripted cowboy flick whose director swore he'd start shooting porn just to make something of himself.

The large woman screamed orders at the assembled cowboys. This fatty who looked like an eggplant with its first creepy purple layer peeled off and possibly whitewashed, then dipped in glue and coated with a random pattern of sequins of all colors and possible variants of pink screamed her fool head off. Her jean jacket appeared random, but upon closer inspection I became aware that the pink actually formed a pattern. It was an American flag out of which a bald eagle holding another star spangled banner in its beaky protuberance flew, talons seeking to crush some non-WASP foe. It was not very well done, because the eagle had the shape of a crow. She was a cowboy all right...a clown cowboy, and one a bull would not hesitate to gore and kick about the air.

"Well, I'll be a goddamned rootin' tootin' monkey's uncle," Malvolio said, keeping in part.

"Do we really want to waste our time with this?"

"It's all we've been doing, and it's all we've got. It's for a good cause."

"A better cause is getting your ass to papa's burial."

"Now you come out and say it. You've really been interfering with my new vocation of being a do-gooder."

"Someone has to do good in the world. If you didn't have as much capital behind you, you'd probably be singing a different tune. It's mine!"

"I'm talking about giving it all up, donating it all away, giving myself just a modest means to advertise my future literary works, and try to live off of that."

"You're a fool. A fucking fool."

"Better to be a fool than be a banker. Or a banker's fool. Or a fucking lawyer writing legal briefs, typing up time with red tape, settling disputes. Don't enter into any disputes if you ask me."

"They're part of life. You live, you get into confrontation. It's part of the business of business. But guess what? Sue me, and I'll kill you," Malvolio said with a grin.

"Lawyers."

"Yeah, your pa hated 'em. Never used 'em. He had other ways to settle his disputes," Malvolio said, grinning underneath that great reptilian head on his hat. Their faces took on the same proportions, a viper wearing a viper.

"What are you saying?"

"Come now, Jackson, don't get upset. It's for a good cause."

"What did you say about lawyers?"

"I don't use them. Your father didn't really either. Oh, he drew up a will when it was time to settle his estate, but he did his business by other means."

"Uh...what other means?"

"You know I can't discuss that. Statute of limitations not expiring and stuff like that. I won't discuss those matters. Let's just say I learned to be Machiavellian from your father, and let's just say that the man taught Mephistopheles his science, which he then imparted to Faust. Let's just keep it at that."

"Yeah, right."

"Oh, there's much you don't know about your father, Master Jackson."

"There you go again."

The thought bubbled up in me like a volcano. I started forming infernal connections in my brain, like a demonical transfer from my irrational to rational brain, synapses firing, going over in my mind what I had somewhat always suspected growing up. My mother was too full of life to ever kill herself. She was a DeBournnaise, from a French aristocratic family. East Coast French. She would have taken on hundreds of lovers before she ever killed herself. And she would have done it like a lady. I just smiled at Malvolio. I didn't tell him my suspicions. He gleamed at me, brilliantly with his burning face underneath that stupid evildoer's hat.

So what did I suspect? I suspected that Mr. Robert Malvolio was quite capable of anything. I just didn't have any evidence other than his insinuations, and I was puzzled at why he would insinuate anything in the first place. Why would he be insinuating that he and my father had something to do with my mother's demise? Did I see him hovering over her? No, it wasn't him. It couldn't have been him. Why would he do this to me right now? I watched him get final instructions from my father. Why didn't my father give me final instructions? Why, if I'm supposed to be the fucking chosen one, didn't my father give me some final fucking instructions? Why not? Why didn't father whisper something to me that was barely intelligible? Just what was on that old man's lips?

"Before we go into this place, you need to tell me what my father told you on his deathbed."

Malvolio smiled. Not quite as demonically as when he told me he didn't deal with lawyers. I was starting to figure him out, that was his insinuation smile, this is his "oh shit, he's on to me" smile. I started to feel the heat rising in my heart. "What the fuck did he tell you, Malvolio?"

Malvolio shook his head from side to side like a child's teeter-totter. I wasn't sure what this meant. Iffiness, perhaps. Now I really got angry. "You tell me what my father told you!"

"Or what?" he shot back.

"Or I'll leave you here."

Malvolio chuckled. "You'll never make it across the state line once you abandon me."

"I can do anything I want. We've surely lost whoever was following us."

"Don't be so sure. You're a very, very wanted man, Jackson. Do you know when you were growing up how many kidnapping plots for you alone I foiled? You owe it to me to get you to Peoria. I'm like your goddamned Secret Service!"

"Oh, fuck you and your security. I'd rather be free than live in a prison of walls and fences and fucking bars!"

"You're born into it."

"Well, fuck it. I'll give it all up."

"You couldn't, and you know it. The world's a prison."

"It is not. Tell me what my father said!"

"It wasn't for you to hear."

"Damnit, tell me. I know he didn't tell you to just watch out for me."

"It was only for my ears. I bet the suspense is really getting to you. Sheldon, it's getting to him. He wanted to know as well. He wanted to know, and he offered me five million dollars to know the night before I left that house. He offered that I should go to work for him in his little endeavor. I'm obligated to your father. I'm contractually obligated, and my obligation only expires with my death."

"I thought you didn't deal with lawyers."

"This goes well beyond lawyers."

"Tell me what he said to you."

"No can do."

"Was it about me?"

Malvolio paused. "Don't know."

"Surely you know. Stop it. Tell me. You work for me now."

"No, I don't work for you. I will always work for your father. I've got a lifetime's of fealty to him. It didn't expire when he died. Actually, it grew stronger. It only expires when I die. Whether I go out in a gun battle with all these fucking bikers, ninjas, whoever else the competition has dispatched against us, I'm bound."

"I can dismiss you at any time. Wait? Are you a Djinn?"

Malvolio laughed. "I'm flesh and blood, like you, but I have some now non-existent thing called loyalty. I can't help it. I promised to carry out your father's wishes, and I'm doing it."

"What did he tell you?"

"That's for me to know. He didn't intend for it to be shared."

"I'll pry it out of you. Torture it out of you."

"Not likely."

"You have a weakness. I'm going to find it and break you."

"Maybe it was gibberish."

"It wasn't. Why would your dad waste his last words on gibberish?"

"He was really, really, really old."

"People are starting to stare at us."

"Make your move. Personally, I've got a bad feeling about this."

"You've got a bad feeling about everything. It's a miracle you even get out of the house."

"Risk management. No unnecessary risks."

"You're just nuts."

"I've never, ever even seen a doctor. You know you're the one nuts here, Jackson."

I opened the door and stepped out, putting the evildoer's eel skin boot on the ground. I wore the uniform of an evildoer, but I'm a prince with a heart of gold. Sometimes you had to dress up like an evildoer to get people to leave you alone. Call it a conundrum, but I'm living in mighty perilous times, or maybe they aren't all that perilous, but we're all bored and feel doomed. Maybe father's last words were rubbish, nothing profound. That's why very rich men hire poets like Ovid to eulogize them. Hell, Augustus got Virgil to do it for him during his lifetime. They just aren't very wordy for everything they receive.

Pa, he was a hell of a businessman. When it comes down to it, when the fat lady sings on this hot little bastard of a planet, will it all just be garbled gibberish? When we're all underwater will the transmission go through? Will anyone be able to decipher the words written on a page? Is it all just for naught? Is it all folly? Or am I supposed to live in the moment like a good dog, like a Buddhist, a Hindu cow, always pondering nothing, trying to fill my head with the nothingness of the void that I will melt into, whatever that means? I don't wear a cowboy suit. I'm not the man in black. Whatever uniform I wear, it's the uniform of a madman. Is there any other way to be? I glanced back at Malvolio. He wasn't following me.

I spied Rebecca and her self-important oaf of a boyfriend. I shot my arm out to shake his hand, which he reluctantly did. We looked each other in the eyes, two tigers about to be in some tiger fight.

"I'm here to be in your fashion show and make a special donation," I exclaimed.

Rebecca sheepishly nodded to me. I think she got a talking to for being herself previously. Don't you dare be vivacious, outgoing, and gorgeous, Rebecca. Don't you dare smile. You smile in your wedding photo with me. If she didn't leave him it would be her fate and the death of more than just her freedom. It would be her choice to be unfulfilled in life, perhaps always wondering why she chose to hitch her wagon to such a dumb, slow horse. I wanted to take the massive belt buckle from the oaf's waist and bludgeon him to death with it. I wanted to be not just her liberator, but also the liberator of women from the idiocy of the modern male; me, the humble anachronist, ushering in an age when men actually treated women with respect. I don't care if we would have to go back to living in caves again. At least there would be some sort of love on the goddamned planet. I realized I had on my person a very large hand cannon. You know what? Maybe I would try to instigate rhinestone cowboy into decking me. Armed with a shiner, I would pistolay whip him into submission. Deadly force. I was afraid for me life, ossifer. Please ossifer, I swear, he's way bigger than me. Did he have intelligence that I was well endowed with a sizeable bank account? Did Rebecca make him play nice? I knew nothing about these people. I relaxed his against his grip and tried to pull my hand away.

Let the dick-measuring contest begin, I thought, as I ran my eyes across her sequined chest, trying very hard to avoid staring for what her dumbass oaf could misconstrue as titgazing. It was really impossible not to. So I glanced over there again, and I looked into her eyes. They were mirrors. Should I stare long enough, I could see my own reflection and object of love. I stared into her eyes, trying not to break a gaze. My eyes weeble wobbled, and I looked away, timid. I thought I heard dumb oaf growl, but it was only him clearing his throat. Then he spit, quite conspicuously, near the toe of my eel skin boot.

"Oops," he said.

This had the makings of a bad Western film gunfight, but I saw that he wasn't armed. Apparently he didn't consider a loaded hand cannon as a proper accoutrement for a sequined cowboy outfit. Keep the damn sequins and bring a proper pearl handled revolver. Make it out of platinum if you can afford it.

I didn't let on that I was armed and dangerous. We're in the Wild West, and it is a fairly safe assumption for a person to make that I'm packing a masterblaster in my pants that I will pull it out and ruin your day with it. Everyone out here is armed to the teeth. I looked around me and saw the fashion accessories of more than a few bikers. A masterblaster is more than a survival tool; it is a fashion accessory. Some of the ladies sport pink Glocks in their purses so they can blow the brains out of any would-be rapist and not be seen as unladylike, not having to be seen in public with an ugly, black, and obscene mangun. No, I doubt I could even get close to blowing stupid oaf away without this entire rhinestone mess pulling out so many pieces that they could have filled me with more holes than an I-80 Nevada whorehouse after a visit by the Harlem Globetrotters.

You know what? I'm going to just play it cool, let simple simpleton have his fun with me. I won't sink to his level. His woman is on a higher trajectory than him, and we vibrate on the same wavelength. I can feel it. So may the better man win out in the end. I didn't even mean to try and attract this damsel in distress, who may not have even been in trouble. Maybe the gene pool in these parts was so shallow that the man she has is the best possible gentleman, and I have just ridden up and sown seeds of doubt about it all, tossed the seeds all over her blissful watermelon patch. I looked back to Malvolio through the great front windows, and he had remained in the Judge, looking down like he didn't want to acknowledge my presence and ready say I told you so when I came back to the car bandied and bloodied, ready to get the fuck out of Dodge.

Done sizing me up, peacocking, and rootin' tootin' like a rooster, the dumb oaf Ben decided to wow me with his way with words.

"The man in black, huh?"

"Yeah, you're darn tootin'."

"Oh, are you some sort of tough guy?"

"Don't misconstrue what I say, oaf. You're a big guy. Who gives a fuck? You'll be plenty of food for the maggots and worms when you kick off. And if you keep that tone with me, you'll be kicking off shortly."

"Sounds like fightin' words."

"No shit!"

Oaf breathed in deeply. It could be seen in every confrontation amongst males of any species. Only I had a gun. I had my two fists as well, though they weren't of much use or importance. I had the great-goddamned equalizer in my pants, and it was in the back of them, not the front. Tension raced across the atmosphere, but things started to slow down for me. Oaf tensed up. I could see it. He swung, wildly. I dodged. Malvolio was out of the car, like a tiger out of his cage. A great, acid spitting, denizen of hell, point focused like a bullet from a talented sniper with great equipment, bent on destroying oaf's testicles. Malvolio burst in the front door, much to the dismay of the Rhinestone assembly.

Malvolio practiced Jimmy Fu, a variant of Kung Fu, not Shaolin or named after any particular animal style. This was aimed purely at causing considerable pain to the other male and possibly rendering him incapable of breeding. It had one flaw: any steel-toed boot could be rendered a moot point by the opponent wearing a jockstrap or codpiece, stuffing their pants with ample socks, or having a tiny frank and beans, also known as a micropenis, which Malvolio could not kick or smash with any accuracy, kind of like trying to shoot a dancing flea with an artillery piece.

Instead, for Mr. Big Dumb Oaf, Malvolio blindsided him with the three times five finger death testicle twister. Well-honed in bar fights in 28 states and used all over Africa on child soldiers, Malvolio could grab testicles through the pants and crush the epididymis this way with his thumb and two forefingers and then twist them free of their moorings with his other hand. Dumb oaf went purple with pain and collapsed to one knee before keeling over.

Typical of a battered spouse or girlfriend, Rebecca rushed forward to aid her abuser. Malvolio's spinning Jimmy Fu was useless against her because she was not in need of an orchiectomy. Instead he punched her in one of her pendulous titties and knocked her off balance, enough for us to escape into the Judge, which was soon surrounded by psychopathic bikers intent on beating the prime finish with chains like incense censers. I am certain that, if we did not punch the gas, hitting at least one fatty leather clad weenie off onto his spiked helmet, we would have been given up to the Gods of Western Nebraska as an Auto de Fe. Whatever Gods there were favored Malvolio and I in the equation, and we were soon cruising a backcountry road towards the East and bumblefuck Iowa.

"It's tough being good. You know, I was really trying to help those people out."

"Fuck 'em, cultural filter feeders. Barnacles. You do what you have to do. We'll leave these Earthworms behind to root through the garbage and detritus of this time. You worry about yourself. They'll call you selfish. Fuck 'em. You do what they're all doing. You care about yourself. You get to Peoria, and you stop your ceaseless worrying. You put pen on paper, or I'll kill you myself."

"After my dad is laid to rest, I'll start my life as an itinerant writer, creator and destroyer of worlds."

We sped off into the sunset like two lone but together highwaymen set out to rob and plunder the decent people of the world, and when the sun went down on us, you couldn't tell the difference between us and the empty, abandoned, and open road. We were driving with our lights out to avoid detection.

XXXXXXXXXXXXXXXXXXXXXXXXXXXXXXXXXXXXXXXXXXXXXXXXXXX
XXXXXXXXXXXXXXXXXXXXXXXXXXXXXXXXXXXXXXXXXXXXXXXXXXX
XXXXXXXXXXXXXXXXXXXXXXXXXXXX

"My boy, tragedy is written from life, and flows to the void. Comedy is the void searching out cheery bits of life, grasping at them. A life preserver it is to be able to laugh at yourself. Which side are you on?"

"Neither side."

"You must choose."

"I can't, and I won't."

"How is this thing going to end up then?"

"No one knows."

"Come on, man. What are you writing next? Another romance?"

"I'm not writing what my agent wants me to write. I'm writing what I want to write, and if it sells, so be it. If it doesn't, oh well."

"Surely you want recognition, babes, cars, all that," Malvolio said.

"I can have that anytime I like. A car is a way to get from point A to point B," I said.

"Are we ever going to get out of this monstrosity of a state?"

"Drive on, eventually it will happen, we'll see the road sign for Iowa go whizzing by."

"It's quite possible. Is that freedom? Driving around in the same old ruts?" I asked.

"I don't see a problem with it."

"You're a fan of security," I said.

"I'm not a fan, I'm a practitioner."

"Who watches out for you?" I asked.

"I look out for myself."

"And you watch out for me."

"Comforting, right?"

"Not really."

"Ha!" Malvolio chirped.

"Want to stop for the night, or just get some coffee, energy drinks, peanuts, and keep rolling on through?"

"Maybe take a rest. I don't know how much of this prairie I can take before I crash into an open field from lack of sleep."

"Where should we pull over? A rest stop?"

"Are you foolish?"

"I think we've already established that."

"You're going to stop at a hotel, and not just any hotel. You're going to stay at a fancy hotel with a pool."

"I want to sleep, not swim."

"I need to soak my tired bones. All this fighting and saving your ass has me tired."

"We'll get a room, but you have to start dishing the dirt on dear old dad."

"No can do. I signed a secrecy affirmation statement. Legally binding."

"I thought you didn't deal with attorneys."

"I didn't. He made two of the biggest bastards who worked for him sign it with me. A way of keeping all of us in check. You tell anything to anyone, and then these two bastards come looking for you. And they wore jockstraps, believe you me."

"Well, you'll tell me what you can about my dad...come on...I'm bereaved."

"Baloney. You didn't talk to your dad for almost ten full years before he took to ailing. Even then you thought it was a ploy to get you out of your rat hole hiding place there on the coast of California."

"I thought about him often."

"Doesn't matter. It's actions people see. We can't read minds. I don't know, maybe you can."

"Don't lecture me."

"Why don't you meet a nice girl?"

"What?"

"Yeah, go out and find a nice girl, settle down with her."

"No."

"Maybe that's what your father said to me."

"He would have told me that himself."

"Maybe he's so used to using me as an intermediary that he couldn't."

"Maybe your inheritance is tied to it," Malvolio said, smiling.

"Just fucking tell me, Robert."

Malvolio took genuine delight in my consternation.

"Tell me," I implored him.

"No way, buddy," Malvolio said.

I sighed.

"Tell me about my mother then."

"Charming lady," Malvolio said.

"No, tell me more about her."

"Like, what do you want to know?"

"Do you think she killed herself?"

He smiled, "Oh, I can't really speculate on that. What did the police say?"

"It was an open and shut case."

"Then that's what it was."

"It was swept under the carpet."

"No, no, no," Malvolio said, shaking his head.

"You said it yourself. My father didn't deal with lawyers."

"What are you trying to say, Jackson?" Malvolio asked with a sneer, much like a wolf, but really coming off much like a Pekinese. The corners of his lips turned upwards and then crinkled into a frown.

"You know what I'm saying. You're not dense. You've been doing your job for so long, that you can't have forgotten everything. I'm saying that my mother didn't kill herself. She was murdered. Someone killed her and covered it up. I don't know who it was exactly, but I think it was you. I think you did it because she was going to divorce my father and he didn't want to deal with a lawyer. My mother's divorce proceedings would have been very, very public, and all the dirty laundry would have been aired out in the open for the public to see. So I think that father may have had you get rid of the problem for him."

"Baloney," Malvolio said with a laugh. "You're truly paranoid. Have you been taking the medication that the doctor prescribed for you?"

"That old quack?"

"The doctor gave you some pills. Where are they? Have you been taking them?"

"You're the paranoiac here, not me. You should be medicated."

"That may be the case, but my paranoia is a job qualification, and yours is a condition that requires medication. So where is it?"

"He never gave me any."

"Or you threw it away?"

"It doesn't matter whether I'm taking my pills or not. What are you, my pharmacist? Just answer my fucking question."

"Don't tell me what to do, boy. I was eating Hezbollah operatives for lunch while you were still in diapers."

I decided to explode on him.

"Right. Mom killer. Snuffer of innocent women, you son of a big, ugly, buttfucking bitch! Bastard progeny of the coupling of a horsefly and a maggot. Your buzzing is much more annoying than your bite, and you remember, I'm armed and capable of removing your scummy carcass from this planet at any time...."

"You wouldn't dare," Malvolio said with a grin.

"I will dare. I'm a daring man, and you've seen it, I know."

"You would have been worm food back there at Saks if it wasn't for me, you petulant boy."

"How do I know that those two old bastards weren't trying to kill you? I'm the target? Everybody loves me! You just burst onto the scene and now all of a sudden, you've got me convinced that there are all sorts of demonical plots on my life. I'll tell you what, Mr. Malvolio, I don't fucking buy it. I stayed in my home, a hopeless fucking closet recluse for nearly ten fucking years. Why didn't they come for me there? What, there wasn't any good sport in it?"

"Drive on, you bastard. I had nothing to do with killing your dead old mama."

"I know my father."

"Oh, really? Do you?"

"What happened then?"

"She offed herself. Not in a way typical of women, but probably the only means available. You should know. Suicides are terribly secretive. You would never have seen it coming. These suicides, they wear masks. They don't want to share their misery, so they don't ask for help. It's part of the disease. They're so diminished and in such pain that they don't think removing themselves will have an effect on the world or the people that loved them. I'm sorry Master...I mean, Jackson, I'm sorry. You just have to accept that."

"I swear to God you're responsible."

"This is a conversation you should have had with your Father."

"My father? My fucking father? He wasn't around for long enough in one place to ever have a conversation with him."

"He had to keep moving. He was a slave to inertia. Why be like the rest of the masses? You know, acting like electricity or water, taking the path of least resistance?"

I gave up my struggle to get answers out of Malvolio for the time being. He was a puzzle, a witty Sphinx. Plains whipped by us, a few silos in the distance ripped across the windshield and retreated like forlorn soldiers, grey and moribund in isolation. I'm not even sure if trains dock in these places anymore to carry their cargos to be made into cattle feed and human feed. Malvolio's words penetrated into me.

No one told my father to go out and do business, that's just how he was. He probably thought building the business into the global powerhouse it has become would be the best way of taking care of his family. Did mother really decide to kill herself? I could never believe it, and I would never believe it. I would never believe it. This man, sitting right next to me was the most likely person to have committed such an unnatural act of matricide, but it wasn't his mother, so he just a lady killer and not a "get in her pants" type, I mean a real dastardly murderer.

I resolved then and there that I would have to off Malvolio, if I were ever to be free of his infernal company. And how would I do it? Wait until he's sleeping and just do him in with a gunshot, like he did my poor mother in with? Or should I challenge him to a duel? Perhaps rapiers, broadswords, a knife fight maybe. I have never fought with knives before, but it can't be too terribly difficult. It's in the movies all the time. Malvolio no doubt probably received extensive training on the subject.

"I think you should take your medicine, Jackson," Malvolio said. "You could conk out, and I can drive for a while."

Surely this was a ploy. I'd conk out, and he'd bury me up to my neck in anthill with honey on my forehead or stake me out on it with the sticky sticky smeared all over my testicles. I saw through his games. Maybe I could buy some time by having him tell me a tale from my father's youth.

"I don't need any medicine. Stories are my palliative panacea. So, tell me one about my father, as you promised.

"Hmm..." Malvolio thought, fidgeting a bit in the passenger's seat.

"Thinking up something juicy?"

"Hardly saucy. Maybe a bit dry."

"I'm only up for lovely stories. I don't want any old desiccated bits, flopping tall tales, fish stories. This had better be brass tax, Malvolio, if you want to live to see another day."

"Ha! So I'm to be your Schezerade now?"

"No. You're going to recount my father's autobiography to me, tidbit by greasy tidbit, or I'm going to fill you full of holes and make your carcass disappear."

"Really? You'd do that?"

I pulled over to the side of the road and whipped the hand cannon out of my inner pocket, real Dirty Harry style. I pointed it right at his nugget. "Yeah, I'll do it, and you know it, so start talking."

"I don't respond well to being at gunpoint," Malvolio said, smiling.

"Damn you! All I want to know is something about my father. You know, what type of man he was for real. I've just been lied to about him my whole life. For fuck's sake, I had to read the society papers just to find out where he was when I was growing up. I can't have him dead and buried without knowing anything about him. If you don't tell me, I will kill you."

"You'll have to take your pea shooter off safety, fool. Do you even have a round chambered? Look, the hammer's not back. You don't even have a round in this. Here... give me that."

He seized the weapon and in one deft movement, dropped the magazine, and seated the shells into the magazine by tapping it against his protruding skeletal cheekbone, the whole time looking at me with his great black eyes, never flinching. He racked the round into the chamber, removed the safety, and handed the pistol back to me. I gulped with nervousness.

"She's got a match grade trigger. Three point one pounds. That's not much of a squeeze. You're going to do it, don't shoot me in the guts. Put it right through my black heart."

"How do I put it on safe?"

"Just flip that lever in the back upwards. It latches in front of the slide and makes sure the hammer can't fall."

I flipped it and lowered the weapon.

"Your father said *save my son* right before he died. He repeated it over and over again. I promised him, I would. That's all he said."

"That's what he said?"

"That's it."

"What the hell does that mean?"

"You tell me."

"We all want our best intentions carried on after we're gone. Maybe that's what he meant."

"Could be. At any rate, that's what I'm doing."

"You could start by teaching me how to protect myself. Show me how to fire this thing."

"I can't believe you carry that around and never knew how to use it. You could have killed yourself, gotten yourself killed, or blown your dick off."

"Teach me how to use it."

"Get off the beaten path. There's no firing this around people. They'll summon the police for sure."

At the next junction, I turned in the direction of the open prairie. A mile down the road, we could only make out a lone farmhouse and a lonely tree off in the distance. A tire swing hung from the tree, held in its death throes by a nearly rotten jute rope, WWII surplus, dangerously frayed at the edges. The grass was lush, save for underneath where it appeared threadbare like the bald spot on a sunburnt farmer. You know, I think that people grow like the corn, only they grow internally. On the outside you cannot tell a seedling from a nine-foot tall, well-watered giant. You also can't tell by talking to them. Some people's souls are so miniscule you wonder if they are truly a human being at all, and not just an animal that walks and talks. I think the people whose souls are immense are capable of casting great shadows on the environment they come up in, fanning out, and taking up great space. And what of the little ones who never quite get enough sunlight across their leaves, and end up withered, failure to grow, failure to thrive, failure to live in that case? We all have to live – you, and me, even Malvolio, and the strange man we're about to meet at this isolated farmhouse.

Malvolio did not take a liking to him, a man who was dressed in the tatters of a rock concert T-Shirt, Styx I think it was, from the 1988 World Tour, but it could have been another band. His clothing was so grubby and stained. The man looked to be a near skeleton, closer to death than Malvolio by far. He announced quite heartily that his name was Winfield, and he wondered what we were doing on "his property" and what we had come to do there, and was it specifically having to do with him, or his "business." He had wild, bloodshot eyes, dry and sleep encrusted. He also revealed to us the reason he hadn't slept for at least four days.

I asked him if his girlfriend or wife had cheated on him or left him, if that was the reason for his shabby appearance. He shook his head no in a maniacal frenzy. I then asked him if perhaps he was an Antechinus and he had been on a fuck bender off in town for the last four days, though I suspect by his appearance he would have to pay for it and it didn't look like he had much money to his name. It appeared he had a touch of the love bug at any rate. The man shifted from one foot to the other, never taking his eyes off of us. He then backed up into the house, like he was trying to escape from ghosts or deadly animals, I couldn't tell which one. Malvolio whispered in my ear, that if he made any false moves that I should blow him away.

"What's a false move?" I shot back sheepishly, unsure of how to take on the role of tough guy. We were dressed tough enough I suppose, but now this called on me to actually be tough, or have the appearance of being tough, besides my clothes which were on all accounts, bad ass.

"You know, if he pulls out a gun, a pipe, a knife, a spackling trowel, you know, something that can do harm."

"I blow him away?"

"Shhh...not so loud, but yeah...shoot him right between the eyes."

"I don't think I can do that."

"What are you scared?"

"No, I've never fired this thing. What are the chances of pulling off some Hollywood number like that the first time I ever fire this thing?"

"Pretty slim."

Winfield appeared from inside the house with a grin on his face, kind of like a child who knows that he's done something wrong and is elated that he has not been caught yet. He stayed on the porch and shuffled back and forth.

"Thank God you're not Messicans," he said.

"Huh?"

"Oh, nothing."

"Do you actually live here?" Malvolio asked.

"Oh, yeah," Winfield said with the same wolfish grin.

"Do you own it? Or rent it?" Malvolio asked, and bolstered his interrogation of our poor strange gentleman.

Winfield didn't answer, but just grinned.

"What are you hiding here, man?"

"Are you two cops? You aren't Messicans, so you might be cops."

"Cops can't be Mexican?"

"Not 'round here they can't."

"We aren't the cops. Do cops drive cars like that?" I asked, pointing to the Judge.

Again he didn't say anything, just sat and fidgeted.

"What are you two doing out here? I don't get any visitors."

"We're looking for a place to do some shooting."

"Uhh...why?"

"We're just looking for a place without many people to do some shooting. Buddy's got a new piece and wants to learn how to use it."

"Hmmm," Winfield said, suddenly looking a bit on edge.

"Man, you look like you're really tense. What's wrong?"

"Nothin'."

"What are you doing out here? It must get awfully lonely."

"Ahh, nothin'. You're on my property; I figured I might as well see who it was. You're not Messicans. That makes me happy."

I saw Malvolio tense up when Winfield was being ambiguous about what he was doing. Malvolio wanted people to be open and honest with him, and he wanted to hide himself away behind a curtain, obscured from the light of day and any line of questioning. He wanted to be the questioner, the seeker of knowledge, without himself being open to question. You could say that Malvolio was the quintessential modern spooky man, wanting to know all without being known about, asking all questions and being so good at deflecting scrutiny that no questions were ever asked of him.

Malvolio, on his external appearance, seemed meaningless, and that was his great power, his forgetableness, and that is what made him dangerous. Maybe the subjects of his interviews were impressed by Malvolio's insistence at getting to know them, because he framed his questions and shot them a smile like he genuinely cared and was trying to get to know the person from the inside out, know them on the basis of their soul. He would have made a fine Human Resources specialist. Any questions asked of him were deflected with sayings such as, "Oh, I matter not," or "I'm a nobody," or the classic and effective, "but, Sir, I'd rather get to know you in your entirety than share my little old self with you." Malvolio wanted to build rapport to such an extent that he even mimicked the accents of his quarry.

This accomplished a double mission, for Malvolio could fully assess the danger or threat the individual represented to Leman Global Industries and eliminate them, and I do mean eliminate them with extreme prejudice; or he could see if they had any use to the Malvolio program, that is, in providing him with information, any sort of information really that Malvolio could put to good use. And by good use, I meant what was best for Malvolio. All his cares were for personal gain, and by personal gain, I mean what was best for my father's enterprises, because he ever was the faithful employee, steadfast and unwavering until the bitter end. Malvolio fundamentally believed in the Aristotelian maxim that all men by nature desire to know. That was in the *Nicomachean Ethics* maybe, or the *Ethics*, or maybe the *Metaphysics*. I don't remember the work, it's all fuzzy, but I remember the saying well. All men by nature desire to know.

Men that did not desire to know, but rather entertained themselves and spent their precious time in wiling away in the tripartite passions of feeding, fucking, and forgetting, were all pawns to be used or abused in Malvolio's framework. He questioned to decide use, and he questioned to decide if you could work for him or against him. I had never seen this fundamental calculus in action yet, but he was now putting our new buddy Winfield on and stretching him against the rack.

"You're doin' something out here," Malvolio said, in his best attempt to mimick the accent: the clean yet slightly hickified stammer that Winfield shot speech through his lips in clean staccato notes. Malvolio did his best to follow Winfield's method of banter but it pained my ears as condescension.

"Don't see why it concerns you none."

"Everything 'round here is my concern."

"Well, I'm really just trying' to mind my own business out here."

"So what's your business, then?"

Winfield hesitated again and again looked like he had something to hide.

"What's your business, Winfield?"

"What's your business, Jack?"

"The name's Robert. Robert Malvolio."

"Don't sound Messican to me. Is that Messican?"

"No. Grandparents were Eye-talian."

Winfield scrunched up his eyes and stared at both of us.

"What about him? Your partner. The weirdo?"

"Oh, we're not together. Not like that. I mean,..we're together, but not together."

"I'm Jackson. We're not together. We're not cops or anything like that. Not queers either. Not that there's anything wrong with that."

"What are you doin' out here dressed like cowboys? That's awfully queer to me."

"What do I look like?"

"I don't know. Some people tryin' to look tough."

Malvolio chuckled, looked at me, and smiled. I shook my head and then looked down towards the ground.

"I respect your compliment, Winfield. I'm neither a cop nor am I one of those things you just mentioned. I'm a man whose business it is to protect things and people from those who would do them harm."

"You're sellin' insurance then. I am not interested in a damn policy. I dun told you people once before. Who you with? State Farm? Mutual of Omaha? I love them damn animal shows. Bring those back. I might buy a policy then. Chimpanzees fightin' baboons fightin' cheetahs. Great times. Used to watch it with my granny."

Malvolio laughed again out of genuine delight. He tossed his head back and chuckled, not evilly this time. Instead, this laughter was unpremeditated and free of malice. I didn't think Malvolio capable of anything unpremeditated, but it seemed that Winfield's genuineness had rubbed off on him.

"We were looking for a place to shoot, so I could train this greenhorn how to handle himself, and you happened upon us."

"So you've got a gun then?"

"We covered that. My buddy has a .45 in his pants. We want to practice somewhere, and thought this place was abandoned."

"Oh, it was. 'Til I moved in."

"So, you're squatting out here?"

"I can't answer that 'til you tell me if you're out here to kill me or not. I figure you're not, 'cause you're not Messicans."

"What? Kill you?" Malvolio asked, startled.

"We aren't petty assassins! Look at us, man! We're built for great adventures, not base murder for hire."

"I've never even harmed a flea. I'm a writer, err...author, and Malvolio here, who's been interrogating you, and I do apologize for that, is my bodyguard and confidant. I'll tell you, if we were rogues, assassins, or thieves; you would have been dead or robbed and hog-tied already. They don't waste time with speechifying or getting to know their targets. They kill. But, I have to know. Why'd you ask that?"

Winfield shuffled back and forth on his feet and clunked his skinny hands in the grimy pockets of his jeans.

"I'm in big damn trouble. Big damn trouble," Winfield said, and it seemed like just making the confession relieved his tension a bit, and allowed him to stand up more upright, like a man.

"What kind of trouble?" Malvolio asked.

"The kind of trouble that don't go away."

"Who's after you? The IRS?"

"Some bad guys."

"Join the club. We're on the lam, too."

"What kind of bad guys? Maybe our bad guys and your bad guys are working together. Or maybe they hate each other. Maybe we can help each other."

A hint of hope appeared in Winfield's face. He smiled at us. His teeth were destroyed like the walls of some city turned battlefield, full of holes and char.

"Tell us your story," Malvolio said.

"I had been praying' for the angels to deliver me from my troubles. It looks like my prayers have been answered!"

"We're no angels, but we're not scum either," Malvolio said.

"We're definitely not assassins," I added.

"Well, whatever you are, if you listen to my story and you still want to help me, I need to get out of here. If I stay here, I'm a dead man for sure.

"What's your story then?"

And shifty Winfield told us a story of love lost, dwelling in the pits of despair, which has marked him until the very time that we showed up. It made us tear up a bit, Malvolio more than myself, as great crocodile tears streamed down his face, for Malvolio may talk like he's tough as nails, but I know that he's a big softie, having never done anything of real importance, just talked a lot. Talk, talk, talk, that modern panacea. Talk about all the ills of the world but do, do, do nothing but fill up the airwaves and idle time with useless, unproductive chatter. Like it on Facebook.

Talk is the blanket over the soul of humanity in a blizzard. It warms you ever so slightly and makes you forget about the storm raging around you, but it doesn't find your way home to the hearthfires burning, and if you stay too long in its comfort, you'll surely freeze in motion, unable to move, unable to grow, locked in a dead sprint towards no finish line. I prefer action. I prefer walking home to your hearthfires. Or carrying them with you.

Listening to Winfield's story, I realized he was a man caught in a trap laid there for him that he could not help but fall into. It was sprung from the moment of his birth, just as my life's adventure hatched from the egg I incubated in and so did Malvolio's for that matter. Winfield spoke to us from the front porch of that rickety old farmhouse. Winfield was a squatter in the midst of all this, a hider out in the prairie where he hoped his vigilant pursuers, the Messican Mafia as he called them, who he used to cook and smuggle methamphetamine for, did not find him.

"And what will happen to you if they find you?" I asked, ever inquisitive towards the ways of those dangerous, nefarious types.

"Well, they use me to make an example out of me to future methamphetamine cookers, and that if you fuck with them and steal what you're cookin', they won't take kindly to it. I suppose they could bury my dead body in a shallow grave and jus' remove me from the rolls of the ever living, do it quietly, but no these people got no tact and they don't like to be quiet about handling people who transgress against them. Most business people, they advertise in the local paper or billboards. I suppose they'll kill me in some heinous way and leave my body in a very public place to be found almost immediately. They'll leave a calling card. But they'll cut off my head and my hands, and I'll be John Doe Number 7 in the morgue, and all the cops will just shake their heads and use my headless, handless corpse photos in police training seminars about the dangers of this Messican Mafia and speak on how it's probably spreading to a town near you."

"Well, we've taken on bikers, cowboy rhinestone gangs, and now we're being pursued by an ancient and secret guild of assassins. Ancient because they are mostly geriatrics...the best kind of assassins because you don't suspect them, but it seems like you are dealing with the worst of the worst, Winfield. Tell me, how do you run afoul of this gaggle of heathens, this cabal of killers, these sombrero wearing gangsters?"

"They don't wear sombreros."

"Oh. I guess it was wrong of me to assume. What's their uniform then?"

"They don't wear uniforms. They're clean-cut businessmen. Worst type of murderers. They're polite. They'll be all nice to you and ask you your name and then stick a knife in your throat before you get to the second syllable of your family name."

"Ahhh, shit," Malvolio said, looking nervous for the first time that I ever saw him.

"How did you cross paths with this insane bunch of evil-doers?"

"It was a business proposition that worked out for a good while and made me very, very rich. Well, rich compared to the rest of the penny pinchers out there. My hands were on the product, and they just handled all the finances. You know, bankrolled my operation and found the lackeys to transport the stuff. My hands being on it, I assumed all the risk. You'd figure that I would also make most of the reward, but no. Do you even understand business principles?"

"Only enough to know I don't care for them," I said.

"Yes, our good friend here is as pure as the driven snow."

"You have to understand them, or they'll end up standing on top of you, crushing you underneath their iron heel."

"I don't care to. I'm an author. An artist."

"What have you written?" Winfield asked.

"Exactly," Malvolio said and shot me a told you so glance.

"You would think that because I was actually producing the product that I would end up with a lion's share of the loot, but I didn't. The people who put the money up to produce the product did. I was taking all the real risk...hell, I could have blown myself up numerous times, putting my neck out there, risking chemical burns the whole nine yards, raids by the police, dying by rival drug gangs. That doesn't count for anything. I didn't put up any of the money for the little adventure. The reality behind the situation was the damn money, the money that everyone puts first, not the dude actually stickin' his neck out there. It isn't the dude doing the work; it's the dude with the money. He's the one risking his neck. Baloney. I'm the one that understood organic chemistry well enough to make mountains of the shit. You think that these dumbass Messicans understood organic chemistry? Hell no. You think the moneymen understand anything besides how to take a pile of money and feed it into a machine to shit out a bigger pile? And they're called a success. They're the risk takers and the fucking beacons of hope for all of us. Fuckin' baloney!"

"You don't have the money. Yours will be a lonely endeavor," I said.

"Your writin' won't sell. You'll be buried with them," Winfield said.

"I don't buy that, not for a dollar. I'd much rather write a precious hidden gem buried under mountains of refuse and trash. I'd rather be that gem than the twenty million billion tons of chirt and volcanic rock, basalt bullshit that it's buried under. Churned out and forgotten, applauded for an instant. I'd rather labor and turn my soul into pure diamond, wrought under intensity and pressure, than ever just be something or someone plain and ordinary. I'd rather, I'd rather...," Malvolio said.

"Just write and be done with it. Crack whatever filter there is, whatever constraint ties your wrists and drowns you, the filter that says, 'oh, I'd better not say that, that might get me into trouble,' that opinion might not be paraded and lauded as a triumphant Caesar to the masses. It won't be a blockbuster, forgotten after a summer. I say the world turns on imagination and ideas and not on money as the stupid and dull-witted, petty peoples of the world think. You've either got them or you don't, and your pockets are full of it or you're living check to check doing the bidding of others, a plucky little slave, maybe much on your mind with fear in your heart, afraid to speak. I say you take that fear and you forge it into a weapon, you strike at the heart of the matter," I said.

"Uhh, which is?" Winfield asked.

'This is all illusion. Smoke and mirrors, fucko. A big dog and pony circus show. All of it, the whole lot of it. The whole vast, stupid, incessantly, blindly trudging forward, bumping into things blind, stuttering, wrecked blobs of humanity," I said.

"We were discussing our friend's predicament, not your predicament, Jackson, Winfield's predicament is your and my predicament. We're all in it together, but we're not. We're all here physically, but some exist on separate plateaus, separated by the ability to pay for separation. That's it. That's what distinguishes us from the animals. That's it. That's the only thing. Blunted, devastated, loved, imbued with special powers, whatever you are, you can pay for separation, or you can separate yourself. The whole time I was traipsing about the merry planet with your father, doing his bidding, I wondered, how can one man do so much? Then I realized in the course of my daily activities that your father never did anything that anyone told him to do. He was a ruler. An orderer, and people did everything for him. If he made up his mind to head in a certain direction, others acted as his eyes and ears, and he was driven there. Your father was just reduced to pure will. He willed it, people would do it, even if it was nonsensical or foolhardy or seemed an impossible gamble. People would do it because he paid them to do it. And much he did was an impossible gamble. Now what of our friend Winfield here, hiding out from dangerous men dressed in upscale business attire? Malvolio said."

"I'd rather die a man than be found in a hole and crushed like a spider," I said.

"We haven't even heard what got him in trouble," Malvolio said.

"We know what got him into trouble," I said looking at Winfield. "He got uppity. He stole from the wrong people. He justified it by saying to himself over and over and over again, 'they don't value me, they don't pay me well enough for my time or my services.' The same calculus runs through the minds of peons everywhere, afraid to take that final leap into the self. Something not valued is not worth investing in. He's not special. Sure, he knows organic chemistry. You can teach a monkey to cook up meth. He's only special to you, Malvolio, because he ran into us. We're men who can deliver him from his enemies. You're lucky you ran into us there, Winfield. You can't get yourself out of this hole, so you might as well allow us to take you away," I said.

"No offense," Winfield said, "but you two don't look like much."

"My granny told me a fable, or maybe it was a Marionite priest in St. Sharbel's parish in the Christian section of Beirut, Lebanon, when I was over there during the civil war, or maybe it was a missionary in Cote D'Ivoire, I don't remember, it all blends together when you've been as many places as I have. Anyway, the story's important, the source isn't. Here it goes. An old woman who complained all of her life died and was buried in a modest plot in her parish cemetery. Instead of being admitted immediately into Heaven, as was her expectation and what she had been anticipating her entire life, she found herself falling through empty space at terminal velocity, straight into the fiery pits of hell. The gaping maw. This woman, in her lifetime, had never asked for help from anyone. She was fiercely independent and also assumed that everyone should live the way she lived, therefore she never helped anyone nor did she ever ask if anyone needed help. She had the means, she lived a comfortable life, and in her prayers she never asked for help for herself or anyone else. She always assumed she was on the straight and narrow path to heaven. She was so alarmed to find herself falling faster and faster towards hell. She flapped her arms like a bird, assuming that it would allow her to fly out of hell. Faster and faster she fell. Finally, as she looked downward and felt the doom approaching, she screamed, "God! Help me! Oh God! Help me!" Time froze for an instant, in exact contraposition to the church fathers, eternity does exist in time, not outside it, and she felt an immediate relief that God had answered what she hoped would be her final prayer outside the pearly gates. Up high above her she made out a distantly shimmering, falling object. From a distance it looked like a great diamond attached to a rope, falling fast, towards her. It grew closer and closer, pure white in color. It looked like a golden ladder she could climb up to the pearly gates. It dropped and hung right before her eyes shimmering in the hellfire. It was an onion attached to a rope. 'An onion? An onion!' She screamed. The onion faded to nothingness, and she fell headfirst in the pit to burn for eternity," Malvolio said, and smiled.

Winfield looked at me with a puzzled look on his face, and I just shrugged my shoulders.

"Now, Winfield, do you really want to question who delivers you to the Promised Land? We might be a couple of onions, but we're all you have."

"But you don't even care about my story," Winfield said.

"Tell us in the car. Right after we get done with this target practice. Sounds like we'll be needing it, dealing with all the assorted scum we're facing."

"Pooling problems don't work," Winfield said.

"We aren't pooling problems. We're helping out a stranger in need. We're god-damned do-gooders. Surely we'll get our recompense."

"I don't got much money."

"We don't need your money."

"That's not a good reason to do anything."

"That's the way the world goes 'round."

"Just people trading time."

"What's your motive, man in black?"

"Jackson."

"What's your motivation?"

"Helping people."

"My best intentions have thus far been laid to waste and blown away with the prairie winds," Malvolio said.

"Oh fuck, so dramatic. Why don't you copy that internal drama on the page and share it with the world instead of acting it out."

"Then I can give it to you, and you can pretend you have talent all over again," Malvolio said, smiling.

"Why don't we just shoot this fucking gun like we said we were going to?" I asked.

"Give it here."

I yanked the hand cannon from the tight form-fitting waistband of my all black villain cowboy suit and handed it over to Malvolio. He dropped the magazine, a 7 shot wonder, and cleared the pistol.

"You see that? That's lesson one."

He loaded the magazine and cocked the round into the chamber.

"You see that? That's lesson two."

He showed me, with his thumb, where the safety was. He pushed it up, and then removed it and pointed the .45 masterblaster at the tree swing.

"Cover your ears."

He pulled the trigger. Nothing. No blast. No bang. Nothing.

"Must be a dud round...happens sometimes."

He cocked the round out of the chamber and slid a fresh round in.

"Cover your ears."

Winfield and I obeyed and covered our ears. Winfield shook, his knees knocking together. I don't know if it was from the cold or if he still believed, in a wee fragment of his brain, that we were Mexican Mafia assassins. Malvolio pulled the trigger. There was a click but no bang.

"God damnit, what's wrong with this thing?"

He dropped the magazine and pulled the handgun's slide to the rear.

"You got to be fucking kidding me!" he yelled right at me, right in my face.

"You realize that if we would have had to shoot our way out of anything, this gun wouldn't work?"

"Uhhh, no."

"It's got no fucking firing pin!"

"Uhh, that's a bad thing?"

"Duh! Of course it's a bad thing! It won't fire without a firing pin! Me pull trigger, me no go pop!"

Winfield laughed like a newborn baby laughs, in innocence, as if suddenly a huge weight had stopped crushing him. He dropped to one knee, as if he were praying, and then fell to the ground.

"What's so funny?" I asked.

"You two can't possibly be here to kill me! The Messicans only send professionals. Sometimes they send thirteen year old boys, but they're professionals. You two...ha! Ha!"

"What are we?"

"Idiots!"

"I'm no idiot," Malvolio said.

Winfield prostrated himself with laughter, digging himself into the front porch. Malvolio glared at me and shook the useless masterblaster in my face. How the hell was I supposed to know it didn't work? Having a gun makes you an immediate bad ass. I didn't know you were supposed to do training and actually learn how to use the damn thing. Guys in the movie just automatically know how to use them. It's easy.

"You idiot. We need to get some guns. Some guns that work. We've got bikers, an ancient assassins guild, and now the fucking Messican Mafia in hot pursuit of us. We've got to get strapped and fast! Where's the nearest gun shop?"

"This is Nebraska. There's one on every corner, I'm sure."

"We've been putting off our weapons purchases for far too long."

I pulled Malvolio aside while Winfield ran to his hideout to grab the remainder of his few precious belongings inside a raggedy bookbag.

"You're compounding our problems by bringing him along. What are you thinking? Don't we already have enough problems?"

"Hey! The assassin's guild after us is going after two people riding in a Judge, or maybe they don't know, hopefully they don't know what kind of car we're riding in...they could have strapped plastic explosives to it already and are just waiting to press a fucking button. At any rate, they've got an entire network of informants out there who will alert their agents whenever we enter a particular location, and they'll unleash hell on us. I know for a fact they've got two agents at each particular truck stop here in Nebraska and a full five at the truck stops in Iowa. We've got to be very, very careful. Travelling with Winfield will not only provide us with some much needed company, but face it, you're pretty boring, so he may also be able to give me some insight into how the Mexican Mafia is infiltrating the United States up to the highest levels. Security is a passion of mine, just like writing, or pretending to be a writer, is a passion of yours. Now that your father met his maker, I'll most likely be out of a job. Quiet now, our guest has arrived."

"I think you're making a mistake."

"Never mind what you think. I'm getting us there in one piece."

"I'll have to search that bookbag, Winfield," Malvolio said.

"Sure thing," Winfield said and tossed it over.

"These drugs?" Malvolio asked holding up several baggies of a white, crystalline powder.

"Yeah."

"We'll be keeping those. You can't have them. It already sucks badly enough with all the people looking for us. We don't need to add civilian law enforcement agencies as well, monsieur."

Winfield's fear leapt back into him suddenly, writing itself in terror shrieks upon his face, but he didn't make a sound.

"I can't live without that," Winfield said, shamed by the weight of his addiction. "I really can't. I mean, you take that stuff away from me, suddenly, without the benefit of tranquilizers, and I might die."

"More trouble than he's worth, Robert."

"Think about the mission we're on."

"My mission? I don't have a mission. You're the one on a mission. I'm going to my father's funeral and going to listen to a will being read at some attorney's office. Then I'm holing up somewhere to write. You're the only one amongst us who's got a mission or even thinks of life as being full of missions."

"I've a mission," Winfield said, sheepishly.

"What's that?" Malvolio asked.

"Well, just to survive another day," Winfield replied, and then curled up in the backseat against the window. He stared at us as if he were staring through us, looking into some great beyond.

"I guess that's everyone's mission," Malvolio said, and with that bade me to drive onward.

"To the nearest shop that traffics in firearms and ammunition!"

"Where's that at?"

"I don't know. Say, Winfield, where's the nearest shop that sells firearms and ammo to evil doers, no questions asked?"

No reply. Winfield was staring out the window, not looking at anything in particular, and looking like he was more worried about not having his crutch substance in a few hours. He looked rather like he wanted to bolt from the vehicle and ask Malvolio for his drugs back. As I drove off, I saw a sense of solace appear on his face, but it was not real peace. Soon he was sleeping like a newborn baby boy laying in the sunshine.

"Ahh, fuck," Malvolio said. "Just Google it."

"That would require me to turn my phone on."

"Shit. Ahh, it's worth the risk. Just don't answer any calls from your sister or that scumbag, Sheldon."

I turned on my iPhone 4S. The familiar and comforting Apple symbol, symbol of the religion of technocracy, the hope that technology would bring meaning to the masses and world, supplant Christianity, Islam, and those other ones as the highest meaning of humanity, and symbol of hope in technology glowed brightly on the screen and then faded to black before the desktop came up. My phone then searched desperately for a signal, any signal out there. I glared at the little display, and I saw my reflection in it. I looked tired and unkempt but pretty good in my cowboy hat, or I dare say, dashing, like I'd been riding the range for a good cause. I eagerly anticipated finding a signal so I could scout out the waypoint to our next destination.

"What the fuck? Are we in Amish country out here?"

"It's the goddamned land that time forgot," Malvolio said.

"Ahh, patience...."

SEARCHING...

"It's folly to wait. We could always ask someone at a gas station."

"Look how we're dressed, you fool. You think anyone in their right mind is going to tell two people who look like evildoers where to stock up on guns and ammo? We're going to be purchasing an arsenal there."

"Like what?"

"You let me, the weapons expert, peruse the wares, and you focus on the driving."

Winfield slept while we drove the main thoroughfare in what I thought was Dingledumpingtown, Nebraska. The sign for the joint whizzed by, and I didn't bother to figure out the name. Could have been Babesville or Corntown or some town named after some dude who did Godknowswhat way back when. This town, in the 1950s, before time froze for it, was probably a happening little place. Then all the cool people moved away, and all the people who stayed just got really, really old. Now, most of the businesses were boarded up with plywood.

"We can't purchase too much at any particular gun shop. That's the surest way to get the Federal monkeys called in on you. Especially considering how we're dressed up as evildoers. That's sure to get the authorities all over us."

We turned a corner, dusky on both sides with abandoned or poorly kept up homes, all really depressing and junky like I imagined a collection of serf's hovels would look like in a Tolstoy novel. We headed south; past some old high schools named after some guy who did Godknowswhat kind of interesting stuff in the 1890s when the now junky looking brick schools were built. There couldn't be any sort of higher learning going on in them. We did pass a lovely high school football stadium, however.

We headed farther South, past all this chintz and junk on a rural route, which really reminded me of a sclerotic vein on the leg of an aged old cow, and not the bovine version, but a really aged, obese American hausfrau. Then we passed a desolate area still on this road leading nowhere fast. There was only one, great beacon on the horizon. It was Wally World, the Mecca for people round these parts, a great vacuum of capital, a giant phagocytizing cancer cell on the rural heartland. And the people, who lived there, if they had a brain to wonder, could wonder why their town appeared so dingy and ill kept. Maybe it was just to outsiders who had actually been somewhere else in the world that viewed these small, uninformed communities of the hinterland with such derision. The only buildings actually kept up were the ginormous Church; named Godknowswhat poppy sounding positive name and wasn't called a Church but rather a Worship Center when we passed it, and the Wally World.

SEARCHING...

"Where's the best place to look for a gun store?" I asked Malvolio, starting to get a little mired into the swampy scenery, feeling as if I was sinking down inside of it like it was an ugly painting that repulsed me so much that I could not stop looking at it.

"This place looks dead like it's covered in mold and fungus."

"There aren't any children scurrying about. Where the hell are they all? It's like 2 o' clock on a Saturday. You'd think there would be children outside."

"It's far too dangerous, what with all the chimos and all," Winfield muttered from the backseat.

"Far too dangerous for children to be outside playing? What's wrong with you man? That's what children do. They play."

"They've got video games and movies and the like, but the outside is far too dangerous for them."

"That's preposterous."

"I do work for families all the time, trying to protect their little youngsters from the hazards of the world. It's a real growth industry."

"Whoever would pay you to protect their children is a fool."

"You're calling your father a fool then. When you care enough to send the very best," Malvolio said, smiling.

"But are never around yourself to make sure everything is up to snuff. How come I never saw you while I was growing up?"

"I always worked behind the scenes. I was never out in the open trying to bask in any glory. You know us security minded types. We always have to be secretive," Malvolio said.

SEARCHING...

"What kind of town is it that doesn't have adequate cell phone service? Hell, I thought AT&T was ubiquitous. I mean, it's fucking American Telephone and Telegraph Company, for chrissakes. They should be everywhere."

"I wouldn't know. I don't own a cell phone," Malvolio quipped.

We came upon another downtown. Maybe it was a dead sister city of the first, joined in the middle by a Wally World.

"Well, isn't this town fucking quaint," Malvolio said.

"What's its name? I didn't see any signs."

"It's Wally World Nebraska East."

"How about 'saw its heyday around the Great War and never changed' town?"

"Oh, come on, I saw a few hotels near the interstate on the way in here."

"We're looking for guns, monsieur, not rooms for the night."

A large cowboy sign loomed on the side of the road, to the front of our car. His arm pointed down a street, reaching out into the distance.

"You got to be fucking shitting me," Malvolio said.

"Yeah, that sign's pointing the way to Buffalo Bill's Ranch. The last goddamned resting place of Buffalo Bill Cody and his Wild West Show. Killed off by the cinema. There's sure to be a gun shop out that way before we get to the ranch."

"It's not his final resting place. He's buried on a mountain in Colorado."

"Winfield, how the hell do you know that?"

"My daddy took me there when I was just knee high to a frog. I remember. It's a desolate place. Well at least it was then."

"His ranch worth seeing? Do they have souvenir pop guns?"

"You two have to be the stupidest people living. They don't sell guns at the Buffalo Bill Ranch. They've got a damn museum and his house that he got by fleecing people who didn't know any better, city slickers and the like, who paid a damn quarter to see his show. You go down that way in search of guns, and you're going to be sorely mistaken about what you find. Down that way is a bunch of blue hairs on a quest for escapin' boredom, heading to where the cotton pickin' sun shines at a greater angle and the snow doesn't fall. Your best bet's to avoid that place altogether. Tourist fuckin' trap. Snowbird trap. If you've got kids, by all means, go there, but if you don't, stay away. They damn sure don't have any guns for sale there. I suppose if you were desperate you could try and steal the display museum pieces, but those would probably just blow up in your hands if you tried to fire them and get you locked away in prison with a cellmate with a coke can sized cock. A long one at that."

"Where do we go then, smarty-pants?"

"Wally World's your best bet."

"We need some serious military grade hardware, man. We're up against professionals here. We aren't going rabbit hunting with grandpa!"

SEARCHING...

"Fucking preposterous, this signal! Remind me to write AT&T and complain."

"Wally World is out. We need hardware. We'll get ammo there, but we need the masterblasters to shoot the ammo first!"

"We got to get strapped," I repeated blandly.

"Time is of the essence, Winfield," Malvolio said, bluntly. "You're either with us or against us, man, so what's it going to be then?"

"I'm trying' to think up a place around here. Why don't you ask for directions to a place? No one is going to think twice about two gentlemen such as yourselves, drivin' the car you're drivin', wearin' the clothes you're wearin', askin' where to purchase firearms. If y'all were black or Messican, maybe. Me, they'd throw me in jail in a second because I look, well, poor and desperate enough to commit some sort of crime in the town. You two look, well, uh...."

"Malevolent, like evil-doers, like we're here to take the town and its minions by force, here to enact some evil plot," Malvolio said, fiendishly grinning, or rather, doing his best to grin fiendishly.

"Nah, you two look like two rich, bored guys. Well, at least you do, Mr. Jackson. Robert here, I can't really say what he looks like, much."

"Dashing, charming, aren't those the adjectives you would use to describe me?"

"I was thinking creepy and old, but trying to act young."

"That's a kick in the balls," Malvolio said, slumping down further in the passenger seat.

"Well I am sort of wanted around here," Winfield said.

"What do you mean 'wanted'?"

"The police want to haul me in for questioning regarding something that happened one of the nights I was last through here," Winfield said.

"Jesus Christ, what happened?"

"I knocked over a church."

"You robbed a church?"

"I stole the offering plate. I figured I needed it more than they did, bunch of fat asses. I was having a hard time finding something to eat."

"You could have asked them for something."

"Ha! Have you seen the miserable state of Christian charity these days? That's a quicker way to wind up in jail than stealing the collection plate. And you'd be in there on a vagrancy charge. At least by stealin', you have some money in your pocket, some opportunity to do better, to pull yourself up by your bootstraps. Nah, a man like me goes to a church and starts askin' for a bite to eat, I'd probably just end up with a job or a job offer or an offer to join their church and get saved. I'll save myself. No thanks."

"You're quite a cynic."

"Don't think so. That comes from years of experience in dealing with these SUV drivin', big screen watchin', science denyin' fat people. I'll tell you somethin', Jack, they don't have a religion but foodn'stuff. They only give a fuck about their fellow man if they can squeeze a buck or a cheap day's labor out of him."

"How'd you do it?"

"Oh, I just sat in church for a couple of days. A couple of consecutive Sundays. I blended in by getting' a nice, fancy suit at the Goodwill in town. Ate out of dumpsters and suffered the rest of the week. Come Sunday, I stationed myself to be near the door, where I had seen the collection plate, all loaded down with cash and checks, would come by. I figured I'd grab all the cash and make for the door. I only had to get by a wrinkly old deacon. Well, that old bastard proved to be as strong as a bull. I grabbed the cash and went to run, and he clocked me a good one right in the jaw that had me seein' stars. How was I to know the old bastard was the 1956 Golden Gloves Champion of the state of Nebraska? Then most of the men in the church started stompin' the shit out of me in a most Christian manner, in that they had dress shoes on and not steel toed workers shoes, Thank God, some of the women even jumped in on my beatdown, but Thank God they didn't have high heels on. Thank God there was an actual lawman in the church who informed the preacher man that they could go to jail for mob action and second degree murder or possibly get it dropped to manslaughter and might as well be in violation of some laws against lynchin' if I met my maker that day. They stopped, Thank God, and the law man escorted me first to the hospital, and then to the jail, the whole time telling me that he knew some prisoners who would make sure that I didn't live another day if I told about the congregants nearly beatin' the life out of me. You know, I agreed to that, seeing that I didn't have much of a choice, and I was a stranger there."

"Did you do jail time?"

"Nah, I escaped from that stupid little jail they have in this town. The holding pen they put me in has a window to a courtyard. Now I may look like a skinny bastard not capable of even lifting a finger, let alone helping myself through the narrowest of spaces, but that's just what I did. I squeezed out into the courtyard and sealed the drain pipe, got on the roof, jumped down the other side, making sure I feel like a fucking acrobat, and then walked away."

"So now we're not only eluding bikers, assassins, and Messican mafiosos, we're also eluding the cops."

"Nah, I doubt it. I gave them a fake name in the holding cell. They didn't have the technology back then to find out who I really was."

"Who are you?"

"Wouldn't you both like to know?"

"It's not the time to get smart, Winfield, if that is even your real name. We're all in this together. I offered to give a ride because I have some underlying faith in humanity, even though I am a security professional, I, err, always like to see the good in people. My friend here is a hapless, hopeless romantic, so much so that he penned a romance novel adored by women the world over. It sold a hundred fucking million copies worldwide. We're on the way to bid his dear, departed father and my former, humble employer adieu in a private ceremony in Peoria, Illinois. We can take you as far as Peoria, but after that you're on your own. Right now, in order for me to trust you, we need to do some full disclosure time. You have to tell me all about you. We're going to be riding together after all. Now I'm going to shut up, and you, Mr. Winfield, you start talking."

"The same is required of you, Malvolio, after Winfield is done, of course."

The corners of Malvolio's mouth turned hideously straight and pursed as if he had just gotten a bite of something foul. Perhaps this look on his face could be called his "eat shit" look or "I have just eaten shit" look. His face gave him away, I had trapped him, and he knew it.

Winfield smiled, and said, "Sure, I'll dish my dirt...if the gentleman here does as well."

"You two shake on it, then start sewing it up," I said.

"Who's first?" Malvolio reluctantly asked in agreement.

"I'll go first," Winfield declared.

"This should be a treat," Malvolio uttered, trying to act bored, now that his pet project had just defecated in his face.

"Well, where do I begin?"

"From the beginning. Tell us all your sordid tales of woe, or whatever happened to you to get you from the time you squirted onto the planet from your mother's besotted womb until now. Right this instant," Malvolio said with venom dripping from his lips, now quite butt hurt about the possibility of having to share his own story.

Winfield, either too pure of soul or possibly not knowing the meaning of Malvolio's words, just looked at the heaving madman askance and said, "I really don't know where to begin."

"Jesus, man! Begin at your beginning!"

"What's his problem?" Winfield asked.

"He likes stories," I said, trying to reassure Winfield that he had not decided to take the worst free ride of his life. "Me, I'm a collector of stories. I'm a writer, so stories are my bread and butter."

"Maybe I could better tell my story if I knew what you wanted to know."

"Don't care about what we want to know. Just tell your story, and make it true. No hiding, no dissembling, no equivocation. Just the facts, ole Winnie, just the facts. We won't judge. I've seen and done things that will make your Mexican Mafia pursuers blush with shame."

"Unsubstantiated!" I yelled at Malvolio.

"Who's on trial here? I'll get to all my deeds and misdeeds soon enough. Winfield volunteered to go first. So he's on the spot now. If you want some help, a little crystal seed for the supersolution of your mind, something to frame your life experiences around, tell me first, who your father is."

Winfield looked Malvolio dead in the eyes and said, "I don't know."

"Ahhh!!!! A fellow bastard! A brother scheming Edmund! Welcome to the club, my dear brother bastard in this world! You're part of a special crew then. The school of harder and hardest knocks. There's a day for mothers and a day for fathers, everyday is a day for legitimate children, but there's no day for bastards set aside to honor them, even though that's how the majority of children come to be, either bastards like us or cuckolds: the products of a stupid, strong lust in the face of societal, eh, boring rationality and convention. So fuck it!"

"You seem to feel pretty strongly about it."

"Shut it, boy who had a father," Malvolio said.

"You had a father, obviously, you're here aren't you."

"He was around for a few minutes I suppose. I never asked my mother about his performance. He wasn't around like your daddy dearest who you didn't appreciate."

"He wasn't around to appreciate me."

"Oh no!" Malvolio said mockingly, "You mean he didn't provide you with the absolute best of everything? He wasn't around because he was traipsing around the world, dispersing capital in hopes of a higher return in the future. And you know he was damn good at it. I'm guessing that Winfield here had it rough, like I did, and that made him the man he is today."

"Yeah, a criminal," Winfield said, and smiled.

"We're kindred spirits, my man, but I'm on the opposite side of the spectrum. However, like I told young Mas...young Jackson here, in order to be able to catch a thief, you have to be a thief."

"Okay. Shut up. Let Winfield tell his story."

Malvolio glared at me and did not say a word. He looked, rather, like he was now actively engaged in plotting to kill me, rather than have me even tell him what to do again.

"Where to begin, where to begin," Winfield muttered to himself.

I glanced at my iPhone 4S.

.....AT&T

"I grew up in Wichita, Kansas. Well, at least that's where the tides carried my sixteen-year-old pregnant mother. Like I said earlier, who knows who my sperm donor of a father was; he's probably alive somewhere, but hopefully he's dead, though not dead from any horrible genetic diseases, but maybe dead from a bar brawl or gunshot wound. Who knows? Mama died young after a life of whorin' and fuckin' and fuckin' and whorin'. Only some of the time she didn't get paid. She had a string of men who tried their best to show me the ways of the world. It seems like right when I started to like one enough to start callin' him dad, and the guy ever broached the subject with my mother, he'd be out the door, his bags packed, and callin' her a crazy ass bitch who didn't deserve a boy as good as me. Some of them even asked if they could come and see me, but she flat out refused. By the end of the week, she'd have another dead beat living with us and a few more cookin' on the side. I'd say she was a master chef, able to balance and manipulate ten different men, usually with the dopiest of all staying with us because he was the last to wise up to her schemes. What a brilliant woman, or maybe she was just fulfillin' her lust. Who knows? I happen to think that women know exactly what they are doin', and it's us men who are the less wise, the ones controlled by our cock 'n balls, runnin' about every which way our boners guide us. Men want it easy, women want a challenge. You know what I say? Focus on whatever you're doing and pay the babes no heed. They'll come flockin' then like ants to honey. Show them you're in need of improvement, and you'll have all the women you can handle. Be successful, and she'll think she can make you all the more successful. She'll do whatever it takes to make sure you keep pursuin' her. That's what my dear old mom did, until one day she just disappeared."

"What? Just vanished?"

"Yep, just up and left without packing anything or saying goodbye."

"I hate to say it, Winfield, but it sounds like your mom ran afoul of some people who didn't take kindly to a woman jerking them around. Someone really probably had a fatal attraction to her."

"That's what I've always feared. So, that's the next part of my story. How I grew up in an orphanage."

"Well, goddamn, Oliver Twist!"

"Did you get in many fights?" I asked, my only experience of orphanages being from movies where the children would always gang up on the new, good kid and beat the hell out of him so that his face looked like a half ripened pomegranate before he was allowed to join their ranks, eventually taking over the gang of sickfucks, achieving a level of sophistication and pickpocketing the richest man in town who falls in love with the little rapscallion scamp and learns the value of selflessness and eventually adopts the boy and makes him sole heir to his airplane parts manufacturing fortune. Then the boy gives all his old compatriots and tormentors jobs at just above minimum wage and earns money hand over fist from their labor. I know I saw it once. It must have been a Hallmark Special.

"Sure, there were fights. Me, I tried to avoid them."

I glanced at my phone again.

....AT&T

Totally useless. We'd have to wait until we reached Lincoln, Nebraska before we could even think of getting a signal strong enough to use GMAIL Maps.

"We're going to have to drive onwards to Lincoln, and hit up a gun shop there."

"Whatever you say, driver. I'm just the navigator."

"You're no Prince Henry. You're a piss poor navigator who doesn't pay attention to much, just your own idle thoughts."

"Just drive. I'll get us there."

"You don't even have a map."

"I know the way to Lincoln."

"Do tell, but finish your story on the way."

Winfield got us back on the I-80 after navigating through a circuitous maze of off, country ass roads where we narrowly avoided the death by collision with farming implement when I spaced out on the fallow rows of corn and Malvolio had to yank the Judge off onto the shoulder to avoid the threshing arm of a great Green John Deere out for a joy ride or doing whatever farmers do in the wintertime besides hunkering down. Why I had never really even seen a piece of farming equipment so huge to know that running into it would produce a catastrophic result. Why, I bet you if you asked two hundred city dwelling scum suckers that a full 195 of them could not even describe how their food was grown. The other five probably moved to the city from the farms for what they thought were better opportunities and more culture besides what they could ascertain from satellite television. The whole time I drove the little avenues through the fallow cornfields, I thought GOOD THING I DON'T LIVE HERE.

I cannot even imagine myself living an agrarian existence. Getting up at the butt crack of dawn to go and milk the cows, the sights, the sounds, and the smell of it all. I suppose if we got out of the car and talked to some of the good people of this place, this highway through the fat, beefy midsection of America, this nearly nonstop string of truck stops and hokey little gift shops and roadside attractions that take you miles off the beaten path to Bum Fuck Elsewhere. How I long for a city, and a city where I can immerse myself into the crowd, feel the comfort of the shopping mall, where I know the price of everything, what everything is worth, and can buy anything I want, and I am less dependent on talking to another living soul for help, information, or even to say hello.

Let's face it, you're much better off being rich and completely alone, than being broke and surrounded by other broke as a joke people. I've tried to think that I'm some great humanitarian, when really it comes down to it; I'd much rather just hide from people as much as talk to them or help them. The majority of them out there are time vampires. I'd happily give the cowboy suit off my back and the boots off my feet to a person in need. But you want me to spend time with you? You better be some-thing really, really special. Maybe that's why I spent the last ten years with a figment of my own imagination. I preferred it to the real people who always let me down and never seemed to live up to my already much too high expectations of them. Don't call me a misanthrope. I don't hate people or human beings for that matter.

"Oh my god. Do you notice that everyone here is equally girthy?"

"You mean fat? Bordering on obese?"

"Yeah."

"The only really skinny ones are us tweakers," Winfield said.

We turned onto the entrance ramp onto the I-80 after we first passed one of the innumerable truck stops, which glittered to the planes that flew over this flyover territory like diamonds, encrusted onto the surface of the Earth. These places are like great diamonds hidden away in a black bag, invisible to all but those who know what they are looking for. I don't take these wonders for granted. Every time I walk into one of these treasures, I immediately feel weak in the knees.

I think about the struggle upwards from the depths of wild natives, to be able to actually put up a truck stop in the middle of nowhere, supply it, and keep all the patrons safe on their journeys throughout the land. They remind me of the inns of old but without the soul and much, much more security.

Perhaps this is what attracts me so much about these little oases. No matter which one I go into, everything, granted regional differences, will be the same. The same is not true of people, and though you can take the time to talk to them, you never really know when someone is struggling to be different, to take a departure from the herd. I want my products uniform. I don't want my people uniform. But isn't that what people are becoming? Mere uniform products? Where is the originality? Doesn't that start with me? With you?

I don't know the pain of never having a thought that didn't escape the level of the average and everyday patterns of thought, of worrying about the future, worry about the mortgage, worry about which school my spawn will attend so they can hopefully be just as well off and continue the chain into oblivion. I guess I can't talk. I've none of these concerns to worry about, so I've more concerns of a religious or literary nature.

For me, literature is my religion; it is my way of life. Just because I don't write now doesn't mean I'm not planning something stupendous. I just need the right spark to set fires, blazing deep from all the potential energy, all the gasoline and coal stored deep down within my black soul. Other people might be contented to light coal pitch ablaze, but I've refined my inner essence to the point of no return. I've raged against myself and turned my innards into rocket fuel. There's going to be no one who can stop me.

All I need is a simple spark. I figure a woman will supply that spark. It always is. Some muse will come along and deliver me from my block. She'll catapult my soul outside of myself to new heights.

I left my train of thought just long enough to catch some of our buddy Winfield's story. It wasn't exactly, all things being relative, a tale of woe from which there was no escape visible for Winfield, but one from which Malvolio and I pretty handily found a solution.

"So during my time at the orphanage for troubled youth, I learned how to steal. We weren't given much outside of our three hots and a cot, so if you wanted any-thing in addition, you had to sneak out and take it. I escaped no less than fifty times in a two-year period. I remember bein' really excited the first time I ever left the orphanage. You know, the freedom. I walked around the little town, until I got a little hungry. Then I realized I didn't have any money. I walked into a small grocery store, they were still small at the time, and I pinched a package of bologna. I remember it felt cold on my cock n' balls, but since then I've had tons of food down my pants. In fact, they've been more chilled than allowed to dangle during those two long years. I remember how terrified I was when the police came and picked me up and took me back to the orphanage."

"Uh huh," Malvolio said.

"The headmaster, he always told us that the cops would take us to prison if they caught us, so that's where I expected to go, so I remember sitting in the car and crying, and the officer saying he was going to take me home and my father would give me something to cry about, those being very strong words during that time for some juvenile delinquents, and I started crying more and more and the police offi-cer thought his scare tactic had worked, but it came back on the dispatch that I was an escapee from the old Hadley Home, and the police officer apologized to me for assuming that I had parents to scold me and even went so far as to say that he made an ass of you and me by assuming."

"Hmm..." Malvolio added, looking out the window, as if searching for something to stare at.

"Well, that was the most cordial visit that police officer and I ever had, because after that he called me a worthless thief and would bend and twist my arms behind my back when he cuffed me after making me take everything I stole out of my pants. Still, he didn't search me that well because I still managed to get a few comic books through by rollin' them around my thin legs in my socks like they were soccer shin guards, but I sweated on them and that made some of the words run together so much that Bobby Frigus couldn't read his Silver Surfer and that caused him to beat me up within an inch of my life. They sent Bobby Frigus away for that. They sent me to the hospital."

"Oh that sucks," Malvolio added.

"Come four or five in the morning, every weekend, I'd be gone up over the wall or underneath it depending on if I prepared that week or not. There were no rats. All the people that could have qualified were on my list, and I always tried to make sure their needs were taken care of before my own...like when Timmy Bartholomew asked me to get him a magazine with big tits in it. I had to walk miles for that one, as all the businesses in town now knew me by face and name and had their rotary phones ready to dial the police, they knowing me to be an escaped child convict. I struck a deal with a few of the kids from the town who took pity on me and let me stay in their basement for a few days in exchange for a Penthouse Magazine. A Hustler could get me a week. Tits were like gold. Muff like Platinum. Cock Going into Pussy...that was diamond. I could trade it for anything. The bigger the titties I filched, the more hardcore the magazine, the more favors I garnered. You know what? I ended up staying in one kid's cabin by the lake for an entire week, fishin' and earnin' my daily bread with my skill and patience. I guess that's what I had been doing all along. Out of all the stuff I stole, I never really stole anything for myself. I always thought about it, but I guess I was so eager to please everyone else that I never even bothered. That's what made ripping off these Messicans all the nicer. That's the first and last time I ever stole for myself. It felt damn good."

"Damn foolish if you ask me," Malvolio said.

"If you have to steal you might as well steal for yourself," I said.

"Spoken words of wisdom by our living saint, Jackson Leman," Malvolio said.

"Jackson Leman?" Winfield asked with more than a pinch of indignation in his voice.

"Yeah, our buddy here is a scion of American Industry. He's never had to beg, borrow, or steal a day in his life. You're the Anti-Jackson. He's the anti-Winfield."

"Well, some people got it good. Some people are lucky to be birthed from the loins of royalty."

"Lucky? How so?"

"You never have to worry about anything?"

"Well, nothing real."

"Malvolio here protected me from kidnapping plots as a child," I said.

"You had the ability to hire him to do just that. We all had to worry about whether the good state of Kansas would feed us. Some of the kids in the orphanage got passed around from pederast to pederast foster parents. Fucking horrible. No I don't think you've ever had much to worry about."

I couldn't say anything to this man. I was too busy going through the furies in mind directed at Malvolio. Malvolio saw fit to bring up my wealth in front of this tweaker who was more likely to rob me, stab me in the guts and leave me for dead, than want to be my friend. Maybe he would ask me for the money to pay back the Mexican drug cartel he stole from. Why should I care about this guy, this stranger? Because our resident paranoid security specialist thinks we should have a third party to avoid detection by all of our pursuers, none of whom I have really seen as of late? The old couple in the mall...I don't know who they were...they could have been two of Malvolio's bungling cronies who refused to retire that he sent to scare me into hanging on to his every word. Just what the hell was he up to?

"Malvolio, what do you plan on doing in the future, now that you're no longer in my father's employ?"

I glanced at my phone after uttering the words and we passed a large freeway sign that stated that Lincoln, Nebraska, was only 80 miles away. The phone had two bars, but no 3G. Suddenly, I wanted to talk to someone else, someone like my sister, and get to the bottom of what was actually happening. I just didn't feel like I could trust just anyone, hell not even myself. After all, I had ridden across the country with two people who were almost fully figments of my imagination: hallucinations of parts of my psyche projected onto the world to fit my deepest desires and make a world that had grown fully out of my control, more controllable, more able to conform and comport itself to my wants.

Much of me wants to return to that car ride with Marcus Hanely, to let this shot of whatever experimental medicine and these fucking hoo haa pills the doctor put me on wear off, and then maybe they'll all come back. Maybe I should just start writing again and ditch these two suckers with their fly ride and head out on the road by myself! Why did I always need a guardian? Malvolio's answer snapped me back into whatever reality existed between the three of us.

"Well, since you asked, I was hoping to be brought in to be your, or possibly your brother-in-law's special advisor, depending on what the will says, of course."

"You mean you'll go with whoever gets the lion's share of the loot?"

"No, I didn't say that. Whoever is in a position to have an advisor, that's salaried, you know, needs one for the course of their duties; I'll make myself available to them. I like to stay busy. You know, work all the time."

"That's the way to be," Winfield said. "One of my foster moms used to tell me that an idle mind is the devil's workshop."

"Ask our writer friend here," Malvolio said with a sneer.

"My mind isn't idle. I'm always thinking."

"Scheming is a form of thought, believe me, I know," Malvolio said.

"No one is scheming. I'm the anti-schemer. I don't care. If you don't care you can't fall into traps laid by people who care. Plus, we're not talking about me, we're talking about you."

"I pledged to your father to protect you from the toils and snares of this big, bad world. However, if you're just going to sit around and write all day, you know, writing your shitty romance novels and not trying to make some decent enemies, not try to get fatwas declared against you, you know try and be some literary esthete, I don't think there will be many people in terrorist organizations out to get you. I'm more in the line of business of security protection and counter corporate espionage and stuff like that. Fairly drudgy, boring stuff. Stuff your father had a use for, but stuff you'll probably never have a use for as an author, writer, or time waster or whatever it is you intend to become."

"I'm already the latter, sitting here with you."

"What would you rather be doing than chugging down this non-snaking highway in the opposite direction from fun in the sun?"

"That's where I'd rather be goin', but I'm a man without a home, and the chances of the Messicans finding me out west is much, much greater."

"No one asked you, Winfield. You don't have a pot to piss in, so you don't count," Malvolio said.

Winfield looked at me with a look that implored me to lose Malvolio at the next stop we made, and I can't say that I didn't agree with our tweaker buddy. Malvolio was, at best, a strange bird and was getting stranger with each opening of his mouth. His time spent in the trenches at the side of my father in global pursuits had forged him into a hardened, paranoid madman who lived in a world of fences and walls, locks, keys, ciphers to be made and broken, packaged security practices, weaponry, rounds of ammunition, spies, cutthroats, knaves, butlers, turncoats, and lady assassins. It was enough to make anyone crazy, and we had not even heard enough of Malvolio's story yet to give him the benefit of the doubt. Maybe that's why he insisted on Winfield traveling with us; to get out of his own debt to me. Malvolio owed me a story. His story.

"Tell us your story, Malvolio. You made Winfield tell us his, and you wouldn't even let him finish, so that he could ride with us. Therefore, *mutatis mutandis*, it's only fair that you tell us your story. Fair is fair."

"Well, I really wasn't done with mine," Winfield said, sheepishly.

"Oh, no one really cares about your story, Winfield. That was just for show to welcome you to this little ship of fools we've got speeding eastward."

"You know how to make a feller feel welcome."

"Not my intent."

"Speak, Malvolio, tell us how you came to be."

"You've got to follow me, Jackson. It shall be our gentleman's agreement. I want to hear every deep dark secret you've got."

"And I want to hear yours, dear Robert Malvolio."

"Promise?"

"I promise that you won't like what you hear, Jackson."

"I want to hear it. Straight from the devil himself."

Malvolio laughed. It started from his belly and spread to his throat like a crow cackling over the corpses of dead youth.

We were now approximately sixty miles from Lincoln. My Phone hit 3G coverage, and started vibrating wildly. Text messages and voicemails poured in. They were from my sister. She had called about fifteen times, and my voicemail box had ten messages in it.

Malvolio glanced at me from the passenger's seat.

"Who called you?" he asked quite evilly, like the Grand Inquisitor himself.

"Oh, no one."

He grabbed my arm. "Jackson, who called you?"

"Let go."

"No. Tell me who called you."

I yanked my arm free.

"My sister, Hannah."

"You can't call her back."

"She said she's going to put in a missing person's report."

"Let her. You absolutely cannot let her know where we are."

"Because she'll dispatch assassins to come and get me, not police?"

"You've got it."

"You two are insane," Winfield said.

"You don't know anything, Winfield. Shut it."

"I know madmen when I see them. You talk and twist around each other like a great ball of knotted mess. You're both mad. So, just drop me off in Lincoln, Nebraska, and I'll find my own way further east."

"Look what you've gone and done now, Jackson."

"You did it."

And then we saw it. Like a great goddamned slice of heaven on Earth. It was as if the heavens opened themselves and a host of angels poured forth to illuminate our path to the Promised Land. It was a single huge, yellow sign with red lettering. Not for a revivalist church in the prairie. No, that would have been perfect for a bygone era when people actually trusted one another and enjoyed meeting strangers. Now we were advertising the new age of not knowing your neighbor and not welcoming people into your home, rather each small home was a Fort Knox unto itself, the new age of untrust, advertised with an entire convention center full of guns and ammunition. GUN HEAVEN! A WONDERLAND OF GUNS FOR THE ENTIRE FAMILY! Thousands of retailers, Cash and Credit Card Welcome!

"Jackpot!" Malvolio screamed.

"Oh, it's today!"

"Just our luck!"

"We can catch the tail end of it today and stay for tomorrow."

"Stay where?"

"I'm sure there are some dingy hotels in Lincoln, Nebraska."

"There might be some nice swanky place that we would blend right into, some place Messicans won't be liable to stay."

"You in or out, Winfield?"

"Ehh...."

"Come on, man. In or out?"

"Yeah. In or out?"

"I'm out."

"You sure? Gun show, tons of guns, handguns, rifles, shotguns, you really want to go out on your own?"

"You two are fucking nuts."

"Says the meth head," Malvolio said.

"I may be a meth addict, but at least I'm trying to do something with myself. You're a fucking hack writer, son of a rich man who doesn't know his ass from a hole in the ground, and you're a psychotic insurance salesman, from what I've been able to determine. I'll take my chances in Lincoln, Nebraska, on my own. At least it'll keep me out of the slammer, which is where you're both headed."

"You need a fix, don't you?"

"What are you talking about?"

"It's not us. It's you. You need a fucking fix. If we give you your ice back, will you stay with us? You're more valuable to us being with us than out roaming on your own."

"Yeah, we'll give it back to you."

There was a silence in the car while we crossed the threshold from the rural nothingness to the outskirts of Lincoln, Nebraska.

Now Lincoln, Nebraska, is one of those gems of the plains where people band together from the snowdrifts in the winter, their houses each forming a small bit of snow break from the blowing drifts, and the snow piles aligned concentrically in the breaks of the houses. Children actually played in their front yards, some building oddly shaped snowmen. There were Lincoln, Nebraska, University of Nebraska Cornhuskers gear, flags flapping the breeze, red and white and yellow, people strolling down the streets in bright red parkas like an ancient lost tribe or migration following a herd.

Most of the people were overweight, not obese as of yet, but a few Christmas parties might send them over the edge, but they were desperately starting that long, drawn out last gasp toward a total decline and bedriddeness. Perhaps not. Perhaps they would take a look in the mirror and tell themselves that they had to do something about their ever expanding waistline, to take some pills, or get their stomach stapled, bariatric surgery or whatever it was called, instead of taking that long walk through pain, working out, through suffering, towards redemption and a slim, sexy body.

You know, I think the main reason that Americans today are so fat is not the amount of food laying around for them to scarf up; that's only a piece of the puzzle. It's really them being afraid to death of any sort of suffering or any sort of setback. It's the feeling that if you do not do something perfectly the first time you do it that it isn't worth doing at all. That if you aren't absolutely brilliant, a master craftsman, a fucking celebrity that you aren't worth much of anything. You know, that's the attitude I had when I wrote my one and only novel *Asymmetric Hearts*. That's the attitude I went into it with. You've got to be the best, immediately. There's no working towards the long off distant goal, because that would involve some struggle.

Did you really believe that the technological level we've reached would actually remove struggle out of the equation? Self imposed struggle? Struggle was to be medicated away with well dosed, easy to manage medication. I was beginning to think... no, I had thought for a very, very long time...that the first company to discover and market the neurotransmitter for joy, to mass produce it, and to sell it, here a feeling easily obtainable, normally only felt by the long sufferers or people who have given birth, achieved a major life's goal, but now obtainable without struggle...this company would soon become the most valuable on the planet. More valuable than Apple Computers. Technological products must be perfect right out of the gate or they fail, die, and are buried. Literary works can stumble at first and die during their age, only to run anew for future crowds.

I looked at the people shambling their way to the stadium, and I realized it was Saturday, it was game day, and they were going to park themselves elbow to tit for a cheering section for a bit of collective experience, a burst of excitement. Something to make them cheer, something to make them cry. To draw in deep breath and hope for a positive outcome, but it was something they played absolutely no part in. They were passive. An Earthworm burrowing through a dung heap was taking a more active role in its self-development through nutrition than these fans would be taking in the course of the football game. They would be a part of the roar. If they weren't there, someone with functional lungs could take their place. So as I watched them walk with seat cushions in hand for their already well-cushioned bottoms, I wondered if a civilization that ran from any sort of suffering and chose only comfort as the highest end of this civilization could hope to keep on going onward and upward. Because that's what you had to do. It was either that or stagnation and death.

I wondered if this sort of yearning could be remedied or if I was witnessing a tailspin of decline and the slow and steady death of an entire culture. I glanced over at Malvolio and Winfield. Something had lulled them off into sleep. Maybe it was the bland uniformity of the plains, the uniformity of the restaurant chains, the people walking to the game, all full of smiles and hee-haws with dreams in their hearts. Knowing that something was at stake, but at the end of the day they would be safe, able to walk to their cars and drive home, and the most that would happen was someone got arrested for DUI or someone got in a traffic accident and the airbags and antilock brakes didn't save them. It was obviously their time to go.

Their warriors were not trying to lift or break a long drawn out, starvation-inducing siege; they were playing pigskin. The crowd witnessed suffering by proxy. Just as any effort of the fat people to lose weight, whether by pill or by surgery was done without the reinforcement of the pain that said, I don't want to go through with that again. I looked at Malvolio and Winfield sleeping peacefully. I glanced out over the oceans of red and yellow fans. I was feeling sleepy too.

You know, driving through the burgh of Lincoln, Nebraska, I wondered where the soul of these United States was. I witnessed the decline almost creeping, like the Charlie grass that grows to take over the yard of Kentucky bluegrass like a cancer, and the whole time it said, "Everything's okay. Just business as usual." I saw beautiful old buildings that housed corporate doughnut shops, corporate coffee houses, all alike on the inside.

I began to fear so much that it crept up slowly inside me. Slowly creeping throughout my own veins, swimming in my bloodstream, up towards my reptilian medulla oblongata where it took root and spread into my forebrain as a more delocalized anxiety. These buildings once housed farmer's banks, implement stores, and hell, I even think I saw a façade for an Indian Motorcycles dealership that now contained a store that sold t-shirts with non-funny witticisms on them and pre-digested and instantly recognizable little tidbits of pop culture.

And this place, this University town, this was to be an incubator for thoughts? In horror, I thought that the people here were all just like the buildings here: old exteriors like the German settlers who stayed here, perhaps too scared to make it to Colorado, too afraid of the red Indians, too tired to make it to California. I looked at the people walking by the shops that were like any other shops in any other part of the country in any little town, and they came and went much like the winds that blew all over this prairie, but they were all possibly, when you peered inside them, they were all quite possibly THE SAME. Full of the same hopes, the same ambitions, the same dreams, all stuck in the same wagon rut heading around and around in a circle.

I was very, very afraid that I had recognized in myself this same tendency toward inertia. I could predict the future. 100 years from now, if you go to any Wally World or football game, the people will be fatter, with stupider looks on their faces. I recognized in myself this noxious weed, this attraction to the already known, digested, and comfortable. The hell with that! To hell with Mr. Malvolio's rut bottled security! The man drinks and slakes his thirst in well-worn wagon ruts. He drinks from puddles. I want to drink from flowing rivers and swim naked in them with wild, bushy-haired maidens. But it isn't happening in Nebraska. To hell with Malvolio and his timid profile. I glanced over him, asleep on the watch. My phone began buzzing. Against all wishes, I answered it. It was my sister.

"Jackson! I'm worried sick about you! Where are you?"

"I'm in Lincoln, Nebraska. Where are you? Peoria?"

"Good God, Jackson! Nebraska? Why are you in Nebraska?" She was almost screaming into the phone, not out of anger, but rather exasperation and fear.

"I'm driving. You know my phobia of airplanes and having my balls felt up by the TSA. Right fascists, they are. Give anyone a mandate, and they'll follow it to the letter of the law."

"Who are you with, Jackson?"

"Mr. Malvolio, and our buddy, Winfield. You know Robert Malvolio, don't you? He was dad's employee, head of security."

"Jackson! You have to get away from him! Do you understand me? You can't stay with that man! He's not a friend. Promise me you'll get away from him."

"He's alright, Hannah. You know, dad hired him to watch out for me."

"Jackson. Dad didn't hire him. Oh Jesus, just Thank God you're all right. Just promise me you'll make every effort to get away from him."

"He's not dad's employee?"

"He was a long, long time ago."

"What happened?"

"Some sort of dispute. He got fired. He kept a horrible grudge. Pathetic little man, he followed father everywhere, still pretending to be in charge of his security."

"Jeez. He was at dad's bedside."

"Find out why. He's very dangerous."

"How dangerous? He's right here next to me."

Malvolio stirred. Yawned his big gaper open and then stared at me.

"Who the hell are you speaking with?"

"Uh...no one."

"So...the gun show is in the Lancaster Event Center and will be opening today, I mean, will be open today."

"What are you talking about?" Hannah asked.

"The Lancaster Event Center, in Lincoln, Nebraska."

"Who the fuck are you talking to?" Malvolio asked, his voice rising steadily in decibels and cracked at the end like a teenager going through the end phase of puberty.

"Oh, dear god, he's right there. Jackson, get away from him."

"Take care," I said and hung up the phone.

"Who were you talking to?"

"I was asking the Chamber of Commerce just exactly where the gun show was."

"No, you weren't."

"I was."

"Show me your caller ID."

"I was talking to the Chamber of Commerce."

"If you want to live, you'll throw that phone away."

"Hell no. How will I call anyone or find our way across the country?"

"Don't you understand that the people after us can find us when you use your smartphone? You fucking broadcast to them that you're going to a gun show in Lincoln, Nebraska. Fuck, they're probably activating their cell here in town to come and do us in."

"No, they aren't. There is no assassination guild; there is no gang of bikers, no secret society out to get us. You're a nut bag, and I don't mean the kind that regenerates the species and dangles behind the cocks of men everywhere. You're insane."

"I second that," Winfield said.

"Shut up, Winnie!" Malvolio screamed.

"Don't yell at him like that. You invited him along."

"I did it for us."

"So I'm a human shield?"

"Yes, Winfield the human shield."

"So you didn't care anything for me when you picked me up? Just when I was thinking I could trust people again."

"At least we aren't Mexicans."

"We're no reason for you to gain your faith in humanity again."

"We're offering you a ride for the cover that you provide us."

"What cover? You idiot, there's probably more people lookin' for me, scourin' under every rock in the entire state of Nebraska, than you two have combined. These are real people, real dangerous people, not some fuckin' fantasy."

The Lancaster Event Center loomed ahead of us. A big, brown monstrosity, like a giant elephant's carcass that lay on its side in the middle of a vast parking lot.

"Gun time! Time to get strapped!"

Malvolio had a one-track mind. It was a broken record that broadcasted, DANGER, DANGER, DANGER!

I swerved to avoid an enormous truck, too big for any man or beast: a great, diesel exhaust-spitting behemoth, and leviathan, not dragging a trailer or hauling lumber to a worksite. A tiny woman, perhaps aged in her mid- to late-forties rolled down the window and called me "a piece of shit cock sucking motherfucker who couldn't drive." It did not befit her status as a member of the landed gentry to call me such epithets. Perhaps she was only a member of the noveau hilly billy riche, one of those farming bumpkins who was getting rich off the whole fracking debacle, or off the corn subsidies, and the increasing popularity of Mexican restaurants and their burgeoning corn chip popularity explosion amongst the do gooders of the heartland. I acted like I couldn't hear her.

"You fuck stick!" she shouted.

"I'll show that old bird a fuck stick," Winfield said, adjusting his dong in his pants.

Malvolio flipped her the bird. Her face went from irate red to insane with rage purple. She came at the Judge, swerving into our lane with her big psycho mobile.

"Holy shit, she's trying to run me off the road!"

"Avoid her! Fucking hit the brakes or step on it!" Malvolio yelled right in my ear.

I rolled down the window as she inched forward with a psychotic look on her otherwise clown makeup painted face, further towards the Judge, and nearly clipped the mirror with her infernal, gaudy, fire engine red, Earth-destroying hell machine.

"Hey!" I screamed. "This car is worth more than your life, slut!"

I slammed on the brakes. She came in the lane ahead of me. Maybe she had a bad day at Wally World or wherever she worked or maybe her husband had a bad day and took it out on her. If she worked, she had psychotic underemployed wife of a constipated Republican plastered all over her bumper. PROTECT LIFE bumper stickers were slapped up against NATIONAL RIFLE ASSOCIATION and DUCKS UNLIMITED and DUCK COMMANDER stickers. KEEP HONKING ASSHOLE!, I'M RELOADING was a testament to her daily road rage. But what was she enraged at? Her comfortable lifestyle? I thought a dog that got used to eating mutton and veal snapped and bit the hand of its owner when it was offered kibble.

Maybe it was our own throbbing hard-on of a muscle car that enraged her. We totally outdid her simpleton, dime a dozen truck that she was supposed to feel proud about, totally burst that bubble. Or maybe, as Malvolio suggested, she was part of the Lincoln, Nebraska, sleeper cell, and she was readying her samurai sword to decapitate us whenever she ran us off the road.

"I'm going to flash the gun at this slut," I said.

"Look where you are, idiot! Chances are she's got a gun that works!" Winfield screamed.

"To the fucking gun show! Lose her in the parking lot."

We turned sharply, and ran in front of a semi...a PETERBILT or maybe a Mack... that blared at us and barely missed clipping our tail end as we leapt the curb through the decorative grass surrounding the pristine brown building. Out of the corner of my eye, I saw the LIFEWAY EVANGELICAL CHURCH, REVEREND BILLY MEYERS GLOBAL MINISTRIES Sticker.

"Oh, sweet Jesus!" I screamed.

"What is it, man?"

The Judge came to a halt after careening between a silver Silverado and a black, five-tired Dodge Ram with Turbo Stroke Cummins Diesel Engine. The owner must take great pride in this because to cap it all off, the Ram had a big tittied profile of a country girl that said, "I'd rather be Cummin' than strokin'," next to an enormous fat Cornhusker Cowboy or whatever he was, pissing on a Longhorn, and Sooner, whatever the hell that was. Winfield was nearly hyperventilating with fear.

"That one, may have been onto me," I said, remembering back to my on-air public humiliation of the Reverend Billy Meyers, put upon by Marcus Hanley, and I remembered the promise that Reverend Billy Meyers told me, that he'd see me in hell. No doubt about it, this irate woman was a listener, perhaps even a parishioner.

There wasn't enough evidence to assume that she was dispatched to do us in, or even if the Reverend Billy Meyers was capable of finding me, but all I knew was, he had a global reach.

"What do you mean, 'that one may have been onto me'?"

"I phoned into Billy Myers' global ministry's live broadcast claiming to be a cured homosexual who prayed away the gay. It didn't go so well for him. He became a bit of a YouTube laughing stock. It went viral. That crazy woman, she had one of his stickers on the back of her hell wagon."

"Oh Jesus! The Reverend Billy Meyers?"

"The Global Ministries Broadcast?"

"Who doesn't know him? This isn't good," Malvolio said, as he gulped his fear to the deep recesses of his chest.

"Here she comes," Winfield announced, bracing himself in the back seat and hiding from any eventual machine gun fire.

The fire engine red hell wagon barreled through the entrance to the parking lot.

We exited the car at Malvolio's behest and ran for the entrance, taking cover from any possible bullets behind the enormous trucks in the parking lot. The truck roared past us as we took cover behind an even larger phenomenon, the monstrosity known as the Ford F650 Supertruck, which looked like a great, bright yellow supernova pus eruption, and rose like Mount Everest in the parking lot.

The truck was a great big "Eat Shit and Die" to the Sierra Club, Greenpeace, and environmentalists everywhere. It screamed, "I don't give a fuck about the environment. You can shove your environment up your ass!" I wanted to show the owner videos of polar bears swimming from ice floe to ice floe and watch him laugh heartily before I shot him execution style. I wanted to show him rising ocean levels, choking carbon dioxide suffocating the planet in a warming blanket of death. I wanted to ask him what kind of world he was going to leave for his children. I expected to hear, "What the fuck do I care? I'll be dead anyway," as his typical response, as he adjusted his pathetic one inch little penis in his Wrangler jeans. That's what these monstrosities were: PCDs. Penile Compensation Devices. I just wanted to meet the owner, who I've assumed to be male, and ask him, "Why?"

The red bitch drove by again. She was a robot, a death robot in scan mode, powered on Christ and condescension. Good thing she was a member of a religion that benefitted from the fruits of science but didn't believe its basic principles nor believed in teaching them to the future scientists, who would dream up the future consumer products. No way they could commission an actual death robot. Most likely they got some lady out of a woman's shelter and turned her into some super assassin with years of training. They never show you the training though. They only show you the assassinations. No one trains to be perfect anymore. They're shot from the womb perfect.

It suddenly dawned on me, that this would be a semi-excellent plot line for romance novel a geared towards bored and horny housewives. It shot into my brain like a bolt from the blue like an arrow delivered by that literary cupid, serendipitously shot into my brain by a crossbow hurled from heaven. No fucking way would my heroine be a religious psycho, stay at home mom with a gun fetish, truck driving hilly billy. She'd be a woman who liked to give it away for free, to the right man, before she offed them. She'd only take contracts on the biggest studs.

Or maybe she'd be a heroine saving the world from utter devastation and ruin, one hot lay at a time. I snapped to when Malvolio tugged at my sleeve to tell me that the slow moving death mobile had parked. We peered over the hood of our cover, and we noticed the woman, quite diminutive, get out of her truck using a stepladder, which descended automatically when she opened her truck door to the elements.

"Why are we hiding from her?" I asked, peeping my head from behind the lemon colored leviathan. Malvolio quickly grabbed me by the shoulder and pulled me down to his level, which was cowering by the wheel well, such as a man of action would do if faced by a fearsome church lady.

"What are we going to do? Just wait her out?"

"We'll wait until she finds the Judge, and then we'll leap out and surprise her."

"Sounds like a bad plan for three guys to attack a woman in the parking lot of an enormous gun show. Might send all the Wyatt Earps inside out with all their steel to turn this parking lot into quite an artillery range," Winfield quipped, never failing to add his two cents into any pot.

"Shut it, Winfield, and get by me. If there's anyone to get us out of this mess that Jackson got us in, it's me."

"How do you figure I got us in this mess?"

"You're the one trying to speak truth to power. You're better off just minding your own business and tending to your own projects than butting your head into some wacko evangelist's operations. So what if he hates fags? What the hell were you thinking?"

"It was funny."

"You think the assassins coming to rub us out in the middle of this godforsaken parking lot, which is at an events center housing the majority of the guns now in the state of Nebraska, is funny? What do you think our chances of ever getting out of here are?"

"Pretty good. I'll walk up and apologize to her for cutting her off. Then she'll go her own way, and I'll go my own way. No harm, no foul."

"She'll kill you as soon as she sees you."

"I highly doubt that," I announced and stood up heartily, full of bravado, and courage.

"What are you doing?" Malvolio asked with a whisper.

"Something that should have been done a long time ago. I'm breaking your spell."

I stepped out into the open. "Ma'am!" I yelled to her.

She spun around in the maze of BFTs and SUVs, dual-purpose semi trucks suitable for family escapades to the waterpark and long distance cross country hauls of citrus products from Florida to Michigan. I lost her for a moment as she ducked behind a gold colored Peterbilt. When she emerged, she had murder in her eyes, or maybe it was mascara. At this distance, I couldn't tell.

"Come back here, Jackson!" Malvolio yelled.

The woman took a powerful stride forward. I stood my ground; confidently smiling, fairly assured that everything would go well, and I would live to see another sunrise. Malvolio wasn't so sure. He was shaking near the wheel well. Either way, I know I could run faster than Malvolio. If not, I would trip him so that I could get away. He was the Secret Service Agent to my President. You know, it was his duty to lay his life down for me. If he disagreed, I could easily make him comply through force or deceit.

I outstretched my arms to appear less menacing to the woman, whose facial expression indicated that she had either lost a great deal of money or that she found out she had a terminal case of cancer. Her face was long, drawn out, kind of like the face of a horse without the benefit of nobility or a shiny mane. She was what I would call an ugly woman. Of course, I wasn't about to tell her that to her ugly face, and I really hoped her personality made up for her face's lack of grace. It didn't. She was every bit as disrespectful and barbaric as her truck was.

"You the fucking prick in the old car?"

"I drive an older car, ma'am, yes," I said trying to make peace.

"You cut me off, you fucking prick!"

"Ma'am," I said, trying to calm her down, "I'm Jackson."

"Wait a damn minute now. You just hold on," she said squinting, appearing to search my face for recognition.

I stood back and grew nervous throwing my head back, trying my best to escape her gaze, horrified that I might be in some mug shot church hit list, my face might have just been passed on to this lady assassin, and now she was ready to smite me with some righteous indignation for making a laughing stock of her Reverend out there in the Global Arena. I think people make laughing stocks of themselves. They don't need my help. I even brought my hands up in a defensive position, ready to block whatever ninja stars or bo staff she wanted to come at me with.

"I know you," she said.

"What?"

"I know you. You're Jackson Leman. You're, like, a famous author! You wrote my favorite book ever!"

"What's that?"

"Silly!" she exclaimed.

I smiled.

"You wrote *Asymmetric Hearts*, silly."

A rush of joy came over me.

"Wait, did you actually buy it?"

"Yes."

"Before or after *Oprah*?"

"Way before. I feel like I discovered you. I saw the book on the shelf. You know what made me want to buy it?"

"What?"

"Your picture on the back. You were quite handsome back then."

I laughed, further breaking up the tension.

"I mean, you're still quite handsome."

"Thanks."

"You writing a sequel? I heard you're writing a sequel."

"Let me tell you the truth about *Asymmetric Hearts*. I can't write. I just discovered for myself that my father's corporation got the ball rolling on the thing by ordering five million copies through secret means to make it appear to be a runaway best seller. So that's the truth of the matter. I can't write."

She looked shocked, appalled that I would share this with her, like she was watching one of her childhood heroes getting into a drunken stupor in public.

"You actually wrote *Asymmetric Hearts*? You didn't have some ghostwriter and pass it off as your own, trying to make a buck?"

"No, I wrote it. Every damn word."

She smiled, "See then, you're a great writer. Women loved that book. Who cares how you got them interested initially. We loved it. We want a sequel, or just anything from you."

Here's where I got sheepish. Excessive praise, maybe she was just drawing me in. Getting me to let my guard down so she could thrust her bitter dagger in my heart. It surely didn't feel like I was a talented writer. I had only written one thing before the well ran dry, if only for lack of practice and maintenance and for me sitting around all day thinking about writing instead of actually putting pen to paper, or in my case whipping out my old laptop and tapping out words on the word processor. So I thought for a split second, as I looked at this woman, and felt her genuine emotion in her praise of my work. I made a promise to her and to myself at the same time. I thanked her for her praise of *Asymmetric Hearts* and told her that what I was about to set out to write would only improve upon that well-laid foundation.

She smiled, showing many teeth, a genuine smile, not one of those phony smiles ordered by a fashion magazine photographer instead of the models looking constipated or quizzical. It was not a smile designed to sell hand lotions or handbags, but it was a smile that reflected that human emotion, happiness. I felt happy too and naturally smiled back at her. I felt a bit of sadness and anger melt from my face at first and then the granite heaviness of my frown blew to bits. I reached out and shook her hand and thanked her heartily.

Her smile suddenly turned to surprise, "But Mr. Leman? What are you thanking me for?"

"I know what I have to do now," I said, and bowed to her like any Archduke of the era of chivalry and big flashy uniforms would and backed up, all to the sound of her laughter at my antics. But they were no antics; this was I not knowing how to express my genuine gratitude. I wanted to jump for joy! To kiss her! To give her a great big hug! Not only did she provide me with the key to liberate myself from a self-constructed prison, but also she did not wish me harm, and she made no attempt to kill me. Malvolio's spell was fast wearing off, and for the first time I made my way to his hiding spot, and he seemed utterly laughable.

"What the hell were you doing, cavorting with the enemy? You're going to get us all killed! You fool," he said as he grabbed my shoulder and pulled me downwards toward him, down there in the muck surrounding the tires of the big fucking overwrought, Earth-destroying truck. I really wanted to see the owner of the big ass truck and ask them, "Why?" Well, chance would have it that we were about to luck into the owner of this lovely big ass vehicle who had forgotten his cellular telephone on the front seat of his enormous ride and was missing out on the comings and goings of his worldwide mega church empire. Who turned the corner and saw us sitting there in the muck and mire surrounding his massive rubber tires that looked capable of running down and crushing a full grown African Bull elephant underneath. It was none other than the Reverend Billy Meyers himself. I saw him, and I gasped. Malvolio put his hand over my mouth.

"The driver of this infernal monstrosity is none other than a man of the Lord."

"Piss on that," Winfield said "Con artists claimin' to be holy...bunch of goddamned mind control specialists. They're the world's best damn dope salesmen, but what they're pushin' in the pens and aisles came well before dope. They're sellin' feelin' good about who you are too, but it's all phony baloney. Feelin' good because you're doin' well, and they tell you what doin' good is. But it's all stacked against each other. In order to be good, someone's got to be bad. The people's that's bad, they're the ones who don't listen, don't believe, don't pray, and don't pay the piper. I fuckin' hate them preachers."

"Better than meth abuse, right?"

"At least mine's honest. I know what I'm gettin'. I haven't chucked my brain aside for someone to tell me right from wrong. I've discovered the wrong. I've lived it. These rich motherfuckers who listen to this scum bag, and then pass judgment on everyone else...fuck them."

"Here he comes."

"What the devil are you hooligans doing around my truck?"

I quickly pitched my wallet underneath the truck before the Reverand could see. It landed in the very center, out of reach of any mere mortal.

"My wallet fell and blew under there, you know, God's providence and all, and we're trying to get it so we can go into the gun show."

"Wallet must be pretty light. Got some money in there, son?"

"No, I try not to carry cash."

"They only take cash or credit in there, son."

The Reverend listened intently to my voice. I hoped he wasn't putting two and two together right here, whilst we were desperately unarmed, with assassins in hot pursuit or maybe not, but nevertheless Winfield was a harassed man, and maybe Malvolio and I were in the clear, but only harassed by our greatest fears.

"Get...Get...Get!!!" The Reverend screamed, his face becoming a shade of magenta I've never seen in a Crayola crayon box.

"Huh?" we said in unison.

"I know your voice you wretched blaspheming heathen."

"How, sir, amongst the billions of sick, humble, degenerate, and fornicating souls can you possibly know this gentleman's voice?" Malvolio asked.

"Once you're humiliated the way this sicko's humiliated me, you don't ever forget the sound of the voice that done did it."

"Come now, dear Mr. Brother of the Holy Spirit, my compatriot here has never wronged you. He's only recognized you from you television show and humbly requests that you move your noble automobile so that we may retrieve his loaded with cash wallet."

"He's not more loaded with cash and currency than the good, great man of what's happening now and the Lord here."

"Oh, well, I do suppose I overreacted."

"Maybe a donation is in order," Winfield suggested, sweetening the pie.

The Reverend's wheels and cogs were spinning in place.

"The congregation does always need to purchase some new protection."

"Oh, yes, think of it as a gift to the congregation."

"A very generous gift," Malvolio added, then winked at me.

"Can you move your truck, good Reverend?"

I knew it was a Christian claiming bastard who owned the infernal death machine. Only a freak who believed the world was a transition point on the way to Heaven, a great global test of good and evil and other assorted nonsense, a waypoint to Jesus and the Angels, could countenance spending almost one hundred and fifty thousand dollars on a massive ego truck, haul absolutely nothing but his wee frame, and if there was anything the Reverend was not, it was wee. The man was a red-faced communion biscuit if I ever saw one, stretched into an exploited tracksuit. Hell, he probably wasted three gallons of gasoline just idling at a stoplight.

"I won't move my car and risk losing my prime parking space. There are all sorts of vultures here just waiting to pounce on an empty spot. Oh, there may not be any now, but this beast of a truck is very difficult to park."

"How about one of us helps you park it after we retrieve the wallet?"

"No! You won't lay one of your hellish hands on my sanctified ride!"

"You're very particular," Winfield said.

"My truck has been sanctified, bonafide, certified, demon free and free of any evil spirits. I can't have riffraff entering and polluting the holy sanctuary."

"I've always thought of my car as a way to get from point A to point B."

"No. You should watch my special, 'Thy Car is Thy Holy Chariot.' Do you know how many people lose their lives in automobiles a year in this great, God-fearing nation of ours? Millions and millions. Do you know why?"

"Uh, drunkenness and stupidity?"

"No."

"Piss poor driving skills? Texting and driving?"

"No, and no."

"Weather?"

"Excessive rate of speed?"

"No! No! No!" Reverend Billy shouted, becoming redder in the face and stamping his boot with each successive shout.

"The problem, my sons, is that SATAN rules the roads! Every turnpike and every off ramp and on ramp is ruled by LUCIFER! From Louisiana to the infernal hippie dope smoking liberal queerdom of California! Mephistopheles, the Devil, SATAN holds America's roads as part of his evil kingdom on Earth."

"How so?" Winfield asked, partially inquisitive and partially baiting the good Reverend.

"I've never stepped away from an opportunity to enlighten, my brothers, to the truth about Satan's infernal conspiracy against God's last bastion of hope for humanity."

Somewhere a cuckoo clock struck 4PM, but we could not hear it. We stood mesmerized that this man could actually command a listening audience of several hundred thousand to a couple of million devotees. He played on their deepest fears, but he was believable because he believed himself. At his core, he was deeply afraid.

"Satan rules the roads, interstate highways, and toll pikes of this great nation of ours because there are so many fatal accidents on them. Satan is always seeking to cause death and destruction, especially of our innocent families. He wants to destroy families at their most precious instant, while they are traveling to the store, the family vacation, or even to church."

"Dude, crawl under the car and get your fucking wallet," Malvolio whispered to me, while the good Reverend continued on his tirade against the Triple A and other communist forces composed of both queers and college professors and sometimes both, but all from the PAC 10 conference, their nexus being at UC Berkeley and Stanford University.

I started to crawl underneath the truck.

"Stop!" Reverend Billy screamed. "I'll do it! No one touches my sled of Angels! Corruption!"

"I'm perfectly capable of getting it Rev...."

"Don't fight with him. Let him get it!"

Reverend Billy Meyers, in his tracksuit, which proclaimed on the back, I AM A MAN OF THE LORD, DEVIL GET BEHIND ME! prostrated himself on the ground and began squeezing his girth under his enormous Supertruck. He wheezed while he shuffled and skinny meth head Winfield offered more than once to take over his duties for him, promising not to touch his great sanctified beast, but Meyers would have none of it. He reached the Wallet, and instead of tossing it out to us, held onto it for dear life, actually opening it to check for his promised donation, not believing that I was a cash carrying Republican. He flipped the billfold to my ID photo, and then he flipped his lid.

"You heathen bastard sons of Satan! Jackson Leman! It's you! You degenerate author! You evil terroristic queer loving queer! Why, you suck more souls away from Christ than all the liberal media combined!"

"Give us the wallet."

"No!" Meyers screamed.

"Give us the damn wallet!" Malvolio yelled at the fat man, now quite stuck underneath his hell wagon.

"No damn you! You aren't getting me to give you anything!"

"Give it to us and we'll be on our way," Winfield added.

"I'm really sorry that I wrote that book."

"That isn't the half of it. Your voice! Damn you. Damn you Leman! You're the one who called in claiming you prayed away the gay."

"Oh, yeah. I'm really sorry about that. It was really childish."

"It was! It was a childish queer baiting prank that lost me most of my BUY GOLD, Share in the seed bank, reverse mortgages, and hell it even lost me my damn gun and ammo sales contracts. You know how much it cost me?"

"No money changing in the temple," Winfield reminded him.

"Money changing? You know how expensive it is helping people nowadays? It costs a damn arm and a leg. Hurting people! That's a buyers market. It'll always be cheap. I have an overhead of tens of millions of dollars in Africa alone."

"It's your fault you lost them. You're the one that spreads hate."

"So what if I think queerdom's an abomination? It is! They just look so fucking happy all the time. No one can be that fucking happy!"

"I believe you can. You could too if you didn't hate on people to think you were good. You're just a coward. A scared little coward," Winfield said. He was turning into quite the meth mouth philosopher. Billy Meyers tried to get out from underneath his Supertruck. He was gloriously and inextricably stuck.

"Oh! Just help me get out of here! Goddamnit!"

"First the wallet!"

He tossed it out.

"Call the jaws of life on your cell phone."

"I can't! It's in my front pocket!" the Reverend yelled.

"You know, if you trusted more and hated less, this wouldn't have happened to you," Winfield continued to lecture him.

"Shut up, you skinny bastard! What, are you on drugs? You're one of those drug-taking demon people aren't you?"

"Oh, can it. You want our help or not?"

"I'll do it myself! Get away from me! I got myself in here; I'll get myself out! Help me, Jesus!"

We walked away, towards the entrance to the gun show, through the sea of enormous trucks, but none was as enormous as that of Billy Meyers, the rich Reverend and gold market speculator who funneled fears of an apocalypse and currency devaluation into driving up the price of gold so that he might reap a bountiful harvest on Earth.

A banner that said "GUNS! GUNS! GUNS! AMMO! Cash! Credit! As much as you can carry with two hands! No wheelbarrows allowed" greeted us at the main entrance. The banner could be seen from the highway to encourage anyone to purchase a masterblaster or Kalashnikov before leaving the great state of Nebraska. Dancing Charlies danced like chickens blown apart with shotguns on both sides of the entrance. A greeter, an older woman with an NRA hat on, handed us a booth display car and demanded our ten-dollar entrance fee that could be applied towards a purchase over five hundred dollars.

"So you're getting a bargain," she said.

"All these guns? For ten bucks? I'll say!" Winfield said, bemused. He handed over thirty for the three of us.

We entered the cornucopia of death and killing. Up front there were rifles, including the scary cool military looking ones. A few fat kids drooled over them, though they were too big for them to carry, and you weren't allowed to touch the rifles if you didn't at least fit the bill for purchasing them. Babes with weapons in front of every booth, most the local big ass, big tits, post-German stock variety, the prairie babes who took naturally to posing with either farm implements, big ass Earth moving equipment, or military grade weaponry. We came upon one, holding what looked like a brown box, complete with a scope.

"What do you have there, dear?" Winfield asked, failing in his meager attempt to seem debonair and dashing. He needed a sidearm, and quick, preferably something shiny, with pearl handles, maybe an exotic wood from the Brazilian rainforest, something really endangered, beautiful, and depleted...something almost black to offset against the bright silver chrome of the gun's body.

She answered him, robotically, "This is a Heckler and Koch G11, gas operated, bull pup design which fires 4.7 millimeter NATO rounds. This is the civilian variant, which is semi automatic only. It comes stock with a Carl Zeiss 10X45 millimeter 4X zoom scope and attachment for a bayonet. Military forces around carried it, exclusively. Until now! Asking price four thousand five hundred dollars."

I couldn't stop staring at her tits in the bikini. Malvolio was staring at the gun. Winfield was doing a mixture of breast gazing and gun gazing. I felt the expression on Winfield's face indicated that he was about to ask a question, but Malvolio beat him to the punch.

"Can I touch them?" he asked.

"Excuse me?" she retorted, dropped from her semi-robotic reading and memorization of the various functions, and spring weights of the G11, her full attention now fixed on creepy Malvolio.

"The guns. Can I touch them?"

She looked at him flabbergasted.

"Can I pick up the weapons?" he asked again, this time more serious.

"Are you looking to buy? We really don't let people who don't intend to purchase handle the weapons."

Malvolio laughed. "Oh, we're looking to purchase. Rather, my friend here is looking to purchase some personal protection."

"Maybe he should be directed over to the little pistols for the ladies," she said smiling, looking at me.

"I can handle big guns," I said.

"Right," she quipped.

The gun show/trade show had the look of a hilly billy fashion show just like the ritzy fashion show I had been to one time in San Francisco. To the majority of the people here, from the gun nut doomsday survivalists to the soccer moms dragged along by their husbands and who sprouted on their faces the same mixed expression of fear and wonder that I had on my face.

"Yes, I'm looking to buy something. What do you suggest?" I asked the bubbly blonde.

She laughed. Her tits bounced heartily like she was in an Earthquake. Wiggle wiggle. I take it that was part of her training. I imagined her sexy frame perforated and bloodied with multiple gunshot wounds. I tried hard to shake the image from my mind once it crept in. I looked at the massive crowds and imagined a machine gun wielding psycho running around the building blowing them all away with a minigun he acquired from an Air Force surplus sale. I suddenly got a bit sick to my stomach.

A salesman, a little, squirrely, slick backed hair, fast talker, literally pushed the buxom blonde to the side saying, "Sorry, Darla."

He pulled me aside, eager to make a sale. You could see the eagerness pouring from his sweaty forehead like a fat kid on a short recess McDonald's binge.

His whole delivery reeked of SALE! And it screamed BUY! It did not care about the consequences of my owning a thirty round capacity, military-grade, human hunting rifle equipped with a scope. He wanted me to own a scope capable of reaching out and touching his grandmother or children.

"What the heck are you lookin' to buy there, chief?"

"My buddy here tells me I need to get some protection."

"Well, by golly, you came to the right place. Our newest model, the one my beautiful assistant Darla's holding, that's a gas-powered, magazine-fed, German piece of Security inducing beauty, the Heckler and Koch G11. We've been selling them like hot cakes all morning long. It's super easy to use. One guy bought a G11 for his wife and also threw down for one for his ten-year-old son. Going to be a special birthday for that little guy. But the reason I'm telling you that is to show you how easy the G11 is to use. Hell, a ten year old can use it! The ammo is absolutely caseless, so do you know what that means?"

Malvolio interrupted, "No shell casings to sweep up."

"Your friend is on it! Whew!"

"How many rounds does it hold?"

"Plenty," Malvolio said.

"Like how many?" I asked the almost out of breath salesman.

"The G11 holds 70 rounds in a prefabricated magazine."

"More than enough to kill every kid on a kickball team and not have to even stay to sweep up the evidence," Malvolio said, as he laughed. It was a maniac's laugh.

"Ha! Heh..." the salesman said, as he started to laugh, but then backtracked, looking at Malvolio with fear in his face, like maybe he was suddenly in the wrong line of work. Instead of a red flag and police report, the salesman continued with his sales pitch, about ready to tell me the virtues of the bull pup design when Malvolio interrupted him.

"Never mind my friend here. He's just a bit apprehensive about purchasing his first firearm. He's from California originally. You know, the state the criminals run to."

"Damn liberals," the salesman said with a laugh.

"He who doesn't want to stand up and protect what he has deserves to lose it."

"Damn right, brother," the salesman, whose name turned out to be Bob, said.

Malvolio mentioned something to me, pulled me aside, and whispered, "Have you seen the five, bald, tatted up Mexican gentlemen behind us? They're been standing there for about three minutes now. I think they've found Winfield."

Winfield was shaking, looked about ready to piss himself, and was as white as the clitoris of an albino Scandinavian.

"Do you sell ammunition too?"

"Of course we sell ammo, in prefabricated magazines."

"I'll take a magazine right quick," Malvolio said.

"You going to get the weapon to go along with the ammo?" Bob asked laughingly.

"In due time, how much?"

"It's not cheap."

"Don't worry. My California tree hugging hippie friend here is rich, and he'll be covering it."

"Why not throw in a couple G11s?"

"Just the ammo right now. One magazine, pronto."

"That'll be 175.50," the salesman said and rang it up on a cash register.

I swiped my Visa Black card and waited for the confirmation. The machine flashed APPROVED to my sigh of relief. Malvolio flexed up and down on his heels and breathed deeply. I hadn't sensed what was about to happen. No one did. The salesman, upset at not having sold enough firearms to me to keep a small African country in a state of civil war for a decade or more, tossed the prefabricated magazine to Malvolio while I signed my name to the line. By the time I had finished, Malvolio had stripped the G11 from Darla. He was so quick that she did not scream. In one deft movement, Malvolio loaded the magazine and made the HK G11 ready to fire. He raised the G11 at the Mexicans and pushed Winfield's scrawny ass to the ground. The Mexicans screamed something undecipherable at him, I don't know what it was, but it sounded like what someone would scream out of utter terror, which came across in any language, akin to the screams of passion with a colinguinist. The Mexicans went for peashooters, ensconced in the waistbands of sweat pants and tight fitting jeans. They fell over each other in a panic, as Malvolio, quick and deadly, shot five times. The Mexicans lay cold and dead, brains blown out on the ground, and in the air still hung a sickly pink mist, which floated downwards. Screaming. It started slow boiling, first from Darla. Then the screaming spread across the convention center. The salesman, Bob, ohmygodded about fifty times.

Malvolio asked him, "What's the used price on this one?"

He tossed the weapon to the ground, and picked up Winfield. "Come on, we've got to get out of here."

In this distance, even through the brick and mortar, we could hear the sound of fast approaching sirens and helicopters. Pandemonium erupted inside the plaza. Women screamed. Men ran and yelled "Active Shooter!" Malvolio struggled to pick Winfield up, but could not do it. "Help me," he said.

The chaos and din amused me. It chipped away at my generally stoic nature. I spied a bunch of other bald, tattooed up Mexicans, probably members of the same gang, who came into the convention center to deal us our dose of death.

"Leave him," I said.

"We can't. I already smoked those five fuckers."

I would never doubt Malvolio's bona fides again. What he just did, and how dispassionate he now is, struck a healthy respect and fear of him in me. The sound of helicopters grew louder and louder. They seemed to be directly overhead. The Mexicans, red eyed with rage or perhaps marijuana, godonlyknows, with veins that bulged in their enraged foreheads, stormed into the room. There seemed to be about fifty of them. Some may have been Eye-talians with moustaches. Screaming and panicked citizenry ran, tripped, and stampeded towards the exits, away from the loud noises. I watched the panicked looks on their faces. Whizz! A bullet flew past me.

"Oh my God, it's all so real." I stood mesmerized.

Malvolio grabbed me down towards the ground, behind the booth. "Of course it's all real!" Winfield, still catatonic, received a hearty slap from Malvolio. "Wake up, Winfield, wake up!" He grabbed up the HK G11, peeked up, and then exploded upwards, and fired the G11. The helicopters grew louder still, and now vibrated the entire building. The roof peeled back and exploded, like a putrescent sardine can in several places. Black clad men descended on ropes. They wielded sub machine guns.

"Oh my God, it's the NAVY SEALs!" A woman screamed from her hiding place.

"Here to save us from these nuts!" her husband shouted.

"Jackson Leman!" one of the black clad warriors shouted.

"The SEALs are here for me?" I asked Malvolio, but he couldn't hear because he busily blasted Mexicans who took up fighting positions in other booths. Thank God someone somewhere had some sense to disallow the selling of high explosives and rocket launchers in this venue. We'd be dead for sure.

"Jackson Leman!" the black clad men started shouting in unison as they fired off rounds at anyone with a firearm, hitting most of their targets with deadly precision. Mexicans dropped like flies that took one too many trips to the punchbowl at an Irish wake. Malvolio was unsure about whether to toss his weapon or to fight them. "Assassins!" he screamed. "They've finally found us!"

In the end, he too tossed his weapon to the ground and pulled me under the table, and we waited.

The men in the black tactical uniforms secured the perimeter of the building, and kept shouting, "Jackson Leman!"

Winfield came to and sat up, dazed.

"Jackson Leman! Are you here?"

"Over here!" Winfield shouted, on impulse.

"Goddamnit, Winfield, shut up," Malvolio whispered at a decibel above library voice.

Two soldiers, SEALs, SWAT team members, whoever they were, came up to Winfield.

"Doesn't look like Mr. Leman," one said to the other.

"No, he's under the table," Winfield said, still dazed.

"Oh, god," Malvolio moaned, and he expected a sudden and swift end from a gunshot wound to the face. The two shined a flashlight at me, right in my eyes, while the others, who totalled about thirty men, formed a perimeter. The sirens got louder and louder.

"Got him. We have to go," one radioed.

They grabbed me up. Struggle was not an option.

"Wait. Who the hell are you, and where are you taking my charge?" Malvolio asked from the darkness.

"LGI CRT, sir."

"What? LGI CRT?"

"Leman Global Industries Crisis Response Team."

"What?"

"Crisis Response Team, mate," another masked man with an Australian accent said.

"Got to go," the man said as he picked me up effortlessly.

"Wait, what about me?" Malvolio asked, half in a panic, half enraged at the prospect of the cops fast approaching.

"Who are you?"

"Robert James Malvolio, long time employee of Mr. Leman."

"Sorry, you're not on the list."

"List?"

"It's got one name on it. Jackson Leman."

The men started running towards their ropes and the waiting helicopters hovering near the roof.

"Where are you taking him?" Malvolio yelled.

The men did not seem to care to answer him. They hooked me up to a contraption like my back was broken, and it hoisted me through the ceiling towards a hovering helicopter. I looked at the opening towards the ground, and saw Malvolio running, leading Winfield towards the Judge. Fire trucks and police arrived. The helicopter throttled forward and I laughed, looking out at the trees, which now looked like broccoli spears, and gazed back at the stern face of one of the CRT guys. I laughed again, wondering if Reverend Billy was still under his BFT. I laughed out loud thinking of how Malvolio would get out of all the trouble he was in, and whether I'd ever see my sexy ride again. The remainder of the helo-ride I did not remember. The CRT Medic administered me a sedative, and I fell into a dreamless sleep.

When I woke, we were landing. From the tiny circular window, where I guess a gunner would gun out of, as we were flying a military type helicopter, the genuine article of some far off conflict, make and model unknown to me, but I guess given the amount of saucy hydraulic fluid and oil covering my badass cowboy getup, that it was in serious need of repairs. I'm just glad we didn't plummet to the Earth and flatten some idle farmhouse. The look on the faces of the security guards or whatever you called them in today's parlance was grim. I doubt that any of them talked the entire way back. They ate seriousness for breakfast, lunch, and dinner. They were not my type of people. I decided to try and make conversation with one of them as the helicopter touched down, bounced a couple of times, and came to a rest. The men loaded me into an SUV, in a convoy of SUVs. Thorn sat next to me.

"Where are we?" I asked as the SUV sped away from the airfield.

"What?" he asked me in response, which barely came over the engine, which the pilot killed and now died a prosaic death. When the deadfall whir lessened to where I could hear some of the other gentlemen joking around, I asked again the man who due to all the insignia and badges on his uniform, and his graying sideburns and moustache, I assumed was the captain of this unit.

"Where are we?"

"You're home."

"Monterey?"

He laughed, "That's right. You've got several homes. Nah, Peoria."

"Peoria's no home of mine."

"Your father's home."

"My father's vacation rental just in case he needed to negotiate business deals with Caterpillar or any of the other companies that call this dusty burg their home."

"That's the only one of note. We're holding here, waiting on cars to pick us up. You must stay put here. Don't try anything."

From his uniform, I discovered that he had a typical military type power name, most applicable for Hollywood roles or cheesy military political thrillers: the literary porn of young men. Thorn. He didn't look like he wanted me to ask him any more questions. This was the type of guy that you would have to beat his first name out of him on a first date, even if you were Miss Universe. He had paranoid, lone wolf written all over his face. He looked like a man who had done plenty of shit in his lifetime, done women in exotic locales, maybe tried more than a few bottles of cheap beer outside of five star hotels and international airports in his day. Instead of talking about him, I decided to see how much he knew about the man I had just spent a little, but strange chunk of my life with.

"Do you know Robert Malvolio?" I asked him.

Thorn paused, flexed the sinewy muscles in his forearms, probably acquired through a tremendous amount of pull-ups or other vigorous exercise that involved tugging and pulling. Maybe it was terribly lonely in all of those third world shitholes these gentlemen had traipsed through. Thorn's face went from a calm shade of lightly tanned and lined, to a shade of magenta, which made him appear like a rare flower in the jungle about to bloom from a bud in the sweet early days of spring. I should have liked to think that, but all I did was set him off.

"Bob Malvolio? You really want to know about fucking Bob Malvolio? The guy is scum with no honor or loyalty, a goddamn excellent soldier, I mean, among the best, but with zero trustworthiness. Oh, yes, he's reliable, he'll get the job done, but he takes things too literally sometimes. He mistakes talk for orders, you know."

"Why are you so angry with him?"

"The guy, he left me for dead in an African shithole. I can't remember if it was Botswana or Burkina Faso, Mali, Mauritania, Sudan, or Somalia. Really, I don't...all I know is that we were sent there to do some things on behalf of your father, and Bob Malvolio, he spooked and left me out there to find my own way out. It's a fuzzy fucking memory now...something I'd much rather forget."

"According to him, he was my father's right hand man."

"That he was."

"Is he still?"

"Don't know. I kind of stopped talking to him after that African fiasco."

"He said my father wanted him to protect me."

"Could have, but from what?"

"Everyone who was out to get us."

"Come on man, there was really no one out to get you. You rich kids and your imaginations. You're so damn gullible. That's why you run off to join cults and become documentary filmmakers. You crave attention. I'm sorry your pa wasn't around when you grew up. Mine wasn't either. I never knew my dad, didn't know my mom much either. When she wasn't in jail for this or that she was at the bar cozying up to whoever would give her the time of day. You should've seen all the type B personalities she brought home who liked to get drunk and take their frustrations out on a young boy. What did I get out of it? You got to look at the positives, man. I learned to fight at a young age. I got to be real scrappy. Sure, your dad was never around, but look at all the money he's going to leave you. Suck it up. Your money will cover up your feelings."

"But it doesn't."

"It helps. You can buy the time to figure it all out."

"Who wants to figure it all out? I just want to get on with my life."

"Don't we all."

"You know, you're right. I'm spoiled. Over-ripened on the vine. I never knew when to pluck myself and fall."

"Fuck, man. Life's incredibly simple. No matter what you do, you're going to croak. You can seek it out if you want, make danger your life, you can live anyway you choose, but you must choose. That's the fucking fundamental problem. Your problem's your money. It's taken away your need to make any decisions or do anything."

"You're more wise than any doctor I've ever talked to."

"I can't speak for them. I can only tell you what I've lived and experienced."

"That's probably a lot. Just like my dad did."

Thorn laughed. "Oh yeah, your old man experienced plenty."

"Malvolio wouldn't ever tell me anything about it."

"Oh, that fucking drama king is clinging to the belief that we're super secret spies. That's your first mistake. Anyone who has ever done anything serious in their life never talks about it. Not one bit. Malvolio's hinting at what he did was designed to make you think he was necessary and indispensable. Tell me. Do fucking ball bearing manufacturers advertise to the general public? Do they have Super Bowl commercials?"

"Never seen one."

"Things and people who are indispensible don't need to court attention. They just operate. Do wheat growers of America put out advertisements reminding people to eat bread?"

"No. Nor do truly talented people crave the limelight."

"Bob Malvolio is a never was. If you remember anything about him, remember that. He's a pathetic little attention monger. Always was, always will be. You want to know more about your father? The real unvarnished truth or at least what I learned during my observations of him?"

"Please tell me."

"Okay. Like everything else in life, it comes with good and bad. There's nothing in this world all good, and nothing all bad."

"Agreed. Please tell me."

"Your father is a hell, or was, excuse me, a hell of a businessman. He didn't micromanage; he didn't get all worried about plans and projects. He simply hired the best and told them what to do. He had ample free time when we were out and about.

"What did he do? Spend it in art museums? Yachting?"

"Ha!"

"Uh, no. Your father's business prowess was probably an extension of his libido, which was fierce and insatiable."

"So he spent his time looking for women?"

"No. He found them. Procured them. Had us procure them. Had them set up in apartments, arrangements signed, nondisclosure agreements, you know, all that legal baloney. Malvolio took care of most of that. He also, well, took care of things if any of your father's lovers got out of hand."

I turned inwards to ratiocination. *Was my mother just the top of this vast pyramid scheme? I hate to use the word like that, but was she just another one of my father's women? She was from a good family. Did my father tell Malvolio to get rid of her when she threatened him with a divorce?*

"What types of women did my father court?"

"Did your father have a type, you mean?"

SUVs appeared in the distance, blowing a cloud of snow behind them.

"Your father was pretty progressive. He didn't discriminate. You could say he was the Baskin and Robbins of his day. If I had to say he had a type, it would have to be pure art."

"Pure art?"

"Yes. Women that were like the classical Greek goddesses."

"Thank God. I thought you were going to say Peter Paul Reubens."

"Your dad was no chubby chaser."

The SUVs skidded to a halt. Thorn grabbed me up.

"Got to go, maybe I'll see you later," he said.

Not likely.

I tried to shake Thorn's hand. The men loaded me onto a single SUV. For the first time, I realized I was in a straight jacket. I yelled to Thorn that I needed to see him later that I needed to know details about my father. I struggled against my straight jacket...fucking Velcro. This shit wasn't advertised either. Maybe in industry publications for fasteners.

Nothing that actually matters is out in the forefront or seems central to our existence. Where there were once sex and death and cereal cults of Earth mother goddesses, now we had professional football and all the adjacent advertising of nothing anybody needs. It all seemed so special. I struggled against my restraints. I raged against them. I grunted and groaned like an animal, but my drivers did not bat an eye or turn around in concern. Soon, I realized that raging was nothing really special, and I lay my head against the tinted window, accepting my fate.

Father's will reading took place immediately following his funeral. I will spare you details of the funeral, which was non-denominational, attended by a few heads of state from various countries in which we held mining interests and who may have just been there to collect their dividend checks instead of actually wanting to pay their respects, but all the same, the security was assured by men who wore designer suits who reminded me of the Secret Service, but better compensated, as they had designer sunglasses instead of the issued ones, and haircuts that looked like they were done by people who knew what they were doing. Their suits were more than a cut above JC Penney or even a middle of the road retailer such as Brooks Brothers.

In my humble opinion, their shoes indicated they were fashion conscious, well-paid guns for hire. They did not appear to be nervous about an impending changing of the guard or possible job loss. They appeared to be well assured of finding a job anywhere. There were plenty of hot and cold wars, like water faucets in city apartments that turned on and off all over the globe.

I didn't pay much attention to the Benediction, the sermon about the value of helping people. Apparently my father had his name on several buildings and several organizations throughout the world that did good works. I guess these things paid for themselves or received funding from private donors who wanted a tax shelter and could not afford to speculate in and donate works of art to museums. The curator of MoMA or maybe the Met or maybe the other museum in New York City, I don't remember, because I just watched this lady who was pretty snappily dressed and had ruby red lipstick that clashed heartily with her pale skin talk about how my father was a great patron to the arts in the United States, just another thing that I didn't know about him and I faintly wondered if he ever supported any artists who were struggling and male or if he only supported female artists who were hot. I didn't ask because I didn't think it appropriate to disparage my father's name at his own funeral.

The woman asked me if I also planned to support the arts, and I told her that I would make every effort to help out young, creative minds in the United States and around the world, for that matter. And I thought, I could probably just give away all my father's money, and not just throw it up in the air, I mean, really design some sort of program to do real good for everybody. I wouldn't have to donate it to random children born with physical ailments that, while good, did limited good. I would set my mind to doing something that would help the maximum number of people. Some would say that just employing all the people that Leman Global Industries had would create the most amount of good. I flashed back out of my fantasy and kept receiving the guests who poured past, some offering condolences that seemed canned, but were brushed off with a smile and a handshake.

Normally funerals are come one come all occasions, but security did a good job at keeping out the riffraff who were just looking for an expensive hor d'ouevre or two at the reception following the visitation, which was held in the Peoria Civic Center. There, the city unveiled a statue of my father, perhaps as a ploy to bring the global headquarters of Leman Global Industries to the city, back to my father's place of birth. Where were Hannah and her husband? They were holed up on an entire floor of the fanciest hotel in town while I stayed in my father's 34-room bungalow on Grandview Drive.

Security had made the decision that if there were a coordinated terrorist attack, that it would be best if we took separate shifts at the visitation and did not attend the funeral at the same time. The actual burial took place under cover of darkness. My father, not being a religious man, did not care to have a ceremony at the graveside, ashes to ashes and all that drizzle zizzle.

Actually, I don't believe his wishes were followed to the letter. He would have been much happier having his body launched out into space or cryogenically preserved in a capsule like Walt Disney. Instead, he was placed into our sizeable family vault where my grandfather, whom I never knew, and great grandfather were entombed, all amplifiers of the wealth passed onto them from the very progenitor, a plucky Frenchman who got to be really good at trapping beaver and sending their pelts eastward. I've got the blood in my veins that could dissolve my sister's husband like he was a baby taking an acid bath.

You know, I slightly care about the will that's about to be read. I'm sitting here in the fancy hotel conference room, all participants have been put through a thorough airport screening by men who did not look like the fat slob TSA personnel. I noticed that they did not grope testicles and more than just a minor brush pass for contraband. There was no lingering on women's breasts, who nonetheless appeared dismayed that they were not trusted.

And then, who walks in the door but Robert Malvolio in a nice three-piece suit without a smacking of cheapness about it. Expense aside, he looked like the suit had been wadded up in his closet for a fornight before he decided to put it on. He didn't even have the common courtesy to lint roll the thing. Malvolio bade Winfield, also dressed up all snazzy, with his hair parted to the side with Brylcream and looking like he had put on some pounds, to wait outside while he went through the security procedures. Apparently, he was named in the will, because only people on the list could get inside with a single guest. I guess to help them carry their loot away. It was a strange affair. Malvolio nodded to me and then smiled. He sat in the rear, even though there were a few seats around me open. I looked back at him, and he nodded at me again.

Another one of the lawyers, a stuffy looking prick, my assumption because he had decided at one point in his youth to submit to lawyering school and because his collar was too tight, cutting off the oxygen to his face, give it a slightly deathlike puce shade, and leaving his neck ever so mushroom shaped. In fact, as he read the will, I could see his neck wobble like a turkey's gobbler. It was hard for me to take my eyes off it. He was in a shabby suit, shabbier than even the security guards could muster, and he looked as if his mother, suffering from advanced cataracts, had dressed him. He was the most appalling of the hangers on. Well, perhaps second to Malvolio, who dressed in his wrinkle-bombed suit looked like he had been through a food processor set on ugly.

The lawyer droned through the opening remarks before he entered into the Leo Tolstoy sized tome that was my father's will. He started with the piddly shit. To my dear Aunt Helen, sister-in-law to my father, and in the event that her demise preceded my own (and it did), to my dear nephew, her heir, Herbert, a 1920s Picasso sketch on a napkin, which the artist later used to serve as the basis for a charcoal drawing, which served as the basis for a mural called something in Spanish dealing with loss, valued in the year 1984 at 10,000 US Dollars."

I chuckled inside. It was probably worth far more now, though it would be pawned for crack in a fortnight, probably before he made the train station in Bloomington-Normal. The list droned on and on. Father saw that no one was left out. He left his personal library to his alma mater, which didn't need any more books, and insured they would end up with another fifteen million dollar Prescott Leman reading room, along with a bust of him. To the head of the legal department, my father left his favorite pen, but it might have been better to leave his writer son the pen, but then again I've a computer to do my work on. The lawyer can have it. It had my father's initials on it and was used exclusively to sign contracts and to impress the locals.

Once they received what they had come for, the legatees departed. They probably secretly hoped for more. My second cousin twice removed got my father's golf clubs. He was less than thrilled at having to cart them through the dingy little airport and pay the extra baggage fee to get them on the plane. Soon, only the lawyer, myself, and Hannah and her plucky husband remained. Malvolio was still sat in the back, waiting patiently. Sheldon looked at me as if this were some moment of truth. If my sister inherited controlling interest, he could manipulate her into ceding control to him and B1 bombers and everything else that father believed the petty bourgeois of this planet profited off would come pouring out of the mouths of our factories like curse words.

I had given no thought to how I would react when the verdict was read. Perhaps I should dance a jig out of the door and hitch a glamorous ride with my security escort to parts unknown. If I secured my inheritance, it would at least guarantee that all these people would leave me alone to do what it is that I did. I looked back at Sheldon. Once I had the freedom to, I would write something that would take the smug look right off his face. His look of embitterment at having been handed very valuable keys to the kingdom and then losing them to me would more than pay for it.

I wasn't smug about it. I was worse! I took it all for granted! My father's dead corpse was not even in the ground and the amount of tears I shed over him was far less than the amount of tears he made me shed for myself growing up. How I cursed and despised him for giving me life! What a vain and selfish act! Would it have been better to never know any of this? To never live? To be as dead as the lawyer's pen, as inanimate? Used by people? As discarded by my father as my mother was? Everything in his life he used and discarded. Look at poor Hannah! A diamond found in the trash heap, claimed as this troglodyte Sheldon's, whose intent is as plain and worthless as the promises of a whore. I looked back to her. She seemed nervous, but not for herself, just to please someone else. Maybe, I think, it just came to me, that she always had this look about her and this need to please other people.

On the whole of me, this need was also entwined in my soul like a malignant cancer strangling my descending aorta. It would not last very long, it would all be unfulfilling, and it would eventually kill me. It would leave me on the road to ruin, trudge me downwards, down muddy, washed out paths that countless, worthless millions had trudged before. These were the thoughts I told myself; trying to get myself to be brave, renounce my inheritance, to declare that I am a disinterested party in the global business enterprise of Leman Global Industries. All I want to do is write in peace. I don't even care to finish. I'll start and go without stopping. Hunt and peck until my bloody fingers rest dead and cold.

I will not look for inspiration in this damn disgusting outer world. I will mine for the golden nuggets of my beautiful soul, and I will make it all the more beautiful, hurling beauty outside of myself, proclaiming to everyone I meet to look inside! Go inwards! Know thyself! Just look! You can bear it! Look like I have looked and see that you are absolutely unique and there has never been anyone like you and there will never be anyone else like you.

Now hurl yourselves outwards, but the entire time mine deep into the depths of your own soul. In a world so obsessed with appearances, trifles, finished product without labor, brand, we forget about the inner light that is fleeting, that is soon to blink out and never shine again. I wanted to scream to Sheldon. I wanted to shake him and say, "You can have it all! It's all yours! The world is your oyster, my boy! Shuck it and throw it over your shoulder. But you remember or don't, Sheldon pal, who made your glory for all to see, which made that possible. You'll be shiny and new, a demigod on Earth or a Giant! A marvel!"

The lawyer called Malvolio to the front of the room and handed him a brown envelope that appeared to contain a book. Malvolio bowed humbly and walked from the room, not stopping to say goodbye to me.

I attempted to stand, but my legs failed me. Any outburst now would not comport itself very well with the assembled attorneys. Better to draft him a fancy bit of correspondence on my monogrammed stationary, congratulating him on his success of marrying well. I could tell him that I wished him to live long and be happy. I decided that I had just better be quiet. I wish someone were here to spur me into action, but whatever meds they had me on kept any compunction at greatness beaten down into the little folds of my soul.

My mountainous thought faded into mere molehills and flat little pathetic fields as the lawyer stopped crossing things off his list and turned to the very last page. He seemed just a genteel country preacher about to deliver a fire and brimstone speech from the book of Revelation of an archaic Gutenberg Bible.

"To my daughter, Hannah, I bequeath the estate in Provence, and an annual stipend of 25 million dollars, deposited into a gift escrow account at the Bank of Mellon, New York, or whatever institution that venerable bank is operating under."

Sheldon gasped and then attempted to crane his head forward as if he desperately wanted to hear something else, but there was nothing. Nothing followed. I could see the bile rising in his throat, shutting it off. He cupped his hand to his mouth and wretched once, went to a knee in his fancy sheen shirt, said, "Oh, Dear God!" and bugled all over his three hundred dollar Hermes tie. Just a trickle at first, but when my sister went to comfort him, he projectile vomited all over her as well. I chuckled slightly, but then the creeping realization of that dire importance seized me, that I, a man who was very used to doing nothing important, was about to be in a very large, very bright spotlight.

"To my son, Jackson Leman, I bequeath the controlling interest in the continuing, ongoing, and future operations of Leman Global Industries with the following stipulations paced upon his exercise of the activities thereof: 1) I declare this arrangement to be null and void if Leman Global Industries is ever made into a Public corporation for trade on any open market; and 2) My son, Jackson Leman, must complete a series of internships of ever increasing complexity beginning with management of the Global Industries Personal Healthcare Prophylaxis line and working his way up to Automotive Subcomponents, Ball Bearing Manufacturing Division, Heavy Capital Goods Division, and finally Global Mining Operations before he assumes the mantle of Chief Executive Officer."

Sheldon had to be wheeled from the room. "What does this mean?" I asked the lawyer. I knew precisely what it meant. Father trusted me most of all to guide the family business, which would remain a family business. He knew the temptations for further fortune were great. I would be the one to keep it private.

"It means a period of learning, and then you will be the overall boss of Leman Global Industries."

"And what if I don't want to be?"

"I don't see you as having much of a choice in the matter. In order for the corporation to remain a private entity there must be a member of the family attached to it in some form. Your father specifically willed you a number of properties, but no inheritance in cash, like he willed your sister. He did that in effect to tell your sister that she will have no business dealings with the corporation and that you will be solely taking the reins. If there is something you don't understand, you can come down to our law offices, and we would be happy to explain it all to you. This, sir, isn't the time to get into discussions about these matters."

"Get me a car, Mr. Lawyer Man. Have a taxi dispatched to take me to your LLP."

"Mr. Leman, you know as well as I do that you don't take the taxi anywhere. They haven't been vetted, and they aren't trusted. From now on you're only to travel with our own security staff. Anyone else could pose a grave threat to you."

"And now, I'm to listen to you lawyers. And who am I to listen to tomorrow, and tomorrow? The doctors?"

"All in due time."

I wanted to live a life unplanned from one day to the next. To live a life of goals, that was climbing on the inside of a domed cage, all the way to the top, where you a can barely hold on, and end up plummeting to the bottom of the dusty floor. I wanted to crawl around a dusty cage of my own creation. A novel is a soul pounded to fit a mold, to be put on display or put under a rock. I wonder if these goons would allow me time to write, or I would have to steal out under a private nom de plume and an alter ego in order to find time to splat these naughty bits of my soul onto the page.

Would they grant me pens, or would I have to dip the tip of my cock into an inkwell, take up the page, and hope for the best?

Any amount of time spent alone, pouring my thoughts onto the page, watching them chatter, pick up their telephones, chatter some more, hold it in their phones longing to talk and text other people even when they were in audience with the pope or some movie star. I would really love to sit in the sun atop tall buildings and look at the miniscule happenings below and be totally uninspired by the exterior world because I find it uninspiring, and just go inside myself, deeper inside myself. Go! Go! Maybe go swimming without drowning, without need for oxygen, my thoughts alone sustaining me all the way to the point when I just blink out. I would never take myself out, just in case you were wondering. I don't know why my mother died, for all things pass, but when we're in pain, we recall the experience of it and it makes us stronger, but we don't recall the actual pain. That's how I know we'll make it in the end.

Lawyers ushered me into a Cadillac CTS. In the coming months, I would learn all the automotive subcomponents that my family's firm supplied to Cadillac to put into this admirable machine. It would bore me to tears to learn all of the planning and intricacy, how many single lines of approval projects such as this involved, but then I would come to learn all of the individual people who's hopes and dreams my family chocked up the capital for in the form of assembly line jobs, management jobs, extraneous associated industry jobs, all the individuals who's very existence depended on our top notch performance and continued stewardship of the most intertwined global industrial corporation in the world. But still, it bored me to tears.

I would not say it bored me to death that would be admitting that I subscribed to the enervating ennui of the age, the bland moneymakers, and the bland movies. Maybe I was suffering from it, having drunken deep of the waters of Lethe on my road trip, because I found it so all uninspiring, the culture, bland, tepid, incapable of fostering any more grand enterprises, other than a steady movement of capital, like a vast machine chewing on itself for spare parts. Perhaps the problem was with me.

These were all the thoughts that I had bouncing around my brain like gas in a cylinder as the security goons drove me northward from Peoria to Chicago. On the way we transited fallow fields of corn, and occasionally I spied a hare in one of these fields, or a crow that sat on a wire and cackled. I liked the driver, who played some club music with pounding bass rhythms that he declared to be all the rage in certain clubs that he frequented, and told me that I should see the babes get down to it. Drop it low, or some such shit. I liked him for his exuberance. He wasn't like all the other gentlemen in the follow on cars at all: the lawyers or the flat-topped psychos in the PSD, all with submachine guns underneath their seats.

The driver talked, never leaving enough of a gap in his wall of speech for even a word spoken on my behalf. I delighted in listening to him recount all of the, what he called, little sluts he bedded on his driving gigs throughout the country. Women here, women there. His main preoccupation was finding women with low self-esteem. He always returned to, "but I would really like to get married some day to a nice girl." That cultural vestige dragging him downwards like an anchor, choking him, urging plainness, urging conformity, urging upon him the necessity to settle like a barnacle on the great blowhole of Moby Dick, and flick your damn little feathery flittering cirri for whatever happens to just drift on by, man, I tell you there is a much better life for you, that you haven't settled. On his fifth regurgitation of the same story, I offered it up to him.

"But I would really like to. I mean, I should find a nice girl and get married to her and just settle down...."

"No! No! No! No! No!" five times for emphasis, I shouted over the modern beepy boppy din.

"You shouldn't because that isn't you."

More really boring stuff happened at the LLP in Chicago. Father made sure to hire a law firm, which wasn't flashy in the least, but really got the job done. They didn't bother to spend money on any corporate art, as the walls were filled only by smiling and sometimes stern photographs of the senior partners in power suits. At any rate, there I found out what the will meant, as if I didn't already know, and I generated a bill for a couple thousand dollars, just for the benefit of having the junior partner go over every detail with me. For each point, I said, "yeah, yeah," and I bet I came off like a real prick. Next stop was the headquarters of something called Leman Information Services Personnel, or LISP. They operated out of New York City and weren't officially on any books, or so the little recent law school graduate told me. When I asked him what they did, he replied, "Ida know."

We traveled, all these security guards and I, by SUV in a long cavalcade, or convoy, as I believe it is called in the modern parlance, past Chicago, past the urban decay of Gary, Indiana, where no one turned their head to even catch a glimpse of the abandoned homes and chessboard vacant lots, little kiddos riding bicycles that they acted like they had stolen; their eyes darted as they weaved in and out of traffic. These little bastards were more suicidal than I. One of the guards nervously or perhaps eagerly fingered his machinegun up front.

Dan Bokavman! This was the same gentleman who I saw at the gate as I was leaving my father's Colorado compound, the gentleman who confided in me about his sick daughter, or maybe it was a son. I couldn't remember for the life of me. I knew that I recognized this man from somewhere, as he is instantly recognizable as on of these secret agent types of Leman Global Industries who are normally only distinguishable and categorizeable into two different versions, Sears or JC Penney, depending on where they bought whatever cheap suit they wore as a daily uniform.

Not that there weren't any women on the LGI Security Force, but they were employed for more nefarious purposes than the prosaic diplomatic and corporate protection jobs. Let's face it, a woman could get a man to talk in more ways than just a smile and a handshake, a round of golf, or a loosening up in a strip club, especially if she had no scruples, which many in the basic materials subsections of the global economy possessed a complete lack of, mainly because their industries were so vital to all of the other industries that they formed an invisible substratum who not many people but commodities traders even noticed, or ever thought very hard about.

No one lost much sleep over whether the two largest plastic pellet manufacturers were publically traded or entered into collusion with each other to fix the price per metric ton of B-P 2 XD polymer plastic chips above the already heavily subsidized at an artificial twenty five cents per pound. No one really cared what the demand for this particular polymer would mean for the burgeoning automobile industry on the Indian Subcontinent.

You see, it's just that boring, this life I was about to lead. These business concerns were to become my main focus in life. I was going to be feeling out the fissures of the economy and making sure that there was a boring Leman Global Industries product out there to exploit these fissures. These prime market niches. These were important industries, not very flashy, but a matter of life and death for someone like my father who wanted to know the price of everything so he could manipulate it in his favor. He didn't know the value of anything.

Towards the end of his life, my father was the head of an intelligence network rivaling that of the United States in the post war years, right up to 9/11. Many of his finest operatives, Malvolio included, as I would come to find out, came out of MI6, and MI5, British Secret Services, or just "the Service," as the stuffy Brits said at cocktail parties to maintain some level of anonymity, and he had a good many CIA, FBI, and other US Government functionaries with chairs constantly waiting to be filled with these governmental service dropouts. We paid top dollar.

Father was willing to pay any sum for information, no matter how insignificant it seemed at the time to the lay uninitiated. Along with all of these professionals, my father maintained a network of gorgeous women, usually culled from amongst the losers of the Miss Pretty Lady Global Beauty Pageant, not all of the losers, but the ones who weren't judged most beautiful, but had really interesting stories to tell (to seduce even the most recalcitrant petrochemical engineer), or possessed skills valuable to the organization, such as driving, paragliding, mini submersible piloteering, military commando operations, guerilla warfare experience, which believe it or not, was often on the resume of Miss Pretty Lady contestants from Northern Ireland, Colombia, and the West Bank or Gaza Strip. You know who I would discover was one of these ladies when I was fully vetted and read on to the entire business practices of Leman Global Industries? That saucy and spicy little tart, Vanessa. The babe who I balled in my front seat, in case you forgot. I haven't.

As we weaved in and out of the labyrinth of Indiana cornfields and crossed through what looked to be a number of ramshackle shanty farming towns named after godknowswho, passed innumerable Wally Worlds, strip malls, the denizens stopped and had looks on their faces of wonder, as if they thought the presidential motorcade had just passed because fuel prices had grounded Air Force One and everyone felt the pain from the austerity measures. I finally worked up the courage to address the guard I met, and even though I never promised to help him out through a large sum of money donated for his daughter's operation. I hoped that my sister had done something about the situation. The whole trip, he had been nervously fingering his gun, flicking on and off the safety, which in my truncated experience with weaponry is not safe to do. None of the other guards paid him any heed, because he rode shotgun.

"Buddy," I said sheepishly.

No one responded, too preoccupied with scanning their lanes of fire for threats.

"My man. You, there," I said and tapped him on the shoulder of what felt like a 130s grade grey wool suit.

He gasped and turned to me, ceasing his flicking of the safety from safe to fire to three round burst.

"What is it, Mr. Leman?"

"How's your daughter doing?"

"Oh, my son?"

"Oh, sorry. Your son."

"He's in a better place."

"I'm really sorry."

"The doctors, they miscalculated. We thought he had more time."

"Oh, Jesus, I'm sorry. Are you suing them?"

"What's the point? He's in a better place. Money won't get him back to us."

"Were you able to raise the money for the surgery?"

"No. We thought we had time. My wife is really shaken up about it."

I recoiled internally, raged against my sister's oversight. If I had called her and told her to do something, she would have done it. Her husband must have poo pooed it. I thought about all the possibilities, not saying anything to the bereaved guard. That's the problem with logic, once there is a contradiction, you can postulate anything, so I did.

"Did anyone contact you about your son?"

"Oh, yes. Someone from corporate."

"Were you offered anything?"

"Yeah. This position, which came with an additional twenty thousand a month salary. You know, I had already applied for it, but they told me the waiting list was long, so I had just resigned myself to prayer and waiting, just like the prayers for my son."

"The Lord works in mysterious ways," the driver said, his eyes fixed on the road and the tail end of the Peterbilt we followed.

"Jesus! And your son died?"

"He did."

"Jesus," I said, my voice synched off in a noose. I could have done something right there and then when I met him. I could have pulled out my fucking smartphone and Pay Palled him the money for his son's surgery like it was a fucking quarter flipped to a bum on a busy city street. Guilt crept into my pores like it was madness. A trifle! A fucking quarter! People in my family would have thought I was double mad, giving all my money away like that to strangers without receiving anything in return.

"Who hired you?" I asked, gasping.

"Some bigwig came down and said it was a personal favor from corporate on behalf of my sick child and all."

"And you took the job?"

"I'm here, aren't I?"

My sister obviously ran my request through Sheldon. In his world, there are no anonymous donations, everything has a price and it is paid for with the toil and sweat from the brows of men. Then all of this labor is covered up, and the much-vaunted product is put up on a pedestal, so that people forgot about the labor that went into it and thought that the product fell, perfect, from heaven. That's technology for you.

That way, you could really jack up the price on the chumps. Sheldon would have never believed the man would truly have appreciated the money, unless he earned it, and since indentured servitude, at least amongst the landed white gentry was formally played out as an institution in the 1700s, Sheldon thought the best compromise was just to offer the gentleman a better job in the corporation, because it was what the man wanted anyway, and Sheldon was in the business of giving people what they wanted, but only if they really deserved it.

Anger drilled through my bedrock heart, sending a great well of sadness up like viscous oil, which my throat tried to catch and tried its best to block. I cried for the man, I cried for his son, and the least I cried for, so much that it was in infinitesimal comparison was my own failure to act. Why do something yourself when you can go through an intermediary? Because it will get done! I swore at that moment, that I would never again not act when I felt compelled by some higher principle or feeling. I would never just descend to some rational calculus to let me get through my day. When I heard its call and pull, I would respond. I stopped my crying because tears for errors are dammed by resolutions. I think the men in the SUV thought I'm soft, a poor leader.

"Nothing to apologize about, sir," the man who lost his son said.

The other men remained silent, looking ahead, scanning their lanes of fire for threats and other hints of danger. It was a boring drive, but I think they were feeling pretty much the same way I was about the situation but had too much steely resolve to allow themselves to be overcome, or for that matter, crack as much as a smile or surrender a frown to gravity below the horizon's parallel. And that was the natural state of man, melancholy, because it's the downward slope, the track that men are on. Being otherwise...that required Herculean labor. I am a coward.

The expression on all their lips was bare, like death. I should, I thought; endeavor to be more like them. Stoic. The thought escaped me as the sun went down, and we got into Pennsylvania, bound for New York City, or it could have been a waypoint off into Wilmington, Delaware. I've no idea. In this car, I am just a passenger. I had driven far too long.

"Why are we driving?" I asked on the outskirts of Greasy Forks, Pennsylvania, home of abandoned textile factories that used to shoot out approximately five million pairs of BVD underwear a year, approximately one fifth the replacement rate yearly for doo doo stained underwear, with the remainder of the orders being filled by factories in China, Malaysia, and India, which eventually eclipsed all the orders of these factories and necessitated them being shuttered by corporate. The factories had been idle for a decade or more, and were now only sanctuaries for pigeons and rats that thought the cotton remainders excellent material for nests. It was a paradise of warmth and sunshine for them, a real rat Crate and Barrel. Restoration Hardware for the birds.

My active imagination spared me the droning monotone of the overbearing driver who switched out with the other driver sometime during the evening, along with the other guard crew. Leman Global Industries policy stated that a guard force member worked no more than a 12-hour shift every two days. Anything longer was a violation of policy and made the guard subject to a harsh rebuke that consisted of being forced to work for thirty-six straight hours, itself a violation of the policy, punishable by what was called a counseling statement. Just like baseball, a counseling statement was a strike on your record. Three counseling statements, and you were sent packing, given a poor worker referral form back to the state unemployment agency, which would follow you the rest of your days like a black cloud or case of VD. At any rate, your next employment, was certain to be lesser in all the metrics quantifying worker satisfaction, lesser in salary, lesser in safety, lesser in "I feel I'm contributing to society", because your employment at Leman Global Industries makes you feel like someone, and Leman Global Industries (at least on their website and recruiting pamphlets, was) "A SUPER PLACE TO STRIVE!"

Not great! That had connotations of phoniness around the dinner table, not a great place to WORK, for Leman Global Industries employees did not do WORK, they STROVE, they STROVE for a better tomorrow, for higher profit margins, for greater workplace safety, of course only through the auspices of the international industrial conglomerate. They were known in corporate boardroom meetings as STRIVERS instead of EMPLOYEES, or that other much maligned S word: suckers. When strivers were let go for no reason other than the bottom line that would not allow for their continued striving within the auspices of the corporation, they were notified via email and their first line Striver Supervisor that they were now known as Severancers, and were promised a glowing recommendation after they signed a non disclosure agreement.

The man who I met at the gate, whose son died, and who had shared personal information with me was given no less than four counseling statements after his shift. One was for sharing personal information that caused visible stress to a corporate officer of higher than executive vice presidential rank. Leman Global Industries welcomed corporate information that did so as a valuable part of business. When your brain was in the safe confines of work, all your synapses were expected to be firing and focused on company business.

The other counseling statements were for sharing personal information, the time and place for personal information was on personal time. Another was for questioning the genuine outpouring of emotion by an officer of higher than or equal to senior vice presidential rank. The other guard force members all signed sworn statements against the gentleman, that his divulgence of personal information made for an uncomfortable and stress inducing trip. The fourth and final sworn statement that served as the nail in his coffin as a Striver was for his generally nervous appearance and flicking the safety on and off in direct contradiction to the training he received via Internet Streaming Video, outlined in the LGI Safety Video: Don't Be A Casualty: Firearms Safety During Corporate Protection Operations.

"Sir, we're about three hours out from New York City, LISP Headquarters."

"What exactly does LISP do?"

"Don't know. I suppose you'll be finding out when you get there. Don't worry, sir. That must have come off as flippant, but we're only assigned to transport you there. We don't know what actually goes on there."

"Compartmentalization. The best method to prevent against corporate espionage, practiced at all levels and facets of Leman Global Industries, so much so that one hand often does not know what the other is doing, save for coded messages passed through the LGI Encryption Algorithm, jointly formulated at MIT and the Princeton Institute for Advanced Studies..." LGI Safety Video: Corporate Espionage, and You: A Corporate Spy is a Vermin Nibbling at the Pure Heart of America.

On the outskirts of Scranton, PA, I saw junk factories on cheap land that no one wanted that melted seamlessly into farmlands then into golf courses, that old standby to drive up the price for otherwise hilly land unsuitable for farming and ensure a steady stream of snooty, rich bores as long as the sprinklers worked and golf ball manufacturers dimple machines still dimpled, for no one wanted to play golf with a cement-filled ping pong ball as the rich were forced to do during the Great Depression. No one. No matter how desperate. Why, they'd dredge every water hazard and chop down every palmetto in Florida to meet the demand of those noxious little, easily lost, plastic excuses for missing church. At Leman Global Industries, who supplied the die for every major golf ball manufacturer, we liked to think of golf balls as an indispensible facet of the global economy of fun.

If suddenly, golf was outlawed, disappeared, or all the golf courses went literally to pot, full of too many divot holes to replace, would anyone drink poison? A few might, but they were already on the verge of it. They were the men who went into the water hazards after the little phantom balls on vacation in Florida while their buddies were screaming that the ball was on the green and old Fritz the alligator still lived in the pond and was hungry for geriatrics.

My father aimed to be indispensible to the modern global economy. Nobody would treat LGI like an old plastic bag to be discarded into the ocean and choked on by an endangered sea turtle that thought it a jellyfish snack. We'd stand as long as the pyramids of CHEOPS and CHOFU, all the while serving more of a purpose than that of a dusty tomb. And that's exactly what I think men have built for time immemorial, whether they were building pyramids for pharaohs or doing their part to contribute to the global economy for pharaohs. They've been building dusty tombs.

We sped through the city of Newark, New Jersey; the guards had been on duty for a full six hours. When we got to the HQ or wherever it was, it would be about time to swap out. If you've seen one strip mall, you've seen them all. They are boring cells along a blood vessel, boring places along a road. If lucky, the strip mall owner will reap the benefit of a heavy traffic and not worry that the red blood cell cars will be diverted by construction to another strip mall just like theirs, possibly containing the same shops, just fifteen feet down the road.

The passengers, carried valuable dollars with them like oxygen, and the most pitiful site in the world was an abandoned strip mall with a for sale sign on it. It looked just like a necrotizing limb on a baby. Sometimes worse, was a single struggling store, which looked like a drowning puppy doggy paddling towards shore in the middle of the ocean. We passed no less than forty five STARBUCKS, seventy five DUNKIN' DONUTS, and twelve struggling, lost puppy mom and pop donut shops who could not withstand the Golden Horde of Krispy Kreme and Dunkin Donuts.

The sameness of all these places was that they were all failing and only pride kept them afloat. Different types of fat people walked into the successful, established brand name places, because everyone wanted to be part of success. Fatness was indicative of success in many parts of the dusky world, but here in these particular burgs it just indicated that you were lazy and made poor food choices. In other parts of the world it indicated that you did not perform heavy manual labor and had plenty to eat. You had made it. But someone had to do the labor, and why not the other person instead of me? Why not the Latin American, before him the Irishman, before him the Chinese railroad laborer, before him the African slave, and before those unfortunates some other spit-upon. I looked out the window at the people who drove, walked, and waddled from store front to store front, and it was a rare sight indeed to see someone who looked like they could run from a tsunami, rebel army, a herd of rampaging elephants, mob of machete wielding apostate psychos, no these people all dug their graves with their forks because there was nothing else for them to do, nothing to worry about really, these real biological worries dissipated, and replaced by all sorts of worries about Godknowswhat and the oil prices that rose, but would come down eventually.

I started counting. I passed no less than 1327 fat people, as we drove past the New Jersey governor's mansion and headed toward a toll turnpike, bound for the Big Apple, the city that never sleeps, where the only porkers I swear are tourists and transplants from Ohio, but they soon slim down. They never look at the horizon but they the whole time look upwards like guppies in a fishbowl, and awaited whatever flashes of brilliance come to them from the fashion advertisements and entertainment choices as ubiquitous as smog, SUVs, and online Universities. A real enterprising gent with a profit motive would advertise plastic, recycled containers full of pure oxygen as a diet supplement. Breathe in; don't eat, the directions would say.

Again, I digress. It is on account of my nervousness at being led by the nose to an uncertain fate that has me worried. But what am I saying? When I had my freedom without stipulations, when I had my unlimited credit card balance, and no questions asked at all, I stayed indoors most of the time, so unsure of what to do with myself, paralyzed by my success, which I discovered was just marketing gimmickry.

To be as indispensible as the sun! Hard wired for all the generations! Shine brightly for the generations like Billy Shagsbeard or Milton or some of the other poets, and LGI 60W light bulb LED diodes. Yes, we supply those too. I believe something is all the more indispensible because it is not necessary, but becomes necessary the more entrenched in thought it becomes, connected through some magic to everything before and everything after.

There is something real phony and plastic about this age where everything has a function, a purpose, a pre-ordained place from time immemorial it would seem, and there is something phony and plastic about my mind, which sees all these arbitrary categories and cannot help but place all things, even the people I come to think of as things into them. I will close my eyes, and not open them until I have banished these horrible, hellish judgments from my consciousness. I'm hoping that this fundamental unwiring comes by the time we get to New York City, because this is really getting to be oppressive. I can't seem to just let all of this pass me by without filtering, without the sheer weight I accord images squashing me flat like a postcard mailed and forgotten, like a photograph devoid of shape pasted on a billboard for gawkers underneath to ignore.

You know, over that car ride, I made some of what I call, Real Decisions. Running a business is nothing that I want to do in life, nor do I have any talent at doing that. My father would be unable to pull any of my strings from the grave. His business would perish with him, or I would appoint someone trustworthy to run it in my stead. I don't care about violating the terms of my father's trust, he should have realized that I was untrustworthy, and had he spent more time with me, he would have realized just that. We crossed over the Hudson River into Manhattan, and the skyline formed a certain harmony of musical notes with the sunlight gleaming off the windows, altogether breathtaking.

The guards seemed unperturbed and only white knuckled their weapons more. The head guard, who was sitting next to me, ordered a certain driver guard to phone ahead to the NYPD that we were coming to the city and to offer us their usual additional protection. We wouldn't be offered a police motorcade. I mean, I wasn't POTUS or anyone significant like that VVIP, but those politico types usually flew direct by helicopter to their appointed rendezvous on the taxpayer's dime. Marine Corps One.

No private individual, save the mayor of this fire gleaming jewel of the coast, this great golden teeming boil of modernity, this nexus of thought, the nerve center of global fashion, this metropolis, a veritable Olympus among the blowing dust I had been through, a real city to stand the test of time, not maintained as a memory to what once was, when the trains rumbled tracks through the hinterlands, spreading diffusements of capital far flung to the sodden peasants who escaped this place. Why didn't everybody out there just call it quits and move to this magical place? A magical place where men did magical manipulations and made currency appear from thin air! Oh Wall Street, I love your alchemy!

The New York Police Department telephoned the guard chief and told him that the most expeditious pathway through the city. Why was this not input into a database and shared with all the citizenry, that's beyond me, but then I realized that if this privileged information was shared, those golden streets would be clogged and privilege would sink right down into the swamp of commonplace knowledge, trite and easily swept away like all the cities, towns, burgs, and villages that we once knew for doing something or other, but what that was only the inhabitants remembered.

It was not marked on the billboards that I passed at seventy miles per hour, and it certainly couldn't be seen by plane. We hurried through the crush of buildings, dwelling in the shadows because it was the fastest way to circumvent the muck. We avoided the tourists and busybodies sticking to the well paved, pot hole-free arteries of commerce.

The New York Police Department did not even know our final destination, but from the outside it appeared to be an abandoned hat factory, last applying felt and silk to chapeaus worn by gangsters, hipsters, hip cats, and finally Eye-talian Avant garde film directors until it shuttered in 1961. My father had purchased the building in a spirit of urban renewal in 1971, cleaned it out, and paid the miniscule upkeep in taxes, so none were the wiser as to what he put on the inside, because that's what's important about a building and a person, for that matter. It's what's on the inside. The city didn't care what he did with it, because at least it wasn't going to be a hangout for a gang or heroin shooter's gallery, or gallery of some unsavory pop artist to shoot low-grade pornographic snuff films. I think Andy Warhol used to work out of Grenwich Village, or maybe SoHo. I don't know.

We entered a garage, and the SUV train halted. The engines tickle-tacked and cracked from the heat that dissipated from them. The guards would go no further. Their mission was complete. Now that I knew where this place was, I wondered why I couldn't have just driven myself in the Judge. The guards bade me enter an aluminum door by pointing to it with severe reverence like priests pointing at some holiest of holies. In the end, they would not be admitted.

"Salut," I said to them.

They backed out of the garage one by one, bound for godknowswhere. It wasn't my business. Yet.

I entered an elevator. Whether it went down or up, sideways, zagged or zigged, I could not discern. I only know that it moved at a high rate of speed, similar to a subway car. The elevator was unlike other elevators with a boxy shape. This elevator was nearly spherical. I sat on a plush couch and listened to the hum. The elevator was without Muzak, I suppose this was so the executives, who did their executions, or whoever actually used this conveyance, could have private conversations within, away from the silly fashionable banter of a bar or the mirth of the streets.

The elevators contained no buttons on the walls or any discernable means of operation; I could only tell that it was moving. Humming ceased. The elevator became translucent. Fifty or so faces assembled in a mock formation with Mr. Robert Malvolio, looking quite more polished with a long coat in his usual black color but probably of a more exquisite cut of cloth from the look and how it shimmered in the light, looking a few thousand steps above the rags we purchased together for the cowboy fashion show. He was sans cowboy hat, and this upset me because I rather liked the rattlesnake head monstrosity. The translucent door opened. I walked into the atrium of which the floor was made of a shiny polished metal, but it had no give at it all, no slipperiness, like it was the exact opposite of a frictionless surface. You could not slide on this surface, no matter how hard you tried.

"Welcome to Leman Information Services Personnel, Mr. Leman," Malvolio said with his arms folded in front of him. His subordinates looked at me with a mixed devotion. Near the rear of the formation, I saw the ravenous, yet ravishing Vanessa, and the man she claimed was her father standing side by side. She broke her position of attention to look at me and shot me a flirtatious smile, which melted suddenly into a simpering look of concern. Her partner, father, whoever he was, nodded to me with an "I know your secret" look of confidence on his face. In his profession, to get one over on the boss ensured job security well past retirement age.

"What am I here for?" I asked Malvolio, who hastily answered me, lest I produce the appearance of not knowing my ass from a hole in the ground to the assembled employees.

"All will be explained to you, and then you can address the troops here."

I nodded my head to them, and like an idiot, at least it appeared that way to me, and probably them as well for I think I heard a few suppressed laughs, some rising to the level of the agent having to cough to avoid laughing out loud, things they would write to other co-workers over social media programs in their spare time, or God forbid not at work lest they be discovered, "that the new boss, who is the old boss's son is an idiot and I almost totally LOL'd when I stood there looking at him."

I looked at their smiling faces. To them I would always be the boss's son, that great, dear, old bastard who everybody looks upon with reverence who just had to go and kick the bucket and bring ruination to the firm by appointing his idiot son in charge of everything. I followed Malvolio like a puppy dog into the board room, which was visible from the outside until we entered and sat at the large heavy wood boardroom table that was rather triangular instead of the classic rectangle to stress the three virtues of any Striver: Courage, Competence, and Loyalty. It was not quite an equilateral triangle, even though father stressed the development of these traits in equal proportion, because he really loathed symmetry in architecture.

Nature never produced a straight line, and much like his life, he garnered a certain level of personal asymmetry in all of his affairs, both business and affairs of the heart. He was a secretive man; only the level of his secretiveness was totally unknown to me before Malvolio produced the envelope, less befitting a champion of industry, than some cheap porno producer who sold tapes out of the trunk of his car. This was no Asian Butt Sluts 55. There was no personal monogram. The envelope came from a police department, filled with its lone content by a crack team of murder investigators who ultimately ruled my mother's death a suicide. They were paid handsomely for their judgment, and no one ever bothered to ask what happened to the security camera tape that recorded the happenings in the room.

"I was supposed to destroy this. I swore to your father the moment right before he died. You know as well as I do that neither of us believe that he is watching us from heaven or looking up at us from the lake of fire, full of rage in his heart. He's dead. He knows no more pain. The time I spent with you in that car, it showed me something: that I had this one thing that I knew it existed, and it's probably the key to whatever is raging around in your brain for all this time, whether you were screaming at the top of your lungs in your therapy sessions with Doctor Quackeroony or in your dreams or your nightmares. I know it's worn a path in your soul, knowing that something happened to your mother."

"What's in the envelope? What do you have in there?"

He turned it upside down on the table. A tape, what looked like a Betamax or maybe some other format, landed with an unceremonious thud.

"What's that then, Malvolio?"

"Surveillance tape from the house the day your mother died. This is the unedited version, delivered by me to your father, following her murder."

"Murder?"

"Yes, your mother's murder."

"Murder?"

"Don't look at me. I didn't do it."

"Who did?"

"That bastard Meriwether, the man that you called Red. Of course, I arranged for it to happen..."

"You son of a bitch!" I screamed. I wanted to do him in.

"Hey! Wait! I didn't know what I was doing! Your father had me call him up and tell him to bring some crabs for a crab boil. It was a fucking code. I didn't know what I was doing. But you saw him, didn't you, Jackson? You saw him crouched over your mother. You saw his red hair, didn't you?"

"No. He was wearing all black with a green stocking mask. I didn't see him."

"But he saw you. I've been protecting you from him this entire time. After that job, he quit us. He went to work for rivals. You know, them."

"I don't fucking believe you. Show me the tape."

"You don't want to see it."

"Show it to me, god damn you!"

"It really isn't for you to see. Jackson, I'm sorry. I didn't know what I was doing."

"Why the fuck did you still work for him, my father, after all those years?"

"You know how hard it is for us secretive types to get a job after we leave one."

"Red did, obviously."

"That was all arranged. These power brokers. They're all in it together."

"God, you people are sick. Why the hell did you show me the tape, then, if you don't want me to play it? Unless I actually see it, that tape could contain anything.

Maybe some of my father's exploits with the tribeswomen of bone in your nose! The fucking wretch!"

"He had to do it."

"He had to murder my mother?"

"Yes, he did, and it had to look like a suicide."

"Why'd he have to do that? Why not just divorce her?"

"I told you. Your mother was planning on going public, to the public that your father didn't own, didn't have in his pay, threatening to bring all the matters into the light, full fucking disclosure of all his marital indiscretions. And you know once the public starts digging, the little burrowing worms, they don't stop. Then the fucking government, of and for the people, gets involved. Those marital indiscretions, those were just the tip of a massive, looming iceberg. The investigators could have crawled out of their holes and poured over every shady dealing and every shady third world contact and palm that your father greased. For fuck's sake, she even corrupted members of my staff for her knowledge about what was going on."

"Corrupted? They told her the truth! They told her the truth about father, fucking curse his goddamned name would he be burning in hell, but he's just dead. He's escaped! Hell would be too fine an accommodation. Why, if he's in the fucking boiler room of hell, shoveling the pitch into the furnace, that would be five stars! Fuck him!"

"You and I both know we don't believe that your father did what he had to do for posterity. Your mother threatened to burn it all, to toss a match to it all, and it was all soaked in gasoline. Still is. He would have done anything for you and your sister."

"Except spend time with us! Fuck him! Show me the tape, and I'll spend eternity burying and cursing his name. I'll dismantle all of his concerns! I'll run the business into the ground."

"Then you'd only bring ill upon your own name. I only showed you this so you can move on with your life and stop blaming yourself for your mother. Stop blaming your mother. No one could have saved her, nothing could have saved her. Your father made the decision, and it was a rational one. He set the machine into motion, and it devoured her."

"And this madman is still pulling strings from the grave like some decayed puppeteer. I refuse! I refuse to be part of his games! Show me the goddamn tape. Show it to me so I can begin setting bombs, to the foundation he built, with my hatred!"

"After I show this to you, it will have to be destroyed."

"And it's the only copy, I suppose."

"We made sure of that. It's not worth a fortune to us, but it's worth a fortune in the wrong hands. This is what the man you called Red was after. He would have gotten it and killed you."

"Did he have to sign a non-disclosure agreement?"

"No. And you know what, paying all the cops off wasn't enough. I'm sorry to say that everyone connected with this tape has met a violent end. They died young. Police officers have such horribly stressful jobs. Violent jobs. The only thing that saved the assassin was going to work for the competition."

"You said it was arranged."

"Yeah. We needed to subcontract out getting rid of the cops to someone."

"Did you kill any of them?"

Malvolio remained silent with the same serious face as if he knew that he too was doomed along with my father, along with every other murderer and foul devious beast that walks the Earth free, while the innocent decorate graves.

"Why didn't you just destroy the film and be done with it?"

"It was your father's nuclear football until the day he died."

"Why not just destroy it and be done with it?"

"I was your father's closest confidante. Jackson, the man, after your mother, was not well. He couldn't destroy it. It served him as a reminder of just how low he had gotten. You know, when I first met him, he was in your shoes. You two are quite the same, really."

"How so?"

"He had no interest in business."

"But he chose it. Serves him right. Why burden me with the truth?"

"You've lived your whole life under a false illusion that your mother was a horrible, selfish person. You berated her in your counseling sessions. You nearly lost your mind asking the question why. You burrowed and burned the question into your soul. I regret that I couldn't tell you while your father was alive. He used to fret too about your condition, but nobody could know. He thought that he caused it. I guess we...did. But he's dead now. And you're alive. You need to live."

"What does that even mean?"

"Do what you will."

"I don't know what that means!"

"You will."

Malvolio approached the Betamax player. Just in case, a Smithsonian worthy complement of nearly every media format player from the last fifty years lay ready, assembled at no small cost to the LISP. Most of the time, it was used by the industrial spies for Christmas parties, because being pipe smoking anachronists at heart, they preferred music that was on LPs and 8 Tracks and preferred their films 8mm and grainy.

"Don't play it. Burn it."

Malvolio paused. "Are you sure?"

"I am. Do it in front of me."

"Are you sure?"

"Yes. I order you to." The words felt good coming from my lips. I had another order in mind, bubbling forth as well, which I would issue this demon, as soon as he consigned my bitterness, my family's path through the world, to the flames.

Malvolio peeled the protective cover back and grasped the tape within. He looked up at me, for my final confirmation, he was such a creature of slavish devotion. I gave him the go ahead, and he pulled the tape out, yard by yard like a man pulling the guts from a rare animal. It whistled against the case, sound almost, but not quite like a bagpipe funeral dirge.

He ripped the tape from its moorings and placed it in an aluminum trashcan. He produced a lighter from his pocket. The tape was only a thin magnetic strip, bits of information now, meaningless, much like the universe, colliding atoms and interacting wave fields, until a reader could make sense of it all. As he lit the end, the plastic smoke hit my nose for the first time, conjuring up images of my mother and all the hate I ever felt for her, abandoning me, soon dissipated much like the smoke. I laughed. I laughed when the fire alarm went off and the sprinkler system engaged, dumb, a program carrying out its functions.

"Has the water put out your flames, good sir?" I asked a sopping Malvolio.

"What?" he asked.

"I want you to go back to whatever pit of hell my father found you in. I don't require your services any more. You are released from your obligation."

He walked from the room, wringing his hands.

I must have stood there for half an hour as the water made all in the room soppy and puddled on the floor like it would in some gentle tropical rainforest island. I laughed and laughed and lifted myself up on the balls of my feet, basking in my new-found freedom. Illusions are the most painful, difficult things to part with because they are nothing. You cannot leave anything in the middle of the night by slipping down the fire escape. You cannot run into nothing on the street corner.

You would not believe my dismay when I was toweled off and shuttled off to our business headquarters to meet with my business handler, who would show me the ropes in my father's chosen for me profession of master of illusions, spinner of dreams, and architect of destiny.

"Richard Avalon!" I shouted to Vanessa's purported father as I walked sopping. "You're in charge now! Your first order of business is bringing Mr. Robert Malvolio back here. Tell him all is forgiven."

"If he wants to stay hidden, he'll stay hidden, sir. This guy has got plans on top of plans from A to Z already waylaid. I'm sure he's enacting them."

"Please track him down."

"I don't know if that's possible."

"Do it!"

"Do you want him eliminated?"

"No. Just bring him back."

They looked at me sheepishly, confused.

"Has this ever happened before?"

Still, dumb stares. A few people looked at each other blankly, like they knew something, like they had been called to secret meetings about wayward rogue agents and done secretive activities on behalf of the family business, but were sworn to secrecy until time immemorial by one of the infamous non-disclosure agreements.

"Listen, I'm in charge now. You can tell me anything. If you prefer to speak to me in private, I'll be in my office."

"In Los Angeles?" one agent asked.

"In Denver?" another shot forth.

"In Buenos Aires?"

My god, I had plenty to investigate.

"The business director is waiting for you at JFK."

"Who cares, I don't know him."

"Sir, you've got to meet him," Vanessa said.

"As long as you come with me," I pointed to her, while all the other agents stared at me like I was some Prince of some wretched third world country with vast mineral wealth, who just pointed at her to come and talk with me in my private quarters.

"Hey, we know each other," I told the assembled agents.

"What's of it, to you all?" she asked them. Leaving the formation, she was no longer a mere employee. I took her by the hand. She would be my personal assistant.

"I had something to tell you anyway," she said.

"What?"

"Let's wait until we get where we're going."

Cell phone rang. It survived its soaking. Confounded distraction. I looked at the wastebasket in front of me. I should have tossed it inside and let it vibrate the trash bags. Instead, I answered it without looking at the caller ID.

"Holy shit! I thought you were dead!"

"No, I made it. Who's this?"

"Ha ha! Have you gotten anything on the new novel done?"

"What novel?"

"The sequel to *Asymmetric Hearts*. Hey, I heard you did some impromptu signings for the 10th anniversary edition. Unsanctioned signings."

"You don't own me, Mr. Agent Man."

"Did you get anything done?"

"You bet your ass I did. I just haven't had much time to work on it. My dad just died and all, and I'm, like, head of the business now. I guess all my shit's getting published. I'm not writing a sequel. I'm doing something different."

"What's the synopsis?"

"I don't know. I'm just going to write it."

"You need to come to my office."

"I don't need to do anything. I know what plot you and my father cooked up for *Asymmetric Hearts*."

"Come and see me while you're in New York City."

"How do you know I'm in New York City?"

My agent, the wretch, didn't bother to respond.

"Just come here, please."

I hung up the phone without agreeing to anything and promptly fished the soppy card for RAYMOND LEFEBVRE, PROBLEMS? SOLVED! From my dingy wallet, that oh so wily leader of the senior biker gang, The Old School Truants, my main man, my compatriot on the open road. After a few moments of reminiscing with him, I reminded him who I was. I told him that I was the gent who owned the 1969 Pontiac GTO Judge. He inquired how the car was doing.

Suddenly, I remembered that the last person who drove it was Malvolio, that bastard, that thief! He probably had already sold it for a retirement plan. I told Ray to ready the troops and please meet me in New York City, and he bought off on it only after I told him that I would compensate them for all the fuel and lodging on the way out, and food in the city. After this, what the biker gang leader called a splendid notion, which was sure to be a good deal of fun for the Old School Truants, their sister gang Gerianthrax, and he told me they would meet me at the John Lennon Memorial, Strawberry Fields in Central Park. I wasn't sure if their Harleys and Can Ams could negotiate the pathways without garnering the attention of the authorities, so perhaps I would have to call in a favor from the humble NYPD who owed my father and therefore me, several favors.

From there we would pay my literary agent a visit and enforce my demand that he let me out of my publishing contract. I could hire some high paid lawyer from some Madison Avenue firm to negotiate the release for me from my contract, but seeing the look on his face when a bunch of silver haired and blue haired killers, with knuckle dusters and brick bats came and barged into his office, would be priceless.

Why, I bet he'll really shit his pants when the old ladies really lay into him, and if he doesn't immediately tear up my contract and all subsequent drafts, addendums, sub statutes from here to infinity as well as grant me exclusive rights without all the various associated leeches, gnats, rats, boll weevils and other literary parasites and hangers-on attached, we'd probably see to it that he fell out of the window tied to his Italian marble desk, bought and paid for by proceeds from my little book, *Asymmetric Hearts*, which he so graciously saw fit to attach himself to.

That is, after the members of the Old School Truants and Sub brigades of Gerianthrax, made a quick and expedient hole in his window to allow in gusts of wind and falling objects to defenestrate. Death by defenestration. I can't think of a more literary or ignoble end! It would be beautiful. I know the law sees fit to try to prevent situations like this from happening, but hiring a legal assassin would just take too much time.

Vanessa and I piled into the car, which careened around the corner as if pursued by Chinese Triad gangsters on crotch rockets. Inside the car there was at least a modicum of silence. Vanessa, ever woman, interrupted it. It did not upset me, because this was the purpose of asking her to accompany me, to see if what really transpired between us was really real or if it was just part of some colossal act to get me to let my guard down enough to be open to suggestion. What suggestion and its context, I could not know for sure. In the grips of paranoia, all becomes pre-conceived notion, a veil, and the world and all its randomness, an impenetrable mind seeking the ultimate goal of your demise.

She acted like she wanted to say something and then motioned towards the driver. I did not know him. He was slim with a bulbous head. Perhaps he was a student at NYU or Columbia University and did this as an unpaid internship. I don't know. I wasn't about to ask him about his background story.

The kid was a good driver, unlike me, when he wanted to do something like change lanes or cut across four lanes of traffic to make a turn; he just did it without hesitation. The automobile appeared to be an extension of his arms and his will. Everything pertaining to driving appeared effortless to this kid who couldn't have been over 20 years of age. Four years of having his license, you don't think he would have had the wherewithal to drive the way he did. Perhaps he was a 35 year old with a rare glandular disorder. He cut perpendicularly across five lanes of traffic and drifted into an alleyway.

"My God, where'd you learn to drive like that?"

No response came from the front. Driving down the one way alley, the wrong way, he came out on a one way street heading the wrong way, but only for the length of a few city bus lengths, before he cut onto a side street which was decidedly built for travel in the direction we were headed, but it was so narrow it wouldn't have mattered much.

"Say there, what's your name?" I asked, definitely directed towards our diminutive driver. Vanessa looked at me with a hint of fear in her eyes when he failed to respond.

"Where are you taking us?" she asked nervously.

Still no response.

"Hey, man, stop this car this very instant!"

Nothing going. I looked at the man again and raised my hand to slap his arm to get his attention, and then I realized there was some wires weaving a trail from his suit pocket to his ears...it was an iPod. Maybe an iPhone. I looked out the window of the SUV, people walking, not talking to each other, not paying much attention save for the ground in front of their feet, insulated from all the pressures and barbs of the world by three feet of miniwire, minispeakers, and a device which Leman Global Industries just so happened to make a key transistor for, through a subsidiary which was headquartered in Shandong, China. That was just another place I would have to visit.

I motioned to Vanessa that we were safe, that there was nothing to worry about because our driver wasn't some maniac bent on doing us harm or some assassin, but rather much like the other people of the fair city, this nexus of information for the new information age, where information in the form of bytes, bits, megabytes and files of music that somewhat sound the same upon a layman's inspection, books on digits, books for children in the hands of every single adult walking about because they were just so distracted and information overloaded between their jobs and everyday life that their brains wouldn't process much more than just a story arc without much complexity.

On the city streets, the people we saw thronging by were part of the all flowing traffic, all iPods and touch screens, people texting, wishing they were somewhere else with someone else, anywhere but where they were, on the way somewhere, full of plans, intentions, worries, the same swum stream, which at once, one time back in the past someone might have stopped another person to ask directions, but now they just pulled out a device and asked it.

I noticed that they passed a panhandler who chose the wrong section of town to beg change from because no one carried change, they carried debit cards, and unless the panhandler had a smart phone with attached little widget to process debit card purchases, he was SOL. He wouldn't make even enough money for a cup of coffee in this dump, especially in one of the many establishments that dotted this urban landscape. The going rate was banker prices for coffee.

Traffic barely moved. The stream parted for the panhandler like a stream in nature would part around a troublesome rock, mossy, shiny on the sides where it was rubbed raw by the flow, stuck in place, ground smooth, worn down. We sat there for two full minutes. I counted not one person who acknowledged the dirty man's presence. These people did not acknowledge each other's presence either, but everyone had somewhere else to be.

I don't think any of them were out for a leisurely stroll, their faces all looked so busy. Their heads never deviated from the selfsame angle, sort of down, sort of looking forward, trudging along. I detected a few smiles in the crowd, but those were in groups of people and they faded as they went trudging on. The businesses along this artery collected a few perspective clients who may have entered because it was a destination along a trail, a waypoint, a respite, or maybe because a sign caught their attention. Where I was headed, I would learn that aspect of our business. Advertising.

Vanessa looked like she had something she wanted to say. I didn't have an iPod to plug in to tune her out so I just looked at her. She held out her hand, and I grasped it. She smiled cherubically, without a hint of malice, and I turned again to look out the window. We arrived on Wall Street, and this kid, who in fact was a kid still, nine years old and from Brazil, maybe one of father's bastard progeny, god only knows, renowned for his ability to navigate and serve as getaway driver for drug lords in some of Rio's most notorious, crowded, and byzantine favelas, discovered by Robert Malvolio who's thumbprint would remain on the organization even if his thumb did not. The kid parked the car and opened the door, like a gentleman.

"Just where are we, kiddo?" I asked the kid.

Before he could answer, a man dressed in a suit provided the answer to me. Ahh yes, always trust the man with the suit on. From now on, we would meet but men in suits who spoke a language, although English, was one that I could not quite understand, because I had not spent enough time in the business of business.

The new English kingmakers and kings language, which I would come to call the New King's English, was designed to provide minimal possible information while also sounding grand and utilizing the maximum possible words to describe something completely mundane, being generally unphilosophical, acceding importance to what among the initiated was not that important.

These were all maxims, which could be summed up with the following mantra: the business of business is business. Its interlocutors were all equally bored, and therefore boring, but all had plenty of money to spend and prices and items for sale to talk about.

Example:

Old King's English: The dog took a shit.

New King's English: The canine, feeling that the gross capacity of its warm feces storage chamber had reached the threshold of maximal fecal content made the decision to flex in contractions of the spasmic variety its abdominal and leg muscles and thus bring its warm feces storage chamber into harmonic balance by forcing removal of the excess processed food. We do not foresee, and this is a forward looking statement, the canine needing to engage in the feces removal operation for at least, but perhaps at most two to three hours given the consumption of food and canine snack treats remains constant.

The suit wrapped gentleman introduced himself as the Director of North American Operations for Leman Global Industries, which I would come to discover, was embroiled in the most boring of all the boring businesses, but probably one of the most essential to global commerce, industry, and manufacturing.

It was so essential and engrained that nearly zero money was spent in the marketing of its products. Suit wrapped man introduced me to suit wrapped man number two whose most distinguishing feature was that his pants were just slightly, ever so slightly high waters, and this was only noticeable to the highly trained eye. These were not exactly clam diggers, but they could have been an inch or maybe an inch and a half longer.

He introduced himself in luminous tons befitting a troubadour as the Corporate President of the North American Manufacturing Association of Ball Bearings and Other Assorted Industrial Lubricants. He was unremarkable except for his title and his bald head, which looked precisely machined just like a ball bearing.

WHERE THE BUSINESS OF THIS BUSINESS CONCERN BECOMES MY CHIEF CONCERN, AND BUSINESS

A whole host of corporate middlemen, all with titles befitting an Order of the Society of Jesus or Holy Orders of some sacred medieval Knights Templar Monastery, ushered Vanessa, whom I introduced as my personal assistant, into the Leman Global Industries Global Headquarters.

"It's a brave new world now, Mr. Leman, and I'm sure you're going to do your father proud and grow the business even more than he was able to," one of the corporate peons said.

"I really don't want to."

"Don't want to grow the business? Businesses either grow or they contract. If you want to remain a going concern, you keep growing and expanding into new markets, find new revenue streams and new product lines to maximize your profit potential," the Corporate Operations Director of Ball Bearings Manufacturing for North America, a wholly owned subsidiary of Leman Global Industries vomited effortlessly from his great steak and potato lunch eating mouth. I detected just the slightest bit of grease on his red tie, which was one of those ties that looked plain but was built of the finest materials to withstand all of the hostile elements in a corporate climate controlled boardroom, even up to a political brouhaha, provided you didn't slop your lunch on it or dip it into a gravy train. Ball bearings being a very precisely engineered manufacturing process, the Chief of Operations was a slob in direct contraposition to his product, which was quite elegant. The other Chiefs of Operations of Leman Global Industries had assembled from their various headquarters around the world to New York City and the building that my great great grandfather built, not knowing fully well how massive an enterprise would flow from these confines.

One corporate Chief of Operations was notably absent as we filled the board room with our prospectuses in hand so that I could learn all the numerous facets of the business or at least as much as I could learn in what would be only a five hour meeting and then dinner in the private dining room of a very exclusive New York Club Restaurant.

The entire time I sat in the boardroom I looked at the empty chair of the Personal Healthcare Products Prophylactics Division Chief of Operations. Apparently, Mr. Gliddenprof saw fit to jump ship as soon as he heard that he would be training me up in the day-to-day happenings of his Division. He had expected all of the positions to just shift up one, much like the College of Cardinals on the death of a Pope. When he found out that eventually, I, the idiot son of Prescott Leman would be taking the reins after he first taught me the ropes, he signed on with a head hunter to get gainful employment elsewhere. The other Chiefs of Operations did not seem to mind, and the Personal Healthcare Operation was one of those that seemed to be able to run without much day to day management.

Vanessa took diligent notes during the meeting, and I played mental games, wondering just why everybody strove so hard to be in the position they were in and how many Machiavellian schemes each of these gentlemen were involved in. They were each equally guarded when talking to me, as if they knew something sinister that I did not, and they would only find out in the near future once they had all ceased droning on and on and brought in the refreshments or dancing girls or whatever else ushered in the conclusion of these ceremonious occasions.

This couldn't be everything. Christ, this was dreadfully boring, and poor Vanessa had to shake her hand from the tension a few times just to keep up with their endless talking back and forth about the gross liquidity of this or zero sum games and other things I really had no idea about. When it came time for the Personal Healthcare Products Prophylactic Division's Chief of Operations to speak, the position now quite vacant, all of the assembled gentlemen just looked at me for guidance. I guess I had assumed the role. I looked at Vanessa, who set her pen down and implored me with her eyes to say something...anything.

I looked up at the men with their stuffy conservative shirts, and with their charcoal suits that they wore to project an image of Corporate uniformity, but to me, they looked like a whole lot of those Puritans you see in the Rembrandt paintings. There wasn't a purple suit in the bunch. I would have to liven this place up a bit. I glanced at them individually, wondering who would break the silence. Then seeing that they were all waiting on me to supply them with some guidance or information, I decided that I was just going to use some of their talking points, but in the end, I decided to do what was perfectly normal for a greenhorn and ask a question.

"Uh. So, that's all very, very, well and, uh, good and interesting. You're all doing a good job. Uh...gross liquidity seems to be in order. Mining operations are on track. Now, well, can someone tell me just what the Personal Healthcare Prophylactics Branch...I mean Division, product is?"

There were a few dislocated guffaws from around the room. Some of the Heavy Industrial Equipment and Capital Goods Chiefs were turning red trying to suppress laughter. The Industrial Lubricants Chief elbowed the Chief of Global Mining to speak.

"Got something to share, Charles?" I inquired like a schoolteacher in a room of unruly children.

"Prophylactics."

"Prophylactics?"

"Male Prophylactics."

"Uhh…."

"Condoms, sir. Male condoms."

"Condoms. Hmm…."

"Yes, sir, both the lubricated and unlubricated. Many sizes, shapes, color, and grades of latex."

"We make condoms?"

"Yes, sir, we've been pumping them out for, about, oh, seventy five years now."

"And this is what I'm going to be in charge of?"

The men in the room stopped their snickers and each looked around at his fellow businessman. They finally realized what I had realized before ever taking this gig on, that I had no idea what I was doing nor did I possess any of the knowledge of the lubricated and unlubricated condom business.

The Chief of Mining Operations spoke up. "Sir," he said, "I'm going to call Gliddenprof back in as a consultant at double whatever the people at that substandard manufacturer of adult novelty items pays him. I'm sure he'll be happy to hear from us."

"Throw in a company car," I said.

"That might not be enough."

"Give him a membership to the golf club, make him feel like we'll welcome him back as a full-fledged chief of operations. Of course he'll just be a consultant, but make sure that he gets a discount on the employee health plan…he'll have to know the option is always available that he receive full employee coverage if he becomes a full-fledged officer again. But for now, he'll remain a mercenary until we determine his loyalty level. He did leave us, remember that."

"Yeah, could be beneficial to know what those schmucks and busybodies over at Fleshsword Sheafing Incorporated are up to.

"Nothing much. Probably still making finger cots and making micropenis condoms again for the preschoolers."

"Kids these days."

It was settled. Frank Gliddenprof would receive an offer of three million dollars for a term of contract of six months, provided he quit his new job and agree to provide his new temporary employer with what he had shared with his newest full time employer, as well as what he learned while on the job for the three weeks he had been away. Fleshsword Sheafing was our main competitor in the male condom business. They were right, competitive bastards.

Upon acceptance of the contract, he would receive a full debriefing by LGI representative at an undisclosed location prior to signing a non-disclosure agreement dispensed by the medicine men at our pluck little pharmaceutical division to see if there were any new insights into the manufacture of ribbed for her pleasure, terrifically tactile, reservoir tipped prophylactics, including whether nonoxonyl-9 could be made strawberry flavored, or would remain that nasty bitter face-inducing flavor of industrial junk. Their prophylactics were manufactured in the same old boring way without innovation, doled out of those huge rolling machines and molded onto metallic lock cylinders, tapered at the base, finally being blown up to the size of a Moby Dick before being deflated, lubricated, and packaged in brightly colored love packets.

I do not know how the condoms are actually lubricated, I only know that the rubber, great mounds of it, fresh from the tree rubber plantations goes in one door and out the other comes boxes of little boxes, each containing one, three, nine, twelve, or up to thirty six condoms in an orgy-sized economy pack.

They are not stamped with our corporate symbol, as we do not actually manufacture anything. The subsidiaries manufacture the products, and we merely sell them and manage the business. The business includes the marketing of the thing being sold. We design our marketing campaigns in house for utmost security, and we refuse to hire anyone external to accomplish these campaigns. "We know our own products best, so how on Earth can someone else sell what you manufactured?" my father used to say. We know the value of the products we offer, so if they weren't valuable, we wouldn't be manufacturing them to the high exacting standards we follow.

Gliddenprof keyed me into all the ins and outs of male condom manufacturing. And that is the man made manufacturing process of the lubricated condom, manufactured to specific tolerances to fit over the vast majority of phalli around the world, with some even manufactured in tiny batches for the abnormally large or abnormally small outliers, mainly marketed towards the pornographic industry for easy money shot yankoffability, as well as smelling like roses when used for particularly vigorous anal gape films. There were tiny batches made for micropenises and to control the wild population numbers of our less endowed simian zoo populations, though they have large testes with ample sperm volume, I'm told they have ridiculously tiny cocks, with the tiniest cocked beast being the Golden Lion Tamarin.

I'm told that some simians in the London zoo have actually learned to open up the shiny packages, but thus far have only taken to rolling the condoms out to their full length, smiling, and then stretching the them back and forth until they break across the chimps' fingers. Upon discovering that this hurt they took to snapping the chimp buttocks of their fellow cage mates, much to the delight of tourists and chagrin of animal right's activists. This was all a ploy by the marketing department to show that microcock condoms, which we originally issued as Mighty Minis..."You're a Mighty, Mighty, Mighty MAN!" booming over the loudspeakers, were able to be figured out and used by our less smart simian relatives, they should be able to be figured out by an entire Irish Catholic parish. Fat chance in that product selling well.

Maybe it was time to bring in a marketing consultant to see which product lines we should axe and which ones to keep afloat as well as maybe design as series of ad campaigns for us. From what I understood, we were due for a complete brand overhaul of our King Kong Dong, Maxtros, Anal Destroyers (ridged maximally for friction's sake, girth extending, ejaculatory prolongers) and also the condoms designed to shroud the testicles from what's known in the industry as "anal slappage", called BALL CRAB DEFENDERS. We even had a condom designed to be worn like a pair of britches to prevent any lower body contact whatsoever, which I found patent infringingly similar to my cock out jeans that I wanted to attempt to market, but you know all great geniuses think alike), and it's so similar that I really want to bring this market under its original name, The Herpes Preventer Pal nicknamed the HIPPIE, and it's lubricated version called the SLIPPY HIPPIE.

From the original 1974 trials, the contraption to a trained practitioner took no less than ten minutes to put on at which time he usually lost wood or his partner left in disgust thinking that the man struggling and sweating to get into this contraption, which resembled the zero gravity pressurization britches from a Russian Cosmonaut's suit, did not trust her enough to even use a regular condom. This made me wonder. The pullout method is an extremely effective method for reducing pregnancy. I think it's about eighty percent effective more than blowing loads in your partner and hoping for the best. Don't most condom sales stem from a lack of trust between two people? You think if people were responsible and decent then they would tell each other if they had something fishy going on below the belt or just abstain from intercourse. There's no sense fucking an untrustworthy partner. Just love yourself, and masturbate.

Speaking of hot fucking, Vanessa and I have been fucking like rabbits everyday, multiple times a day, for weeks. Even though I'm the acting head of operations for the world leader of prophylactic manufacturing and sales, I never wear the things. Wearing one is like a man wearing a pink leather-racing suit to a Hell's Angels rally. You're there to take risks. Nature is founded upon it. You either trust her or you don't. If you don't, you shouldn't be talking to her because there's a lot worse she could get you involved with than a couple of bumps on the tip of your cock. I explained this conception to Gliddenprof the first day of his job mentoring me on all the ins and outs of LGICD - The Leman Global Industries Condom Division. I renamed it from the Prophylactic Division. Might as well call a spade a spade. I decided to change all the names from their obscurantist titles, which Gliddenprof did not agree with.

He also really didn't like my ideas for the marketing campaigns of all our various Condom Brands, LEMAN GLOBAL INDUSTRIES FAMILY OF CONDOMS, IF YOU USE THE OTHER BRANDS YOU'LL GET AIDS. Or HOW DID MARY GET A BUN IN THE OVEN? TED DIDN'T USE A LEMAN BECAUSE HE WAS A CHEAPSKATE, AND NOW HE'S GOT A BABY TO TAKE CARE OF. HOPE YOU CAN MAKE YOUR CHILD SUPPORT PAYMENTS TED! I think my marketing schemes are brilliant and true, but he explained to me that I couldn't just go about insulting the other firms and saying their products will fail in the prevention of disease and unwanted pregnancy. He told me that firms were like people, and you had a right to sue other firms if they made disparaging comments about you that weren't true. It was called slander or libel or some such bullshit.

Yes, Vanessa and I are dating exclusively and officially, and I'm in love with her. We spend all of our time together, and we fuck like jackrabbits, royally and mightily, without using condoms. Instead, I pull out and leave it all over her stomach. I've yet to leave a direct hit in her belly button, because as you might remember, I'm a dribbler and not a powerful shooter. To become a shooter, you have to practice and do kegel exercises and all that, but I don't have time to practice because I'm trying to manage a corporation with quarterly gross profit of 12.65 billion dollars, and that's Billion with a B, and not Million with an M, thank you.

Ray Lefebvre called me on the eve of my planned trip to visit the Lubricated and Unlubricated Condom Factory in Thailand and told me that the troops were ready and in order to depart the Great Plain States to converge upon New York City. He told me in his pocket he carried a trump card. Vertical Hell, a newly formed Segway gang, would be joining the Old School Truants and Gerianthrax. Vertical Hell was probably the fastest growing collection of Hell's Angels retirees, and they had a chip on their shoulder that smoldered and grew day by day because their doctors had forbidden them to ride Harley Davidsons. The good vibrations are bad for old bones.

Gerianthrax and the Old School Truants rode strictly Harley Davidsons and BMW Motorcycles, usually the cruiser variety with one of the cargo compartments stuffed full of foodstuffs and the other full of war implements to remind them where they came from and the violent summers of their youth, out on the prairie before it became butter soft, untilled, and the rugged farmland was sold for miles and miles of strip mall after paved fishbowl in every town and city with no overarching industry, and you'd see the factories where these men who formed the biker gangs worked, abandoned in favor of places where customer service skills were required. A place where telling someone to fuck off and shove it up their ass was the chief sin among the cardinal sins.

No, these retired persons came from a different era where people were not afraid of taking a massive risk because they were adequately bored, but not bored enough to give into the ennui of 5000 channel television, just bored enough to sell everything and strap themselves in a motorcycle and hit the open road.

What Lefebvre promised us with Vertical Hell was a new incarnation of the time-honored tradition of American mob violence. Dispossessed people whose only possession were their two wheels. Not motorcycles, no, not wheels arranged on an X axis, wheels aligned on the Y axis to enable the rider to stand vertically and amplify the rage they felt in their hearts. They rode vertically, eyes fixed on the infinite horizon in hate. Eyes on the mission, no mission too large, because if they failed they were dead anyway, and they didn't believe in that false American dichotomy of winners and losers that every Sunday football game and election seemed to perpetuate. They believed only in the dead and the living. They believed in the present act of busting heads and in the future act of preparing to bust heads.

You could say they were composed of military service veterans but these people really saw only a piece of the conflict before they were tossed out on drunken disorderly misconduct, served up a big chicken dinner, and otherwise disenfranchised and tossed out on the street to make their way in the world. Some were college boys who failed one too many rhetoric papers because it so bored them to tears, and they didn't have enough sense to just man up and play the game because everybody's watching and rooting for you to fall flat on your face. And sometimes, when these geezers rode their Segways into combat, some did just that.

They were Vertical Hell and they rode Segway Personal Transporters in violation of several New York City Ordnances. They hailed from small towns in the New England states and the blood of militiamen flowed in their veins or from the Great Plains States and the blood of pioneers coursed and eddied in their arteries. They came from all over the States where men were still rough and rugged and chomping at the bit for action. And now they were ready for our own little adventure this Saturday, for I've been invited to a little literary gathering: a coming out debutante party for a previously unknown author who just wrote a book for kids that every woman and her teenaged daughter just seem to love, but her name escapes me.

I was invited to the party, but I would be crashing into it like a tsunami wave crashing into Hampton's balsawood beachfront property after an asteroid the size of Texas hit the Atlantic Ocean. My agent wouldn't know what hit him. What would I do? Act like the Manson family and terrorize and kill everybody, write names in blood of popular rappers who inspired me, chop the fetuses from wombs, toss it all out the window, and scream to high heaven my rage? No, I would not do these things. Those games are for sickos with no moral compass. I merely wanted to fire my agent and tell him that he is no longer necessary because I no longer desire to write anything anyone else wanted to read prior to my writing it. Once I did this, once I had my final break, I could free myself of all these demons, wily, cunning, scheming for control, that had been manifesting and testing themselves in my rabid mind.

I had a thought today: I cannot escape my thoughts. They are as much a part of me as my arms and legs, my fingers and my toes, and my great swinging dick. Just as I cannot escape my thoughts, I also cannot censor them. I can act in a certain way and give credence to my thoughts for I would like, love to, in fact, go about smashing things, including people's faces who looked at me, who just gandered in my direction, but that would mean that I actually was a madman instead of having what I think, are the thoughts of one.

My thoughts might be quite tame to someone who actually is a violent, depraved, a maniac person, writer of literature, fucker, and schemer after rich widows, adulterer, the whole host of human goodness and depravity. It all coheres in thoughts, rises in thoughts, finds its roots in someone dreaming it up and giving it a voice in action. I have a voice in this matter, and I'm going to proclaim it.

It was seemingly innocuous once the geriatrics began arriving in small droves. Soon, when hundreds of geriatrics who rode Segway Personal Transport vehicles began to descend on Manhattan, the police were certain to know that something was up. I thought about asking the Vertical Hell leadership if they could stash their Segways elsewhere and just descend on Manhattan on foot or by taxicab or Subway like everyone else. For Ray Lefebvre, this was totally out of question, and not even up for discussion. They were Vertical Hell, not Bipedal Hell. They would ride their Segways or not ride in at all. Vertical Hell would as much die as walk anywhere. It was agreed to.

The night of the soiree and coming out party for the lady who's name I forgot, you know, author of the book which tons of people out there read and liked though they forgot the reason when they sat down, much like McDonalds fills the belly but doesn't satisfy your soul and potato chip bags litter the dumpsters of Wally World but are forgotten when the wind blows. This lit chick was rich. And I suppose that was why she was being celebrated. I just have never heard her name on the lips of the people, but I'm sure she's the talk of the Internet for several months now, and her book is, like, really fine and dandy and well received by the kiddies, but who knew? I for one, cannot remember her name.

Vanessa and I decided that we were being highly irresponsible using the pull-out method as a form of birth control and decided to start employing Leman Global Industries' several brands of condoms into our sex life. Really, I never told her this, but we were totally beyond the natural lusty sex and sweaty fucking phase of our relationship and well into the point at which many healthy children are brought into this world through unintended pregnancies which used to result in a couple years' duration marriages but now just result in paternity tests and Maury Povich show visits. Welfare and child support payments. Still worse than those calamaties, was unwanted children. An invite to a party you did not want to attend.

We decided not to be like these people and to do the responsible thing, which was to wrap it up. We were no longer in the sweaty, dripping, rambunctious phase of our relationship and were instead in the well-planned out, rehearsed, sometimes taking on sub/dom roles phase. Sometimes I dressed like a knight and she dressed like a damsel in distress, and at other times I would engage in her rape fantasies after I slid the default blue colored condom down the shaft of my cock. Each time I did this, I lost a slight bit of pressure in my erection, but quickly regained it when I tossed her on the bed and forcefully stuffed in her holy, gushing lady temple. You know, I could get used to this.

Still, I was not large enough for the King Kong Dong, Man's Man, or Trident XL brands and had to settle on Meager Jimmy Value Brand, because going any smaller put me into nearly the kid's sizes for the prepubescent, sexually active youngster or the training models for toddlers. It's not like the big dong versions aren't tapered at the end. I could wear one if I wanted to. This was a point of contention between Gliddenprof and me; I told him that condom sales were in no way shaped by the marketing that goes into them but instead shaped by the individual's perception of themselves or the reality of their wiener size. All the money we dumped into marketing was better spent educating people of the truth of why they should wear a prophylactic, and all he was responsible for as creating a great deception with smoke and mirror tricks.

It went something like this. Gliddenprof and I traveled to the airport to visit our Lubricated and Unlubricated Condom factory in Thailand, which incidentally also filled orders for thirty five inferior brands of prophylactics, all of which we owned and sold to their packagers and distributors.

"It doesn't make any sense that we spend 3.5 million dollars to put a Mr. Happy Big Dong advertisement on during the Super Bowl when it's already our most popular brand in India under the Brand name Shiva Would Be Proud. I mean, we're selling condoms here; we don't need to advertise them. Word of mouth will be enough."

"You've got it all wrong, Mr. Leman. During the decisive moment, whether it be in the bathroom of a bar, a bowl of condoms put out at the doctor's office, or waiting in line at the pharmacy, the people want, err, men to think about Leman Global Industries Brand Condoms. We don't want them thinking about any other brand for safety, reliability, comfort, elasticity, quality of lubrication, scent, or any other qualitative feature. We also don't want them thinking of the price they will have to pay for our condoms is out of line with their pocketbooks. We want them to be comfortable paying that inflated price. We want them to wear our condoms and feel like a king, a prince, like it's a luxury item."

"You don't get what I'm saying. They're strips of rubber that you put on your cock to keep it from the woman's vaginal juices and to keep the juicy bits of your cock from her mucous membranes. It protects against HIV and other diseases. It keeps a man's swimmers from meeting their target. Why do we spend so much damn money advertising this without actually talking about that? Why not ask our customers, 'Think about it. Do you really want children to tie you down?' or 'Want some AIDS with that beer?'"

"We're selling people an experience."

"Why not tell them the truth?"

"The truth is bleak, so we have to sell them something in addition to the truth. We have to add value to the truth. It will be the truth in brilliant palatable packaging."

"An illusion."

"Yeah, so what? As long as they sell, fly off the shelves, and put money in our pockets, so what?"

"It's stupid. What you do with your life and your time is stupid."

"Rebel in your own time, but remember you're on the company's time right now. Whatever doesn't improve the bottom line should be discarded. That includes people."

"Spending three million dollars for a Super Bowl ad for something that is already our top seller is ridiculous. We could donate that money to someone."

"Wow. Now you're talking."

"We should."

"I don't think so."

"Why not donate it to AIDS research? Say that on the box. It will remind the people more that they should be protecting themselves."

"AIDS is such a mood killer. We want to be thought of as foreplay. It's helping our competition. That would be like telling people there's a coupon for a free vasectomy in every hundredth box."

"Face it, condoms suck. They're like snow pants."

"They're a money maker. You'll come to see that. They also serve a vital function. You'll come to see that. They're scientifically manufactured. You'll come to see that too."

"You still haven't answered my question. Why can't we just make our condoms and not advertise them?"

"Because we're asking to be buried!"

"We're not going to be buried. You told me we make the highest quality. So why do we have to advertise them. Won't people just be able to tell that?"

"I must bite my tongue so I don't have to scold you for being so, so, well, ah damnit, stupid! Are you kidding me?"

"It's just a question. You don't have to get all bent out of shape."

"Tell me, you're a writer...are you just going to dump your next novel of yours out into the world without marketing it at all?"

"Yes. And the one after that, and the one after that, and so on until my pen falls from my cold, dead fingers. I may not even put them into final form, but instead just write them and not care what becomes of them. I'll just care what I put into them, for the craft, the act, not the reception by the public too blunted and dulled by advertisements to comprehend anything with any depth to it. So what if the public loves what I've written, it will be as shitty as whatever is selling right now. If that's the only thing it has going for it, no thanks! It's a sham. I'll just be as desiccated and lame as the phony condom advertisements you hawk. Real, natural things that are fulfilling should just sell themselves once a few people hear about them. They shouldn't need to be hoisted up and dangled over the masses!"

"My ads resonate as the most memorable condom advertisements of an entire generation, boy! Mr. Happy Big Dong? That's mine! King Kong Dong? That's mine! The Mediocre Johnson? Mine too! I'm a fucking genius of condom manufacturing and marketing! You can't take that from me!"

"It's stupid. And if you ever call me boy again, you'll find yourself out on your ass in the street, and I'll make sure you never surface to write another rubber jingle."

"Well...I never...."

"Never heard that from my father? Tell me, how was he? Maybe I can piece his biography together by interviewing all of you twerps."

"You've got a lot to learn about business."

"I don't care to learn it. The science of getting things done. Covering your ass. You're so deluded that you can't even see what's in front of your face."

"You're the deluded one. We both know it."

"Sign away your business then, and go off and spend your millions."

"You'd love that."

"We would all love nothing more than for you to go away."

Instead of teaching me the business as he was supposed to do and had been paid a sizeable sum of money to do, Mr. Gliddenprof took to inciting me to rages in a report he would promulgate for the board to attempt to arrange for my dismissal, as if he could actually do that.

The other board members knew that I had several kinks to work out, and they told me this on a nearly daily basis via email and conference call. Still, business went on as usual. I think they thought I was worth keeping around. I was easy to manipulate and keep in check because I didn't know anything about the business or my father's true holdings. All I did know was that I had been having very strange dreams as of late, dreams that began when I rolled off Vanessa and fell into a deep sleep while cuddling her. I had never really dreamed before, or perhaps I never really remembered my dreams because they were of no consequence.

Maybe it's because I'm stressed out, and prior to this I lead a relatively stress free existence that I did not dream. Or maybe I dreamed and they were not as vivid. For instance, I had a dream where I was a little boy again. In this dream I was walking down a crowded street, following a man whose face was always turned from me. I followed him and tried to get close to him but people in the crowd were always bouncing off of me chattering nonsense at me. I followed this man to a darkened doorway and went inside.

I entered a maze, following him, but never quite catching up to him. The walls of the maze were covered in paintings, all remarkable, masterpieces. I wanted to stop to look at them, but I kept following the man. In the center of the maze, I found him painting a naked woman, the man lost in trance, sweating heavily, painting an exact reproduction of her beauty on the canvas. While he painted, and they both did not notice me observing them, she sang and I heard her voice through the dusty, incense smoky haze:

My beauty is my meaninglessness

Your beauty is your meaninglessness

My strength is that I am not a thing

Your strength is that you are not a thing

All else is a cage, a trap, and a snare

Designed by men for men to feel

Safe in their beds when the Earth spins on its axis

And the lights go out.

Men have built a superstructure to replace our Eve of time

It will fail, crumble, and bury them.

And time, a snake, will slither on.

I closed my ears to the sounds, not wanting to hear anything.

I awoke in a pool of sweat, and I wrote my dream down. I woke and Vanessa woke. I told her the contents of the dream in rambling incoherent babble.

"It's nothing," she said. "You were dreaming of nothing."

"I didn't. Surely it means something."

"No it doesn't. A person's dreams don't mean anything. It's the meaning you give them. Your dreams mean nothing before that."

I would come to discover what meaning this dream had for my life. It would not come for some time in the future after many trials and tribulations. Vanessa was a wise woman, well wise beyond her now twenty years. Twenty years of gorgeousness and study, not resting on her laurels, or content to just be another pretty flower flapping in the breeze. For now, I took it that I am nothing until I stop struggling to overcome fear and begin by not giving into it from its very inception like the mad painter in my dream, just blazing forth through the crowd to my favorite activity.

I came to realize that the only way I would be free of fear is if I were constantly distracted, not distracted by the ash and smoke and noise, but distracted by my own thoughts, my own intentions, in accomplishing what I willed. Right now, at this very instant, I will myself to be a literary artist, to write, to experience, and to share my experiences through my pen until my pen falls from my cold, dead fingers.

Notice I said nothing about happiness, for that too is a distraction that comes without our input. Happiness is an addition to states of affairs. So, I gave up on happiness or what I thought happiness was going to be, because I found it merely safety, mundane, boring mediocrity, or not even mediocrity, but deep risk aversion and not just failure, but rather unwillingness to even try, and I determined to myself that I would distract myself and my own din would rise above the din of the world and the modern age, and I would cast pen to paper without thinking, writing what I wanted, creating. This may seem contradictory to you, but much of what we practice these days is as well. Contradictory. Without merit.

When I awoke and Vanessa stirred beside me, she asked me if everything was good, and I was all right. I kissed her, kneaded her breast, and woke her fully by making love to her gently, which lasted about five minutes. Afterwards, as she snoozed, I showered and solidified my intention to quit the world fully in my mind. I said it over and over and over to myself, that I would have nothing more to do with any of it.

All of its systems, all the hopes, all the dreams, the collective terrors that moved the people to and fro, sent them careening all over the world in search of long lost love and newfound freedoms, the madness, the deep profound hope that the thought of which and feeling kept them all ticking, and in line, it was going to all be behind me. I was going to kill it in myself. I wasn't going to go out like my mom had gone out. I was too good to consider suicide. I mean, wait, she was murdered.

To do that, I would have to have all the answers. I don't. I'm not Jesus Christ. I'm Jackson Leman. I don't care about much, but I do know what and whom I care about, and I don't care about anything, anyone, or any other activity besides those. If you do an inventory of what you really actually care about, not value, because value attaches itself to things far beyond your ability to control or influence them, if you do an inventory of what you really truly care about and only pursue those cards, you will have a great deal more freedom and more mental space, and you will actually be a genuinely caring person.

So, as the water beat off my skin and washed the sweat from my lovemaking away, I decided what I really cared about, whom I really cared about, and what could be let go. Leman Global Industries did not make the cut.

You may think me insane for desiring to sell off and flush down the toilet, an organization that employed hundreds of thousands of people globally, had global profits in excess of 20 billion dollars annually, and consistently turned out products that came to seem like necessities and were in fact necessities etched fully into modern life...not to mention that it generated me a nearly infinite expense account where I could buy all the toys and fashionable clothes and trips anywhere in the world that I wanted.

Every young man's wet dream, right? My only thought was my absence of care for wanting to keep seeing it going on as a concern, my absolutely nihilistic confidence that I did not wish to see myself continue on with that enterprise. And why not? I can't really explain it any more than you cannot tell me that blue is your favorite color or why purple is not your favorite color. I just don't care about Leman Global Industries. However, I do care about the employees, so I won't just willy-nilly fire everyone and tell them to go home and find another job. I'm going to let the managers take the company public and give it a different name totally unrelated to Leman. I haven't thought of one yet, perhaps the board of directors can just hire some business consultant firm to brainstorm possible names that convey the message we are trying to convey.

Personally, I would vouchsafe MONAD INDUSTRIES, because we are reflected in pretty much everything else made in the world today, but that is somewhat obscure, and you have to be acquainted with the philosophies of Leibniz to understand it. I wouldn't expect my readers of *Asymmetric Hearts* to understand. This, I will bring up in front of the board. It is not that I want to go against the dying wishes of my father, but I suppose I can introduce into the corporate charter for the new public corporation, that the company can never perform any functions or imbed itself in the supply chain, any supply chain, or parts manufacturer for the industries for war or defense, if that is even possible these days. We would be a great black hole to defense contractors and only lend our products, which are present in pretty much anything, anyway to the pursuit of peace. I'm sure the board would find these terms amenable.

Like I told you, I'm getting out of my literary contract because it is based on a sham. Prior to this, I did not write what sprung from my soul; I did a marketing survey and wrote something just to make a fast buck once it was discovered. I didn't need to be discovered because father made sure his agents buying it would put it to the top of the New York Times Bestseller lists within a fortnight.

Add to the mix, a young, handsome author who was not inclined to give interviews and an inclusion in *Oprah's Book Club,* and voila a literary phenomenon was created. I don't know if that same strategy would suffice today, but I wasn't going to try it. I would bury my manuscripts under rocks if need be, waterproof them, and hope against hope that someone, somewhere would read them and find value in them for their life. This would probably be after I'm long dead, and if someone in the future finds worth in any of the books and the thoughts I have written down, it's worth all the glory, fame, long lines at book signings, young women throwing themselves at me, interviews in magazines, being photographed to be a somewhat brainy intellectual type in scotch and cigar ads, and in general making money hand over fist on the whole endeavor. I will be free to write the truth, as I perceive it and say it no matter the consequences – be it notoriety, no sales, or dying completely unknown. I won't write bullshit anymore.

What is success anyway? To me, it's just the act of doing. The remainder is all perception on the part of others. Even if everyone else in the world calls you a success, you can still think yourself a miserable failure, especially if you're not doing what you want to be doing.

As an artist, you will hate the finished product and love the act of bringing something into being from nothing other than the recesses of your imagination. Business people care about this finished product and artists care about process. I doubt the two can cohere in the same person. Comparing apples and oranges, if Vincent Van were still alive today and saw his paintings selling for hundreds of millions of dollars, he would by necessity change his style so he was again original and people once more thought his paintings no good, poorly executed trash because it clashed with their sense of the good and proper, because it was so new and ran so far ahead of everything that the people who cared about art and bought it for investment would think him again a degenerate hack artist.

But the pejorative "artist" still applies. Let posterity judge you when you're long dead and decide if you've added anything of value. What's the alternative? To add nothing? To consume? Only the Art Institute of Chicago cares who bought what painting and donated which collection to the museum. No one else does. While I'm at it, I'll donate father's art collection to a museum, and I won't name a wing after him. I'll name it after my mother.

Where should I go? There's much to see in the world, and I feel I have limitless options because I'm young and have my health. I tickled Vanessa on her ribs to try and get her to wake up.

"Let's travel while we're still young."

"Let me sleep."

"We can sleep while we're dead, honey."

"Ugh...what's with you and all this talk of dying? Just let me sleep."

"It's an expression. I've got some business to handle. You sleep."

She sprang up. "You don't need me?"

"No, I've got it covered today."

"I can come to the office if you need me."

"It's not very important. Plus you aren't really my personal assistant, and every-body knows that."

"What am I then?"

"My lover."

"So this is the talk, then."

"I guess it is."

"You don't know where you stand."

"I don't."

"You have to hear me say something."

"I think I'm entitled to that, because...."

"Why?"

"Why?"

"I'm with you aren't I?"

"But you never tell me anything. You never tell me what's going on in that head of yours."

"What? I do too."

"No, you don't. You don't share anything with me."

"I'm here, aren't I?"

"Yes and no."

"What are you getting at?"

"You never tell me what you're thinking."

"I don't know half of the time. My thoughts come and go. I get about half of one formulated, snared, horseshoed, then it's off to the races again. I'm sorry. It comes from being alone for so long."

"But you had friends on the trip with you."

"No, I didn't."

"You were looking for them when we found you."

"If I had friends, they weren't real."

"Oh, they were just acting like they cared about you and acting like they were your friends, but they were really using you."

"You could say that."

"I'm sorry."

"It's okay. I've got you now, and you're real."

Gliddenprof was not pleased that I canceled our upcoming trip to Thailand.

"Just how are you going to learn about the manufacturing, distribution, and marketing of lubricated and unlubricated condoms in the third world? We were to go to follow on trips to Shanghai, Beijing," he said.

Ah, yes, where our condoms are distributed as Happy Man With Smile Brand after first being purchased after a cheap discount, nearly at cost, and then distributed by People's WAU TU Company for Healthcare. This was all a way for my father to keep the Chinese out of the Lubricated Condom manufacturing business, which they would surely overtake and flood the burgeoning markets of East Asia, Africa, and India with an inferior and cheaply priced product. By selling them prophylactics at cost we insured that we were doing our patriotic duty of keeping Red China at bay. It was important for them to have quality in keeping with their one child policy.

That could be a marketing ploy: nothing gets past the KEEPER. Perhaps they'd be more popular in Brazil, South America, or some African countries where futbol resonated more with the populace. Confucius say, "if you don't want your dragon to breathe fire, you must keep him dry in the rain." It could possibly make it past our cultural response panel and be in magazines and Internet advertisements within the week. I didn't come to write advertisements, though; I came to drop a bombshell on all these moles. They'd at least be happy to have me out of the way.

"Call a board meeting, Gliddy," I said.

"Whatever for? We're not doing that until the end of the month. Everyone's scattered all over the globe."

"Let's go to VTC then. I need to have a word with everyone."

"You're calling an emergency meeting? What's the emergency?"

"Just call it. You'll find out soon enough."

"This has to be an actual emergency for you to call it."

"Who says?"

"Well that's how...."

"My father did things? Call the meeting. Send them emails. Have your secretary call their secretaries. Just do it now! Damn you!"

"Yes, sir!"

We brought five seventy two inch plasma screen televisions in and arranged them around the mahogany board room meeting table where the stuffed suits would normally sit, as they waited for my announcement, but for now the large, high-definition screens would have to suffice. On their end, my face, terrifying, bulbous, and on the day of the video teleconference, I hoped it was oily, full of blackheads, and pimply.

I would not even wear the makeup that Gliddenprof suggested. This would not be akin to briefing of the 2003 Invasion of Iraq by the Bush Administration. Just another farce. This was not political theater, meant to convey a message. It would be me giving the assembled gentleman my true feelings and time to come up with a plan to take Leman Global Industries into the public. I would try my best to not appear like a deer in the headlights. I would try my best not to seem like a dyed in the wool greenhorn in front of all these sharks. I hoped I wouldn't look like Dubya.

They would have questions, I'm sure. Questions like, "What's going to happen to all of us?" The smart ones would couch their concerns within the concerns of the overall business, saying, "What's going to happen to Leman Global Industries?" Nothing. The madmen would get their chance to take the business public. I'm sure they'd love the sexy stock options, the shareholder meetings, selling their stock to institutional investors, shopping it around to pension funds as the blue chip of all blue chips. Something guaranteed to keep increasing and gaining in value over time. Let's face it. I'm not a manager.

My father was a fool to ever leave the corporation to me. He probably figured that I would give it away. Wait! Maybe this is what he wanted me to do all along? Perhaps this was all a ploy. If he had wanted to continue this business ad infinitum he would have handed the thing to Sheldon to run.

Or maybe he didn't want me to run it into the ground, but rather succeed at something besides just sitting there staring down my writer's block, thinking about pulling out my .45, which apparently I had also left somewhere. In the car! With Malvolio! You know what! I think after this whole VTC is over and done with, I might just try and look him up, see if I can find him on Facebook. Richard Avalon certainly hadn't located him. Dipshit. The only person Gliddenprof had hired was an interior decorator to make sure that the VTC "studio," as he called it, was as nice looking, and by nice looking he meant symmetrical and without a white background or I would appear washed out in it. The background would be green, which the designer Emilio selected amongst all the other symbolic colors because it symbolized new beginnings. But it just looked green to me.

On the green brocade, he painted a dainty pattern with paint containing real gold. Emilio brought heavy, medieval looking curtains and drapes and commissioned a tapestry for the wall behind me that five computers attached to digital looms could print out in approximately two or three days. Emilio promised it sooner because he had an "in" with the company who made the tapestries. What this "in" was, I couldn't guess. Every time he talked about this "in" he did so in a flirtatious manner, putting his hand on his hips and winking his eyes at me. Gliddenprof left the room, and Emilio kept talking about his "in" in the company.

"Who's your in?" I asked.

"He's a friend of yours too."

"Who?"

"Robert Malvolio."

"What?"

"Yes. He wants to see you, stud."

"How do you know him?"

"I just do."

"Where should I meet him?"

"Just make yourself available."

"What's that supposed to mean?"

"You ask a lot of questions. Where did you meet him the first time you met him?"

"He sort of found me when a couple of people were trying to kill me."

"Well go out there and get into trouble, I guess."

"Do you really know anything? Does anyone really know anything? What am I supposed to do?"

"I wish I knew. That's all I was told...to tell you to seek out Robert Malvolio."

"That evil bastard, I'll seek him out alright."

I knew what I had to do.

"Gliddenprof! Let's get this started!"

"We don't have the tapestries yet!"

"Do it with the blank, black walls. We don't need any tapestries!"

I turned the camera on as Gliddenprof frantically called the other Chiefs of Operations. My face looked huge on the screen like some psychotic dictator or a giant planetoid's surface glistening with ice. One by one the screens flickered to life with stone poker faces. The Chief of Mining and Earth Reclamation Operations, Charles Wendig III, appeared to be sweating heavily, on the verge of a massive coronary.

"I'm stepping away from the company," I said. My voice boomed over the loudspeakers.

Still poker faces remained, from Sal Singlehammer, head of Modern Consumables, makers of toilet paper, tampons, and ink printer cartridges, I detected a slight smile, and then he caught himself and resumed his poker-faced expression. Everyone was so serious, almost to the point of death.

"I've decided that I really have no business acumen and any attempt on my own part to gain any business acumen was just a farce and the overarching fact and feeling that I really don't give two shits about all this. I've been wasting my time concerning myself with things that shouldn't concern me, so therefore, I'm stepping down to pursue my writing career full time."

"What's going to become of Leman Global Industries?" they asked me in unison.

"I'd like you to take it public. Take into consideration that my father's wishes, that it never get involved with the defense industry, in no part of it, from logistics to even providing the nuts and bolts for a toilet paper dispenser in an aircraft carrier are respected. His wishes must be respected, even though I could not respect him as a man. None of this is me. It never has been."

"Take the corporation public? Have an IPO?"

"Yes. You know, have an IPO. Sell it off. Break it up. Whatever you will."

"Sir, as a public corporation, we won't be able to engage in our other activities."

"So what."

"We're provided a highly useful advantage by remaining a private corporation. No accountability," Charles Wendig III said.

The dissent was not well received, and the Chiefs bantered back and forth amongst themselves gruffly.

"I didn't ask your opinions on the matter. This corporation is a tyranny. You follow orders to the letter. My orders. I'm really not a tyrant, and I refuse to be one. I'm an artist. I am a member of one of the most maligned professions ever. The profession on the totem pole right below spies and prostitutes, though you businessmen at least thing those two groups of people are at least useful. You malign us in our lifetimes because you think we aren't doing anything productive. We aren't contributing to the GDP, frittering away our time in meetings, dreaming up products, managing things. No, we're not doing anything like that; we're making life bearable. It would be nice to be known and make tons of money, but our profession doesn't really lend itself to that, unless you've had help like I've had, unless you've got financial backing, or unless you won the jackpot when you were born. I'm...you know what I am...I'm a crusader against boredom and ennui. I'm trying to add a little bit of light into this overly dreary dream world, which doesn't have to be this way. It's the world we've made. Well, I don't want to make it that way anymore. I'm stepping aside. Standing down. Dropping out. Arrange to sell it off. You hear me? Do it as soon as you can!"

There were smatterings of chatterers who claimed that I was not mentally stable enough to make the decision but there was no clause in my father's will regarding mental stability. I wouldn't be taking the company public; they would be. They could change the name before they did so it had nothing to do with the Leman family name. If need be, I'd stay on as a controlling shareholder and just attend shareholder meetings. If art without industry is the realm of the hobbyist, then call me a hobbyist.

I'll be a hobbyist until the day that I die, if I can get away from these money bent pushers of product and thieves who would feel comfortable selling garden hoses or gardenias as long as they provided a retirement income and a large pad somewhere near the equator, but not quite at the equator, for that was too hot, uncomfortable, and prone to civil disturbances. The highest end of humanity is not to buy and sell things to each other in perpetuity. I'm talking about a culture here. The soil that we all take mental nourishment from is what binds us all together.

If the highest exemplar of our culture is a hedge fund manager, a person talented in making a small sum of money into a larger sum of money, then we need to tear it all down and pack our bags with the scraps. I'm here for the hidden ones, the ones that operate in twilight, sharpening their knives in the darkness. They are staring at me right now. I am heaving. I do not know how much I will profit from the Initial Price Offering of godknowswhat they decide to call the Corporation. I only know that I will give most of it away. Not all. I need something to be able to live off, and earn my daily bread. God knows it probably won't be writing.

What? That sudden fear at the prospect of being absolutely penniless? I think it's because most people do not live. They move in mental space from one acquisition to the next. Experiences become acquisitions for them; they become things. So, it all starts with me.

"Let me know how the sale goes, gentlemen," I said, and walked out the door in search of Bob Malvolio.

"Sir, wait!" Gliddenprof screamed. "You need to name a successor."

"You mean, which one of these apes should be king?"

"Yes, sir."

"I don't know."

"Mining Operations generates the most revenue," Charles Wendig III said proudly.

"What's the least important?"

"Research and Development. That consumes money."

"Who's in charge of that?"

"Herr Fritz Reindorfer, uh, me, sir," the slim looking blonde man said with a heavy Bavarian German accent.

"You're in charge, Fritz. If we're going to change the world, we might as well start here."

"You've got to be kidding me," Charles Wendig III, Chief of Mining Operations boomed.

"Turn him off. Turn them all off. I have spoken," I said, quite like a pharaoh or at least high priest of Ra.

It was settled. Finished. Legal drew up contracts. The PhD in mathematics was elevated to CEO. An egghead with minimal experience in management. It was quite a coup d'état hailed in business journals as a splendid gamble. The Chief of Mining Operations, that colossal prick, Chas Wendig III, quit and was immediately hired by Anglo American to serve as head of their African Operations. Whoopy ding.

We replaced him with another scientist. I would much rather have people who deal with truth than spinners of illusions at the helm. Illusion is comforting while it lasts, but it is nothing, and when it becomes apparent and you're faced with the truth, it seems jagged, puncturing, and deadly. We must be inoculated to the truth in small doses. That is why an artist is so important. We feel the jagged edges and don't smooth them. I was all set up for my next sally into the world outside the office, where I would do my damndest to run into one Mr. Robert Malvolio. I had an idea of where he would be hiding out. Anywhere that money pooled and intrigue mounted and rumor of war was whispered in bathrooms and dusty hallways.

492

Here's the deal. I'll tell you straight up. We artists deal with abstractions and bring them to the ground, making them natural. The businessmen deal with the ground and make the natural world into an abstraction to be chopped up, priced out, and sold off. I will never feel guilty for pursuing art again.

I sought Malvolio out and found him almost immediately. Unable to gain employment at a corporate firm probably because his secret work had removed virtually every trace of his work experience, and human resources directors of the firms that he did manage to get interviews at quickly tired of his strange beady eyes and smiling and way of saying, "I cannot answer that question," to nearly every question about his background and work experience they asked him. His only real reference, my father, was dead.

Everybody else the human resources people called would disavow knowledge of even who Robert Malvolio was, afraid it was just another one of his loyalty tests. I walked around the fashion district in SoHo until I came across my long missing automobile parked precariously in a ten dollar a day lot. There still was not a scratch on her, though she had a healthy coating of dust to camouflage the fact that The Judge was a 47,000-dollar car.

A few birds had shat on the window because Malvolio saw fit to park it under the only tree near the parking lot. He had a job as the doorman at the Louis Vuitton. He was impeccably dressed in a Louis Vuitton suit, which he paid off in small increments from each paycheck. He had gotten a haircut and a shave and looked about ten years younger than when I saw him last. He looked good. He was not surprised to see me.

"You've been busy," he said.

"So have you, it looks like."

"Been keeping tabs on me?" I asked.

"I have been. My work is never done. Even though you fired me, I still had made a promise to your father. Just one of several."

"What other promises were there? I suppose you're in the mood to talk to me now."

"I want my old job back."

"What's that?"

"Being your shadow. I quite like you."

"We'll see. Dish."

"That's why I called you. I wanted to tell you. I'm glad you've come. I also wanted to return your automobile. I don't know why you didn't inquire about it sooner."

"When do you get off?"

"I'll leave whenever I want to. Now that you're here, I don't need this job anymore."

"I haven't hired you yet. What do you want to show me?"

"A safe house."

"Your apartment?"

"No. Your father set up a network of safe houses throughout the United States, Europe, Canada, and Africa...well throughout the world. He hated hotels. They were too public."

"I think you told me this before."

"Well, now I'm going to show you one."

"Where is it?"

"A rougher part of town. Queensbridge."

"Nice."

Being in the Judge again was a comfort. Malvolio drove. Just how out of my mind I was when I took that trip came galloping back to me like a waking nightmare. I reached under the seat; there was no .45.

"Where's my masterblaster?" I asked.

"I took the liberty of selling it. They're quite illegal in the city, plus we both know you won't be needing it anymore. It sold for a tidy sum. I'll wire you the proceeds."

Malvolio drove on. He took a circuitous route to avoid being followed. A brownstone with a busted up exterior and a fake no vacancy and condemned sign were pasted on the front wooden door. For a moment, I thought Malvolio was bringing me to an abandoned home to kill me and bury me in the basement, but when he opened the door I recognized the exterior as one of my father's dingy disguises. Inside, immaculate furniture sat under dustcovers. Malvolio turned on the light.

The walls were covered in paintings. All different styles. All of different women painted exquisitely in various poses and all in the nude, some hiding. One curiously looked like my mother at a young age.

"Who did these?"

"Look at the signature there," Malvolio said pointing to the painting that looked eerily like my mother.

They were all unsigned. Only my mother's painting had a signature.

PRESCOTT LEMAN III

I gasped. "My father?"

"Yes."

"He painted all of these?"

I gazed at the innumerable pantings. They claimed all available wall space.

"Yes."

"God, he was talented."

"It was his one real love in life...painting."

"Why didn't he pursue it then?"

"He did. You're looking at them. All the other apartments are the same."

"I mean, out in the open. Why not pursue it in the open?"

"He was a secret artist."

"A gift like this should be shared!"

"He didn't want anyone to know."

"Why show me?"

"It's up to you to share it."

"Why did he hide it?"

"Your father was a man torn between two worlds. When your mother died...when he ordered it...well you know...all of this died with him. He had firmly chosen one side. The side his father had chosen for him. Did you know that as a child your father would make drawings, and your grandfather would beat his hands? When he would find drawings in his school notebooks he would take them out and burn them in front of him? 'No son of mine will enter a world so fickle,' your grandfather would say. Your father was a born artist but the desires of his father, social pressures, marrying rich and staying rich, and business got the better of him. He had a choice. Quit that life, you know, totally go Gauguin and be disavowed and cast out into the darkness, or choose a third way, become a secret artist, a painter of secret loves and secret things. His paintings would never see the light of day, not even when your grandfather died, because by that time, your father had already made his choice."

"How did he have time to run the business?"

"Come on now. He hired the best people and paid them well. They ran the business."

"While he went off and painted."

"And did other things."

"Philandered."

"Your father never should have been married. He never should have been born to an industrialist. These paintings are the work of extreme pent up frustration. He hated his father."

"I admit. I hated mine, too."

"It's like this everywhere. The moment he was alone, well not totally alone, I was there protecting him he would get to work. He couldn't be seen buying painting supplies, so the models, his lovers, would bring them in as well. All this, for something that would never see the light of day."

"He took his talent and shoved it under a rock."

"He had to."

"No, he didn't."

"You don't understand. The times, they were different."

"The pressures of money have always been the same. You can brush them off because they're only your desires."

"If your father would not have been a secret painter, he would not have been a painter at all. All the frustrations of his life manifested themselves in his gift. Without that tension between the two parts of him, he would not have been able to create all of this."

"But then he quit."

"After you mother's death, after one part destroyed the other, yes, he quit."

"If he wasn't painting, what would he do?"

"Not much of anything. Stare off into the distance?"

"So all you told me before, it was all a sham?"

"Frightfully, regrettably, yes."

"I'm going to give my father what he never wanted: a public showing. I'm going to take all of this and fling it up in the air for the world to see and judge."

"If you think these are well done you should see his later pieces, when the tension in his soul was at its highest, right before your mother's death. These were only the beginning."

"Where do I go for that?"

"The Villa in Athens. The murals he painted cover the entirety of the walls."

"Have someone trusted box them all up."

"That's no small feat. He turned out a painting a day for nearly fifty years."

"And he just hung them up on the walls of his houses?"

"That's it. And only he and I know the locations of them all."

"What a fucking waste."

"Wait until you see them."

An army of laborers began the painstaking process of boxing up the collective output of my secret artist father, Prescott Leman III, once Malvolio gave them the locations of the paintings. They were discovered in storage facilities in far off locales, in secret rooms in taverns once used by resistance movements, and in apartments in the dank and dreary subsections of the world's great cities. After that, an Army of realtors began listing the properties for sale.

I had no interest in seeing them. I had no interest in my father's personal effects and anything else other than his art. I felt very badly as the boxes began arriving. At the house in Mumbai, located on a hill surrounded by a teeming slum, and rumored among the locals to be the final resting place of a mad wizard, a defunct ice factory housed the paintings that my father did of Greek gods and goddesses, warriors, and denizens of the underworld. He used as a model a voluptuous Indian woman who also bore him four or five sons before she disappeared into the mists. Her Diana the Huntress featured her with muscled breasts full and obscured behind animal skins, but the focal point were her eyes, black as midnight and in them my father was able to paint ghostly images of a doe and a buck.

In his painting of the virgin huntress, he reaffirmed women's mastery over nature and the men who pursued Diana and could never quite seem to catch her sylvan beauty, sleeping in the background, pale, perhaps dead, perhaps slumbering and dreaming of her, yet too afraid to pursue her for fear of what they would find. All of these emotions swept through me as I viewed my father's handiwork, and I broke down in tears as painting after painting, all masterpieces in their own right, came off the truck.

The art critics came to view the works and many were left speechless and shook their heads and ohmygodded at the trove. Father had it all down: originality and technique. When they inquired about the artist, I told them that it was my father, Prescott Leman, a simple businessman who never wanted to shame his art with the world during his lifetime. They said that he must have patronized talented artists the world over and didn't confirm that it was in fact one artist until they looked at the brush strokes under special lenses. Malvolio was able to construct a general period in which the paintings were painted according to the house they were found in.

A fine New York Gallery, Lippman and Sons, managed to have a showing, but the paintings were not up for sale. They were to be donated to a museum along with my father's amassed art collection. They would go into a wing with no name, paintings with no name. The only painting he had signed, I sent to my sister Hannah as a peace offering.

My father's art seemed to come from nowhere. There was no discernable inspiration. It seemed to be born in a vacuum, straight from the perturbations of his mind. His final painting was of a Christ figure standing in a brilliant garden on one side of his body and on the other a decaying rotten forest that looked as if a fire or pestilence had ravaged it. Christ stands on the path that forks between the two entrances to both kingdoms: that of the blessed and that of the damned. His face is illuminated by the entrance to bliss but is gazing into the shadows to the entrance of death and despair. I realized that Christ's face was my father's face and he had painted himself. Like all the other paintings, this one was not signed. His final brushstroke had been to add a little shadow to Christ's foot, meant to indicate motion towards the side of evil.

My final instructions to the workers were that the paintings should be boxed individually and released at the rate of one per year for one thousand years. That way, people wouldn't have any recollection of him as a man when his final painting was released and would judge him as a talent based on what he had created. If something were beautiful in itself, anonymously releasing it would only add value to the world. I feel this is how my father wanted it to be.

I would not be attending the opening of the gallery. I did not care. I had witnessed the paintings as they trickled into the warehouses, and it was enough for me. I could barely move for days. My father is dead and gone and he cannot paint anymore. I am still alive and can put pen to paper.

I granted Malvolio the right to the Judge, as it would suit him better, and I released him from any future filial obligations. Still, he stuck around, glimpsing at me from the shadows.

That evening, it was a Saturday, I met the hundreds of members of the Old School Truants, Gerianthrax, and Vertical Hell at Strawberry Fields in Central Park. From there we would head directly to my Agent's home in Central Park West for the literary soiree. After the Segways stopped to recharge, we worried that the NYPD would cite their owners for violations of the city ordnance, but no one seemed to care, and everyone just pointed at all of the cute old people as they rode Segways and clogged up traffic. No one suspected they were a terrorist mob. We arrived forty-five minutes late. I entered first, and downstairs, Gerianthrax members tied up the front doorman and promised him that no harm would befall him if he just buzzed everyone else in. He complied and buzzed everyone in with his foot. Ray Lefebvre followed me closely.

"Everyone wait out here in the hallway. If I need you, I'll let you in."

I knocked at the door and a sparkling, bubbly blonde answered. The hubbubs poured into the hallway like froth from a lukewarm beer, slowly cascading, bubbling forth, and becoming liquid.

"Jackson Leman."

"Are you on the guest list?" she giggled to me.

"See this place, sugar? I bought it, so I think I should be."

She giggled again. Some security. "I'll go check," she said.

She slammed the door in my face.

"You need us, Leman?" Ray called from around the corner.

"Not yet."

The door opened. My agent, fifty pounds heavier, answered.

"Jack Leman, buddy, how the hell are ya?"

"Tannenbaum."

"You look...good."

"Thanks. You too. Real healthy."

"It's been a wonderful year."

"Good to see the world's treating you well. How's the literary business?"

"Come in. Come in. I was just about to ask you the same thing. I've got someone you should meet."

I walked into his palatial apartment, much like Augustus Caesar's mansion at the Palatine of Rome. All this from hustling words. My God, I'd have to get into this business.

"Love what you've done with the place," I said, offering the usual platitudes.

"How's business?"

"Quit."

"I hope you didn't quit writing."

"Nope."

"Good. You had us all really worried about you. Anyways, here's who I wanted to you meet."

I walked past his wife, the bubbly blonde. Everyone who was on the lips of modern art gallery owners, a *New York Times* Bestseller list, and who happened to be in New York City was there.

And who did Tannenbaum introduce me to but Veronica Gilb, the "it" author of the moment, who partied separate from everyone else, a party within a party, and was doing enough blow to make a Colombian coke mule dry heave, all whilst being sandwiched by two well muscled ballet dancers with moustaches, who did not seem to take offense that we were gazing at their perfect forms as they writhed against hers, and she had all of her clothing on, with a pen in her teeth and notebook on her lap, with words scrawled upon the page. What a strange method!

She looked up from their passionate embrace, and they were mainly going after each other, but she blocked the way, cock blocker par excellence, without even a hint of malice in her eyes and looking slightly Castilian Spanish, like one of those strange looking members of inbred royalty from the Habsburgs, or other royal family I know not which. I'm getting to asking her a little bit about herself, but the situation is really uncomfortable because the guy's cocks were out, they were erect, and they were trying to perform a docking operation, all veiny like, and she didn't seem to take the slightest notice, but just sat there writing little scribblings in her notebook.

"Veronica Gilb, this is Jackson Leman."

"Hi. I was greatly inspired by *Asymmetric Hearts*."

"Thanks. Um...who are you?"

"Tannenbaum's latest and greatest."

"Greatest, eh?"

"My novels sell very well."

"Price point is right, women aged 14 to 18 are snapping it up. Women aged 19 to 35 are starting to take notice. We've got a spread in *Cosmopolitan* next month, unfortunately no more *Oprah* show, but we're going to do an aggressive marketing campaign to them. We discovered that as long as something is popular, people will buy it, no matter the content," Tannenbaum said.

"I know, I've been meaning to ask you about that."

"What happened, Jackson? What do you mean?"

"I saw the warehouse you so desperately wanted to tell me about."

"Jackson, that doesn't mean you aren't a good writer."

"Well, Tannenbaum, we're through. I want out of my contract. You're going to release me."

"He's the best agent going! What are you insane?" Veronica asked. The two ballet dancers achieved geosynchronous orbit above her.

"Shut up, you neophyte," I told her.

"Ha! What have you even written? Recently? You're all washed up."

"I've taken some time off. Anyway, I don't know who you are."

"What, have you been living under a rock?"

"This is Veronica Gilb!"

"Doesn't wring a bell."

She broke into tears. The men stopped writhing and lost their erections. Her notebook fell from her lap.

"Away! Away! Now!" she shouted to the men. They scampered away, naked with their drooping erections waving back and forth like the flags of a defeated Army.

"We better get out of here. You've upset her. What were you saying, Jackson?"

"She's awfully temperamental."

"Yeah. She is. Hell of a writer though. These young girls really snap her stuff up."

"Is she any good?"

"I think so."

"You ever read any of it?"

"No."

"But it sells."

"Yeah, like hotcakes. We're overjoyed at her success. We've got a movie deal. Prefigured audience. Every 14 to 19 year old girl in the country will want to see it."

"Great."

"So you want out of your contract?" Tannebaum asked, lawyerly.

"Yes. I do."

"Why?"

"I don't want to write the bullshit you think is going to sell anymore."

"I know what's going to sell."

"I don't want to write it."

"Why not?"

"What sells...it's sort of trashy. I'd much rather just write something from myself."

"Do it, then. I'm not holding you to any particular form."

"You sign away all your rights to *Asymmetric Hearts*."

"Can't do that Jackson, sorry."

"You will."

"I won't. I'll be able to find another writer to continue the story line, now."

"You will."

"I can't, and you can't make me."

"You're serious! You're going to count yourself blessed in heaven by producing the trash that coke slut back there writes! Face it, man! You're supported by hacks! You sell dross of hack writers to fucking kids who don't know any better!"

"And what do you write, Jackson? What makes you so special?"

"Not that."

"I forgot. You don't write."

I made for the door. I whistled at the collected members of the Old School Truants, Gerianthrax, and Vertical Hell. Vertical Hell rode right into the apartment on their Segways and guarded the exits to prevent escapes.

"Cell phones in the fucking bag," Ray yelled. His troopers gathered them up in a pillowcase. New York's finest were perplexed about the newest uninvited guests. A notable pear-shaped critic dressed in a checkered tuxedo wheezed, "Is this a robbery?"

"You're going to let me out of my contract and sign over the rights to *Asymmetric Hearts*," I told Tannenbaum.

"You're trying to extort me now? This is quite criminal, and I've got all these witnesses."

Ray slapped Tannenbaum in the face, though not hard enough to knock him out. Just a slap, really. An artful slap. "You think we're joking now, you fucking lawyer piece of shit?!"

Tannenbaum fell to his knees.

"You're only as popular as your latest work, bwwahhh," he gasped.

"It's mine, fucko. I wrote it. You have no right to it anymore."

"We printed it. We distributed it. It would have been buried under a rock if not for us."

"Do you want us to throw him off the roof, boss?" one of the Vertical Hell members asked.

"Just give them what they want, dear" his bubbly blonde wife droned.

"Your wife is a wise woman," Ray said.

Veronica Gilb came into the room, coked out of her gourd, and stark naked. Everyone forgot what was happening and looked at her.

"Why do you need this loser? You've got me, Roland."

Roland Tannenbaum lifted himself from the floor.

"You're right. You haven't written shit for a decade, Leman. You're finished."

"Release me."

"You'll never publish another damn thing in this town, Jackson, you're finished."

"I learned Tannenbaum, I actually learned something. If you decide to be an artist, you have to go all the way."

"Go off and be an artist, then."

"I know you keep my files here. My contract. Tear it up in front of all these people. Then we can forget we ever knew each other."

"Get it!" Ray Lefebvre shouted to Tannenbaum and made to punt him in his exposed ribs with his steel-toed riding boot. He stopped just short when Tannenbaum opened his mouth.

"Get it!" Tannenbaum shouted to his wife, who complied.

"You're nothing but a hack, Leman. *Asymmetric Hearts* never would have seen the light of day if it wasn't for your father's support."

"Who cares. The sins of the past won't be repeated."

His wife produced the contract that was ceremonially burned in front of all assembled, including the heir to the illusory crown, Veronica Gilb, who squeezed her nipples haphazardly and rubbed her reddened nose. We burned it, and no one shed a tear as the document went up in flames. I was a has-been, a hack. The wave had broken in favor of other people. I did not care. My freedom was my own to decide. Mr. Tannenbaum was no longer necessary. Who needed him?

We beat a hasty retreat before the police were summoned. I doubt Tannenbaum called them; he was too shaken up. One of the models must have smuggled a phone past Lefebvre in her pussy or jail wallet. When the cops arrived, they found enough blow in the place to book everyone on major distribution charges. It was quite a literary scandal for a fortnight, and then what's-her-name made another porn tape with what's-his-face, and it all sort of blew over amongst the people who cared about entertainment news.

So...

I was free. Free to pursue my own ambition. Free to pursue my own course in life. I was free, and it was terrifying. Do you know the terror of freedom, of knowing what it is you want to do and actually being able to do it? Or do you struggle daily in your self imposed slavery, going from dopamine, or is it serotonin burst to serotonin burst, like some cocaine addict in the hunt for acquisitions? You know why I gave all the money up? No matter what I did, the money was there to remind me that there was something bigger and better I could be doing. And guess what? No one, not even a spendthrift, wishes to be labeled a spendthrift.

My talents in life do not include spending money like some Saudi prince. Everyone now has a talent, they may just hide it, or not spend the time to discover it, in favor of working some job to practice the primary talent of the day, acquisition by spending money. That's what I think freedom is: pursuing your internal talents no matter what the universe decides to throw in your way. It was the way of Hercules; it was the way of Odysseus. Life is a quest that is internalized searching and refinement at first, but then, when put into practice, your freedom is not so much what you have the ability to do, but what you actually do. You have the right to put into practice that which you bring forth from your innermost being, and even if you never discover it, you needn't die in frustration because, at least you tried. At least you made the attempt.

Call it God-given or a product of nature or a combination of both, but you're nothing if you don't attempt to bring it to the surface; you're nothing but the bitterest of all slaves in this world in that you have the opportunity to at the very least try. This brings me to what I would like to believe is the advent of a Golden Age. You're mistaken if you think that they just happen, that the right mix of ingredients was present to make sure that this hyper flourishing just happens.

I'll tell you what I'm going to do. I'm going to take the steps to make sure that one takes place. I will add something to this world of ours and help and encourage others to do the same. A Golden Age comes about when the rich, the well off with piles of surplus cash, which could be put into generating more piles of cash, through the application of finances to business, put their money into the radical arts. Instead of growing the business, they get the strange notion that they have enough money as it is and they actually want to go about improving the world they live in.

They do this when they are reminded of their mortality through authentic art. They don't burn it up in election campaign finance or serving their own bitter self-interest. So, guess what I'm going to do. I'm going to spend the rest of my days practicing my art, and I'm going to travel the lonely highways and byways seeking out other individuals to uplift. I'm going to tell them, anonymously of course, to spend their time, their one and only life, creating beauty! Then I'm going to give them a grant that increases based on their production. As long as they produce, money winds up in their pocket. I don't care for any sort of return. I just want no other person to wind up like my father, but instead become what he could have been. Contented. Dare I say, happy! I'm not looking for the already established. I'm no MacArthur Genius Grant. I'm looking for talented nobodies.

The weather in New York City has turned towards the muggy heat of a South American effluvial swamp, and it is high time that I head back towards the west where the breeze is cooler in California. I will go back to my home there on the beach, and along the way I will discover and gather my companions and progenitors of an American Golden Age. I know the rest of the world considers Americans backward and provincial, but I tell you this land, all of it, from your most impoverished strip mall degeneracy town that time forgot to the very boroughs of New York City has the potential energy to create something that will really be remembered. You can call me insane if you want to. You can read over the stories of my life and decide you are so much better off having never known me.

You may be confused, and I don't blame you; I'm a confusing fellow. Just allow my words to sink in and decide for yourself if they are better left in the trash, aborted, and you aren't the slightest bit ennobled as a human by my tale. I'll tell you what. I will travel west. You may hear about my travels; the future is unwritten. Nothing is written! I will toss what I write backwards into time to play out in the reels of my memory. You may judge me a fool and a man without good sense, but I ask that you at least read my words and tell me that I wasn't well within my rights to at least try to tell my tale before I am cold and dead. I cannot scream from my tomb. Tombs contain no screamers, only cold sleepers.

LUBRICCCATED CCCONDOMS

"*T*hrown Backward Into Time..."

That I was born, that I underwent a series of events, many of them beyond my cccontrol, this is all known to me. What remains unknown, and therefore cccompletely uncccertain is just what part of me remains to be cccompletely cccertain about, in that I have cccome into cccontacccct with so many people whose authenticcccity as genuine human beings of flesh and blood to me remains suspeccct. They have not identified themselves as human beings, though they are cccapable of speaking my language, I see them - they are cccapable of walking, bumping into objects, laughing hystericccally at events I do not find in the least bit funny or mildly entertaining, they cccry at funerals; in short, they do things they are supposed to do. You may ask yourself the question "just who are you, my humble (or perhaps not to humble) narrator?" Well, allow me to be frank with you, dear reader. My name is Marcccus Hanley, and I have existence as a ficcctional cccharacccter, with as much substancccce as a Madison Avenue advertisement, as much of the glitter, flash, and a good portion of the fame of the Kardashian sisters. Should you see me on the street passing you by in a hurry, you probably should not stop to ask me my name, even if you are very cccurious to discccover what it is.

I look smashing in a suit, though I don't own any. Everything I do ccclaim to be mine was appropriated to me by the mindful generosity of my faithful cccompatriots who see fit to keep me ccclothed in the finest silks and ties and the nicccest oxford cccotton dress shirts. In other words, they pretty me up for their important funccctions in whiccch they require some good-natured arm cccandy. I do look like a male escccort, but not too much because I have a very diverse, very discccrete ccclientele with very discccriminating tastes. These ccclinentele favor discccretion above all else, but I may have already told you that before.

Discccretion because they are very often powerful women who perform vital funccctions in our socccciety and to have it known that they often required the servicccces of a professional who could servicccce them heartily, with reccckless and feccckless abandon, mucccch like a well hung eunucccch to the Emperess Dowager of CCChina or some Roman noblewoman. I am a well-trained male escccort at that. I'm fluent in a few languages, knowledgeable of cccustoms and cccourtesies, and able to fix a flat tire and do automotive repair without getting as mucccch as a spot of grease on my lily white Frenccch cccuffed shirts or a pang of cccumpunccction on my lily white ccconsccciencccce. I am in succch great shape that nary does a drop of sweat break forth from my hypermasccculine brow line with fiercely symmetricccal eyebrows that never need plucccking or separation, nor from my jutting ccchin or aquiline nose, which I inherited from my mother, my father being a tall lithe-limbed half Native Americccan who had not quite escccaped the reservation when he enscccconccced my ma with his cccoccck and balls in the baccck of her cccar, she being a teacher of English to poor illiterate injuns, but mainly taught Adventure Stories.

I inherited from this woman, a woman of fierce breeding, prone to violent passions and dead at a young age from godknowswhat cccause. The broke ones said it was too much drink and fun, the gentry accccccused her of laying about and letting the idle nature of a veritable plowshardded fifteen furrows of rumor and innuendo, sin, and bad behavior run through her mind, to whiccch she finally succccumbed when I barely knew how to raise up my head and cccall her mother in any way intelligible besides that cccutesy baby talk. Her passing did not affect me much in the way of my psyccchology, given that my cccome to be ccchosen profession was to be very pleasing in the short term to the ladies. I often don't accept repeat cccustomers, because for them, I cccannot perform. If I've dipped my bucccket in a singular well oncccce, that well has up and run dry for me. Oncccce I've up and cccarried my horse cccoccck to pasture, that pasture bears me no more familiarity.

My trouser snake shrivels to a pantaloony grub in sight of previously plowed fields. You may have heard of this cccondition by where a man has a mental bloccck for a woman he has already accchieved cccconquest of and cccan no longer accchieve erecccction and take advantage of her feminine cccharms. I used to think there was something wrong with me, and the women thought there was something very wrong with them, yet still they paid me for my time, of cccourse at a heavy discccount, enough for cccab fare baccck to my dingy apartment, whiccch was dingy acccccording the standards of the female CCCEOs, and occccccassional princcccess of some dumpy royal family I entertained.

However, it started getting really hairy (no pun intended) when women would arrange to fly me acccross cccountry so that I cccould serviccce them while their husbands were away. You cccan imagine my ccchagrin when the wife of a well ccconnecccted, herself well ccconnecccted, CCCEO of a major European Bank (the name of whiccch I shall not mention becccause you will know immediately who I am talking about if you read succch publicccations as Forbes, and the London Financial Times, and Der Spiegel, and perhaps La Monde), whose wife I met when I was vacccationing in Italy, while I was walking through a Roman piazza, a woman who literally ran from her cccafé seat and dragged me down to her level to sit with her.

This woman was an Italian munccchkin, approaching 50 years old, who had the body of a perhaps 25 year old who didn't take cccare of herself well enough to be cccconsidered a total hardbody, but who was round in all the right placcces and somewhat tight like a 25 year old should be. She told me in exquisite English of many of life's frustrations and quoted Dante and some other Italian poets I don't know and have never heard of, explaining each line to me without boring me to tears, telling that Roman blood, the blood of the nobility, whatever that meant, not of the hoi polloi, whatever that meant, flowed through her veins, that she was a very passionate and hot-blooded, fiery, stereotypicccal Italian woman with shocks of hair dyed slightly blonde to set herself apart, black though at the roots, possibly evidencce of her laziness or perhaps inability to keep an appointment at her salon, or maybe that was the ongoing trend in Italia, to look ever so slightly like a trashy American trailer park ho, but for some reason I doubted that. I had a sense, and it is a well-honed sense, that she was fishing, so I decccided to go with it and test her out.

"You get my blood up," I said.

"CCCome with me then, Marcus," she said.

"I cccan't stand up. Not yet."

When my boner subsided, it's always out of cccontrol the first time ever, even though this mama was as old as my dear departed mother would have been, I wanted to feel her beneath my weight, getting cccrushed underneath, I wanted to feel her squirm, look at her faccce winccce as I pressed forward on her. I wanted to have her. From the moment this woman made her existenccce as woman present to me, that is, she talked to me and let me know that she was a real person and not merely some sort of astral projecction or movie advertisement cccome alive to breathe and succck the blood from the living, as soon as she encccouraged me of that, it was my sole objeccctive in life, never mind the other tail I was pursuing to the bitter end, it was my sole goad in life to have her. I am very good at separating my goals into time moments and small sequences of my life, snippets of life if you will. That way, no sort of guilt, no sort of hope for the future enters into each small facccet of my life, they are all distinct facccets of a single harmonious diamond, unfolding into time as I live.

So I floated with this woman back to a seedy dive hotel, as seedy as they could be in Rome so as to avoid deteccction by her husband's loyal goons, hotels where faithful Monday to Friday husbands went to fuck their mistresses on Saturdays, present them with a week's worth of gifts, and go on their merry way, but not before hearing her implorations to leave the old bag and get with the new like what he did now wouldn't happen to them in fold. This Italiana, she behaved as a man might, but it was I with the thrusting member, and quite a magnificcco one at that. I recccall her parlanccce while I thrusted and squeaked the mattress before flipping her over to tongue her glorious spunk-drenched pussy and taut brown Italian balloon knot.

Being polyorgasmiccc, a quality normally assigned by the Lord to women, who gave them the cccurse of pain in ccchildbirth but the great joy of being able to particccipate in gang bangs, trains, multiple orgasms with no annoying, refraccctory, flaccccid, shrivel diccked one hour, whiccch becomes longer and more bothersome with age like it is never going to cccome up again ever. I cccould shoot multiple loads and still maintain my ereccction without pain in the glans or cccoccckhead for you uneducccated goons out there. It must have been a fault in my wiring, a doccctor told me oncce, but I told him that I ccconsidered myself and my ability to fuccck for days on end, provided enough water, snacks for nourishment, and lubricccation existed, as being part of a new evolution to a muccch higher humanity.

If I cccould populate the world with an entire gang of Marcccus Hanelys, there would be no need for television, cccinema, or other things that are a mere paltry substitute for nature's best free accctivity. When women ask me, I tell them that my cccoccck was always that way as long as I cccan remember. I never knew a time, not even the first time, when I was not in cccomplete cccontrol of it. Most men are barely able to cccontrol themselves on even getting a whiff of a tight, wet fuccckhole and end up dribbling on their balls before they get ensheafed. Men shoot in their pants in strip ccclubs all the time. They barely get a kiss in before their spasticcc cccoccck sees fit to inseminate their BVDs.

I'm the anti-man of the modern age. I'm a boy toy to the riccch, the famous, and powerful women, and I'm proud of it. The Lord our God made me this way. He blessed me with the ability to be polyorgasmiccc and also induccced in me the inability to ever be with a woman more than onccce. Doccctors have accccccused me of having some deep-seated attaccchment issues, but that's all phooey. It's been this way for as long as I cccan remember. They told me that was the meaning of deeply rooted attachment issues, but I just blew them off and cccontinued being who I am. I have no need for them and their ccconspiracccy to rob me of my polyorgasmism, or whatever you cccall it. So what if it doesn't cccomport itself to a relationship; the doccctors are always whining and moaning about a relationship. I tell them I've got to jam in a lifetime's worth of fuccks in a fortnight. So we did.

The bella Italiana rolled off me after four hours of baccck breaking sex, cccomplaining that she would have to put her pussy on iccce, really iccce down the beef cccurtains, as if she had particccipated in one of those absurd, over five-hundred fat bastards with little dicccks gangbangs for video and publiccc ccconsumption.

"I'm but one man," I said.

She just shook her head as she pulled up her skirt and shuffled bowlegged towards the hallway, but not before I gave her my businessccccard hoping to drum up some business, secccretly hoping she wouldn't cccall me, but secccretly hoping she would becccause I liked staring at myself in her cccaramel cccolored eyes and the mirror and felt that our intertwined bodies were a perfect fit, my cccocccck the perfeccct angle, my shaft able to penetrate fully without all the baccckstraining involved with boinking American babes who I found to be either unnaturally skinny or unnaturally hogged out, too fat for my liking.

Don't get me wrong, I'll still fuccck them, but don't expeccct me to enjoy it too mucccch. And here is this Italian woman, delightfully plump, round in all the right placcces, happy with her body, not a prey to music videos or Saltine cccraccker advertisements. Oh my, Americccan women, I'll try any of them out provided they approacccch me first and step out of the shadows, introduccce themselves as people to be respecccted and not just some empty-brained pretty face, too timid to say anything really real and cccontent to hide behind whatever mask they decccided to paint on that day, which I also do sometimes, but just for shits and giggle and not because I'm accctually am attempting to tailor my personality to fit anyone's particcccular predileccction.

There are some women who ask me to dress up like a cccowboy and say "ride 'em cccowgirl!" while they're bucking on my cccocccck like it was a happy fountain of youth in a forlorn valley of death. The most I usually do is scccrew them with my cccowboy boots on, nice exotics, and alligators like, maybe cccrocccodile; I have no idea, really. They were a present from the first requestor of this particcccular fetish. This particcccular grand dame had a fairly elaborate fantasy about riding the open range and getting used and abused by every two bit, hard-dicccked cccowpoke, outlaw, and cccattle rustler going' by.

She asked me that I pretend that she was some lonely prairie wife that had been abandoned in a mucccky prairie house by a husband muccch older and wrinkly than her, whom she was married off to at the age of 14 not only becccause it was quite cccommon during those times for men to get a hankering after a young pieccce of ass but it was perfeccctly legal if the parents signed away their rights to just another hungry mouth. And she went into this poor little "woe is me, lost sccchool girl" look, even though she was a grand dame of about 45 years of age.

She told me her story, married off at the age of 14 and never really wanted to, didn't even look at the boys before then, but she had to because he offered my father a stolen horse and four blankets and a few bottles of whisky and paw he loved the old rye more than the ccchildren, especccially the girls, and I had to submit myself to a cccruel old man whose faccce was like a bitter leather over tanned by a subpar tanner, too heavy on the acccid, and this man he had a beer gut, and stinky whisky and rotted meat breath, but so happened to be a cccrack shot with a pistol and who would kill anyone who looked at me even sideways, but who just so happened to be driving our prize steer to market in town a few days journey from here, who had already been gone for a few days, but you, you lonesome stranger, who just so happened to ride up in search of Godknowswhat and just so happened to find me this flaxen haired beauty, bathing, bare breasts bared in the scorching prairie sun, shining like two fierce cccantelopes, yet you don't want too look at me because your dear old, fiercely Puritan CCCambridge, Boston, Mass, mother raised you the right way, the old way, to be God fearing, and taught you to respeccct money and the Americccan way, but your father, a soldier cccum brigand affected by the great war between the states, maybe an officer of a regiment that distinguished itself with ccconspicuous gallantry against Johnny Reb, and stormed the pickets, and skirmished with the greycccoats until they broke, and shot and slashed them with pistol and saber, with wild hair, eyes, and moustaches, and those little bugles trailing into the distanccce, your battle scccarred father, unable to hold down a job, encccouraged you to be a ne'er-do-well, an outlaw perhaps, because fighting on the side of law and order meant that you would probably end up unfulfilled, frustrated, and probably do things you didn't want to do and not in your own interests all the time.

Your father had a sense of duty, but thought phooey of it all now that his sense of duty earned him nothing but blown out eardrums and images he'll never be able to get from his head, no matter the booze he piccckles his brain with. If you lived the life of an outlaw, at least you cccould do whatever you wanted, and people would know who you were instead of treating you as harmless and invisible. Women would be scccared of you, but at least they would know who you were and secccretly they would all want to fuccck you. This dual nature would form a ccconstant battle in your soul. The need for law and order and the need to sow your wild oats and cccomitt wanton acccts of random violenccce, random fuccching, random talks with random men, randomness in general and your world would be a veritable microcccosm of your homeland.

Pursued by lawmen who are just as immoral as you but don't let on they are becccause they don't cccurse, don't ccchew tobacccco, and don't assocccciate with loose women out in the open, but like Wyatt Earp tried to be bad and decccided they cccouldn't and had to toe the line by donning a ten gallon hat, a tin badge, and a gun, duly deputized and given leeway to cccomitt wanton acccts of violenccce at the behest of the state. You cccome upon me, and we play the following role to a tee, don't deviate, stay with me, and by God dress in your cowboy uniform, you rogue, and make sure you get the acccccccent right. You're from Boston, but you refused to study at Harvard becccause your old drunk of a father gambled all of your family's money away, so you decided to just leave and ride a rail out west.

You sold your cccollecccction of Greek and Roman CCClassicccs to a notable dentist in Topeka, Kansas, for a small sum with which you bought your CCColt Peacccemaker, and did your first really heinous accct, whiccch still galls at your ccco-nscienccce (whiccch incccidentally takes on your mother's voiccce, but diminishes in time to take on that of your drunken slurring father) you stole a horse, and not even a very good horse at that, more a yearling, or a starter horse, of the ricccchest man's son in that fine town of Topeka, or maybe Abilene, a boy just like you whose father didn't spend the family's money frivolously and instead engaged in the lucccrative pracccticccces of being a cccattle baron and hiring a bunch of cccoolies to be part of a railroad gang building a great line out west.

You figured this man wouldn't miss the horse becccause he had several horses and this one wasn't very special looking. You didn't even steal a saddle; hell, you rode barebaccck. You stole the saddle from some other sccchmuccck in another town over but not before you realized that most of Bloody Kansas was after you, and you're being pursued hotly, when you cccame upon my little farm. You're all alone. You're a notorious outlaw, but I don't know this because I haven't talked to another soul, save my drunken, bleary-eyed, foul-mouthed and breathed hubby for months, maybe years. And I'm dying of loneliness, and I'm quite naked for you right, bathing in the small cccow pond behind our mud shacccck of a home, and it cccannot cccover my womanly virtue more than a dollar cccould cccover the US trade deficccit with CCChina.

I'm quite naked, so I guess I should just go ahead and get in role and get naked, okay so I'm quite naked for you right now but I'm cccovering up with this blanket and I will go ahead and get quite naked for you when you go ahead and dress up in your blaccck cccowboy outfit with your boots on and, wow swell moustacccche, I did tell you to grow that because what's a cccowboy without a moustacccche, and we see each other, you and I, right and our eyes meet and the attracccction is irresistible, but still I'm a married woman, why my husband would just kill you and me if he knew that I had set eyes upon such a rough, yet handsome stranger or allowed that stranger to see me all dressed and prettied up like Eve. So read your lines, and pay attention to your cccues, and goddamn it, put some timbre in that manly voiccce of yours boy:

EVE (E): Who gave you permission to stare?

MARCUS (M): Uh, it's a wide-open cccountry, ma'am. I do apologize.

509

E: Don't just stare. You look like a man of accction.

M: What do you want from me?

E: Whatever you want to give to me, willingly of cccourse. There aren't any thieves in this household.

M: I don't have anything, really, just my horse, which isn't rightfully mine, and my gun.

E: Is that your gun?

M: Bought and paid for.

E: Oh, it looks niccce and shiny, barely used.

M: I've never shot it.

E: Do you even know how to use it?

M: I reckon I cccan figure it out, ma'am.

E: Well, get off that horse, then.

M: I'm afraid he'll run away.

E: No, he won't. We'll tie him up.

M: Have you got a hitching' post?

E: I'm sure we cccan find one.

M: The gun might spook him.

E: Guns don't spook cccolts, maybe a mare, but not a cccolt. Never a cccolt.

M: How do you know?

E: I've been around horses my entire life. All 21 years.

(thunder lighting, booms in the distanccce, streaks acccross the ccclouds, and riccchoccchets off the prairie ground)

M: Storm's brewing'.

E: You better hitcccch that horse and cccome inside. Don't want you getting' wet.

M: Put some ccclothes on, ma'am. I cccan't have anyone think I'm taking indecccent liberties.

E: Who would say that? We just bumped into each other. There's not another soul for miles.

M: Aren't you scccared of me? I'm a bad guy.

E: No one as handsome as you has ever truly been a villain. You're a hero, and I know it. Maybe if you had an eye patch or some horrible scccars on that sweet faccce of yours, I cccould cccconsider you devilish.

M: Dunno, ma'am. I might have some hideous scccars round here.

E: Where?

M: Oh somewhere. (whistles)

E: Show me!

M: Where's that hitchin' post?

(inside, by the fire, a furious storm blows outside)

M: Ma'am, cccould you oblige me and put some ccclothing on?

E: It's my home. If I want to walk around perfectly nude, I will do so. It's just that my husband is usually so drunk that if I wear multiple layers he won't be able to unwrap me in time to violate me before the booze sends him to slumber. He gets tired of peeling baccck the layers at around layer three, not to mention if I have time, I haphazardly squeeze these ample breasts into a cccheap whale-bone cccorset, which is too cccomplicated for him to get his drunken fingers into the little nooks and cccrannies to undo all the hooks and fasteners. He usually tried to rip them off, not that I wouldn't mind having it ripped off, but not by that drunken, old, cccallous, disgusting, good for nothing old man. Do I need to say it again, just how filthy, dirty, filthy...oh god! I cccan't take it. Hold me, good sir!

(she runs into his manly cccowboy arms, strengthed over days of holding the bridle of a highly aggressive, promiscccuous cccolt)

E: You've got to help me! But I don't even know what to cccall out for you when I cccry out for you to ease my sufferings?

M: Marcccus. My name is Marcccus.

E: Oh, Marcccus! Marcccus! Were you named after Marcccus Antoninus, that Roman guy?

M: Uh, no.

E: Oh, he is so dreamy in that play by the Englishman with the baldhead. What was his name? I read it in my little prairie gradescccchool so many years ago....

M: Shakespeare?

E: That's the one! Handsome! And smart, too!

(She grasps him, fiercccely thrusting her full breasts into his ccchest, well ensccconccced into his blaccck, grimy cccowboy shirt, full of man sweat and pheromones, whiccch of these prairie yokels had no ideas as to the cccauses, only the effecccts. Marcccus attempts to resist, and pulls back slightly.)

E: Marcccus! If you're a man, you'll ravish me! Then you'll wait here and keep ravishing me until my husband cccomes home and finds you ravishing me, and you'll let him draw on you, and you'll shoot him dead becccause you're so handsome, smart, and such a good quick draw with your big, new gun.

M: It's new because I've never used it. I don't know how to use it, really.

E: Oh, it doesn't matter. I'm sure you're my ccchampion.

M: I need pracccticcce.

E: Pracccticcce on me.

(Marcccus shrugs, you cccan see in his expression he figures what the hell...)

E: That's it. If you're a man, you'll do this for me.

M: We won't be able to stay here. We'll be on the run for the rest of our lives.

E: Oh, it will be worth it! You'll take me away from this horrible place.

M: The future won't be cccertain.

E: It is cccertain here! It will be horrible!

M: You're sure?

E: It's already been seven years I've wasted on this degenerate!

M: Okay, we'll do it. Got to put the world to rights.

E: I knew you'd be my hero.

M: I'm a villain. Everyone who hears this tale will cccount me amongst the greatest of them. You too.

E: What's the point of being good and doing good? Nothing! What becccomes of good people? The wicccked do them in! Just like my husband wants to do me in!

M: You're being dramaticcc.

E: Just wait until you meet him! Then you'll see some drama!

M: Enough talk.

E: Take me, Marcccus. I'm yours for all time.

(he seizes her roughly by the hips and draws her ccclose to him, before throwing her on the bed)

M: Wheewee, I feel like a regular outlaw.

E: You're good with your gun.

M: I hope so.

E: Want to praccccticcce some more?

M: I'm more a fan of the real thing.

E: You don't need any praccccticcce. Why are you bad men so good at everything you do?

M: We have to be. Soccciety doesn't cccut us any breaks.

E: Oh, to be a man! To be able to do what you want, on what, whenever you want, wherever you want. I have to stay here tethered to this one place! A beautiful flower, never to really see the light of day!

M: I'm taking you with me.

E: It cccan't cccome fast enough. I ever thought I'd say this, but I cccan't wait for that wretcccch to cccome home so he gets what's cccomin' to him.

M: What's your husband's name?

E: Pete. Friends of his cccall him Deadeye. Some call him Killer. Over in Sussex County, they cccall him the Hammer.

M: (gulps) Why all those names?

E: Oh, back when he was a young man he was kind of a big deal. Not anymore. Believe me.

M: He sounds right dangerous.

E: Oh, don't worry. What he hasn't lost being an old geezer, the whisky has blunted. It frays the nerves. Why, I doubt he cccan even shoot straight anymore.

M: But you don't really know.

E: Why, just last week he shot three wild dogs dead that had been getting' at our free-range ccchiccckens. Must have been around forty, maybe fifty yards away.

M: Fifty yards away? What kind of dogs were they? Big dogs?

E: No, just some old lap dogs that escccaped from Old Lady Weatherington's estate. You know, that old real estate magnate Weatherington's widow? Yeah, they escccaped and turned to a life of cccrime. A Pekinese and a Pomeranian, both led by a vicccious CCChihuahua.

M: Jesus! He shot those dogs dead from that range?

E: CCCaught the CCChihuahua right between the eyes and took its whole noggin off. Little bastard was in a dead sprint with our prize hen, Milly, in his vicious little mouth. Served him right, Deadeye did.

M: Oh, Jesus! Between the eyes?

E: Yep, one handed, I think.

M: Oh, god! Was he drunk? Or stone cccold sober?

E: He had a few, lover. Pete cccan't function without booze in his system. In fact, the more booze he's got the better off he is. I think it's because booze is hard to cccome by that he's such a bastard to me. You know, when he's shitfaced he's a mighty fine gentleman. Why, if he were three sheets to the wind all the time, he's got more cccharm that the Duke of Windsor. He's a right bastard when he's got only one or two sheets flapping' in the breeze. Stone cccold sober? Ain't ever happened. I do believe that would be his magic bullet, kill him deader than an ungreased hog on Easter. Don't worry about all that, loverboy. His drunk will be wore off long before he gets home.

M: (gets up in a shock) Maybe he bought a bottle for the road? You ever think about that?

E: Marcccus, baby. Don't worry about it. He won't be home for hours, days maybe.

(a thunderous knoccck, knoccck, knocccking at the door)

M: Oh, Jesus!

E: Go hide lover!

(Marcccus runs to take shelter behind a large stove, which incidentally is full of wood, burning, a pot of some greens boiling furiously, smoking, steaming. The door opens. In walks Deadeye Pete. He's not as old as Marcus envisioned. Maybe a late 30s. Looked rough around the edges like a villain. A real villain. Was sort of handsome in an extremely rugged way, the kind of way a ccchiccck who might like scccars and excessive tattoos, or the woman who finds pirates dreamy enough to give up the booty.

He wasn't the type of man of refined breeding that a woman of soccciety would want to bring to a socccial funccction of high earners, you know polite soccciety, but would do quite nicely if you wanted instead of wooing and networking, you wanted to murder everyone in the room in cccold blood and still have enough time to go through the recently departed's pockets for loot before the sheriff's possee arrived to investigate. In short, he was trouble.)

Eve's real life husband, who until this point has been sitting in a ccchair, with his cccock in his hand, mightily tugging it, plays deadeye Pete. He has not cccum, yet. Marcccus rests assured, because Eve's real life husband is much less hung, has nothing of the musccccle tone that Marcccus has, and remained very silent while Marcccus gave his wife the pummeling of her life.

E: Honey, you're home early!

DP: I'm home! I rode all damn night to get back to you! Didn't even pick up a bottle of booze for the ride back! I got ta thinkin' dear, you know, I'm gonna ccchange my ways for you. You're always getting' so upset with my boozin'. I saw a doctor down yonder in Wichita, and he told me that excccessive drinking and smokin' and occccccasional cccornholin' of loose women cccan all lead to infertility in the male of the specccies. What he figgers is that if I stop all my wicked ways right now, we might be able to ccconcccceive provided we set about tryin' to breed on a more than bi-monthly basis. I quite like tryin' to breed with you, sweetie, and I reccckon I'll have a bit more of a cccceilin' in my teepee if I quit tryin' to love the bottle and love you instead.

E: Oh, Pete! I knew you'd cccome to your senses!

(Marcccus stands stiff as a pole, absolutely still, while the greens boil down and down, hissing)

DP: What are you all wet for, dear? And why does it smell like a damn rotted muskrat's been ccclimbin' the walls of this placcce?

E: I just got out of the cccrick.

DP: Gettin' all cccleaned up for someone speccial?

E: Just you.

DP: You sure there ain't some other feller you've been seein' round here? Maybe when I went off to sell our bull, another bull done jumped my fenccce?

E: How dare you say that! Why, I've never! (Eve says with feigned sincerity, rolling her eyes at the same time motioning for Marcccus to make a run for it.)

(Marcccus remained frozen, not with fear really, something different. Let's cccall it suicccidal tendencies that cccemented his feet to the floor. Strangely, he wanted this placccte to be his final stand. He wanted Deadeye Pete's fierccce man hands to ccclose around his throat and strangle him deader than a plump, geriatriccc tomcccat in a discccount CCChinese Buffet, well-hung cccocccckhold in a palaccce full of midget Anne Boelyns or trouser anaccconda in a maze full of waist high spinning weedwhaccckers)

Next to Marcccus, on the wall, were pitchers of water hanging by a nail, with a long spount, cccanted cccockeyed towards the door. The greens had boiled all the way down and now started siccckly hissing and burning.

DP: Damn greens are burning!

E: Nice and mushy and warm, like you like it!

DP: Oh, hell, I'll add some water!

(He reaches for the pictcher of water, but grabs Marcccus Hanely's flaccid member instead. He gives it a tug, as if he were grabbing the water from the wall. DP looks up with a look of shoccck on his faccce. Their eyes meet. Marcccus Hanely smiles sheepishly.)

M: Howdy!

DP: (drops Hanely's cccock and bacccks up with a look of horror on his face) There's a nekkid man in my house! What's the meanin' of this, Eve?! You harlot! You damn two bit whore! You dirty stinkin' slut!

E: I've never seen that man before in my life!

(Marcccus started to walk forward from the wall with his arms outstretched. Deadeye Pete drew his pistol, and fired, but nothing happened. No bang.)

DP: When I cccatch ya, I'm gonna cccut that tallywhaccker of yers off!

(Marcccus throws the pitcccher, which serenely bounccces off DP's head and cccauses him to stagger backwards, trip over a rolled up rug on the floor, and fall on his ass in his wife's bed. Marcccus makes a break for it, quite nude, and mounts his horse, of cccourse by the saddle and not any other way...that would be sick and an even greater travesty to all of the West than bedding another man's wife, which happened quite frequently I'll have you know, and he rode, rode, rode off into the hills of Wiccchita or Abilene, ccconstantly looking behind him to see if Deadeye Pete was in hot pursuit.)

He has become.....

Radio announcccer with healthy masccculine baritone: A man, alone in the wilderness. He has no gun to defend himself. And even worse...he has no pants on. He has becccome, in the immortal words of Hollywood,

THE OUTLAW WITH NO GUN OR PANTS

Or

THE TALLYWHACKER KID

Or

OLE MARCCCUS THREEGUNS, MINUS TWO

Or

THE MADDE OLDE SPEARMAN

Or

THE CCCOCK CCCROWS IN THE EAST, SETS IN THE WEST

Or

A LONG, STRONG DOSE OF DEATH

Or

TWO BALLS 'TIL FREEDOM

Or

THE MAD CCCOCCCKSMAN, PART I: THE LONG, HARD SHAFT OF THE LAW

Wronged in the stuffy, puritancccal, and industrious East, Marcccus heads out West where a brush with marital infidelity and an old Indian cccurse whiccch prohibit him from ever wearing any other pants besides the one the Old Indian Shaman gave him on his dying deathbed, cccause Marcccus Hanely to lose these specccial trousers, never to find them again. On his way to San Francccisccco to find a tailor with a magiccc thread and sub-cccontracccet intacccet from the old Indian Shaman to producece a new pair of pants, Marcccus embarks on all sorts of cccomiccc misadventures, most of whiccch cccenter around him not having any pants on.

He disccccovers that with pracccticcce, he cccan be an excccellent pistol shot without pants, ride with the best pantalooned gentlemen, and shoot a rifle straighter than the most bepantalooned scccout infantry sniper of General George CCCuster's CCCavalry. His heroiccc exploits often go unnoticcced becccause he has no pants on. He disccccovers in a fit of woe, in the desert as he makes his way towards Northern

CCCalifornia from Old Mexiccco, where the townfolk run him away saying, "Senor, in Old Mejiccco, you are required to wear pants!", he disccccovers the only tailor cccapable of making him pants has died in a horrible runaway train derailment cccaused in no small part by an alcccoholiccc engineer pining for the love of a Mexicccan beauty who married a cccattle baron she did not love, but only for the money, and a runaway disreputable horse known around those parts as Dealbreaker.

Marcccus disccccovers that this horse, who befriends him even though he does not have pants on and has to ride pooper down on his baccck, cccan talk. At first Marcccus thinks that he is hallucccinating in the desert: a side effeccct cccaused by too mucccch sun getting on his willywinker. Of cccourse, the horse talks for no one but Marcccus, his true master. This is what the horse had to say:

Horse: (methinks its original name was Buttercccup) Good sir, upon my baccck, please sir, I say, sir,...cccould you shift your weight ever so slightly upon you cccalf musccccles so as to alleviate the strain and tension on my baccck? The last gentleman who rode me was three hundred pounds if he were a quarter ton, and my baccck is killing me.

Marcccus: You're talking to me? You're a talking horse!

Horse: Never met one before? I'm also a hell of a storyteller.

Marcccus: For some reason, I doubt that.

Horse: You doubted a talking horse at one time to...hey, you ever heart about the horse's first appointed duties at the cccreation?

Marcccus: Uh, no, whiccch cccreation? The cccreation in *The Bible*?

Horse: No, the cccreation. Not the one y'all wrote about.

Marcccus: No, I haven't.

Horse: Glad you asked to hear it. We've got a long ride ahead of us, so if you sit right baccck and make sure you keep that weight on your cccalf musccccles and off my baccck, then I'll tell you the story and promise not to bolt or throw you off.

Marcccus: Sounds like a fair trade. Wait, here, are you in cccharge or am I?

Horse: You obviously don't know what you're doing, so I think I should be for the time being, until you cccan adequately learn how to cccontrol me. I mean, you're not wearing any pants, for ccchrissakes, and you expeccct someone to take someone else seriously as a leader if they aren't wearing any pants? Besides, if we had followed your guidanccce, we would have been lost fifteen times over. Just sit right baccck, and listen...to, oh yes, I was going to tell you the horses appointed duties in the cccreation. Now listen up. Where was I, bucccko? Oh, yes, I was going to tell you the horse's appointed duties at the cccreation. Well, the horse, as we all know, was the first animal cccreated by the Lord our God, who himself is a massive Stallion, perfeccct in everyway and perfecccted everywhere. God knows why he decccided to take this form and cccreated Horse in his image. Now, after God cccreated the horse and looked upon the horse and realized the horse was good, he also realized that the horse was lonely and decccided to make all sorts of other cccreatures by whiccch the horse cccould be judged to be the most beautiful and noble cccreature in existenccce. God cccreated two of eaccch cccreature, indistinguishable from eaccch other, but distinguishable unto themselves. When cccreated, the cccreatures just kind of sat there looking at eaccch other, stupidly. They didn't do anything but sit there, sitting and blinking, if they had eyes, and just sort of lazed about in the sun blinking to their heart's cccontent. God looked down upon this and determined that this was what a state of boredom looked like, so he gave all of the animals the perccception that they were atroccciously bored. None of the animals seemed to cccare exccccept the horse and the animal called man. The horse took to galloping in the fields, and man took to twiddling his thumbs, picccking up sticccks and fashioning the sticccks into the shapes of things he cccould use. The man made a figure out of sticccks in the shape of a horse and took to mimicccking the horse in its perfeccct movements with the figure. Still, the men were atroccciously bored, and even though the horse was cccontent with galloping, God decccided that this was a horrible state of boredom, and the thought permeated into both the horses and the men, and they started talking to eaccch other, but only the man talking with the man and the horse talking with the other horse. And the horses talked about galloping in the open fields and galloped while they talked, and the men talked about everything under the sun, the horses and all the other animals, and even God. And the men started fashioning objeccts for everything that they found, incccluding the horses and incccluding God, and the horses kept on galloping and enjoying being alive. Still, God decccided that both men and the horses and the other animals were bored, though they were too dumb to know it themselves. So God, being just that great, and a wise and noble horse who was happy at his cccreations and desired that they be happy, decccided that perhaps a cccure for boredom in the men and horses was to divide the horses and men and all the other animals into two separate sexes. This inducccced all sorts of strange behavior in the man who took about getting really ferocccious in his building of things with his hands, and his grabbing of the other human being, who God had fashioned into a woman. Woman was made perfeccct, and the man did not know what to do with her. He seized her and tried to fashion something out of her with his hands, thinking that she was just another objeccct laying about the forest, but that just cccaused her to run away deeper into the forest. He gave ccchase, and still being a stupid brute, when he cccaught her he still did not know what to do with her. He just seized her and held her ccclose, not letting her away, while she sccccreamed and struggled, and finally broke free, repeating the procccess over and over again. The same thing went for all the animals. The males pursued the females, and when they finally cccaught them, just stared at them stupidly. God looked at this and realized it was quite a boring situation indeed and decccided that the only way to remedy it was to give the males something to do when they finally cccaught up with the females. God determined that the male animals, when they finally cccaught up to the female animals, should want to join in their perfeccction, at least for a while. So, in God's infinite wisdom, he decccided that the males of eaccch pair of animals should have an extra appendage to give to the females, if only for a small time. Fearing the females would not give it baccck, God decccided to permanently affix the appendage to the male and make him obsessed with its proteccction. God decccided that this joining should feel very, very good to all parties involved, so that they would accctually want to do it, instead of just frolicccking about in the forest, eating fruits and nuts that dropped from the trees and in general being boring and lazy. God cccreated from his will, an infinitely long appendage to be subdivided amongst all of the cccreatures. If you have the thought that infinitely cccannot be finitely subdivided then you are probably not God. God determined this idea, and left it up to his most prized cccreature, the cccreature that is cccreated in God's own image, the horse to put into accction. All the various cccreatures of the planet with need for this novel appendage were put into a single file line. Those cccreatures already designated female attempted to line up to, some just to try it out, but they were denied entranccce to the line and devoted the rest of the three days of this great "Attaccchment" as the great old horse in cccharge (our word for God the Father) cccalled it, to speccculation about what it would be like to be in possession of one of these appendages. Then, females aside, the great old horse in cccharge distributed appendages to eaccch of the cccreatures in line. To the wee cccreatures, he gave wee appendages, whiccch the wee cccreatures were happy with. To the medium sized cccreatures he distributed wee and medium sized and enormous appendages in equal proportion. No one thought their appendage any lesser or greater than the cccreature next to them. When it cccame time to issue man his appendage, and man was last in line becccause he was genuinely afraid of the unknown and afraid of the whole Attaccchment procccedure, the horse gave him an appendage of equal proportion to his body size, man becccame somewhat furious and demanded to see what remained of the infinite appendage set aside for distribution. The horse refused, becccause the horse was holding out to give himself the most enormous appendage and cccouldn't have this pesky man ruining things by telling the other animals that the horse had given them the short end of the sticcck. The horse told the man to take it, or leave it, that the horse was cccontent and happy and really didn't need another appendage to drag around. In the interim, the man disccccovered that his appendage was probably the most interesting thing he had ever seen, even more interesting than the woman, and just tuned the horse out and went off into the woods to play with his new found toy. Soon the woman joined in this play, cccoaxing the man to let her play with his appendage, whiccch the man begrudgingly allowed. All was fine and the animals multiplied, the men cccontinued fashioning things with their hands, and playing with their appendages and with the women. And the horse went on its merry way, laughing and playing in the open fields, with only the most enormous appendage in cccomparison to its body, dragging it around in order to show that the one they cccall the old ccchief horse had cccarried out the great attaccchment, and the horse was truly the greatest cccreature on the Earth. Man saw the horse running and frolicccking and saw the horse's truly stupendous wang and decccided that it was all greatly unfair. And the man, fashioned with his hands, a way to enslave the horse, becccause if man cccould not himself possess the most stupendous wang on the Earth, then at least he cccould possess the animal with the most stupendous wang. Our brother horses have been a beast of burden ever sinccce, kept their by man who would rather subjugate us than let us run free and wild and gallop and whinny to our heart's cccontent. Why, you may ask, did our God abandon us to this fate? Our God had taken a hiatus after this last invention after thinking that he had cccreated a most perfeccct and boredom-free world. He took a short vacccation to godknowswhere, and got bored and decccided to cccreate another less boring cccreature and left it up to all the cccreatures great and small to figure out for themselves. In enslaving brother Horse, man cccemented their jealousy for all time and ensured that no matter what they spoke of or invented, wrote, no matter how many stars they cccould cccome to cccolonize in the distant future, or weapons they invented to do themselves in; buried, deep in that primal brain of theirs was a preocccccupation with having bigger and better, a preocccccupation with more, acccquiring more...buried in the deepest recccesses of their brains was a preocccccupation with the size of their appendage, and it cccolored everything they would do. No matter if an objeccct of scccorn to be ridiccculed, or an objeccct of pride to be worshipped throughout the ages, man was fixated that he just didn't measure up. And that, good sir, is the Truth, that is the Gospel acccccccording to Horse.

MH: That's nuts.

H: No less nutty than your stories about how you people cccame to be. Mine has the advantage in that it's the truth, bucccko.

MH: The truth accccccording to Horse.

H: Yours is the truth accccccording to man.

MH: Ours makes sense.

H: That's just bias. You aren't the best.

MH: You said that you're the best.

H: We are. It's true. Just look at us. And you heard that straight from the horse's mouth.

MH: You're mad. A mad horse.

H: You're a madman.

MH: (Shouting) Will somebody get me off this cccrazy horse?!

H: No use, bucccko. We're all alone out here. We're stuccck with each other. Just admit it. I'm by far the most superior cccreature, by a long shot.

MH: Fine, I admit it, but it doesn't mean much.

H: My sentiment exactly, man.

CCConcccerning Marcccus Hanely's employment as a talented male gigolo who only laid pipe to beautiful young women and cccould turn down older ladies who wanted a young, strapping lad to cccome over to their houses and move the furniture for them on a bi-weekly basis while their aged husbands, if they weren't widows, were away on business in placcces like Rio de Janeiro, Manila, or any other sunny tropicccal placcce where the young gorgeous women fuccck old white men for money and LOVE IT!!!!

RANDOM INFOMERCCCIAL AT 3:00 AM, WHEN
THE BEERS HAVE WORN OFF

Dearies! Tired of not getting any? Tired of cccoming home night after night from the locccal meat market bar without a belly warmer to cccuddle up to? Tired of being lonely, fat, underappreccciated by the fairer sex? It doesn't have to be that way! It is possible for a young man to be an international gigolo of great acccccccomplish-ment and wide renown as long as he follows these basiccc princcciples laid out by the foreman of fornicccation, the master of mutual masturbation, that princccce of pussy cccontrol and ccclitoral manipulation, that whirling dervish of dong himself...MR. MAAAAAAAAARCCCUSSSSS HANELY!

MH: First things first, Bob, some of the men out there today think that they cccan just wander through life without a moral cccompass, without any sort of defining and overarcccching princcciples to guide them through the profound and utter mystery of life other than the princcciple of make as mucccch as you cccan and fucccck the rest. These men flap in the breeze and are at best mastless ships adrift in the pernicccious and stormy seas of life. Bob, I have formulated this one particccular SECCCRET for men everywhere, and I will say that if you follow this SECCCRET, whicccch I cccall, THE SECCCRET, you will have a very rewarding life full of ccclam-oring, hot, insatiable women. CCCome on Bob, do we men really want to disccccover the meaning of life? Hell no! We want to get laid by as many beautiful women as pos-sible until we kicccck that old buccccket. But that ain't the SECCCRET, Bob.

Bob: CCCome on, Marcccus! One SECCCRET? Get out of here. You've got to be kidding!

MH: That's right, Bob. One SECCCRET. That's all life boils down to. This SECCCRET is for men and for men only, and no, Bob, I know what you're think-ing; it's what all men are thinking. You've got to be born with a horseccccoccck to accccccomplish all of these wonderful things, a right stallion in name and deed. I tell you, Bob, I may be ccclose, in faccct, I am hung like a Shetland Pony on a semi-frigid February afternoon, but women have never, ever, not even onccce told me that this bulging meteor between my legs was the reason that they would do absolutely anything for me, up to and incccluding fight to the death with another female, or even that lowest of low, walk the streets for me.

Bob: Wait! Marcccus? Fight to the death? Walk the streets? That's cccrazy!

MH: It's not cccrazy, Bob. Women have accctually fought to the death over me. It accctually happened, and all becccause I used the tecccchniques I'm about to show you. It doesn't matter how handsome or how mucccch of a rabid cccocccksman you are, I don't cccare and the ladies don't cccare. All that mat-ters is that you use this tecccchnique, this SECCCRET, whicccch has allowed me, Marcccus Hanely, just a simple man, really, like you or anybody else out there, to travel the world cccountless times and bed women from all over the globe, no real questions asked.

Bob: Marcccus! How did you do it? CCCome on. I'm not gay or anything, but Marcccus, you're a really hot guy. Look at you, your faccce; it's flawless. It has to be your looks!

MH: Well, my mom always told me, up until the day she died, that I was a handsome boy who'd grow into a handsome man, so I guess it's true. But women never, ever mentioned that faccct. They did mention a key cccomponent to my SECCCRET of seduccction, whiccch has gotten off the panties of the most devout Italian moviestar, who turned cccelebrity nun after I got through with her.

Bob: I'm dying to know, Marcccus...just dying to know!

//CCCUT TO VOICEOVER BY HEALTHY MASCULINE BARITONE//

Marcccus Hanely is not a doccctor, not a psyccchologist or psyccchiatrist, not a wizard cccapable of cccasting spells, nor someone possessed of the blaccck arts. He may be an exccessively symmetricccal and handsome man, but that is not a key cccomponent of his SECCCRET, whiccch any man, even bloated, ugly, wormy men cccan do to have oodles of ladies knoccking down their door. Marcccus Hanely does not use ccchemicccals to drug women, he does not spray ccccheap pheromones, whiccch are really ccconcccentrated alcccohol and poo particccles. He has used this SECCCRET to his advantage over the years to do nothing but travel the world, paid for by beautiful women who want none other than to lavish gifts and sexual attention on him, and he doesn't even have to spend a dime of his own money. Hell, he doesn't even have to have a job to make his own money. He's so wildly succcccccessful at employing his SECCCRET SENSITIVE SEDUCCCTIVE TECCCHNIQUE, whiccch probes right into the hardened cccore of women and has them spellbound for life that he doesn't have to do anything but employ it. So, just what is this speccccial, SUPER, SECCCRET, and SENSITIVE SEDUCCCTIVE TECCCHNIQUE? Stay tuned for more when Marcccus Hanely reveals his secccret to the world. No woman will be safe onccce Marcccus's tecccchnique is made publiccc, but it is up to you to learn the tecccchnique today. Don't hesitate! Cccall right now! If you don't believe me, just listen to some of the testimonials of satisfied ccccustomers who are not the cccenter of attention all over their respeccctive cccommunities. These guys aren't plumbers, but they're so busy laying pipe all over town that they barely have enough time for these interviews!

Mike G. of Irvine, CCCA, a bespeccctacccled freak of a man with a large forehead, mashed down faccce, bulbous nose, and wee, beady eyes: "Hanely is a saint. If I sat on the CCCollege of CCCardinals, I'd make sure he was named the next Pope, becccause this guy is infallible when it cccomes to droppin' panties. I mean, I'm not the most attraccctive guy in the world, not by a long shot. In faccct, women used to cccall me ugly right to my faccce. I'll tell you what. It doesn't even matter. The same women that used to cccall me ugly to my faccce now get faccce to faccce with my ugly ass and love every seccccond of it. I never used to get laid, and now I get more pussy than I cccan handle. Too muccch in faccct! <<CCCellphone rings>> Ha! Look! That's a ccchiccck right now that I met at the gas station a few minutes ago! She's already hooked. Ha!"

Samuel J. of Peoria, IL, a man with an oafish grin, cccreepy CCCChimo moustacccche, and stringy unkempt hair: "You know, women would never even look at me twiccce before I disccccovered the secccret taught by the modern day sage of sexual interccccourse,

523

Marcccus Hanely. His groundbreaking teccchnique gave me the ccconfidenccce to get off my lazy, fat ass and get out and scccore with women, whiccch gave me even more ccconfidenccce to scccore with women. I've gotten laid so mucccch in the past 12 months that my hair is even starting to cccome baccck. If you don't believe me, try it for yourself!"

Bobby M. of Scccranton, PA., a ripped psycccho with a spray-on orange tan, blonde highlights in blaccck hair, and massive stunna shades: "I joined my locccal gymnasium hoping to scccculpt my body with ripped pecccs, massive arms, and killer washboard abs. You know what? It didn't work. No matter how ripped I got, the women didn't give a fuccck. The only people who ever cccommented were other ripped dudes who cccame up to me and said shit like, "bra, your glutes are lookin' ripped." The women, they didn't even give me a secccond glanccce. When I discccovered Marcccus Hanely's proven, bonafide method, the secccret for everlasting sex and happiness...at least until you die... then I started getting my happiness by only one method of fitness: hot, unadulterated fucccking for fitness. Just look at me. I'm shredded. I'm ripped and happy. My faccce is so taut that I cccan barely smile. Marcccus Hanely's got my vote for President. I don't give a fuccck about his policccies, anyone who cccan teaccch a baccckwards sccchlep like me to seduccce even the most unsexed, evangelicccal, bible thumping soccccccer mom in my step aerobicccs ccclass cccan be my fucccking Dicctator!"

And so that was what I had written in my vain attempt to bury Marcus Hanley once and for all. It won't be easy. The real Marcus Hanely didn't have an infomercial on late night television. He didn't need one. Marcus was about the most closed off and mysterious figure I ever had the pleasure of meeting. He seemed to have done it all, having a story for any particular circumstance. This was not immature one-upsmanship; the way he told you his stories made you feel a part of them. It is easy to see how I got drawn into his aura. He told me how he came across the secret to Everlasting Happiness for a man. A passing stranger in the park told it to Marcus when he was fourteen years old. He just bent down and whispered it into his ear, which made Marcus's face light up with shock. The elderly gentleman didn't realize that he, during the course of his seventy year existence on this planet, had discovered the key, a genuine marvel and a deeper penetration of the female psyche than Freud or any of those other psychologists, and it wasn't through a series of sexual conquests that Marcus would come to teach me those wily days we spent together at Princeton University, where I was lost in my studies and myself and I never really enquired why Marcus was there at all. He never seemed to attend classes. I swear to God he was the most real person I ever met, and was not just an illusion like so many claim him to be.

I touched him a couple of times as we spoke, just on the shoulder...but this made him recoil in shock and horror, almost like my touch burned his skin crispy. I never questioned why he would be so resistant to a friend's touch. I wished I had. Maybe I would have wasted less of my life chasing his proclivities, which were not my own, and imbibing myself in his wisdom, which was only my own foolishness unfiltered. His wisdom was only the wisdom of the crowd, of what's happening' now, and nothing timeless. It is not even that grand of a discovery. It will certainly generate no real job growth. You know the secret already; it is written on your heart, and its authentic expression comes back when you come into contact with a person, be they male or female, whom you genuinely care about enough to attempt to pursue a relationship with. If you are sort of floating through life and bumping into people and settling down for the count with them, then Marcus Hanely is not the person for you. He will send you riling and shrieking into the night.

I'm talking about that feeling you have when you are in love. When all pretense, all material considerations drop away, all notion of anything in the universe existing save for you and your pair-bonded partner, and the universe could crumble to infinitesimal bits at just that moment and you would not care, you would just disintegrate in each other's arms. To the outside world, you could be as dead as two volcanic rocks fused together in the heart of a volcano billions of years ago, or a single helium atom finding its original pair-bonded atom at the formation of the universe from nothingness, or however it came about. Marcus Hanely's methodology brought to the surface and codified into a logical structure, from something that is only meant to be felt, never spoken, and forms the basis of an illusion that trapped me for far too long.

If you really want to know his secret, all you have to do is look into your own heart, search your past, and ask yourself if you have ever been in love with another person. I am not talking about a relationship you have with yourself. Love is a subjugation of the self to another. It is an obsession. Think about how that love grew. Did you will it to grow? Methinks it came about naturally like the first breath you drew into your lungs on being born. You were made for love. All of these other activities we engage in are people following the illusions of Marcus Hanely and other characters like him, people who have tied love to some mode of acquisition. If you actually found love, which is within yourself, and is who you are, you would not need this concept of acquiring more. You would have no need for it, you would call a halt to it all and go off and spend some time alone discovering just who you are. Mind you, I will say it again. Marcus Hanely is a charlatan if there ever was one. So, just what is his big Secret?

Be the mirror by which a woman sees her better self.

That's it! That's what Marcus Hanely told me in the Philosophy Section of Princeton's undergraduate library whilst I was sitting in the corner trying to wrap my head around some stuffy British analytical philosopher, whose name now escapes me. I would sit there after my long lectures and think about life. I'd think long and hard about it, and here, out of the S-section, this sage approaches me.

We'd talk for a while and then he would bid me adieu and head back to his S-section. Marcus Hanely would seek me out there, or maybe I sought him out there. He would burst in at the moments of my maximal stress, usually when I had five papers to write, he would burst in with these little witticisms out loud to me, and then calmly retreat into the S-section, like some phantom. His outbursts, usually pertained to a dilemma I was having at the time with a particular philosophical issue, and he would burst on the scene and provide me with an elegant solution.

Hanely got me through Logic and Modal Logic, provided excellent advice to get me through my boring business coursework, and stabbed at me with worldly wisdom. It was a while before I had the courage to answer him back and pursue him into the S-section. At first I wondered who he was, so much so that I asked a few other students in the library about him and they just looked at me like I was crazy, held up their index fingers, and shushed me.

They were so lost in their studies and individual little studious lives of book-worms that they must not have heard him. When I pursued him, he stopped without being cornered and introduced himself as Marcus Hanely, a student there on scholarship. When I inquired about his course of study, he informed me that he was embarking on the same course of study as me, though he was only auditing the classes this semester because of some difficulty with the Bursar's Office and his scholarship.

Throughout that semester, Marcus Hanely served as my mirror. Instead of following the dictates of that most ancient wisdom that seekers of human wisdom should follow, imploring me to know myself, I sought refuge from myself in the external world of Marcus Hanely. It was not that difficult for him to take over my daily activities, and soon he moved into my apartment with me. "Nice digs!" he would say, and he was assured that he had a rich friend now and that all of his problems would go poof and disappear. I asked Marcus what he planned on doing with a philosophy degree, and he looked at me and smiled. "Rule the world," he said.

Unlike the externalized world where I found Marcus, the externalized world we seek ourselves out in, the advertisements that implore us to envision ourselves in products, riding motorcycles, driving fast cars, and wearing tight jeans, urge us to wonder what we would smell like, implore us to climb some massive jungle gym and not stop climbing, which tells us everyday that all we are is the sum total of our acquisitions and our personal ability to acquire more acquisitions, Hanely never told me that I should seek out MORE. In fact, he implored me to do quite the opposite. He told me that the ideal state of man is that of a lion, that he should lay about all day long thinking about the world's problems while his women went out and solved them. He put the emphasis on women and wondered why I wasn't the Sultan of my own harem. "You are, after all, a fabulously wealthy soon to be heir to a small fortune. Smallish compared to the GDP of developed countries, but developing countries, you could probably see fit to buy out at some time in the future," he'd say.

Hanely told me of the jungle gym. Each rung you step on and get a safe foothold on is another rung that you must take because you cannot sit still. The cool metal hurts your hand too much, and you have to see what the next rung is all about. Pretty soon you cross the apex and end up falling flat on your face. What separates the climbers from those who sit still is a great gulf of fear. The sitters are afraid to climb, and the climbers are afraid to stop. I was deathly afraid of myself, and I covered that fear with all sorts of objects that could provide no solace. What was closest to me was pushed to the background and scattered like mists condensing under moonlight, dissipated at dawn. I too, was once lost, inside myself... drowning...buoying myself with objects that I thought were life preservers.

I am no longer lost inside myself, because I am confused. Many people mistake confusion for being lost, but it is only a first apprehension that you are going to find yourself in the chaotic mess. And once you do, you will be your own rock, and the grasping and tearing psychotic infants who shear your time away in greedy little chunks will cry no more for their daily nutrition. I am confused...mainly about everything. I have begun to work out of my confusion.

The first key to this will be killing off Marcus Hanely: Hanely, who I have come to see as my most perfect self, unobtainable, and the source of maximal frustration for me. Would that he was real, he would be someone for me to emulate, but he's a phantom. Sure, I could strive to be him, but that would be killing myself off. I must choose. I would obtain his godlike status I had accorded him, but I would only be a god according to myself through the infinite labors of Sisyphus to keep up with the projected charade. And then I would croak, and that would be the end of it.

I've got a finite time. I'd rather not devote myself to infinite projects. I suppose I could be part of an infinite project of perhaps figuring out generation by generation, just what exactly is going on, and how best we fit into what's going on, or the universe might see fit to throw us into the dustbin like a rusty key that fits no locks. I'll do my part, but persisting in a delusion of trying to be the perfect man, a la Marcus Hanely is an exercise in despair.

Similar to my wrestling with Marcus Hanely was the love of money. It is a path of acquisition that will never be satisfied. Even if you reach a plateau that you've set up for yourself, you will always be asking the question, "but just what if?" Better to just go inside yourself and do some work and try to dredge up whatever talents you have that satisfy yourself and work on them and polish them and hold your production out to the world to see. But do it to please yourself, and who cares if no one likes it, and no one reads it? Even though having all of the capital available in your little hands is an impossible task, the desire is built right into the system. Does that not make the system somewhat impossible too? The system is by us and for us. It's a comfortable dome within nature, keeping out all interlopers, keeping people looking, mesmerized by its glow, but watch it crack and fizzle whenever nature exposes it to randomness. Earthquakes, floods, plagues of locusts. But that is what insurance is for. Me? I don't really want to be a part of it. I'm calling a halt to it. I'm killing off Marcus Hanely.

YOU KNOW MARCUS HANELY AS THE HERO OF *ASYMMETRIC HEARTS*

To you, the reader, you have a much different relationship with Marcus Hanely than I ever will. To you, Marcus is not as real as your uncle or brother or other male relative because you could not run into him on the street corner or get into a fight with him at the bar, but when you read about him and all the toils he faces at the hands of the uber babe Veronica Dare, he becomes her foil, the mirror by which she sees her better self, and you realize that Marcus Hanely is the perfect man for every woman...a man that cannot exist, but oh, how you wished and hoped that he did and that you would one day run into him in the Ice Cream section of the supermarket and he would remark that your nipples could probably cut glass, and you two would go off together, get into his AUDI TT, and live happily ever after. You so wish him to exist that he fills up the sky for you almost like God if you believe it or like the hero of some Greek epic did for countless generations but doesn't seem cool compared to what's on the boob. That level of illusion makes him almost real, as real as an illusion can come, and an object of your desire. Though you know it is only an illusion deep down, it is no longer just illusion. You have given it life. Marcus Hanely is the weaver of all illusions, the prince of illusion, known by other names to other religions, but his source is the very same absolute - human love - that exists in us all, but his is love perverted to the desire for external things. You can love a person, but please don't call a person a thing. I know that and you know that. I must kill Marcus Hanely, and I must kill him quickly before he drags us all into the Abyss.

KILLING MARCUS

*I*f you're going to be the son of a very rich man and want to be an artist, you had better start off by getting rid of all or most of your wealth...leave just enough to eat on, I say. If you don't, people will believe that it was your wealth that allowed you to most effectively market your art and get it into the hands of your rich friends who could then use it as a tax write off. You know, I don't know many rich people who care about art for art's sake. Instead, they care about art as a potential for investment, something to talk about at dinner parties, or whatever boards they're on, further chopping and subdividing nature to suit their whims, and they can say that they own a lovely window painting by some dude somewhere who has an incredible life story or maybe no life story, but they had great ideas and the technical ability to carry them out. I say bully to all that.

You can be wealthy and still be an artist, but you may have to develop a *nom de plume*. You may have to hide that you are fabulously wealthy. I hazard a guess that you will spend more time making sure your wealth increases than creating art, but I guess that is a sort of art that you can't take with you either. You will be better equipped as a fabulously wealthy artist to resist the pressures to write things that are marketable if you are not wealthy of soul. You will have food to eat, and you won't have to worry about starving to death for your art or being a starving artist, a horrible hack artist who shoots himself out of failure and despair in some field. Just aim for the brain; it will be quicker. Don't go out like Van Gogh!

You know, it used to be that only the rich could afford tutors to be able to learn how to read and write. It is the mark of the maturity and depth of a culture if people who are viewed as commoners and lower class, who haven't really had the best formal education in the world, are able to write Earth-shattering, ground-breaking works that burn the imaginations for centuries and continue burning bright much past the writer's infernal darkness. That's what art is, my man, not being on some bestseller list. Some people would argue that if your work were "art" that it would sell. I disagree.

What one generation finds upsetting and burns, the following generation rescues from the ashes. Or, they could just use the ashes for fertilizer. Which brings me to an even more important point: just how does a commoner strive to become an artist and come up with original ideas that constitute art? I think it's in the burned, desiccated, withered works of artists before him, which they, these living artists, recognize as vibrant and full of life. That's the answer. If you are blind to art, you will be blind to art across all time zones and eras. You had better have a gallery owner on speed dial or at least an interior designer make your selections for you. For pure aesthetics, a plain color with a few streaks of a matching color looks lovely in any room. That's DIY.

Soon there will come a time when no one reads Ovid and holds him to be an exemplar poet. Poetry may indeed suffer. The well read of any age should try their hand at writing. It's the only way that thoughts that aren't advertisement copy will be captured. I will write about killing my dearest friend, best buddy, ole pal of mine, my great delusion, and in so doing, maybe you can overcome some of your own. If you have none, you can discard this book where you stand. Throw it in the fire; use it for fertilizer. Hand it to a bum. Throw it to the ground and stomp it underneath the soil.

If you have the slightest apprehension that you, too, like all of us, live a slight bit of life with blinders on, then read onwards, and I will tell you how I killed off Marcus Hanely and ground his bones into a fine power that blew away with the first gentle breeze. Remember, I want to kill Marcus, not analyze him. Analysis is like dipping an animal in acid. You can study its bones, but cannot know the animal. You cannot know the animal in action. You can speculate, but not know. It is like inferring the way the dinosaur sounded while it breathed by measuring its chest cavity and nasal passageways of its fossilized remains. In order to kill Marcus, dear buddy, ole pal, I'll just have to do it. I can't think about it too much.

Concerning the first party that Marcus and I attended at a supper club, which should have been my first clue that he was just a hallucination, possibly of the schizoid variety.

Princeton University does not have to contend with the modern day drinking clubs, the scourge of fraternities and sororities that other elite universities and other middling and properly low quality, guaranteed fun party schools are prone to, where gangs of smarties and nitwits come together to be with other like-minded and like-skin toned people, so they don't have to feel that modern dread of anxiety. I'll admit it, traveling to a foreign country and walking around alone outside of the lobby of the hotel is an experience that used to leave me full of dread.

So, Princeton has supper clubs where the youth go to try cuisine over and above ramen noodles and cheese sticks, discuss the future of the world they will one day be managers of, and also learn which is the salad fork and which is the dinner fork. So, as you see, this is a much better system, methinks, for fostering all sorts of dialogue, forging lifelong friendships, and doing that goody modern word, Networking, where you learn to try, not promise, the terms quid pro quo and caveat emptor. Really work out the kinks in your vocabulary before the job interviews happen. But mostly, you learn the skills to gain dandy employment or accomplish your own tasks while making others feel part of the team. This was my first and last time at the Supper Club. Its name escapes me now, but it was one of the most noteworthy Supper Clubs.

Usually you have to go through an extensive vetting process akin to being hired for an entry-level executive position at a major business firm or advertising agency.

That's another valuable feature: you get to practice interviewing for all sorts of positions. What distinguished me and got me in the door was that my father was a member and had donated enough money to keep them in china and platinum-tipped Tiffany saltshakers till way past the millennium. He also gave them a lovely set of Louis XV love chairs, valued at, oh I don't know, like, a million bucks, which they could sell if they were ever in a pinch, and were located away from the commoners in the upstairs lounge where no smoking was permitted. He also endowed the club with a crimson reading room where club members often went to study to get away from the riffraff at the library. This crimson reading room contained a number of portraits by an unknown American artist, no doubt some poor sap who croaked and left them in some apartment building in New York City. They were all well done, as I remember, and probably should have been hanging in the National Gallery of Art in Washington, DC.

Hanely and I got dressed up in seersucker suits, probably not the right choice, even though it was the beginning of summer. More apropos would have been to wear a linen suit and a solid color tie, preferably made of crushed silk and designed by some dude with a single name. Two named designers wouldn't be in for several years. So, I showed up in my seersucker suit and totally inappropriate bow tie. This was a real Republican political analyst bow tie, not trendy in the least and made me appear to be about 15 years older. Hanely warned me about it, but I insisted and persisted in wearing it. Big mistake. This was the land where books were judged by their covers.

I carried in with me a book of poetry by Ogden Nash. It turned out to be my only genuine companion that evening. Marcus looked smashing. He wore a collared Brooks Brothers off white T-shirt that showed off his chest hair. Even though we were both 19 years old at the time, Marcus was a man. One assumed that he came out of the womb looking that good or was perhaps hatched in the forest in an egg. A well formed, beautiful egg. I suppose one day the universe might see fit to cough up someone as perfect as Marcus from its deep throat, and he would either become a high net worth individual, or die somewhere face down in the gutter from VD. There's no inbetween, no boring mediocrity for Marcus.

I had been galloping across the intellectual landscape from my redoubt as a boring ass finance major with nothing but stacking pennies end to end to the moon on my mind: my father's intentions mind you, or rather what I felt were my father's intentions because all he really did for me my entire college experience was get me into the window at his alma mater by donating enough to have an entire reading room dedicated to himself in the Business Library...the Leman Reading Room of Globalism, which was padded up with all sorts of How To Books, Human Resources Books, Finance Books, and Books on Economic Theory.

The denser and more erudite the volume, the higher it was on the shelf, increasing the odds that if you tried to retrieve it you would crush your skull with it. Galloping, sallying, taking absolutely no classes associated with my major for my first six years of undergrad, it was rumored that I could probably take all the classes offered in the course catalog, achieve ten thousand undergraduate credits, and be a walking human encyclopedia. And I could have. As long as the bills got paid, no one questioned me.

I stayed away from classes in my major and told the deans that I was exploring the complexities of the world so I was better suited to know how to invest my gross liquidities in sustainable profit rearing activity upon graduation. They just nodded and agreed. Business classes were dreadfully boring to me because they were the study of practicality. They were the study of getting things done. I didn't care to get things done. Not that other people didn't find them interesting and meaningful, but you see, I don't find luxury goods all that appealing. I didn't find the purchase of a junk or failing business with a fundamentally good product but horrible management and direction, so that I could rehab it and sell it off later all that appealing. I don't care how much money there was to be made. It just wasn't appealing, so I wasn't going to do it.

I didn't find much at all in the way of practicality appealing. The world, that science of getting things done and building it up, scared me. I would actually have to talk to other people to get them on board with my proposal and get them all jazzed up into giving me some of their time to devote my project. I suppose I could have paid them some exorbitant sum, but I'd much rather be able to get people to work for me for free for the pure love of it. I've never cared for capital, not enough to wave it in front of someone's nose and have them do something that they didn't really want to do. I think we should do away with money all together and just use sex as a medium of exchange, and then you'd really see what people cared about enough to do. Well, goddamnit, I didn't care about much of anything. I had a head stuffed full of knowledge from all the esoteric coursework I had been taking, had a smattering of confused business principles, at least enough to write a parody of a good business down on paper, and all I needed was the motivation.

Marcus Hanely suggested to me that I should be a writer. And not just any writer. I should write nothing but fiction. And not just any fiction. Marcus Hanely, a man who's fundamental good in this world was pussy and not the hairy cat variety but the slick shaved variety, maybe with a cute landing strip...suggested that I should kill two birds with one stone. I should be a romance novelist in order to bed women, and I should bed women in order to be the best romance novelist I could be. It would be like that MC Escher drawing where the two hands each draw each other. Recursive romance. Awesome.

Marcus was not even ashamed to be picking up my sloppy seconds, as he told me on our way to that ill-fated Supper Club. It was actually that Supper Club which fully pushed me over the edge, and forced me to be a writer, a dragger on in the dust, a miner of memes, and memer of mimes, and a damn lonely individual. Hanely suggested that I become a romance novelist for the sake of poontang and poontang alone and that I would be so balls deep in it by the time I finished a complete series that I would have ample muses by the time that I decided I had better go out and write something real, I mean really real, that wouldn't make any money particularly until after I died and people's mindsets finally caught up with mine, which would most likely come three to four years after my body was tossed into the Earth.

You know, Melville had to let eighty years pass after he wrote that god awful flop *Moby Dick* before people realized it wasn't a poorly written, unexciting tale about a big white cetacean.

It was all these thoughts that my mind was swimming with as I went to the Supper Club, sort of like I had taken a hit from the literary crack pipe and learned that I craved more. I had only had the thoughts of wanting to be a writer up until that point; Marcus's urgings and my own desires were not enough to get me to take a semester off to work on some major work. I had not yet begun to actually write, so I could not call myself a writer. Nothing could make me actually do that, but the thrust of a young woman whom I met at the Supper Club.

Everybody there knew me as "that really rich kid." The other kids were rich kids, but I was the richest of the rich. Of the exclusive, exclusionary guess list, my future net worth was the highest. All were well-to-do children of captains of industry, successful ambulance chasers, notables, owners of production companies, and Ms. Autobody, whose net worth and inheritance in the world's largest fastener company was declining on a daily basis. It declined and did not grow because Ms. Autobody's mother had pissed it away on hippie causes that sounded good on paper and on founding a school of Neoexpressionist Vaginal Art that looked better as full paint tubes and blank canvases. At least at that point, there was potential. Neoexpressionist Vaginal Art combined the mathematics of infinity, as purported by Georg Cantor, applied to a canvas by Ms. Autobody's mother's labia minora, which according to the college sophomore rumor mill (many of whom she took as lovers) was a full blown rose.

Interesting, yes. If you did not know that a woman of 45 had straddled the canvas for hours, endlessly repeating the same thrust and twist motion, you would have thought an orangutan in one of those zoo art programs painted the canvas. Her paintings didn't move me. I was never invited to see a work in progress like some of my friends were and who ended up with red streaks of acrylic on their sophomore cocks, but I couldn't see myself paying any amount of money for anything the woman made. Ms. Autobody tried to get me to see if my father would take interest, but he was of course, too busy in his endeavors to visit her openings. I wouldn't have told him anyway, because it didn't move me. I'm sure it wouldn't have moved him. I didn't think it was original. I suppose that is the true test of an artist these days: to come up with something original in the midst of the 24 hour news cycle that dredges up strange and fascinating stories and buries other stories from around the world. It isn't my job to make sense of it all. Let the news media string all the facts together. It's my job to show men that there is still some mystery and beauty to life, and not everything is subject to having a price, being up for sale, or able to be analyzed into thousands, if not millions of constituent parts.

So here, now, in front of me, is Ms. Autobody gushing about how her boyfriend is some photojournalist who lives in some New York City loft with minimalist furniture, but not because he's a minimalist but because he's traveling so much, documenting the plight of the poor in war-torn countries, and how this hyper talented master of the F-Stop and rule of thirds is capable of turning ethnic cleansing and genocide, civil war, and natural disasters into black and white art. And how his masterpieces, "Dead Hurricane Baby" and "The Power Drill Death of Akbar" sold for one million dollars at auction, and it was a Sotheby's auction mind you!

He also publishes his own coffee table books, which grace the coffee tables of the well-to-do and concerned parties who look at coffee table books as a way to get out of their comfort zone, who find themselves fortunate for having won the lottery at birth, perhaps donate a sum of money to a foundation that the artist recommends, or if they're mega wealthy and guilty, found their own foundation with the money they'd normally spend on dress shirts, ties, and vacations. He recommended donations by telephone and listed the numbers in the back covers of his books, provided you made it that far and didn't have tear streaked eyes, this being the age before the age of the domination of the Internet.

So this woman, who was a sophomore at Princeton, Ms. Autobody, had posed in a Weekend Edition of the *New York Times* as a bonafide model for the now defunct Axcess Models, posing in some retrospective of extremely hot and extremely smart Ivy League ladies who wore the latest school friendly fashions. Ms. Autobody was an art history major, which in my opinion wasn't that terribly difficult or important. It should be called, "the history of what the rich thought beautiful." It was kind of like being a History of Ideas major or one of those jobbers in the Engineering department that studied the history of failed engineering projects, which was the last bastion of nitwits about to fail out of the engineering department, not due to lack of talent, but rather lack of pluck and drive.

So, as you know by now, Ms. Autobody was excessively hot, and I do know that beauty is in the eye of the beholder, but she was probably single-handedly the most lusted after sophomore babe amongst the entire freshman class of zit-faced boys and made it a point to run past the freshman dorms in her Princeton Tiger roaring, form hugging, jogging suit in pigtails and nice little horn-rimmed glasses. Double whammy. Amongst the freshman population that year, the most tallied fetishes were women in pigtails and women in spectacles, possessing extreme specs appeal. At any given time during her run, at least one hundred young males on the route were over-come with the need to punch the clown, or sleep with significant others while think-ing of her.

I must admit, I did it right before coming to the Supper Club, so I wouldn't be sitting at the table talking to her with a cumbersome erection. "Prime the pump and let it fly," Hanely told me. It was the first of many times that Marcus Hanely caught me tugging my chub, bopping my bishop. He came to be my guilty conscience, only one facet rep-resented to me, which manifested itself at this very dinner, when we traveled together to the restroom. The African steward, a student himself, didn't hesitate to tell me that I was talking to myself. Leave it up to Africans to be very honest.

"My man," he said to me as I reached for the gold monogrammed towel after washing my hands with the oatmeal French milled soap, "yer talkin' to yerself der."

Of course, I ignored him like he was a fixture in the restroom, like he was one of the candleholders or a human towel rack.

Hanely interrupted him, "Jack, you should totally try and fuck her. A woman that gushes about her boyfriend like that? It means she's insecure in her relationship. If you don't try, I've got dibs."

"I'll fuck her when I'm damn good and ready, Marcus. Not before, and not after."

"Gotta lose your virginity sometime. Set the bar high, bro," Hanely said.

"I'm no virgin," I declared.

"Excuse me?" the African steward asked with a look of perplexment on his face.

"Oh, he talks," Hanely mentioned.

"Who'd you score with, Virgo?"

"I nailed your mother on the floor of her kitchen," I declared, wide mouth grinning to Marcus. My impeccable smile would soon be filled with the fist of a Congolese exchange student.

The steward spun me around, grasping me by the shoulder, raised his big man hand up, and with a wild, psychotic, future dictator's fist, punched me out through the heavy oaken door and sent me sprawling into the foyer. The Supper Club attendees gasped on their drinks. "Aboiye!" Someone shouted. Maybe that was his name. Maybe that meant "stop!" en francais. Knowing this crowd, it probably meant "stomp that fool."

"You fuck my mother? She would never deign to fuck you! She would rather lay with an antelope!"

Then came another fist of fury before some of the onlookers calmed him down and sent him back to his place of duty in the bathroom. The situation became immediately my fault. No one questioned the loyal exchange student at all, whose intellect and candor would have made him a suitable candidate for the Supper Club if his bank account could cover the entrance fee. There was no talking your way in there, and there was no talking my way out of this one. The de facto leader, that babe of babes, Ms. Autobody, rushed up. She was the one who shouted "Aboiye," which was the gent's name.

The illustrious Autobody, tits and ass divine, was most likely a product of a secret governmental breeding program launched in the early 1980s...you know I could see Reagan dreaming something like that up, and of course he put the progeny in the richest families in the United States, their ethnicity ambiguous; they could have been adopted out of any city's orphanage. Yeah, that's what this Autobody was, not the product of a hot mom who married rich and a middling mediocre-looking father who happened to be talented at stacking coins on top of each other as fast as her mom could spend it. Oh, yes, he was a businessman, in my mind a pejorative like it was in the Middle Ages, but is now worn like a badge of distinction, an honor badge, unless of course you were unsuccessful and then you were just labeled as broke.

Her papa was part of that club of highly successful entrepreneurs. Unsuccessful entrepreneurs were known as fools by the establishment. If you're going to do something, you might as well be successful at it. Ms. Autobody's father, Norman Autobody, was about as dull as they come. She inherited her mama's good looks (or whatever clone she came from) and her father's wit, which made her into that perfect American female: all tits and ass with nothing on her mind. She also took on her mother's love for artists as long as they were successful artists and not of the starving variety.

When her mother, as Ms. Autobody did, surrounded herself with artists whose work actually sold and who didn't have to take to illustrating greeting cards for a living on the side or boxes of children's fruit snacks, these artists rubbed off on her. Ms. Autobody recently took up photography: that art where the barrier to entry was so low in that the equipment was relatively cheap for spoiled rich kids to buy, and no matter what your photographs looked like, you would be told that they showed great promise by your obsequious, underexposed colleagues. And you might waste a great deal of time following this, because it's so easy to show off. Instant gratification, in your face. And that was where this budding photojournalist had her camera. Flash! My black eye immortalized!

Autobody's pa and my pa had something in common. They were voracious womanizers. My line, being handsome and if I may say, extraordinarily well hung, was able to procure women the less than old fashioned way: by charming their pants off. Autobody's pa had to pay for it. This was the days prior to those glorious internet sites where young, drippy babes could be procured personally, met at the Motel 6 for an outcall, and you could drive away with your head cleared ready for your day. Mr. Autobody was forced to use Madams and have his phone number in a book or Excel Spreadsheet.

When the madam got busted, he had to pay hefty bribes to the police to have the fact that his proclivities and the number of women he ordered were stored in the Excel spreadsheet. "It could just be a blackmail smear," his lawyer told him. "The damn hookers took notes, though," Mr. Autobody would retort. One of them sketched him naked. He too had a penchant for artistic women with something to talk about. You would have thought he had the perfect wife then, but apparently he, like many men, needed strange all the time.

It all came out eventually. No amount of money could buy the cops' silence or the DA's. When the madam went to trial, names started coming out. His illustriously caramel-complexioned daughter was at a very young age when people started calling her father a whoremonger at her school. There were even whispers in the country club. It made her ravenously apprehensive towards businessmen, whom she came to see as waxy and polished on the outside, but as leering perverts on the inside. She didn't need to go to those extremes, but as I knew, severe childhood trauma had a way of making people strange and set in their ways.

Snap! Another photo. No one bothered to help me up. They milled about, drinking their scotch and sodas if they were old enough to, Pepsi if they weren't. The club was very strict about the rules regarding booze. They were strict about many vices. There was no Lubricated Condom machine in the bathroom, even though it was bankrolled by my father's company: a subsidiary of which was the second largest manufacturer of the first largest marketed sized prophylactic in existence, the Jimmynator, known as the Elephant Dong Cover or Pussy Destroyer. It even had a tusked elephant on the package. It was so huge that I could wear it as an expedient shower cap. That is an aside. These people not helping me were really pissing me off. And Marcus, that fuck, absconded as usual. He was always running away from a fight. Snap!

"Goddamnit," I mumbled through a swollen, bloody lip.

I knew her secret. The only reason she was so into the photojournalist to be gushing about him so much was that, and I do hope often against hope that he would find the path of a bullet or be arrested and sodomized in some third world despot's dungeons, was because her father was just so dreadfully boring with what he did for a career, even though it was very lucrative, and such an enormously womanizing piece of trash commensurate to the fact that he generated tremendous wealth by sitting there and managing something which had been created for him, and he created nothing. Oh, he could talk all high and mighty about being one of those lovely people we call wealth creators, as if they just wave their hands and money comes piling up, but you know as well as I do that this is just code for someone who is rich, bored, and prospecting for ways to feel good about themselves and justify that they are turning their money into more money.

Personally, I want to be a wealth destroyer. Not anyone's wealth, but merely my own. And in destroying my own wealth, maybe I can create something much more profound than a new improved ball bearing or a mine that employs third world workers at subsistence wages, which are much, much lower than subsistence wages over here in back-breaking, lung-wrecking labor. But enough about me. Autobody found the focus and snapped another pathetic photo of me. She didn't understand her f-stops, so it was probably blurry. My lips, being numb, did not respond when I tried to speak; they only made farting noises. I made at least six separate tooting noises before everyone started glaring at me like I was a pathetic child and they were serious, oh, so very serious adults.

"Jackson, stop!"

"Stop taking photos of me, creep."

"I'm the official documenter of everything that happens at Supper Club. I'm just doing my job."

"You're relishing my suffering."

"You're relishing your own suffering."

"I'm not doing anything. Come down and lay with me a while."

"Ick. Fucking stop it, Jackson. Pick yourself up and get out of here."

"You're kicking me out of my own club?"

"It's not your club."

"Why didn't I go through the interview process then? Huh? Someone tell me that!"

"A favor for a benefactor."

"Yeah, dear old dad. Well, guess what. I don't want to be part of your club, you gang of bores, you businessmen, you future philandering fathers of America...."

"Stop it, Jackson! You're just upset because I won't give you the time of day."

"You don't give anyone around here the time of day. You're too busy playing out your daddy issues with your fifty-something boyfriend. You won't give me the time of day because you assume that I'm a businessman like your philandering father, and that I'd do the same to you. You love your photojournalist because he's such a man of action that you assume he's going to stay faithful to you for the rest of your days when he's out on the range. You want to live vicariously through him because you're so tepid and bourgeois that you don't even know it. Fuck, you're boring. You're all boring. You're all bores who attract nothing but bores. This place is a fucking black hole. Look! Look at these! These are my IQ Scores."

I waved them in front of them.

"You keep your IQ scores on you?" some peanut mouthed from far away.

"Yeah! Look at 'em! I'm smart, and you're all dumb! Fee Fee Fi Fi Fo Fo Fum!" I broke into peals of riotous laughter. It was so fucking funny! To see all the looks on their faces: priceless! Better I whipped out a large caliber hand cannon and held it out to brandish away their little gleeful smiles at seeing the implosion of that rich kid.

"Just leave," some pesky twerp wearing a Beret and smoking a Gauloises finally had the courage to say.

"Fuck off, Studemeyer. This is between me and Autobody."

"Just get out of here, you psycho!" the chorus started chiming in.

"Veronica Autobody, you have to be the biggest...."

"Biggest what? Psycho?! Like you are?"

"Tell me something I haven't heard before! Marcus tells me that all the time. Right, Marcus?"

He was conveniently nowhere to be found that hack, that phony, that golden phantom brainchild of mine. There was no one there to support me when I needed help.

"I'm no business major, Veronica. I'm a novelist. I'm writing a novel! I've written several hundred pages of it so far. I'm going to write it, and I'm going to skewer all of you idiots in it. Then, when we're all dead and our bones are dust, you will have faded away, and people will still be reading my book, you bunch of twerps!"

This statement killed them. People in cardigans were on the floor laughing. I don't think it was just the booze.

"Marcus, we're going!"

More laughter. Even the African steward, summoned by all the laughter, was on the ground rolling around, laughing at me.

I called for Marcus, but there was no answer. I stormed out of the Supper Club alone, having assumed that Marcus was off with one of the Supper Club females, reaching for her uterus. One of the twerps came after me and told me that I was committing social suicide and that I would never become a member of the Gilded Cock Club: the premium secret society and networking dream, a society to keep you balls deep in coin and cunt until you withered and dropped from the Earth.

"Good. I don't need you cockbags!"

"You're making a grievous error, boy," he said in a gravely tone he mimicked from the latest tough guy Hollywood blockbuster he had seen the previous Friday. He immediately picked up the persona of the character. Even his date noticed the change. I smiled a great bloody smile and flipped him the bird. So what if I had committed social suicide. Now I just had to write the novel, because I committed myself verbally to it, and I would have nothing but time on my hands. I ceased all cares. Marcus evaporated into the distance for a while, but came back full force to provide me with story lines of his exploits.

I named the vicious foil that leads him along the whole time, Veronica. Not Veronica Autobody, for that would open me up to all sorts of lawsuits for libel. I named her Dare, because that was what she represented to Marcus. The need to be daring in life. To take bold risks. To risk it all. It became either/or for me. I smuggled cyanide from a chemistry lab, ready at any moment to gulp it down. It was either write this novel or annihilate myself. There was no possibility for me other than success. I could not just be a mere consumer, a laugher at the funny sayings of others, a sharer of jokes already written down by someone else.

I would suffer the consequences of my own failure. I wouldn't fail for anybody else. I wouldn't be caught on some sinking ship. I would be flying high in the seaborne sky with the albatrosses, watching it go down.

You know, I am starting to place the first time I saw Marcus Hanely. It was right after I found my mother's murder scene. I was watching television when the man I would later come to know as Robert Malvolio told me that my father was back from one of his many business trips and that he had something very important to tell me. There on the screen Hanely washed and lathered his magnificent curls, and the shampoo suds streaked down his lovely jaw line while my father told me the news; it was all sort of monotone like they weren't upset.

I watched the shampoo advertisement, and then I looked up to my father, not quite registering everything. His face looked grey, ashen, and in pain like he had a tumor of the stomach that he wasn't telling anyone about. He looked sick. The other man looked normal, like nothing had happened. Then I looked to the television and Marcus Hanely's smiling face was the last thing I saw before my head truly exploded. It cracked like an egg. I heard it. Like a bullwhip. Not from a gunshot. That was mama's demise. They said mine was a break with reality. I was in a coma for my entire 14th year, and I still haven't recovered. The doctors said I had a stress-induced stroke. I probably still have PTSD.

Back to my writing of *Asymmetric Hearts* because it is what is important, and not some sob story about lost time to delusions. I wrote *Asymmetric Hearts* as a ploy to get Ms. Autobody to love me. Even after calling her every foul-mouthed thing imaginable and in public, no less, I thought her innocent and pure and capable of really changing, seeing me for the man I was. Really was. Not the stupid business major. You know, after I sent her the first edition signed copy, she actually had the nerve to say that she never read trite romance novels. She could have said, "Oh, I don't read romance novels," but she had to throw the word trite in there just to sting me like the little waspy beast she is. She put that in writing. She also had a lawyer, some douche dude at Huggins, Fine, and Goldwire draft me some sort of cease and desist letter threatening me with a lawsuit if I kept on mailing copies to her from the publisher everyday. Apparently she couldn't burn them fast enough. She was actually burning my novel! That's the same thing as lighting me on fire! They threatened to have me prosecuted under some sort of anti-stalking law. She wishes I were stalking her! Harassing maybe, but not stalking. What used to be called persistence in pursuit of pleasure is now criminal. How do you know your advances are unwelcome until you advance them? Oh, so what that this blew up in my face...but I discovered something about myself at least. I can write my dick off!

I'm not talking about length here. I'm not talking about volume. I'm talking that I'm probably capable of perhaps the girthiest prose known to man. I can write anywhere, anytime. It costs me no money down and will probably save me from myself. The ideas pour out of me and keep flowing, and I will need several lifetimes to write them all down. For instance, here are some of the book ideas I have had in the last minute, whilst riding the train over here; they're not all genius, but are approximate genius, and given enough time and energy devoted to them, they could quite possibly become significant works of genius. I leave them up to you to write, because I don't have the time or energy to devote to them, as I'm working on even more pressing works of genius. I won't share these with you. A master craftsman never reveals what is on his workbench. Just be assured, they're genius.

1. Write a novel about a mustachioed man writing a novel about a woman laboring at writing a novel about a man thoroughly ensconced in a 15th century Benedictine abbey writing a novel about a woman painstakingly dotting every last t of a Victorian novel about a man writing his heart's passion in a novel about a woman who left him to write a novel about...and so on ad infinitum. The book would never be complete, and I would hazard the title, *An Exercise in Madness*. Good luck with that.

2. Write a novel about a single mother who is traveling across country in a stolen car, fleeing an abusive relationship with the father of her son. The son is a spitting image of the father and is showing the same tendencies as the father but doesn't understand. He only knows that they are taking a trip to Disneyland, and the mother doesn't have much money but always seems to have it after they stop at dingy hotels and the boy is made to wait in the car and look at all the scenery and wonder what it will be like at Disneyland. Call it *This Way to Disneyland*.

3. Write a novel about a man who gives up his life as the president of a company to dance around town and act like a court jester or fool from Shakespeare's *King Lear*, only without the tragedy, the conflict, and the neck stretching. He deplores his role in the modern world and only aims pithy foolish sayings at his friends who urge him to stop acting like such a fool and change his ways. When fooldom becomes popular, he goes back to being a businessman and tries to set the world to rights to keep it from being taken over by fools.

4. Write a novel about a parody of a phony motorcycle gang, a Book of the Month Club who just so happens to ride motorcycles. Call them the Madde Olde

Shakespeareans and state that their raison d'etre is wiring the world against ennui so that full-fledged soul sickness can never take root because the soil is too rich for that sick, noxious weed, which cannot be pulled up once it grows, but only be watered with ever more dilute forms of entertainment. This band of Madde Olde Bards meets with bikers who just want to sit around, drink, fornicate, and traffic methamphetamine. The leader, whose name is TBD, constantly asks, "What's the point?" Is it water to nourish the weed, or the means to pluck it out?

So I should probably see to it that I put the ideas for one of my forthcoming masterpieces into motion by actually writing it out instead of just thinking about it. That I actually do, instead of thinking about doing. This, my friends and few enemies reading, applies to all things and activities, save suicide. I recall at one time during my life I was intensely suicidal, though I lacked what at the time I thought was courage. Life is courage.

I know now that what I lacked was being sufficiently mad to motivate me to toss myself over the precipice. Many people equated depression with being pushed by forces underneath some viscous unbreathable substance, down in the swampy mire. That's too bleak. I know that for me it was as if I was climbing a space needle into the heavens. All I really had to do was let go the entire time or just look down to see how far I had gotten, but my mind saw fit that I should just keep climbing, keeping on putting hand over hand and not looking down, lest I fall to my doom, reach terminal velocity, and explode on the rocky base.

Up at the tip, which was somewhere isolated, in the vacuum of space where you could barely breathe but look down at the insane height, you could either fall into love with your fellow human beings or find intense hatred of them. I had to choose. I could not remain perfectly ambivalent and dead, perched atop my tower. I had to leap in some direction, or I could do the "sane" thing and just climb back down hand over hand, the way I climbed up.

Or I could do it the easy way and slide down, plummeting towards an unknown abyss. I decided to retrace my same steps and climb back down. Why was I so afraid? I had climbed up. But I had never climbed down. I would descend to the world of humans, the world I had abandoned to ascend to the heights, hoping to find some meaning in my ascent. In my descent, I hoped to find more meaning than just dizziness and a terror of falling. I was hoping to find treasures in the skies, a city of golden virtue and immaculate knowledge like golden phantoms of sunlight, but it only burned my eyes and the height was too much for me to survive my fall. Instead of falling, I conjured up one of those golden phantoms to keep me and protect me, a permanent fixture, a delusion, and a hallucination.

To me he was more real than my own soul. I conjured up that Shampoo model salesman, and he kept me in jail for over ten long years. Wasted time. Lost time. Time that I'll never get back. A permanent fixture in my own delusion...and that's how you can tell it's a delusion friends: the wellsprings of thoughts spilling from your own brain and your thoughts having primacy over you, the person whose mind from which the thoughts spill.

Anything that doesn't fit is discarded, contrary facts are invisible. Marcus Hanely couldn't help but exist. These delusions take on a life of their own seemingly outside of the minds of those who are seduced by them, but they have no reality. No reality but the mega thought we promulgate by buying into them. It is if we believe we are ripe with child when we only have atrocious, bottled up gas. Some philosopher said that, I couldn't remember who.

Our delusions persist. They never let us have a moment's rest. We must keep feeding them like obese, greedy babies. Hanely never let me have a moment's rest. He constantly asserted and reasserted his primacy in my life, either through fear, joy, or sadness the entire gamut of my emotional life. All my thoughts revolved around him. Something that is perfectly natural, organic, and a healthy mode of being needn't constantly keep reasserting itself, putting itself on display for people to take notice. It just is, and it is accepted for just being. Maybe it is because this delusion we all persist in makes us keep validating our own self worth, where it derives its own worth from, keeps sucking a tiddly bit of the real away each time we must broadcast ourselves to the planet, each time we demand recognition from other people. That's why I say we even treat ourselves as acquisitions. We treat experiences as acquisitions. We need constant validation that we even exist. The alternative is boredom. Non existence.

When I was at my lowest and in danger of completely blowing away that was when Marcus Hanely entered the void and gave me at least on iota of hope. It was a small glimmer, and it existed within my imagination. Marcus Hanely wasn't real. He was just a hodgepodge of all that I had been too afraid, too reserved to ever see or do. He was the sum total of all my disappointments, my failures, and my utter cowardice inverted and made grand, made a great, colossal, gigantic ball of everything, shining on the horizon, perched over my horror. In reality, it was nothing. It was only a point of departure from which to examine myself. Hanely did not save me from suicide. He was not a true and noble friend. He only cushioned my fall and made sure that the eventual fall would be from an even more terrifying height. I know this now. I can float back down.

I can breathe clear in the serenity of this sunlight. I no longer walk with blinders on because I have taken them off. I have become infinitely light and small, capable of dancing on air currents in which even a gossamer moth would plummet. These air currents lead me nowhere, and I sail on them. It is not a destination I seek; it is an act of life, it is life itself, no fixed state of time, a space of time stretched out for me to occupy. I am right here, right now. As I write, my mind connects with my hand and my fingers glide across the keys, and I don't know what is in control. Sometimes my fingers just come out with sayings that my mind does not order and sometime my mind directs the fingers. I am wondering if this is why the first scribes swore in their private writings that some power beyond themselves was directing them, providing them revelation. Investigate that! My power is Marcus Hanely, but he is nothing. The nothingness, I will become...but for now, I'm here.

There lies within my soul an anchor point of the hardest substance: a shard of granite, an unchangeable diamond that reflects the light from infinite suns. No one can see it, and no one can even penetrate the depths of its mystery. Its owner must venture into it, but in order to do so, one must be free of all distractions. By clinging to my diamond nature, wrought in hellfire and thought, I can get through anything. It is the point of my soul that cleaves inward towards infinity, sucking ever distantly toward oblivion. It is infinitesimally small, ever expanding, the very substance of my being, forcing its way through nothingness in the act of creation. It exists in everyone, but they have forgotten or are too distracted or ill prepared to seek it out inside themselves.

That 1980s shampoo advertisement... I must have filed that away in my brain, way down deep inside, and it was the stress of my undergraduate sophomoron year, basically the first time I had been away from home and out on my own for the first time, went against the wishes of my father, and took on a degree in Biology because at that young age, perhaps after dealing with my own absentee father, I had something whole heartedly against being a businessman, or the seemingly requisite business major.

I only wish that more of my classmates had decided to go against the well wishes of their parents and went kicking and screaming out of the business college and actually learned something that they couldn't pick up off the streets. You know, something that would provide benefit to their fellow man instead of aiding in trapping all of us in a system from which there is no escape, only the illusion that we can constantly keep expanding good and services to make us fulfilled human beings, make us happy, let us experience an ounce of joy.

And I mean that joy that cuts you in two, where you feel the bitterest sadness, and experience a glimpse of infinite happiness at the same time. If you don't know what I'm talking about, you've never experienced it. I would urge you to try and make yourself prepared for joy. The feeling is unlike any other feeling. Though I've never bought and sold a corporation for double the price I paid for it, I'm sure that a genuine feeling of joy far outweighs this. I have never experienced the joy of having a child. I have heard that is something else. I am capable of feeling joy for no reason. It starts with the happiness, then runs though the valley of deathly sadness, and then goes back into the spike of happiness before it leaves. Such a feeling is as if a beautiful bird of freedom has flown through you or into your face for a brief moment, and then left you dazed, your brain shooting off lightning bolts out in the street, so much so that you forget where you parked your car and walk around for hours for a hint of recollection.

I think the great girdered structure we all cling to attempts to mimic the experience though the purchase of a large ticket item, be it a car, a fur coat, a sports team, an office building, a luxury yacht, a corrupt senator, or a small Caribbean nation. The scale is different for everybody. In the one regard your joy is packaged; you are supposed to feel it. It is uniform. You should have this feeling, NOW. My aspect, you are unprepared for. It floors you. You are reeling for weeks. You have to be prepared for it. It doesn't reach out and greet everyone like an insurance salesman. I don't know the actual pathways in my brain, as I nearly failed Biochemistry but managed to cram for the final and get a C. I doubt there is a chemical that people could take to experience this feeling, which I consider the fount of all feelings, and beginning of them all because it is the feeling of freedom and the perception that it will all come to an end in time. It is infinite happiness and sadness all rolled up into one.

I flushed the cyanide that I had smuggled out of the Biochemistry laboratory down the toilet and watched the bowl turn a bright sickly blue as it went around and around. That would have been my color, had I swallowed it. I thought that Marcus would discover me, but it probably would have been a really long time, and I would have started to stink. I imagined myself a rotted corpse, lying on the bathroom floor. I shook the vision as soon as it started. With Marcus Hanely, I chose the slow suicide of isolation and loneliness of a man of letters, always thinking. I wrote. Hanely encouraged me, and I wrote without thinking according to the parameters of writing what would sell. I didn't write what I thought would sell, I wrote what I knew would sell. Hanely encouraged me to write something beautiful, short, and easy to read, market it to women because they were the only ones who actually took the time to read in great droves anymore.

Plus, being a famous author amongst women would really drive the point home to Ms. Autobody (yes she was an obsession) that she really had no business snubbing me for a run of the mill, absolutely untalented hack of a photojournalist. What paper did this fruit even work for? Agency France Press? Who cared if he was French. I don't even know why there's the perception that French men are superior lovers; maybe they are more patient than Americans. Maybe they know the female equipment better because they get more experience with it. I personally think it's marketing, just like the French have sold *La Jaconde* (*The Mona Lisa*) to the world as a masterpiece for a hundred so years. All marketing. This thing isn't that profound. I've seen it. Up close. It's about the size of a couple of postcards end to end. I've heard that women like Autobody date older men like le photojournaliste because they have deep seated daddy issues. I don't know about all that. I can only read the contents of my own soul.

As a child I often stared at rocks and wondered if the rock had an internal life like I had an internal life. I felt them against my skin and wondered if the rock could feel me back. I knew that I was different from the rock because the rock just sat there for (billions of years according to my pa) or had been bashed about by events happening on it. The rock had never made a decision to go anywhere nor could it make a decision. It could not remember where it has been. It was cold to the touch, lifeless, dead. I remember when I went to my grandfather's funeral at the young age of maybe two. This was around the same time that I was having the thoughts about the great rock in my expansive front yard. I reached out and touched my grandfather's face in his coffin and found it cold, lifeless, and dead, much like the surface of the rock.

My auntie scolded me and told me that it was not proper to touch the dead. I asked her why, and she could not provide me any sort of answer that I accepted; I merely asked why to each answer she proffered. I was trying to find out the answer to the question of "Why?", but my auntie got annoyed with me and just walked away. I realized that my grandfather had become just like the rock, which never knew anything that ever happened to it over its multibillion-year existence. It did not matter if fragments chipped off the rock as it tumbled down the sides of mountains, drowned in streams, baked in the sun, or had a dinosaur shit on it. It didn't matter. It could lie at the bottom of the ocean. Unmoving, uncaring.

We could do nothing in death but just lie there like the rock, getting chips taken out of us. What mattered was what we did in life. I don't remember much of my grandfather. He was gone all of the time, much like my father, but from what I learned later, he stacked away entire banks full of money to leave to my father who did the same to leave to me. At that point, I became totally unafraid of death. What I grew afraid of more and more each day was that blank spot within me that no one but myself could tell me how to fill. I was terrified of my utter freedom. Even now, as I write these words on my maladjusted computer, the terror bubbles up within me. Because I feel it, I know that I am alive. My words fashion my freedom into a sword that I wield against crushing infinity.

I have given up. I have ripped myself from the cycle of trying to fill up my void with objects that I acquire, and instead, I have decided to push outwards. I push outwards with my words, which bubble forth unabated and unfiltered. There is nothing, no man, nor beast, nor foul conspiracy that can stop me. I push forth with my discovery of my own completion, and that is I. Too much emphasis has been laced on the acquisition of comfort through items, and nothing has been placed on the acquisition of talents, or the uncovering of that which we have talent for. And if you find you are not talented at any activity in existence, invent one to be talented at and show it off. This dreary place, and it is a dreary place, will be made all the richer.

Now that Marcus Hanely has disappeared in a poof of confusion, my only regret is that I wasted so much time in pursuit of the golden phantom. I was free to write my story. I would write it with no real beginning or no real end. I would start it as an artist begins an oil painting...as a series of smudges that slowly come into focus to present a whole. I would be the focusing lens on my own work. What the painting would come to be, I have no idea.

Viewed from a distance it could be something entirely different than when viewed from a speck's distance away. I would love for an individual period in the work to be a microdot, which was actually the entire work shrunken down. Inside that microdot would be the same individual period that would be a microdot shrunken down, and so on. Any one of these periods you have read thus far could be the one. Hidden from view within that would be the entire message over and over again. It could be this one. Or this one. Or this.

I would probably begin my story somewhere near the beginning. I would probably end my story somewhere near the end. The end would reach all the way backwards and embrace the beginning like a familiar lover. And the beginning would reciprocate and their coupling would give birth to a beautiful child, which would be the meat of the story.

So...here I am. I have gotten rid of my delusions, and it has proven to be quite a painful experience for me. Now, the only trick is how to get others to give up their delusions about this not being their one and only life without causing them too much undue harm. Getting rid of a delusion is probably one of the most painful experiences a person can go through. We humans have the luxury of forgetting a physical pain after we go through it. You only remember that it hurt. You do not re-experience the pain. That trip to the dentist, or breaking our arm when we were a child, getting tortured as a prisoner of war, we can only remember that it hurt; we don't have to keep reliving the pain over and over again. We cannot summon it up. This is not the same with mental anguish. We are forced to relive the same experiences, which produced in us that mental anguish. I will be forced to relive finding my dead mother over and over again...if I choose to keep replaying the tape. We can invent all sorts of packaging for it, delusions being the brightest and prettiest decorations, but all in all, it is the same mental anguish we are putting ourselves through by giving these delusions energy.

I gave an awful lot of my own creative self to Marcus Hanely and his various incarnations that we met on that trip across the United States when I should have just bit the bullet and consented to having my balls groped by the TSA when I boarded a delusion free flight. I would have gotten to spend more time with my father. Perhaps he would have been able to tell me all about his secret art habit and offered me some advice about what to do in the future in regards to the family biz. My father's delusion was that in order to feel constantly alive, my father had to be constantly on the move, always seeing something new.

The old and familiar became, for him, something dead, something without substance. Only the new moved him. He used experience as a possession. These possessions we take to be extensions of our beings may fill the same role. I will do without them. I will have a few tools with which I can shape my own world, but I will be using them; they will not bury me.

You might think me somewhat mad, but I have to tell you that until you have ceded nearly 15 years of your one and only life to a golden phantom, given it every credence to being the only real thing or person in this world, and then discovered that the person was, in fact, just a phantom, albeit a beautiful phantom, that calls to you softly to just embrace it, to forget about your own ambition, to just go under into the calming warm waters with it where the things underneath all glimmer, but you drown. No thanks. I'll be a madman in the sun. I'll walk without blinders on. I'll go in my own direction.

I'm going to give the vast majority of my fortune away to complete strangers. This is not going to be entirely at random. That would be the work of a fool. These people who I give money to must have attempted in the past to show themselves capable of original thought. You may consider that arrogant of me to consider myself an arbiter of what constitutes originality in this great expansive cultural morass we're all trudging through. But I'll tell you something: better me than someone else. I'm not looking for a savior or something to change my perceptions. I'm looking for things to spark me to think. I'm not looking for meaning. I'm looking just for evidence of thoughts. If an object can inspire me to think, that is all I need. (So many artists these days have become interior designers or website designers.) Salesmen.

So...here I am. I've gassed up the Judge, which my buddy Robert Malvolio saw fit to park in a location known only to him, which was the parking garage of a Wall Street Security firm with whom he was in negotiations with for gainful employment. I decided to hire him back in my employ. He followed orders to a tee, just like a faithful Cerberus. Ask him to do anything, and he would do it. He absolutely didn't talk unless it was to right some wrong, and he was fiercely loyal to me. He wouldn't question my motives in giving my and my father's fortune away. I have gotten rid of any capacity for revenge against his person. He, after all, made the admission. I wouldn't have had a clue, and I would have hated my mother, an innocent in this whole situation whose only crime was marrying my father out of naiveté and her father's wishes.

Malvolio admitted his guilt, and he did it without provocation, without being under oath in front of some Congressional panel that grilled him for hours. He didn't take the coward's fifth. He helped me rid myself of my hatred toward my mother, which allowed me to extricate myself finally from Marcus Hanely. I am not a man given to violence. I am a man given to forgiveness and love. Happiness doesn't dwell under the sun; it dwells in us, and if you're looking for the key, you can't go looking outside yourself. It starts with a decision.

Well, I made a decision to forgive Malvolio, and I made him my traveling companion. He's really the only one mad enough to embark on this journey with me from Coast to Coast, up and down the great Continental Divide, driving through mountains, badlands, plains, and effluvial swamps. Driving through all the various geographies of this land, this planet, where I can set my car a driving, through the landscapes of my mind. I'm forever moving, because I'm my father's son.

My father, who was laid to rest, never found peace in his waking hours. I don't know the secret forces that wound his clocks and set him into motion. I know my secret heartstrings, and I know my motivations. I am not motivated by anything, and it is profoundly not a thing, it is the anti-thing, and that means my motivation is love. It does not rest, it stays in constant motion even if between two people. I will stay in constant motion because my being is an act of love; I am love incarnate. That is my new delusion, but it feels natural to me, like it was my composition at birth, and the remainders of my personality are an amalgam of genius etched on my soul, airy and light, but non-existent.

I have sent my lover ahead on a flight to our home in Monterey. Vanessa announced three months ago that she was pregnant. I did not ask her that foul question that so many women hear from the wretched curs of today's age: "Is it mine?" I had no reason to ask the question. A baby isn't an it. As my personal assistant, we were together all the time. She never had occasion to go and get plowed by someone else. She doesn't have anyone else. Neither do I. We talked about it several times. She is the most beautiful woman I have ever met, though I don't know much about her interior. I guess I haven't asked, or she hasn't shared.

Sometimes I have the paranoid thought that she is still working for someone out there, spying on me, or that she was sent to bring me home. I dismiss the former and put all my confidence in the latter. Every man who loves women needs a good woman in this world, and I have found one in Vanessa. Just her name flits off my tongue when I say it. It dances around my mind as Malvolio and I make our way West. Thus far, I have given one million dollar grants, anonymously of course, to a talented poet I met at a coffee shop in Peoria, Illinois, and a painter from Iowa City, Iowa. I have saved them the dregs of ever having to be a corporate tool and thinking of their profound talent as a mere hobby.

It seems to me that everything is on its head. Someone, no matter what they do, should first and foremost be an artist and love their creation, and they should consider moneymaking as a hobby. I am investing in a woman who owns a small theatre company in BFE, Nebraska, who had the courage to write her own plays but doesn't have the capital to make a move to New York City or somewhere with a more appropriate venue. She has tried, I am told, to get some of the Nebraska gentry interested in sponsoring her production company, but I am told that they just don't see the potential for profit in it. So, I will probably swoop down and make an anonymous donation with the caveat that she fulfills what she has discovered she is supposed to do in life.

Malvolio is an excellent driver. He is mad enough to stay up for weeks on end, driving straight the line on our search for talent, on our way to Monterey and my woman whom I will make my wife, and he never questions the wisdom of the decisions I make. We are perfectly content, seeing the countryside, making this countryside all the richer. We care not for the present. Our wills are bent towards a future outside of us. If you are to be alive today and tomorrow, this is the most proper attitude. We hurtled over the Rockies. I began a file on a troubadour I met on the corner in Five Points, Denver, Colorado. An Old Veteran, methinks.

I'm dispatching the people my father formerly had assassinate troublesome individuals owning mining stakes who wouldn't sell, the crew that my soon to be wife was part of. They're searching the United States for talent as well, and they forward it to me with videos. The troubadour had given up any hope of worldly success and played his guitar because he loved it. He, too, had given up. I hope the name and email address he gave me weren't fake.

The limelight is there for people who need aid in shining, who need to make themselves into marketable objects, summarized by taglines. I, for one, don't care. Maybe someone, somewhere, godknowswhere will discover this text under a rock and find some inspiration within. They will find it dusty and unused, lurking in the corner of a used bookstore, if any of those still exist. They will find it encrypted on the cloud server of some league of malcontents and possibly see fit to give it a read. They may seek to understand me, but they will never know me. That is for me to know. Epitaphs do not need to be written for troubled times. Memory of those times will suffice. But how we forget...

Monterey is not like the last time I was here. I feel less a piece of kelp washed up on the rocks and dragged back out to sea: an endless cycle of decay and reconstitution. I won't say I feel whole or complete; that makes no sense to me. I don't know what that means. I feel at peace in this season, knowing that for half of the next year, I will drive the open road in another car with the same traveling companion. The Judge garners too much attention. Artists have started speaking of a mysterious black car that comes in the middle of the night and drops off parcels. They only know it as a muscle car, so we are safe for now. The Judge is not fuel-efficient. I will trade it for a fleet of more incognito autos. I will seek out other seabirds that fly the open seas, searching. I will stop briefly and chat with them, and I will go on my merry way, spreading my wings, flying.

A new day follows a new day follows a new day...an endless string of possibilities that I know will end. I am so full of hope that it is crushing me. I must share it with others. I have a budgetary hope surplus in this world of deficit. Hope is my currency and dreams are my savings account.

Vanessa gave birth to our daughter on a December day, a foggy December day where it sort of lingered like a tired old friend on your doorstep who was bound to depart for home. I named my daughter Marjorie, after my mother. Her eyes are blue like mine, blue like the Pacific, our backyard.

I sat on the deck with her the other day and the sudden compulsion came over me to walk to the very side of the Earth. I held Marjorie tight to my chest as I walked through the rough scrub pines and aloes. I made my way to the edge of the cliff, and the surge battered the rocks below to pebbles, the pebbles to sand. The salt air stung my eyes like teardrops. I held my daughter up in the air and looked into her tiny face. Her eyes opened, as blue as the sea, and stared at me with surprise. She cooed and smiled. I smiled back at her. I heard a resounding voice with each breath of the sea that bashed its might in waves upon the rocks. *Do better. Do better.* That is all I can do. I pulled her close and held her tightly to my chest. As I held her, tears broke from my eyes, and sent torrents down my face. It is okay for a man to cry. I would do better. I really would. That is my hope. That is my dream. My most solemn vow.

A scene at the very ending...

www.ingramcontent.com/pod-product-compliance
Lightning Source LLC
Chambersburg PA
CBHW081131020726
47504CB00010B/2045